WITHDRAWN
Damaged, Obsolete, or Surplus

Jackson County Library Services

Modern Jewish History

Robert A. Mandel,
series editor

Commodore Levy

Portrait of Commodore Uriah Levy, U.S. Naval Historical Center
Photograph, National Archive ID # 48113
(PD-USGOV-MILITARY-NAVY).

Commodore Levy

A Novel of Early America
in the Age of Sail

Irving Litvag

Edited by
Bonny V. Fetterman

Texas Tech University Press

Copyright © 2014 by IL Family Publications, LLC

All rights reserved. No portion of this book may be reproduced in any form or by any means, including electronic storage and retrieval systems, except by explicit prior written permission of the publisher. Brief passages excerpted for review and critical purposes are excepted.

This book is typeset in Minion Pro. The paper used in this book meets the minimum requirements of ANSI/NISO Z39.48-1992 (R1997). ∞

Cover designed by Kasey McBeath.
Cover illustration: *USS Constellation*, (cropped) painting by Rear Admiral John. W. Schmidt, Navy History and Heritage Command, National Archive ID # 428-KN-2882 (PD-USGOV-MILITARY-NAVY).

Library of Congress Cataloging-in-Publication Data
Litvag, Irving.
    Commodore Levy : a Novel of Early America in the Age of Sail / Irving Litvag, edited by Bonny V. Fetterman.
        pages cm. — (Modern Jewish History)
    ISBN 978-0-89672-881-3 (hardback) — ISBN 978-0-89672-883-7 (e-book) 1. Levy, Uriah Phillips, 1792-1862—Fiction 2. United States. Navy—Fiction. I. Fetterman, Bonny V. II. Title.
    PS3612.I885C66 2014
    813'.6—dc23   2013050896

14 15 16 17 18 19 20 21 22 / 9 8 7 6 5 4 3 2 1

Texas Tech University Press
Box 41037 | Lubbock, Texas 79409-1037 USA
800.832.4042 | ttup@ttu.edu | www.ttupress.org

Excerpts from James Inderwick's journal are quoted from *Cruise of the U.S. Brig Argus in 1813: Journal of Surgeon James Inderwick* (New York: New York Public Library, 1917; available on Google Books), 15–19, 25.
    Excerpts from Uriah Levy's speech to the Court of Inquiry are quoted from Benjamin F. Butler, *Defence of Uriah P. Levy: Before the Court of Inquiry, Held at Washington City, November and December, 1857* (New York: W. C. Bryant, 1858); reprinted in *The Making of the Modern Law: Legal Treatises, 1800–1926* series (Farmington Hills, MI: Gale, 2010), 11, 87–89.

For our grandchildren
Jakob, Isabella, and Jordan

Contents

Acknowledgments

My husband, Irving Litvag, passed away prior to the final editing of his then 1,350-page manuscript of *Commodore Levy*. Knowing how much it meant to him after over five years of research and writing, I embarked on a journey to see his book published—and so it has come to be. I want to acknowledge the people who encouraged me to see it through and provided insight, guidance, and support: Howard Schwartz, Alice Gleason, Rabbi Jeffrey Stiffman, and Harvey Blumenthal.

This book would not have been published without the dedicated work of our editor and agent, Bonny V. Fetterman, who edited Irv's manuscript with great skill and appreciation for his research and writing. Keeping true to his vision, she brought the novel to its present form. A big thanks is due to Robert Mandel, the publisher of Texas Tech University Press, who believed in the novel from the start and steadfastly supported it. And of course to our children, Julie and Larry Dyson and Joe and Lisa Litvag, who were instrumental in advising me along this unfamiliar course.

Irv wanted to dedicate this book to our grandchildren: Jakob and Jordan Litvag and Isabella Dyson. Although he only knew Jakob, he knew there would be more, and this book is for them, too.

Ilene Litvag

Commodore Levy

Prologue

Uriah Phillips Levy, deposed captain, United States Navy, awoke from a troubled sleep with a desperate start—certain beyond doubt that he had heard the drums beating to quarters. He was reaching out to his trousers, ready to heave on his clothing and rush up the gangway to his station, when he looked around him and hazily saw the now-familiar surroundings of his hotel bedroom.

He sank back on the bed with a groan. He put his hand across his eyes until they could open fully to the sunlight pouring through the two big windows. The rattling noise that had awakened him, he now comprehended, was a heavy dray hauling something to Centre Market down the way.

Uriah lay there for a while, watching the dust motes rise and fall in the beams of morning sunlight. He silently cursed the drayman for his noisy wagon and also the proprietors of this august hotel for locating it at such a busy intersection. *Why is it*, he wondered, *that European hotels in the great capitals were quiet and secluded, with peaceful courtyards and silent lanes around them, while all the hotels in Washington City were barbarically located on busy intersections along Pennsylvania Avenue, "The Avenue," the busiest thoroughfare in the city?* And here he was at Willard's, possibly the noisiest of them all, right on the main channel to the city's old marketplace.

He didn't care a fig where they stayed, so long as it was reasonably clean and the food edible. But Virginia had insisted on Willard's. "It is *the* place in Washington City," his young wife had beseeched, "and everyone in the government gathers there. Please, my dear, say that it will be Willard's!"

He was fully awake now and turned his head. Virginia was still asleep, a faint smile at her lips and an occasional genteel snore lightly tipping the quiet in the room. It was still warm for late October, and she had thrown back the heavy comforter.

Uriah climbed slowly out of the thick, soft hotel bed. As he washed and shaved in the tiny bathroom, he could hear the increasing volume of morning sounds coming from the streets, two floors below. The capital of the nation was known to be a late-rising city, but surely that applied only to the government workers and the chief clerks who supervised them. The laborers and haulers, the cleaning people and drawers of water, were at their jobs as early and noisily as in any other city.

Dressed now in a severe black broadcloth suit, Uriah walked into the adjoining parlor and sat in a chair at the big circular table. He glanced despairingly at the pile of white paper on the table, next to the waiting steel-nibbed pen. "Just as blank as they were yesterday," he muttered, and picked up the pen. He dipped it into the inkwell and tried to formulate his opening words.

Fifteen minutes later, he had neither moved nor written a syllable. He sat staring ahead, waiting for the right words to come. He could feel the red fury rising in his head. He damned Ben Butler, his lawyer, for sentencing him to this torturous task.

It was hard enough to write a simple report to a squadron commander or a newspaper article on a naval topic. But to write one's own life! And to write it so excellently as to convince a naval court of inquiry that the writer is competent to hold the exalted rank of captain, highest in all the service! Impossible! Well, perhaps not impossible to write . . . but apparently impossible to *begin*.

"I was born in old Phila-dell-phy-ayyy and I chose to be born there because I wanted to be close to me mither." *Wonderful*, he thought. *I can begin with that old Paddy joke and we'll see our whole case sink right to the bottom.*

He sat at the table, unmoving, for another ten minutes. Finally he put down the pen and covered his face with his hands. He rubbed his eyes. It was not yet eight o'clock in the morning, and he felt as tired and empty of thought as if he were coming off a double watch on deck.

He wondered if a brisk walk might unclog his mind. He smiled at the thought. It was the same feeble hope with which he had arisen each morning for the past week, since their arrival at the Willard. And each morning he had taken a spirited walk in the fresh morning air, returning to the hotel as bereft of opening words as when he had departed. Well, he would try it again this morning. Ben Butler had warned him that he must have some material ready for him to read at their meeting this afternoon.

Uriah quietly closed the parlor door behind him and walked down the stairs to the lobby. The big, carpeted reception salon was still quiet and almost empty. He came out into the warm fall morning and walked down the hotel steps to Pennsylvania Avenue. A Negro hack driver, parked in front of the entrance awaiting hire, called to him questioningly and politely raised his hat. Uriah silently shook his head and turned westward, walking briskly along the sidewalk under the ailanthus trees that lined The Avenue. This was the favorite promenade of Washington City, and by mid-morning it would be thronged with people greeting each other, darting in and out of the hotels, watching for famous government leaders.

"Wind's southwest by south and veering west," Uriah muttered to himself. "Change in the weather coming. Rain by sunset."

As if to confirm his thought, a cat's paw of wind flicked his face with a stinging load of dust. *Damned primitive city,* he thought as he wiped his eyes with a handkerchief. Mud-swamp streets in every rain. And when it was dry, so full of blowing dust that people had to walk with cloths tied around their faces to avoid suffocation. Washington City had been the capital of the nation for almost sixty years now, and it still looked like a country village—and a damned strange and ugly one at that. A few piles of government marble scattered here and there, like icebergs floating in a sea of desolate fields, shanty houses, and cow path roads.

As he neared the White House, he realized that he was ignoring the major purpose of this walk: to clarify his thinking about the story of his life that Butler demanded for the defense. *I will begin with the receipt of my warrant as sailing master from President Madison,* he thought. *That is the proper place to start. No, no. If I start with that, I will eliminate all of my training at sea. And that certainly is important. It must be included.*

That much decided, he gazed at the president's house across the street. Uriah glanced up at the windows at the end of the second floor. Sometimes when walking past like this, he had seen the president at his desk, wearing a dressing gown, head bowed over official papers, a long cigar clasped in his lips. But today the curtains were drawn.

He walked up to the fence that separated The Avenue from the White House grounds and stared intently through it. He studied, as he always did when he walked this way, a big bronze statue in the circle before the north portico.

"Goddamned bird dung!" he said aloud. He startled a prim young schoolteacher from Boston, who stood a few feet away looking at the president's house with the rapt adoration of a first-time visitor. She didn't hear his profanity, or she immediately would have retreated, but only the exasperated tone of his voice.

"What?" she said timidly.

"The birds!" Uriah repeated sharply, his eyes still fixed on the statue. "They're covering up the top of his head. It's a damned disgrace!"

She was somewhat offended by his cursing, but he was an elderly, well-dressed man and she decided to ignore it. She followed his stare to the statue. "Please," she asked, "who may that be?"

Uriah looked at her finally, irritated that she did not know. "It's President Thomas Jefferson, of course. Our greatest president. It's *my* statue, you know. I commissioned it and I gave it to them. Only government statue ever given by a private citizen. They moved it over here from the Capitol in '45. Didn't even ask my approval."

The young teacher went slightly pale at the man's apparent ravings and gave a quick look around to see if anyone might be near to come to her aid. "Oh," she replied vacantly.

"'Course I wouldn't expect you to know about that," Uriah went on. "That I gave 'em the statue, I mean. Nobody knows anymore. Or cares. Good day, ma'am." He raised his hat to her and went on his way up the street. *It's still a damned beautiful statue*, he told himself, *dung and all.*

Uriah made the left turn onto Seventeenth Street. It was noticeably less busy than The Avenue. He welcomed the respite from the dust and noise thrown up by the passing carriages and drays. To his left, clerks hurried along the gravel paths between the White House and the adjoining War and Navy Buildings. The public also used the president's lawn as a throughway; fences bordered the north and south boundaries, but the rest was open to access by all.

There it is, Uriah thought to himself: *the seat of power—the headquarters for the mighty martial forces of the United States of America.* Ahead of him were two small, almost identical brick buildings, each three stories high. The northern building, now at his left, was the War Department.

Uriah stopped on the sidewalk for a moment as he came abeam of the southern of the two buildings, the Navy Department. He turned to face it. He knew that he might well be recognized from within, but he didn't care. Somewhere among those third-floor windows was the hearing room. There he soon would fight the climactic battle of his life: the combat for his honor. His jaw tightened, and he tilted his face upward slightly as he appraised the enemy. Then he abruptly turned and walked on.

An ever more overpowering stench told Uriah that he was approaching the old city canal. The well-kept presidential lawn on his left degenerated rapidly into a perverse marsh as it neared the canal. Just scant yards from the bed of the president of the United States lay this rotting, fetid swamp draining into a once-busy canal, now clogged with sewerage, that ran its diseased way across the southern end of the city from the Potomac to the eastern branch of the Anacostia.

Uriah held his nose and quickened his pace. The smell was sickening, even to a veteran of the berth deck on a man-of-war where mingled the aromas of seven hundred unwashed sailormen.

On this warm October morning, he had taken this nauseous route for his walk because it was the most direct line from his Jefferson statue to the Navy Yard, his eventual destination. *Why*, he wondered, *did his walks around this city inevitably take him to the yard?* There were few old friends there anymore. Yet . . . he was drawn there. He would walk silently around the coils of rigging and the old horse blocks and somehow feel at home—more so than anywhere else in this city of politicians and their clerks.

He crossed the high iron bridge over the canal at Fourteenth Street and wended his way on the open ground that the city planners called "The Mall." It was messy, unpretty terrain, not helped by the lumber and coal yards hanging just across at the northern bank of the canal. To his right, as he walked south before making the half-turn onto Virginia Avenue, was the sick-looking stump of the monument to George Washington. First proposed in 1800, the construction of this grandiose stone column had finally begun in 1848. It would be a seven-hundred-foot-tall obelisk, they said, and the eyes of the world would be on it. By 1855, however, the money had run out, the arguments raged heavy, and all work came to a stop. Now, two years later, the stump sat alone, one-third completed, and was ignored by all.

He recrossed the canal, this time on the Virginia Avenue Bridge, and left that part of the city known as "The Island" because of its separation by the smelly stream. Now he was in the Navy Yard section, an isolated, semirural neighborhood peopled by those who worked at the yard. Ahead of him he could see the two masts of a steam sloop under repair at the yard. The still-ambivalent navy fathers powered most of their ships with steam these days, retaining the masts and sails for the engine failures they were certain would occur.

High in the distance to his left was the marble pile of the unfinished Capitol, scaffolding strung around its slowly rising dome. By next year, they said, Congress might be able to move into its new halls.

He was feeling better, by God! For once the walk had served its purpose. Somehow, in some mysterious fashion, the jumble inside his head had begun to order itself. The events had been clear in his mind, but he couldn't seem to think of the proper words to relate them. This bright morning, though, the walk had done him some good. He felt invigorated now, mentally prepared to pick up the pen and set to work. He would stop briefly at the Navy Yard, then hire a hack and return quickly to the hotel. He would have some pages for Butler to read at their four o'clock meeting today, and tomorrow he would work all day until it was finished.

And the question that had so plagued him, of how to begin? Why—he would just begin at the beginning.

Part I
Young Sailor

1

The three of them bobbed along Front Street, pointing occasionally at the wooden structure that billowed skyward ahead of them. They walked gleefully and excitedly down the quiet streets of Philadelphia, heading for Southwark. Despite the disparity in their ages, there was an ease and mutual joy in their companionship, born of many hours spent together on expeditions just like this one, save only for its destination.

The occasional pedestrian or householder watched them go past with a smile: something warmed the heart in the sight of this husky old man with the loud voice and emphatic gestures as he strode past the redbrick houses with his escort of two small boys. Their faces were etched with expectations and their eyes were wide. They obviously were on a mission of great import.

The old man was Jonas Phillips, merchant of dry goods and sundries on Second Street above Arch and esteemed past *parnass* of Mikveh Israel Synagogue. Trying to keep up with him and peppering him with questions as they went were two of his grandsons: eleven-year-old Mordecai Manuel Noah and five-year-old Uriah Phillips Levy.

"Look at it!" piped Mordecai, pointing again at the towering wooden spectacle. "It must stand five hundred feet high!"

"Or maybe a mile!" added Uriah for good measure.

"*She*, Mordecai, *she*. You have to refer to a ship as a lady," Phillips reminded him, "or Mr. Humphreys will have your head on a platter."

Mordecai was too excited to acknowledge the correction. "Look, Papa, it even rises above Old Swedes' Church. I have never seen such a giant ship!" He was tall for his age and thin, with a mop of unruly brownish-red hair that matched his exuberance. Uriah, his younger cousin, walked with an erectness that was almost a stiffness and kept his thin lips tightly compressed in intense concentration.

"Poys! Poys, quick look!" Phillips's German accent always thickened when he became excited, and the "b" of his words exploded into a sharp "p." "Poys, down the street—here comes the vice president!" The boys turned to follow his pointing arm down Front Street. They saw a large bay horse cantering regally down the street. In the saddle was a tall, rawboned, redheaded man. He was bare of hat and nondescriptly clad in a faded brown riding coat, a red waistcoat, corduroy breeches, and short brown boots, above which could be seen woolen hose.

As the horse approached the place on the sidewalk where the old man and two boys stood, the rider stared vacantly into the distance. Then, as if some instinct told him that they were watching him intently, he turned his face to them, smiled, and nodded pleasantly.

"Good morning, Mr. Jefferson!" said Phillips loudly. He stood as if at attention. The two boys looked on, openmouthed. Living in the nation's capital, they often had seen high public officials riding past in carriages or standing on distant platforms. But it was unusual to get so close a look and to be given a personal nod.

"Do you know him, Papa?" asked Uriah.

"I have shaken his hand," Phillips replied. "But I do not have the honor of saying I know him." They watched silently as the bay continued his solemn canter down the street.

"He is a good friend to us, to our people," Phillips said thoughtfully. "He understands that in the United States of America, every man is equal. No matter what the man believes." The horse now was almost out of sight. "Remember this day, boys. You have seen a great man."

"Papa, is Mr. Jefferson going to see the ship, too?" asked Uriah.

"Naw," Mordecai broke in. "He and the president and all the other cabinet people wouldn't have waited this long, until it's almost finished. They've probably seen it lots of times already." Mordecai already had a vital interest in politics and the leaders who dominated it.

They continued along the brick sidewalk, past whale-oil lamps at intervals on the curb, until they finally arrived at their destination: a high brown fence ending in a big wood and wire gate that was propped open. On the gate was a small, neat sign: WHARTON & HUMPHREYS, SHIP BUILDERS. They passed through the gate.

Directly before them, between them and the Delaware River, towered the hull of a gigantic ship. It lay in a nest of wooden stanchions and frames, its keel resting on the inclined ways that soon would carry it into its own element on the water that glistened in the late morning sun.

"Well, the right honorable Mister Phillips! About time you came to call on my lady!" He was a short, big-headed, barrel-chested man of about forty-five years, dressed in rough workman's clothes. He was standing near a small superintendent's shack near the ship when he saw them, and his loud, rasping voice echoed up the sloping ground to the gate. He finished giving orders to a carpenter and then walked toward the old man and the two boys.

Phillips made the introduction: "Boys, meet Joshua Humphreys, builder of the frigate *United States*." The boys gravely shook the shipbuilder's gnarled hand. "Joshua, you have met Mordecai at my store. And this is another of my grandsons, Uriah—the son of my daughter Rachel and her husband, Michael Levy. Uriah is the family's expert on ships. He spends most of his time on the Front Street docks, admiring the view."

"Someday," Uriah proclaimed, "I'm going to have a store like my father and also be captain of a big ship. Probably this ship right here." He pointed to the enormous hull in front of them. The two men laughed, but Uriah was serious and nodded vigorously.

"So? What do you think of her?" asked Humphreys, his voice eager.

Jonas Phillips looked up at the big frigate and studied the hull for a time before answering. He had been to sea only twice in his life and claimed no mastery of ships. But he was a merchant in a busy port, and talk of the sea and ships surrounded him. He had learned a few things, enough to let a ship's form fill his eye and to make a judgment as to whether that form was fair or awkward. The stillness of the moment was punctuated now and then by the sound of a hammer or saw or by the ring of metal on metal, but the shipyard was much quieter than it had been in months. The work on the frigate was substantially complete.

"The question is, will she float?" Phillips always had a bit of fun prodding Humphreys, who regarded each of his ships as a daughter and spoke of them with affection and utter, unwavering seriousness.

"Will she—? Why, this is the finest and fastest frigate in the world!" Humphreys's face was beet-red, and he gestured wildly as he spoke. "She's bigger and tougher than any of the British or French frigates and much faster than their 74s. Why, she's a good twenty feet longer than any of the English frigates and four feet wider. Look at her lines, man! She's—she's downright magnificent! And she's going to change the look of naval warfare . . . she and her sister ships. She's going to stand with the *Great Harry* and the *Henry Grace de Dieu* and the *Sovereign of the Seas* in the history of ocean combat. I think she's going to stand higher than any of them."

He took a deep breath and went on. "Look, Jonas, we learned some hard lessons in the War of Independence. Oh yes, we had known a few things about fighting in ships. My own father, you know, was the master of a privateer in the old days. But they were like toys against navies such as the English and French. We had a few successes in the late war, like Captain Jones and the *Bonhomme Richard*, but we also learned some things that we could *not* do." He scratched his head with both hands at the same time and then looked down at the ground, as if to summarize the ideas churning through his mind.

"We learned that we cannot compete against England, nor France for that matter, in number of warships or weight of metal thrown. Impossible! They have too much of a start on us. We cannot match their fleets. But what we *can* do is to build fast, powerful single vessels that can pick and choose their fights. Don't you see? To build a 74-gun ship-of-the-line is not the answer. They cost too much to build and to cruise, and our enemies have dozens of them.

"Ah . . . but what we *can* do is to build long, sleek, fast frigates like my lady here that will carry a powerful punch!" He cackled with delight at the thought. "A 74 can never outsail her. She's much too fast. Look at the run of her, man, look at her length! She has an overall length of more than two hundred feet, forty-three feet in the beam, and she'll displace over fifteen hundred tons. Her masts, when we set 'em, will be almost two hundred feet high!"

He paused to grab his breath. Phillips decided to risk asking the question that was on his mind: "Joshua, some people say that in fact she might be too long. That she is likely to hog."

"Not so, not so." The response from Humphreys was milder than Phillips expected. "We have here, in front of you, a long frigate that is strong and will not hog. This will be no broken-backed lady! And this length will give her the speed we must have, plus . . . *plus* the space needed for the armament that we must have. A history-making ship, Jonas, I assure you."

Phillips looked up at the vast oaken hull with new appreciation. "How many guns will she carry?" he asked.

There was a noticeable change in the tone of Humphreys's voice: it had a darker hue. "She is a 44-gun frigate; that is her design. But she will be made to carry up to 52 guns. God help us if that load of metal changes her sailing qualities. It will undo all my work. It will ruin everything."

"Will you be the captain of this ship," Uriah asked, "and ride her on the ocean?"

Phillips let out a roar of laughter. "Captain? This one? Hah! He only builds the ships. He has never even been to sea. The farthest he has ventured is the middle of the Delaware River, and even then he was shaking like a dove!"

Humphreys joined in the laughter of the old man and the two boys. "All right, so I am no sailorman. But I know ships and how to build them. Boys, did you learn in school about the *Randolph* in the Continental Navy? That was my ship. She, too, was a frigate, but nothing like my lady here."

Phillips was enjoying the bantering. "So, if she is built for 44 guns, why must she carry more?"

"Why, you ask? Because the experts—," and he gave the word a hard, biting stress, "the great fighting captains who know so much more than us humble builders, they are not satisfied with that. 'More guns, more guns!' I hear the infernal cry in my sleep!"

"So, how many?"

"They talk now of thirty long 24-pounders and twenty-two 12-pounders. That would give her more than 490 pounds weight of metal to the broadside. She's just not designed to carry such a load and yet retain her speed. Think of the weight—oh, think of the weight!"

Phillips could not resist yet one more jab of the needle. "Ah, sad to hear a Quaker speaking about guns of war. A follower of George Fox and William Penn, going on so about the instruments of death. So, so sad."

Humphreys shrugged his shoulders ruefully. "Ex-Quaker, you mean. Didn't you know I was expelled by the Friends for working on a ship of war? But I still follow the Inner Light, no matter what they think of me."

"You know what a Quaker is?" asked a new voice, lilting, with a touch of brogue. "He prays for his neighbor on First Day and preys upon him the other six!" The speaker came out of the superintendent's shack, a tall, husky, affable man with brown curly hair, wearing the impressive blue dress uniform of a captain in the U.S. Navy.

"Ah, the tormentor himself," said Humphreys. "I was just speaking of your incessant demands for more guns, more guns. And here you come to bedevil me some more." He turned to Phillips and the two boys. "Gentlemen, may I present Captain John Barry, who will command my beautiful ship one day and meanwhile is assigned here by the secretary of war to make my life miserable with his constant interference." Barry smiled broadly at the comment.

Jonas Phillips again stood erect, as he had when Jefferson had ridden past. "I am honored, Captain Barry," he said. "I followed with great interest your exploits on the *Alliance* and the *Lexington* in the late war."

Barry nodded politely in response and moved forward to shake hands with Phillips and with each of the boys. Mordecai was especially impressed. He knew all about the captain. "Sir," he said, "isn't it true that you are now the senior captain in our navy?"

"Aye, lad," Barry answered, "and me but a broth of a lad and in my prime at age fifty-two."

"Halloo!" A hail came from the shipyard gate, and they all turned to see a slender young man with dark skin, prominent eyes, and jet-black hair striding down the hill.

"Ah, young Decatur!" said Barry with a smile. "Come to supervise the supervisors and make sure the work is being done aright."

Decatur was a youth of about seventeen, neatly clad in gray coat and breeches, white silk hose, and well-polished slippers. "Gentlemen, aday!" he boomed in a strong voice. "And how are you treating my frigate today?"

Humphreys introduced the newcomer to Phillips and the boys: "I think you know his father, Jonas. Captain Decatur is master of the ship *Delaware*." Phillips nodded. Stephen Decatur, Sr., was a well-respected master who had commanded a privateer, the *Rising Sun*, to good effect in the War of Independence.

"Young Decatur, Jr., here is a clerk with Gurney and Smith, our purchasing agents for the frigate," Humphreys went on. "He seems to have some sense about ships, and I foresee that he might someday make a designer and builder. But he is blind to that. It's only the navy that he wants."

"Aye," added Barry, "despite all my efforts to dissuade him."

"The navy it shall be," proclaimed young Decatur. "And the *United States* shall be my first ship. I await only my midshipman's warrant to sail away with Captain Barry. And then we shall go out looking for adventure, and woe be to any Frenchman or Englishman who gets in our way!"

"Listen to him!" shouted Barry. "The bravado of the young and ill-informed."

Humphreys had been staring up at the great hull of the frigate, shaking his head again in admiration and wonderment at his own creation. "Look, Jonas! Look at those timbers. She has the body of an English ship-of-the-line. I demanded live oak for her. Told 'em I wouldn't build the ship without live oak from the seacoast of Georgia. It's the only wood that compares to the English oak. Three years it took, but we got it. Look at those frames! I even had to send my own boys to Georgia to cut wood when the yellow fever had emptied the cutting crews."

Barry stood a few feet away from the others, hands on hips, half-listening to the conversation. He was a fine figure of a man in his blue navy coat with its bright gold epaulettes, sparkling white breeches tucked into short leather boots that glowed each morning when he arrived but quickly were covered by the thick dust of the shipyard. He, too, looked up at the frigate from time to time, as Humphreys did, with love in his eyes. Humphreys rightfully could boast that the *United States* was his lady. For now. But soon she would belong to Barry and he would take her away. Humphreys was her father, but Barry would be her bridegroom and their lives would be intertwined as those of a real man and wife.

The handsome navy captain, the honored warrior, nodded in pride as he ran his eyes again along her spar deck bulwarks. The masts, the yards, the rigging—they would find their places after the launching. And then she would truly be a man-of-war. He smiled. *What a strange way we mix our naval genders*, he thought.

Now, at last, his dream was coming true. The United States would have a real maritime fighting force, an honest-to-God navy worthy of the name. In the War of Independence, it had been called the Continental Navy, but that was a joke. Yes, the Continentals had fought with a few good ships, a few good men. And he would include himself in that group. But it could not honestly be called a navy, not in the same breath with the awesome fleets of the English, the French, and the Spanish.

Then the war was done and independence was won. And the Founding Fathers, in their wisdom, decreed that war never again would trouble the nation's shores. The little batch of ships was sold, and the officers and men of the Continental Navy were told to seek gainful employment for themselves. And thankee, men! You did well, but you're no longer needed.

The Founding Fathers quickly were disabused of their peaceful dream. In the hot summer of 1785, before we even had a constitution, the corsairs of Algiers seized two of our merchant ships and held twenty-three American seamen for ransom. What could we do? We had no navy. Barry's stomach tightened as he thought again of the insult to his nation. His old frigate *Alliance*, the last ship of the Continental Navy, had been sold just eight weeks before the merchant ships had been captured.

Yet wise men in the government continued to proclaim that standing armies and navies were the playthings of tyrants and the causes of wars. Let Crazy George and Fat Louie have their military toys; such is not for the United States of America, protected by the wide ocean and destined to live in eternal bliss! And the American sailors remained in the dungeons of the Dey of Algiers, worked on his rock piles, and felt the bite of his lash. Then one died, and then another, and another. The months of imprisonment became years.

By December 1790, even Jefferson, the secretary of state who regarded standing armies and navies as tools of the devil, was enough moved by the plight of the American captives in Algiers to propose to Congress that ships be assembled for a Mediterranean Squadron. The response of Congress was to generously raise the ransom offer to Algiers and to promise that someday, when the country could afford it, perhaps we would form a fleet. By then, seven of the twenty-three American prisoners were dead.

Meanwhile Congress continued to debate the wisdom of having a navy. Articulate, well-meaning men warned repeatedly that the establishment of an American navy would be the first step down the road to ruin, that we might as well ready a crown for a king. George Washington used all the influence of his presidency to persuade Congress that such was not the case, that a navy was essential, even if it must be a gradual creation, by degrees. "To secure respect to a neutral flag," he told them, "requires a naval force organized and ready to vindicate it from insult or aggression."

Finally, finally, it was done. A bill "To Provide a Naval Armament" was passed on March 27, 1794. It established a U.S. Navy of 2,060 officers and men and authorized the construction of three frigates of 44 guns and three more of 36.

On June 28 Secretary of War Henry Knox, who would supervise the building of the new navy, appointed Joshua Humphreys of Philadelphia to serve as naval constructor of the 44-gun frigate to be built in that city. He already had been hired to do the designs and build the models for all the new 44s and 36s. The work began, and Humphreys dispatched cutting crews to the Georgia coast for his precious live oak.

But as President Washington's second term was nearing its end, U.S. diplomats met peacefully with the Dey of Algiers and signed a treaty with him, calling for the payment of money and gifts by the United States to total $1 million in value and to be followed by annual tribute of twenty-two thousand dollars to ensure that American vessels would enjoy safe passage in the Mediterranean and Atlantic—unless, that is, they were marauded by the corsairs of Tunis or Tripoli, who were not parties to this agreement.

As soon as the treaty was brought back to America, Congress began debating the fate of the six men-of-war under construction. The anti-navy forces prudently had inserted in the 1794 bill a proviso that, in the event peace should be struck with Algiers, Congress would have the right to nullify the plans for the six new warships and scrap all work already completed.

Joshua Humphreys sat in the visitors' gallery of the hot, smoke-filled House chamber in Congress Hall one April day in 1796 and listened to a persuasive new voice call in Europe-accented tones for a cessation of the construction. The speaker was Albert Gallatin, the Swiss-born Pennsylvanian who had come to Congress only the year before. A loyal follower of Jefferson who shared his abhorrence for a professional military service, Gallatin persistently called for government frugality. We can't afford these ships of war, he said over and over, and now we do not need them.

After Gallatin's impassioned address, Captain Barry—also a visitor that day to hear the debate—walked outside for fresh air. On the stairway, he found Joshua Humphreys standing alone, tears coursing down his rough cheeks. Humphreys could not say anything, but only stood and shook his head and cried.

But other voices also were heard in the Congress. Some were Federalists who would fight anything advocated by Jefferson and his followers. Some were men of Jefferson's Democratic-Republican Party who warned solemnly that the peace with Algiers did not diminish the need for a navy. England and France were battling each other in Europe, and each of them was threatening the neutral ships that traded with their enemy. Hadn't French cruisers and privateers, unafraid of interference, captured British ships within American territorial waters? Hadn't the insolent French even the gall to take American ships? Congress erupted into angry debate and catcalls, the Jeffersonians defending the French and the Federalists demanding that the navy be finished so that punitive actions could be taken.

In May 1796 it had been resolved with a compromise. Three of the planned six warships would be cancelled. But the other three—the *United States*, 44, at Philadelphia; the *Constitution*, 44, at Boston; and the *Constellation*, 36, at Baltimore, would be finished as planned.

Humphrey and Barry, among others, gave thanks to God on that day. The new navy would be only half what it would have been. But one arm still could strike a hard blow, and better that one than none. The *United States* herself had been spared. She would survive to carry forth the news that America no longer could be trifled with.

As the men discussed ships and politics, Stephen Decatur, Jr., good-naturedly showed the young boys around the frigate. They were awed by this handsome youth and his seemingly limitless knowledge of ships. And they were awed by the immensity of the *United States* as they walked around it. They had stood high on the frigate's lofty spar deck. Now they were back on the ground again and studying the great depth of the vessel, with its draft of some twenty-three feet.

Decatur tapped the frigate's copper bottom. "You see that tough copper sheathing? Under that is the false keel, and then, between that and the keel itself, is more copper sheathing. The shipworms will not eat of this lady! And the barnacles can't grab the copper as well as they can wood, so she'll always be a fast sailer." He put his hands behind his back like a captain on his quarterdeck. "You can say, boys, that this keel is mine, in a sense. You see, I myself procured the keel pieces for Mr. Humphreys."

They stood now at the edge of the river, near the frigate's larboard bow. Decatur pointed upward. "Look, boys! Look at her figurehead! Ain't she beautiful? She's called *The Goddess of Liberty*, and she was carved by the great artist William Rush. He did the figure for the ship *Ganges*, and it's called *The River God*. When the ship *Ganges* came into the fairway at Calcutta, India, thousands of Hindoos rowed out in boats and worshipped the ship's figure like it were a real god. Come, lads! Onward and upward! I'll show ye the rudder!"

Decatur walked quickly back up the hill toward the frigate's stern, followed closely by Mordecai Noah. Uriah Levy stayed where he was. He looked up at the *Goddess of Liberty* for a moment more and then let his eyes run the entire length of the ship's larboard side.

The five-year-old whispered to the unfinished frigate as if to a new friend, "Some day, I will be your captain. We will sail together to the seven seas and all the lakes in the whole world!" He stood there for a few seconds more and softly patted the copper bottom, as Decatur had done. Then he scampered up the slope to catch the others.

2

Philadelphia, 1797

Rebecca Machado Phillips paused for a moment as she set the places for breakfast and wondered where all her children had gone, where all the years had gone.

The house seemed lonely these days and almost empty, even though at least six sat for each meal and sometimes more if married children and grandchildren stopped by, as often they did. Rachel's little Uriah, for example. It seemed as if he ate more meals here than he did at his own house on Cherry Street. Rachel, in fact, had told her mother that Uriah's father was irritated over the constant absence of his son. And for the perpetually silent, almost phlegmatic Michael Levy to show irritation, there must be ample provocation.

Ah well, Rebecca thought as she carefully placed the dishes and spoons on the big wood kitchen table. Uriah worships his older cousin Mordecai and wants to be with him as much as possible. Her husband, Jonas, in turn, regarded the two grandsons almost as his own sons. He was like a young father again. He took them everywhere with him. Between those constant expeditions all over Philadelphia and Uriah's obsession with watching the ships dock and depart at the Front Street wharves, it was no wonder that his father complained that the five-year-old was never home.

She finished setting the last place. It almost made her cry to see the six settings, lost on the expanse of the big table. She longed again for the days when the kitchen had been filled with the laughing noise of a large family at the morning meal. Phila had been home then, and David and Rachel, of course, and Naph and Benjamin and all the others. Oh, the work had been hard, fearsomely hard, to cook and clean for them all. But her mother had been younger and stronger then and had helped, as had the older children. Would she have the strength now to take care of that great brood of children? She was fifty-three years old, not an old woman. But she had borne twenty-one children, and the years and the rigors had taken their toll. Though her face remained unlined, her hair was gray and her slight figure was stooped.

Mordecai and his sister Judith, four years younger, came into the warm kitchen with its aroma of fresh-baked bread. "Good morning, Grandma," they piped, almost in unison.

"Good morning, children," Rebecca responded. "Sit down at your places and wait quietly. Grandpa and Uncle Zaleg should be here in a moment."

Her eyes softened as they always did when the two little ones came into her kitchen for their breakfast. Poor little orphans. Their father was God knows where, probably dead by now. And their young mother, her own sweet Zipp, also gone. Rebecca busied herself at the breadboard and vigorously sliced the fresh loaves so that the children could not see the tears in her eyes. The worst punishment that God could inflict on a parent was to see a child die. And she had lost so many, most of them in childhood or infancy. *Oh, how it hurts to think of them*, thought Rebecca as she tried somehow to keep her hands busy preparing the food. *Where are you, my babies? Are you safe with God?*

But, she reminded herself as she fought down the tears, *we've also had many blessings. Eleven of our little ones lived to become adults, and now some of them have families of their own. God has taken away, but he also has given us in abundance.*

Listening to the giggling talk of the boy and girl waiting patiently at the kitchen table, she thought again of her daughter Zipporah. She had been named for her grandmother, the aged woman who sat now in the corner bedroom of this house, unsure where she was or what she was expected to do in the soft morning light.

It was in this very kitchen that Zipp had come to her with her two babes in arms and said quietly, "My husband has left. He has run away. The business failure was too much for him. I fear he has lost his mind." Indeed, Manuel Mordecai Noah had departed for places unknown, leaving his wife and two babies dependent on Jonas Phillips for their support.

And less than two years after that, Zipp herself died, far away in Charleston, where she had taken little Mordecai and Judith to visit their great-aunt Esther. Rebecca never would forget standing on the Front Street dock and watching the two wan-faced children slowly walk down the gangplank from the ship that had brought them home to Philadelphia, accompanied by a solemn distant relative who had to be paid for his trouble. From that day on, Mordecai and Judith had lived with their grandparents in the big house on Second Street that now was almost empty of children, except for Zalegman, Rebecca's last-born.

"Rebecca! Where is the meal? It's late, I have to get to shul!"

The impatient voice of her husband jarred Rebecca Phillips from her reverie.

"Yes, Jonas. Sit and I will put the food on the table, then I'll go and get Mother dressed. Where is Zalegman?"

"The last time I saw him he was standing halfway down the stairs with his face buried in a book, muttering something in a foreign tongue." Zalegman, now a strapping youth of eighteen years, was immersed in his studies at the university and was preparing himself to read the law. "Zaleg!" Jonas shouted. "Breakfast is on the table!"

Zalegman walked into the kitchen, murmured a "Good morning," and sat at the table, his eyes focused on his book and his hand running distractedly through his curly hair.

Rebecca put the simple breakfast on the table: milk and water for the children, coffee for the adults, served in a tin cup, and for each person two large slices of fresh bread, heavily covered with butter. Not for the house of Jonas Phillips were the rich breakfast meats and sauces of other well-to-do families. Bread and coffee had been good enough for his father's house in Buseck, Jonas frequently proclaimed, and it would be good enough for his own house in Philadelphia.

For several minutes, the two children and the two men ate silently. Rebecca had gone to dress her old mother and to bring her into the kitchen.

"Well, Mordecai," Jonas suddenly began, "next week you will start your apprenticeship with Hookstra, the carver and gilder, eh?"

"Yes, Papa," Mordecai replied. He would have preferred to continue working as a messenger boy at the federal auditor's office, but that job had been only temporary. Anyhow, Papa had told him that it would be better to apprentice in a good trade than to rely on the government for a job. Politicians always were hiring their friends and firing their enemies, Papa said.

"Good, good," Jonas went on, his mouth full of warm bread and butter. "Meanwhile, enjoy your last few days of idleness. And perhaps study harder for your bar mitzvah. Hazzan Cohen tells me that your last lesson was not so good, eh?"

"Yes, Papa," said Mordecai.

"If you study hard today on your Hebrew readings, tomorrow I'll take you and Uriah to see Congress in session. And perhaps, if the weather is good and I can be spared from the store, we'll also walk up to Shackamaxon to see the elm tree where Penn signed the treaty with the Indians. Would you like that?"

"Yes, Papa. Especially seeing Congress. I like listening to them yell at each other."

"Good. Then it's done, *if* you study hard today like a good boy. And remember, next week is the launching of the *United States*. All of Philadelphia will be there. If Mordecai Manuel Noah wants to be there, he had better have a good lesson with the *hazzan* this week!"

"Yes, Papa."

Rebecca led her mother into the room and to a chair at the table. "Come, Mama. Sit and eat your breakfast."

Zipporah Nunez Ribeiro Machado looked around in bewilderment, as if wondering who these people were. Then she remembered and smiled a greeting at them.

"Good morning, Great-Grandma," said Judith, and Mordecai said it, too, his voice echoing a split second behind his sister's. Jonas threw a sharp look at Zalegman, who, without looking up from his book, softly said, "Good morning, Grandmother."

Jonas said, "Mama, I hope you are well this morning?"

The aged lady, dressed all in black as she was each day, looked at him in surprise, as if trying to recall what he had asked. Then she smiled and nodded again. Her mind slipped quickly into and out of lucidity; one moment she was here in the room with them, the next she was back in Georgia or even in Portugal.

"All right, all right," Jonas proclaimed happily. "A good breakfast, Rebecca, to begin a good day. Now I must get to shul and then to the store. Mordecai, will you be coming to morning service with me?" The boy quickly gulped down the last of his milk and water and stood up to leave with his grandfather.

"Shul, shul!" muttered Grandmother Machado, shaking her head angrily. Her white hair, carefully arranged by her daughter, came loose from its bindings and swung wildly against her head as she glared at Jonas and continued to shake her head, quietly uttering imprecations in Portuguese. "*Tedesco*," she grumbled. "*Tedesco*."

"Jonas," Rebecca gently chastised him, "must you forget? You know how it upsets Mama when the synagogue is called a shul. Please humor her."

"Papa, why does Great-Grandma always look at you and say '*tedesco*'? What does it mean?" asked Mordecai.

Jonas smiled broadly. "It means I am her inferior and she is my better. None of which I deny. '*Tedesco*' is what the Hebrews of Spain and Portugal—the Sephardim—call the rest of the Hebrews . . . especially the Hebrews from Germany, like me. They call us that to remind us, whenever we need reminding, that they are the aristocracy of the Hebrew people and we are the peasants." All this was said in good humor. Jonas accepted without malice the Sephardi view of the Israelite people as a great triangle, with the descendants of ibn Gabirol at the apex and the rest of the Israelites somewhere down below.

Rebecca offered a more careful explanation: "Whenever your grandfather refers to our synagogue as the shul in the German fashion, it upsets your great-grandma very much. After all, Mikveh Israel always has followed the Sephardi *minhag*. It is wrong to call it a 'shul.' If anything, Grandfather should call it the *esnoga*."

"Great-Grandma forgets that we all are children of the same God," said Jonas. "But at her age she is entitled to forget a few things."

"She was the wife of a great *hazzan*, Mordecai," added Rebecca, "and she is very proud of her tradition."

"And she knows that she must live in the house of a *Tedesco*," said Jonas. "She would much prefer that her son-in-law bore the name of Seixas, Lopez, or Cardozo."

"Jonas, don't say that! Mama always liked you."

"True. But she would have liked me more if my line stretched back to Cadiz or Lisbon. Come, Mordecai. God awaits our prayers. Zalegman, I don't suppose you care to join us at the *esnoga*?"

Zalegman looked up from his book. "If I pray today, it better be to Zeus. Only he can help me with this awful Greek."

Jonas and his grandson left the house to walk the short blocks to the synagogue. Rebecca began clearing the breakfast dishes as Zalegman continued to study for the day's examination in Greek.

Zipporah Machado stared at the whitewashed kitchen wall. She was puzzled. Her son-in-law had mentioned Lisbon. Were they going to Lisbon today? She would love to journey to Lisbon today to see the colorful Baixa market with its thousands of stalls.

The old woman reached into the pocket of her black silk dress and pulled out a string of beads. Fingering them in shaking hands, she began whispering her morning prayers. So had her mother taught her to pray, rosary beads in hand, in case the agents of the Inquisition should burst through the door and accuse them of being secret Jews. They lived always in dread of a day when the agents would line them up against a wall and scream at them the dread word, "Marrano!" It was a Spanish word that meant "pig." The Christians of Spain long had used the word to describe Jews who had become conversos, converts to Roman Christianity, but who had remained Jews in secret. They tried so desperately to portray themselves in public as good Christians that it was said of them, "They would eat pork in the streets." And so they were labeled with the word for pig.

The secret Jews of Spain and Portugal never called themselves conversos. To each other, they were *anusim*—the ones who were forced. Many of them left these sunny lands of their forefathers. Somehow they found a way to escape . . . to England, or the Netherlands, or some warm island in the southern ocean that would permit them to stay.

Those left behind, and those who chose to stay, were to find that hell would be a paradise compared to life under the Inquisition. In December 1497, all Jews, including recent refugees from Spain, were given ten months to leave Portugal. At the next spring's Passover, before most of them could leave the country, the forcible baptism of all their children was ordered. Rather than be separated from their children, many parents converted. From that point on, the newly converted were constantly in danger of being accused of "backsliding" to Judaism, tried by the Inquisition, and burned at the stake.

A few converso families managed to survive, and some even prospered, because they were convincing enough in their roles as Christians—and because they were important in some way to the Portuguese crown. Such a family was that of Samuel Nunez Ribeiro, physician to King John V. His forebears also had been physicians to the House of Braganza.

For several generations, the Nunez clan managed to guard their secret Jewishness more closely than their jewels. They hollowed out secret little niches in their furniture to store their siddurim— their Hebrew prayer books—and tallitim, the prayer shawls. On the Sabbath, the family gathered in a darkened room and softly repeated the ages-old service as one stood watch at the window, ever on guard. The girls were taught to say their daily prayers in Hebrew silently, with the rosary beads wrapped tightly in their fingers. Eventually they were no longer able to say the prayers without the guiding beads.

The privileged status of Dr. Nunez and his family ended one Shabbat in 1732 when, somehow, their watchfulness failed. A Dominican friar, his eyes wide with fury, burst into the house with four soldiers and found the family at Sabbath prayers, the telltale Hebrew writings in their hands.

They expected to die after long torture, but neither death nor torture occurred, thanks only to the king who had been saved from death several times by Dr. Nunez. They were jailed for several weeks, but treated with civility. Zipporah then was twenty years old and a virgin. She was certain that she would be violated in jail—the fate of Jewish women at the hands of Portuguese prison guards was well known—but the Nunez women were not harmed.

They were sent home with a stern warning. If they again were found practicing Judaism, their possessions would be confiscated and they would be put to the fire at once. Two agents of the Inquisition henceforth would live with them and would watch them at all times.

Dr. Nunez understood that they had to leave Portugal. Almost immediately he began making plans. There were, among his loyal patients, those whom he could trust and who would help him.

On a golden spring day, an English ship dropped anchor in the Tagus, below the Nunez estate, and the family was smuggled aboard. As soon as the party was on deck, the ship set sail for England. The captain pocketed the thousand gold moidores that had been promised to him, and the Nunez family went below with whatever jewels, gold, and silver they had been able to hide in their clothing. They stayed for a time in London, where they reconnected with other Jews from the Iberian Peninsula. And they went in wonder and awe to the Holy Congregation Shaar Hashamayim, the great Sephardi *esnoga* in London, where they became the first members of their family to worship openly as Jews in almost 250 years.

But Dr. Nunez, once having broken from his homeland, was determined to leave Europe behind him. He wanted a new beginning for his family. Members of the London Sephardi congregation had been working on a project to secure land grants for Jews in the New World colony of Georgia. General James Oglethorpe, who recently had been granted a royal charter for the colony, had said it would be a refuge for debtors and other unfortunates, to populate the colony and protect it from Spanish incursion.

But the elders of the London synagogue were not certain that Jews would be welcome in this refuge. So they acted with daring: they chartered a vessel and found forty members of the congregation who were willing to make the journey, including the Nunez family. That they were allowed to remain and prosper in Georgia was due entirely to the kindly Oglethorpe, who ignored protests both from England and from other settlers in the colony.

Another member of that group of forty who endured the stormy, dangerous Atlantic crossing was a pious young man named David Mendez Machado, also from Portugal. When his older brother was burned to death by the Inquisition, David's zeal to secretly remain a Jew became almost an obsession. Somehow he managed to procure Jewish books and sacred texts and to study them in the cellar of his family's house. His great dream was to be a Jew without fear and then to become a *hazzan* and to chant the service in an *esnoga* in one of the great cities of the world. As he sat in the dark cellar in Lisbon, reading by the light of a single candle, it seemed a foolish dream.

David Machado surprised himself by confiding these precious hopes to Zipporah Nunez during the long talks they began to have aboard the brig taking them to the New World. In Portugal he had known of her only as a daughter of the renowned physician to the king. Now they would sit for hours, their backs pressed against the heaving bulkhead, and tell each other their hopes for the new lives they soon would begin.

In Savannah, a few weeks after they landed, they were married.

Less than four years later, David Mendez Machado was appointed *hazzan* at the Sephardi congregation Shearith Israel in New York City. He would officiate at services in the congregation's new building on Mill Street, the first structure in North America built expressly to serve as a synagogue.

Great-Grandmother Zipporah looked around her and saw that she was sitting in the warm, fragrant kitchen of a large brick house. She put her prayer beads back into the pocket of her dress. Who was this pleasant gray-haired lady speaking to her in such kind tones? *Why—why, this is my daughter Rebecca!* Slowly the haze faded from Zipporah's eyes and she knew again that she was sitting in the Philadelphia house of her son-in-law. He was a *Tedesco*, yes . . . but a good man. She nodded with a smile to Rebecca. Yes, she would have some more coffee. The warm sun felt good as it shone on her through the glass. She would sit here a while longer and think about the old days . . . and about David.

Jonas Phillips was the recipient of respectful greetings from all sides as he strode into the sanctuary of Mikveh Israel, his grandson Mordecai at his side. Jonas was not universally beloved by his fellow Hebrews of Philadelphia, but he possessed their respect. He was admired for his courage, depended upon for his leadership, honored for his patriotism, and feared for his fiery temper and ear-splitting denunciations in a dispute. Even Hazzan Cohen took a moment from his preparations for the morning service to walk over and shake hands with Jonas and wish him a good day, giving him the deference due to one of the *esnoga*'s leading elders and its former *parnass*.

Jonas looked up and caught the eye of his son-in-law Michael Levy and gave him a friendly nod. Michael was a quiet man, and some thought him very shy. He may have been a bit frightened of his bluff, hearty father-in-law, although the older man always had treated him with courtesy. Now that Jonas no longer was *parnass* and did not sit upon the *banco* for the services, he sometimes wished that his silent son-in-law would sit alongside him, but Michael always preferred to sit by himself in a back row. Jonas sighed softly and sat down with a thump on the wooden bench. Mordecai sat next to him and began talking quietly to a young friend in the row behind.

Reaching under the bench, Jonas withdrew a siddur and his tallit. Then he took out the worn leather case enclosing his tefillin. He carefully placed the tallit, the big white prayer shawl, around his shoulders. The siddur rested on his lap while he opened the little case and took out the phylacteries with their leather straps. The familiar scent of the straps and phylactery boxes was sweet in his nostrils. He stood and nodded a greeting to some friends as he tightened and wound the strap the required seven times around his forearm and then wrapped the remainder of the strap around his palm. He did not speak to anyone as he completed the placing and adjusting of the head tefillin, for the law forbade idle conversation or even the uttering of prayers while one was laying tefillin; full attention must be given to the holy task. That task now completed, Jonas opened his siddur to the morning service and waited for the opening prayer.

Each morning, in the last few moments before the *hazzan* walked up to the *tebah* and began chanting the blessings for this new day, Jonas enjoyed looking around him and reflecting on the blessings of being an Israelite in the United States of America. What a miracle it was! To worship freely and openly in this bright little building, right on Cherry Street in the nation's capital. Oh, it *was* a little building right enough—a far cry from the fine, spacious Christian churches that dotted this city of forty thousand souls. But it was good enough for the Hebrews of Philadelphia, who numbered only about one thousand men, women, and children.

On the outside, it was a two-story redbrick building, looking much like the houses on either side. On the inside, it was a beautiful little Sephardi synagogue. The men of the congregation sat on the hard wooden benches on either side of the *tebah* in typical Sephardi fashion. A Sephardi Hebrew from London or Amsterdam would feel at home here, as would any Hebrew who still remembered the old congregations in Spain or Portugal. Above, on three sides of the building, was the women's gallery, occupied on this morning by a half-dozen sleepy-eyed old women.

These people called the synagogue the *esnoga*, instead of the shul, as he and his people always had done. And the way they pronounced the Holy Tongue! The popping of the Sephardi "t" sound whenever there should rightfully be a good hissing "s" was an affront to him. It took him a long time to get used to people greeting him with "Shabbat shalom" instead of "Good Shabbos!" on a Sabbath morning.

When Jonas came to the United States and found that the synagogues in New York and Philadelphia and Charles Town all followed the Sephardi ways, he was disappointed but accepted the fact. He worshipped in the new style that gradually became familiar to him. He became accustomed to the Sephardi ways and even picked up a few words of Ladino, the Spanish-Jewish dialect. His mother-in-law did not like to hear it, however, for her people had considered it beneath their standing to use it. They would speak only English or Portuguese.

The Sephardim long since had been outnumbered in the larger American cities by newer Hebrew arrivals from other parts of Europe—Ashkenazim, as they were called. As the number of newcomers from Central and Western Europe increased in Philadelphia, the Ashkenazic Jews wanted a shul where they could hold their own Shabbos and daily services and hear a familiar German or Yiddish phrase. So in 1795 they formed their German Hebrew Society and began holding services in the Ashkenazic fashion.

The German Hebrew Society invited Jonas Phillips to become a member, but he declined. He had been a member of Mikveh Israel for twenty-three years, almost as long as the old synagogue had had its name. And he was highly honored here. On the first day of Rosh Hashanah, he was called to chant the haftarah. And every Yom Kippur, with the small sanctuary packed to the very windows, Jonas Phillips, as bearer of the name Jonah, had the honor of reading the book of Jonah in the afternoon service. No, this was the place for him, this old Busecker, in the *esnoga* of the Sephardim.

Hazzan Cohen walked to the *tebah* to begin the service. When the hourlong service was completed, Jonas would walk to his store for a long day of work. But that was later. Now, as the *hazzan's* ancient chant echoed through the *esnoga*, Jonas Phillips prepared single-mindedly to pray to his God.

3

The Jerusee, *1802*

Jonas Phillips was startled into wakefulness by a noise somewhere out in the darkness beyond the flickering glow of the candle on his table. He had been sitting alone in his store, going over his account books as the twilight faded into night. He had felt himself become weary and slipped into a light doze.

When he heard the noise, Jonas jerked up in his chair, his eyes suddenly wide. The mist in his head cleared, and he knew where he was and realized that he had heard a rap on the store's locked front door. He went to see who was there.

His grandson, Uriah Levy, stood at the door, shivering in the spring dampness.

"Well, Uriah, what brings you out on this night? After that fine birthday supper, I thought you would be hard asleep by this hour. Or, now that you're ten years, do you plan to roam the streets at night?"

The boy's face bore a look of great seriousness. "Papa, I must talk with you. It's very important. Can you talk with me now?"

The jesting tone left Jonas's voice. *Perhaps something is wrong.*

"Come in, lad. Take the chair there, alongside my table."

Uriah sat in the chair, rubbing his palms together to return some warmth to his chilled hands. His grandfather took the moment to study the boy in the candle's light. Uriah was small for his age, but his shoulders were square and hinted of a husky build to come. His hair was dark and curly, and his eyes also were dark and intense. Since he had learned his first words, Uriah had been a blunt, direct child, speaking what he had to speak in a forceful way, devoid of shyness. Now, as Uriah sat beside his grandfather's worktable in an otherwise dark store, his face was set and grim.

"Papa," he said, "I want to go to sea."

Jonas nodded, still unsure of his ground. "Yes, I know that. I have seen your interest. But when you are grown, you might—"

The boy shook his head impatiently. "No, Papa. I mean *now*. I want to go to sea *now*."

Jonas did not reply for a moment. He must be careful. Put a halter too quickly on an unbroken colt and it bolts and runs. Care must be taken.

He spoke softly and calmly. "Uriah, what has brought you here? What has happened? Is there trouble at home?"

"No, Papa, no. Nothing like that. I have a chance to go to sea at last. It's what I've dreamed of for many years. But I couldn't go without talking to you about it."

"So. At ten years of age—it seems like only yesterday that you were just nine—your dream of so many years is coming true? What is this big chance?"

"Do you know the *New Jerusalem*, Papa? It is a trim little snow, Captain James Wilkins."

Jonas tried to lighten the leaden feeling in his stomach. "A 'snow'? What is a 'snow'? A ship that sails only in cold weather?"

Uriah did not smile. "No, Papa. A snow is a kind of brig."

Jonas didn't understand any of this, but he said, "I see." He paused and then went on: "I have met this Captain Wilkins. He has been here in the store. He seems an honorable man. His ship is a coaster, I believe."

"Yes, Papa. Its home port is Savannah, and it sails to Boston and back, with calls here and New York and other ports as well. They are short of crew, Papa, and they are hiring in Philadelphia and they need a cabin boy."

Now Jonas understood. "A cabin boy. Ach, now I see." He stopped, gathering his forces, trying to find some words that might dissuade this child from turning to the cold, hard life of the sea. Oh, what would this do to his poor daughter Rachel?

"I talked with Captain Wilkins today, Papa. And he is willing to take me on. He said that he went to sea at ten years also, and he has never regretted it. I will never regret it, Papa, I know."

"Have you talked with your parents about this?"

"Oh no, Papa, no. You know they would never agree. I don't want to hurt them, but I have to do it. I'll just leave them a note when I go."

"And how soon will that be?"

"The *New Jerusalem* sails at first light, Papa. If I want the berth, the captain says I must be aboard by no later than four o'clock this morning."

"So soon?" Jonas felt desperate; he felt as if he would weep. "Why do you come to me now, Uriah? What can I tell you?"

Uriah had been speaking in fast bursts, like a drummer trying to close a sale. Now he sat silent, as if trying to find an answer. At last he spoke: "I don't know what you can tell me, Papa. But I hope you will give me your blessing. And . . . and I just couldn't leave without telling you good-bye. I know you won't tell my secret. I *know* you won't." And again he fixed Jonas with that piercing, dark stare.

"How long before the ship returns to Philadelphia? Did Captain Wilkins tell you that?"

"The voyage is two years, Papa."

"Two years! *Mein Gott!*"

"I'll be home in plenty of time to prepare for my bar mitzvah, so you don't need to worry about that. And I'm taking my Hebrew book with me so I can practice my reading. And Captain Wilkins said that, if I find out the life of the sea is not for me, he'll put me ashore at the next port of call and send me back home on a stage. But I know that won't happen."

Jonas studied his grandson's face and tried to remember how he looked as a babe in arms. He took a deep breath and continued, "Uriah, I want you to make me a solemn promise. Promise me that you always will remain a Hebrew. I beg you to swear that to me now and never to forget that you have taken this oath. Will you do this?"

Uriah's eyebrows rose in surprise at the request. "Of course, Papa. Of course I'll remain a Hebrew. What else would I be?"

Jonas impatiently shook his head. "Oh, that is easy enough to say. Easy enough when you're ten years old. But when you are older, there will be many temptations. So many of our Israelites in America are leaving us . . . marrying out or accepting Christianity or refusing any religion and proclaiming themselves to be atheists."

Uriah listened politely, but the warnings had little meaning for him. His mind was full of sails and rigging and the glorious life of a cabin boy.

Jonas's voice took on new urgency, rasping intensely, "Swear to me, Uriah, swear to me that you will never forsake the faith of our fathers. Swear it!"

"I swear it, Papa. And I never will break my oath to you."

Jonas sat now, his head down, as if drained of spirit and will. Finally he looked up again and softly said, "There is nothing I can say to stop you? You could not wait a few years?"

Uriah's answer also was quiet, but very firm. "No, Papa. I can't wait. They don't want twenty-year-old cabin boys. They want them at my age so they can teach them to be good seamen. And that is what I want to be most of all. A good seaman."

Jonas sighed. Suddenly he felt very old and tired. "A good seaman, eh? Like your heroes Truxton and John Paul Jones, I suppose. Ach! Uriah, it is a hard life and a lonely one. And it is not easy for a Hebrew out there, separated from his people. You will encounter men who—ach, never mind. A good seaman." He shook his head. "Your father looks ahead to the time when you will learn his trade and take his place in the shop as my sons now are taking my place here. What will he say? What will he think?"

Uriah leaned forward in his chair, his dark eyes burning across the candle's glow at his grandfather, his voice again assuming the insistent drummer's pitch. "I have five brothers now, Papa," he answered confidently, "and surely that should be enough help for my father in the shop. I have never wanted anything but the sea. And now is my chance!"

Jonas nodded and said the words that must be said: "And if, somehow, this chance is denied to you—if we tie you to your bed or something like that—you will find another chance a week from now or a month from now, won't you?"

"Yes, Papa, I will," Uriah softly answered. "I *have* to do it."

There was a long silence. The mournful cry of an oyster vendor could be heard out in the street and then the clopping of horse hooves as a carriage rushed past through the night.

Jonas sighed again. "Tell me one thing," he said. "Does a cabin boy have to climb all the way to the top of those masts like all the other *meshuganehs* do?"

The boy smiled for the first time, recognizing the Yiddish word for crazy people. "I don't know, Papa. I hope so. But mostly I think a cabin boy carries messages and cleans the captain's cabin and things like that. I'll soon find out."

Jonas stood up and walked slowly around the table. The boy was conscious, really for the first time, of how old his grandfather was and also noticed that he limped slightly as he walked.

"Will you do one last thing for me before you go?" Jonas asked. "Will you stand up and let me give you a big hug? I know one doesn't hug an able seaman, but with a cabin boy perhaps it would be all right?"

The boy stood up, and his grandfather clasped him in his arms and held him tightly for a long time. How barren his walks around the city would be without this bright, curious child at his side! How still would be the afternoons without the blunt, well-formed questions about history and politics and the nation's leaders. Among all his children and his burgeoning band of grandchildren, how empty would be his days without this special one.

"Papa, do one thing for me?" Uriah had stepped back and turned his face up to his grandfather's.

"Yes?"

"Tell my mother that I love her and I am sorry for the hurt. I am very sorry for the hurt."

He backed another step into the darkness of the room and then he was gone, his absence announced only by the soft closing of the outer door and the gentle tinkling of the bell.

Jonas sat down again and remained sitting for a long while, even after the candle had guttered and then gone out. Finally he stood up, put on his tricornered hat, and walked out of the store, carefully locking the door behind him.

"I had better get about my business," he said to himself. "I must find this Captain Wilkins and have some clear understandings with him. Only after that will I be able to have any sleep this night." And then he strode purposefully down the dark street toward the pungent smell of the docks and the river.

Uriah Phillips Levy, newly inscribed on the vessel's station bill as "Cabin Boy and Assistant Cook," stood at the taffrail of the *New Jerusalem* and looked back up the Delaware River at the receding buildings of his home city. The sun hung low over the New Jersey flats and bathed the redbrick buildings in a fresh, warm light.

In one of those buildings, his mother probably was rising to begin cooking the family's breakfast. Soon she would call everyone in to eat; his absence would be noticed and the note on his pillow would be found. His chin trembled as he thought of their alarm and anger.

Behind him, the main topsail popped as it caught a dawn freshet of air. His stomach again felt sick, as it had when the men of the

New Jerusalem cast off the lines in the blackness just before sun-up and the ship was taken by the current and began to move out into the river. He knew then that this was no game of make-believe. He was leaving for the sea and he wasn't sure he wanted to go. He wasn't sure *now*, that is, when hot rivers raced through his stomach, though scarcely a half-hour before he had been shaking with excitement and joy.

"No good lookin' back, lad! No good to look back on your first voyage! Look for'ard, look downriver to see what's ahead." It was a big, booming voice, worthy of a commodore at least, but it came from a husky, open-faced, sandy-haired young tree of fifteen years—newly minted ordinary seaman James Wilkins, Jr. It was this exuberant son of the ship's captain whom Uriah had succeeded as cabin boy, for young Wilkins had completed his own apprenticeship and now was ready to assume the duties and responsibilities of a sailor. It was he who had shown Uriah to his bunk when the new boy first came aboard and he who would be his mentor and guide on this passage.

"Come along, 'Riah," boomed Jamie Wilkins. "I'll show ye round the ship, now that there's light enough to see. She's an honest ship, the old *Jerusee*, a worthy sailer and at her best when beatin' to windward and that, says the cap, is the best test of any vessel. And if the cap says it, it must be the gospel truth!"

Jamie most often referred to his father as "the cap," though sometimes he called him "the old man," as did the other sailors. He did not, however, speak of him as "the Giant." The other men on the ship did so whenever they were awed by something the captain had said or done. He stood six and a half feet high and wore a long, red beard. He reminded Uriah of the pictures of Moses that he had seen in books at Mikveh Israel. Young Jamie was nigh onto six feet tall himself and gave promise of growing to his father's height when he was a full man. The other sailors spoke of him as "the little giant," and Jamie took it as a compliment.

"Here now, Doctor, here's your new helper." They approached

the ship's galley just abaft the forecastle, and Jamie addressed a small, totally bald black man who smiled as he worked and showed a shiny gold tooth in the middle of his mouth. "Doctor, meet Uriah Levy, the new cabin boy. 'Riah, this is the Doctor, who feeds us well and keeps us happy and plump."

"Are you really a doctor?" asked Uriah as he shook hands with the black man. The cook and Jamie howled with laughter.

"Ships' cooks have been called 'Doctor' ever since there have been ships' cooks, I guess," explained Jamie. "Don't know why. Suppose because without the cook, the men would starve and be in fierce need of a doctor."

"You know how to cook, boy?" asked the Doctor.

Uriah gulped. "No, sir. But I made coffee once for my grandma and everybody said it was right good. I—"

"No matter," interrupted the Doctor. "I teach you. Soon you be fine cook. Almost good as me. You better be. If not cook good, sailors throw you over the side. Hee, hee, hee!"

"Don't pay him no mind," Jamie laughed, just as Uriah felt a stab of fear in his chest. "He does all the cooking. You haul water for him, that's all, and bring meat up from the barrels in the hold, and maybe pound biscuit for the 'scouse. That's all the cooking you have to do. You'll—"

"This the new jay?"

They all turned at the sound of the high, squeaky voice and saw standing before them a tiny, incredibly skinny old man with spiky gray hair darting out from his head at crazy angles. He stood planted to the deck, arms akimbo and feet spread wide, appraising Uriah, who was almost as tall as the old man, with a fearsome look.

"Sails!" shouted Jamie. "Didn't know you were on deck. Meet Uriah Levy, the ship's new boy. 'Riah, give a howdy to old Sails, who's gonna larn you the ship and the sailor's life. Like he larned me."

Uriah didn't know whether to shake hands or not, but decided to wait until the little man put out a hand. Sails, though, didn't move and kept his wrists planted firmly on his scrawny hips.

"Levy? Levy?" rasped the old man. "What kind of name be that?" He stared hard into the boy's eyes. "You ain't be a Finn, be ye?" he demanded, a touch of fear creeping into his voice. "I can see ye ain't swivel-eyed, and that's to the good, but if ye be a Finn, then ye be a Jonah and I don't want to sail with ye."

Uriah stared openmouthed, not knowing what to say. He didn't know what a Finn was. It was something on a fish, he thought. Was he a Finn?

Jamie was laughing uproariously. "Sails, heave to and relax. He ain't no Finn. He be a Jew."

"A Jew?" Sails looked at the boy with renewed interest. "I ain't never seen a Jew sailor. Wonder if a Jew is a Jonah." He shook his head and then suddenly straightened as he remembered his task. "Oh, the cap'n wants to see the new boy. In his cabin."

"Whyn't you say so, Sails?" grumbled Jamie. "We stand here blatherin' and the cap'll have my hide for not a-comin' on the run. Let's go, 'Riah! The cap don't like to be kept waitin'."

As they started to walk aft, Jamie grabbed Uriah's arm and guided him over to the port side of the deck.

"Always walk aft along the leeward side of the deck," he said.

"Why?"

"I don't know. That's just the way it's done. Lots of things on a ship you do because it's always been done that way. But if you want to get along, you do it just the same way."

As they made their way to the captain's cabin, Jamie explained that old Sails was the ship's sailmaker. In addition to keeping the sails in good order and repair, he handled all the regular duties of a seaman on the ship's larboard watch. And, as tradition dictated, the sailmaker was responsible for the training of the ship's boys, of which Uriah now was the latest and only one. He was a good teacher, Jamie affirmed, and not a cruel one, but he demanded hard work and obedience. And there was no better able seaman on the *New Jerusalem* than Sails, who had shipped with Jamie's father for many years.

"What's his name?" Uriah asked. "Past 'Sails,' I mean."

Jamie laughed. "Ya know, I never thought to ask him. Just 'Sails.' That's what he's always been."

They had reached the door of the cabin after hastily descending the lee gangway. Jamie loudly knocked on the door. A voice inside shouted "Come!" and they entered.

Captain James Wilkins sat at a small table to the side of the cabin and studied his ship's cargo list. There was something still not quite right about the loading plan. The distribution of the cargo in the hold would affect the vessel's speed through the water and possibly even its safety. It must be right.

The captain's legs were so long that, even with his feet firmly anchored to the floor, his knees rose high in front of him. A bushy red beard erupted from his face and spread down his chest. Above the beard he was clean-shaven and looked somehow like a boy peering across the top of a thick hedge. When finally he looked up and spoke, his voice was amazingly deep—much deeper than Uriah remembered from his previous interview with the captain. It sounded to Uriah like the vibrant bass tones of the steam organ he had heard played in Philadelphia.

"Wilkins," said the captain to his son, "when I direct you to come to my cabin, I expect you not to dawdle amid ship."

"Yes, sir," said Jamie, licking his lips. "We—we, uh . . ." He thought better of it. "Yes, sir. Sorry."

"That'll be all, Wilkins. Return to your duties on deck." Jamie nodded and left the cabin.

The captain looked for the first time at Uriah, who stood before the table and felt his entire body shake with fear. "Sit down, Levy," the captain said. "We will talk."

Uriah took a chair near the captain's table.

"Gear all stowed? Find your bunk?"

"Yes, sir," answered Uriah in a quavery voice. "Your son . . . uh, that is—Jamie Wilkins showed me where I sleep."

"Good, good." The captain did not speak for a moment and studied the boy in front of him. His eyes softened as he remembered the little lad coming aboard at the Philly wharf and pleading to be taken on as cabin boy.

"Well, me lad, we have covered some miles and put some water under our stern since our first meeting in Philly, eh?"

Uriah, not knowing what to say, simply nodded. His heart pounded. His knees felt weak as jelly. He thought for a moment, unaccountably, of his mother, and his chin trembled. Then the captain began to speak again, and Uriah gave him full attention. Thoughts of home vanished.

"Well, ye have your wish and ye are now cabin boy aboard the *New Jerusalem*. She's a good ship for a coaster, and our crew is treated well, if they do their jobs, and fed well. 'Tis a good ship on which to learn. A boy on my ship, Mr. Levy, is not merely a scullery maid and a pan washer, though there is some o' that. A boy on my ship is an apprentice sailor, and he learns the tricks o' the trade. You'll be crumb bosun for the cook and help him. 'Twill teach you respect for the food you eat at sea. Lubbers turn up their noses at our ship's food. That's cause they don' know anything 'bout it. After helpin' the ship's cook, *you'll* know. And you'll be glad for what you get to eat. When someone among the crew is sick, you'll be the loblolly boy and bring him food to his bunk and help him make his way to the head. And clean up his slop, if necessary. That'll teach you humbleness and something of the hardness of the sea life.

"And, meanwhile, if the cook don't need you, you'll stand watch with the larboard watch under the first mate, Peder Konopka, and with ol' Sails, who will teach you everything there is to learn. And when we tack or wear ship, you'll help the cook work the foresheet. Do ye know what is a foresheet, lad?"

"No, sir," answered Uriah.

"Ye soon will. And after a while, when ye get your footing, you'll go aloft and Sails will teach you to hand and reef. You'll learn to splice and reeve, to draw and knot yarn, to slush masts and work the log reel, and to loose and furl the light sails. Some day we'll teach ye to steer. 'Course now," and the voice took on a darker tone, "it ain't all exciting things like those. You'll also pull your weight at the windlass when we weigh anchor and you'll holystone the deck like any other sailor. And of course, the most important duty of all"—he smiled for the first time since Uriah had met him—"ye will make up my berth each morning and sweep my cabin. You wouldn't be much of a cabin boy without doing that, eh? Eh, lad?" And he laughed aloud, his booming roar echoing across the small cabin.

Uriah had known for a certainty that he would not sleep—that he *could* not sleep—in this foul compartment in the forecastle, crammed with narrow bunks and ditty bags and reeking with the smell of strange bodies. He had climbed into his bunk and lain there, cowered really, and thought of his warm home and his brothers and sisters. He whimpered softly. Within moments, snores rendered the air in the forecastle. The ship was nearing the Delaware's mouth and she pitched and rolled with the tide. His stomach began to churn. His eyes felt hot and sleepless. Above the snoring, loud and clear, a long fart rose and then fell across the dank cabin, sounding almost like a musical instrument. The boy was positive that he never could sleep in this stinking room, among unknown, hard men. He wondered if someone his age could exist for two years without sleep. He wondered if Jamie was asleep. The splashing of the water against the ship's planking seemed to surround him like a soft blanket. Then . . .

A piercing, metallic voice tore through the predawn darkness: "Larbowlins, do ye hear the news? Rise and shine! Up, me hearties, and face the day! 'Tis the mornin' watch, and God is waitin' to see your shiny faces!"

Around the cabin, dark figures began slowly to rise from their bunks, moaning and groaning and cursing those who had disturbed them. Meanwhile, other derisive voices of the starboard watch came hurling down from the deck:

"Come, me hearties! The cap'n hisself is waitin' to serve you a nice hot breakfast on the quarterdeck!"

"You've slept enough, you lazy bastards! Get up here and relieve us starbowlin angels!"

Uriah pulled on his clothes, groping for them in the blackness. He realized that somehow, despite all, he had slept. He had survived his first night at sea, even if it had been passed running down the

Delaware River. Now his first full day as a sailor was at hand.

"Uriah! Be ye dressed?" It was Jamie's voice. "C'mon then. We must be on deck within four minutes or the mate will start screamin' like a banshee."

A moment later, they stood shivering on the deck. Uriah saw the faint, low outline of land off the port beam. The sky ahead was just beginning to lighten.

"Awright, larbowlins, heed my words!"

Jamie whispered to Uriah, "That's Konopka, the mate. He's all right."

Konopka strode about in front of his men, slapping his arms against his sides for warmth. "The cap'n says the ship has carried away a coat of Philadelphia dust and he wants it to shine. So let's set to with a will this morning and make 'er gleam. Have at it!"

Within seconds, the head pump was rigged and the mate manned it, washing down the decks with the thick water of Delaware Bay. Meanwhile, the other men of the watch—Jamie and Uriah among them—picked up brooms and old pieces of sail and began a careful scrubbing of the entire expanse of deck. Back and forth they went, sluicing the grime off the planks. As they did, old Sails walked among them, scattering sand across the deck from a rusty, battered bucket.

"All right, enough!" screamed Konopka. "Bring out the stones!"

In another minute, the seamen, working in two-man teams, were energetically swinging the holystones across the wet, sanded deck. The large, soft, flat-bottomed stones were guided by a rope at either end and swung back and forth, polishing the deck and cleaning it at the same time. Uriah and Jamie, meanwhile, had taken possession of smaller stones called "prayerbooks" and used them to get into the crevices and corners where the holystones could not go. The work continued for what seemed to Uriah like endless hours. It was fully light by now.

Finally Konopka's voice bellowed again: "Belay!" The sailors began picking up the holystones and prayerbooks and returning them to the locker from whence they had come. The head pump was rigged again and another stream of water shot across the deck, rushing the sand through the scuppers and out into the bay.

When the pump stopped, swabs were used to dry the deck, and after the mate had deemed the surface to be acceptable, the hoelike devices that were called "squilgees" were brought out and used to push the last drops of water off the deck.

The *New Jerusalem* did indeed gleam, as her captain had demanded.

"How often is this done on a ship?" asked Uriah, his back aching and his legs near exhaustion from all the bending and crawling.

"How often?" Jamie laughed. "How often you say? You think, maybe, it is done only on the cap'n's birthday or maybe once every other month? No, me lad, we do this each and every mornin' of our lives."

Uriah was incredulous. "Every day? Every single day, the ship is cleaned like this?"

Jamie nodded vigorously. "Every solitary day. The cap always says that any ship that ain't holystoned each dawn is a sad-lookin' ship. 'Course, our watch don't have the job every day. Tomorrow it'll be the starbowlins' turn. And we'll have the joy of shoutin' pretty things down at 'em from the deck at eight bells o' the graveyard watch to let 'em know it's time to rise and shine. Jest like they did to us this mornin'. It's one of the great joys of the sailor's life, rousting that other watch out of their nice warm beds. 'Specially in the middle of winter when they's two inches of snow on the deck and more fallin'. Ah, that's real fun!"

"So there ye be, boy!" It was Doctor, the cook. "Come with me to the galley—'tis time for your first lesson in cooking at sea."

Uriah went forward with him to the galley, and they stopped in front of the two huge copper kettles in which the ship's meals were cooked.

"The lesson for today," said the Doctor, a huge smile on his face, "is that we cannot boil coffee for breakfast until those coppers are nice and shiny and clean. And that is your job."

The boy was puzzled. "But . . . but—how do you clean them? They're so big!"

"The first thing you do is climb inside one of them. Here, I'll give you a boost."

When Uriah was inside the cauldron, the top of which came about to his chest, the cook handed him some small pieces of soapstone. He was told to rub the inside of the kettle until the grease from last evening's supper was gone and the surface shone just like the deck of the ship. Uriah sighed softly once and then got to work, rubbing the stone up and down against the cauldron walls.

Later, Uriah sat with Jamie and ate his breakfast at the rough table near the crew's sleeping bunks. He ate with good appetite although the food was crude, simple fare: a chunk of stale bread—the last of the fresh bread brought aboard in Philly—some strange-tasting butter, cold salt beef left over from the last meal of the previous day, and hot black coffee. The beef was fat and greasy, but tender, and Uriah quickly devoured it. Jamie smiled as he saw the younger boy wipe up the last streaks of meat juice with his bread.

"The sea air and the hard work do somethin' for the appetite on board, eh, 'Riah?"

Uriah, his mouth full of sodden bread, grunted in assent. He took a big swig of the coffee then and almost choked. It was not only still very hot, but it had an acrid, overpoweringly bitter taste. Uriah somehow downed the mouthful and then retched.

"God," he gasped. "I have never tasted coffee like that before! What makes it taste that way? It 'most tore my tongue off!"

Jamie cackled with delight. "Strong men need strong coffee," he said. "It's probably the onions you're tastin'. Cap says they give the Doctor's coffee real character. They put raw onions in the coffee to help prevent scurvy. That's what ol' Cap'n Cook of England used to feed his sailors, and they never sickened at all."

Uriah shrugged. "Well, if the scurvy don't kill you, I reckon the coffee will." He held his breath and took another, smaller sip.

Jamie stretched luxuriously, his stomach pleasantly full. "Well, we're off watch for four hours now. Me for the bunk again and some more sleep. And as for you, me young laddie, time for you to get to the cabin and make the cap's bunk and sweep the place out real good. Oh, and be sure not to touch the charts or other papers on Cap's table. He don't like for nobody to touch his papers. When you're done with that, you can come below and go back to sleep if you like, or do whatever strikes your fancy. We're not on deck again 'til meridian and then it's all hands until dark. Some vessels go watch and watch all twenty-four hours, ye know, which means four hours on, four hours below all the time—save for the dog watches, o' course. But on this ship, we have all hands from meridian to dark."

Uriah stood up slowly. His entire body ached. "I feel like I've been working for twenty-four hours already," he said.

"I know," nodded Jamie. "But you'll get used to it. It'll make a man o' ye in no time, I promise. You'll be a man before your time . . . and a sailorman, at that."

Uriah sat with his back to the starboard bulwark and breathed deeply of the cool afternoon air. The *Jerusee*—a week out of Philadelphia now—was thrashing her way southward with all sails set and the wind off her port quarter. A few miles off the starboard beam was a low coastline that Jamie told him was Carolina. There was a long swell beneath them, and the ship rose and fell with a gentle regularity. It was lulling to the boy and sleep provoking, and he found it increasingly difficult to keep his mind on his Hebrew reading. He took another deep breath and forced his attention back to the worn book in his hands and to the biblical excerpts that he had read in their ancient script hundreds of times.

After the first word of each phrase, he could recite the rest with his eyes closed, so familiar had they become to him. But he knew that two years away from Hazzan Cohen and his Hebrew lessons would scrape all memory of the phrases from his mind. He had vowed before he left home to take his Hebrew book with him and to go over his readings at least once a week.

It was Sunday afternoon, and the ship's crew was at leisure, subject to call only if they were needed at stations for tacking or wearing ship or some other duty requiring their arms and legs. Some of the sailors were, like him, enjoying the fresh air and sun on the foredeck. Some were sewing their clothes—"Jewing" they called it, and Uriah reddened when he first heard it said. A couple of the men read books, and another was carving on a piece of wood with a long, dangerous-looking knife. Two others were stretched out on the deck and loudly snoring.

Along the deck, striding in a no-nonsense way with incredibly long legs flinging forward, came the captain taking his constitutional. His face was set in that peculiar, expressionless, almost glassy-eyed mode that Jamie referred to as "Cap's quarterdeck face." It was the face of a commander, the master of a ship—intense, concentrated, stern, yet not angry or cruel.

Captain Wilkins pounded along the deck planks, his huge feet making slapping sounds as he briskly made his way forward. He reached the bow, turned in almost military fashion, and headed aft once again. The men lounging along the rail looked up at him as he passed and nodded in respect. He did not acknowledge their greeting.

As he strode along the weather side of the deck, the captain suddenly glanced across and saw Uriah sitting with his book. He broke stride, angled over to the leeward deck, and stopped in front of the boy.

"Well, Mr. Levy," he said. "You have been to sea for a week now. You are getting along, I presume?"

Uriah didn't know whether to stand, but to be safe he quickly rose and touched his hand to his cap as he had seen the sailors do when the captain addressed them. "Yes, Captain, thank you."

Wilkins nodded. "The cook tells me you are a willing worker and you follow his instructions and do not talk back. Good, good. Keep it up and you'll be all right. Work hard and follow orders. That's all it takes to be a good seaman. You'll see, you'll see."

Was he expected to respond? Uriah nodded, touched his cap once again, and stood mute.

Captain Wilkins seemed about to resume his walk when he

glanced down at the book in the boy's hand and noticed the strange printed characters. Without a word he gently took the book from Uriah and stared at it, a puzzled look on his face.

"What in tarnation language is this?" he asked.

"It—it is Hebrew, sir," responded Uriah, wondering if he had committed some error by bring aboard ship a book not in English.

The captain's eyes widened. "Hebrew, is it?" he said, his mouth pursing in surprise. "So this is what Hebrew looks like. The language of the Bible. I have never seen Hebrew writing before." He pulled the book up closer to his face and studied it closely, almost suspiciously. "No . . . no, I cannot make out even a word. It bears no resemblance to English a'tall. You read this Hebrew language, do you?"

"Well, sir, I—I more study it than I read it. I don't know what all the words mean. But I aim to keep practicing whenever I can so's I don't forget how to read it. That way, when I get home—"

"I see," interrupted the captain. "A worthy aim. Be sure you don't forget to study." He clasped his hands behind him and looked out across the ocean for a moment or two, as if inspecting the Carolina beaches. "You see, I am a Bible-reading man. I have my Bible in the cabin and I read it often, and most certainly on Sundays. Just this morning, I was reading in the book of Lamentations: 'What shall I liken to thee, O daughter of Jerusalem? What shall I equal to thee, that I may comfort thee, O virgin daughter of Zion? For thy breach is great like the sea and who can heal thee?'" He paused for a moment and smiled slightly. "'For thy breach is great like the sea'; I rather liked that. Often times, I have wondered what my Bible would sound like in its Hebrew voice. What would be the sounds of that ancient tongue?" He paused again, as if thinking upon a decision. "Would you perhaps be willing to visit me in the cabin of a Sunday and read to me of the Bible in your Hebrew tongue? It would be of great interest to me."

Uriah was taken by surprise. He felt himself blushing. "I . . . I would be happy to, sir. Though my Hebrew instruction book contains only little bits of the Bible here and there. And I fear I don't read as well as you may think I do."

The captain held up a huge hand. "'Tis good enough, I warrant, for me to get a taste of the sound and rhythm. I would be obliged. Now, good day, Mr. Levy, and please resume your studying." With that, his arms swung out again and he resumed his thumping pace down the length of the shining deck.

The water already was bubbling in the cauldrons as Uriah picked up great chunks of salt meat, fresh from the harness cask, and lifted them gently over the top and then down into the water to boil. The meat had a slightly different color than usual, and he detected an unusual smell to it.

"What sort of meat is this?" he asked the cook.

"Salt pork, of course," answered the Doctor. "What you think? We not serve salt beef all the time. Other days we serve salt pork. Dee-licious!"

Uriah's face fell. "But I can't eat it."

The cook was incredulous. "What you mean, you can't eat it? Why not? My salt pork good as any ship. Better than most. Why you can't eat my salt pork?"

"Because I am a Hebrew," the boy said quietly. "And Hebrews are not allowed to eat pork. Any kind of pork."

"Who not allow? The captain? He don't care. He eat it hisself and like it. He even tol' me so."

"No, not the captain. God. He told the Hebrews not to eat pork. So I can't eat it."

The cook shook his head in dismay, drops of sweat flying off his glistening brow. "Hebrews is Jews, right? You Jews sure unlucky people. Not eat pork, you miss lots of good eatin'." A new thought struck him and he smiled, his gold tooth brilliant in the sun. "Anyways, who's to know? I pray, you pray—okay, we don't tell God you eat pork. Maybe he don't know. Then it be okay. Okay?"

Uriah sadly shook his head.

"Okay," sighed the cook. "No pork for you. Pity. Well, if you no tell anybody, maybe I give you extra potato in your kid and even extra biscuit. Then you fill your belly even without the meat. Okay?"

A half-hour later, Uriah was helping the cook pass out the pork to the dinner-bound crew. The sailors filed slowly past the galley, kids in hand, to receive their portions. Uriah was glad now that he had held to his vow not to eat any forbidden food because the pork had a grayish color and a slightly rancid smell.

The second mate, Murray, a fleshy, buck-toothed man with a perennially sour expression and a viper tongue, picked up his portion of meat and held it up as if to inspect it, the juices dripping through his fingers and down to the deck.

"C'mon, c'mon!" the cook shouted. "Pass on along. They's hungry men behind you and you keepin' 'em from their dinner. Pass on along!"

"Do ye hear it, boy? Yet do ye hear?" Sails's voice took on a note of impatience, a teacher pushing hard on a slow pupil.

"I'm *trying*, Sails," the boy said, a quiver in his voice. "All I can hear is the sea."

Uriah strained so hard to hear the vagrant sound that his head ached. All was silent to him, however, except for the wash of water against the *Jerusee*'s bow.

Sails took his arm, and they moved to another position on the deck, just aft the foremast. It was a sunny afternoon, and a strong, cold wind blew from the northeast. "Here," Sails said. "Mebbe you'll hear it over here. Lissen with both ears this time."

The tumult of water creaming past the bow subsided just a trifle as the wind backed slightly. And in that instant, Uriah heard—in the very corner of the universe of sound around him—a remote tinkling, gentle like a tiny harp.

"I hear it!" he whispered urgently. "I hear the rigging sing!"

"Aye," said Sails. "I knew ye would soon. It's time. Your ears are losin' their lubber habits. The ship is beginnin' to accept you. She's a-singin' to you like she's been a-singin' to me for eighteen years.

Lissen well, boy, lissen well. The song'll change as the wind and the weather change. It'll go up and down like the lady singer at the Swantigo Theater. And when it does, you pay heed. The change has a meanin'. The *Jerusee* is confidin' in ye. The riggin' sings almost all the time, and the smart sailor pays heed. The shrouds sing in a deep tone, like a big strong man, like the voice of the cap'n hisself. And the runnin' riggin' pipes away in a high voice like Abby Adams a-callin' to her John. Hark, lad!" He stopped suddenly and grabbed Uriah's shoulder.

"What be this?" he asked, pointing to a thick rope.

"Brace!" responded Uriah quickly.

"'Brace'? Tarnation, boy, *which* brace? That ain't good enough."

Uriah glanced upward at the mast and at the way the ship was lying over. "Lee brace," he quickly amended.

"Good." Sails nodded, then pointed to another rope.

"Fore royal weather sheet!" This time the answer was brisk and complete.

"And this?"

"Foretopmast backstay!"

Sails nodded again and clapped the boy hard on the shoulder. "Aye, lad, aye. You're a-learnin'. Faster than some I've taught, 'specially for a lubber lad."

Uriah reddened with pleasure at the praise.

"Now don't be gettin' all filled up with yourself, boy. You're still just a cub. Tonight, when we come on deck for first watch, bring a good long kerchief with you."

The boy looked at him in puzzlement. "A kerchief? Why?"

Sails smiled. "'Cause tonight we start all over again on pickin' out the riggin'. Only tonight you'll be blindfolded."

Uriah was incredulous. "Blindfolded? I got to know all these different ropes without being able to see 'em? I don't see how I can do it. I barely been able to learn 'em with my eyes wide open."

Sails gave him a cold stare. "How you think you do when you're on deck in a night storm and the water is pourin' across the masts and it's black as the inside of the Doctor's crotch? How you gonna pick up the right piece of riggin', eh? How you gonna pull-haul when you in the pitch dark if you don't know the riggin', eh? Tonight, you bring a kerchief and we really start to teach you the riggin'. Everything up to now been just baby school. Tonight, boy, you start learnin' to be a blue-water sailor!"

"The onny time I ever saw anythin' bleed like that is when I slaughtered a pig at me uncle's place back o' Plymouth. I tell ya he bled in quarts. *Quarts*, I tell ya!"

Murray, the second mate, looked around at the faces in the cabin and nodded emphatically. "I saw the worst punishment any man can suffer on this earth. I never saw so much blood in my life!"

Uriah listened, openmouthed, and felt sick in his stomach at the graphic description. The sailors were sitting about the cabin and ragging about life at sea. The talk had turned to the navy and to the punishment of its miscreant sailors by the lash. And Murray told them of the time he had witnessed, while he served in the British Navy, a man who was flogged 'round the fleet.

Few of them liked Murray and usually paid his talk no heed. The second mate of a merchant ship seldom was liked, mostly because he was neither lion nor lamb, neither an officer nor an able seaman, but somewhere in between. The place he occupied was like a ditch, for both the officers and the men looked down on him. Besides, Murray was an altogether unpleasant man. He had buckteeth that came well down on his chin; a protruding stomach; greasy, thinning hair; and a snarling temper that became sniveling weakness in the presence of the captain or first mate.

Now, though, with his account of the copious blood spilled in a British flogging, the larbowlins for once gave him their unbroken attention, and Murray reveled in it. Uriah sat in his bunk, a small white face stuffed away back in the corner darkness, listening raptly to the chronicle of gore and suffering.

"I was foretopman on the *Defiant*," Murray began. "'Twas in '98 and the navy was in stays and broached to because of the mutiny at the Nore and all the officers was crazy with fear. Every time a belayin' pin dropped to the deck, they thought it was the mutiny all over agin.'"

"What was you doin' in the Limey navy anyhow, Murray?" asked O'Rourke, a waister from Boston.

"I was pressed o' course," answered Murray, a kind of pride in his voice. "A press gang caught me in St. Kitts after I shipped on the brig *Lucy Q* out o' New York."

"Git to the point, Murray," growled Kartawicz, a big Pole who intensely disliked the second mate. "I wanna git some sleep tonight."

Murray gave the sailor a look cruel as death, then continued his tale: "An old sheet-anchor-man from a ship-o'-the-line was charged with strikin' the second luff of his liner. They found him guilty and sentenced him to be flogged 'round the fleet. I never knew what it was until I saw it with me own eyes."

What was it? Uriah wondered. It must be terrible because the cabin was strangely quiet now and the men were hanging on each word from Murray. At other times, the second mate's efforts to tell stories or make comments were rudely interrupted and catcalled. This was different. Murray made the most of it. His voice dropped almost to a whisper. Uriah crept toward the front of his bunk to hear better. He clasped his arms around his legs and leaned forward.

"They seized the sheet-anchor-man up in a barge," Murray hissed, "and sent him out from his own ship with right pleasant companions: a few men at the sweeps, o' course, a marine drummer, and a nice surgeon to see to the health o' the prisoner. O' course, the surgeon was so drunk he didn't know where he was, and all the time laughin' like a banshee. And so they set out on a sweet visit to all the ships in the squadron. All the decks o' all the ships was filled to the bulwarks, o' course, 'cause we had all been ordered on deck to witness punishment. And sailors were hangin' from the shrouds and spread out on the yards like a flock o' birds in the trees. But it was quiet as a church . . . quiet like the weather side of a quarterdeck with a mean captain. Nobody said a word. And across the water, you could hear the old prisoner a-cryin' and a-moanin'."

"The barge came to the next ship in line from our ship and ran under the counter and they grabbed the falls. Then a big boatswain's mate climbed down and stepped into the barge. The drummer began to beat out the Rogue's March, and the boatswain's mate started a-swingin' the cat. He gave him fifty lashes in all. After the first couple of lashes, the sheet-anchor-man was a-screamin' and a-callin' for someone to help him. After twenty-five lashes, he was only just a-moanin', and after the last twenty-five he was just a-groanin' so softly you could barely hear him, and we was on the next ship to him."

The larbowlins had grave looks as they listened in the bleak, dim cabin. Uriah winced and grimaced in his bunk as he pictured the cat-o'-nine-tails coming down again and again on the bare back of the shackled, seized-up old seaman.

"After the fifty strokes, the drummer stopped and the boatswain's mate went back up the falls and the oarsmen began movin' the barge on to the next ship, my own ship. The surgeon walked over and pulled up the prisoner's head so's he could look into his face. He was still breathin' 'cause the surgeon laughed so loud we could hear it up in the foretop. Then they rowed over to our frigate, tied up, and our boatswain's mate went down, cat in hand. The drummer started up again, and the whole thing was repeated."

"Fifty more lashes?" said one of the sailors, reluctant to believe.

"Aye, another fifty," answered Murray. "And a hard fifty, because this was a fresh swinger and he had been ordered to swing well. And he did. And that's when I saw all the blood. The old man's back looked like a fresh raw side of beef hung in a butcher's shop in New York and a river of blood poured down off it. There was blood all over the drummer and the surgeon and on the sweeps and the men who held 'em. And then they moved on to the next ship, and then the next one after that. Two ships down the line, I could see the oarsmen actually bailin' blood. I guess they were afeared the blood would sink the barge. I swear, I never knew one man could have so much blood."

"How long did this go on?" asked Kartawicz.

"'Til he had been flogged at every ship in the squadron," replied Murray, his eyebrows lifted as though in surprise that the Pole didn't know. "He was dead, o' course, by the time they was done with him. It ain't suppose to be that way. The surgeon is suppose to check the prisoner after each flogging and stop it if he looks like he's gonna die. Then they wait until his back heals up and they can send him out in the barge agin so's the punishment can be finished. But this ol' surgeon kept lookin' him in the face and laughin' like hell and orderin' the barge to go on to the next ship. I heerd later that the guy was dead two or three ships before they finished with him. But they kept hittin' him and he kept bleedin'. I didn't know a dead man kept on bleedin' like that. When they took him off the barge, I hear, his back was as black as the Doctor's, like it had been roasted acrost a fire."

Uriah leaned weakly back against the planking that formed the wall of his bunk. He was afraid for a moment that he would be sick in front of his shipmates. He put his hand over his mouth and tried to quell the rising nausea.

"I hear they sometimes order 800 lashes when they flog through the fleet," said one sailor softly, as if talking to himself.

"Yeh, they order that many," said Murray with authority, "but nobody ever took more than 350 and lived to tell the tale."

"*Ashray yawshvay vaytecha*," chanted Uriah in the singsong way he had been taught by his *hazzan*. "*Awd ya hallaloocha, selah.*"

"And what does that mean?" asked Captain Wilkins.

Uriah gulped in embarrassment. "I don't know, sir. I only know how to read a bit of Hebrew. I don't know what it means. I know that we sing it at morning prayers."

The captain nodded. "No matter, no matter. It is a strange-sounding tongue, but a noble one. It has a kind of . . . of majesty."

"Yes, sir," said Uriah, who did not know exactly what "majesty" meant and couldn't grasp the captain's meaning.

The boy sat stiffly on a chair drawn up to the big chart table in the ship's main cabin, his knees primly together and his shoes not quite reaching the deck. There was just one chair in the cabin. The captain sat on his cot, his Bible open on his lap. His legs were so long and the cot so low to the deck that his thighs and knees sloped sharply upward from his waist, forming a bony lectern on which the big scriptures rested.

Uriah did not know whether to continue reading or to sit in silence. He had soon learned that, when in the presence of the captain, a sailor does not speak until spoken to. He sat and waited. For long moments, Captain Wilkins read silently from his Bible, his face bent low over the pages to catch the light from the swaying oil lamp that hung above the table.

His voice suddenly pierced the silence: "Whatever might be said against your people—the House of Israel—and justice requires that some such things be said . . . I say that all such things are overcome by the great gift you have given the world in this book." He thumped the Bible with his huge hand. "This book is the salvation of the earth. Your people took it from God Almighty and then gave it to the nations of the earth. Don't ever forget that, boy! Be proud of it always!"

The captain cleared his throat, then went on. "Can you—is it possible that you can read to me in the Hebrew tongue from the New Testament? Do you also study that?"

"I don't know what that is, Captain."

"The New Testament is the second part of the Holy Bible. It is the story of our savior Jesus."

Uriah thought for a moment. He had heard of Jesus from his Christian playmates at home and knew that they worshipped this man. But he knew nothing of this new—new . . . what was that word? "No, sir," he stammered. "I don't think I know any of that in Hebrew. I suppose Hazzan Cohen will teach me that part when I get back home. I'll have a lot more Hebrew to study for my bar mitzvah."

Wilkins looked again at the cabin boy sitting mutely in the chair, obviously very ill at ease, his eyes shyly turned down toward his feet.

"Are you happy on my ship, Mr. Levy?" he asked kindly. "Are you being treated well?"

Uriah's face brightened. "Oh yes, sir. I'm being treated fine. And Sails says I'm learnin' the rigging as fast as any lubber boy ever has."

The captain smiled. "Good. That's good. Sails is a fine teacher. He has taught me a great deal about the sea."

"You, sir? But . . . I thought—"

"You thought that the captain of a ship was born with his seamanship, eh? That he took it in with his mother's milk, eh? No, I had to be taught like anyone else. And a good captain still learns from his crew, even though they serve under him. Sails has been on my ship for almost twenty years. And he has taught me much."

There was silence again. Then a new thought struck the captain. He looked at the boy and put his finger to his lips, pondering. "In a few weeks, we dock at Savannah," he said. "We tie up there for several weeks, and I can see my wife and daughters again. We have to find a place for you to stay."

Uriah didn't understand. "Sir? Can't I stay here on the *Jerusee*, same as always?"

Wilkins shook his head. "My ship will be careened at Savannah and her hull scraped and she'll be smoked out good. Get all the vermin out and the rats, too. Nobody can stay on the ship. And I'll not have you staying in a sailors' boardinghouse. You'll fall into bad company there. No, perhaps I can get you into the Bethesda Home for Boys. It is a fine orphans' home, the food is good, and they read the Bible to the boys twice a day. It would be a good place for you."

Uriah couldn't keep the doubt from his voice. "An orphans' home, sir?"

Wilkins didn't hear the question but continued musing aloud. "Or perhaps we can take you into our home. I'll speak to Mrs. Wilkins about it. Of course, we won't careen the ship for several days after we land, and you can remain in the forecastle until then."

The captain nodded, as if ratifying his own decision. Then he again swung open the big volume on his knees. "I would be obliged, Mr. Levy, if you would let me hear some more Hebrew words before you rejoin your watch mates on the spar deck. I can hear them doing some Sunday skylarking, and I'm sure you would like to join them. In a few minutes, I'll let you go. But for now, please to continue."

Uriah reopened his worn Hebrew lesson book and found a new passage.

He began to chant, "*V'al koolam yeetbarach v'yeetrohmam. . . .*"

As they came within two days' sail of the *Jerusee*'s home port of Savannah, the ship's crew was thrown into a fever of activity, making the vessel all ataunto, all shipshape and Bristol fashion. It was a matter of great pride, Jamie explained to Uriah, for the captain and mate of a vessel to have her looking her best when coming into any port, but especially into her home port. "Everyone on the wharf will take note of such things," he told him. There wasn't a man jack on the *Jerusee* who didn't want to earn the admiration of the shore-bound observers.

They began by setting up and tarring all the standing rigging and then rattling down the lower and topmast rigging. Then the *Jerusee* was scraped, fore and aft, top to bottom. A platform was rigged to hang outside the bulwarks, and crewmen clambered out on it to first scrape and then paint the hull down to the waterline. This done, paint was applied to the rest of the ship, a dark brown on the masts and yards, green for the bulwarks. All the brightwork was polished and then polished again. Then the work parties were sent below decks to scrape and paint the cabin and forecastle and to lay varnish on the decks.

Through all this, the men worked with a will and a spirit. They sang their favorite old work chanties as they labored: "Cheerily, Men" and "Jack Crosstree" and endless choruses of "Time for Us to Go." One man sang the line—usually Kartawicz the Pole with his booming bass voice—and all the others joined in the refrain. They were happy and aching for sight of the Savannah River. Some of the men had wives waiting for them. Others would purchase their companionship. But each one was eager.

Even the captain, usually a stolid, intense, silent figure upon the quarterdeck, had shipped his homeward-bound face.

"My daughters are a-pullin' on the tow-rope, boys!" he shouted as the ship bounded through a heavy sea in the sunny, windy afternoon. "Heave hearty, lads!" he bellowed as the ship tacked. "I can see my wife a-wavin' me home!"

O'Rourke, the Boston Irishman, was almost babbling in his happiness. "Wait'll you see them Savannah bimbos on the wharf," he laughed to Uriah as they hauled together on the foresheet. "Savannah has the finest bimbos on the southern coast." He laughed again at the boy's puzzled look. "Don't you worry none, laddy. We'll find one for you, too. They got 'em all ages on the Savannah wharf!"

Uriah looked all around him, openmouthed, an innocent in a garden of earthly delight. As the warm, moist air of Savannah embraced him, he wondered if this place might be the heaven that his elders at home so often mentioned. It was unlike any other place he ever had seen. It did not even resemble drawings of the great cities of Europe that he had seen in books.

He walked a few feet behind Jamie Wilkins, who had taken the boy ashore with him. The distance between them kept widening as Uriah stopped to look this way and that, his eyes rounded with astonishment.

Jamie had stopped and was waiting for him. "You keep walkin' backwards like that, 'Riah," he said with some impatience, "and you're either gonna foul one o' them trees or else fall right on your ass!"

Uriah reluctantly faced forward again and quickened his pace to match that of the older boy.

They stood on a grassy esplanade that centered a broad avenue leading from the riverfront wharves and up a gentle rise toward a neighborhood of fine homes. All along the lush green esplanade were gigantic oak trees, their huge butts forming long columns. But even more awesome than the great tree trunks were the waterfalls of Spanish moss that festooned the oaks and virtually flooded the air around them. Uriah felt as if he was walking in an enchanted forest. After all the days and nights in a cramped vessel on rough, churning seas, he was unprepared for this scene of mysterious loveliness.

"Now, see that there house?" Jamie asked, pointing with authority at a pink mansion ahead. "That there house is made of what we call 'tabby' in Savannah. They make it out of oyster shells, lime, and sand, and mix it with water in some way and paddle it all up together and then we build houses out o' it. Shore is lots prettier than all those red bricks you got in Philadelphy, eh?"

The avenue now was lined on either side by large homes, and Uriah's eyes widened again as he looked at them. How big they were! Everyone in Savannah must be rich! Why, his father's house and his grandfather's as well would fit with ease into just one of these castles, with their odd light-colored walls. He puzzled over their balconies with the black iron filigreed railings. Why did they have such big front porches? He marveled at the wide stairways that led directly from the ground to entrances on the second floor.

Oh, he would have something and a half to tell his brothers and sisters and Mama and Father . . . and Papa. Especially Papa. He couldn't wait to see the excitement in Papa's face when he told him about the strange Savannah houses and the giant oak trees with their long shawls of gray moss.

When the *New Jerusalem* was finally careened and her crew scattered to find temporary homes ashore, Uriah was taken by Captain Wilkins to his own home. He had spoken to his wife, he said, and she would not hear of Uriah being sent to the Bethesda Home. He would be good company for Jamie, she said, and no doubt could stand some home-cooked meals.

For the next two weeks, Uriah would once again taste life in a loving family home. He was well fed and shepherded by Mrs. Wilkins and alternately spoiled and teased by Alicia and Huldah, the two daughters. He was handsomer and more mannerly than their own brother, Alicia proclaimed at dinner one day, and she wished him to be her second brother. Jamie laughed and took no offense. He continued to take Uriah on long walks around Savannah, proud to show off his hometown to his appreciative guest.

One had only to glance at the faces to understand. All the officers and men had shipped their going-away faces, and they went sadly about their duties as the *Jerusee* prepared to hoist anchor and sail away. Uriah noted that Captain Wilkins shouted the same orders as he ever did when the ship prepared to depart an anchorage and he shouted them firmly enough, but clearly lacking in them was the ringing tone, the spirit that marked such orders at all other times.

The topmen were aloft, led by the nimble Sails, and they loosed and then set all sails. The mate sang out the command to back the head sails. Uriah was called to help man the windlass, and as he rushed forward to grab a handspike he saw the captain glance again at the distant wharf, where his wife and daughters still stood, waving and blowing kisses, three recognizable dots of pink and white and blue, calling good-bye.

Every few minutes the captain would look again to see if his family still watched from the wharf. He did not wave back to them, but his jaw muscles clenched and his face took on an even sadder look as he turned away and shouted another order to his crew.

"Heave hearty, men! Heave with a will!" beseeched the mate. The windlass slowly began to turn, then faster, bringing the *Jerusee* up to her anchor. Uriah joined the Doctor on a handspike and bent his legs to apply maximum push to the long wooden bar.

"How about a song, men?" pleaded the mate. "Kartawicz, how about some 'Cheerily, Men' or 'Jack Crosstree'?" But Kartawicz remained silent and walked stolidly in a circle on the deck, his giant arms extended to his handspike. The sailors all wore a sullen, almost dazed look. Why, it hardly seemed like more than yesterday that they had dropped anchor. Now, a wink and a flash later, and here they were a-haulin' once again. *I'll heave and push*, they seemed to say, *but don't ask me to sing. Not now.*

"Hove short, sir," called out the mate, as the anchor cable tight-ened and went vertical. "Straight up and down, sir."

"Very well, Mr. Konopka," replied the captain. "Break her out!"

The windlass continued to turn, and the anchor broke ground and began its climb to the surface. The *Jerusee* swung slowly about, canted by her backed headsails. As the bow pivoted around to the proper downriver course, with the helmsman taking care lest she swing too far, the captain at just the right moment shouted the words that would send his ship gliding down the wind and out to the sea again: "Brace the topsails! Square away!" The sailors ran to the braces and began swinging the big yards around. The top-sails caught the fresh breeze and filled with it, and the *Jerusee* fairly leaped ahead.

"Sails, to the chains!" the captain ordered. "I want the lead hove every five minutes!" The old seaman hustled for the starboard chains, shouting, "Aye, aye, sir!" as he ran. It would not do at all to get hung up on a shoal in full view of their home port.

Now the ship relaxed a bit and the men could stand still for a moment or two, their daubers still down, their faces inclined mo-rosely toward their feet. The gear must be cleaned up and then ar-ranged all Bristol fashion, like the captain wanted it. There would be time for a breath or two and a smoke, and then after supper the same old watch-and-watch would begin and another day at sea would be upon them.

Uriah started forward to the galley to help the Doctor begin the evening meal. He glanced behind him and saw the captain standing at the taffrail, looking as the city of Savannah and all it held for him faded slowly into the pinkening western sky.

The *Jerusee* was plunging along through a heavy sea off the north-ern coast of Spanish Florida. Spray hurled high above the bulwarks and gave the two boys and the old sailor a good wetting, but Sails did not once interrupt his soliloquy on the weather and its ways. After a few minutes, his gray head was drenched, but he never once even paused to wipe away the sea spittle. Sails was a born teacher, and once he got to teaching he could not be deterred by the sea, the weather, or even the denseness of some students.

He put one hand roughly on Jamie Wilkins's neck and the other hand on Uriah's and bodily swung them around and tilted their faces upward to the sky.

"There, my young cockies, be one o' the truest guides to the weather o' tomorrow," he proclaimed. "Mark it well. That red-eyed sun. A red sun has water in its eye. Remember that! If red the sun begins his race, be sure the rain will fall apace. Red sky in the morning is a sailor's warning, red sky at night is a sailor's delight. Words of wisdom, young childer, and not to be ignored 'less it be at your peril. Heed what I say now. We'll have rain, and lots o' it, by the morrow."

Jamie, his neck set free again, looked across at Uriah and smiled a message: Let's humor the old top with all his superstitions and sailors' proverbs. Sails intercepted the transaction.

"Oh?" he said, arms akimbo. "Ordinary Seaman Wilkins doubts me word. Ordinary Seaman Wilkins, who has the bountiful experience of two or three voyages, is sayin' that these old warnins carry no truth. Eh? Well, when it rains tomorrow, I'll see Ordinary Seaman Wilkins out on the foredeck with pail and squilgee, a-moppin' up the rainwater off the deck and placin' it gently in the pail. Then mebbe you'll larn not to doubt me."

The smile had vanished from Jamie's lips. "And if it don't rain tomorrow?" he asked.

"It will," replied Sails. "It will."

Kelly of the starboard watch came toward them. "Sails, the mate wants ya."

"Mind what I tol' you," Sails said to his two students. "And don't forgit it five minutes from now. When I get back from the mate, I'll tell you how to read the weather in the moon and also how to tell the winds from the porpoises. It pays to know the comin' wind, and the porpoises will tell you, if ye have sense enough to watch and lissen to 'em. Stay here and think on what I told ye." He walked rapidly aft to see what the mate wanted of him.

Jamie laughed again and shook his head. "That ol' Sails," he said.

"Him and his ol' sailor tales."

"I reckon you won't be laughing tomorrow if it rains. You'll be too busy wiping up water off the deck."

"Shoot," Jamie answered. "I've seen lots of red suns, and the next day was dry as a whalebone."

"Jamie, what do I have to do to be an ordinary seaman like you?"

"Well, you got a long road afore you can think about being rated an O.S. See, an O.S. has got to hand, reef, and steer—except mebbe in bad weather when the cap'd want an A.S. at the helm—and he's got to know how to work the ship and make sail and take in sail. He's able to pass a common seizing and splice all the small ropes, at least. Oh, and that means knowing a whole raft of knots, like the clove hitch and the timber hitch and bowline knot, and the like."

Uriah shook his head and sighed. "If you know all that stuff and you're just an ordinary, then what does an able seaman have to know? Seems like you already know everything there is to know about a ship."

Jamie puffed his chest a bit. "Well, I know a hell of a lot, all right. But that ain't beans to what an A.S. has to know and do. Why, he's got to make all sorts of splices in the largest of the ropes and pass seizings and make every sort of knot ever invented in every sort of weather, make rope-yarns into lashings, and jury-rig a mast or a rudder. And an able has to go aloft in the middle of a hurricane and stand up there on that footrope and hand and reef like it was a sun-shiny Independence Day. When you can do things like that, you can ship as an able seaman and they'll call you a 'deepwater sailorman.'"

"Jamie, when do you think they'll let me go aloft?"

"I dunno. Why don't you ask Sails?"

"I don't mind slushing masts and helping the Doctor and making up the captain's cabin. But you ain't a real sailor until you go aloft."

"That's true. But ain't you scared? It's a long ways up there."

"Were you scared . . . the first time you went up?"

"You bet your ass! 'Course I wouldn't have admitted it then, but now that I go aloft all the time, I don't mind sayin' that I was truly scared. My first time up, I stopped for a minute about halfway up the shroud and bawled. 'Course nobody else saw me."

"You were *that* scared?"

"Hell, yes! You get up there the first time and you'll know what I mean. You'll probably brown your britches."

The nightly argument was raging with gusto in the forecastle. Some of the sailors stretched limply in their bunks and snored loudly, deaf to the roaring, profane opinions of their shipmates. Others sat on the deck and sewed their clothing back to good repair, looking up now and then and sometimes nodding in agreement or shaking their heads in silent protest.

Uriah sat, as usual, in the back of his bunk, knees drawn up and arms wrapped around them, listening to the debate. He never spoke unless spoken to, except when he was with Jamie or Sails or the Doctor, whom he regarded as his special friends. And this night he was below decks with the starboard watch. He had remained above and helped the Doctor scour the galley while his own watch was below deck. Now he was off-duty with the men of the other watch. Come morning, he would resume watch-and-watch with his own larbowlins.

Murray, the second mate, was shouting his opinions of the American presidency through the cabin, his face bright red. His vocal antagonist was the bantam rooster Kelly, usually an obliging confidant of the second mate and something of a groveler. But when the talk turned to politics, or the superiority of the British Navy to the French, or anything suitable for a resounding clash of opinion, little Kelly suddenly became a fighting cock.

"They don't call him 'Mad Tom' for nothin' I tell ya," Murray snarled. "He's in the pay o' the French. For why else would he be doin' what he's doin'?"

"Our noble president in the pay of a foreign power?" Kelly feigned horror at the thought. "And, pray tell, what is he doin' that frightens ye so?"

"Why, you dumb turd, don't you read the newspapers? If you're too iggerant to read 'em yourself, at least have someone read 'em to ya. Mad Tom is plannin' to disband our navy, is what. I tell ya, he's made a deal with his pals, the Frogs, so they can come over and capture these United States and rule 'em right from Paree."

"Aaah, you Federalist pigs is so busy kissin' King George's bottom, you don't even know what's happenin' in the world." Kelly's voice took on a hard, knifey edge.

"Who don't know?" Murray screamed. "I know that the U.S. sent the sloop of war *George Washington* to Algiers, but Tom Jefferson had no stomach for a fight. So the Dey of Algiers commanded—*commanded*, I tell ya—our Yankee ship to carry tribute and two hundred of his stinkin' Algerines to Turkey. He even made our sloop fly the Algiers flag. Oh, we have a real fightin' president, do we not?"

"Why, Tom Jefferson warn't even president when that happened! Adams still was. And anyway, they hauled down the Algerine flag as soon as they were out of range of the Dey's guns. You don't know nothin'!" O'Rourke chimed in.

"I know that ol' Adams was a fightin' president. He fought the Frogs on the oceans for over two years. But I say that Mad Tom Jefferson is sellin' out his own country to France!"

"You can't say that about Thomas Jefferson!" The childish voice cut through the thick cloud of argument like a silver knife through a bowl of suet. "He is the greatest president you will ever know!"

The two men turned in surprise and searched for the source of the voice. In a lower bunk at the side of the cabin, the cabin boy was sitting on his haunches, an unaccustomed look of anger on his face.

"Was that you, boy?" Murray demanded. "Was that you said that?"

"Yes, it was me! And I say again: Don't you insult President Jefferson like that. What you say is a lie! He is a good and honest man!"

Kelly cackled with laughter. "And pray tell, little fart, how do you know such things?"

Uriah climbed from his bunk and stood on the deck. "I know

because my grandfather says Thomas Jefferson is a great president and he is the smartest man in Philadelphia!"

Murray was enraged. He bent over and shouted full force into the boy's face. "Why, you little Jew bastard, what do you know about anything? Your grandfather is some slick Jew tailor or moneylender, sucking blood from honest folks. If he says Jefferson's good, it proves how bad he really is. Whichever way a Jew goes, I goes the other way!"

Uriah felt his legs tremble and his head swim. He saw a red cloud before his eyes. His mouth felt hot and dry. He would not be spoken to like this!

Murray straightened up again and laughed an angry laugh. "You little piece o' Jew shit, don't you ever break into my talk again or I'll throw ye to the sharks. I never liked your face anyways. The captain's pet, be ye? Not here in the foc's'l. He ain't here to wipe your nose and clean your pants. You interfere with me again and I'll break your mouth!"

"To break him, you'll have to break me first." The bass voice was soft, but it spun across the cabin from a lower bunk in the corner, its tinge of foreign accent giving it a muted menace. Kartawicz the Pole slowly uncoiled himself and stood up. Murray was not a small man, but Kartawicz towered above him.

Murray stepped back. "You keep out o' this. It don't concern you, Polsker."

"I make it my concern. You are scum and not fit to sail with honest sailors."

"He's a damned Jew and not worth my trouble or yours!"

Kartawicz did not reply. He merely lifted a powerful hand and rammed it into Murray's shoulder. The second mate shot backward, slammed painfully against a bunk frame, and then dropped into a sitting position. He glowered there and rubbed his aching shoulder.

"I tell you again and for the last time," Kartawicz said, a look cold as icebergs on his face. "Leave the boy alone. If any harm comes to him, I will kill you." Then he returned to his bunk, climbed in, turned on his side, and closed his eyes.

Uriah stood silently for a moment, then returned to his own bunk. He crawled back to his accustomed place against the ship's side. He sat there and rocked back and forth. He wondered how long it would take for him to stop shaking.

Sails stood on the quarterdeck and waited for his captain to dismiss him. Captain Wilkins had called the grizzled sailmaker to him to direct that a new suit of canvas be bent on the morrow. They were off Cape Romain now, bound for Norfolk, and Wilkins wanted his best suit bent to meet the onslaught of stormy weather that usually awaited them in these seas. The order was given and acknowledged, and Sails was ready to return to his duties in the sail locker, but the captain did not release him. He stood and stared out to sea, a pensive look on his face. Then he turned back to Sails.

"The cabin boy, Sails. Mr. Levy. He has been aboard for over a year and a half now. How does he, these days?"

"He does well, sir. A bright and willin' lad, and with spunk."

"Good. Is he ready to go aloft?"

"Aye, sir." There was no hesitation in the sailmaker's voice. "Ready and willin'. Perhaps a bit more willin' than ready, but ready all the same. He's been badgerin' me for weeks now."

Wilkins nodded. "Very well then, Sails. Take him aloft."

"Aye, aye, sir." Sails turned to leave but was stopped by another word from the captain.

"Sails, go along with him and watch the boy. The first few times are always a risky try." He smiled slightly. "You see, I was warned by the boy's grandfather before we left Philadelphia that if anything happens to the lad, he will personally break my arms and legs. So . . . see that he comes to no harm, eh? For my good and safety."

"Aye, sir, aye," chuckled Sails. "I'll do that, sir."

A scant quarter-hour later, the sailmaker stood in the ship's waist with an excited, near-breathless cabin boy, euphoric at the long-awaited chance to climb the great wooden stick that soared into the sky.

"This is a good day for your first voyage aloft," Sails was telling him. "The sea is calm and the wind is talkin' softly. Now, lissen to me as we go up the shroud, lad, and heed my words. And do not try to go too fast! Get your footin' and larn the feel of the ratlines afore ye try to move too quick!"

He put his hands on the boy's shoulders and looked directly into his eyes as he spoke softly, urgently to him. "Hear me, boy. This is no child's play. A fall from above means death almost for sure. If ye don't die, ye'll be hurt so bad ye'll want to die. If ye hit the deck, your body'll be broke in fifty places. If ye hit the water, chances are ye'll drown afore we can loose a boat and seek ye. So pay heed to me.

"Remember always the first rule o' the topman: *One hand for the ship and one hand for yourself.* Never forget that rule as long as ye go to sea: One hand for the ship and one hand for yourself. Do ye understand those words? Are ye sure? Keep that one hand firmly clasped on the right thing. Not jest anythin' that feels solid, but the *right* thing. Catch aholt of a yard or a mast or standin' riggin'. All right. But never catch aholt of *runnin'* riggin'. First ye know, it'll run and that'll be the end o' ye. Oh yes, and be sure when you're up on the yard, never to let go o' one rope until ye have holt o' another."

Sails paused for a moment and scratched his head, trying to remember what else he should tell the boy. He had instructed many boys over the years, but he was getting forgetful these days. Then he continued, "When ye get to the futtock shrouds, ye have a choice to make. Ye can continue like a sailorman, which means hanging back and down until ye get up to the topgallant shrouds, or—if you're too scared to do that—ye can keep goin' up through the lubber hole. No one will rag you this first time or two if ye do that, but it is lubberly and you can't keep doin' that if you're to be a sailorman. Mought's well larn to climb the futtock shrouds right now. When ye get to the yard, stop and wait for me to tell you what to do. And mind your steps on that footrope. Remember, it's sized for full-growed men, not a small one like yourself. Grab onto your yard with both arms and feel your way along the foot-rope until it starts to know your feet. Oh, yes. Should ye fall from aloft and land in the ocean, try to keep calm. Turn your back to the wind and the swell and jest paddle about. Raise your hand every now and then to help guide our boat to ye. Do not waste your strength by screamin' or tryin' to swim back toward the ship. Do what I say and mebbe ye'll stay alive long enough for us to pull ye out."

He peered into the boy's eyes to see if his careful instructions and dire warnings had cooled the fire. But the boy still breathed hard and strained to prove himself. Sails released him: "All right, slowly now. Up ye go."

With no word, save a little gasp of excitement, the boy sprinted for the nearest shroud and was already a few feet above the deck when he was halted by Sails's shout of anger: "Where ye going, ye young fool? Belay that! Off the shroud and on the deck!"

Crestfallen, a bewildered look on his face, Uriah climbed down to the deck and walked back to the sailmaker. Sails stuck a bony finger in his face and shouted a hoarse warning: "Never, ever, go aloft on the lee shroud! It's unseaman-like and lubberly and jest plain stupid! Look—if you go up the lee riggin' and a strong wind blows, it blows you *off* the riggin'. If you go up the windward riggin', the wind blows you *onto* the riggin'. Use your head, boy! This is no business for iggerants! Understand? When ye get aloft, if ye need go to the lee riggin', ye can cross over then."

Uriah, chastened and somewhat subdued, walked more slowly across the deck to the windward shrouds, Sails at his heels. Together they mounted the bulwark and climbed out on the shrouds, and together they slowly began to ascend the ratlines. Uriah climbed carefully, deliberately, not fearful but striving to avoid another angry blast from his mentor. The hemp rigging felt rough and solid under his fingers and feet. He grabbed it hard. It was his friend; it made him feel sure, stable. He started once to look down at the deck that slowly fell away beneath them, but Sails—watching his every twitch—quickly warned him to look level or above, but never down.

"Stop here a minute," Sails ordered as they neared the futtock shrouds. "One more thing that I almos' forgot. Never wear mittens on the riggin'. No matter how cold the night or how icy the wind, ye must go barehanded. For the riggin' would feel different to a covered hand, and that difference could mean your death. It is your familiar touch that will keep ye safe. Now, the futtock shrouds are up here. Are ye game to try 'em, or is it the lubber hole for ye this day?"

The boy said nothing but pointed at the futtock shrouds, and his meaning was plain. Sails nodded, pleased. He went ahead, slowly but easily, a supple sureness to his every move. He hung back downward as he climbed the futtock shrouds. Uriah followed, after only an instant's hesitation. He closed his eyes, relying on his hands and feet, and it wasn't so bad. Sails softly called advice to him as he went up.

In another moment, they were standing on the topgallant shrouds. Sails patted the boy gently on the shoulder. It was unspoken, but it was the most eloquent praise the old sailorman could offer.

Then they stood on the yard, their feet swaying slightly on the footrope that hung a few feet below the thick horizontal timber. Uriah was surprised to find that he was not scared and did not feel dizzy or sick to his stomach.

He looked out at the flat blue sea and saw the masts of another ship on the horizon. He felt a sudden, overwhelming sense of kinship with that vessel and with the men aboard her. "Hello, shipmates!" he wanted to cry, in the ancient greeting of sailors to their brethren. "I am aloft like you. I, Uriah Phillips Levy of Philadelphia! From this moment, I am one of you!" All these words coursed through his mind in the sun-swept silence, broken only by the soft hiss of the wind and the occasional flap of a sail.

Following Sails and holding tightly to the yard with both his arms, Uriah edged his way out on the footrope. Sails stopped at the middle of the yard, and they stood there for several minutes without any words so that the lad could drink in and absorb the sound, the feel, the very soul of this sailor's workplace, high above the benches and plows of landbound men.

Then Sails began speaking softly to him again: "This here place, lad, in the middle o' the yard, is called the bunt. And it is here that your best topman is stationed, for it is here that the hardest work is done in furlin' a course or a topsail. On a man-o'-war, the captain o' the top is always stationed in the bunt. And in a merchantman, it is the best sailor ye have. This used to be my post, for I was always the best man—first aloft and first back on deck if I willed it. Now—," he stopped for a moment and gazed out to port at the coastline—"now, I'm too old. Someday, perhaps ye'll be the best sailor on a great merchantman and the station bill will have ye in the bunt."

The boy nodded silently. Oh, he would soon enough be furling and reefing sails on yards like this. And he relished the thought of those times to come. But they would only be waiting times, learning times. For he had his eye on the quarterdeck. Aye, it was there he finally would walk some day, the master of his own vessel. And, much as he loved the *Jerusee*, it would not be a small coaster like this one. No, he would command a great man-of-war . . . a frigate like his beloved *United States* or even a giant ship-of-the-line, which surely his own country would someday have. This was his old dream, and nothing had happened to change it. He lifted his chin, closed his eyes, and let the sun and the breeze stroke his cheeks. Standing here, more than a hundred feet above the deck, suspended in the air, his dream was more real to him than ever before.

Three bells had just been struck in the afternoon watch, and Uriah straightened up from his odious task of slushing the mainmast. His fingers were black with tar. It was a cloudy day, and the winds were erratic; all hands had been called to tack ship three times in the past two hours. The *Jerusee* was heeled over sharply in the stiff wind, and it was difficult for him to hold his balance on the wet, slippery deck. In his first weeks on the ship, he had several times lost his footing completely and slid roughly across the sloping deck. Now, at least, he had learned to keep his feet on this steep hillside of a deck, albeit still with difficulty.

The *Jerusee* seemed to be climbing the sea, one wave at a time, heeling over with the swell, then corkscrewing madly into the trough.

He heard the captain's deep voice echo out from the quarter-deck: "Ease her two points farther off the wind!" The helmsman acknowledged, "Two points farther off the wind, sir."

For no reason save to stretch his muscles, contorted and wearied from long bending over the slush bucket, Uriah straightened up and looked out to starboard, where—over the bulwark—he spied a low coastline. Land to starboard? But that should not be, unless. . . . He quickly turned and looked over the port bulwark. A more distant shoreline could be seen. Land on both sides of the ship. That meant they had weathered Cape May and already were up into Delaware Bay. It was homeward bound, then, and Philadelphia's spires and red bricks were only hours away. Thoughts of his parents and grand-parents, of his little room at home, suddenly flooded his mind. His eyes filled with old pictures, almost forgotten in these many months at sea.

Sails had climbed into the chains and was chanting the depth. Already he was soaked with spray from the heavy sea and from the water cascading off the dipsey lead. "By the mark twenty!" he shouted to the quarterdeck. There now were only twenty fathoms of water under them.

Uriah felt a wave of sadness wash over him. Oh, he loved this faithful little ship with her clean lines and her great white pyramids of sail. Soon he must leave her and his friends aboard her. For them, the stop at Philadelphia would mean only another passage, one of many. For him, it was voyage's end.

The gusting wind brought plaintive, harplike songs from the weather rigging. The boy marveled now that he could so plainly hear the music of the rigging to which he once had been deaf. He told himself that the *Jerusee* was singing this farewell melody just for him and that not another man on the ship was privy to it. He listened for a moment more, then sighed and bent again to his work at the mast.

The *Jerusee* fit as pleasantly up against the wharf as if she were nest-
ling her head upon the shoulder of an old beau. Her sails all were
neatly furled, the bunts brought up to a cone proper enough to
please both the captain and the mate, yard-arm gaskets and bunt
gaskets tightly affixed. All in all, a good harbor stow.

Uriah stood in the waist, waiting for permission to go ashore.
On the deck beside him, a few feet aft of the gangplank, were his
ditty bag and a small canvas sack filled with trinkets that he had
purchased in ports of call for his family.

He had said his good-byes to Jamie and the Doctor and most of
the other men, who were working down in the hold, lifting cargo
for unloading.

"Well, Mr. Levy?" The captain stood beside him. "All packed
and paid, I see. Hardly seems two years since you came aboard." He
paused, as if groping for words. "We shall miss you. Jamie especially . . . but all of us. You are a bright lad and obedient and willing to
work. You have the makings of a good sailor. A few more voyages as
a boy, and then I think you would be ready for an ordinary's berth.
When the time comes, Mr. Levy, that you are ready to go back to
sea, let me know. You can write to Mrs. Wilkins in Savannah, and
she will let you know when next we will anchor in Philadelphia.
There is always a berth for you aboard my ship."

"Thank you, sir. I would rather sail with you and the *Jerusee* than
with any other ship on the seas."

The captain smiled slightly and nodded in response to the lad's
strong feelings. "Oh . . . and Mr. Levy, I thank you for the pleasant
Sunday hours when you read from your Hebrew testament to me.
It was most enlightening. Now I can feel that I am familiar with the
sound of the ancient language of the holy scriptures. Luck to you,
Mr. Levy. And my felicitations to your grandfather. Tell him that I
faithfully kept my end of our bargain."

The captain nodded again in farewell and then strode down the deck to the gangway, en route to the hold to check upon the un-loading.

Uriah wondered what the captain meant about a bargain with his grandfather. He bent down and picked up his possessions. He supposed that the captain's dismissal meant that he had permission to leave the ship. The quarterdeck and waist were empty of people now, save for a pair of larbowlins polishing brightwork near the gangway.

The boy looked up and around him, taking a last look at the ship that had been home and schoolroom and workplace to him for the past two years. He turned and moved for the gangplank and then saw Sails standing alongside it, a look somewhere between a smile and a frown on his wrinkled face.

"Here, you wasn't haulin' anchor and I gettin' under weigh without sayin' farewell to your old friend, was ye, lad?" he said gently.

"I couldn't find you, Sails! I looked everywhere but I couldn't find you."

"Aye, I had to run up to the victualers to see to our provisions. I was afeered I'd miss you." He scuffed loudly to clear his throat and wiped his nose with a quick swipe of his arm. Then he brought his other hand up and offered a small package wrapped in muslin. "Aw, here's a bit o' scrimshaw I thought you mought like to have. Keep you remindered of old Sails. I larned scrimshaw when I berthed on a spouter years ago. Bought the bone from a whalin' man when we anchored at Gloucester a few months back. Been a-workin' on it ever since. Thought you mought like to have it."

The boy nodded and took the carving. He didn't know what to say. Without thinking, he dropped his bags on the deck, shoved the scrimshaw into the pocket of his pea jacket, and stepped forward. He threw both arms around Sails. The ancient little man, his wispy gray hair blowing in the river wind, clasped the boy tightly. Uriah felt his eyes fill with warm tears.

Sails roughly cleared his throat again and then slowly took his arms away.

"Good lad, good lad," he said gruffly. "Get on with ye now. Your family surely would like to know that their sailorman has come home."

Uriah again picked up his bags; gave one last quick glance at the sailmaker, who nodded to him; and then walked briskly down the plank and onto the familiar streets of Philadelphia.

4

Philadelphia, 1804

They wondered, these small children playing in front of their house on Cherry Street, who was this young man walking up to them, dressed in the garb of a sailor and wearing a broad smile on his face?

Eliza, the eldest Levy child, was watching the small ones play, keeping them from underfoot while her mama prepared the family dinner. Curious, she watched the young sailor approach the house and wondered why he looked so familiar. Then she shrieked, "Uriah!"

Without saying a word to Uriah, she turned and fled into the house to spread the news to her mother and the other children that their long-lost brother had come home from the sea. Her excited calls could be heard in the street as they echoed through the small house.

The little ones simply stood on the curb and stared at him with open mouths. Uriah stood in front of them, hands on hips, a smile on his mouth, and savored the moment. *Ah, this would be Amelia, who would be eleven years by now . . . my, how she has grown! And here are Morton and Joseph—their faces look much the same. And this blond boy,* who has returned to his digging in the dirt after a moment's curious glance at the smiling intruder, *this must be Isaac,* who still was in diapers when Uriah had left. Where were his big brothers, Louis and Benjamin? He couldn't wait to brag to them about his high adventures.

From the house he heard his mother's familiar voice as she approached the door. He had time to say only, "Hello, Mama, I'm home," before she had swallowed him in her eager embrace.

They marveled over how much he had grown and filled out; over the brownness of his skin, which bore the sailor's perpetual tan; and over his shaggy, unkempt hair, which had not been trimmed at all since Sails had taken a scissors to it on a quiet day at anchor in Norfolk. He could not unpack his bag nor present his gifts, much less venture from the house, until his mother had sat him at her table and personally seen him properly fed as, she insisted, he had not been these many months away from home.

His father had returned home from his shop by now, accompanied by Louis and Benjamin, who helped him there. Michael Levy was no more talkative now than he ever had been, even in this emotional moment, but there was no doubt that he was joyed to see his wandering son home again. His strong embrace and thumping on Uriah's back had made that clear soon after he walked through the door. He listened intently at the table, but said little, as the older children plied Uriah with questions about the life at sea and the ports he had seen and the men of the *Jerusee*. After a few minutes of this, the younger children lost their shyness and awe of this brother-stranger, and their piping voices also filled the air with questions of their own.

Rachel Levy sat at one end of the table, near the cooking fireplace, alternately listening to the questions and Uriah's confident answers and refilling the food bowls. Her face was suffused with happiness. If the questions of the children should run dry, she had a few of her own. She didn't really care about the answers; she wanted only to gaze into the face of this bold son she had so many times despaired of, whom she had pictured so often, in midnight dreams, in an ocean grave. What a joy to hear his voice again, to see him hale and strong, to watch him devouring her dinner!

She wanted the questions to continue, to keep on and on—for

this meal had become a feast, a holiday. She wished it would never end. She wished that God would spare her from having to break the boy's heart on this day of his homecoming.

Uriah basked in the attention. He answered each question fully and with careful gravity, even the ones from the smallest children. He tried hard not to be boastful or arrogant. He wanted to share his two years with his family, but he hoped they would not resent him or think him playing the lord. He ate until his stomach pained. Food had not tasted so good since Mrs. Wilkins had roasted a turkey at the captain's home in Savannah. Only now would he admit to himself, if never to his family, how sick to death he had become of salt beef and hardtack and scouse and even of plum duff, which had seemed early in the voyage like the food of kings. Oh, how good it was to sit at this familiar table in the warm, sweet-smelling kitchen and to eat his mother's delicious lamb and the fresh vegetables that came from her own little garden behind the house. How good it was to come home!

The thought came to him, as his mother brought out a fresh-baked raisin cake, that there had not been a single reprimand since he entered the house, not even a reproving look. He had worried much about that as the *Jerusee* had sailed up the broad Delaware toward the city, wondering if his homecoming would be spoiled by tears and anger at the way he had departed two years before, in the dark and silence of night, without a word of farewell save an apologetic note and a consoling message left with his grandfather. He need not have worried. All was welcome and love. Soon, in a quieter moment, he would talk with his mother and father and tell them how sorry he was over the hurt he had caused them and the worry. But he would also tell them that he had not made a mistake. He loved the sea and the life aboard its ships. Oh, it was the life for him!

He finished the last crumb of cake and then stood up resolutely and said he must hurry over to Papa's house and tell him he was home. He was anxious to answer the many questions that he knew his ever-curious grandfather would ask him. How he had looked forward to this moment, to see the pride in Jonas Phillips's eyes at his grandson home from the sea!

Uriah heard footsteps behind him as he walked across the parlor to the door. He turned to see his mother and father standing together with solemn faces. Behind them, in the kitchen, he could see his brothers and sisters clearing the dishes from the table and sluicing the plates with water from the pump.

"Stay a moment, Uriah," his father said. "We must have words with you."

Words? What words? Would the angry reprimands come now? Uriah looked at them, at their suddenly joyless eyes, and waited.

"He is gone, Uriah," said his mother. "He is gone now."

He knew. He knew instantly. But he asked anyway, "Who is gone?"

"Grandpa Jonas." His mother's voice was so soft, it almost was drowned by the noise of a passing carriage. "He is dead, last January a year." Her face bore a look almost cruel, it was contorted so with sympathy for him. She always had known what they had meant to each other.

Uriah's head swam. He felt himself moving backward as if he would fall, and then he sat down suddenly in a stiff wooden parlor chair. His face had gone stone-white. He shook his head, then again. Everything . . . *everything* had gone according to plan, just as he had dreamed it so often aboard the ship: the loving homecoming, the first meal, the chattering of the little brothers and sisters. But this? He never had thought of this. His reunion with Papa always had been the centerpiece of his homecoming fantasy. And now . . .

He sighed and looked up at his mother. "How . . . how did it happen?"

"Grandpa just died in his sleep. His friends said he had just wore out from a long life of hard work and caring for his family. Grandma found him in the morning, in his bed. . . ."

"How is Grandma? How has she—?"

"She is well, thank God. Mordecai and Judith still live with her.

They are good company and help her take care of the house. And she has so many friends. Every Shabbat, after prayers, they all go from the *esnoga* to Grandma's house to wish her a good Shabbat. She and Grandpa had so many friends. She is not forgotten."

Uriah stood again. His face was filled with pain, but his chin was firm, and when he spoke, his voice was steady.

"I am going to the burying ground," he said. "I want to say good-bye to Papa."

"He is not here, Uriah," said his mother.

"What? What do you mean?"

"He is buried in the Shearith Israel burying ground in New York City. He is not in Philadelphia."

Uriah seemed insulted by this news. For the first time, raw emotion showed in his voice, anger: "Why? For God's sake, why? *This* was his home."

His mother nodded and held up a calming hand. "Yes, but you see, Grandpa—." Suddenly she smiled. "You know how he was, Uriah. Oh, he had some temper, my father did, and when he felt he was right, there was no power on earth could change his mind. After you left, he had another of his disputes with the *adjunta* of Mikveh Israel, and he told them he never would forgive them. And he made Grandma promise faithfully that when he died, he would be buried with his old friends in New York, rather than here. What could Grandma do? She had to keep her promise to him. You know how he was." Michael Levy nodded firmly as if to endorse his wife's statement.

"I will go to New York then. I'll go at dawn. I have to say good-bye to him."

Rachel started to protest: "But you've just come—" Then she stopped. "All right. Your father will rent two good saddle horses from the livery, and he will go with you." Her husband started to object but stopped at a look from his wife. "You may be a brave sailor, but you are still not old enough to travel to New York City alone."

Uriah nodded. "Thank you, Mama. When I get back, we'll have

plenty of time to talk. Now, I want to go see Grandma and Mordecai and Judith. I'll be home soon." And he was gone.

Rachel and her husband were silent for a moment, looking at each other. They felt relieved. They had dreaded this revelation for so long.

"He did not even cry," she said, wonder in her voice. "Not a single tear. And he loved him so much."

"It is the way they are taught on ships," her husband said knowingly. "It is a hard life, and they are taught not to show their feelings. If a man is killed or badly hurt, they just shrug and go about their business. That is how they are taught."

She knew better. "No, he is still a child. He will cry. Perhaps when he sees my mother for the first time, perhaps not until he stands at my father's grave. But he will cry."

They roamed the old streets of Philadelphia, talking without stop. Stories endlessly came roiling from their lips; when one would stop for breath, the other took up the slack. Their arms waved as they measured and drew pictures in the air of what had befallen them in their months apart.

Nothing is more endearing than the recovery of an old friend, and that is what it was for Uriah. He had renewed ties with his red-haired cousin Mordecai Manuel Noah and found that he had a new intimate, a trusted chum with whom he could trade dreams and fears as he had with Jamie Wilkins during his months aboard the *Jerusee*. In the years before he had left, Mordecai had been merely an older cousin who had shared his devotion to Papa. But still there had been little intimacy between the two boys. After all, they were seven years apart, and those years loomed larger then.

Now Mordecai was eighteen years old and Uriah one day shy of twelve, yet things were dramatically different between them. Perhaps it was Uriah's time at sea, with all that does to a boy and to the way others regard him. The teacher-pupil feeling had vanished forever, and now they were two old, fast friends.

Today, without planning it, they were retracing the old walks they had taken so many times with Papa. They strolled, almost oblivious to their surroundings, down Elfreth's Alley and Front Street and Cherry Street and Market Street and told each other rollicking stories of where they had been and what they had done.

Uriah pulled him down to the Delaware wharves and pointed to the ships tied there to illustrate his perilous adventures in the rigging and his hard toil at the *Jerusee's* capstan and to show him how an anchor was catted and how the cut of one vessel's jib differed from another's. And he told him of the men: of the quiet giant of a captain and old Sails and the smiling black Doctor who had fattened him up by fifteen pounds.

As they headed back uptown, Mordecai told him about his own travels through New York State and Canada as an apprentice to Hookstra, a gilder and carver, who roamed like a nomad selling his wares. Times were hard, and he did not want to be a burden to his grandparents, so when Mordecai failed to find a job in government, he signed an indenture that bound him as apprentice to Hookstra until he was twenty-one. But there was light at the end of the road: it would not be much longer until he could buy his release from the indenture, he confided.

It wasn't long before they got to talking about Papa. Mordecai said that he felt like he had lost his own father, for he could hardly remember his real father, wherever that lost soul might be now. He had stood with Jonas's children before the coffin and said good-bye to him, like the youngest son of the family, for he suffered as if he were.

Zalegman had said a brief eulogy for his father, there in the parlor of the old house, before they had taken the coffin out and put it in the back of a sturdy wagon drawn by two gray horses and set out for New York City and the burial. Jonas's sons accompanied their father to his grave, Mordecai among them. The daughters stayed home in Philadelphia with their mother because of the Sephardi tradition that prohibited women from being present when a body is committed to God's ground.

And in New York, in the little enclave where the sons and daughters of Congregation Shearith Israel had been laid to rest since 1682, Jonas Phillips took his place, mourned by all his sons and old friends by the score. For the Hebrews of New York City had not forgotten loud, hard-minded old Jonas. His old ally from the days of the Revolution, Hazzan Seixas, was there to say the prescribed words over the grave and to lead them in the prayers.

And then it was Uriah's turn to describe to his cousin the long horseback ride across New Jersey with his father on the day after his homecoming and their visit to Papa's grave. Hazzan Seixas joined them there, and the three of them whispered prayers for Papa. It was a rainy, cold day, and Uriah told Mordecai that he had the strange feeling that God himself was weeping . . . for Papa and for them.

Uriah did not tell Mordecai about his father's odd remark as they left the burial ground. Hazzan Seixas had said good-bye and bade them a safe return to their home. They mounted their horses and began moving toward the Hudson River ferry. Michael Levy glanced back at the cemetery and then said to Uriah, "He was a good man. He is missed. But maybe now you will understand that I am your papa." Then he fell silent and said little more during the long ride back to Philadelphia.

Uriah Levy looked out at the congregation on his bar mitzvah day with no joy in his heart. There was pride, surely, for today he would take up his own religious responsibilities and relieve his father of that burden. He was proud that, two days hence, he would become thirteen years and that today, on this Shabbat morning, he had received for the first time an *aliyah*, a call to the *tebah* to say a blessing over a part of the weekly reading. He was now among the men of Mikveh Israel, and he stood straight in this knowledge.

But he could not feel joy, for missing from his old place on the front bench was the husky man with the bushy gray hair who had always roared his way through the prayers and earned reproachful hints from his neighbors to sing more quietly. Oh, how Jonas

Phillips's eyes would have gleamed when it was time for the *maftir*, the last and most honored call to the *tebah*, and the call was for his grandson, Uriah Phillips Levy, to come forth and chant the haftarah.

And chant it he did, slowly, sweetly, and without hesitation. For the past year, ever since his homecoming, he had prepared carefully for this day with Hazzan Cohen and his son Abraham, who had gone patiently over the Hebrew passages with him again and again in the Cohen house on Cherry Alley. The boy had insisted from the outset of his instruction that he would chant the entire *sidrah*, the weekly reading from the Torah, even though it had recently become the custom for the bar mitzvah to chant only a single *parasha* of the *sidrah*.

He stood now at the *tebah*, grave and unsmiling, and pulled his tallit closer about him as the *shamash* chanted. He chastised himself: He must stop thinking about Papa and feeling sad or else he would ruin this day for his parents, who were so excited about it. He looked up and saw his mother and grandmother beaming down at him from the women's gallery. With them sat their friend Rebecca Gratz, who worked so hard with them and other women in collecting funds for and operating a soup house, where poverty-stricken women and children could find sustenance—the grand ladies of the Female Association for the Relief of Women and Children in Reduced Circumstances. He nodded to them and smiled slightly.

In the back row of the men's section, as usual, sat his father. Michael Levy was proud of his son; you could tell that by the way he looked around the room and studied the faces of the other worshippers. His pride overcame his irritation at having to again sit here in the old *esnoga*. Soon after his father-in-law's death, he had resigned from Mikveh Israel and cast his lot with Rodeph Shalom, the new German synagogue. He was no Sephardi, he proclaimed, and he wanted to pray with his own kind, in the Hebrew that was comfortable for him, and without the strange Spanish-Portuguese customs that always had made him feel an outsider. Now he worshipped with his fellow German Jews in the rented room on Margaretta Street where Rodeph Shalom had made a home.

But on this day, Michael Levy sat again in Mikveh Israel and listened with quiet satisfaction as his seafaring son chanted the entire *sidrah*. He nodded in affirmation at the end of each verse and looked from the side of his eyes at the admiring faces on the benches around him.

Uriah cleared his throat and prepared to chant again. *It was going well*, he thought. Hazzan Cohen looked pleased. He hoped that, somehow, Papa could hear him. It was almost over. Tomorrow, at the morning service, he would pray like the other men, with tefillin wrapped around his head and arm. Religiously he no longer was a child. Suddenly Uriah realized that he had not thought of himself as a child for a long time.

The *shamash* nodded to him. Uriah took a breath and began to chant once more. His high, reedy voice soared in the ancient tropes, carrying clearly through the crowded hall, up to the beaming, approving women in the gallery, to the street beyond, and hopefully to the heavens above.

It was sad that Philadelphia no longer was the nation's seat of government. Uriah walked past the imposing building at 190 High Street in which first Washington and then Adams had rented quarters while they controlled the destiny of the thirteen united states of America that now had increased to seventeen and might someday go as high as twenty-five. Right here, just a few blocks from his family home and the lots where he and his friends had played their childhood games, had lived the general in chief of his own vast nation. It was a heady feeling!

But now the capital had been moved to the malarial swamps on the Potomac River, and the distinguished old house in which Washington and Adams had lived was a hotel. Nearby, the State House, where judges of the Supreme Court had pondered the nation's laws, sat silently among its arcades.

Uriah headed for the long, low buildings of the High Street Market to buy the fresh fruit his mother wanted for dinner. He also wanted to find the pants merchant who reportedly had opened a stall in the market and offered strong gabardine pantaloons at respectable prices. Uriah was sprouting like a young tree and needing larger clothes often enough to keep a perpetual harried look on his father's face.

While I am here at the market, he thought, *I will see about those new right and left shoes that have become all the rage.* At first he had considered it somewhat frivolous and wasteful to buy shoes that were made differently for each foot, but he had seen a newspaper advertisement by the shoemaker William Young, who had invented the right foot, left foot shoes, and was intrigued. Young advertised a variety of styles; he had "Suwarrows, Cossacks, hussars, Carrios, double-tongues, Swiss-hunting, fall dress, walking, York." If he bought a pair, Uriah vowed, he would buy the ones designated for walking, because that is what he aimed to do in his shoes. What those other styles were intended for, he couldn't imagine.

As an old man walked toward him, coming out of a market door, Uriah was struck first by his antique appearance: he wore a wig, knee breeches, silk stockings, buckled shoes, and a long wool coat, all in the older style. Jonas Phillips, were he now living, would be dressed like this. On the man's head was a good old tricornered hat, not one of the high-crowned round hats that topped the heads of all the Philadelphia dandies and fops in this summer day of 1805. Breeches? My God, every good Republican donned trousers these days to dramatize his support for the Republican Party of Mr. Jefferson and, in many cases, to show ongoing solidarity with the revolution in France, though many were beginning to wonder whether Bonaparte would not eventually lead that nation back to a monarchy or empire.

It was the old-fashioned dress that first captured Uriah's eye, and he looked at the oncoming man only with a mild, rather fond curiosity. But then he was struck by the thick barrel chest and the head that seemed to overbalance the body, and he had just started to strain to remember who this might be, when suddenly he knew it was Joshua Humphreys, master draftsman and builder of ships.

He was astonished at how much Humphreys had aged. It had been perhaps four or five years since he last had visited the shipyard with Papa and Mordecai, but what was four or five years? This appeared to be an old man. He walked slowly and peered ahead with nearsighted eyes. He was slightly stooped. His face bore a grimace, as if he walked in pain.

"Mr. Humphreys? Hello, is it Mr. Joshua Humphreys?"

"Eh? Yes, yes? Who be ye?"

Uriah respectfully took off his hat. "You may not remember me, sir. I am Uriah Levy, the grandson of Jonas Phillips. We used to visit you at the shipyard during the time that—"

"Oh, yes, yes! My goodness, yes!" A gentle smile replaced the look of pain on the shipbuilder's face. Even his voice had aged. He no longer rasped like an adz; he no longer roared. He spoke softly now, with the caution and weariness of the elderly. "My, you have grown into a young man, Mr. Levy. I would never have known you. What are you up to these days?"

"Now I am working in my father's shop, Mr. Humphreys. I have been to sea for two years."

The smile faded from the face of Humphreys. "To sea? Oh, yes. I seem to remember that you always were in love with the sea."

Uriah laughed. "Well, that love disappeared on the first stormy night aboard ship. It really was the ships that I loved and not the water, and that hasn't changed. I'm sure you understand what I mean."

Humphreys nodded but did not reply. He stared rather vacantly over Uriah's shoulder as if preferring that their eyes did not meet.

"What ship do you build now, Mr. Humphreys?" asked Uriah.

"I build no more ships. I live quietly now in Haverford and tend my flowers and puff my pipe. No more ships. Ah, but my son Samuel is still building ships. He is partnered with Penrose. They built the *City of Philadelphia*, you know."

"Yes, sir. I did hear that." He hesitated before speaking further. "I—I am sorry about the ship's final end."

Humphreys nodded sadly. "Yes, but it was better to burn it than let it be used by those devils in Tripoli. And this country got itself a new national hero. Can you imagine that young rapscallion Decatur, who used to run around my shipyard and criticize the way I was building my ship—that audacious young pup is now our national pride and treasure, the hero of Tripoli?"

"It was indeed a daring sally, sir," agreed Uriah. "To take that small force of men into Tripoli harbor, faced by over one hundred heavy cannon and twenty-five thousand Arabs and Turks, and to burn the *Philadelphia* right under their noses. An amazing feat!"

"Aye, 'amazing' is the word. And Decatur deserves all his glory. Oh, but that was a beautiful frigate that Samuel built. A real beauty! Such a waste, such a waste."

The harsh look of silent sorrows had returned to Humphreys's face. Uriah tried to change the subject.

"And how is your other son, Clement? Is he, too, building ships? I remember him from that day in your yard—"

"Clement is dead." It was said so quietly, so matter-of-factly, that Uriah wasn't sure he had heard correctly. He said nothing, thinking he might have misunderstood the old man, but raised his eyebrows in question.

"Yes, my boy Clement is dead," Humphreys repeated. "Like you, he couldn't wait to go to sea. He had a berth on a merchantman that went down with all hands in ought-three. And then this year, my wife, Miss Mary, upped and died on me. She was merely forty-seven, you see. Far too young to die. So I am left with only Samuel, who stays very busy at his shipyard. I have my flowers, of course, out in Haverford." He nodded as if to himself and stared into the distance.

Uriah didn't know what to say. "You are a great builder of fighting ships, Mr. Humphreys. Surely our country will call on you again. We are needing ships and—"

A touch of the old fire came back into Humphreys's eyes. His face grew flushed. "Needing ships, are we?" he barked. "Not this nation. Not this president. Jefferson is a good man, but sometimes good men can be fools. They think all men to be angels and they pet night dogs on the head and expect them to purr like house cats. It was the frigates that won us respect on the Barbary Coast—the *frigates*! And what does Mr. Jefferson propose? That we build tiny little gunboats to protect our harbors—little piss-boats that will be swamped by the first good wave. Aye, with twelve ships-of-the-line, we would be a match for any naval power on God's earth, save possibly the English, who already have more liners than Philadelphia has trees. And what says our president? 'Give me teeny gunboats!' With all respect, when it comes to our navy, Mr. Jefferson is a pain-in-the-stomach fool!"

Uriah bridled inwardly a bit, as he always did when someone criticized Jefferson. But he could see that Humphreys's caustic comments were less an expression of hatred for the president than a cry of fear for the country.

"Speaking of frigates," Uriah said, "how goes it with the *United States*? I have always thought of her as *my* ship, you know. And it is still my dream to command her some day."

Humphreys showed no reaction to Uriah's sentiment. His eyes again assumed their faraway look. "The *United States* does well enough, although they have let her fall into deplorable condition. I see her now and then. Of the eleven frigates in our navy now, only the *Constitution* is in fighting trim. The others are slowly rotting away."

He paused, sighed deeply, and shook his head. Then he went on: "She never recovered from the launching, you know. Were you there? All of Philadelphia was there. She went down the incline too fast and bent her false keel. I worked night and day all summer to fix it and thought I had. But she never again sailed as she should. And do you know what the navy men call her now? 'The Old Wagon.' They say she is the slowest of all the six frigates built just before the century. I don't wonder. We broke her back that day, and my lady will never be the same again."

An awkward silence hung between them. Uriah felt sad. Humphreys must still be less than sixty years old, though he looked aged.

There was no interest in his eyes. And, except for the moment of fire when he had questioned Jefferson's policies, he seemed always to dwell on death and loss and disappointed hopes.

"Well, sir," Uriah said, "I must be going to the market. I seek some shoes and also some food for my mother."

"Yes, yes, of course. You must be about your business. What is your plan, Mr. Levy? For the future, I mean."

"I plan to return to sea, sir. I am sure of that. I promised my parents to stay home for a time and get more schooling. But soon, I'll be seeking a new berth."

The old builder looked directly at him again. Now there was urgency in his eyes. He pointed a finger at Uriah's chest as he spoke. "Stay here, Mr. Levy," he said. "Stay with your father and become a merchant like him and your grandfather. Forget the sea. Forget your beloved ships. In the end . . . in the end, they will destroy you." His eyes watered as he said his final words, "As they have destroyed me." Then, with no farewell, he walked slowly on his way.

Uriah sat in his parents' parlor, an expression of stunned surprise on his face. In the flickering light of the fire, he glanced again from his mother's pale, drawn face to his father's, on which played the usual tight little smile, perhaps a bit cheerier than usual as he enjoyed the effect of his pronouncement.

The boy's dark-complected face was flushed with emotion, and he ran his fingers nervously through his curly black hair. He had fully expected a battle here tonight and indeed had well armed himself with words, arguments, pleadings. What had materialized instead could not even be called a skirmish. It was an abject surrender.

"Do you really mean that, Father?" Uriah asked, not quite prepared to believe what he had just heard.

"I mean it," answered Michael Levy. "I will arrange your apprenticeship with John Coulter. You can go to sea. I realized months ago that your mind was made up. There would be no changing it. This does not have my blessing, you understand, nor even my approval.

But there is no point in standing in your way. It serves no purpose. In the end, you would do what you must do."

"Uriah?" His mother's voice was low and calm, as usual, but it trembled.

"Ma'am?"

"Is there no persuading you? Your father has consulted me about this, of course. I knew his decision. But—tell me, please, that you will think about it some more. I want you to have more schooling. We have such a fine university here. You could study surgery—or the law. And if not that, there is always a place for you in Father's business. . . ." She shook her head, as if she knew there was no point in continuing. She looked down at her lap and shook her head again.

Uriah hated the tortured look on his mother's face. He hated more the thought that he was responsible for it. If only he could do as she wished!

"Mama, believe me, I have thought about it. I have worried it again and again, ever since I came back home. But I keep coming back to the same result. I want to live under sail. That's all that I want. Always the same answer."

"Then let us worry it no more," said his father. "There is no point. If you must go to sea, let it be on an honest, sound ship operated by a decent owner. I've known John Coulter for years. He has made a great deal of money from shipping because he is a good business-man and knows the value of a dollar, but also because he hires good masters who treat their crews humanely. He has a reputation that few other owners can boast."

"And he will find a berth for me on one of his ships?" asked Uriah, still finding it hard to believe that the long-anticipated struggle of wills had been resolved so peaceably.

"He says he will. He has seen you at work in the shop and says you seem industrious and bright. He will be in Baltimore until Tuesday, inspecting a schooner for buying. On Wednesday we'll go to see him and work out the details."

John Coulter's shipping offices occupied several rooms on the second floor of a Front Street building overlooking the teeming wharf and the river crowded with vessels. Several harried-looking clerks scurried around with manifests, provision lists, huge ledgers. Piled on a table in the corner of one room were designs and specifications for a brig being constructed for Coulter.

Michael Levy and his son waited in Coulter's private office. The voice of the owner could be plainly heard from a nearby room as he concluded a lengthy and passionate discussion with the brig's shipwright over the quality of the work being done by the sawyers who cut the timbers and the adzmen whose job was to transform the rough timbers into the smooth strakes needed for the outer skin of the brig. Coulter kept himself under control and never became loud, but the strain in his voice was evident as he demanded better supervision over the yardmen. The strakes had not been properly smoothed, he insisted. They must be hewed further.

On the wall behind Coulter's desk, between two windows that framed the masts and furled sails on the river, was a portrait of Coulter by Charles Willson Peale. Uriah studied the face. The image showed a man in his middle years with confidence in himself and in his future. The smile on his face fell somewhat short of arrogance. It would better be described as a look of benign pride in oneself. On the other walls were paintings of ships—merchantmen, except for one man-of-war that Uriah instantly recognized as the frigate *United States*. He would know those lines anywhere. On another wall was a small fireplace in which logs cheerily burned. On the mantle was a wooden model of a bark. The model, Uriah surmised, was of a Coulter ship, and the pictures also must show Coulter ships of past or present.

The conversation in the other room had ended. Uriah cleared his throat. In a moment, Coulter bustled into the room, apologizing for the delay and asking to their health. He sat down behind the desk, leaned back, clasped his hands behind his head, and wasted no more time on inconsequential talk.

"So, Master Levy, you want to follow the sea, do you? It is a hard taskmaster, you know. The men are rough fellows, and the living is not easy. Nor is the work."

Uriah was ready to relate his own experience with sea life, but then he realized that Coulter was not waiting for an answer.

"I presently operate five ships," Coulter continued. "I own three brigs and a bark, and I co-own a schooner. Another brig is being constructed for me by Green and Sons. My ships are sound ones, good sailers all and dry vessels in a storm. My crews are well fed, worked hard, paid according to the standard prevailing, and each family provided a small bird at Christmas. My captains are the finest on the Atlantic coast. That is why my ships are known in all their ports of call as reliable vessels which make their way safely and in due time."

All of this had been stated in a perfunctory monotone, the hands still clasped behind the head, the body leaning backward in a state of repose, the eyes focused on the wall beyond them. Now he brought his hands down, sat forward, and stared intently at Uriah.

"I understand you were two years along the coast with Captain Wilkins in the *New Jerusalem*. Cabin boy and assistant cook, I believe your father told me. Correct?" Uriah nodded. "Wilkins is a fine captain, known far and wide as a fair and honest man. I offered him a ship, but he won't make any voyages to Europe because he's a family man and won't be away that long. Pity. Will you go out again as a boy?"

This time, Uriah could see that he was expected to answer. "Yes, sir," he said. "I'm not quite fourteen years and willing to take another voyage or two as a boy, for I know I've a lot to learn. But after perhaps two more, I would expect to ship as an ordinary or not at all. I am anxious to get rated as able and then become a mate. I have no wish to be a common sailor forever, sir. I have hopes of someday captaining one of your ships for you."

Coulter nodded, pleased with the boy's show of ambition. "Good, good! Commendable! You stay with me, young man, and do well and work hard and someday you can be not only master of a ship of mine, but you may well co-own it with me. I am setting up a new plan to bring my captains into partnership. It will ensure their loyalty to me and certainly fatten their purses. It is important, by the way, that you learn something of the business of running a merchant vessel, and you'll learn that crewing on my ships. It is not only being a foretopman or a pull-and-haul man. You'll also learn how to load the cargo for the ship's best trim, how to purchase victuals in foreign ports, and how to buy and sell cargo, among other things. Aye, a young man who trains on a Coulter ship becomes not only a good sailorman, he becomes a businessman of the sea."

Uriah's head was swimming with possibilities. Did this mean that he was hired, that he had a berth? On which ship? And leaving when?

"Then it is settled, John?" asked Michael Levy quietly. "You can use him?"

"Oh yes, we'll find a berth for him." He rose from his chair, and his two visitors did likewise. "Master Levy, hold yourself in readiness for a summons from me. It may be a week or as long as two months. I must confer with my captains as they arrive in Philadelphia about their needs for new crew. I have my eye on a particular ship for you. It is the big schooner *Rittenhouse*, Captain James Moffit. He is a fine teacher, much in the manner of Wilkins. You'll profit from sailing with James Moffit. But his ship is not due here for several weeks yet. Hold yourself ready, Master Levy, and heed my call when it comes. I'll have a berth for you, I promise. Then good day, gentlemen, good day." He ushered them expansively to his outer door, brushing away the proferred thanks of father and son.

As they walked down the stairs to Front Street, Michael Levy placed his hand on his son's shoulder, an unaccustomed gesture. "When he has a berth for you," he said, "Coulter will insist that I bind you to him as apprentice for four years. He will not take you on his ship without such an agreement. I hope you understand. You will be his bound boy for four years. Are you sure that is what you want?"

"Yes, Father, I'm sure. If it will get me back to sea and help me learn of ships, that is what I want."

"Very well. Then you shall have it."

5

Uriah Phillips Levy, the boy who left on the schooner *Rittenhouse* in late May 1806, swaggered a bit as he walked up the hill to his family's home almost a year later. He had added both inches and pounds during this year and now could be taken for a man, though he was only scant weeks past his fifteenth birthday. It was "Ordinary Seaman Levy" now and no longer boy. He had served as a boy across the stormy North Atlantic and showed Captain Moffit that he could hand, reef, and steer. He could heave a log or lead with the best of them. They called at Liverpool, and four days later, as they prepared to haul the *Rittenhouse* up to her cable and sail away, the captain quietly told young Levy that he had been promoted to an ordinary. He was a sailorman, for sure, now and drew a sailorman's pay.

They called at Irish ports then and listened to the Irishmen keen their hatred of the English. They even dipped into L'Orient in France and then beat their way back across the Atlantic toward the Gulf Stream, that great quiet river of warm water flowing gently to the north and east. Uriah carefully watched Captain Moffit chart the trade winds—the latitude and longitude at which they were encountered, and how long they lasted—as well as the Horse Latitudes with their sickening calms. And the soft-spoken master patiently showed the curious youth the mysteries of the parallel ruler used in navigation and the calculus that made it work. Uriah listened for as long as the captain was willing to speak and never tired of being instructed.

After miles of clawing and clambering across the heaving ocean, they began to slide, as if down a child's toy, into the quieter waters of the West Indies and hove to at Antigua and Port au Prince. These were weeks of peace, prosperous trading, heat and wetness, and giant clouds of mosquitoes and gnats. Other ships reported men going down with bilious fever and intermittent fever and even the dreaded Yellow Jack, but the *Rittenhouse* seemed to live a charmed life.

Then, in the Windward Passage—that narrow channel thick with the ships of all nations, between Haiti and Cuba—the *Rittenhouse* fell in with a French privateer which cared not that America was neutral and taking no part in the struggle between Bonaparte and King George.

The Frenchman fired two shots across the *Ritt*'s bow, sent a prize crew aboard, and calmly sailed the schooner into Santiago de Cuba. There a magistrate placidly heard Moffit's tirades of protest, scratched his head, and announced that the *Rittenhouse* would be free to depart, providing that its captain would post a bond of good conduct. Oh . . . and of course, her cargo would be confiscated. Moffit, whose choices were extortion or a Cuban jail, really had no choice; the bond was paid, and the *Rittenhouse*, high and light upon the long swells, made an easting and was hull-down on the horizon as soon as her crew could get her there. It was east nor'east then, to Grand Turk Island in the Turks Island group ninety miles north of Hispaniola. Captain Moffit knew that a cargo could be obtained there, and so it quickly was. They hauled anchor, bound for home, but trouble secretly had booked passage with them. The French prize crew had treated the *Ritt* roughly when taking her into Cuba and had skinned her on some reefs. Her bruised seams began rapidly to open after she left Grand Turk. She began to ship water and within a matter of minutes was foundering. The crew was well-drilled and well-ordered and quickly put boats in the water with all hands aboard.

They were in the boats for several days, and it took all of Moffit's navigation skill and sea experience to finally bring them to a safe landfall on what seemed to be a deserted island somewhere in the Bahamas chain. There was despair at first, for some of the men thought they would die here on this hot beach as soon as the water ran out. Young Levy remained calm and obedient to orders and was highly praised afterward by Moffit for his coolness under trial.

A few hours of beachcombing led them to the discovery of a wrecked schooner, much smaller than their lamented *Rittenhouse*, but—or so Moffit assured them—seaworthy with some repair. Her masts and sails fortunately were intact. They spent weeks working on the wreck, using driftwood and fine wooden pegs as nails until finally they had the little schooner in good enough shape to try the surf. Sail she did, and they soon found their way into New Providence harbor for rest and food and further repairs to their rescue vessel. Then on to Eleuthera Island, where Moffit made sure the trip would not be a total loss by procuring a cargo of fruit. Then back to Philadelphia, to the stares and unbelieving derision of the wharf rats, to be succeeded by huzzahs and applause when the full story of the epic trip became known.

Uriah Levy had learned enough about the sea and its ways to realize how much he yet had to learn. He was no conceited fool. But the voyage had proven him, had made him show his mettle. He had been tried and was not found wanting. His zest for the sailor's life was undiminished; indeed, it was stronger than ever. And now he knew, beyond all doubt, that he could give whatever his captain and his ship might ask of him.

Uriah was walking fast, a near-run, down Cherry Street and was within fifty feet of the *esnoga* when he heard himself hailed. It was Joe Nones, also bound for Mikveh Israel and also late for services, who was calling his name. Joe was ten years old, and he reminded

Uriah of himself at that age: enchanted with ships and panting for the day when he could go to sea. He wearied Uriah with his obsessive queries about ships and seamanship, but the older youth was patient with him. For one thing, he saw too much of himself five years before to be short with the boy. Also, Joe was the son of a man much respected: the merchant Benjamin Nones, who had fought with great bravery in the Carolina battles during the Revolution and was part of Pulaski's regiment in the siege of Savannah.

The Shabbat service already had begun; he was late enough now, and a conversation with young Joe Nones would make him even later. Uriah had assured his mother and grandmother that he would attend the Shabbat worship on this Fourth of July before wandering over to the festive Independence Day fete on the square. Since his latest return from the sea, the girls of Philadelphia viewed him with new interest, and the square would be full of pretty girls on this gala day.

"Uriah! Uriah!" Joe Nones had caught up to him. He was panting, and his face was flushed with excitement. "Have you heard the tidings? Have you heard about the disgrace? The war may start soon!"

"What war?" he asked the stammering boy. "What tidings do you mean?"

"It is spreading all over the docks!" His breathlessness made it hard for Joe to speak. He had to pause for a moment to gather his wind. "The disgrace of the *Chesapeake*! They say Jefferson has a declaration of war on his desk, ready for signing."

Uriah was losing patience. "Joe, stop it! Catch your breath and tell me what the hell you're trying to say!"

Joe took a huge breath and started again: "It's the naval frigate, the *Chesapeake*. It happened off Virginia. She fell in with the British ship *Leopard*, 50-guns. Captain James Barron commanded the *Chesapeake*; a Captain Humphreys, I think, commanded the *Leopard*. The British sent an officer aboard, supposed to bring dispatches, and he demanded the right to search the *Chesapeake* for British deserters. Barron refused to allow the search, and the English lieutenant went back to the *Leopard*. They knew there would be a fight, but they say the *Chesapeake* was not ready and the gunners did not even have their rammers or gunlocks. The *Leopard* opened fire and poured broadsides into the *Chesapeake* for fifteen minutes. A lieutenant on the *Chessie* somehow managed to fire a gun, but that was the only shot she fired. Barron brought down his colors! The *Chesapeake* had three killed and eighteen wounded, and the British searched her as they pleased and pulled off four sailors who were taken away. The *Chessie* came limping in disgrace into Hampton Roads. They say Barron will surely be court-martialed. Washington City is mad as hell, and Congress is demanding war against England!"

Uriah had listened to this tale with a sense of growing anger. "My God," he said, "what a horrible disaster! If the *Chesapeake* was as unprepared as you say, they *should* court-martial Barron!"

He walked with the still-breathless Nones boy into the synagogue and sat down on a back bench. As he put on his tallit and adjusted it around his shoulders, his thoughts remained on the *Chesapeake* and the likelihood of war with England.

Well, he thought, *one thing's for sure. If we truly are on the verge of war, I will not be going to sea any time soon.* John Coulter, ever the careful, conservative businessman, would never let his ships sail out on the eve of war with Britain. The English naval fleet, so they said, had ballooned to a strength of six to seven hundred ships. To send unarmed merchant ships into the Atlantic against a force of that size, with our own navy reduced to only a handful of ships worthy of the name, was tantamount to handing them over to the British. Coulter never would chance that, in spite of the profits awaiting him if a ship got through.

Uriah had spent a pleasant summer at home, resting up from his voyage and shipwreck adventure and getting to know his family again. He was now the fourth-oldest of ten children, and the two youngest were almost complete strangers to him. Little Frances, whom everyone called Fanny, was three years old now and had warmed to him from the moment he had walked back into the house. And tiny Jonas Phillips Levy had been born only scant weeks before his return. It gave him a chill of pleasure to realize that once again there was a Jonas Phillips in Philadelphia.

His elder sister Eliza had married and had children of her own. His brothers Louis and Benjamin had moved away from the family house, too, although they still worked in their father's shop.

As warm and content and relaxing as the summer had been, Uriah was awaiting the day when John Coulter would summon him back to sea. He hoped to fill an able seaman's berth on a departing Coulter ship. He was anxious to continue his progress up the seaman's ladder toward the mate's rating, working toward the day when he would receive his master's papers.

Now though, with war in the air, it was hard to say when that day would be. But if war was declared, he somehow would have to persuade his parents to let him join the navy in whatever capacity the navy would have him. He was as game as anyone to represent the United States at sea and to give the Brits a strong taste of the American fist.

After England's apology for the *Chesapeake-Leopard* fracas was received in Washington City, the frantic war fever suddenly subsided. Coulter sent his little fleet back to sea and resumed his busy trade with partners throughout Europe and the West Indies. Uriah's next ship, *Polly and Betsy*, hove short and brought up her anchor in early September.

Uriah Levy had stepped aboard *Polly and Betsy* as an ordinary seaman, but Captain Silsbee soon promoted him to rank of able seaman. Now he looked forward to a voyage of a year or more and to some profits for himself, for he, with the other able seamen, had been given a patch in the hold as his own, to buy a bit of cargo and carry it for trade or sale.

As Americans sauntered on blissfully amid the fighting, the patience of the combatants was wearing thin. Soon steps were taken to prevent these carefree neutrals from supplying their enemies. Napoleon, with his consummate egomania, issued his Berlin Decree, declaring a blockade of Britain, though it was only a year since his disastrous defeat at Trafalgar.

The arrogant, hot-tempered George Canning had become Britain's foreign secretary and complained bitterly that the United States had not only failed to help England in its death struggle with France but was trading with the enemy and filling its ships with British deserters. Indeed, the American trade boom had suddenly raised a sailor's pay from eight to twenty-four dollars a month. How many suffering British seamen could resist this shower of riches?

Canning could take no more of this and declared that, since Napoleon had broken international law, Britain would follow suit. In November 1807 the cabinet approved Orders in Council declaring that Britain forthwith ban all trade with France and countries allied with France unless the neutral ships passed through British ports and paid duty to the Crown.

In response Napoleon issued his own Milan Decree: If any neutral ship allowed itself to be searched at sea by a ship of the British Navy, France would no longer regard that ship as neutral and would seize it.

The vise began to tighten, and the United States found itself securely caught. French men-of-war began to capture Yankee merchantmen and escort them into French ports. British warships flew down upon American vessels and demanded the right to search for deserters. Any men deemed by the British commander to be British subjects, no matter their protestations of American birth or any other proof of U.S. citizenship, were summarily hauled aboard the English vessel and impressed into the British Navy.

Jefferson no longer could look the other way. His flag was being spit upon from Sandy Hook to Brest. Congress screamed for a response.

On December 18, 1807, Congress authorized the construction of another 188 gunboats.

On December 22, 1807, Jefferson signed into law an unlimited embargo on all foreign commerce. All U.S. naval vessels were recalled from the Mediterranean and positioned along the coast of the United States.

When news of the embargo reached Philadelphia, John Coulter sat with his head in his hands and thought he would be ruined. Shipowners and traders in New York and New England called protest meetings and drafted memorials to Jefferson and Congress, demanding cancellation of the embargo. Jefferson answered that the embargo was necessary to teach the warring powers to respect neutral commerce. Port collectors at all Atlantic ports were instructed to prevent any ship from departing for a foreign port.

The *Polly and Betsy*, fresh from a quick sugar-and-molasses passage from the West Indies, was anchored in Baltimore harbor when the express rider from Washington City arrived with the news. Plans for a sailing to Liverpool and on to Copenhagen were quickly discarded, and Captain Silsbee brought out his coastal charts. It was back up the Delaware again for him, and into home port. And Uriah found himself back in his parents' house for the foreseeable future.

The bustling, teeming docks of Boston, Philadelphia, New York, and Baltimore became still. Seamen soon began going hungry, as did other citizens whose livelihoods depended on the ocean trade. Angry sailors staged fire-lit parades in the country's port cities. Soup kitchens were set up to feed the famished in Salem, Massachusetts, and other coastal towns. In New York a few sailors were put to work building the new City Hall and others labored at Wallabout Bay, where a Brooklyn Navy Yard was being built on the old site of John Jackson's shipyard. Men who longed to climb a weather shroud once again were reduced to hauling dirt from New York City's hills and throwing it into the Collect, the old freshwater pond that now reeked with garbage and was being filled up.

Meanwhile, five hundred ships sat idle along New York's docks and wharves, their hatches tightly battened down. Another fifteen hundred ships rotted in other U.S. ports. For every sailor who had some kind of work, a hundred others were idle and penniless. The country's economy was in tatters: sugar cost three times as much in Baltimore as in New Orleans, and flour was twice as dear in Boston as in Baltimore.

All of this, Jefferson assured his advisers, would force the British to stop their harassment of American shipping and their impressing of American sailors.

Uriah could not bring himself to join in the sailors' near universal condemnation of Jefferson. Oh, things were in a bad way alright. He knew full well himself, for he hadn't a day's work as a sailor since the *Polly and Betsy* had tied up at the Front Street wharf after the embargo had been declared. At least he had a family with which to live and food to eat. Every day he saw hungry sailors walking the streets, their usually ruddy faces now gaunt and white. He ached for them and for himself, sharing their yearning to be long away on a sound ship, but he did not—could not—bring himself to join their screams of rage at Jefferson and their calls for his downfall. Somehow, some way, Jefferson would bring this crisis to an end and the seas would be crowded again with billowing sail.

February 1808

Sitting in the presence of Coulter's ship models and paintings, Uriah wondered why the shipowner had sent for him. Surely there was no good news from the federal city. If anything, two months after the Embargo Act was passed, Jefferson was still tightening the embargo. Uriah's grave mood hadn't lightened upon his entrance to Coulter's outer rooms, the usual realm of clerks and assistants. The bustle and activity of his last visit here had been replaced by a depressing quiet. Only one aged clerk sat at a table in the first room, writing slowly in a ledger, one hand propped under his chin as if to keep his head from falling in slumber upon the polished wood tabletop.

"Ah, Uriah, it's good to see you."

Uriah rose. "Mr. Coulter. Good day, sir."

"Sit down, sit down." Coulter took his place behind his desk.

"I've been down at the dock inspecting the hull of the *Polly*. She's taking water at an alarming rate. She'll have to be careened, I fear, and freshly sealed. God knows where I'll find the money to do that. This damnable embargo is destroying my ships."

"Any chance of it being rescinded, sir?"

Coulter sighed heavily. "Ah, the chance at present seems small. Last month, you know, thousands of jobless sailors marched through the streets of New York City. We'll soon have a rebellion on our hands. I hope our honored president will come to his senses. Meanwhile I come closer each day to ruin. And you, my young apprentice, how are you standing this idleness?"

"I want very much to get back to sea, sir, but I have no strong complaint. I do odd jobs in my father's shop, and my mother keeps my stomach full. And I manage to visit the docks every day or two and go up and down the ratlines to keep my hand in."

"Yes, yes, good man. Let me tell you why I summoned you here. I've been keeping my eye on you, you know, and your progress has been very rapid. Silsbee was most impressed. He predicts you'll be a second mate in another voyage or two. I would say you have a bright future with me if this miserable embargo ever stops darkening our days."

Uriah didn't know how to respond to this praise, so he kept silent and merely nodded respectfully.

"It occurs to me," Coulter continued, "that you should not waste this idle time on the beach if we can find a profitable way for you to spend it. Profitable, if not in an immediate sense, then surely for the future. Do you get my drift?"

Uriah didn't, but he nodded in agreement.

"I know you wish someday to become a ship's master," Coulter went on. "I hope it will be on a ship of mine—perhaps one in which you will share ownership with me. Let us, then, plan for that day. You must, of course, know the mysteries of nautical navigation—an arcane science that is totally impenetrable to me. It must not be for you. I would like you, during these weeks of enforced idleness, to attend a good navigation school. Are you willing?"

"Why . . . why, yes, sir. Of course! But—"

"Oh, I neglected to add: Of course, I will pay the fee. You are my apprentice. It is my responsibility. I regard it as a good investment in my company's future."

"I am honored, Mr. Coulter. I don't know if I'm smart enough to master all the bookwork, but—"

"Nonsense! You'll excel, I'm certain. Very well, then. Of all such schools in our city, I believe the best is operated by Mr. Talbot Hamilton. He is an elderly codger, a former lieutenant in the British Navy, and a genius with charts and sextants and all those odd things they use to keep from getting lost at sea. You'll learn a great deal from him. I shall speak to him about you, and we'll find out when his next class begins."

March 1809

Uriah braced his feet comfortably on the footrope and gave careful study—leisurely, as would an eagle from his aerie—to the moribund port of Philadelphia. The wind blew stiffly at him, but the sun was warm. His arms loosely encircled the yard, and his chest pressed against it to further bind him to his lofty resting place.

It had been months since his graduation from Talbot Hamilton's navigation school. Though it still was winter by the calendar, this day in March had the smell of spring, with the sun glistening and the birds chirping in the tall masts. Aye, that's what the masts were used for these days—as nesting for birds. They were of no use to sailors. From ahigh, he could see grass growing in places on the wharf. The sailors were hidden away, or perhaps all dead of hunger by now. The wharf rested quietly, dully.

He climbed the rigging at least once a week on one or another of John Coulter's rotting merchantmen. He went aloft and stayed awhile out on a fore- or mainmast yard in order to think, for there was a peace and aloneness up here that he could find nowhere else. He felt very much at home up here, standing on a thin cord of twisted hemp, his hands holding easily to a long splinter of pine, suspended calmly 150 feet in the air above a white oak and yellow pine deck. He felt easy on this perch, and it was a feeling he had earned. He had paid for it with hundreds of hours, some of them passed in sheer terror, on other yards and footropes, furling sails, reefing sails, bending and unbending sails, putting on gaskets, taking off gaskets, skinning canvas at the weather leach in driving rain.

Uriah's thoughts of the future today were set upon the U.S. Navy, as they often had been of late. The embargo had killed the Yankee merchant fleet; it existed now only on paper. A few bedraggled coasters were the only vessels permitted to leave the Atlantic ports. All the other merchantmen rotted at anchor, like this Coulter brig on which he stood. Jefferson had only a few more days in the presidency, and yet he stood firm on the embargo. The farmers of the South, their grain piling up on the ground and their cattle growing old and tough, joined with the merchants of New England in sending memorial after memorial to the president's house, begging him to reconsider. Jefferson was silent.

Uriah shook his head in frustration, the movement scaring into flight a bird that had lit behind him on the main topyard. The breeze freshened and blew his black hair. He shivered. Winter was reasserting its reign. He had climbed up here hatless and wearing only a light jersey.

Any man thinking of a career as a seaman or officer in the U.S. merchant fleet must be low in spirit on this day. The only hope for finding sea work lay with the navy. Jefferson finally had been persuaded to abandon his dream of defending American coasts with little gunboats, the "Jeffs" as the president's detractors called them. Some silver-tongued soul—there were those who insisted it was James Madison—had convinced Jefferson at last that the gunboats provided no defense against British or French ships-of-the-line or frigates. Reluctantly—all the old fears of a military autocracy rising anew in his bosom—Jefferson signed an order recommissioning three old frigates and a corvette and increasing the navy's complement of men and boys from 1,425 to 5,025. Hungry sailors stood in long lines at navy receiving ships in desperate hope of finding a new berth at last.

Uriah had given up many hard, sleepless hours in the night to thoughts of the navy. It offered his only chance of getting back to sea. But he still was shy of his seventeenth birthday, and the navy would not look at him as an able or even as an ordinary seaman. He would never go back again to being a ship's boy. The only other path open to him was that of midshipman. True, this would start him on the ladder up to an officer's commission. But a midshipman was not much more than a glorified boy, and the arrogant young "reefers" were roundly hated by the common sailors. It was not a role he fancied for himself, even should he be able to obtain such an appointment.

A sound startled him from his meditation. It was fortunate that he retained a solid hold on the yard because he twitched without volition and might have fallen had his grasp been a casual one. The call from below was just a muffled "ooh-aye-uhh" at first, but then it was repeated and someone was plainly shouting, "Uriah! Come down! Uriah!" He looked down and swept the deck, searching for the caller. Finally he saw the lone figure standing abaft the mainmast. It was his father.

He wondered what brought his father down to the wharf on this quiet Sunday afternoon. Uriah decided to show off his prowess in the rigging by sliding to the deck, rather than taking the slower way down the ratlines, the reverse of his ascension. He edged his way along the footrope, moving farther out along the yard until he could grab the brace. With a firm hold on the brace, he swung out into the air and wrapped his legs tightly around the thick rope, then slid slowly and under control, in one continuous, rhythmic surge, down to the deck.

Michael Levy's face wore its usual blank expression, with perhaps an extra touch of dourness on this day. He walked down the ship's plank ahead of his son, and then they strode together along the deserted wharf.

"What brings you here, Father? Is anything wrong at home?"

His father shook his head. "Nothing wrong at home. Some news has come that I knew you would want to hear." There was a pause, as if Michael Levy was reluctant to share the tidings. Uriah said nothing but walked on in silence.

"I was taking my constitutional," Michael went on, "and was near Congress Hall when a rider came fast along Sixth Street. He stopped in the square and shouted that he brought news from Washington City: Jefferson has ended the embargo. The Congress has passed a new bill, which they call a Non-Intercourse Law. The rider said that all ships will sail again as soon as the owners can round up crews. In a few minutes, I suppose, there will be drunken sailors all over this dock, shouting and celebrating. The news is spreading over the city like wildfire."

Uriah was trembling with excitement and elation. "So Jefferson finally has agreed! In his last days as president, he wipes out the embargo. What a dramatic stroke! But what is this new law? What will it mean?"

"Who knows? There are all sorts of stories. I saw your cousin Mordecai soon after the rider arrived. He thinks himself an expert on all political matters, as you know, and was only too glad to give me his opinion. He says this Non-Intercourse Law will continue to prohibit trade with England and France until they lift their restrictions on trade with us. It also bars their armed vessels from entering our harbors. But it allows us once again to trade with neutral nations."

"God, that's great news!"

"Yes, but there are still problems. Jefferson and Madison continue to negotiate with Canning of England on a settlement of the *Chesapeake-Leopard* affair. Mordecai says it is rumored that Canning has offered to rescind the Orders in Council if we will open our ports to English trading ships and close them to the French. He knows, of course, that Jefferson never would agree to this, especially as Canning wants the right to seize any of our ships that continue trading with the French. I daresay Madison will reject such an agreement also. So our troubles with England and France continue. War still seems possible. In fact, I fear it is coming."

As they walked up High Street, heading for home, they were meeting an increasing number of pedestrians—churchgoers returning from afternoon service. Two young, pretty women came down the street toward them, walking arm in arm and giggling softly in a shy, fetching way. As they drew closer, however, the shyness seemed to vanish; with tight smiles on their lips, they stared provocatively at the Levy father and son. Uriah stared back, appraising them openly and appreciatively. His father looked away from the streetwalkers and shook his head in disgust.

"I suppose this news means that you will be going back to sea as soon as you can?"

Uriah nodded, his face solemn now. He could feel what was coming: another appeal from his father to forget the sailor's life and to settle down and learn the watchmaker's trade.

"I won't try to change your mind, Uriah," Michael said. "I fear it is much too late for that. I only beg you, for your mother's sake, to think about the risks of going to sea these days. War is coming, Uriah. I don't want you killed on the deck of some ship. If you are called upon to fight for our country, then do it with our militia so you will go to war with your friends and neighbors."

"Dying is dying, Father. Whether it happens among friends or among strangers—I don't see the difference."

Michael Levy sighed and lapsed again into silence, his customary mien. Only in his beloved shop, trading with his customers, did he really come alive. There he smiled a great deal and sometimes even joked. He called it his "business face." But his wife and children sometimes thought that the long hours in the shop were the only times that Michael Levy truly enjoyed himself. He had come armed today with logical arguments. He still hoped to convince this recalcitrant son to give up his risky wanderlust and find a safe life in the shop and in the bosom of his family. After only a few words, though, he saw it was no use and the arguments were put to rest. Michael Levy set his chin and walked the rest of the way home in silence, his thoughts turned back inward.

Uriah stole a look at his father as they crossed High Street and turned for home. The youth was surprised, as if seeing the man for the first time in years. How old he looked today! Tired and wan. The last time Uriah had looked—really looked—at his father's face, he had seen a man still young. Now he was aging. Uriah wondered: What had happened to the years in between?

6

The Vermyra, *1809*

Uriah Phillips Levy, second mate on the Coulter brig *Polly and Betsy*, under the command of Captain Silsbee, took a long sip of coffee from the black mug and pondered his good fortune. At the bar, Rosie and her "daughters" busied themselves, the air fluttering with their charming patois. The youngest of them, a slim chocolate beauty, would glance at Uriah every so often, a slight smile at the corners of her mouth, her eyebrows raised. Then she would shyly return to her polishing of the oaken bar top.

Surely no other seventeen-year-old lad in the world could feel better than he did on this day, Uriah thought, as he leaned back against the wall and let the tart, chicory-flavored coffee slide down his throat—to be able to relax here, among friends, in his favorite place in the Western Hemisphere; to enjoy this fragrant Virgin Islands coffee; to bask in the warm trade wind that flowed easily through the open windows. Most of all, to look out to the roadstead and see the proud little brig on which he second mated. Oh, he loved that speedy, faithful little vessel as he would a child of his own. And in her hold lay several hundred pounds of sugar that was personally owned by him, and on which he anticipated turning a tidy profit at some oncoming port of call.

It had been a long time since he last had been here at Road Town on the island of Tortola. He loved this tiny settlement with its gentle breezes blowing straight across from Portugal that kept the temperature at a steady eighty degrees, no matter the season. He loved the still gentler people of these islands, with their quick speech that belied their unhurried movements. He even loved the brawling sailors of a hundred different seafaring nations, who jammed the taverns along the settlement's dirt road and kept the air alive with their shouting and flailing.

He also would watch with more than a little envy as the sailors walked upstairs with Rosie's "daughters," their arms around each other's waists. But he could not bring himself to climb those stairs; their low heaven was not for him. He always had a great fear of getting the pox, especially at sea, far from surgeons or hospitals. It was that fear that made him desist, in spite of the smiles and looks directed at him by the young island beauties.

He looked across the water now to Virgin Gorda and saw the outline of the portly woman reclining on her back that had given the island its name. And from that name had been taken the name of this small group of islands as Virgin Islands. Just a few miles distant were the Danish West Indies, with their St. Thomas, St. John, and St. Croix. Cap Silsbee liked to gibe that this was the holiest region on the face of the globe—all saints and virgins.

Uriah wished he had many more days to spend on this beach, but he had only a couple of hours more until the gig would come in from the *Polly* to pick him up. He had been instructed to wait on the beach until 4 p.m. in hopes that the *Henry Freeling*, the mailboat that made regular circuits among the islands and was due at Road Town today, might have brought mail for the ship's crew. On arrival at the agent's waterside office, Uriah had found the packet of mail already awaiting him; the mailboat had come before dawn and was already gone again. With a couple of hours to wait for the pickup gig, he had walked lazily down to Rosie's for some of her excellent coffee. There he contentedly read his own letters from home.

"Cap'n Levy?" The soft voice of Rosie McClaverty broke into his thoughts. "You gone drown in my coffee if you drink any more."

She was a tiny colored woman of indeterminate age who treated her favorites among the sailors with the tender concern of a surrogate mother, but who could turn suddenly into a vengeful, cursing harridan when tempers frayed and brawlers threatened to damage her furniture. Uriah, a polite lad who seldom tasted hard liquor and sat pleasantly at the side of the room, was one of her favorites.

"How come you don' visit my rum bowl?" she asked. She motioned to a sideboard near the bar, where stood a huge bowl of rum punch, holding several gallons of that potent delight, with tumblers scattered around it.

"A few tastes of your rum punch, Rosie, and I'd forget the name of my own ship."

"Good, mon! Then you stay wit' us awhile. Okay, then Rosie fix you good suppa, eh? You stay with Rosie and eat good!"

Uriah was mightily tempted. He had not eaten since breakfast, and Rosie's offer of supper was enticing, to say the least.

He was trying to make up his mind when a slight sound from down the beach caused Rosie to suddenly lift her head and listen. Her relaxed smile was replaced by a hard, vigilant look. The distant muttering grew louder. A sailor ran past the open shutters, heading down beach as fast as he could go. Two more tars went hurtling past a moment later, their eyes wide with excitement. Or was it fear?

Uriah was about to ask Rosie the cause of the fuss when she looked at him and put her finger to her lips. She listened for a moment more, then nodded to herself and said softly, "Press gang. You go now."

Uriah didn't quite understand her. "What? Press gang? What?"

There was greater urgency in her voice and she spoke louder. "Press gang off the *Vermyra*! They come down beach looking for sailors. You go now or they take you! You be Limey swab if you no go!"

"You don't understand, Rosie," he explained. "You don't need to fear for me. They can't touch me. I'm an American citizen. I have my protection paper here in my money belt. It's ironclad. They dare not touch me. They are only after British deserters, and sometimes they take Americans who were born in England. But I'm in neither class. They can't touch me."

Rosie shook her head mournfully. "You see, you see. You nice boy, but you soon be jack tar on Limey man-o-war. No place for nice boy like you. You see." She shook her head again and walked over to the huge punch bowl and slowly stirred the rum punch, her eyes watchfully on the door.

In a moment, the tramp of marching feet was heard on the dirt pathway outside and then a squad of British marines, all pipe-clayed and polished in scarlet coats with plumed shakos on their heads, marched into the tavern. Each man carried a musket with bayonet fixed. There were eight in all, led by a small, stocky sergeant with a gigantic red mustache.

He halted the squad and gave them parade rest, then glanced quickly about the room. His eyes stopped at the punch bowl, and he and Rosie exchanged malevolent glances.

"Only one pigeon left in this coop, eh?" he muttered. "All the others have flown, but we'll find 'em." He walked over and stood in front of Uriah, who remained seated. He was relaxed, still confident that the press gang would pass him by when his citizenship was established, yet he was conscious of his heart pounding in his chest.

"All right, lad! Up with ye, and let's have a look, eh?" The sergeant made a no-nonsense gesture with his hand, brusquely ordering Uriah to stand.

Uriah was not disposed to take commands from any British press-master, but he decided not to offer a provocation. He rose and stood silently.

"Let me see your papers, eh? Ye look to me like a good Englishman."

Uriah did not reply but opened his shirt and withdrew from the money belt around his waist the oilskin packet containing his protection. He had carried the document, signed by the deputy collector of the Port of Philadelphia, since his second voyage on a Coulter ship. It established that he was a native-born citizen of the United States.

The thick-bodied sergeant took the paper and quickly read it. "What sort of name is this? Levy, or is it Levee? I've heard of a tax levy. Be ye a tax collector?" He laughed harshly. "What sort of name do ye bear?"

"I am an Israelite, if that is what you mean," Uriah replied quietly. He tensed. He didn't like the direction this interview was taking.

"Israelite? You mean you're a Jew? A Jew sailor? We don't have such things in England, ye know. All our Jews are peddlers or blood-suckin' moneylenders."

"I'm not an Englishman. I'm a native-born American citizen, as my protection shows. I'm second mate of the brig *Polly and Betsy*, anchored now in the fairway. And I am soon to return to my ship, so if you are finished with me—"

The sergeant laughed again, but there was no mirth in it. "Second mate, be ye? A Jew officer? No wonder American ships are such poor sailers, with Jew peddlers as their officers, eh?"

He laughed again and turned to his men, still laughing. As he turned, Uriah's fist crashed against the side of his jaw, knocking the sergeant roughly against the last marine in the file.

The enraged sergeant started to bellow an order, but his men anticipated him and quickly moved to his defense. They formed a circle around Uriah. He raised his arms to defend himself, but before he could make another move, the heavy wooden butt of a nine-pound Brown Bess musket pounded against the back of his head. He felt the room going dark about him and, very strangely, the floor seemed to be rising up to meet his eyes. . . .

It was the stench that first hauled him back to consciousness—an acrid, pungent, nauseating smell that pierced the fog in his head and forced him to open his eyes. It was dark. Shadowy figures crouched near him. A knifelike pain went through his head, and in reaction he closed his eyes again as he winced. Instinctively he covered his nose with his hand in an effort to block out the awful stink, but there was no blocking it. It was the king of stenches and it heaved across him in waves, like the pain and nausea that also afflicted him.

Minutes passed. He slowly opened his eyes again but was careful this time to leave his head in place. The sharp pain held off. He realized now that he was somewhere in the bowels of a British man-of-war, probably the sloop of war that had been anchored in Road Harbor. He remembered smashing the loudmouthed British marine sergeant in the face and then the air had exploded. Then he had awakened to this. Obviously they had bashed him and carried him off to their ship, protection or no protection.

He swallowed a couple of times to keep down the hot juices that rose up in his throat and threatened to pour from his mouth. He decided to attempt another look around. He raised his head very slowly, bracing for the ripping pain that must follow. He just had time to be grateful that the pain was far duller than before when a hatch was thrown open and a grayish light gave a cloudy illumination to his foul prison.

Three marines and a sergeant—not the one from Rosie's tavern—climbed down the hatchway. The sergeant banged loudly against the bulkhead with his colt, threatening to use the whip for encouragement. "You there! Get up! You're ordered on deck! On your feet!"

Uriah slowly climbed to his feet and managed to stand, trembling and wobbly kneed. The sharp pain had disappeared, but his head now ached with a throbbing soreness. He saw others stand. He counted seven besides himself. One of them, he saw, was the sailor who had been sleeping at the bar in Rosie's until the approach of the press gang. They must have caught up with him later.

The marines, aided by an occasional ungentle shove with a musket butt, pushed the prisoners ahead of them through a berth deck that smelled almost as bad as had the orlop, and then up another hatchway to the spar deck. There they were herded to the ship's waist and formed into a ragged line.

The sun was just dipping below the hills of St. Thomas to the west, and the air had grown much colder. The men were shivering. Three of them had been wading in the surf when the press gang grabbed them and were shirtless.

Uriah looked over the sloop's port bulwarks and there, some four hundred yards down the fairway, lay his own *Polly and Betsy*. For an instant he thought of screaming for help, of bringing his shipmates to his rescue, but he knew immediately that it would avail him nothing. They would not make out his shouting even if they could hear him. And what if they did? Cap Silsbee had no way to force this British warship to surrender his second mate, especially in a port that flew the British flag.

"Stiffen your backbones, you scum! Shut your mouths! Lift your hats to the lieutenant!"

As a British lieutenant approached them from the quarterdeck, the small line of frightened, bewildered men stiffened into attention, and those wearing caps lifted them above their heads under the menacing stare of the marine sergeant.

The lieutenant was a young, fair-complected man. Above his trim blue uniform with its single gold epaulette, he wore a fore and aft cocked hat. He stood before the prisoners and looked them over for a moment or two. Then he clasped his hands behind his back in quarterdeck style and addressed them in a firm, clear voice:

"I am Mr. Hobson, first lieutenant of His Majesty's sloop-of-war *Vermyra*, Captain Scovil commanding. You have been interrogated by a press gang acting under orders of Captain Scovil. You have been found to be British subjects and therefore fit for duty aboard this honorable vessel. Prepare, then, to be sworn as seamen of the Royal Navy. You will raise your right hands. If you have a cap or hat, you will uncover. Boatswain, hand me the oath!"

Uriah said a silent prayer and took one step forward. "Sir!"

The lieutenant turned back in surprise. "Get back in line, sir, or I shall have the marines tie you in place."

"Sir, I beg to address you! I wish to appeal!"

Lieutenant Hobson sighed wearily. The protester looked like a callow youth among this collection of motley old tars. He couldn't be much more than sixteen years or so. And he did have starch in him, to step out like this. . . .

"Very well, then. State your appeal. And quickly!"

"Sir, I am a native-born American citizen. I am second mate on the brig *Polly and Betsy*, which is anchored just down the harbor there. I showed the press master my protection from the Port of Philadelphia, but he would not honor it. I have never been a British subject in my life. They had no right to impress me. I appeal to you, sir, to free me to return to my ship."

Hobson said nothing. He studied the youth's face. Impressment was a dirty business, all in all—seizing Englishmen off the streets of Liverpool and Plymouth and carrying them off to warships to serve on voyages lasting years. Many of them never had walked a deck before. Suddenly they were sailors in His Majesty's fleet. The sound of their crying and moaning for their wives and children was standard music on every man-of-war going to sea. Much less bothersome to Hobson's conscience was the seizure of British deserters from neutral ports or, if necessary, from the decks of neutral ships. These traitors either would honorably serve the King or they would be hung from a yardarm as the deserters they truly were.

"Well, native-born American citizen, if you are really such, we have no claim to you. The Royal Navy does well enough with its own. It does not need Yankees to pull and haul for it. What is your name?"

"I am Uriah Phillips Levy, sir."

Hobson nodded coldly. "You are the Jew who struck our press master, eh? So your case is not quite so simple as you would make out."

"Sir, with respect, I struck the sergeant only after he insulted me and my religion. I cannot take such insults from any man."

Hobson's face reddened. "It is of no concern to me whether you will or will not accept insults. But I say that you will not strike a British sergeant of marines and get away with it. You will be lucky indeed if you escape a flogging!"

Uriah's stomach churned and he felt momentarily dizzy. His rage back at Rosie's, no matter how provoked, might see him soon tied to a grating and writhing in agony under an English cat. He wished profoundly that he had a better cap on his temper.

Hobson saw the youth's face go white and he relented slightly: "As to your appeal, Levy, I can tell you just this: your claim is complicated by your rash action in striking Sergeant Crossland. I shall discuss the matter with Captain Scovil. Your disposition shall be up to him. Meanwhile, take a step back in line with your comrades and take the oath with the others. Remove your hat at once!"

Uriah saw the lieutenant turn and take a worn Bible from the boatswain. It would be passed down the line, and each man in turn would swear on it his fealty to King George and Captain Scovil and to the Cross of St. George that flew from the *Vermyra's* maintop. He took a deep breath, held his ground, and raised his cap as he again spoke out: "Sir, again with respect. I am an Israelite. I cannot take an oath on the Christian Bible, nor can I swear with my head uncovered. It is against the principles of my religion. I cannot do it."

Hobson held his temper with difficulty. "I don't give a damn about your principles, nor do I give a damn about your oath and its form and shape. Swear without the Bible, then, and keep your cap set. Just swear and swear quickly, or I'll have you in darbies if you protest another word!"

Uriah nodded in silent thanks and stepped back into line. The man on the end began softly repeating the oath.

The moment came, as the last fringes of pale whiteness still lightened the western sky, when Uriah almost lost the quiet confidence that had maintained his spirits ever since his capture several hours before. Eight bells had just been struck, and the *Vermyra's* boatswain mates were telling the news that it was first watch. Uriah and the other victims of the press gang stood forlornly on deck, dry pannikins in hand, and waited for the cook to dig out the last dregs from his greasy cauldron and give them some supper.

He looked across the port bow, and there, close enough it seemed to be touched by an extended arm, was the *Polly and Betsy*, slowly sliding under double-reefed topsails out of the harbor toward the Virgin's Gangway. As the brig slid across his field of vision, passing the *Vermyra* from port to starboard, she was close enough that Uriah could identify the sailors by the way they ascended or descended the shrouds. He almost could see their faces, although this was more his imagination. They knew where he was, all right—Rosie surely had told them what happened when they went searching for him on the beach—and they were heading for home without him. There was nothing else to do.

Watching his own ship sail for home without him, Uriah—for the first time since he was a green cabin boy—had to fight back the tears. Could it be that he would have to spend years of his life in the naval service of a foreign country—all because of a rash throw of his fist? He felt panic well up in him and looked at the nearer bulwark with the thought of diving over it and swimming for his life. He quickly thought better of it. He swam well enough, but it was too far for him to swim to shore. He could aim for another ship, but these Brits would have a boat over the side and after him long before he could reach safety. Such thoughts were useless. He worked to calm himself and to reassure himself that the commander of this ship surely would release him when he heard his story. His attack on the sergeant could not, by any fair judge, be considered unprovoked.

In the morning, eyes bleary from lack of sleep after a night in a swaying hammock stretched in the smelly, crowded berth deck full of coughing, farting, unwashed men, the impressed eight were assigned to watches. Their names were added to the quarters bill and the tacking bill along with their posts and assignments, and they were set to work with the other sailors in holystoning the decks. The ship settled into its usual in-port routine.

His inevitable maritime curiosity forereaching his weariness and worry, Uriah had the chance, as he slung a prayerbook around the deck, to study the ship. The *Vermyra* seemed a taut enough ship; her decks were cleaned and her brass shone. Uriah quickly noticed, though, that she was not a happy ship. The tars went about their work sullenly, grudgingly. The boatswain's mates were free with their rope ends and more than one man was beaten into a proper performance. Perhaps it was too much to expect any man-of-war to be a happy ship and especially was this true of a British vessel, for the inhumane conditions in which the English sailor lived were common knowledge among those of the seagoing fraternity.

Uriah's watch was called to breakfast after the holystoning was completed. There he got his first real taste of the carrion that the British Navy called food. The bread was moldy and ridden with weevils, the water from casks that never were cleaned was greenish and full of moving things. By dinnertime he was ravenously hungry, but the salt beef was so tough as to be virtually inedible. An old waister explained to Uriah as he tried to tear the meat with his hands into bite-size, or at least swallow-size, pieces that the navy insisted that the oldest meat be utilized first. So a provisioning ship loaded its harness casks with the same meat that had gone unused by another ship on a previous voyage.

The waister, named Blore, was a plump man of late middle age with a head bereft of any hair. He had been a clerk for a London merchant when he had been impressed in '94, he told Uriah, but had voluntarily enlisted for several hitches since then. He had nobody ashore, he said, so what difference did it make? His ship became his home.

Uriah's pannikin was filled with a brownish liquid that the cook's boy told him was "Scotch coffee." The boy said it was made by boiling burned bread in water and then adding some sugar for taste. It almost gagged Uriah when he ventured a swallow. The drink accompanied a kid full of cold burgoo that smelled vaguely of bilge. He ate a spoonful or two, then put it aside, queasy and disgusted.

After the men hastily had gulped down their dinner, or what passed for it, they lined up for their ration of spirits at the painted grog tub. A lieutenant and two petty officers guarded the tub to make certain that no one got more than his proper ration.

When Blore found that Uriah was a nondrinker and would not claim his ration, he begged him, almost tearfully, to stand in the line and then turn his pannikin over to his new friend when they had returned to their seats along the port bulwark. "Without me daily grog," Blore assured him, "life would not be fit for living—at least aboard HMS *Vermyra*."

The following day, Uriah was ordered aloft with the foretopmen to help in the task of setting up the rigging, which had become slack. Seizings and coverings had to be removed, a tackle brought into play, and the rigging bowsed taut enough to satisfy the demands of the *Vermyra*'s eagle-eyed sailing master. The work consumed much of the afternoon, and Uriah found himself begrimed and weary when it ended. A deep mood of discouragement began again to settle upon him.

With the other foretopmen he was heading for the scuttle-butt, just forward of the berth deck hatchway, for a drink of water, when a stiff little midshipman, who could not have been older than twelve years, approached him and curtly ordered him to report immediately to the captain. The stony-faced middie pointed in the direction of the quarterdeck, then walked away.

At last! The *Vermyra*'s captain would grant him the audience he had demanded since his first conscious moments on this damnable sloop.

Uriah hurried back up to the spar deck and then to the quarterdeck. Three lieutenants stood near the port bulwark, their eyes fixed on a distinguished-looking man wearing the blue finery of a British Navy captain. Captain Scovil stood atop the horse block, an oaken rostrum perhaps three feet by three feet, edged in a shining brass railing, that provided the necessary clear view over the high bulwarks for a deck officer. Uriah came to a position of attention out of respect for rank, even if it was that of a foreign navy. "Sir, I am Uriah Phillips Levy of the American merchant brig *Polly and Betsy*. You have sent to see me."

"Take off your hat to the quarterdeck, Yankee!" snapped Lieutenant Hobson, one of the nearby officers. Uriah hastily complied and held his cap in a hand at his side.

The captain walked down the three steps from the horse block and stood before Uriah, a grave expression on his face.

"Mr. Hobson tells me you have appealed your impressment on the grounds that you were taken by error. Is this true?" The voice was not friendly, nor was it unkind.

"Yes, sir. I am an American citizen, native-born, with a certificate of protection. I should not have been taken and I ask for release."

"If you have a signed protection, then you should not have been impressed, I would agree. Unfortunately, you have greatly complicated your case by striking a British sergeant of marines, a serious offense. Had you not done so, you would be back on that beach right now, enjoying the favors of Rosie McClaverty's 'daughters.' I do not have the authority to release you. Your fate will be up to Commodore Cochrane."

Uriah didn't know if he was allowed to speak further, but he ventured, "Sir, when may I make my petition to the commodore?"

"We shall weigh anchor in two hours and rendezvous with the flagship at Kingston port in Jamaica. At Kingston I shall place your case before Commodore Cochrane . . . and then we shall see."

"May I ask, sir: How long to Kingston?"

"I would estimate a sail of two weeks, since we must do some training en route and there will be gunnery practice, of course. Until then, Levy, you will continue with your regular duties as a member of this ship's crew. I am told that you are nimble on the ratlines and footropes and seem to know your way among the rigging. Very well. Perform your duties faithfully, and I promise you a just hearing with the commodore. Return to your watch!"

"Yes, sir. Thank you, sir." Uriah's voice was soft and husky with misery. Two more weeks at least aboard this miserable vessel, with its screaming boatswain's mates and arrogant, cold-eyed officers. Even the midshipmen were snot-faced and curt. Well, he thought, as he walked back to the foremast to rejoin his watch, at least he could try to put this time of captivity to good use. He would observe as closely as he could the working of this British warship and strive to find weaknesses. He was their prisoner, true, but his eyes were free to roam, and his mind could not be prevented from remembering.

The *Vermyra* thrashed along under a clear blue sky and brisk, ever-shifting winds. The erratic changes of wind brought frequent tacks, and the short boards had the crew weary and grouchy. The seas were high, and great torrents of spray washed across the decks, keeping the pull and haul men constantly drenched and caked with salt.

They had gone on watch-and-watch every day since the *Vermyra* put to sea. Uriah didn't mind the regimen, for it was second nature to him by now. But he was constantly weary, for he found it extremely difficult to sleep in the fetid berth deck. He was used to sleeping in a forecastle berth and could not accustom himself to swinging to and fro in a hammock suspended from the stanchion.

Often, in his hours off watch, Uriah walked the spar deck, being careful always to keep to the starboard side, since the port side was reserved as a sort of corridor for the ship's officers. He carefully studied the *Vermyra*'s cannon, in an effort to learn more about these huge guns and how they operated. All of this would be valuable to take back to someone like Decatur, although he doubtless already knew much about British artillery.

The *Vermyra* carried eighteen guns. With the help of shipmates, he was able to identify them as four long 6-pounders, twelve 32-pound carronades, and two shifting 12-pound carronades. He was fascinated and awed by these great, fearsome guns that rested on powerful oak carriages along the spar deck bulwarks. One only had to look at them to appreciate the roar they would make when fired and, more importantly, the devastation they could bring, if well aimed, to another ship.

Uriah had been assigned to the crew of a 32-pound carronade, but he had not the faintest idea of his duties there. Until now, he had seen such guns only from a distance and never had stood close to one being fired, much less being capable of helping to fire it.

Finally, on a bright midweek afternoon, a swarthy tar with long, greasy hair accosted Uriah and identified himself as his gun captain. He led Uriah to the carronade to which they were assigned and gave him a quick, semicoherent explanation of the gun and its workings, and the duties of its crew.

Their station was on the port side of the quarterdeck, the gun captain reminded him, and right under the captain's eye, so each man had best do his job well or he would soon face the cat's lash.

"We got nine men operates this gun," the gun captain, whose name was Driscoll, told him, "and each tar gots his own job. If somethin' goes wrong, we bloody well know who to blame for it."

The carronade's range, Uriah knew, was far less than that of a long gun, but it fired with tremendous force and was capable of great destruction in engagements at short range. The effective range of his gun, Driscoll said, was about 150 yards, although a ball sometimes could travel more than 300 yards if conditions were right. A 24-pound long gun, on the other hand, with its iron tube ten feet long—twice as long as the carronade—could propel a shot perhaps 600 yards.

"She's a real smasher, she is, ol' Betsy 'ere," said Driscoll proudly, as he tapped the black snout of the carronade. "She'll beat the livin' 'ell out of any bloody ship that gets near 'er."

"And what happens if you fight another ship with many long guns?" asked Uriah. "She will pound you from a distance, won't she, and not allow you to get in range to do harm?"

"That's the captain's problem," Driscoll answered testily. "Admiral Nelson hisself always said that any British ship worth its salt would get in close enough to destroy the enemy. Ol' Man Scovil will get me Betsy in so she can do 'er job, I promise ye."

Driscoll finished the short lesson in gunnery by telling Uriah about the different projectiles that the carronade could fire. The mainstay was a 32-pound cast-iron ball of slightly more than six inches in diameter. But there were all sorts of devilish variations. There was chain-shot—two balls linked with a chain—and bar-shot—an iron bar joining two half balls, which would play havoc when fired into the masts and sails of an enemy ship. And there was grapeshot, a mass of iron balls wrapped tightly together in a strong canvas bag that would fit into the cannon's bore. Grape could be fired down the length of an enemy deck when the *Vermyra* was in position to rake and would do terrible destruction to the human beings walking that deck.

"When do we practice with the great guns?" Uriah asked. "Is it a regular thing?"

"Not near often enough to suit the captain," Driscoll answered. "But their mighties, the Lords of the Admiralty, wants to save powder and balls, so their orders is to shoot the guns almost never. If 'twere up to the captain, Yank, you'd be hearin' ol' Betsy's voice every bloody day."

Uriah also watched with interest the activities of the contingent of marines assigned to the *Vermyra*. They had ongoing duties, of course, as the ship's guards, but in battle their task would be to drag their heavy boots up the shrouds and to take up stations in the fighting tops, where they would fire their muskets down on the enemy decks and try to pick off a captain or, at the least, a lieutenant.

The marines, apparently not so closely bound by the directive to save powder and shot, held musketry practice three times a week, firing their heavy Brown Bess muskets from both the tops and from the spar deck itself, aiming at a wave-top for want of a better target.

Uriah watched the musket firing, noting that the weapons were terribly cumbersome and slow to operate. He counted almost twenty separate actions needed in the reloading process. The marine would use his teeth to rip open the paper cartridge and would pour a bit of the powder into the musket's firing pan, then would hurl the rest down the muzzle. He would use a ramrod to push the powder, wad, and the round lead ball down into firing position. As the musket was fired and the barrel became fouled, the process became more difficult and took longer. Every few minutes the marine had to stop and change his flint.

There seemed to be great variations in the firing skills of the marines. The fastest of them were able somehow to complete the entire reloading evolution with a series of quick, smooth movements and could fire a ball every thirty seconds or so. The slowest of the marines seemed to take an eternity between shots.

Uriah swung miserably in his hammock and awaited, with no discernible enthusiasm, the summons to breakfast. He was gathering his muscles to jump from the hammock at the first scream of the boatswain's mates. Each man was permitted only twelve minutes from the first call in which to pull on his clothes, gather up his hammock and place it in its allotted slot in the nettings along the spar bulwarks, make a hurried trip to the head, and then report on deck.

On this morning, however, things did not proceed according to pattern. At what Uriah calculated was about seven bells in the morning watch—perhaps thirty minutes before breakfast—the sound of running feet was heard on the spar deck above. Suddenly the hatchway gratings were hurled back, and just as the boatswain and his mates began their insistent shrilling with their pipes, there also was heard the loud, ominous, compelling sound of drums— rattling the air with a strange, unforgettable rhythm.

"All hands to quarters!" screamed the boatswain's mates and pealed their pipes once more. "They're beatin' to quarters. . . . All hands rise and shine!"

Uriah jumped from his hammock and quickly pulled on his clothing. He began to unhook his hammock but saw that the other men were leaving theirs in place and were running up the ladder to their battle stations.

Were they going into battle with a French ship—or, God forbid, an American man-of-war? What if war had been declared and he was stuck here on a British deck, firing a British carronade? He would sooner throw himself into the sea than to help fire on a ship flying the Stars and Stripes. He climbed the ladder with a sick feeling in his stomach and ran to the quarterdeck carronade to which he was assigned. As he ran, he looked quickly over the bulwarks to sight the other ship, but he saw no vessel.

Uriah was one of the last of the gun crew to arrive at the big carronade. Driscoll was already busy directing his men in tailing onto the tackles and slacking away the breechings. He reached over and pulled out the tompion, the big black-painted plug of wood that fills the muzzle end when the gun is not in use. He hastily looked down the barrel to be sure there was no obstruction. Then he replaced the tompion to await further orders.

"American," he hissed at Uriah, "your job today is to stay out of our way. This will be a real firing, our first in a long time. We'll put you to work 'elpin' the powder boys, if necessary. Just keep out of our way!"

Uriah, now that he realized this was a drill and not actual combat, was a bit chagrined that he would not play a role in it. He stepped back a pace and tried to be inconspicuous.

In another moment, all noise on the spar deck ceased, except for the flapping of the ensigns on the mastheads in the morning breeze. A lieutenant screamed for attention and then withdrew in favor of his captain.

Scovil walked just forward of the helm and binnacle and addressed his men. His usually soft voice roared out with authority and was plainly heard, even by the most forward of the gun crews.

"Men, today we shall fire the great guns for practice. We do not do this often; let us make the most of it. We shall begin with broadsides, port first and then starboard. I want a ripple-firing, bow to stern. Any gun firing out of turn will have to deal with me. Afterwards, we shall fire for effect at a target. Mr. Hobson, run up your guns, if you please."

Lieutenant Hobson screamed out an order, and immediately the ship thundered with the earthquakelike rumble of the great gun carriages being moved forward. The gun ports were raised with a sharp, percussive sound, and the big black muzzles poked out toward the flat, enamel-green sea.

A flash of red caught the corner of Uriah's eye, and he turned to see the marines making their clumsy way up the fore and main shrouds to the fighting tops, where they took up their sharp-shooting posts, muskets leveled.

The ship's boys raced across the spar deck with huge buckets of sand and laid a thick coating of the grainy material on the deck planks to ensure footing in the blood and gore that would spread across them in battle.

Uriah glanced behind him, fascinated with the hurried yet smooth-running battle readymake. He saw that the captain had turned the direction of the ship over to the sailing master, who stood abaft the wheel and quietly gave orders to the quartermaster who hung to its spokes. The master would control the ship during the fight, under orders from his captain, of course, while Scovil gave his attention to the more important task: the winning of the battle.

The powder boys, directed by a young lieutenant, had run forward and then came hurtling back aft, each carrying a tub containing a long, sputtering slow match. Each tub was set near its gun, where a long reach would find it.

The men of the gun crew bent to their work with a will. There was more spirit shown in this action than Uriah had seen before on this ship, where everything was done sullenly under compulsion. It was as if the men realized that their very lives well could depend on how they did with these huge guns.

The crew, in addition to Driscoll, consisted of a loader, a sponger, a shot and wad man, a crowbar and tackle man, two handspike and tackle men, and two powder boys. The sponger was taking a position astride the gun-port sill, with his right leg hanging outside.

The comparative stillness was shattered again by the stentorian voice of the young gunnery officer:

"Silence! Cast loose your guns!"

The muzzle lashing was removed by the tackle men, who then quickly slackened the side tackles.

"Take out your tompions!" The gun captains reached as one to again pull the black plugs out of the muzzle ends and laid them on the deck.

"Load with cartridge!" A powder boy passed a flannel powder bag to the loader and then ran quickly aft to get another from the magazine below.

"Ram home your cartridge!" The loader pushed the powder as far down the muzzle as he could reach and then turned to the shot and wad man to receive a mass of cotton waste, which he pushed down after the cartridge. The sponger took a long felt-tipped ramrod and inserted it into the barrel, pushing home the cartridge and wad.

"Shot your guns!" The shot and wad man reached down to the rack inboard of the bulwark and pulled up a 32-pound ball. He quickly pushed it down the barrel and it, too, was rammed home, with another wad for company.

"Pick and prime!" screamed the gunnery officer. Driscoll ran a sharp-ended wire into the gun vent to puncture the powder bag.

"Run out your guns and point your guns!" The earthquake sound was heard again as the great guns were run out through the port sills. The handspike and crowbar men used their metal tools to lift the breech so that Driscoll could insert a wedge-shaped quoin far enough to control the muzzle's elevation.

The gunnery officer looked back and forth along the deck to make sure that every gun was ready. Then: "All right, ripple fire, bow to stern. Each gun in order, or we shall know the reason why. Lower your match!"

Each gun captain picked up the coiled, sputtering slow match from his tub and lowered it to near the touch hole.

One more quick look down the deck and the officer screamed, "Fire!"

The 12-pounder bow-chaser carronade blasted out, and acrid smoke poured over the deck. An instant later, the forward 32-pound carronade fired with a mind-shattering roar. The entire ship shook with the force of the blast. A second later, the next of the port carronades fired with another pounding detonation, and then another, and another. Uriah felt as if he were transported into the very heart of a violent thunderstorm. The entire spar deck was covered now with thick blue and gray smoke. It was almost impossible to breathe.

Then his own carronade roared with a shock and blast that seemed double the force of all the others. Uriah swayed as if he had been physically struck by the concussion.

"Stop your vent!" screamed Driscoll. Then: "Sponge your gun!" The loader put his finger, which was protected by a piece of leather, over the vent to prevent the escape of postfiring sparks. The sponger climbed back astride the sill, took a long-handled sponge that he thrust quickly into a pail of water, and then cleaned out the barrel to drown any sparks that might remain therein.

In a moment, the gunnery officer blared out, "Load with cartridge!" and the entire evolution began again.

In a few minutes more, the guns had warmed enough so that the locks could be used, and instead of the slow match, the gun captain could fire by yanking on a lanyard that activated the flintlock mechanism.

"Well done, men!" It was the voice of the captain again. He turned briefly to the sailing master and gave him a quiet order, then resumed: "That was a nice ripple. Carry on!"

Uriah noted that most of the men in his crew had black faces now, their skin stained by the discharge of fumes from the gun's vent.

After two more broadsides, the gunnery officer ordered the gun captains, "Level your guns!" Again putting to work their handspikes, quoins, and strong backs, the gun crews hauled down to a level firing position, with the quoin jammed as far under the breech as Driscoll could push it.

The next round of firing, with all the port guns laid level, involved skipping the shot along the even surface of the green sea in long, straight bounces. This tactic produced a greater range for the shot and a high degree of accuracy, but it was an artifice that could be employed only when the sea was flat as a billiard table. In water of any height at all, Uriah noted, accuracy would be destroyed and range would be left totally to chance.

By now Uriah had a fearsome headache from the noise and fumes, but he was becoming more accustomed to the deafening pounding of the guns and to the bone-jarring roar of the carriages moving as the guns were run in and out for reloading. Even the thick, sulfurous smoke cloud that bathed the entire deck in a stinking fog did not choke him quite as wrathfully as it had during the first broadside. He found that, by dint of careful watching, he even was able to pick up the long arc of the shot as it left the barrel and sped out over the sea. It was only a slight movement through the air, a hint almost, but he could find and follow it, at least most of the time.

After the surface firing, the gunnery officer called a brief respite to allow a small sailing crew to put a boat into the water and tow a small target, consisting of four casks lashed together with a tiny flag flying from them, out to a place perhaps two hundred yards distant.

Scovil meanwhile ordered the sailing master to wear ship, and the *Vermyra* came smartly about to the opposite tack so that the starboard guns could be exercised. The gun crews moved across the deck to their opposite posts and quickly readied the new carronades for firing.

"We shall fire in order at the target, beginning with Number Two gun and moving aft. The first gun that blows the target out of the water will earn its crew an extra ration of grog at supper. The next round, we'll let Number Sixteen gun have first shot. Aim well, gun captains, but if you take more than your allotted time, you will lose your turn. Fire when ready!"

Uriah was amused at the implication in the gunnery lieutenant's comment about the next round of firing that he did not expect any gun to hit the target on the first round. He was right. Great splashes of water rose up all around the floating casks, but there was no hit. Each additional miss brought increasing roars of irritation from the officers assembled near the helm. Scovil was up on the starboard horse block and used a glass to better gauge the degree of miss.

All of the starboard carronades and the 6-pounder had fired twice and there still had not been a direct hit, bringing now imprecations and curses from the quarterdeck. The face of the gunnery officer was bright red with shame and anger. He would hear about this dismal performance from Scovil after the exercise.

Finally, Number Six carronade blew the target to bits with a direct hit, bringing loud huzzahs from its thirsty crew and a general feeling of relief over the entire sloop. Soon after, the order was passed to run in the guns and secure them. The gunnery practice was concluded.

When his watch went below, Uriah sat by himself in the port chains and gave thought to what he had witnessed. He pulled a scrap of paper from his pocket and his carefully guarded lead and noted a few observations: Each British gun crew seemed to rely heavily on its gun captain. If one such as Driscoll were killed in battle, it was his guess that confusion would result at that gun. It was important, he could see, that each man in the crew be familiar with every other man's job, including that of the gun captain, and be able to fill in immediately. British marksmanship seemed quite poor, probably due to insufficient practice with real ammunition. The marines in the fighting tops did not fire very rapidly and indeed seemed even slower in the drill to complete their reloading cycle than they had been in the practices on deck. The *Vermyra*'s marines were able to fire only in desultory fashion, with long pauses between shots. At a critical point in an action, that could be a severe handicap.

The wind was backing and freshening. Uriah held up a wet finger and guessed it was now south-southwest, a foul wind for Jamaica. He climbed from the chains and looked out over the bulwark. Far off the starboard bow, looking eerie and mist-caught in the low-slanting afternoon sunshine, he could see the peaks of Domingo and Haiti.

He thought once more about the fading day. He long had wondered how he would fare in battle aboard ship, whether he had the stomach for it, the nerves for it. Today he had experienced, though certainly not the real thing, at least some of the sights and sounds of a naval fight. He had stomached it well, he fancied. In fact, he had found it positively exhilarating.

Uriah sat rigidly on a thwart in the *Vermyra's* second cutter as it was rowed across Kingston Bay toward the flagship. Outfitted in a clean blue jersey and white trousers that had been grudgingly provided for him by the quartermaster at the captain's order, he sat now in the cutter and pondered over what he might say to the admiral to gain his favor.

The water was choppy, and the sullen sailors did not handle the cutter smoothly, making the trip a rough one. The boat dropped smartly and resoundingly into the trough of each passing wave. Uriah felt a trace of nausea. He was prone every now and again, under certain sea and wind conditions, to seasickness. Apparently, riding as a passenger in a clumsy cutter in a high surf was one of those conditions. *God, please prevent me from puking all over this fresh suit of clothes*, he prayed under his breath.

He tried to distract himself by looking roundabout him, at the awesome display of British naval might in this long harbor, which also was crowded with merchantmen. He raised his eyes. It was a sunny day, but the air was hazy. The Blue Mountains, towering three thousand feet high to the north of Kingston town, were shrouded in an azure mist, but their lushness was apparent despite the haze.

His gaze wandered back to the harbor. The admiral's flagship was the *Invincible*, 74, a gigantic ship-of-the-line. Uriah looked with admiration and more than a little envy at its three long rows of gun ports outlined in yellow against the black sides of the ship—the famous checkerboard pattern favored by Horatio Nelson and now standard for all British warships. He estimated that this vessel must be about eighteen hundred tons and must measure at least 175 feet. What a huge and powerful weapon of war she was!

As the cutter ran in under the *Invincible's* counter, the coxswain shouted, "Oars!" and all the sweeps were lifted straight up. The bow-sheet rowers grabbed the falls and straightened the cutter so that

Uriah could climb up. He was quickly taken in tow by a quarter-master, who obviously had been awaiting him.

The quartermaster said nothing to him but motioned him to follow, leading him down a ladder to the berth deck and then aft toward what was obviously the great cabin. At its door stood two large marines, each looking stonily straight ahead, his musket resting alongside his leg at a precise angle.

The quartermaster stopped just inside the door and knuckled his forehead. "Sir, Ordinary Seaman Levy of the sloop-of-war *Vermyra.*" Then he turned and left.

Uriah stood by the door and waited until he heard the command, "Come." He entered the cabin but did not know if he was to move forward or not. The commodore sat looking pensively at some papers on his writing desk. The cabin was smaller than Uriah might have expected. It was two rooms: a nicely furnished office and conference area and, just beyond, a small sleeping compartment.

The commodore continued silently to read his documents. A brown bottle and a half-filled glass were at his elbow. His uniform coat, with its heavy bullion epaulettes, was on a chair, and he was wearing only a linen shirt above his white breeches. The cabin was humid and warm. Uriah suddenly remembered that he had a cap on his head and quickly whipped it off and held it in his hand.

Uriah estimated the commodore was around fifty years. His hair was gray, and he appeared to be short and rather stocky, almost chubby. His hair was cropped short, but his eyebrows were thick and black, and he wore his sideburns long, down the curve of his cheeks.

Suddenly the commodore lifted his head. "Come forward," he said. "Let us have a look at you." Uriah walked to a place near the writing desk and then followed the quartermaster's example in raising his hand to his forehead in what seemed to be the prescribed gesture of respect.

"You are—eh—Seaman Uriah P. Levy? Is that not so?" asked the commodore, glancing down at the paper in his hand. It was then that Uriah realized that the officer had been reading some sort of report on his case.

"Yes, sir, I am he."

"Very well. I am Vice Admiral Alexander Inglis Cochrane, commodore of His Majesty's Caribbean Squadron. I have read your case." There was a long pause. Uriah wondered if he was supposed to say something, perhaps to offer a plea in his own behalf. But Admiral Cochrane put another stern look to the paper in his hand and Uriah decided to remain silent.

The commodore finally looked up again and stared at Uriah for a moment. Then he went on: "I am inclined to agree that you have suffered an injustice. You should not have been impressed at Tortola. Oh, there are some hard mouths among us who argue that every Yankee is still a Briton, because 'once a Briton, always a Briton,' don't you know? And there are others of more legalistic bent who insist that any American born before 1783 must be considered an Englishman and subject to impressment. But it is obvious that you are not that old. How old are you, young man?"

"I am seventeen years, sir."

"As I thought. Well, under any reasonable definition, you should not have been impressed, since you carried an American protection. I am not one who feels that Britain should break the law of the sea out of desperation in our fight against Bonaparte. Although I agree that your country has given us considerable provocation.

"I trust that the protection you carry is an authentic one, but you will admit, I am sure, that such protections can easily be bribed from port collectors in your country. You see, our marines had some reason to question your document.

"Now, as to your physical encounter with a sergeant of marines: I am willing to overlook that, given the fact that you were virtually kidnapped. I am willing to call it an act of self-defense."

Uriah felt his knees weakening again. He was overcome with gratitude. He feared that he might burst into tears.

"Sir," said Uriah, his voice quivering, "does what you have said mean that I am released from service with the *Vermyra*? That I am free to go?"

"Oh, yes . . . yes, indeed. You'll return to the *Vermyra* with my letter of release and orders for Captain Scovil to put you ashore in a boat. You'll have to find your own way back to the United States, I'm afraid. I have no ships going that way."

"Yes, sir. Thank you, sir. I'll find my way back. Have no fear of that!"

The commodore took a long drink from the glass on his desk and then sighed with deep satisfaction. "Ah, Appleton Rum," he said. "None finer. Some prefer the Haitian rum, but I think this is the best."

The commodore put down his glass and his face grew serious again. "Before you depart, Seaman Levy, a word. I am told by Captain Scovil that you are a sailorman of some experience in spite of your tender years, and that you served as second mate when our press gang encountered you in Tortola." He paused and glanced again at the report on his desk. "You have attended a navigation school in Philadelphia, I see. . . .

"You have both voyages and schooling under your belt, Mr. Levy. You would appear to have a future at sea. I invite you to spend it with His Majesty's fleet. If you sign papers for a three-year voyage, I will commission you on the spot as lieutenant in the navy of Great Britain, subject of course to final approval by their Lordships of the Admiralty. You can go right back to the *Vermyra*, if you choose, and put on the uniform of a lieutenant and serve under Scovil. Or—if it's not the *Vermyra* for you—we'll find you another berth in our squadron. Almost any of our vessels can use a qualified officer."

Uriah was surprised and confused by the commodore's sudden offer. The darkening fear came into his mind that perhaps the entire release was contingent on his acceptance of this commission.

"Commodore, I am honored by your suggestion. It is flattering to think that you deem me worthy to wear the epaulette on one of your ships. But—"

"Yes?" said the commodore, stonily.

"I must refuse your generous offer, sir. I owe and always shall owe my allegiance to my own country. I could not think of serving in a navy other than her own."

"Yes, yes, of course. That is understandable and praiseworthy. But I beg you to consider the situation between our two countries. War is coming, young man, and there is no doubt that Britain will win handily. I urge you to join the winning side now, when you have the chance to do so."

Control, Uriah, control yourself! Do not answer back in anger. You will go back to the Vermyra *and spend the rest of your life on that accursed ship. For once—hold your tongue!* He stood silently, the only sign of his inner resentment being a slight reddening of his cheeks. He finally spoke in a calm tone:

"That may well be, sir. But if my country is to lose this war, then I must go down with her. There is naught else that I could do."

Cochrane nodded. "Well said, lad. I trust that I would say the same, were I standing there where you are. Very well. I shall make out your letter of release and an order that you be paid for your service, and you can carry them forthwith back to the *Vermyra*. Then you can get started on your voyage home."

7

Philadelphia, 1812

Uriah sat silently in the chair for a while and listened to his father's harsh, irregular breathing. It took some time for his eyes to adjust to the darkened bedroom. In the gray solitude, it was an effort at first even to distinguish the outline of his father's face in the bed. Slowly, shapes began to emerge in the room, the old familiar shapes of this room that he had known all his life.

When he had come into the room to spell his sister Eliza at Father's bedside, she had nodded a silent greeting but said no word. They did not want to disturb Father, for his doctor had said that rest and sleep would be as good a tonic as any other. In another room, their exhausted mother also was getting some rest. She had borne the weary burden of constant care for weeks now and was at the point of collapse. Yet she could not sleep the night through, for every sleepy whimper, every sound of movement in the sickroom would bring her on the run. Her sons and daughters urged her to rest, but she could not. Now she slept the blurred, edgy sleep of exhaustion.

On the small bedside table at Uriah's elbow stood a glass of foul-smelling liquid, a remedy that the physician had promised would "thin and incrassate" Michael Levy's blood and thereby help his fever. The medicine had a smell that would stun a dog in full cry, and Michael Levy no longer was forced to take it. It had taken the combined efforts of Rachel Levy and at least two of her children to force the yellow liquid past his lips, and as he gagged and retched she had finally vowed "no more" and ordered the glass set aside.

Now Michael Levy lay in the dimness of his bedroom, watched over in turn by each of his sons and daughters, passing in and out of consciousness, too weak even to move his arms.

It had been almost three years since Uriah's impressment on the British sloop *Vermyra*. His parents had begged him to give up the seafaring life, but within months he was sailing again as a berth mate on John Coulter's ships, and when he had the opportunity to purchase a schooner, along with two partners, he started a brisk business running cargoes to and from the Caribbean islands. On this trip, however, he returned in a weary and heartsick state. After unloading a cargo and picking up a new one in Tenerife, Uriah had proceeded on to the Island of May, off the coast of Africa, where his schooner was stolen by three piratical crewmen. Although the thieves were apprehended and were awaiting trial in Boston, it was still uncertain whether the insurers would make good on the loss of the schooner. He had no ship anymore, nor the promise of one.

When he had walked in the door of his parents' house, he found his brothers and sisters gathered and had known at once that someone was very ill. His younger sister Amelia, always calm and measured in any storm, took him quietly aside and told him that their father's health had continued steadily to decline. He was suffering from what the doctor termed "a slow or nervous fever" of undetermined origin, as well as gout and dropsy. He was in no great misery but seemed to grow ever weaker and more feeble. The physician had ordered rest, quiet, and a bland diet. When this created no improvement, he had tried purgatives and sweats and even had drawn blood from the feet. The yellow liquid in the glass by the bed had been the latest remedy.

Uriah quietly lit the candle on the bed table and in its flicker softly unfolded the long letter from Cousin Mordecai. It had awaited him upon his return from his latest trip, and this was his first opportunity to read it. He found the several pages of closely packed handwriting a bit forbidding and started to put the letter back in his pocket, but then reconsidered. Perhaps word of his cousin's new life in the South would divert him for a few moments from the enveloping sadness of this house, from the draining, mournful pall of oncoming death that hung over them all.

Mordecai Noah's letter from Charleston was written with his usual flair, a manic mixture of bravado and self-deprecation. In the first few words, he assured Uriah's rapt attention by writing that he had "come within a hair's breadth of being killed and even closer than that to killing another." He had continued as a political activist in his new city, supporting Henry Clay and the Democrats as they demanded war with England. Meanwhile, he was writing a column of gossip and politics for the *Charleston Times* under the mysterious pseudonym of Muly Malak.

In one such column, Mordecai had ridiculed a Federalist sympathizer, one Joshua W. Toomer, who promptly responded by challenging Muly Malak to a duel. As Mordecai recounted in his letter,

I conferred with my political friends, who assured me I must indeed fight. They found a carriage and rushed me out to the countryside for pistol practice. Since I had never before fired a gun in anger—in fact, had never before fired a gun—such practice was well advised. I had no anger for the Toomer—I did not even know him well—but I could not evade the duel without being branded far and wide as coward.

The performance was scheduled for four in the afternoon at the local racetrack and a flatteringly large crowd was anticipated. I therefore dressed in my finest suit and polished my boots to the highest gloss. I took special pains with my toilet and trimmed my beard to within a soupçon of perfection. They would at least see M. M. Noah die at the peak of his appearance.

On the way to the racetrack, we were among a huge and festive crowd of duel-bound people. Ladies crowded

the carriages and gigs. My Republican cohorts assured me
that, upon my death at the Toomer's hands, I would be in-
terred with full honors. As you can understand, this greatly
relieved my concerns and I bantered with them the rest of
the way, wondering only why my jokes seemed to issue in
a treble voice much unlike my own. The distant booming
of cannon that caused me wonderment for several minutes
turned out, upon reflection, to be the pounding of my own
heart. Other than that, I was calmness incarnate.

The spectacle of the duel ended in anticlimax. Friends of the two participants reached a last-minute agreement, and the fight was cancelled. "The disappointment at the race track was so pervasive," Mordecai wrote, "that I, too, joined in the groans and moans. Ah, how fortunate the Toomer was!"

Another unhappy reader of Noah's newspaper columns also called him out a few days later, but this time the duel was postponed indefinitely when the challenger fell ill. "There were those," Mordecai wrote, "who foully alleged that I tainted his food."

The climactic moment in his sudden career as a warrior came a few weeks later and, most surprisingly, against

A fellow Hebrew, a brother Israelite who stared down the bar-
rel of his gun at my chest and bade me die. Yet die I would
not, for the strength of Samson and Deborah and Barak rose
up within me. (Gad, that is powerful prose. I must save it and
find some profitable use for it.)

The scoundrel was one John Cantor and he, too, called me
to fight a duel with him. This time there were no late nego-
tiations and Cantor proved to be in remarkably good health,
though I kept looking for some telltale sign of lassitude or fe-
ver. So, assured by my enthusiastic friends that they would
provide horse, carriage, and weapon, I made arrangements
for a surgeon to attend me. On the night before, I tried to sleep
at the house of a friend, but could not . . . being awakened
by such distractions as the hammering in of a black crape

medallion on the door. Everyone was most encouraging and assured me that I would have a burial that would be remembered for years to come.

We drove to a sweet little valley for the fight. As the challenged party, I had the choice of weapons, positions, and distance. Overriding my impulse to command mud balls at fifty paces, I heard my voice sternly call for pistols at ten paces, with the parties to stand at this distance facing away from each other and to turn and fire at the order to fire. I chose this mode for several reasons. It was in consonance with the rules of honor, which do not necessarily claim a victim by a direct and deadly aim; it also gave a chance for both (or neither) to escape; and besides, I did not wish to incur the stern gaze of my antagonist: a deadly scowl, tossing off the hat, and some melodramatic action for effect, to throw me off my guard or shake my nerves. Not seeing my man until brought face to face by the word fire, and the sudden wheeling gave no advantage to either and was deemed by all, considering the slight cause of offense, as proper and expedient.

I hurriedly whispered a prayer (I think it was the Shema, but in my stunned state I could not be sure, it may have been a Hail Mary) and marched off the ten paces. I felt like weeping—not for myself, but for the world, which was about to lose one of its most promising talents. "Gentlemen, are you ready?" came the cry. We both grunted something and were told: "Wheel and fire!"

I whirled in what I believe was a lovely pas de jete or some other classical figure and, before I knew what had happened, my pistol roared. Cantor screamed and flopped in the dirt. My ball, it seemed, had penetrated the calf of his left leg. Blood was pouring out and surgeons rushed to attend him. There was no thought of him firing back, for he could not even sit upright to aim. And so the duel ended, and I was borne off in triumph by my friends, all rumors of my lack of bravery having been put to the lie.

As I write this and look back upon the event, much of it seems ludicrous and laughable and I laughed aloud myself as I wrote this account. All duels seem to me to be comic affairs, yet many do not end so weakly as did mine. Most find one or more of the participants—like poor Alexander Hamilton— lying dead, their lives ended prematurely over some small insult, real or fancied. It is a barbaric custom and one that I truly despise. I shall ever write and speak against it and I vow that, unless my back is surely to the wall, I shall never again be importuned into fighting a duel.

My love and respect to your parents and all of your family and mine, as well. A special kiss, please, to Grandmother from her loving grandson and your faithful cousin, who wishes you ever well—

M. M. Noah

His father stirred as Uriah finished the last lines of the letter, and he folded the thick batch of papers and returned them to his pocket. He bent to see in the darkness if his father's brow needed wiping or there was any other thing he could do for him. Then the small stirring ceased and Michael Levy gasped once or twice, and then he fell back into the rasping slumber, as before.

The candle near the bed was guttering and flickering, and the smell was growing foul. Uriah blew it out and got up to find another one. The door to the room quietly opened, and his sister Eliza entered.

"You can go stretch your limbs," she whispered to him. "I'll sit with him. Mother is coming back here in a few minutes."

"But she just took to bed for some rest. Why doesn't she stay there and sleep?"

"She won't. She can't. She says that she will not waste her husband's last minutes on earth, that she will spend them at his side."

Uriah nodded silently. Eliza sat in the chair he had vacated, near the head of the bed.

He wanted to leave, to get out of the darkness and into the warm light of the parlor or the kitchen, but he tarried. He looked at his father's face with its thin cheeks, at the sparse gray hair on his head. He wondered how his father had aged so quickly. He remembered him as a young man, with thick brown hair.

"Eliza," he said softly. "Do you think he loves us? He has never said."

She nodded. "Yes. I know he does. When I sat here yesterday, he woke for a moment or two and suddenly he said in a strong, clear voice—'Amelia'—for he thought I was our sister—'Amelia, I dearly love you and all my children. Louis and Joseph and Uriah and all the others. I cannot remember all their names,' he said, 'but I love them all. They are my treasures.'"

"He mentioned my name among them?" There was a note of wonder in Uriah's question.

"Yes, he mentioned your name," answered Eliza.

"I wish that I could tell him now that I, too, love him and that I am sorry for the worries I have caused him by going to sea."

"You can tell him. But I'm afraid that he can no longer hear you."

Even if the face—with its long features, prominent eyes, tanned skin, and wavy black hair—were not so well known, the demeanor, the aura of command as he swung along the street in his handsome uniform, would have attracted all eyes, as indeed they did. The whispers—"Decatur . . . there goes Captain Stephen Decatur, hero of the *Philadelphia*"—filtered along the curbside. They certainly were loud enough for him to hear, but he gave no notice, merely continued purposefully on his way.

A few forward souls shouted greetings to him, and he answered with a quick smile and a wave of his hand but he did not stop to talk. Every man on the Atlantic coast, it seemed, now claimed him as a friend, and he did not have the time to separate these claimants from the real old friends of his home city.

Until, that is, a slim youth with curly black hair stepped in his path and stuck out a hand to shake. "Captain Decatur! It is an honor to greet you, sir!"

Decatur nodded politely and extended his own long, slender hand to the youth; he would not be so rude as to pass by the proffered shake.

"Captain, I know you will not remember me, but we have met before—at Joshua Humphreys's yard, while the *United States* was a-building. I believe you knew my grandfather. He was Jonas Phillips."

Decatur now gave his attention to the youth's face for the first time. It was a rather handsome, open face that featured, obviously with much pride, a curling, well-manicured mustache.

"I remember your grandfather well," Decatur said. "And you must be one of the little boys who asked me so many questions when you toured the yard. Your name, sir, if you please?"

"I am Uriah Phillips Levy, Captain."

"Ah, yes, you are Michael Levy's son. I read of your father's death the other day in the *Freeman's Journal*. My deepest sympathy, sir, to you and to your mother and family. And how does your mother?"

"She grieves deeply, Captain, but she does well, considering. And I thank you for your kind wishes. But obviously I am detaining you. I merely wanted to greet you and to offer my good wishes to you for the days ahead."

"Yes, yes, of course. Come. Walk with me a ways. I have heard stories of your schooner's theft at the Isle of May and would like to hear more of it. I am on my way to the Three Irishmen for a last drink with Charlie Stewart. Then we go our own ways to our ships. He commands the *Constellation*, you know, while I have the *United States*."

Uriah matched his pace to the quick step of Decatur. How honored he felt to be invited to accompany this great national hero down a Philadelphia street as bystanders turned to stare and whisper.

"By God, I envy you, Captain!" he said, then felt immediately embarrassed at his overloud show of emotion. He lowered his voice a bit. "Ever since I saw the *United States* in Humphreys's yard, I have wanted to sail on her. I thought of her, when I was small, as my very own ship. I still feel rather possessive about her, I fear."

Decatur smiled. "Yes, I understand. I feel much the same way, having been involved in her construction and then sailing with her on her maiden voyage. Charlie Stewart also was a midshipman on that voyage. He and I were boyhood chums, and we remain close. He's a skillful and brave commander. His brig provided cover for us, you know, when we went aboard the *Philadelphia* at Tripoli."

Uriah could not believe his luck. Here he was, hearing from the very lips of the hero of Tripoli a memory of that action that had stirred the blood of every American. He hoped Decatur would not mind if he ventured to ask about the current crisis.

"Sir, may I ask: Do you think there will be war?"

"No doubt of it. Any day now. The president went before Congress two weeks ago and summarized the crisis. I was in the gallery and heard him speak. When he told of the grievances against England—the ever-worsening impressment situation, the continuing interference with our trade, the stirring up of troubles among the Indians, the efforts from Canada to foment disaffection in New England—all those things heated the faces of tired old congressmen, I assure you. Madison's war message will come any time now, and I have no doubt that Congress will handily approve it."

"That's good news, indeed, sir! Then we can get about the business of thrashing these Limeys and teach them that the United States is not to be trifled with!"

They reached the tavern, and Uriah prepared to bid Decatur farewell and to thank him for the honor of being permitted to accompany him. The captain, however, took Uriah by the elbow.

"Come in," he said. "Charlie will not be here for a time yet, and I still want to hear your tale of piracy at Maio. Be my guest for a glass of cider or, if you choose, rum."

"I accept with pleasure, sir," answered Uriah, "and cider would be fine."

The tavern was well filled, and there were a few shouted hallooes to Decatur, who answered loudly in kind. Then the patrons took no more note of him and resumed their earnest quaffing. Two large glasses of cider were brought to the table by a plump barmaid. Decatur took a deep gulp and then cast a hard look at Uriah.

"So, my lad, you hail the start of this war, eh, and look for a quick victory over the British upstarts, do you?"

"I don't know about 'quick,' sir, but I do look for a sound victory and a certain one. They are strong, but we are stronger. We proved that in the Revolution, and we'll do so again."

"I wish I could share your confidence."

"Sir?"

"Oh, your spirit and your patriotism are quite commendable, Levy. Many Americans have been screaming for war, and they have every right, given the provocations we have suffered. But, like you, they expect that all we need do is fire a volley from our muskets and perhaps a carronade or two and the Brits will strike their flags. Let me tell you a few facts, my lad. I wish I could stand on the roof of this good alehouse and shout out these words and have the whole country hearken to me: *It will not be that easy!* Our army, Mr. Levy, is small and sadly trained, and its officers are so poor that I would not allow one of them to command the bread locker on my frigate."

Uriah was taken aback by the pessimistic tone. What could have happened to warrant such a voice of doom from one of the nation's foremost commanders on the eve of a new war?

"But, Captain, our navy! We have a fine navy that is a match for any power in the world—"

"Ah, yes, our navy," interrupted Decatur. Again he took a deep draft of cider. "Oh, we have some good ships and many brave men. And our officers are better than most. But we are a David, Mr. Levy, standing forth against the earth's maritime Goliath. Ten years ago, the United States Navy had over fifty men-of-war. At this time, my dear young friend, we have the grand total of sixteen or seventeen seagoing combat vessels. Do you know how many England has? Over a thousand, and more than a third of them are ships-of-the-line or frigates. With all of the vessels they are employing against Bonaparte, they still have over a hundred men-of-war plying the Atlantic between Halifax and Cuba. In the past ten years, our peace-loving national fathers have augmented our navy by two sloops, two brigs, and four schooners. And, let us not forget, we now have over sixty of those wonderful little gunboats that Mr. Jefferson favored so much, and which are now as much use to us as sixty mosquitoes! We have a navy of just over fifteen thousand tons, Mr. Levy, while England has almost nine hundred thousand tons. We stand out with some 442 guns, while England can point 28,000 guns at us. We have just over 5,000 officers and men—brave souls all— while good King George has over 150,000 men in his fleet. Does that sound to you, my flag-waving young friend, like a fair fight?"

"Captain, I did not mean to suggest—"

"Ah, Mr. Levy, there is more to this tale. There is so much appreciation in Washington City for the importance of our naval mission that President Madison and his aides recently have suggested that we lay up our few frigates in the national harbors, take down their upper masts and spars, and use them as stationary floating batteries in support of the harbor fortifications, with Mr. Jefferson's little gunboats flitting around them in an awesome show of defensive strength!"

Decatur's voice had risen, and his face, under its deep tan, was red with anger. Drinkers at nearby tables hushed their companions and turned to listen.

"And will this terrible scheme be carried out, Captain?" asked Uriah.

"At the moment, it appears not," said Decatur, his voice subsiding. "Charlie Stewart and Captain Bainbridge managed to get an audience with the president and appealed to him at least to give our frigates a chance to get to sea, rather than shackling them to the harbors. Madison seemed to give his agreement, but who knows what tomorrow will bring? All I know is that, after my farewell drink with Charlie and a last kiss to my family, I shall board a fast horse and ride to New York, where the *United States* lays fully manned and waiting. She is part of Commodore Rodgers's squadron, which is about the only seaworthy squadron we have to oppose them. No, my friend, it will not be easy, though with God's help we may yet prevail in the end. Oh, what these politicians have done to our navy, though. It makes my blood boil!" He paused and thirstily took another long drink of cider, draining his glass and raising his arm to signal for another. "And so it stands, Mr. Levy, as we prepare to go to war, the nation applauding and cheering us on and expecting us to speedily show the British just who is the best man on the water of the world."

Uriah didn't know what to say. He had no idea that things were so bad, that the nation had been allowed to grow so weak.

"Well, dear countrymen, we shall give it an almighty good try," continued Decatur. "Ah, young Levy, I see that I have filled you with consternation. Well, the picture is not wholly black. Thanks to good Preble, we have a sound little navy, well-officered and well-manned. And we shoot well, as the Brits soon will discover. We exercise our men at the great guns every day while at sea. The English do so only when they get bored. That should tell in a fight. If our leaders will turn us loose to roam the seas at our will and to look for trouble, I think we will give a fair account of ourselves—and probably bloody a few English noses in the bargain."

Uriah looked up to see a thin, flaxen-haired man, also garbed in the blue double-breasted jacket of a naval officer, approach their table.

"Ah, Charlie," said Decatur. "Meet young Phillips Levy, a merchant sailor and captain who has recently had a foul experience with thieves among his crew."

"As which of us has not had?" said Stewart, as he shook hands with Uriah and pulled up a chair.

Uriah did not want to interfere with this farewell talk of two senior naval officers as they prepared to go to war. He stood up and put on his hat. "I must take my leave, gentlemen. I am expected at home. I wish you both Godspeed and good fortune. Captain Decatur, I have hopes of making my own contribution to this war. I have thought of seeking a lieutenant's commission, or if that fails, a midshipman's. Or perhaps a warrant as sailing master. But if war comes, I assure you that, once the trial of my thieves has been completed, I shall volunteer in some capacity. Perhaps we will meet again."

"Yes, Mr. Levy," said Decatur. "Perhaps our paths will cross on some deck somewhere. If I can be of assistance to you in your dealings with the Navy Department, do inform me. If I still live, rest assured I shall do all I can."

"I shall remember your kind offer, Captain," said Uriah. "I shall certainly remember it."

Uriah protectively took his mother's elbow as the street ahead of them stirred with activity and excitement. Knots of people filled the sidewalk and the street, talking and gesticulating. The crowd slowed their progress as they proceeded to the *esnoga* for the Shabbat afternoon service.

"What is it, Uriah?" his mother asked. "What is happening?"

"I don't know, Mama, but the crowd is gathered in front of the office of the *Freeman's Journal*. There must be some news, perhaps from Washington City."

"Dear God, do you suppose—?"

They entered the melee of people. The faces were a strange mixture: jubilation, fear, sorrow, joy. Someone handed Uriah a handbill. "Here it is," the stranger said. "The actual words."

They passed through the noisy crowd and stopped for a moment in a quieter place to look at the handbill. The black, thick print stood out starkly on the white paper:

Saturday, June 20, 1812
One O'Clock

AN ACT
Declaring War between the United Kingdom of Great Britain

and Ireland and the dependencies thereof
and the United States of America and their Territories

BE it enacted by the Senate and House of Representatives of the United States of America in Congress assembled, that WAR be and the same is hereby declared to exist between the United Kingdom of Great Britain and Ireland and the dependencies thereof, and the United States of America and their territories, and that the President of the United States be and he is hereby authorized to use the whole land and naval forces of the United States to carry the same into effect, and to issue to private armed vessels of the United States commissions or letters of marque and general reprisal, in such form as he shall think proper, and under the seal of the United States, against the vessels, goods, and effects of the government of the same United Kingdom of Great Britain and Ireland, and of the subjects thereof.

APPROVED June 18, 1812

JAMES MADISON

"So it has come," Uriah said softly.

"There was no way to avoid it, I fear," his mother replied, her face pale. "The clamor was too strong."

"Clamor in answer to England's acts of war, Mama. We can't forget that. They have left us no choice but to fight them."

"This means you and your brothers will be going soon," she said.

"We are Americans, Mama. We fight alongside our comrades."

"Dear Lord, I have just lost my husband. Now must I lose my sons as well?"

"Don't worry, Mama. The Levys are a hardy breed. You don't have to worry about us."

He wondered, as they walked the last steps to the door of Mikveh Israel, whether he really felt the confidence of those strong words.

Brown's Hotel, New York City
January 9, 1813

Dear Mama,

These last few days have been the most exciting of my life. I want to tell you about them, but I don't know if I have suffi-cient words to do them justice.

This city has burst with joy over Decatur's capture of the English frigate Macedonian and has opened up its hearts and all its doors to that brave warrior and his intrepid officers and men of the United States. (I hope old Joshua Humphreys knows of this news. How proud he can be! His "lady" has lived up to all his hopes for her.)

My arms and my eyes are weary as I sit to write, for I have been indulging with all the others of this city in the celebra-tion of recent days. Let me tell you some of the things that have happened.

New York City first became aware of this latest American win at sea on December 5th, when in stately fashion the Unit-ed States sailed down Long Island Sound. Following meekly in her wake was the Macedonian, of 38 guns and known as one of the great frigates of the English fleet. She was immedi-ately recognizable by her famous figurehead of Alexander the Great of Persia. She was sailed in by a prize crew commanded by Lieutenant William Allen, a fine officer who is said to have been largely responsible for the prowess of Decatur's crew at the great guns.

I was sitting in the Phoenix Coffee House at Wall Street and the East River, enjoying a beverage when we heard a roaring noise, growing louder and louder, like a gathering cy-clone. We rushed outside to see hundreds of people running to the river, waving their arms and screaming like lunatics.

Then we saw!

It was the United States and the Macedonian in trail on the river and everyone knew at once the meaning of their appearance. People were jumping up and down and strangers were embracing and crying. The sailors on the two ships were briskly waving and shouting to the people on the shore and they were as excited as we. Resplendent in my new uniform, I was the recipient of hugs and kisses and expressions of thanks (though I hardly merited such) from dozens of people. It was not difficult to suffer through such torture, especially as some of the celebrants were pretty young women.

As you must have heard by now, Decatur fell in with the Macedonian a few days west of the Canary Islands and brilliantly defeated her in a fight of less than two hours. The difference, I am told, was the splendid cannoneering of our men. They fired so rapidly, it is said, that the enemy was deceived by all the smoke into thinking that our frigate was afire. Decatur raked cleverly (this means he maneuvered his ship to pour fire down the length of the enemy's deck) and within minutes, the Macedonian was severely hurt and suffering many casualties. The carnage on the deck was pitiful. When it was done, more than one in every three on the British ship was a casualty, 43 of them dead. The Macedonian quickly struck her colors and it was all over.

One of the officers on the United States was a Lieutenant Hamilton, son of the Secretary of the Navy, and he was given the honor by Decatur of bearing news of the victory to Washington City. He carried with him, as a memento of the fight, the Macedonian's colors. He arrived in Washington City at the height of a ball and gallantly placed the colors at the feet of Mrs. Madison.

New York has been in a whirl of excitement ever since and has been making feverish preparations to properly honor the men of the United States. Several nights ago, Decatur was fa-

vored with a public ball in his honor. I attended. It was glorious! The great hall at Gibson's City Hotel was decorated like the court of a palace. Along the walls was a massive colonnade made of ships' masts, from which flew bunting, laurel, and flags of many countries. Several of the tables contained tubs of water in which floated small models of the United States.

Yesterday the celebration reached its height when the 400 officers and men of the United States paraded along Wall Street to the music of a French military band that had been performing as prisoners aboard the Macedonian until liberated by Decatur. The roar of the crowd was deafening and came near to the noise of that glorious day when the ships suddenly appeared on the East River. I think the proud Americans lining the street would gladly have removed their clothes and given them to the seamen or laid down in the mud and let them walk across their backs, if that had been their wish.

The parade continued on Pearl Street and on Broadway until it arrived at Gibson's, the selfsame hotel where the ball for Decatur had been given.

Again the great hall was opened, and to the tune of the boatswain's shrill whistle and the music of the band as it played "Yankee Doodle Dandy," the men of the ship filed into their seats. They were welcomed in great style by an Alderman of the city and his speech was acknowledged by the boatswain, followed by loud unison cheers by the sailors. Then at the front of the hall, a huge ship's sail was hauled up, uncovering a magnificent transparent painting depicting the heroic battles of the Constitution and the United States, and also the recent victory of our sloop Wasp over the English sloop Frolic in October. The sight of the transparency caused the sailors to burst forth in a fury of cheers and huzzahs, some of them standing on chairs and tables, some dancing with joy. After quiet was restored, a fine dinner was served and enjoyed by all. Soon Capt. Decatur and Lieut. Allen entered the room and fondly greeted their men and offered toasts to them. The toasts continued until six o'clock when the men marched to a theater where they were royally entertained through the evening by a chorus of lovely actresses. It was a night to remember and I shall do so forever.

I have been reporting faithfully each day to the office of the port commander and begging a duty assignment. I truly have been making a nuisance of myself, hoping they will relent and at last assign me to a man-of-war so I can begin practicing my trade. So far, to no avail. I shall be at their door bright and early tomorrow to renew my quest. I had thought the Navy desperate for experienced sailing masters such as myself. It begins to appear that I overestimated the desperation.

Meanwhile, I enjoy the benevolent society of the people of New York, both friends and kinsmen. Uncle Naph and Aunt Rachel have given me supper on numerous evenings and beseech me to come even more often. Hazzan Seixas has been a concerned friend, always asking after my welfare. I attend Shabbat services at Shearith Israel and sometimes morning service as well. Hazzan Seixas often speaks of Grandpa, what a fine man he was and how much he misses him. I miss him too and think often about him. How is Grandma doing? Give her a kiss and hug for me. Have you heard of Mordecai? I have not had a letter from him in a long time.

My eyes are closing as I sit and try to write. I must get to sleep. Kiss my brothers and sisters for me and offer them my love. And a special hug and kiss for you, for you are ever in my thoughts. I know you worry about me, Mama, but please do not worry too much. I am doing what I must do and want to do. I will be all right and will return to you as a conquering hero of a victorious country. My love to all.

Your loving and faithful son,
Uriah

Part II
A Navy Man

8

New York Harbor, 1813

He sat solemnly on a bench near the Southwest Battery, huddled in his greatcoat against the chill, and looked out upon the harbor of New York. These gray waters were said to constitute the world's most perfect harbor . . . fairly gentle of mien, resistant to fog or ice, opening hospitably like a wanton woman to the traders of all nations. On this cold winter day, however, the waters looked uninviting, sallow, treacherous. It was the sullen doorway to a country at war. Out there, just beyond range of sight, hovering somewhere off Sandy Hook cruised an English squadron, ready to pounce on any Yankee who ventured out of sanctuary.

As he waited for the cutter to collect him and transport him across the East River, Uriah pondered the new directions the war had been taking. England had been astonished and humiliated by the two monumental losses in the frigate battles and the further insult of the sloop action. The upstart nation that she had regarded as only a trifling nuisance would have to be taken more seriously—and that England was now doing.

The U.S. Army, such as it was, was stumbling about on the northern frontier, fighting little battles at the edge of Canada, accomplishing nothing. The honor, indeed the fate, of the United States seemed to rest squarely on the back of its navy. And how was that navy to do its job when it seldom managed to slip through the blockade and get out to blue water?

Uriah shivered in the cold and wished the cutter would arrive. He had only to cross the East River to the Navy Yard at Brooklyn. He had assured the harbor commander that he would be only too happy to ride across on the Fulton Street Ferry, but that worthy would not hear of it. It would not be fitting for a sailing master of the U.S. Navy to ride a ferry, he sputtered. No, a cutter would pick him off the Southwest Battery at three hours past meridian promptly and transport him to his duty ship.

It was now twenty minutes beyond three hours past meridian, and there was no sign of a navy cutter coming to fetch him. He stood up and stamped his feet on the dirt and waved his arms in small circles, seeking to stir up some warmth in his body. He was all alone on this little point. On spring days of sunshine, this place was a favored promenade for the young ladies of the city and their beaux. Even the street criers were nowhere to be seen today. On almost every day, warm or cold, the air rang with their raucous offerings of watermelon, sweet potatoes, strawberries, and "Here's your fine Rockaway clams!"

Ah, what he would give right now for a sight of that round little black woman who sold the delicious mulled wine. He would give a month's pay for a cup of that good, hot, spiced wine. It would put the blood back into his limbs.

His gaze ran gloomily out along the two-hundred-foot-long rock causeway that connected the point on which he stood with the Southwest Battery on its little island of rock. The circular battery had gigantic sandstone walls of red that looked to be at least six feet thick, perhaps eight. Out of the ports peeked the black tips of twenty-eight cannon. Today, though, the harbor was almost empty of ships, and the battery was unmanned and lonely.

A boat came clawing around the point from the Hudson River side. Uriah jumped again to his feet, sure that this must be his cutter, but he quickly saw that it was one of the little schooners in which young Cornelius van Derbilt ferried passengers over to Staten Island. After dark those same schooners were used to carry provisions to the men in Castle Williams and the other forts around the island. Young Cornelius, who still hadn't seen his twenty-first year, was fast growing rich from his thriving day and night business.

Here came the cutter now! It was dipping its bow into the angry water, and though the sea was a fairly flat one, it reared and plunged like a runaway horse. *It's roughly handled*, Uriah thought, *and I'm in for a bone-shaking ride to the Navy Yard.*

The cutter dipped its sail and swung into the wharf. Within a minute, Uriah was seated in the sternsheets and headed back out across the toe of the East River. It had taken some skill to swing the cutter in so quickly and as quickly out again in this chopping wind. *It is handled better than I realized*, he concluded, as the cutter again took up its rearing course.

The coxswain was a wizened little boatswain's mate named Finnegan. He nodded happily to Uriah and lifted his cap respectfully as the young sailing master took his place on a thwart.

"Nice day, but a bit chilly," Uriah ventured, as a way of passing the time.

"Nice day indeed, sor," smiled Finnegan, revealing a mouth absent any teeth, "but 'twould be much nicer in Mary's Tavern on Joralemon Street." He giggled shrilly above the noise of the flapping sail.

The cutter rapidly was forereaching on Wallabout Bay, where a flock of small navy vessels was anchored at the Navy Yard—gunboats, most of them, and a sloop or two. The cutter was sailing well on the wind, and Uriah's practiced eye noted the old coxswain's deft hand with the tiller and the way in which he merely raised his hand and the other three sailors on the boat quickly adjusted the sail so that the cutter could keep its luff. Finnegan knew his trade, no doubt of it.

"Why do they call this bay 'Wallabout'?" Uriah asked him.

"The land over there beyond the yard was owned by a Walloon back in the Dutch days," answered Finnegan. "The Dutchmen called the bay 'Wallenbogt,' meaning 'Walloon Bay,' and it came to be called Wallabout from that." He pointed out at the water. "This here was where the Limey prison ships was anchored during the Revolution. This was where they was, all right, the *Jersey* and them other hell-ships. They was so full of disease that the Limeys towed 'em over here and anchored 'em so's they wouldn't sicken the city. They killed ten thousand good Americans on them ships, they did. They bragged that their prison ships killed more o' us than their whole damned army. Lousy bastards." He shook his head and spit over the side.

Uriah's eye was caught by a rotting hulk tied up to the wharf of the Navy Yard. It was a man-of-war all right; he could see the gun ports, but they were empty and staring, gaping pocks in the ship's side. He was surprised that this old waterlogged relic should be left hanging to the wharf instead of being taken away and cut up. Perhaps that is what it was doing there: waiting for the workmen's saws.

"What is that old corpse of a ship over there?" he asked Finnegan, as the cutter began curling into the wharf to put him off.

"That, sor, is the prize *Alert*, now a receiving ship of the United States Navy."

"Good God in heaven!" Uriah felt his stomach tighten and a wave of depression passed over him. *That stinking piece of driftwood is the* Alert? And this was to be his first ship in the navy? *Surely there must be some error. God, there had to be!*

"Are you certain that is the *Alert*? You are not mistaken?"

"No, sor, not one bit mistaken. I was aboard her only yestiddy. She was an English ship sloop carrying twenty guns and was captured by our frigate *Essex*, under Captain Porter, in August. She came in as a prize, but she was so old and decrepit that she was tied to the wharf and used ever since as a receiving ship. If you thinks she looks bad from here, sor, you should see her from aboard. . . . It's even worse. How she stays afloat is a wonder. The men draw lots to see who can be the first lucky enough to get off her." He laughed again, that high-pitched whinny.

Uriah did not laugh in answer. He was in misery. His dreams of

serving gloriously on a proud, beautiful American fighting ship—
like that trim brig over there—what had happened to his dreams?
Had he annoyed the harbor commander so much with his requests
for assignment that the man had put him on the *Alert* as revenge?
If so, his revenge was bitter indeed, for Uriah would rather be in a
navy jail somewhere than to do duty on this disgraceful clump of
marine rot.

He could not bear to see the *Alert* any more and turned his head
away.

"What is that pretty brig over there?" he asked softly.

"That, sor, is the brig-sloop *Argus*, just back from a three-month
cruise under Master Commandant Sinclair. She took six prizes and
was chased for three days by a Limey squadron. Her boats and anchors were cut away in the chase and her water was started, and she
got away. And you know what, sor? While the Limeys was chasin'
her, she fell in with a Limey merchantman and took herself still
another prize. While they was chasin' her!" Finnegan shrieked with
laughter, his toothless mouth working and slavering.

"The *Argus* is a ship to be proud of," Uriah said bitterly. "The
man who serves on that ship is a lucky man. The man who serves
on the *Alert* must be either a rascal or a fool."

Finnegan looked at him and nodded, and his laugh shrilled out
again. Then he gave his men orders to brail down the sail and prepare to land.

On that day and the days that followed, Uriah found that conditions
aboard the *Alert* were as bad as Finnegan had painted them—and, if
possible, even worse. The rotting old sloop was falling apart as she
stood in the water. On top of that, she was filthy and ridden with
lice and rats. There was no discernible effort to change the situation.

The ship was the temporary home for seamen and a few unlucky
petty officers until they could be assigned to their ships. Some were
forced to stay on board for only a day, others for a week or two until
they mercifully were freed. Because the ship was only a way station,

little effort was made to enforce discipline. The nominal commander of the vessel, Uriah found when he reported aboard, was a master's mate who stayed ashore as much as possible and during his brief hours on the *Alert* was usually so drunk that he neither knew nor cared what was happening.

The master's mate greeted Uriah respectfully enough but could only scratch his gray head in confusion when asked what duties Uriah was expected to perform.

"I don't rightly know, Mr. Levy," he said. "Bein' as you a sailin' master, you might want to check on the rigging and such things. Beyond that, I don't know what you'll do since, as you see, we are tied to the wharf and no sailin' orders is expected."

As he walked about the hulk and then looked below decks, holding his nose against the stench, Uriah found his shame and disappointment replaced by a feeling of rage. How dare they do this to him? He felt like storming back to the harbor commander's office and telling him what a travesty this receiving ship was. What use did an old barnacle that would sink to the bottom of this bay before it ever sailed another yard have for a qualified sailing master?

His anger rose and quickened as he strode the deck, and his red face drew stares from the seamen standing about. He began practicing the harsh words he would use as he stormed into the harbor commander's presence. But he knew even as he planned the dramatic confrontation that it never would take place. It would earn him a quick court-martial and likely dismissal from the service, if not a sentence for insubordination. No, there would be no profit for him in such a scene.

The saving grace for him, as it turned out, was that no one cared or seemingly even knew whether he was on the ship. He reported faithfully to the *Alert* each day, checked with the master's mate, if present and if sober enough to converse, and quickly inspected the vessel in hopes of finding her taking on water. Then he returned to his room in the city or sought out friends for pleasure or cultural pursuits. In this way, he kept his sanity as the war went on without him.

There were about two hundred men and boys on the *Alert* each day, most of them destined for a new group of gunboats that some-one had dubbed the Flying Squadron. It was being formed to buzz, mosquitolike, around Long Island Sound. The men were a poor lot, rum and whiskey lovers all, who waited with pathetic eagerness for their tot of grog to be passed out to them at seven-and-a-half in the morning. Most of them stayed drunk the day long. At night, they were too overcome by drink to climb into their hammocks and slept sprawled about the wet decks in the cold January air. As a result, the decks trembled with the constant barrage of coughing. Almost every man and boy aboard was sick in some way, and the faces of many of them burned with fever.

One morning, as Uriah descended the main hatch to the berth deck, he found a frozen corpse lying there. The man had died sometime in the night, and the body had been ignored since then, though dozens of men had climbed past it, up the hatch, to get their morning ration of whiskey. The corpse would have lain there, star-ing with open eyes up at the stanchions, until doomsday had not Uriah, trembling with disgust and near to vomiting, rounded up some men and screamed orders at them to remove the dead man ashore.

At night and sometimes during the days as well, whores from the dockside bars came freely aboard to ply their trade with those conscious enough to patronize them and to steal from those who were not. Uriah threw them off the *Alert* whenever he encountered them and threatened them with arrest, but they only laughed and plotted to return when he was gone. In the night, loud drunken fights were common, and the women freely took part.

On one freezing, intensely clear day in mid-February, when the sun seemed to pierce the iced air with amazing brilliance, two puny midshipmen came aboard the *Alert* and began walking back and forth the length of the spar deck, screeching, "All hands to witness punishment, ahoy!" The loungers on the deck and the curious few who poked their heads up the hatch seemed to take pleasure in ig-noring the orders of the reefers. They gazed without expression at the caterwauling boys but made no move.

In a few minutes, however, the midshipmen were joined on the deck by two husky boatswain's mates armed with thick rope ends. The mates added their robust lung power to the piercing treble of the middies and waved their colts to emphasize. Quickly the loungers scrambled to their feet and the deck began to fill from below with the motley crew of the receiving ship.

Some of the sailors showed an eagerness to view the spectacle and climbed the nearest shroud, taking their lives in jeopardy as they did so, for the ratlines looked frail enough to part at the slightest weight.

Uriah had been within his second circuit of the spar deck when the midshipmen suddenly had appeared from the wharf. He had outlined for himself a daily regimen of three circuits of the deck, during which he inspected the rigging visually for signs of chafe. Seeing none, he sought out the master's mate in charge, paid that worthy his compliments if he could be located, and then vacated the sickening ship until the next day when the procedure would be repeated. Meanwhile, he would ride the ferry back across the river and find some way to pass the day's hours. He found his role degrading and shameful, but he knew of no way to change it. The navy apparently had forgotten him, and he seemed destined to be stationed on this hulk until the glorious day came when it would slowly and finally sink beneath the river's surface.

Now the high-pitched demands of the middies ricocheted through the ship, interspersed with the rasping baritone summons of the boatswain's mates. Uriah had a sinking sensation of what was to come. He would have liked to stride down the gangplank and hurry back across the river to the pleasant bustle of New York, but it was impossible to do so. All around him, men were forming up on the deck for the commanded assembly.

He noticed that several officers stood off from the people, near the mainmast on the starboard side. He decided that it would be seemly to join them, though they all were strangers to him. He quietly walked across and took a position behind the others. A tall, pimply faced lieutenant nodded at Uriah as he passed, in apparent recognition, probably mistaken.

The mumble of conversation among the hundred or more men and boys on the deck suddenly ceased. A pathway opened up, by some internal magic, through the crowd. Two young sailors, darbies shackling their wrists, were led down the narrow road by a master-at-arms in civilian clothes, accompanied by a marine. One of the handcuffed sailors was crying in fear, the other stared straight ahead, his face taut and expressionless. The crowd was quiet now, and all eyes were on the prisoners.

Then: "Pucker up, me boys, you'll soon feel the cat's kiss!" The voice came from somewhere in the depths of the crowd. Uriah thought it sounded much like Finnegan, the old tar who had hauled him to this accursed post.

"Clap a stopper on your mouth, you bastard," roared out the master-at-arms, "or I'll see you at the mainmast with these two!" There were no more outcries from the deck.

A noiseless stir went across the ship's waist, and the pathway through the massed bodies, which had begun to disappear, suddenly re-formed, wider than before. Down it, looking straight ahead, strode Captain Wolcott Chauncey, senior captain of the Flying Squadron. He was a short man with broad shoulders and a pointed jaw. When he spoke, his deep voice rang across the deck like a gun's report.

"You blackguards were absent without leave from your ship and remained ashore until returned by a search party! What have you to say?"

Speaking at the same time, the two youths began to mumble convoluted explanations of their absence. Their words jumped and mixed together like two strands of smoke in the air. They could not be understood, drowning each other out like this, yet neither made an effort to stop and allow the other to proceed. After a few seconds of this awful incantation, the captain raised one blue-jerseyed arm.

"Enough!" he shouted. "Your ridiculous excuses are refused. You are guilty of the charges against you. You will pay the penalty!" He turned slightly to face the crowd of men on the deck and elevated his chin to project his booming voice through the freezing air: "Attend me well, men! I believe in giving you everything the law says, but when you break the law, by the eternal God above, you will pay a fit price for what you have done. You break the law of my ship and I swear I will see your backbone cut out of your body. Boatswain's mate, rig the gratings and seize them up! Six dozen lashes for each!" At these words, the tense-faced prisoner groaned loudly and his companion screamed in fear. The latter then slumped and would have fallen to the deck in a faint had not the marine guard grabbed him and held him up.

Uriah leaned his face toward a middle-aged sailing master standing next to him. "My God, six dozen lashes," he murmured. "I thought the law said no more than a dozen without a court-martial."

The other master glanced at him, then returned his gaze to straight ahead. "On this ship, the law is whatever the cap'n says it is. And you'd better keep quiet, or he'll have you seized up with the other two."

Two square gratings with their wooden bars were hurried to the deck by a pair of quartermasters and were laid, ends down, on the deck planks. The prisoners were brought forward, and their coats and shirts were removed. They were visibly shaking, but it was from fear of the cat rather than from the cold. The quartermasters took short lengths of rope and tied the ankles of the prisoners to the crossbars of the gratings. Their arms then were raised over their heads and tied tightly to the hammock nettings inside the ship's bulwarks.

"Holy Mother of God!" screamed the lad who had been faint, revived now by his abject fear. "Save me from this, Mother Mary! I meant no harm!"

His companion said nothing, but as he was tied his lips curled back from his mouth and his teeth showed in a snarl of animal-like defiance and hatred.

A boatswain strode forward with a big black bag and from it

brought out two cats. Each was given to a husky boatswain's mate. Each mate hefted the wooden pole and took a good grip on it, meanwhile combing out the nine leather cords of the cat with his other hand.

"Get on with it, by God, you boatswain's mates!" screamed Captain Chauncey. "On with it or I'll have you up there in their places. Begin punishment!"

The screaming prisoner let out another echoing, pitiful yell that scattered the seabirds wheeling about the vessel. Then he subsided into choking sobs.

The boatswain's mates combed out their cat's tails for the last time. Then each of them swung his cat back around his head and with all his strength brought the cords down upon the bare back before him. The screaming lad shrieked again and asked God to deliver him. His companion yelled angrily and cursed. Then he was silent and not another sound came from his lips.

After three lashes, the crying, praying youth fainted dead away. The cords rhythmically continued to slash his back with a loud, metallic sound.

The flesh on both backs reddened, and swelling could be seen. As the lashing continued, blood began to ooze down the raw backs, which took on the appearance of veal in a butcher shop. The flesh began to fall off the backs in long strips.

A stir in the crowd caused Uriah to turn his horrified gaze away from the carnage before him. A young sailor in the front row had fainted, and another, older tar nearby also was slumping to his knees, his face white, his eyes glazed.

Uriah began to feel an overpowering desire to run to the bulwarks and vomit into the river. Hot liquids were pouring up into his throat. He felt like his bowels were full of bile and ready to explode. He felt like crying. His eyes pained, his vision misted over, his head began to spin. Desperate to regain control, he raised his eyes and stared grimly, ashen-faced, into the sky, watching the soaring gulls and the floating clouds, trying to dull all his senses. He could not, however, blot out the never-ending sound of the cat's tails falling, again and again and again.

The silent lad stood and took the lashes, his head down on his chest, his lips still pulled back in the grimace snarl. He had taken two dozen lashes, and a new boatswain's mate had grabbed the cat from his exhausted predecessor. Suddenly the prisoner fainted and his knees buckled. His taut arms held him in place.

"Stop the flogging on that man!" the captain bellowed. "Revive him. He has a bad attitude. I want him to feel every kiss of that cat. Revive him, I say!" Water was poured over the head of the prisoner until he regained a semblance of awareness. Then the boatswain's mate was ordered to renew the flogging until the full sentence had been carried out.

When the six dozen lashes had been administered to both men, an eerie silence fell across the deck. Uriah could not resist looking at the prisoners. Their backs were now coal-black as if they had been badly burned in a fire. Neither one could stand. They were cut down and silently carried away.

Captain Chauncey ordered, "Pipe down!" The shrill wailing of boatswain's pipes swelled around the masts, and the crowd slowly began to dissipate.

Uriah stood fast, unable to move, afraid that any motion would cause him to vomit all over the deck and disgrace himself.

"My God," he said softly. "My God."

The other sailing master looked at him again. "Your first flogging, I daresay. Well, it won't be your last if you stay in this man's navy for any time."

"But so much? So many strokes! It . . . it was brutal."

"Brutal? Yes, I suppose 'tis. But the commanders say that it must be done or we would have anarchy on the ships. These sailors are rabble, they say, and you control rabble only with the whip. Hell, you think this is bad? You have heard of Captain Carden, that noble British gentleman who commanded the *Macedonian* when Decatur captured it? That warrior who fought so gallantly that Decatur refused to accept his sword? Well, last year a seaman on his frigate was accused of stealing. Carden found him guilty and sentenced him to be flogged through the fleet . . . 300 lashes *plus* a year in prison. He took 220 lashes and then the surgeon ruled him not fit for more. So Carden allowed him a few weeks for the scars to heal up a bit and then insisted that the remainder of the punishment be given. The additional 80 lashes were applied, and then the lad was toddled off to do his time in prison. That seaman will never take another step in his life without pain, and his back always will be a nest of stripes."

Uriah shook his head in misery. "But that is the British. Everyone knows they treat their sailors like dogs. This is the American navy. We are supposed to be different."

The older master laughed. "Different? I think not. Our sailors call our ships 'floating hells' just like the Limey tars do. A member of our Congress who passengered to Europe aboard one of our men-of-war said later that he saw more flogging done on that single passage than he had seen during ten years on his plantation of half a thousand African slaves."

"My God," Uriah said again. "I have heard of these things before, and I have accepted them. But until today I had never seen it. It is barbaric!"

"Barbaric it may be, my friend," said the other master, "but it is the way of our navy. If you're a navy man, you must go with it."

"Perhaps so," answered Uriah, "but I promise you this, sir: If I ever command my own vessel, there will be none of this. I will find other ways of enforcing discipline."

"Find them, if you can," said his companion. "All power to you. But the best minds of the navies of the world never have been able to do so."

Of all the young women, and there were many, who had given companionship to Uriah Levy during these past months of harbor drudgery, he was perhaps most attracted to Sarah Carvalho, a tall, dark-complected daughter of a physician. He had seen her from afar in the women's gallery at the *esnoga*, and it had not been difficult to manage an introduction at the tea following Shabbat morning service. They had since spent many happy times together, promenading with other young people on Broadway and on the shore by the Southwest Battery, or past the beautiful new City Hall, or attending a performance at the Park Theater.

There were other girls in his life and thoughts, some from the respected families of Shearith Israel and others whose families lived in tight-packed flats along Coenties Slip or Beekman Slip. The Israelite girls were cheerful, vivacious companions for his afternoon promenades on Broadway. The riverside girls were warm and giving partners in their small beds in their dark rooms.

Sarah Carvalho was by far his favorite. He found her witty and intelligent and above average in beauty. And her passion for kissing and embracing almost matched his own. He found himself lying awake at night, perfecting schemes and strategies to take her to bed, but all of these came to ruin when faced with her grim determination: the inner sanctum of pleasure beneath her skirts would be breached only by the man who stood with her under the marriage canopy. He was tempted, sorely tempted at times, to speak the words that would bind them together, but he could not quite bring himself to do it. He told himself it was the war; he could not tie himself to anyone when he might not return from the fighting, or return any time soon. But in moments of quiet and clarity, he knew it was not the war that held his tongue. In truth, he didn't know what he wanted.

"My parents will arrive home at any second," Sarah said, as she returned to the parlor, having quickly brushed and combed her hair and straightened her tousled clothing. "It is fortunate that they didn't return early and catch us. We would both have been disgraced. As it is, my father will be very unhappy when he finds us here alone together."

"We shall be sitting primly in the parlor," Uriah replied, "talking of philosophy and the progress of the war, and all sorts of serious things. There is nothing wrong with that. Anyway, it's not my fault that Hazzan Seixas's dinner ended so early. It was my duty to see you home and into the house, was it not? And to wait with you for your parents? Your father should feel honored. How many young men are privileged to take his daughter to dinner at the home of our esteemed *hazzan*?"

"Yes, and then return home and try to have their way with her?" Sarah answered with a trace of a smile. "So how goes the war, Uriah? What is the news?"

His face grew serious at once. "I don't know. God, I don't know at all. Here I am in the navy and I sit in Wallabout Bay on a derelict ship with a crew of drunken scum. And nobody tells me anything. From what the newspapers say, though, the war has taken a serious turn. After Bainbridge and the *Constitution* destroyed the *Java* in December, it began to seem that we had the British on the run. After all, it was our third straight frigate victory. But the latest reports from the north tell of the English forming giant squadrons off our New England ports to extend their blockade.

"The Brits still have gigantic resources. Our frigate victories have done wonders for our good cheer, but I have the feeling sometimes that our throat is being held within two powerful English hands that are slowly beginning to tighten. Our troops have captured York in British Canada and burned some buildings there. But I don't think it means much. Both sides have only weak forces on the lakes, and all the fighting is inconclusive. This whole damned war seems inconclusive. Our army muddles along, winning a skirmish here, losing one there."

Sarah sat down next to him again. She took his hand. It was obvious that her question about the war had depressed him. "And what about you, Uriah? Any success in your own battle with the navy?"

He sighed deeply. "No—at least, none apparent. Congress finally has learned the importance of having a strong navy. They are now building four 74-gun ships-of-the-line and six more 44-gun frigates. Perhaps then, finally, I'll get my decent chance to serve on a fighting ship when those new ones are launched. But only God knows when *that* will be. Perhaps by 1815, if we're lucky. If the war still rages then, I'll finally get my chance to fight. And I'll be an old man."

Sarah laughed. "Old indeed! All of . . . what? Twenty-one years? Old man, indeed! You are so anxious to taste the war that your reasoning is weak. You'll get your chance soon. I'm sure of it."

"I'd better. Each day that passes, by God, I regret more not having signed onto a privateer. I'd be months at sea by now, capturing Limey merchantmen and at least doing something to help win the war. For now, though, I have one last hope."

"And what is that?"

"The brig *Argus* lies anchored not far from my vessel at Wallabout. It is commanded now by William Henry Allen, a master commandant. He served for two years as first lieutenant under Decatur, and it was he, they say, who drilled the gunners on the *United States* so well that they broke the back of the *Macedonian*. He also was the man who managed to fire the lone shot when the *Leopard* shamed the *Chesapeake* back in 1807. Were it not for Allen, the *Chessie* would have struck without firing a single shot. How I long to serve under a commander like him! I want it so much I would go without food and drink to do so.

"In any case, I hear at the Navy Yard that the *Argus* soon will make an effort to slip through the blockade and get to sea. I have hopes, Sarah, of being able to convince Captain Allen that I am his man. I'm sure he already has a sailing master, but perhaps he is willing to carry another. Some time this week, I plan to order up a boat and visit the *Argus* and put in my request. On bended knees, if necessary."

"I see," Sarah smiled. "For that you would get down on your knees!" Suddenly she stood up. "I hear father's carriage!" she whispered. "Quickly, go sit in that red chair on the other side of the room."

The cutter's passage out to Sandy Hook, latest anchorage of the brig

Argus, had been a slow one, for the wind was veering and mostly foul and the cutter was a slow sailer. There had been some benefit from the tedious passage, though. As the brig's outline grew larger and larger over the cutter's bow, Uriah had a long chance to study the ship's lines and appraise her sailing qualities. Just as men gauge a woman's outline and evaluate her rounding charms, so do men of the sea carefully peruse a vessel, and most especially one in which they are soon to sail.

Uriah had no certainty that he would have a berth on this brig, but he planned to plead earnestly for such. In anticipation of possible success, he looked her up and down, bow to stern, and judged her capabilities, the way her rigging hung, the manner in which her sails were furled, the curve of her wales.

He could see from the cutter that the *Argus* was rather full-bodied for a brig, although fine aft. Her sheer was lovely. Her rigging he would describe as lacy or airy—light and high and somewhat narrow. She reminded him of a speedy merchantman brig of the type sailed by John Coulter, and he guessed that her displacement was more than ample to carry the necessaries for long cruises in foreign waters. Her lower masts, he saw, were somewhat longer than he would have expected, and her yards a bit shorter. She would go, he told himself, about three hundred tons.

The cutter swung into the brig's lee and under her counter. Uriah grabbed the falls and, with a boost from one of the cutter's crew, climbed quickly up to the entry port. He asked the boatswain's mate at the port for an audience with Captain Allen, and the mate went off to find the officer of the deck.

As he waited in the ship's waist, Uriah had a chance to look about him and view the spar deck of this flush-decked vessel. Everything in good order, he noted quickly, brass shined to a high finish, running rigging properly coiled, deck planks freshly holystoned and gleaming. It took only a moment's narrow-eyed study of this spar deck for him to know that this was a taut ship, well-commanded and disciplined.

He glanced aft and saw no sign of any officers approaching. He decided to quickly pace the length and breadth of the deck to better gauge her size. He marched off the steps, counting under his breath. She would be better than ninety feet between perpendiculars, he decided, and probably closer to ninety-five. She would be twenty-seven or twenty-eight feet in molded beam and perhaps eighty feet on the keel. Blocky as she was, she would have a depth of hold of at least twelve feet. . . .

"Well, Sailing Master, what think you of our brig?"

The voice from behind him was not blatantly loud, but breaking into his mental calculations as it did, it startled him so that he visibly jerked. He turned and found himself in the presence of Master Commandant William Henry Allen, Esq., with a grinning lieutenant at his elbow.

Uriah quickly brought his feet together and raised his hat. "Excuse me, sir, for leaving my back to you. I didn't hear you coming, sir."

"I expect not," said Allen. "You obviously were completely occupied in judging my ship. Tell me, does she pass your muster?"

Uriah felt like a fool. How he had hoped to make a favorable first impression, but now . . . "She is a fine ship, sir, and well put up. I would be proud to sail on her."

Allen put his hands on his hips and gazed at Uriah, his eyebrows raised. "Tell me, Sailing Master, what of her lines? Does her silhouette entice you, or no?"

Dear God, how to answer? If he said a word to offend this man, his hopes would go for naught!

"Sir, she fills my eye very well. She does strike me as rather full in line and she carries quite low in the water, but I'm sure that—"

"And what of her rigging, sir? How does that strike your wandering eye?"

"I would say, sir, that her rigging is rather thin and high for a fighting brig, but in spite of that—"

"Well said, Sailing Master! Mr. Allen, we have a man here with a good eye for a vessel. He has described the *Argus* fair and square, with no quarter given." The lieutenant nodded in agreement, and Captain Allen continued, "You are quite right, Sailing Master. The *Argus* is somewhat full in line, but nonetheless she sails well and we are making her sail even better. And the lightness of her rigging is deliberate. She was designed, you see, at the time of our troubles off the Barbary Coast. Commodore Preble himself supervised the design of this brig, and she was built to fit the sailing conditions in the Mediterranean. Our heavy-draft ships had been having great troubles in the shoal water there, you see." He patted the ship's bulwarks. "She is an honest ship and true, and will never let us down. She was built in Boston town by Hartt, builder of the *Constitution*. She has sailed under Isaac Hull against the Algerines and Tripolines and under Arthur Sinclair against the English, and never has she disgraced herself. And never she will." He looked fondly up at the mainmast and nodded, as if confirming his proud words. Then he came back to the present moment. "Now, sir, you have requested the captain. I am W. H. Allen, captain of this brig. What is your business here, sir?"

"Sir, I am Sailing Master Uriah Phillips Levy, stationed at present and for the past months on the receiving ship *Alert*, tied up at the Navy Yard. Sir, I sincerely and urgently request that you consider me as a member of your brig's complement. I . . . I would be honored to serve under you, sir."

"Ah, but I already have a sailing master and am authorized only one."

Uriah's stomach suddenly clenched, and he wet his dry lips. He could tell that his face had gone pale with his emotion. Before he could think of a reply, however, Captain Allen spoke again:

"Tell me something of yourself, Mr. Levy, and of your experience."

Uriah quickly related his years at sea with Coulter's various ships, his brief and ill-fated ownership and mastering of his own vessel, his time spent at Talbot Hamilton's navigation academy, and his dreary, wasted months in the East River since receiving his warrant as sailing master. Allen listened patiently, nodding once or twice at salient points.

When he had finished and stood silent, the captain stared at him for a moment or two, his finger thoughtfully resting upon his lip. "So. Went to sea in a secret way, did you, as a wee boy? So did I. I was afraid it would give my father an apoplexy. He was a general of militia, you see, and expected that I would get liberally educated and then join the army. But, like you, I longed for the sea and joined the navy as midshipman when I was not yet sixteen years. Within three months I was on the frigate *George Washington* and cruising to Algiers."

He was silent for another moment or two and continued to stare levelly at Uriah, who found the long gaze most disquieting. Then the captain reached a decision and announced it: "Very well, Mr. Levy. I like the cut of your jib and your keen eye for a ship. You speak straight out. It can never hurt to have an extra sailing master on hand, though you must understand that Mr. Hudson is our official master and you will be subservient to him. I can classify you as a volunteer aboard the *Argus*, and I don't think the high chiefs of the navy will object too much. Our normal complement is 140 men, including 32 officers and petty officers, but it is quite customary for us to sail over complement. We'll be needing extra men for prize crews, I'm sure. Very well, Mr. Levy. You shall be our assistant sailing master. I'll sign the papers. I shall want you aboard by tomorrow at the latest. We have much work to do before we weigh anchor."

Uriah was overjoyed. He couldn't believe it! He certainly had not expected the matter to be settled so quickly, with such dispatch.

"Thank you, sir," he stammered. "I do thank you. And you will not be sorry. Sir, will you inform the harbor commander? I am posted to him."

"Indeed I will. Mr. Allen, dispatch a message on the gig this afternoon. That fine gentleman owes me more than one favor. He won't disappoint us. Now, Mr. Levy, may I introduce our second lieutenant, Mr. W. H. Allen?"

The lieutenant, a tall brown-haired officer, had a wide grin on his face. He stepped forward and shook hands with Uriah.

Uriah was thoroughly confused. He had thought the officer he had been addressing was W. H. Allen. But this lieutenant had been introduced as . . . but wasn't the commander of the *Argus* a master commandant, not a lieutenant? Were these two playing some sort of cruel joke on him?

"Ah, Mr. Levy, I see by the look of utter foolishness on your face that our little trick has worked once again. It is one we delight in playing on each new officer aboard our brig, and it never fails to amuse us. I am, you see, William *Henry* Allen, holding the rank of master commandant and captain of this brig-sloop. This handsome, grinning worthy is my second luff, who was christened William *Howard* Allen. Our first lieutenant, by the way, is William H. Watson, so if someone aboard our happy ship should call for 'William H.,' he will be answered from every quarter of the vessel. Well, I have work to do and have socialized long enough. We welcome you to our little family, Sailing Master. We shall look for you tomorrow, ready to sail."

"I'll be aboard, Captain. Ready to sail."

●●●

New York
June 14, 1813

Dear Mama,

I sincerely hope this letter finds you and my brothers and sisters in good health and of good cheer. My love also to Grandmother and my uncles and aunts and cousins and friends. I miss them all.

By the time you receive this, we well may be at sea. This letter should be in your hands four days from now and we are expecting to weigh anchor sometime around June 18th. Please don't fear for me! I am aboard a strong ship, well built, and carrying 20 powerful guns. She is commanded by one of the finest officers in the Navy and has a brave and generous group of officers and men. She will come to no bad end, I assure you.

I was pleasured to dine and spend much of a day with Mordecai two weeks ago, just before he sailed to his new diplomatic post. He gave me a minute-by-minute description of his dinner with President Madison in March and of how kind and friendly Mr. Madison was to him and how encouraging. It was not a week after his dinner at the President's House that he received official word of his appointment as consul in Tunis. He is as proud and puffed as a bird of plumage! But I only tease: I cannot take offense at Mordecai. He is ever dear to me and I am so happy for his success at last, after many years of idle dreams that never seemed to come true for him.

As for me, I am very tired, but very satisfied. Mama, I could not have desired a finer ship on which to serve my country. Captain Allen and the other officers are of a kind: strong men, but fair; good companions around the wardroom table but all business on the deck. I am proud to call them friends and shipmates. Mr. Hudson, the Sailing Master, is an older man, in contrast to the officers (Captain Allen is but twenty-eight years and Watson, the First Lieutenant, is about the same age) and is a good mentor to me. The ship's surgeon is James Inderwick, a young man who attended Columbia College. He has only recently joined the Navy, having been at New York Hospital for the last year.

We have moved around much in the weeks I have been aboard, anchoring for a time at Sandy Hook where I boarded, then near Staten Island, in the Narrows, and off the city itself. We sailed out the Sound briefly. Off Block Island, we sighted several sail, probably blockading Britishers, but we made no effort to run down to them, as our cruise was only for training and fitting out. The ship handles decently. I feel comfortable with her.

I have a small cabin to myself off the wardroom. It is so

tiny that if I scratch my head, my elbow is out the door. But I have had worse on other ships and I do not complain. The lieutenants, the surgeon, etc., have no better.

We have been told that we will be carrying an important figure in the government on our cruise, but the Captain has not said who that may be. It has become a mystery for all to consider. We should know the solution soon.

My love and blessings to you. I must finish this letter now as it is almost my watch. I pray you do not worry too much. The next time I see you I will be able to tell you of all my fine adventures.

Your loving son,
Uriah

The *Argus* was almost two hours out from Sandy Hook, and the hard-edged tension that had stiffened all their backbones was beginning to ebb. It appeared that they had slipped through the English picket line. A strange sail had been sighted hull-down on the horizon, and the lookout on the maintopgallant mast thought it might be a British frigate, but the lookout on the other ship must have been asleep and the three distant masts soon disappeared. After that, they had the ocean to themselves.

The brig rode gently on a following sea and had all her sails spread to the studdingsails. The captain would not dally here, not with those accursed Limey squadrons roaming off the coast. He had stood vigilantly on the quarterdeck throughout the two hours, ready at the lookout's cry to put the ship at general quarters. Now he, too, was perceptibly more relaxed and made a small joke or two with his first lieutenant. Then, in a more serious tone, he directed Lieutenant Watson, "Assemble the officers. It is time they were introduced to our honorable passenger."

In a few minutes the ship's small corps of officers was assembled in two lines on the quarterdeck. Uriah stood at the end of the back row and wondered the reason for this unusual assembly. The captain was absent, but he came striding aft on the spar deck a few minutes later, accompanied by a tall, fair-haired man wearing the boots-and-breeches garb of an aristocratic planter. They halted in front of the formation.

"Gentlemen," said Captain Allen, "I have the honor to present to you our most distinguished passenger, Mr. William Crawford, late member of the United States Senate from the State of Georgia. Mr. Crawford is our nation's new minister to France. The *Argus* has been signally honored by the secretary of the navy in being directed to convey Mr. Crawford and his party to France to take up his new duties. Mr. Crawford, may I present the officers of the United States Navy brig-sloop *Argus*."

Crawford stepped forward and nodded his head, a slight smile on his lips. "Gentlemen, it is an honor to meet you and a privilege to sail with you. I look forward to becoming better acquainted with you during our voyage, both here on deck and around the wardroom table." Then, Captain Allen at his elbow to provide introductions, Crawford began slowly moving down the line to learn the name and shake the hand of each officer. As Uriah greeted the new minister plenipotentiary to France, he couldn't help thinking of the letter he would later write to his cousin Mordecai.

9

Uriah was bending over No. 7 carronade to check a lashing that looked suspiciously relaxed when the sharp tapping of a bony finger on his backside startled him such that he came close to falling across the cannon muzzle. He turned angrily to find out who had rapped him so and saw before him a dark man of cadaverous thinness, garbed in a motley and rather threadbare collection of clothing. The man's eyes were wide with pleasure, and a big smile was spread across his face.

"Who the hell are you and what do you mean poking at me?" muttered Uriah. His rear end hurt, and it was all he could do to resist sliding a hand across it to soothe the pain.

"Hi thar, Mr. Levy, sar!" came a high-pitched voice of amazing loudness. "I be Simon McDeal, and I be assigned to you as your boy. I'm reportin' for duty, sar, and ready to do my bit." He nodded enthusiastically, and the smile, impossibly, spread even wider.

Uriah stared in astonishment at the skeletal figure. He hadn't known that he would be assigned a boy, though Hudson had one to assist him. But even so, this—*this* was a boy?

"In God's name, how old are you, man?"

"Why, I be twenty-seven years, sar, and it hain't another boy on this here ship that can beat that. No, sar!"

"You are twenty-seven years and serving as a boy? Surely there must be some mistake."

The man vigorously shook his head. The smile never left his face. "No, sar. It hain't no mistake. I don't know 'nough about sailorin' to be a sailor and they had to find somethin' for me, so they done made me a boy. I'm proud to be your boy, sar, and I'll foller your orders just like I was hearin' 'em from my own pap."

"If you know nothing about the sea, how did you get taken aboard?"

"Oh, I done begged and stomped 'til they gave in. No man can keep me out of this here navy. It's what I allus wanted to do."

Uriah sighed. A lot of use this lubber would be to him. "Where do you come from?" he asked.

"I come from the Ohio territory, sar, but we was original from Pennsy, back on the Juniata. When the game started to give out back thar, my pap took the family across the Ohio River and back into the big woods. Acourse, if you go back futher, we—the McDeals, that is—we come from Maine. That's the northern part of the Bay State, you see. That's where I came by my love o' the navy and the water."

"You lived along the ocean, then?"

"Wal, sar, I cain't rightly say. I cain't even 'member Maine. But my grandpap has told me stories about the ocean all my life, and he's the one who filled my ears with talk o' the navy and how great it fights. That's why, soon's I heerd there was a war with Europe, I done walked out of the woods to York State and signed myself up."

"You walked, you say, from Ohio State to New York? Did I hear you right?"

"Yes, sar. It war a pretty distance. That's why I warn't ready to fight the war 'til now. . . . It took me a time to get here. But here I am and they done assigned me to be your boy and that's what I aims to do. Tell me, sar, how do I start a-boyin' for you?"

Uriah could not repress a smile. "Well, Simon, you probably are the oldest boy in the entire United States Navy. But we'll find work enough for you. For now, I suggest that you join the other boys in swabbing down the berth deck."

"Yes, sar! Thankee, sar! I'll git right down thar!"

With that, the apparition ran to the nearest hatchway and quickly disappeared from view. A loud crash followed, indicating that he had made the last few feet of his journey in vertical flight.

Uriah shook his head and bent again to tighten the lashing on the starboard carronade.

It was the third straight day of harsh storms. The *Argus* heeled far over under the wind's onslaught and plowed madly through the waves even though her sails were triple-reefed. Two quartermasters were at the wheel; the captain would not chance the ship sliding out of control and perhaps getting caught in stays. Mishandle her in this heavy weather and there was danger of her getting pooped, with monster hillocks of water slamming across her taffrail and breaking her to pieces.

Uriah was halfway across the slick deck, which sloped at a steep angle to the howling wind, when he felt his feet giving way. Uriah knew better than to fight against it; he had learned the hard way through many gales at sea that you just went where the ship took you. He went sliding down the steep incline until his feet slammed painfully against the lee scuppers. Then he carefully arose and, hanging as best he could to the hammock nettings, continued his slow progress forward.

He didn't like such weather. No seaman did, for they well understood the dangers presented by these seas and winds. But the discomfort itself, the endless pitching and corkscrewing, did not particularly bother them. The land people, however, were prostrate in their berths. Mr. Crawford and his entourage of three servants and a French escort had not set foot on the spar deck since the gales had begun. Uriah felt especially sorry for poor Simon McDeal. The floor of his thick Ohio forest never had lurched or shaken, and the "boy" was green with seasickness. Though he had eaten next to nothing since the deck had started to fling about, he was constantly running to the bulwarks and retching into the wind. As miserable as the woodsy felt, he asked no quarter and stayed forever at Uriah's elbow, asking plaintively "if anythin' I can do?" Simon was determined that if anyone could win a war through sheer willingness, he would be the one.

Uriah wore his sou'wester and the shiny black gear helped protect him, but the rain was driving at him in such torrents that some water was running down his neck and soaking him to the skin. He had just wiped his face with his hand to clear the rain from his eyes when the hoarse, dreaded scream echoed from the mast above him: "Man overboard!"

He looked up and caught just a glimpse of a body falling past the top of the weather bulwarks. Because of the deck's incline, he could not see the body fall into the water, nor did the scream of the gale allow the sound of impact to be heard.

The scream was repeated, again and again, all over the deck: "Man overboard! Man overboard!"

Uriah and other men inched their way up the deck, using their hands to lean on the planks and help keep their balance against the steepness of the ship's heel. Topmen joined them, sliding rapidly down the braces and stays from their perches aloft.

They finally got to the bulwarks and peered over, but could see only great green waves, churning high into the gray, dismal sky. There was no sign of their shipmate.

"Who was it?" someone yelled.

"It was James Hunt," answered Barnes, captain of the foretop. "One of my best men. I saw it. He was helping take another reef in the foretopgallant and lost his hold. He pitched straight down. There's no saving Jimmy Hunt now. He'll sleep with the fishes tonight." He shook his head and walked away. Simon McDeal, for once, was speechless.

● ● ●

Lieutenant Watson stretched and lifted his face to the warm sun. Two days ago, Independence Day had begun with a continuation of the storms, but suddenly the glass had begun to rise and soon breaks began to appear in the clouds. In a short time, the massive bank of black cumulus had disappeared over the horizon and the swells under them began to subside. Since then, the weather had been perfect: they were alone on the Atlantic, and it was like rowing a whaleboat down the river to Aunt Nellie's house . . . a Sunday excursion.

"Bring her two points further off the wind."

"Two points further off the wind, sir," echoed the helmsman.

Watson's voice, as he gave the order, rang out almost musically across the deck. It was a happy day, a fine day at sea, with a bright sun and a flat ocean, and a wind from the nor'east that was backing round and gave some promise of becoming a fair wind. The *Argus* sailed well on a wind, in any case, and was making a good nine and sometimes ten knots.

"Good morning, Mr. Watson, and a fine morning it is!" The captain's voice also had a chirp to it.

Watson lifted his hat. "Morning, sir. Any orders, Captain?"

"Gun drill, Mr. Watson. This morning and again this afternoon. The weather has put us behind schedule in our training. Blank cartridges this morning, and we'll practice broadsides—both ripple-fire and concentrated fire. This afternoon it's target practice, and we'll keep at it until we do it right."

"Aye, aye, sir. I'll inform the gunner."

"Very well. As you go, send Mr. Levy to me."

"Aye, aye, sir."

In a few minutes, the assistant sailing master came hurrying to the quarterdeck and stood before Captain Allen, raising his hat in respect.

"Reporting as ordered, sir." Uriah looked a bit worried. He had been supervising the transfer of several water casks from one place to another on the orlop deck when he had been summoned. He wondered if he had done something wrong to be ordered suddenly to the quarterdeck.

"Mr. Levy," the captain said, "take the con. It is time to see how you handle this ship—how you handle *any* ship. Mr. Hudson has a touch of fever today. Let us see what you are made of."

"Aye, aye, sir." Uriah picked up a big brass-ribbed speaking trumpet and took his position near the helm, ready to order changes in steering as directed by the captain or to shout directions to the crew. Captain Allen took up a position on the windward horseblock and stood silently for about fifteen minutes, gazing out at the placid sea. Occasionally he would look up the mainmast to see how the sails were drawing. Uriah anxiously followed his gaze, checking carefully to see if anything looked out of place.

"Full and by, Mr. Levy, if you please."

Uriah repeated the order to the helmsman. Now they were sailing as close to the wind as they could. Both Uriah and the helmsman kept a careful eye on the weather clew of the main royal and they knew that the captain was doing the same. If the *Argus* slipped too close to the wind, the first sign would be a shaking of the weather clew and soon the entire weather leech would be slatting. Before that happened, however, the quarterdeck would shake to the captain's roars of anger. No, Uriah would make sure that the ship stayed on that razor's edge called "full and by" so that the weather clew would be seen to just barely lift, poised at the very outer limit of close-hauled sailing. He had an instinct, he had learned, for such sailing. He could sense, long before the shaking of the weather clew, that the ship had reached her limit. In some ineffable way, the ship—any ship—would whisper in his ear and he would hear the gentle sigh and take corrective action. He had little fear that the *Argus* would betray him.

"Mr. Levy," sang out the captain's voice from the horseblock. "Tack ship, if you please."

"Aye, aye, sir. Tack ship."

He had done this hundreds of times, thousands of times if you counted his years as seaman and mate. Why, then, did he stiffen, and why did his stomach contain a large block of ice? Because this was the first test of his seamanship, and they all were watching him, waiting to judge. The captain had stepped down from the horse-block and stood aft the wheel. Lieutenant Watson had returned to the quarterdeck, along with Lieutenant William Howard Allen. They stood together near the port bulwark, watching with interest.

To tack ship . . . to steer the ship's head through the eye of the wind. It sounded simple enough and, done properly, it was simple. But it required the skill and coordination of a good crew to do it properly, a crew responding to commands given at precisely correct instants. There was no ship's maneuver more pleasing to the practiced eye than a tack properly taken; there was none uglier, nor more dangerous, than one done clumsily.

Uriah picked up the speaking trumpet and took a deep breath. "All hands!" he bellowed. The boatswain and his mates took up the call and raced to the hatches to rouse the watch below decks. From throughout the brig, sailors raced to the places specified for each of them on the tacking and wearing bill.

Uriah looked sternly down the length of the spar deck, making certain that everyone was in his assigned place. A group of men, led by the sailmaker, stood near the taffrail to take care of the spanker. All pull-and-haul men seemed to be in their spots at the braces.

Although he knew he needed no additional order to proceed, he still glanced quickly at the captain, who said nothing, but merely stared at him and waited.

"Ease her slightly off," Uriah ordered the helmsman, who quietly acknowledged the order. Uriah wanted the *Argus* to pick up a bit of speed to make sure that she would shove her head vigorously through the wind when asked, even with her sails aback.

He waited and waited more. He glanced up at the sails again, watching that telltale weather clew, judging the brig's way through the water by the manner in which her sails drew.

"Ready about!" he squalled through the trumpet.

This was all, this was everything—the precise moment. If the ship were to turn across the wind without sufficient momentum, there was every danger that she would be caught in stays, stopped dead in the water, her sails aback and useless. Then God only knew what could happen. She would gather sternway and flirt with disaster—and he would be disgraced.

He felt the air with his face, seeking with every instinct that he possessed for just the right instant.

Now . . . now . . . NOW!

"Down helm!" Responding to her rudder, the *Argus* began to turn smartly into the wind.

"Ease your foresheet and jib-sheets!"

He turned 'round and barked an order to the poop gang: "Haul your spanker!" The spanker was hauled to windward, aiding the ship to pivot sharply across the wind that now blew at her straight on.

A mighty roar went up from the masts as the sails began madly to slat, their shaking creasing the sunny air with their rattling. Then the sails were taken full aback. Yet the bow continued to pivot, drawing on the reserve of momentum that Uriah had built up before beginning the turn, helped by the pressure of the aftersails.

Now, again, a delicate balance had been achieved. The exact moment again must be chosen. . . .

"Mainsail haul!" he screamed, to be sure that no one missed his command.

Pull-and-haul men were hauling on the lee sheets of the head sails, which began drawing wind again and helped in keeping the bow swinging around.

The bracemen were running along the deck with their ropes, bringing the yards on the fore mast around to their new tack. Fore-and-aft sails had been sheeted to the lee side.

"Trim those fore yards!" shouted Uriah, his voice boosted by the trumpet and echoing hollowly over the deck. "A better trim there! That's it . . . belay!"

He looked up into the masts, his heart pounding. It was all right. The foremast sails were starting to draw on the new tack; they had a good purchase on the wind. The mainmast sails remained aback, helping the brig finish the last of her swing. Now they would greet the new tack: "Let go and haul!" Smoothly the main yards swung around, and those sails as well began to fill with a loud, pleasing pop.

All was well. He had odds and ends to oversee: the buntlines should be overhauled, the trim of the yards wasn't quite to his satisfaction yet. But the *Argus* sailed now on her new tack, heeling sharply as she was caught by the freshening wind and dipping her bow into the creaming sea as if to express her own gratification with this noble day and her thanks for being so alertly handled.

"Full and by on this tack, Mr. Levy," demanded the captain.

"Aye, sir, full and by," Uriah responded, a crisp tone of assurance in his voice.

"Oh, Mr. Levy—nicely done."

"Thank you, Captain." Uriah put his speaking trumpet back in the rack and stood on his quarterdeck, hands clasped behind him in proper command fashion. His face reddened with pleasure at the compliment.

"That was mighty slick, sar!" boomed out a voice at Uriah's elbow. "That was slick as bar grease!" Simon had walked up behind him and stood there, a proud grin creasing his long face. He had adopted Uriah as his patron saint, and today his saint had done something to earn the praise of the captain and pleased nods from the other ship's officers. Simon didn't know what it was that Mr. Levy had done, but he felt it only right—as the assistant sailing master's boy—that he, too, should step forth and offer congratulations.

Uriah looked around in embarrassment. Everyone on the quarterdeck had heard Simon; indeed, his voice was loud enough to be heard by the lookout on the foremast, who was gazing down in puzzlement. Captain Allen and Lieutenant Watson wore smiles, greatly enjoying his discomfiture.

"Uhh, ahem." Uriah cleared his throat to gain composure. "Thank you, Simon. Uh, perhaps you can make yourself busy by checking the sandglasses against each other for me. You'll find them in the binnacle."

"Proud to, sar," boomed Simon. "And what might it mean—to check the sandglasses?"

"Oh, yes, I didn't realize that you—well, the larger glass is a half-hour glass by which the ship's bell is struck. In other words, all the sand should run through it in precisely thirty minutes. Every so often, we must check the glass to be sure it is running accurately, and we do this by checking it against a one-minute glass. Next time the bell is struck, which should be in just two or three minutes, you keep turning the one-minute glass each time it empties. Mind you, do a mark on the slate each time so that you won't lose count. If everything works as it should, you should have thirty marks on the slate just when the half-hour glass empties out. Is that clear?"

"Yes, sar! I'm right good with slates and figgers. I had teachin' back in Pennsy afore we took out for the deep woods. I kin handle it!"

"Very well, then," said Uriah, glad to divert his boy from further effusive roars of praise. "You can begin at the strike of the bell."

"Deck, there! Sail ho!" The voice seemed to float into their midst from nowhere, yet everyone, except for Simon and a few lubberly sailors, knew at once its origin. All faces turned up, toward the look-out on the foremast. A strained silence came over the entire ship. No one moved except for the captain, who ran quickly to the ship's waist and called up to the lookout, "Whereaway?"

"Off the port beam, sir. Can't tell yet what it is."

All eyes went to the sky above the port bulwarks, and several officers ran to the side to peer out. Lieutenant Watson climbed the horseblock with his glass and studied the horizon in the area denoted by the lookout. He saw nothing.

The captain looked back at First Lieutenant Watson, who merely shook his head. Captain Allen, impatient for more knowledge of the strange sail, immediately sprang up on the weather shrouds and, with a speed and agility that surprised those on the deck who never had sailed with him before, hurried up the ratlines to a vantage point on the mainmast. He had carried a small glass with him and peered through it.

"It's a schooner!" he shouted down to the deck. "From the looks of her sails, I'd guess a Limey. Mr. Watson!"

"Sir?"

"Beat to quarters!"

"Aye, aye, sir!"

This was it then. The first sighting of an enemy sail on this cruise. The *Argus* immediately was transformed from a rather placid vessel snoozing across the Atlantic on a most pleasant day into a man-of-war. As soon as the command for quarters was hurled down from the masthead and repeated loudly by Lieutenant Watson, an ordered sort of pandemonium possessed the brig. The pealing of the boatswain's pipes was a treble harmony to the pounding of the marine drummers as they hammered again and again the famous drum roll that for generations had roiled the blood of men on fighting ships. *Boom-boom-BOOM, boom-boom-BOOM,* roared the drums in the stirring melody known as "Heart of Oak." Throughout the brig, men raced to their battle stations, some delirious with excitement at the prospect of action, some fighting the urge to vomit and dreading what might come more than they ever could admit to another man.

Below decks, hands were knocking down the screens and bulkheads, clearing for action. Surgeon Inderwick and his mates were busily occupied in the after cockpit. The floor there was painted red to discourage, in the heat of battle, disheartening reports of bloodshed. Saws and other instruments of amputation were neatly laid by, along with buckets to receive severed limbs and a ration of rum to help the wounded tolerate their pain.

On the spar deck, a cordon of boys, Simon among them, ran the length of the ship, scattering sand on the planks from large buckets. This would keep the deck walkable, even if it was covered with a slippery mixture of blood and loose powder. Above them, the marine sharpshooters slowly, clumsily, made their way up the shrouds to their posts in the fighting tops.

Now the boys became powder monkeys, dashing from the powder magazine below to the guns, their buckets full of cartridges.

A water bucket was brought to each gun, for use as a swab-wetter and also in case of fire. The boatswain, meanwhile, assembled his firefighting party in the waist and quickly checked the head-pumps and the hoses piled up in the scuppers.

Hurrying back to the helm came a red-faced Sailing Master Hudson, out of his berth in sick bay and determined not to leave his ship to an unproven new master. Mr. Levy would stand at his elbow this day and be ready to take over only if he became a casualty. Hudson yelled to his skeleton crew of yardmen, topmen, and pull-and-haul men to be ready for orders; they would work the ship in the fight while the rest of the crew handled the guns.

Uriah felt a mixture of emotions churning within him. He was excited, curious even, over this impending event that he had so long heard and read about, and now was to experience. He was anxious to do well, to earn more praise from his captain, to carry his share of the load. And he was frightened, too, although he never would admit this to another living soul. How would he react to the noise and the sight of battle? Would he panic? Would he run, God forbid? A man never knows the depth of his own courage until it is sorely tried, and his trial was soon to come.

He stood near Hudson, trying to keep out of that worthy's way as he strode about the wheel and yet to remain close if needed. He found it interesting that he was able to retain the presence of mind, in all the tension of battle preparation, to observe the captain and his lieutenants, to watch just what they did in these breathless moments, to note their reactions, their manner of speech. He knew that such observations would serve him well, contributing to his fund of experience for future battles, even for future wars.

Captain Allen stood now on the larboard horseblock, his glass to his eye. "It's an English schooner, all right," he called out. "She's been running down to us very nicely, but now she's shortening sail, wants to know us a bit better before she comes any closer. Very well, then, let's tell her who we are. Mr. Watson, run up the colors!"

In a moment the big gridiron flag, its fifteen stripes and fifteen stars flapping audaciously in the brisk wind, went soaring up to the mainmast peak.

The captain's voice swelled with excitement: "There she goes! She's seen our flag and she's hauled in her sheets and is beating to windward as fast as she can go! Mr. Hudson, make all sail! Let's show her the speed of the *Argus*!"

With Hudson bellowing commands through his speaking trumpet, the crew quickly loosed and set all sail to the studding sails and the *Argus* surged through the sea, her bow dipping and plunging in a regular, metronomic rhythm. The fleeing schooner was now straight ahead of the bowsprit, and the *Argus* rapidly was forereaching on her.

"Mr. Watson, open your ports!"

A loud slapping noise, almost in unison, came up and down the deck as the gun ports slammed up against their stops.

"Run out the guns!"

For the first time in the heat of actual battle, Uriah heard the thunderous earthquake sound of the great gun trucks rumbling over the deck planks as the gun crews heaved the carronades forward. In a moment, the black muzzles peered hungrily out through the ports.

"You men there," yelled Uriah to the firefighting party. "Close the scuppers, quickly!" This would enable an inch or two of water to pool on the deck and lessen the danger of fire.

"Mr. Levy!" It was the second lieutenant, William Howard Allen.

"Yes, sir?"

"Check 'round the guns, make sure all equipment for boarding is there as it should be—pistols, boarding pikes, cutlasses."

"Aye, aye, sir."

The *Argus* now was off the schooner's starboard quarter and forereaching rapidly enough that a few men could be seen running about the chase's decks. The schooner, too, had gun ports up, so she was armed. It would be a real enough fight.

"Captain? Is there anything I may do to help?"

It was William Crawford, the distinguished passenger, who—it seemed to Uriah as he hurried past him to return to his post—had dressed in his most resplendent finery for this occasion.

"The best thing you can do, Mr. Crawford, is to return to your cabin and attempt to keep out of harm's way. Your work begins when we land you in France." The captain's words were not said unkindly or discourteously, but their meaning was clear: Please leave me to do my job here as I shall leave you in France to do yours. Crawford nodded and walked without another word to the hatchway and returned below decks.

"Mr. Watson, have our port bow chaser fire one ball. We'll let her know we mean business."

"Aye, aye, sir!" A few seconds after the order was relayed down the deck, one of the 12-pounder guns sticking through the bridal ports let out a loud roar as it was fired.

The race, if it could be so called, was practically over. The bowsprit of the *Argus* was abreast of the schooner's starboard beam, and within a few minutes the American brig would be in position to fire a full broadside.

"Mr. Watson, ready the port guns for a broadside. Full ripple, front to back!"

Throughout the ship, the stentorian commands of the gun captains roared out, the myriad different voices almost assuming the guise of a single hoarse bark: "Cast loose your gun. . . . Take out your tompion. . . . Load with cartridge. . . . Ram home your cartridge. . . . Shot your gun. . . . Ram home your shot. . . ."

It was then that Uriah fully understood for the first time the reasons for the constant drill at the guns, the long hot hours spent at both gun drill and actual firing. Now, in the real thing, the precision, the timing of these crews was palpable, a feast for the eyes. This was a most formidable fighting vessel, and its captain had created it.

"Deck, there!" It was the voice of the lookout again. "The schooner is striking!"

All eyes were turned back to the bulwarks and across at the quarry. It was true! The British flag was slowly coming down from the peak. The schooner, knowing she had but a few moments left before being blasted into eternity by an *Argus* broadside, was very wisely surrendering.

Cheers began to sing out from the crews at the forward guns, and the huzzahs spread back along the deck. Uriah looked up. The marines in the tops were shouting and cheering, shaking their muskets in the air.

Uriah could not help feeling a tinge of disappointment. The battle would not take place. His own testing and the testing of his ship must be deferred, at least for a time. But he knew that the tests indeed would come. And, meanwhile, the cruise had yielded its first prize.

The two ships hove to and drifted side by side. Captain Allen sent a boat over to accept the surrender of the schooner's commander and to bring the prisoners across.

In a short time, the captain of the schooner—an elderly British Navy lieutenant—and his sixteen crewmen, for that was his total strength, stood on the quarterdeck of the *Argus* and formally surrendered their ship. The vessel was the *Salamanca* of 260 tons. Captain Allen smiled broadly when he was informed that the *Salamanca* formerly had been the *King of Rome*, out of New York. "Well, we have retaken one of our own children," he said. Although pierced for sixteen guns, the *Salamanca* mounted only six. She would have been no match for the *Argus*, and everyone knew that there had been no cowardice in the quick surrender, only a bowing to reality in order to save the needless loss of lives and limbs.

"Mr. Watson, take the prisoners below and see that Captain Eliot is provided with suitable quarters. And I'll have a party sent to the schooner immediately to burn her. Let us not tarry here any longer than necessary."

"Captain, if I may suggest—?" The words had come from Uriah's mouth even before he thought, and he wondered for an instant if he had committed a terrible gaffe in speaking up like this. But it was too late to withdraw the words.

"Yes? What is it?" Allen looked at him with raised eyebrows.

"Sir, would it not be possible, after the schooner is fired, to permit our guns to fire on her? The men have not had the chance to fire at an actual, moving ship. It would be excellent target practice—much better than a floating cask."

Allen was silent for a few seconds and his face showed no expression. Then he curtly nodded. "Yes! Splendid idea, Mr. Levy. Why waste this chance, especially as the men already are at the guns? Mr. Watson, see to it, please. Mr. Levy, you shall have the honor of firing the schooner."

"Aye, aye, sir!"

Uriah soon climbed into the pinnace with a hastily selected crew, and the big sweeps bore them back to the abandoned schooner. They carried with them boxes of oakum soaked with grease from the galley and tins of varnish and other combustibles. In a few minutes they spread the materials all over the schooner and below decks as well and then, at Uriah's shouted command, set her afire. Then they dashed to the pinnace and rowed quickly back to the *Argus*.

As soon as they were back aboard and the pinnace stowed again amidship, the *Argus*'s yards were braced and she gathered way. With Hudson barking commands to his deck crew, the brig wore around the schooner's bow and then the port carronades roared in unison, sending a devastating raking fire down the length of the schooner's deck. The *Argus* continued to wear around until it again stood alongside the schooner, this time on her lee side. Again the port guns fired, and the deck was choked with acrid black smoke. Through the thick cloud, the schooner was seen to heel over under the assault of nine 24-pound balls smashing into her hull.

"Good shooting, men! Good shooting! There'll be an extra tot of grog for each of you at tomorrow's ration!" Up and down the deck, gun captains pounded their men on their bare backs and the darkened faces were wreathed in smiles.

Fire could be seen all across the schooner's deck now, and flames were climbing her mast. She was taking water rapidly; apparently several of the balls had entered at the waterline.

The gunner came running up to the quarterdeck. "Did you want to order another broadside, sir?"

"No, it would be a waste of good powder. Mr. Hudson, edge around her stern and put us in position to rake again. Gunner, let starboard guns Five and Seven rake her. Might as well let the star-bowlins share in the fun."

"Aye, aye, sir. Guns Five and Seven, ready to fire!"

The starboard gun crews were doomed to disappointment, however, for at that moment the fire reached the schooner's powder room and she exploded with a magnificent blast. Flaming wreckage littered the sky. In another instant, her bow drank deeply of the ocean, and the burning remnants of the *Salamanca* headed mercifully for the bottom.

"Mr. Levy."

"Sir?" Uriah, caught by surprise, had been standing at the taff-rail, enjoying the beauty of the sunset and pondering the meaning of the low-banked clouds in the western sky for tomorrow's weather. He was trying in vain to remember some of the weather proverbs uttered by old Sails on the dear *Jerusee* of his boyhood, for Sails had a proverb and a prediction to suit every conceivable look of the sky or sea.

He had been addressed by William Howard Allen, the young second lieutenant. They hardly had spoken two words to each other since the start of the cruise, but this Allen had nodded in friend-ly fashion to him whenever they crossed paths on the deck and seemed a most agreeable sort at the wardroom table. The similarity of his name with the captain's still posed a problem for Uriah. In his own mind, he tried to clarify it by thinking of the captain as Henry and the youthful second luff as Howard. In this way, he gradually was able to separate their names in his mind.

"I thought you would want to know," Allen went on, "tonight, after supper, in the wardroom, the captain will speak to us of the *Chesapeake* and the *Leopard*."

Uriah thought for a moment. He almost had forgotten that the captain had participated in that infamous surrender back in 1807—the incident that had aroused the temper of the nation and made all Americans ashamed that their frigate had so ignominiously given up.

"This is a rare opportunity," Allen continued, "for he does not like to speak of it. We will hear exactly what happened by one who was there. I should not miss it, if I were you."

"I'll be there, I promise you, Mr. Allen. And I thank you for the notice."

"No thanks necessary. All the officers are most welcome. Oh, by the way, you did very well yesterday—both in working the ship and in your actions during our engagement with the schooner. The Old Man was impressed—both with your seamanship and your handling of men. I thought you might want to know that."

Uriah felt himself growing red. "I do thank you, Mr. Allen. I'm very happy that the captain approved of me. I hope I can continue to win his approval."

Allen smiled at the young sailing master's embarrassment and his rather formal, stilted acknowledgment of the compliment.

"I don't have any concerns about you, Mr. Levy," he said. "I observe that you're a most worthy addition to the *Argus*. You fit in with us, fair and square. Just relax a bit and get to know us. We're a good sort. You'll do just fine." With that, he clapped Uriah smartly across the back and paced back to the helm, where he was serving his watch as officer of the deck.

Uriah turned back to the western sky. He was full of joy and gratitude that he had been taken aboard this brig. What a fine group of men they were, and how he longed to prove himself worthy of them!

The levity and sparking around the wardroom table ceased suddenly as Captain Allen entered the room from steerage. He had, as usual, taken supper alone in his own cabin. A quick tour of the deck then, with his first lieutenant at his elbow, to be sure all was in order for the night watches. Then he descended the hatchway to the wardroom.

The steward, wondering at all the suddenly solemn faces and wondering also at the number crowded around the table this night, made haste to finish clearing away the last of the supper dishes and to retire. Something unusual was happening here tonight, and he wanted to be out of it.

Indeed it was a most unusual gathering. All of the ship's officers and warrant officers were gathered in this room at one time, along with several fortunate petty officers who had been invited as a reward for exemplary performance of duty. All of the midshipmen were present, with the lone exception of Midshipman Richard Delphy, who was above on the spar deck, serving as officer of the deck and nominally in command of the brig *Argus*.

William Henry Allen took his place at the end of the wardroom table. His usually placid countenance bore now a look of strain. His short-cropped hair glistened as if he had just thrown water across his face. The long sideburns that curved down each cheek and came to a point near the chin looked freshly trimmed.

The room was completely quiet as they waited for him to speak. The captain stared straight ahead of him, as if gathering his thoughts.

"From time to time," said the captain softly, "in our moments of relaxation and social intercourse, one or another of you have asked me questions about the ill-fated incident of the *Chesapeake* and the *Leopard* in the year 1807. I felt it would be instructive for you to hear the full account of this moment of shame for the frigate *Chesapeake* and all aboard her, for our country, and for me personally. I wish it were possible for every officer of the United States Navy to be instructed as you will be tonight. When I have told you the story, I ask that you do me the honor of remembering it always. And then—let us not speak of it again."

"In the spring of the year ought-seven, the 36-gun frigate *Chesapeake* prepared at the Washington Navy Yard to cruise to the Mediterranean, where she would relieve the frigate *Constitution*. Captain James Barron came aboard as commodore, while the *Chesapeake* herself would be commanded by Captain Charles Gordon. Meanwhile, the British were angrily complaining that more than thirty-five British citizens were among the *Chesapeake*'s crew and that, in fact, three of them were deserters from the British frigate *Melampus*. The three men were questioned by their superiors and denied they were English. The British request for their return was then refused. The British admiral Berkeley, unknown to us, directed his ships to stop the *Chesapeake* outside American territorial waters and to search her for the supposed deserters.

"The preparations of the *Chesapeake*, such as they were, continued. The frigate was provisioned for a cruise of twelve months. She was well-supplied to fill the stomachs of her officers and people, having over 60,000 loaves of bread, 3,900 pounds of cheese, 225 barrels of beef, and the same of pork. And, of course, more than 4,500 gallons of spirits.

"But, gentlemen . . . it is worthy of note that, under the careful eye of her commodore, as the ample foodstuffs were stored aboard, only seven of the fifty-four powder horns aboard were even filled. Only one of every eight powder horns was even *filled*! Such were the preparations of this great fighting ship.

"I was assigned as commander of the second division of guns. There was no love between Commodore Barron and myself. He regarded me, so I was told, as a most vindictive rascal. I was a friend of Commodore John Rodgers and made no pretense otherwise. He and Barron had long been on the verge of a duel over old matters. But nothing of this sort would keep me from performing my duties to the best of my ability.

"On the twenty-second of June at 7 a.m., we weighed anchor from Hampton Roads, the tide being against us with a heavy swell from the eastward. During the morning, as we made an offing, we observed an English 74 and a frigate lying at anchor in Lynhaven

Bay; also another ship of war, apparently English, standing out the bay, and a second 74 lying at anchor. The ship of war kept near us and appeared to be standing to the eastward under easy sail. At half past two, the English ship about one-half a mile on our weather bow veered and stood for us. At 3 p.m., she hauled her wind about a cable length on our weather quarter, backed her main topsail, hailed, and informed the commodore she had a letter for him.

"The commodore replied that we would heave to and the English could send their boat on board. At one-quarter past three, an English lieutenant was shown into the cabin. Soon after, he returned to his ship. We later learned, of course, that the letter was a demand to search our ship for British deserters and that the commodore had refused the demand. We then observed the British frigate—it was the *Leopard*, 56 guns, Captain Salisbury Pryce Humphreys— training its guns upon us with the tompions out.

"I ran to my station on the gun deck and, with some of my brother officers, attempted to clear our guns, although we had no orders of any kind.

"Now, gentlemen, let me give you an account of the state of preparedness for battle in which we found ourselves at that moment. In the first division of five guns on the starboard side abreast the after bitts was standing the armorer's forge and bellows. On two of the guns were piles of boards and on two others a carpenter's workbench. In the second division, two ranges of cable lay on deck as far aft as the after part of the main hatchway, and nine sick men hung in their hammocks over and abreast the guns with their bags between them. Gear lay everywhere on the decks. Rammers, wads, gunlocks were nowhere to be seen. The guns were secured by seizings on the breechings and tackles. Not a—" Here his voice broke and his chin trembled. He paused to collect himself. "Not a match, sponge, or powder horn was at any of the guns.

"Midshipmen and gunners were ordered below to get the matches and horns. The drum and fife was heard to beat to quarters, but then the commodore himself ordered the beating to stop. We went on loading our guns, but we could not prime them without powder nor fire them without a lighted match or a hot loggerhead, and of these we had none.

"Suddenly a gun on the other ship fired and at the same moment she hailed us. The commodore bellowed out, 'I do not hear what you say!' In another moment, the *Leopard* fired a broadside into us.

"All was confusion on the *Chesapeake*. We thought we heard an order to fire, but of course we could not do so without powder horn or match. One of our lieutenants was finally able to get a horn of powder. He primed a gun and endeavored to fire with loggerheads, but they were not hot enough. So he took a coal of fire in his fingers and managed at long last to fire one gun in reply. At that moment, the commodore screamed out from above, 'Stop firing, we have struck!'

"Begging your pardon, sir," broke in a hapless midshipman, "but was that not you who fired the gun with the live coal? That is what we have always heard."

The captain did not answer the question, nor did he even acknowledge it. He continued to stare straight ahead, his jaw working, his face pale and distraught.

"Until our colors came down," he went on, "the *Leopard* kept up a constant fire upon us with round grape, Langrage, cannister, and musketry. When we struck, the Englishman sent an officer on board us, who mustered our crew and took with him the three men they claimed to be deserters. The commodore requested Captain Humphreys to take possession of the *Chesapeake* as a prize of war, but Humphreys refused. He then made sail, leaving us there with four feet of water in the hold, twenty-three shot through our hull, our foremast disabled and the head shattered, our main and mizzen masts badly wounded, and the sails and running rigging cut to pieces.

"And much more important, gentlemen, we were left with three men dead and twenty men wounded, twelve of them severely. In my own division, two men had each lost an arm and one lost a leg. Another was struck in the chest by a ball and died at my feet. There was blood all over the guns and all over me—the blood, gentlemen, of fine American sailors who had no chance to fight back. No chance, gentlemen, because our colors were struck so quickly when, in perhaps three more minutes, every one of our guns would have been at work.

"My country's flag was disgraced. We stood on that gun deck mortified, humbled, cut to the soul. We would forever have the finger of scorn pointing to us of the *Chesapeake*."

Tears ran slowly down the captain's cheeks as he spoke. Uriah's eyes moved from person to person around the long table. Almost every one of them had wet faces, and several cried openly. Uriah found his own eyes quite full, and he gulped several times to clear his throat of silent sobs.

"I would have died," Captain Allen continued slowly, his voice choked and reduced almost to a hoarse croak. "I gladly would have immolated myself had that meant that the shame of my country, my ship, and myself might have been erased. But there was no erasing it. And ever since that infamous day, young American naval officers have vowed, 'Whatever happens, whatever the circumstances, we must never again permit ourselves to be . . . Leopardized.' Yes, gentlemen, the shame of the *Chesapeake* has been immortalized by a navy expression: to be Leopardized . . . to be caught by surprise, to be grabbed by the short hairs . . . to be disgraced."

The captain put his head down and sat in silence, his fists slowly beating in agony upon the tabletop. For long minutes he sat thus, and there was not a sound in the wardroom. No one was heard even to breathe, and to cough or sneeze would have been unthinkable.

Finally Captain Allen raised his head again. His eyes were dry now, and he seemed to have regained full control over his emotions.

"Shortly after the episode," he continued in a normal tone of voice, "I was summoned by the commodore to his cabin. There I found Captain Gordon, Lieutenant William Montgomery Crane, Lieutenant John Creighton, Lieutenant Sidney Smith, and Sailing Master Samuel Brooks. Commodore Barron ordered his servant to leave and to shut the door behind him. He then said to us: 'Gentlemen, I have sent for you to know your opinion as to this affair.'

There was a pause. Captain Gordon then stated that he felt the striking of the colors had spared the effusion of blood, given our lack of preparedness, but that it would have been better had we given her a few broadsides. I then spoke up and stated that, in my opinion, we had disgraced the flag. The other officers agreed with me. The *Chesapeake* then returned to Hampton Roads, where we anchored.

"In the fall of 1807 a Court of Inquiry was held, at which the officers and myself testified as to the facts of the incident. The Court of Inquiry ruled that a court-martial must be summoned. The Navy Department formally charged Commodore Barron with negligent performance of duty, neglect to clear his ship for action on the probability of an engagement, failure to encourage his officers and men to fight bravely, and failure to do his utmost to take or destroy the *Leopard*. Under the Rules for the Better Government of the United States Navy, an officer convicted of these charges shall suffer death or whatever other punishment shall be decreed by a court-martial.

"The court-martial, with eleven officers of the navy acting as judges, was held in the great cabin of the *Chesapeake* while anchored at Norfolk. After long and involved testimony, Commodore Barron was found guilty of one charge: neglect to clear his ship for action. His punishment was to be suspended from all commands without pay or any other emoluments for a period of five years. Master Commandant Charles Gordon and Captain Hall of the marines were reprimanded. The gunner, poor soul, was cashiered.

"Barron, it is said, lives now in Denmark, where he relies on the charity of the United States Consul to survive. I am tempted now and again to curse him anew, but while he possesses the power of recollection, no curses can add to its own tortures. I leave him to his own conscience.

"My own life, gentlemen, in whatever portion God chooses to extend it, will be devoted to atoning for the shame of the *Chesapeake* and to wiping the stain of dishonor from my forehead. Before God, I pledge you this."

He looked keenly at their faces for a moment, as if he was seeing them for the first time since he had taken his seat at the table. Then, without another word, he rose and walked to the hatchway, then up the ladder to the deck.

Long after the captain had disappeared, no man moved or spoke. Each stared ahead of him, caught somewhere deep within his own thoughts.

Simon McDeal groaned softly, but Assistant Sailing Master Levy was concentrating so carefully on their slow progress down the Blavet River estuary that he didn't hear. They were off-watch and stood leisurely on the forecastle, enjoying a rare chance to relax in the balmy evening air and to watch the French coast recede from the stern, its cliffs reflecting the low-angled rays of the setting sun. The Isle de Groix was hard off the port beam now and the other island outpost of the twin ports of L'Orient and Port Louis—Belle Isle—was visible off to the south.

The nine days at anchor had passed quickly. Uriah had been kept busy seeing to the filling of the water casks and the reprovisioning of the brig. He had to make certain that the new supplies were loaded and stored exactly in conformity with the diagrams so carefully drawn by the captain, who was a stickler for proper trim of his ship.

There had been liberty hours when parties of ship-stale sailors went raging into town, but Uriah stayed on the ship, too tired usually to even think of carousing. His loading duties were hard, and he had also to check all the ship's rigging for tautness. And he had been troubled since the first hours of the cruise with recurrent stomach pains. They were of no great moment, but they kept him from the full enjoyment that was usually his lot at sea. He thought sometimes that his stomach problems might be traced to missing some meals, for he still refused to eat the salt pork that formed almost half the meals on the ship. He wondered if his loyalty to the old dietary code of his people was bringing him a misery in his gut that would continue to plague him. He was tempted at times to eat the food, but just a look at the greasy, fatty pork was enough to ensure his continued faithfulness.

The *Argus* had weighed anchor and made sail and now was carefully picking her way down the roadstead from L'Orient and nosing into the Bay of Biscay. Uriah suddenly realized that he had no inkling whatsoever as to what course they would set when they left this roadstead. Would they head back toward the United States? Would they make a northing and cruise the English Channel? Would they seek British sail off the Canaries or the Azores? He had heard nothing of their orders after they had delivered Crawford to France and had not inquired of anyone.

His train of thought was broken by another soft groan from Simon, this time a bit louder than before.

"What is wrong with you, man?" asked Uriah, a bit grumpily. "Are you seasick? If so, go below to your hammock."

"No, sar," replied Simon. "I hain't sick from the sea. It has a terrible achin' in my feet. I still hain't used to wearin' shoes, and these navy shoes is fierce on my toes. I be much better off in my skin feet."

"Well, the captain wants the crew to wear shoes, so you'll have to oblige him. Maybe if you—," he looked down at Simon's heavy brown shoes, bought from some dockside peddler. *There is something strange about those shoes*, he thought. *They look strangely wrong somehow. They look as if—*

"My God, man!" he shouted. "No wonder your feet hurt you so. You have the left shoe on your right foot and your right shoe on the left foot!"

"You mean," said Simon, wondering if he was being ragged, "that one shoe is only good for one sartin foot? And t'other shoe's good for only another sartin foot? Hell's bells, sar, I allus thought you could put a shoe anywheres long as it was big enough. Wal, I be jiggered!"

Uriah looked to the sky in amazement. "For God's sake, take off your shoes and rest your feet, if that will stop your groaning. If an officer complains, I'll make it right for you. Although I'm not sure anyone will believe such a reason."

With great sighs of relief and gratitude, Simon quickly unlaced and removed his huge brogans and stood on the wet planks of the forecastle, curling and uncurling his toes, the cool evening air acting like a tonic on his beleaguered feet.

"Oh, sar, thankee," he said. "I feel good agin like I was a-standin' in the ole trace near our cabin, a-diggin' my toes in the mud."

There were a few moments of blessed silence then and Uriah resumed his easy contemplation of the French hills and alternately of the sun dipping to meet the western horizon. Then, to his surprise, Simon suddenly began to sing out lustily in an unexpectedly melodious voice:

> It ofttimes has been told that British seamen bold
> Could flog the tars of France so neat and handy, Oh!
> But they never met their match 'til the Yankees did them catch—
> Oh, the Yankee boy for fighting is the dandy, Oh!

> The Guerriere, a frigate bold, on the foaming ocean rolled,
> Commanded by proud Dacres, all the grandee, Oh!
> With as choice a British crew as a rammer ever drew—
> They could flog the French, two to one, so handy, Oh!

> Come fill your glasses full, and we'll drink to Captain Hull:
> And so merrily we'll push about the brandy, Oh!
> John Bull may toast his fill, let the world say what it will!
> But the Yankee boy for fighting is the dandy, Oh!

Uriah found himself joining in the singing, unable to resist the contagious joy in the voice of this strange man-child from Ohio. Gradually other voices joined in the refrain from further aft on the spar deck, and soon a veritable chorus was hurling into the lowering night the song that had taken the country's tongue after Hull's dramatic victory with the *Constitution*.

They were in the midst of the third or fourth of the many verses when a midshipman came to the forecastle and quietly told Uriah that all officers must report immediately to the captain's cabin.

Uriah was one of the first officers to arrive at the captain's cabin and took an empty chair next to William Howard Allen. The handsome lieutenant nodded a greeting to him and asked his health. The captain sat staring straight ahead, his desk empty except for a file of white paper neatly centered before him. In a few moments, Lieutenant Watson and Sailing Master Hudson completed the group with their arrival, having remained on deck long enough to be sure that Midshipman Edwards showed steadiness and a grasp on his duties as acting officer of the deck. Boatswain McCloud, a veteran and resourceful seaman, was quietly ordered to hover unobtrusively near the quarterdeck to be sure that the *Argus* safely completed her departure from the estuary and her entry into the Bay of Biscay.

"Gentlemen," began the captain, "I trust you are all refreshed by your hours ashore and are ready now for some serious and challenging business.

"First of all, a bit of news: I interviewed the American consul at L'Orient to determine if there were any new developments in the war. None of consequence, I am sorry to say. The English blockade is tightening, especially along our southern coast. Cotton and rice are rotting on the wharves for lack of buyers, and meanwhile the price of sugar has gone up by four and the price of tea has more than doubled.

"There has been some minor skirmishing on both land and water in the Great Lakes, but to no conclusion. Oliver Hazzard Perry, a master commandant of my acquaintance and a worthy young officer who was considered for command of the *Argus*, has been given the task of regaining Lake Erie for us. At last word, he was diligently working at Presque Isle to build a small fleet for that purpose. The frigate *Essex*, under Captain Porter, has doubled Cape Horn and is cruising in the Pacific off South America, where she supposedly has taken many British prizes, mostly merchantmen and whalers. Otherwise, there has been little major action on the oceans since our leave-taking."

Captain Allen stared fixedly at the bulkhead for a moment, as if pondering what he would say next. Almost as an afterthought, he half-whispered, "Mr. Watson, we have more fresh water now than we truly need. Give the men permission to wash clothes on the morrow."

"Aye, aye, sir."

The captain was silent for another interval. Then it was as if he had decided to rejoin the group. His eyes came alive and his voice spoke in its usual animated tones:

"Gentlemen, when we weighed anchor in New York, I revealed to you only that our mission was to deliver Mr. Crawford and party to L'Orient. That has been done. However, you will be happy to learn that the *Argus* is more than a mere passenger ferry. There also was an ulterior purpose in our orders from the secretary of the navy. I am ready now to reveal that ulterior purpose. I trust that you will find it most congenial. Our orders read as follows. . . ." He picked up the folder and began to read in a precise, carefully enunciated manner:

"'You will proceed upon a cruise against the commerce and light cruisers of the enemy, which you will capture and destroy in all cases; unless their value and qualities shall render it morally certain that they may reach a safe and not distant port. Indeed, in the present state of the enemy's force there are very few cases that would justify the manning of a prize; because, the chances of reaching a safe port are infinitely against the attempt, and the weakening of the crew of the *Argus* might expose you to an unequal contest with the enemy. It is exceedingly desirable that the enemy should be made to feel the effects of our hostility, and of his barbarous system of warfare; and in no way can we so effectually accomplish that object, as by annoying and destroying his commerce, fisheries, and coasting trade. The latter is of the utmost importance, and is much more exposed to the attack of such a vessel as the *Argus* than is generally understood. This would carry the war home directly to their feelings and interests, and produce an astonishing sensation.

"'For this purpose—'" He stopped reading and looked up at their faces, a small smile on his lips. . . . "'For this purpose, the cruising ground from the entrance of the British channel to Cape Clear, down the Coast of Ireland, across to, and along the northwest coast of England, would employ a month or six weeks to great advantage. The coasting fleet on this track are immensely valuable; and you would also be in the way of their West India homeward fleet, and those to and from Spain, Portugal, and the Mediterranean. When you are prepared to leave this ground, you may pass round the northwest of Ireland, towards Fair Island passage, in the track of the Archangel fleets, returning home in August and September.'"

Captain Allen paused again and listened with pleasure to the excited murmurs in the cabin. Then he raised his hand for silence and read the final words of the order: "'Your talents and honorable services are deeply impressed upon this Department and will not cease to excite its attention. Wishing you a prosperous and honorable cruise.' It is signed, of course, by Mr. Jones, the secretary of the navy."

"By God, sir," said Watson jubilantly, "this means we'll be cruising right in the enemy's backyard!"

"Backyard?" growled Hudson. "We'll practically be in bed with 'em."

"Do you realize the history implicit in these orders, gentlemen?" demanded the captain. "We will be sailing in the wake of John Paul Jones and the *Bonhomme Richard*, sailing in the same waters in which he wreaked such havoc against the Limeys almost thirty-five years ago. We are given the chance to have our names and the name of our ship writ in the history books alongside that of Jones. We shall make the most of it, I warrant!"

A prickle of shudder ran down Uriah's spine. It was action he had craved and the chance to put his love for his country to the test. Well, it was action he would get, for they were sailing into England's home waters and they would be crowded waters, not only with prizes waiting to be taken, but also with Limey men-of-war. The *Argus*—one speedy little brig of 20 guns—would be sailing alone, like a cat with sharpened claws into an arena filled with hundreds of mean, watchful hounds. If they came out of this alive, after having tormented British shipping as their orders demanded, they doubtless would all be heroes for the sheer audacity of what they had done. *If* they came out of this alive . . .

The captain summoned his steward and ordered him to break out a cask of fine Madeira and to bring some glasses. The officers toasted their orders and their ship and wished each other good fortune. Amid the toasts came cheers and huzzahs for their captain and for their flag.

Six bells had just been struck in the first watch. Uriah stood silently and watchfully on the quarterdeck. The night's silence was broken only by the ship's soft sounds: the gentle harping of the rigging, the squeaks of the masts as they gave slightly under the tug of the wind, the light groan of a cable as it strained on a tackle. The night was a dark one, yet he could not keep himself from peering constantly into the blackness, just in case a running light might be seen. They now were just off the mouth of the English Channel, and anything or anybody might be encountered here. Vigilance was a necessity, and he had just impressed that fact again upon the two lookouts posted at the bows.

"All quiet I trust, Mr. Levy."

"Captain! I'm sorry, sir. I didn't see you approach." Uriah began to walk toward the lee bulwark, giving up the weather side of the quarterdeck to the captain, as protocol required.

"Stay, Mr. Levy. It's all right. I'll only be here a moment or two. Couldn't sleep. I tried to write a letter to my sister in Rhode Island but bogged down in that as well. So I decided to step on deck for some air."

"We're keeping a close watch, sir."

"Yes. What think you of our orders, Mr. Levy? Do you share the sentiments of your fellow officers?"

"Yes, sir. Very much. I'm excited about our prospects . . . and a bit nervous as well."

"I shouldn't wonder. You would be less than honest if you said you were not. Any thinking man would be nervous at the thought of striking into the heart of his enemy's waters."

"Yes, sir."

"Mr. Levy, I have a particular assignment in mind for you in the weeks ahead of us."

"Yes, sir?"

"You demonstrated resourcefulness and ability when you were asked to destroy the *Salamanca* after we took it. I expect to take many more prizes in the waters around England. In most cases, I shall place you in charge of boarding and destroying those vessels. As you will remember, our orders state that we are to destroy, except in rare cases where I deem it necessary to put a prize crew aboard the vessel and sail her to a French port. When we capture a ship, I want her crew removed and the vessel put under the water as quickly as possible. It is a job calling for agility and coolness under danger. I would think you are well suited."

"I thank you, sir. I will do my best."

There was silence then on the quarterdeck. Uriah did not know whether to move to the lee bulwark or to remain at the captain's elbow as before. He glanced at the captain, who was looking pensively ahead, down the length of the brig's deck toward the bow.

"Think you, Mr. Levy," said the captain suddenly, "that a battle aboard ship is a time of drama and cheering? A time when the spirit quickens with love of country and gunners sing patriotic songs as they wield the rammers?"

"I . . . I had not given thought to that, Captain. I have never been in battle."

"Let me assure you, then, that it is nothing of the sort. Most of the time you are too sick at your stomach to think of patriotic songs.

It is the blood, Mr. Levy . . . the *blood* that turns everything into an outpost of hell! When we fought the *Macedonian*, their decks ran with blood. Crimson rivers poured out of their scuppers and turned the black side of that frigate into a ghastly pink. Their cockpit, where the surgeon operated, had so filled with severed limbs that men were detailed to carry them to the spar deck and throw them overboard so as to give the surgeon room to work. I have been aboard ships that resembled a slaughterhouse after a battle. I have seen great mats of blood on the bulwarks, on the masts, on the coils of rope. I have seen fragments of hair and skin adhering to the ship. I have seen dead men lying everywhere. I have seen severed heads roll across the deck like round shot. I have seen human fingers protruding from the bulwarks as if they had been forcibly jammed through the side of the ship.

"The worst peril is not the shot from the enemy guns, Mr. Levy. That is the fantasy of men who never have seen such carnage at sea. Oh, the cannon fire is bad enough, but it is the splinters, Mr. Levy, the *splinters* that serve as the devil's swords. These slivers of wood are hurled across the face of the ship and stab and maim as they fly. I have seen them penetrate a sailor's eye, and he was just as dead as if shot by a musket. Someday, perhaps, we'll have ships of stone or iron to sail, but meanwhile we are condemned to ride these great floating logs, and when they are struck by cannonballs, they rupture into damnable splinters. I have seen a cloud of splinters sail as high as the maintopmast in a battle.

"When a fight is ended, Mr. Levy, even in victory, there is no glory on the deck and no huzzahs. The men still living are bandaged and splinted, many of them, and their clothes are red with blood, their own and that of their shipmates. Their faces and arms are blackened with burned powder. The more seriously wounded lie on the planks, groaning or crying with their misery. Pieces of bodies are visible everywhere.

"I remember one fight—it may have been aboard the *United States*, perhaps it was in the Mediterranean—they all seem to run together in my head. After the battle was over, a poor little sheep ran squalling about the spar deck, all covered with human gore. It was intended as a meal for the officers, but no one would eat an animal that had lapped the blood of our shipmates. It would be an act of cannibalism. So the sheep was thrown overboard."

Uriah had listened to the captain's grim recital with a feeling of horror at what was being described, mixed with growing wonder at the unusual revelation. Why was Captain Allen telling him all this? Was it to test his mettle? Was he watching to see if Uriah showed fear? Or was it possible that the captain could not restrain himself, that he felt the need to voice these torturing images that haunted his sleep in the hope that perhaps he could exorcise them? On reflection, Uriah felt that the last explanation was closest to the truth, though there may also have been an implicit testing of himself.

A few more minutes of polite civilities and then Captain Allen bade him a good night and returned below. Uriah walked slowly forward and breathed deeply of the brisk wind that blew from the starboard beam. The sails billowed out, great blossoming white flowers of the night, peaceful and settling to his eyes. His mind kept going back over Captain Allen's words. He knew that such scenes would likely be seen on this very deck in the days and nights ahead. He took a deep breath and asked God to prepare him and to give him the courage to face such agony and horror like a man and like a patriot. He reached the forecastle and looked down at the water, creaming in the darkness as it rushed past the bow. The night was silent, save for the rush of wind past his ears, the rustle of water, and the muted grunts of a poor constipated sailor sitting on the head and seeking relief.

In his cabin, Captain Allen sat again at his desk and picked up the quill pen. He must draw this letter to his sister Sally to a conclusion. In reality, it mattered little. When would he have the chance to post it? Perhaps when they finished their work here, they would call at a French port to water? No, no. Their orders directed a return home around Ireland, in the track of the Archangel fleet.

Well, he would finish it with a flourish and carry it on his person.

Then, when he was home again and likely a hero with stories of conquest to tell, he would hand it to her and they could read it together and laugh over it, along with their brothers, Tom and George.

He was determined to end this letter on a cheery, even humorous note. But he sat long and could think of nothing to say. He began to think again of the battle scenes he had described to young Levy. Why, why had he gotten onto this subject with a raw, untried sailing master? Probably had scared him out of his wits. The familiar sadness began to come over him.

He picked up the pen once more and slowly wrote the last words: "When you shall hear that I have ended my earthly career, that I only exist in the kind remembrance of my friends, you will forget my follies, forgive my faults, call to mind some little instances dear to reflection, to excuse your love for me, and shed one tear to the memory of Henry."

He signed the letter with love and sealed it. Then he blew out the guttering candle and lay down on his cot, resolved to get some badly needed sleep.

The days that followed were busy ones for every man aboard the *Argus*. But in a few free minutes every day, Surgeon James Inderwick managed to jot hasty notes of each occurrence:

July 23d Friday at sea

Cruising off the mouth of the English Channel. Captured this Evening after a few hours chase the Schooner Matilda from Brazil and bound to England—formerly an American Privateer.

July 24th Saturday at sea

Captured this morning a large brig from Madeira for England laden with wine, got a few ½ pipes of the best on board intended for use of the Countess of Shaftesbury—£8,800 ster-

ling—Stove nearly all the rest. On account of 2 Lady Passengers we gave her up to the Captain—Sent all our Prisoners on board her—Manned the Schooner with 14 men under the command of Mr. Groves. Lat 49 50 near Scilly.

July 27th Tuesday at sea off Ustend

Captured a large English Brig the Richard from Giberalter in ballast. Took out the Capt. and Crew and a female passenger & burnt the brig.

August 2d Monday at sea

Captured this afternoon a Cutter rigged vessel laden with butter and Hides from Limerick for Liverpool. Called Lady Francis—took out some of the Butter—She kept near us during the night.

August 3d Tuesday at sea Lat 53 6

It blowing a heavy gale with a high Sea were unable to board the prize—Mr. Allen displayed a signal we lay too 'till he came within speaking distance—found he had no Quadrant on board & was afraid of a separation—Slung a Cask containing a Quadrant-Navigation book &c & veered it astern which after some difficulty he contrived to get on board—he remained by us all night.

August 4th Wednesday at sea

12oClk The gale still continues—unable to board the Prize on account of the Sea—4 PM Gale continues Sent Mr. Levy in the Gig with men to relieve Mr. Allen and crew.

August 5th Thursday at sea

Lat. 53 15
11 oCk The weather has moderated. A heavy sea remains. Every prospect of bad weather again. Prize in Co. 4 P.M. board-

ed the prize—took out Provisions & water and set fire to her. Wind increased to a heavy Gale.

The *Argus*, under reefed topsails, crept slowly and carefully through the fog that laid upon her like a great dark blanket. Four bells would soon be struck in the churchyard watch—it was almost 2 a.m.—and the *Argus* was quiet, the watch below snoring softly in their hammocks, the watch on deck murmuring anxiously as they kept a close lookout on all sides.

Uriah was officer of the deck and had given orders to heave the lead at every glass. According to the charts, there should be no shoal water around them, but he would take no chances with it. They could have been blown off-course in this pea soup and might have wandered onto shoals. Unable to use their sextants, it was impossible to be certain about their position. The captain was a genius at dead reckoning and Uriah felt that he could work a chart with the best of them, so there was little chance that they really had blundered into the shallows, but by God, he would take no chance of running this brig aground. And so he kept a poor leadsman busy in the chains where he would be constantly drenched by the spray and the clammy fog. He also had the log hove at short intervals as well, so the slate could be kept current with the speed they were making through the water. Dead reckoning could lead a ship badly astray unless her speed was fed frequently into the calculations.

Uriah heard the telltale pattering of bare feet on the deck planks and knew that a sailor was running aft with some news. On this damp night, when the deck was slick with moisture, the men had been given permission to doff their shoes and to run barefoot as they would in battle, the better to hold their footing.

It was Ahearn, a maintopman, breathing heavily with excitement.

"Sir," he reported to Uriah, knuckling his forehead, his whisper sharp with urgency. "We can see sail to windward. Looks like four of 'em. Close aboard."

"Very well. Inform the captain at once. But go quietly!"

"Aye, aye, sir."

The sailor scurried off and disappeared through the hatchway. In a few minutes, the captain and the first lieutenant came rushing up to the quarterdeck. Uriah noted that they virtually tiptoed across the echo-prone planks and held their swords tight against their outer thighs to prevent any clanging.

"Mr. Levy," ordered the captain in a hoarse whisper, "awaken the midshipmen. Have them join the boatswain and his mates in awakening the entire ship. But *softly*, for God's sake. I want no talking until further notice, unless absolutely required. I want total silence aboard until we can determine what we have wandered into. With luck, when dawn comes, we shall find ourselves alone once again."

"Aye, aye, sir." Uriah went to carry out the order.

The next three hours passed tensely, amid a desperate silence. Officers and men tied rags around their shoes to muffle their steps. Cabinets were opened gently to avoid a telltale click. The *Argus* held steady on her course, for a change in direction would require a shouting of orders, which was not to be risked. The galley was silent as well, as the cook deftly prepared a cold breakfast for the ship.

The black fog, curling in wisps and tentacles about the masts, began finally to turn to a dark silver and then to a lighter one, as the sun began its slow ascension. The fog took on the guise of smoke, foaming and moving in great luminescent circles as it was touched by the rays from the eastern sky. It remained near-opaque, however, and there was little more to be known about the peril, or lack of it, of their position.

Uriah and Sailing Master Hudson stood together on the quarterdeck, waiting any orders from their captain. Allen stood calmly near the binnacle, hands clasped behind him, once in a while thoughtfully stroking his chin.

"Sir!" It was Lieutenant Will Howard Allen, fresh from the forecastle, breathing deeply from the exertion of his quick yet silent run back to the quarterdeck. He lifted his hat to the captain and reported, "We are in the midst of a British squadron! The fog is starting to lift. We saw through a break a frigate within musket shot. She hasn't seen us or, if she has, doesn't realize who we are."

"She soon will!" snapped the captain. "Mr. Hudson, wear ship, if you please! I want the weather gauge and we'll make a run for it. If we weather her, I think we can outrun her."

"Free to use my trumpet for orders, sir?" asked Hudson, not daring to break the silence unless directed by his captain.

"Yes, free to function normally."

"Aye, aye, sir. All hands wear ship! All hands wear ship!"

Hudson's voice went soaring and billowing across the decks, propelled by the long brass-speaking trumpet. Several poor sailors were startled into near panic by the sudden blast of sound after the hours of enforced quiet. The decks resounded quickly with the noise of running feet and the screaming of the boatswain and his mates to the watch below.

The quick maneuver enabled the *Argus* to gain the weather gauge, and she began to pull rapidly away from the frigate, which now could be plainly seen. In a few minutes, the *Argus* was beyond range of the frigate's long guns. By this time the frigate had realized that this brig was running from her (and doubtless had guessed her identity) and was making all sail to chase. She was making signals also and Uriah could see the tiny balls running rapidly up her halliard and then, at the twitch of some signalman's hand below, breaking free and displaying varied colors to the other ships of the squadron. Off to leeward, a British brig, obviously a man-of-war with the usual checkerboard pattern about her gun ports, broke off her course and also gave chase.

The chase did not cause undue alarm aboard the *Argus*. The officers and people were confident that Allen could outsail most other ship commanders. He quickly had gained the weather gauge and opened a long lead before the frigate even knew what was happening. More to the point, the fog had settled thickly down around them again, and it would be a fairly simple matter to lose themselves in the milky whiteness that provided an unlimited hiding place on the open sea. So it was, and in a short time the *Argus* reduced her sail once more, confident that she again was alone and anonymous.

Three hours past her narrow escape, the *Argus* was back at her usual work of tormenting British shipping. Surgeon Inderwick wrote in this day's journal:

> *About 8 A.M. sent our boat aboard a Schooner The Cordelia from Antigua for Bristol, one of a fleet of 400 sail. Destroyed her Cargo consisting of Sugar & Mollasses. Put all our Prisoners aboard and sent her as a Cartel. While engaged with this vessel another Frigate passed close to us. The fog clearing a little below we could perceive her hull and ports but not her Masts or rigging. She did not observe us.*

The *Argus* was a much happier ship after the captured schooner had been sent in as a cartel, for she carried away with her the six masters and forty-two seamen who had been transported as prisoners aboard the American brig and had crowded her decks, lowered her supply of food and water, and forced badly needed Yankee sailors to remain below as guards when they should have been at work aloft.

Soon after the schooner beat her way to the east toward Cove, a sharp-eyed middie spotted a member of the *Argus* afterguard wearing a coat that had been seen on the back of one of the prisoners. The wretch quickly was brought before the mast on charges of stealing from a prisoner. Captain Allen was scrupulous in his treatment of his prisoners, particularly as they were merchant seamen and no way accountable or to blame for what had befallen them. All personal property of his prisoners was returned to them.

Allen was enraged, therefore, when informed that one of his men had stolen or taken by dint of threat a coat from one of the departed Englishmen. The afterguardsman admitted how he had come by the coat and was sentenced by the captain to a dozen and a half lashes.

Once again Uriah was forced to stand with the other officers in the vanguard of the ship's company and to watch the flailings of the cat, accompanied by the screams and groans of the miscreant. He did not feel sick to his stomach as he had on the *Alert* in the East River, but he still felt compelled to avert his eyes so as not to actually see the tails of the cat bite into the man's tanned flesh. The screams and the sight of the retching, rubber-legged sailor being carried below by his shipmates after the punishment were bad enough in themselves.

It was such a day as makes the crew of a raider ship feel as if it had sailed straight up into the maw of heaven. Oh, the day itself was fine enough—a bright sun in a sheer blue sky and the air brilliant with clarity. But it was the results of the day that made the tired crew of the *Argus* forget their aching bodies and lack of sleep and reach a mood of euphoria.

They were beating up toward the Bristol Channel. Land's End bore due easterly when they began sighting one sail after another. It was the same gigantic fleet in which the schooner *Cordelia* had held a position before her ill-fated introduction to the *Argus*. From what Captain Avery of the schooner had divulged, this mass of four hundred or more sail was almost all merchantmen, with hardly a man-of-war to watch over them. The British felt quite confident with the cliffs of Cornwall visible only a few miles to starboard. Here was a flock of plump English hens ripe for the pounce of the *Argus*, a hungry fox let loose in this crowded Limey chicken yard.

One of the nearer chases was a large ship, and she became the first quarry. Captain Allen ordered all sail set out to the studding-sails, and the *Argus* tucked up her skirts and set out in enthusiastic pursuit.

Uriah stood on the quarterdeck with Sailing Master Hudson.

"Trim that foretop yard!" shouted Hudson through his trumpet. "Brace that yard, you men! I want 'er trimmed fair and square! Belay! Good."

He turned to Uriah and pointed to the chase. "She's a fast enough ship, though she's low in the water with a full cargo. We won't be catchin' up to her so soon, I think. Mebbe a few hours."

Uriah nodded. He was never fully at ease in the presence of the gray-haired, grizzle-bearded sailing master. Hudson was a man of few words, and they usually were spoken gruffly in a hoarse voice. He was a straight enough man and fair with Uriah, though their conversations together had been few. He never had seemed to resent the presence on board of a younger man designated as his assistant, even though the brig's normal complement called for only one sailing master. He instructed Uriah when it was called for and corrected him on the few occasions when he felt the younger man had erred or had overlooked something. Their relationship was correct and distant, though not unfriendly and never contentious.

"Look there, at that craggy point to starboard," Hudson pointed with a long, bony finger. "That is Land's End, where England sticks her toe out into the Atlantic. Between Land's End and the Scilly Islands"—his thumb jerked to point back over the stern—"it is said there once was a land full of forests and thick with game. There King Arthur and his knights are said to have lived amongst a gentle people called the Lyonnese. On the day that Arthur was mortally wounded in battle against the treacherous Mordred, the land of the Lyonnese sank beneath the waters and lies now at the bottom of the ocean separating Land's End from the Scillys."

"You seem to know this land well," commented Uriah.

"Aye, I lived in Cornwall for three years. I know those little villages like the toes of my own foot." He pointed to the coast, where a string of settlements could be seen plainly in the crystal air. Each little cluster had white cottages and stonewalls, with fishing boats bobbing in the harbor below. "Penzance, Newlyn, Zennor, St. Ives. I know them all well. There is a place called St. Just, with a little gray stone church that sits in a lovely garden of flowers and ferns. Many an hour we sat there." He shook his head, as if to clear away a painful memory. "And Sennen Cove, where mermaids have been seen. I did not see them myself, you understand," he added hastily, looking at Uriah to see if he was being laughed at. "But there are those who have claimed to see mermaids in that cove."

"It is a rough land and a rocky coast," said Uriah. "I would not want to be cast on that lee shore in a gale of wind."

"Aye," agreed Hudson. "Many ships have come to their end on those rocks. Too many to be counted. Pillagin' wrecked ships has made a good livin' for many Cornish people these past centuries."

"You mean they scavenge the wreckage and depend on that for their living?"

"Aye, though many are hardy fisherfolk and sailors as well. But wreckin', as they call it, always tempted more than a few. They tell a story of a ship fightin' a losin' battle with the sea and a-headin' for the rocks. People on shore was tryin' to figger where the ship would come to rest, so's they could get a quick start on lootin' it. Seems it was the Sabbath, and church was in meetin' when news began to spread around that a wreck was a-comin' in. The story has it that the dominie begged his congregation to remain in their seats long enough for him to take off his cassock so's everyone would git a fair start."

"It seems so strange," said Uriah, "for us to be cruising here, just a few miles away from the villages of our enemy, within their very sight. And they sit there in their cottages, apparently not even knowing we're here."

"Oh, they know well enough that we're here," replied Hudson. "Don't fool yourself about that. There! Look there! Just to the left of that little cove where the green fisherboat is anchored. You see that tall, gaunt structure with the black circle whirrin' about its head? That circle is made up of three long black arms, which are whirlin' madly about, and they are sendin' signals by so doin'. There is another such semaphore device, which they call a 'telegraph,' down the coast a few miles, just within seein' distance, and another beyond that, and so on. You can be sure that we have been seen and probably identified, since we are becomin' quite well-known in these parts, and the word is rapidly proceedin' along the coast to the nearest naval anchorage. They know we're here, all right. But by the time they manage to get a man-of-war to where we have been, we are somewhere else. At least, that has been our good fortune to date. Whether it will last, no one can say."

"You say we are well-known? How is that?" asked Uriah.

"Why, Levy, the *Argus* is developing quite a name for herself in England. The last couple of masters that we captured told the captain that the London newspapers have been writin' about our exploits and we supposedly have caused somethin' of a panic among the insurers of shippin'. The rates suddenly have pushed up to exorbitant levels, and news of our captures is fillin' Lloyd's list as well as the newspaper columns. The English Navy has come under severe criticism for its failure to catch us, and, say the masters, special instructions have gone out to hunt us down. Several cruisers, they say, have been dispatched to this area with the sole mission of findin' and destroyin' the *Argus*. Our presence along their coast is not only provin' destructive to their shippin', you see, it is like a punch in the King's mouth."

"The captain is getting his wish, then," responded Uriah. "We are taking a page in the history books alongside John Paul Jones."

"Aye. That we are."

Hudson's prediction of a fairly long chase proved correct. It was four hours before the prize was overtaken and boarded. It was the ship *Mariner*, bound from St. Croix to Bristol and laden with sugar. Lieutenant Allen and a prize crew were sent aboard the ship with orders to stand after the *Argus*. From the quarterdeck, a dozen more sail were visible to leeward, and the *Argus* wasted no time in going after them. She ran down quickly to a brig and cutter and after another long chase managed to take both of them: the *Betsy*, a brig also laden with sugar, and the pilot boat cutter *Jane*. The good hunting continued. Soon after, the *Argus* fell in with the brig *Eleanora* and the cutter sloop *John and Thomas*, bound from Poole to Liverpool with clay.

The *Argus* finally hove to, with five prizes gathered around her like chicks seeking succor from a mother hen. She could not afford to sit here for long, for this hostile sea was no peaceful nest in a coop, but would become their immortal resting place if a British cruiser caught them here like this.

Midshipman Delphy, a tall, good-natured lad, came rushing to the quarterdeck and told Uriah he was wanted urgently in the captain's cabin. Uriah walked briskly to the hatchway, plotting in his mind meanwhile the difficulties of burning so many prizes in one fell swoop. He would have to take the pinnace and load her to the wales with oakum and varnish if he was to accomplish his mission without wasting time to row back to the *Argus* and replenish his supplies of destruction.

Captain Allen sat at his desk and was coloring in a diagram of his ship, showing the loading of provisions and ammunition. On the outline of the brig's hull, he colored in the areas from which provisions had been drawn, as well as powder and balls. He must remember to order that beef and pork be drawn from the forward casks for a time, and water as well, so as to return the ship to her proper trim. As it was, she was a bit down by the bow, which would in no wise improve her speed—and she would need all the speed she possessed, what with the entire British home fleet seeking her.

Uriah stood before the desk and lifted his hat. "You sent for me, sir?"

"Ah, yes, Mr. Levy. Sit down, please."

Uriah was puzzled by this. He had anticipated a quick order to destroy some or all of the prizes and was prepared to acknowledge the order and urgently go out to gather his men and begin the mission. He had not expected to tarry. He took his chair and felt some foreboding. Had he failed in some way? Had he forgotten some duty in the press of action? He was very tired, like everyone on the *Argus*, and was not thinking with his customary clarity, but he could recall nothing that he had failed to do. He was rapidly running down a list of his regular duties when the captain finally raised his head from his chart and put down his pen.

Allen looked frightfully weary. There were new lines in his face, and his skin was gray and wan. His eyes were red with lack of sleep.

"Mr. Levy," began the captain, his voice dull with exhaustion, "I must give you a rather unexpected mission. The brig that we took this morning"—he consulted a paper on his desk—"the *Betsy* she is, out of St. Vincent's. Her main cargo is sugar. Were it just for that, I would gladly burn her with the others. But we also found a surprising treasure in her hold: she's carrying ten lovely brass long 9-pounders. I can't take the time to transfer them over here, it would take all day. You know how short we are of cannon at home. There are privateers waiting in every port for guns so they can get to sea. I must send this brig and her cannon into France as a prize. We'll hope they can find a man-of-war to escort her home with those beautiful brass treasures. I want you to board her with a small prize crew and run her in to L'Orient."

"Me, sir? Leave the *Argus*?" There was dismay and disbelief in Uriah's voice. It was an unforgivable breach of discipline, but he couldn't help himself, so surprised was he by the order.

"Yes, *you*, Mr. Levy!" There was sharp irritation in the captain's voice. Then he sighed deeply. He fought to overcome his spiky weariness, for he well understood the young sailing master's emotions. "Look, Uriah. I know how you must feel. We have all developed quite a friendship for each other on this ship. I am aware of that. You surely do not want to leave us now, at this point in our cruise. And I don't want to give you up. You have done a fine job for me, so much so that I have been tempted to name you acting lieutenant. But we have sent in several prize crews already, and I am down to only about 110 men from our original complement of 140. It is important that the brig get safely to France with those cannon, and there is no one else I can spare to do the job. For the same reason I can give you only a handful of men for the brig."

Uriah felt like weeping. But what could he do? "Sir, I will do anything you order. And I'll do my best to get the *Betsy* to L'Orient. But, having done so, how will I rejoin the *Argus*?"

"I'm afraid, Uriah, that this must wait until we complete our cruise and return home. You and your crew will have to find passage on a man-of-war or a merchantman to take you back to America if you are not selected to take the *Betsy* back. When we get back and have our merry reunion, there will be a place for you on my vessel. I assure you there will always be a place for you. That is a promise, Mr. Levy."

"Yes, sir. Thank you, sir." Uriah looked down at the desk. There was nothing more to say then. "Very well, then, sir. I'll get my gear and round up a few men and have a boat take us over to the *Betsy*." He lifted his hat. "It has been an honor and a privilege to sail with you, Captain. I look forward to our reunion."

"Good-bye, Uriah." The captain extended his hand, and the men shook warmly. "Godspeed." He picked up his pen and returned to his earnest perusal of the *Argus* loading chart.

It took Uriah only a dozen minutes to collect his gear from his cubicle off the wardroom and to round up a prize crew. He picked a half-dozen of the most trustworthy and all-round experienced men and then asked Lieutenant Will Howard Allen, officer of the deck, to have the tackles pigged and a boat readied to be swung over. There was no time even to bid good-bye to his fellow officers, who were scattered about the ship and among the prizes hovering around them. Will Howard seemed to know what Uriah was about and solemnly lifted his hat to him and nodded in farewell. Uriah lifted his hat in return and gave him a wave that left nothing more to be said.

He was about to swing himself down the falls when he saw Simon running frantically across the deck toward him.

"Sar, sar!" Simon called. "Sar, hain't you a-goin' to take me with ye? I hear you's a-leavin' aboard that air two-mast ship. Cain't I go with ye?"

"I'm sorry, Simon," Uriah said, kindly but firmly. "I can take only a handful of men to sail the brig, and so they must be men of long experience on the sea. Each of them will have to do the work of two until we reach France."

"But, sar," cried Simon, his chin trembling, "who'll do your boyin' for ye?"

"I suppose I'll have to do for myself, Simon. I'll manage."

"Yes, sar, I knows ye will. When'll we find each other agin, sar?"

"Soon, Simon. We'll find each other again soon and you can boy for me once more. You are the best boy I've ever had."

"Thankee, Mr. Levy. A good luck to ye, sar. Don't let them Limeys git ye!"

Uriah swung quickly down the falls. He jumped into the stern-sheets and ordered, "Boat away!" The sweeps began their great bites into the waves, and the boat gradually pulled away from the brig *Argus*.

The English merchant brig *Betsy* proved to be a sweet and docile sailer and made fairly good speed in spite of high seas and generally foul winds. She beat southward past Land's End and on toward the distant coast of France and sanctuary. That the *Betsy* handled easily was a godsend to Uriah and his skeleton crew, who had to do without sleep, save for short catnaps. She proved to be a dry ship as well, but Uriah didn't come to this conclusion until a number of orders to sound the well had each time brought out a rod that was as dry as his own throat. So at least the *Betsy* was a tight ship and a fairly fast one. That would improve their chances of getting in.

At 4 p.m., Uriah had just returned to the spar deck from a session with the coastal charts nicely provided him by the brig's late captain. The voice of his lookout came piercing like an arrow to the deck:

"Deck, there! Sail ho!"

"Whereaway?"

"Off the port quarter! And running down to us by the look of her!"

Uriah could not wait for more information. He ran past the wheel to the port shrouds. As he went by, he noticed the stricken look on the helmsman's face. This was what they all had been dreading since the minute they came aboard this captured brig.

Uriah vaulted up the ratlines and scurried up the rigging to a point where he, too, could clearly see the sail that was making for him. *Oh Lord, she was a big one*, a frigate perhaps. She was close-hauled and from the look of the cream at her bow was a good ship on a wind. She was looming larger every minute, a sign that she was closing fast. He raised the glass through which he was peering and studied her sails. They were gray with age and use. An Englishman, no doubt. A French ship, ducking out of port to slip through the British blockade, would have a white suit on her yards, fresh and clean.

The *Betsy* already had all sail set, so there was not much more Uriah could do. He and the men busied themselves hauling up buckets of seawater and dousing the sails. Wetting them would allow them to hold the air a bit more and give them a knot or two more of speed. At the least, it gave them some diversion from the oncoming man-of-war, for the telltale yellow around her gun ports made it clear that she was that.

He looked back again over the taffrail. The Englishman was rapidly forereaching on them; that was plain. He ransacked his brain for every trick that he had ever learned or ever read about that might provide some additional headway for the *Betsy*. He could knock out the wedges in the steps of the masts; that sometimes speeded up a ponderous ship, but the *Betsy* was hardly that and it would be of small help. A man-of-war in this position, fleeing for her life, could drop her food overboard to lighten her and open her hogsheads and start the pumps to get rid of her water. But the *Betsy* was only lightly provisioned for this short passage, and this would not help much. As a last resort, the man-of-war would throw overboard her guns, but the *Betsy* carried no guns save for the unmounted brass 9-pounders in the hold. The small, exhausted crew would need a miracle to bring them up in time. It was not even worth trying. He ordered the brig's gig and cutter pitched over, which was quickly done. The Englishman continued to run them down and now was only a couple of leagues distant, dipping her head in the *Betsy*'s wake, as if scenting her prey.

In the end, he tried a few last-desperation measures and wondered from where he had got them. He ordered every moveable box and piece of furniture laid on the weather side of the ship's waist in an effort to stiffen the brig a bit. The yards were laid flat against the braces, and the sails were drawing their deepest breaths of the surging air. He thought for a fleeting moment of sending his men up in the weather shrouds. He had heard that the expanse of bodies in the shrouds would provide additional resistance to the wind and perhaps lend them an added stride or two. But he knew, almost as soon as he thought of it, that this would work only with large numbers of men. With this pitiful little band of sailors, their few pieces of skin would make no difference.

Finally he called the men aft and bade them remain there. Their weight would help set the brig a bit more by her stern, and most vessels of this type would sail a bit faster if slightly down at the stern.

Standing with them around the binnacle, watching the British vessel—which now was plainly seen to be a frigate—ease ever closer to them, Uriah urged his men to be of good cheer, though his own head was full of misery and his face plainly showed it. He wanted desperately to be with his comrades on the *Argus*, continuing to pick the pockets of England's maritime trousers. But he knew that his fate now would be to lay somewhere in an English jail.

In a few minutes more, the frigate was sailing alongside the *Betsy*. Her gun ports were open, her guns run out, and the tompions had been removed. A single word from her captain and the frigate could fire a devastating broadside against the defenseless brig. Through the open ports, they could see the faces of the gun crews, peering curiously through at them.

The expected ultimatum was not long in coming. An officer on the frigate's quarterdeck pointed a speaking trumpet at the *Betsy*, and his voice came through the air with startling clarity: "Heave to! Right now! Or we shall sink you!"

"Heave to," Uriah resignedly ordered his crew. "We are striking."

Even in the stale darkness of the after-hold of the frigate *Leonidas*, Uriah was able to tell that something of consequence was happening. The solid *boom-boom-boom* of feet running across the berth deck above them and up the hatchway indicated that all hands had been called, or the captain had ordered general quarters, although the telltale beating of the drums was not evident.

The frigate, which whined constantly with a loud timber creaking, groaned more noisily than usual. By the swing and sway of the vessel, Uriah surmised that either they were wearing ship or perhaps had hove to.

A few minutes later, he was further perplexed by the distant sound of loud cheering, repeated over and over again. What could the Limeys be celebrating? There had been no fight; the prisoners in the hold would of course have heard the roar of guns. Perhaps some personage had come aboard, or perhaps someone had brought them some news.

The frigate was bound for Plymouth, Uriah had been told during a brief meeting with the ship's commander, a Captain Seymour. He and his men would be put ashore there and sent to a proper prison. They could look forward, Seymour assured him, to peacefully enjoying the remainder of the war, until Britain's certain triumph, in the quiet of a nice English gaol. Meanwhile, they could make themselves comfortable in the after-hold. They would be treated with mercy, Seymour told him, so long as they offered no problem. He had kept his word, and the prisoners were given the same meals as those served to the frigate's own sailors. It would be a compliment, Uriah thought, to call this food "slop," and he was able to eat only as much of it as necessary to keep him from starving. But he consoled himself with the thought that almost four hundred Limeys on the decks above were forcing down the same stale, maggot-filled meat.

He had just set down a greasy kid after forcing down a few swallows and was trying to fight back the waves of nausea that accompanied each sickening meal. Suddenly the hatch was thrown back and a dim light from the berth deck burst into the after-hold. Even the feeble light was enough to make the prisoners blink and shield their eyes, for the hold was immersed in blackness.

Dim figures began slowly to climb down the hatchway. The frigate's marine guards, no doubt, coming to carry off the dirty kids and the water cups. The bodies moved slowly, heavily down the steep ladder and stood at the bottom in apparent confusion, looking dazedly about them.

Uriah looked up, curiously. Why were the marines not moving briskly about as they usually did, stepping unconcerned on hands and legs of the sprawling, filthy American captives? Why were they standing about so strangely?

"Will! My God, Will—is that you?"

"Who is that? Uriah? Good Lord, have they got you, too? Lord, what a disaster!"

The hatch snapped back into place, and darkness resumed its dominion over the after-hold. Uriah took William Watson, first lieutenant of the *Argus*, by the hand and gently led him to an unoccupied place on the dirty deck. In the brief moment of dim light, he had seen a bloody bandage covering most of Watson's head. His uniform was ripped, and there were smudges of blood on the sleeves and chest. The sickening truth of it all was flooding Uriah's brain. Now he knew why the crew of this accursed English frigate had been cheering so madly. The gadfly *Argus*, the brave little feather that had tickled King George's nose, had been taken.

"Ah, dear Lord, my head hurts something fierce," Watson groaned. "And those Limey bastards near ripped my arm off when they pulled me up to the entry port. Those sons of bitches!"

Uriah waited until Watson's frantic, angry breathing had quieted. In the darkness, he could hear murmured conversations with the other new arrivals, several of whom he had recognized from the *Argus*. If the voices in the after-hold became too loud, the marines would be hurrying down the hatchway, smashing at them with musket butts.

"Will, tell me: is it done—is it all over?"

Watson sighed deeply. "It's all over, Uriah. The cruise of the *Argus* has ended."

"What happened? Are you able to tell me about it?"

"We fought an English brig yesterday—the *Pelican* she was, a huge brig—and she took us. That's about it."

"How bad was it, Will?"

"Casualties, you mean? We had six killed. Twelve wounded, I think. Some of them very badly. The captain among them."

"God. Who are the dead?"

"Two midshipmen. Edwards took a ball in the head. Delphy had both legs almost shot off at the knees. He lived about three hours, screaming in agony. Then he mercifully died. The others were seamen: Jones, Gardiner, some others. I can't remember the names. Good men, all."

"And you, Will? Are you all right?"

"I'll live, according to Inderwick. A grapeshot tore away my scalp right to the bone. But it's bandaged and the bleeding has mostly stopped."

There was silence in their little corner for several minutes. Uriah felt more empty than sad. His head was light. Bright circles formed in his eyes. He found it difficult to swallow. And that proud little brig of theirs? Did it lay now at the bottom?

"Will, could you—would you mind telling me how it came about? I don't mean to plague you with it. But it would mean a good deal to me to at least know what befell us."

Watson sighed again. "I'll do my best, Uriah, though thinking about it again is very hard—very hard, indeed. I'll try.

"The thirteenth of August had been a busy day and a good one. We caught and burned two ships at six in the morning. That night we copped a large brig—the largest prize of the entire cruise, I think—and we set her afire and stood from her to be sure she went under. It was that fire, I think, that was the death of the *Argus*, for the flames must have led the *Pelican* to us. It was so stated by Maples, their captain, when he boarded us after the fight. The *Pelican* had been specially assigned to find us and to cruise St. George's Channel in search of us. Well, she had hunter's luck. We were in St. George's off St. David's Head, which is on the Welsh coast and bore east maybe five leagues, I think.

"Oh, we saw her coming, all right. She was standing down under a press of sail on our weather quarter. She was much heavier than the *Argus*, almost five hundred ton, I would judge. We could easily have outrun her. But William Henry always told us that he would hide from superior strength, but he would never run away from another two-masted ship. So we shortened sail and ran easily, waiting for the Englishman to come down to us. At 6 a.m., she was almost up to us and she had the weather gauge. We wore around. We heard the crew of the *Pelican* give us three cheers. Then we fired our port guns and the battle began in earnest. We were running side by side now, perhaps two hundred yards apart, and giving each other full broadsides.

"No more than four minutes after the fight began, a round shot shattered the captain's left leg. He refused to go below but remained on the quarterdeck, hanging on the binnacle for support, his leg gushing blood, calmly directing our fire. Finally he fainted and was carried below.

"The *Pelican* was firing with accuracy, Uriah. The Limeys must be working on their shooting. They already had shot away our main braces, main spring stay, gaff, and trysail. I did my best, but our balls were either not hitting them or at least not doing very much damage. About that time, I was hit by grapeshot and lost my wits. I was carried below, and Will Howard Allen took command. He did a fine job, I was told later. The *Pelican* tried to rake, but Will Howard luffed into the wind and threw all aback and outsmarted her. He now was in position to rake, but our guns somehow just didn't get the job done. I came back on deck about six twenty-five, and by this time it was about over. Our spritsail yard was lost, our wheel ropes and almost all our running rigging had been shot away. We were out of control. The *Pelican* kept up her heavy fire while we fell off before the wind. She raked us fore and aft. For fifteen minutes, she . . . she . . ." Watson was weeping now and he found it difficult to continue. "She cannonaded us for fifteen minutes, while we could offer little in return except some musket fire from the tops. I tried . . . I tried to rally a boarding party, but it was no use. The *Pelican* had lashed to us by then and they had boarders coming over all our bulwarks. I ordered our flag struck. I had no choice. It would have been a slaughter. A slaughter."

"My God. My God." Uriah could do nothing except to stupidly repeat the phrase over and over. He had convinced himself that the *Argus* was uncatchable, unbeatable. And she had been vanquished.

"At least they didn't sink her," he finally managed to offer by way of scanty consolation.

"No, they didn't sink her. But she flies the Cross of St. George now."

"You said the captain was wounded but alive. How does he fare? And where is he?"

"His wounds may be mortal, Inderwick says. He and most of the crew are still aboard the *Argus*, being taken by a prize crew into Plymouth. When they encountered this frigate, they decided to transfer some thirty of us over here . . . to ease their burden of guarding, I suppose. Anyway, we are all bound for the same destination—a Limey hell-hole of a prison."

"God, Will, I am so sorry. Perhaps the captain will survive somehow and live to lead us again so that some day we can get our revenge."

"It's all in the hands of God now, Uriah."

"Will, did you happen to notice the whereabouts of Simon Mc-Deal, the man who was assigned to me as a boy? Is he still on the *Argus*?"

"Simon McDeal? Oh yes, I remember him—a lubber, but a cheery and obliging fellow. He is among the dead, I am sorry to say."

Uriah gasped. "Simon was killed in the fight?"

"Aye. A round shot tore his head clean off as he was running cartridges to a port gun. Poor fellow. They had to throw what was left of him overboard. No time to say the prayers or give him a proper burial at sea. Poor fellow."

Uriah climbed unsteadily to his feet and felt his way to a distant corner of the hold. There he vomited and retched and finally grasped his abdomen and wound it with both arms in an attempt to halt the violent pains that assailed him.

•••

The contingent of prisoners from the *Leonidas* stood on the wharf in the mild morning sun of Plymouth. Under the baleful stares of their marine guards and the curious eyes of a few hangers-on, they waited for their battered *Argus* to complete her anchorage. When the brig had lost headway and been made fast to the wharf, they would join their compatriots and assist their wounded fellows.

As the British sailors on the *Argus* threw hawsers to other tars on the wharf, Uriah studied the brig with an appraising eye. As much as it hurt to see her now in the hands of the enemy, he found himself assessing the degree of her wounds in order to understand the severity of the fight she had been through. Most of the damage, he saw at once, had been done to her rigging, but her hull and masts also were cut up. Her foremast had been left almost unsupported and even a cough of wind might knock it down.

"'Ere, you idlers!" screamed a Limey marine corporal. "Come 'elp carry the cot of your captain!"

Uriah, Will Watson, and several seamen ran to grasp the sides of the cot and gently lower it from the gangplank to the wharf. Captain Allen lay with eyes that were open, but glazed and languid. He was frightfully pale. He stared at something off in the distance.

Suddenly he looked up at the men carrying his cot and seemed to recognize the faces. He raised himself on an elbow and said, softly but clearly, "God bless you, my lads. We shall never meet again." Then he lay back upon the cot and closed his eyes.

The sad, bedraggled procession continued on its way through the dismal dockside streets of Plymouth, bound for Mill Prison.

Surgeon Inderwick had taken a place next to Uriah and helped carry the cot, so as to keep a close watch on his patient.

"Joseph Jordan, the boatswain's mate, died this morning," he muttered to Uriah as they walked. "Just before we anchored here. Almost his entire thigh had been shot off. I gave him large anodynes and dressed his wound, but it was hopeless from the start."

"How is the captain doing?" asked Uriah softly, trying to keep his words from being heard by the semiconscious patient.

"He has no fever, which is in his favor. He has been having

spasms in his stump, but I am giving him anodynes for that. He is greatly bothered with dyspepsia. I don't know. We'll just have to hope."

"Will they let you care for him at the prison?"

"Yes, I think so. And I'll have the aid of their surgeons, if necessary. They have a hospital of sorts, I am told. I hope all of our wounded will get some decent care. On the ship, those English bastards gave us no peace. They were running drunken all through the vessel in celebration of their great win. They even stepped right on our wounded as they lay upon the deck. Bastards!"

Surgeon James Inderwick sat down with a weary sigh and made the following entry in his journal:

> *Capt. Allen—9 P.M. Pulse feeble, frequent, interrupted, skin covered with a clammy moisture—Vomiting continues unabated notwithstanding the use of anti Emetic remedies— Since last report has taken Alkali & lime juice administered seperately is now using Soda Water supersaturated with Carb. Acid Gas.—He is extremely restless, desireing often to have his position altered—Comatose Delirium with startings—subsultus tendinum.*

He closed the journal with a flick of his wrist and, with a nod to Dr. Magrath, the prison doctor, he proceeded to the cell area to examine several of the walking wounded from the *Argus*. He had been unable to pay them much heed these last two days, having spent most of his hours at the bedside of the faltering commander of his ship.

When he entered the big cell in which many of the *Argus* prisoners were kept, they gathered around him to seek news of their captain. Inderwick looked grave. Uriah couldn't help thinking that this young surgeon still bore the face of a boy.

"He is surviving, but barely," the surgeon told them. "His sickness of stomach and vomiting has become steadily worse over these two days. We are giving him wine every hour and that and the anodynes seem to help the vomiting, but then it begins all over again. He is very languid, very weak. I fear for him. We do all we can."

"My God, Doctor, you must save him!" cried an old seaman in the back of the cell. "You can't let him die! For God's sake, find something to save him!"

"Please, please," said Inderwick. "We do all we can. I promise you: We are doing everything that we know to do for him. Pray for him. . . . That's all I can suggest to you."

Two hours later, Surgeon Inderwick returned to the big cell. At the sight of him, a low moan went up from several of the men, and others covered their eyes as if the devil himself stood before them.

"Gentlemen," said Inderwick, "it is my sad duty to inform you that Master Commandant William Henry Allen, captain of the brig *Argus*, passed from this life at eleven o'clock this evening. God rest his soul."

The funeral procession of Captain Allen left Mill Prison at noon. A guard of honor, composed of two companies of Royal Marines commanded by a lieutenant colonel, saluted as the coffin was carried to a hearse. A velvet pall covered the coffin and over it was spread the American ensign. On the ensign were Captain Allen's hat and sword. The procession slowly began to move ahead, a military band striking up the mournful and affecting "Dead March in Saul." The hearse was preceded by the marines and the band and by the vicar, curate, and clerk of St. Andrew's Church. Behind the hearse, tears flowing freely down their cheeks, marched eight seamen from the *Argus*, their arms bound with black bands of crepe tied with white ribbon. Then, in respectful tribute to their departed foe, came eight captains of the British Navy with hatbands and scarves. After them, faces composed and stolid, came the officers of the *Argus*, walking two by two, in full-dress uniforms with crepe sashes.

The remainder of the procession was made up of Americans

who had served in the consulate prior to the outbreak of war, officials of Mill Prison, and additional British Navy captains and marine and army officers, followed by townspeople who also desired to pay their respects, for the English gave full deference to a foe—especially a foe on a fighting ship—who had fallen in battle.

At the church, the marine guard halted, clubbed arms, and formed single files through which the remainder of the procession passed into the sanctuary. The vicar read the solemn rites of last commitment. Then the procession re-formed and passed again through the files of guards and out into the bright sunshine of a late summer Saturday.

Captain Allen was laid to rest in the churchyard of St. Andrew's, next to Midshipman Richard Delphy of the *Argus*, who had been buried the evening before.

As the procession slowly wound back to the prison, Uriah felt suddenly weary . . . weary to the point that he could barely find the strength to walk. He turned his head slightly and murmured to Will Howard Allen, who was paired with him in the line, "I feel as if my own father had died."

"He was the father of us all," answered Will Howard.

"You know, I was thinking this morning: Never once since I first came aboard the *Argus* did Captain Allen, or anyone else for that matter, say anything about my being an Israelite."

The lieutenant glanced at him with surprise. "Why is that so remarkable?"

"Take my word for it," Uriah answered with a deep sigh. "It is most remarkable. But he was a most remarkable man."

"Yes, he was that. He *was* that."

They continued in silence, each wrapped in his own thoughts and memories, until the gray prison walls loomed up in front of them once again.

10

Dartmoor, *1813*

As the column of American prisoners left the gates of Mill Prison in Plymouth and walked through the city streets, large crowds of the curious gathered to watch. Surprisingly, the onlookers did not taunt the prisoners or scream insults at them. Instead many of them ran up to the marching men and offered them ale or cakes or fruit . . . for a proper price, of course. The prisoners silently waved them off; they had no appetite on this day.

They were headed, they knew, for the war prison at Prince Town—the great granite camp that had become infamously known among all American seamen simply as "Dartmoor." There the human prizes of the war with France had been confined since the prison had opened in 1809. Now, increasing numbers of Americans were being pushed behind the high walls, there to await a resolution of the war.

Uriah marched in couple with Will Howard Allen. They attempted talk but were roughly reprimanded by a soldier who warned them that another sound would bring them the pinch of cold steel. So they contented themselves with a careful study of the landscape around them, but the bleak, barren landscape of southern England's moors provided little consolation.

It was a high country of rolling slopes. The hillsides looked strangely infertile; there were few trees or shrubs, and it seemed doubtful that even grass would grow on these moors. There was only bracken and heather. Yet the land must be capable of supporting a crop, for every so often they passed a farmer's cottage. Always the same—steep-roofed, with a single door and a single window. Around each cottage were little patches of cultivated ground guarded by walls of the granite stone. Sheep grazed here and there in the fields, and a few cattle. There were ponies, too, powerful little black ponies that dragged sledges loaded with stones from the hillsides and carried dung to the fields in pots on their backs.

The otherwise silent march was enlivened now and then by a scream of pain from a lagger who had been hurried along by a British bayonet. As the route of march lengthened, a few sick prisoners began to stagger and fall by the way. These were roughly seized up by the soldiers and hurled bodily into the trailing baggage carts, where they rode, groaning in misery, the rest of the way.

They had walked, Uriah estimated, some eight miles when they came to a village that, a signpost informed them, was Yelverton. There they were halted for a brief rest. The military escort was relieved and began its march back to Plymouth. From here on, the prisoners would be escorted by a detachment of soldiers from the Prince Town prison.

As they stood wearily in the muddy street of this bedraggled village, a group of women passed them, bound for market in Plymouth. As the two groups came abreast, the women began screaming imprecations at them in their strange Devonshire patois, of which Uriah could grasp only an occasional word. But it was enough to get the drift: the women were accusing the Americans of being renegade Englishmen, of being traitors to their own land. One toothless harridan did not waste her strength in screaming but busied herself by spitting frantically in the direction of the prisoners as she hobbled past the halted column.

"Ah," muttered Will Howard Allen, "British womanhood in full flower."

In a moment more, the detachment commander yelled the order to move, and the slow, painful procession of prisoners gathered headway once again.

The soldiers that made up their new escort were a different breed from the others. They were old hands at guarding prisoners and were considerably more relaxed about it. Oh, they too were not reluctant to use a bayonet to prod a slow walker when necessary, but they conversed easily with the Americans and did not anticipate a revolt at every step, as had the edgy warriors who had walked them the first half of the way.

"We have several thousand Yanks at the depot now," a husky, red-faced Irishman told them as he walked alongside. "And many more to come, for at the rate you lads are losin' the war, we'll have all your army and your navy within our walls before much longer." He grinned widely as he watched their faces go pale with anger. "'Course the place is still full of Frogs," he continued, "and they're a crazy pack. Ah, but they're a sight easier to guard then you hardheaded Yanks. We'd rather keep watch on twenty thousand Frogs than on a thousand of you people."

"How much farther?" asked Uriah, whose legs were much more attuned to scrambling up and down ratlines than to hiking endless miles over a vast terrain that seemed to stretch emptily to a far horizon.

"Mebbe another six or so," answered the Irishman, who told them his name was Willow and his home was Belfast. "You be lookin' up ahead for Sheepstor. That's a marker. That tells us we're gettin' close. Soon you'll be seein' Vixen Tor far off to the left. That's beyond the depot. So that means we're nearin' the end of our little stroll."

"God, my legs feel like pieces of rock themselves," Uriah complained. "I have never been so tired out by a hike."

"You are not only hiking, laddie, you are climbing," the Irish soldier told him. "By the time we get to Prince Town, we'll be fourteen hundred feet above the level of the sea. And you've climbed every foot of it. You have reason to be tired. But think 'pon it: soon you'll have years and years to do naught but rest." And he laughed and laughed.

Another half-hour of steady walking brought them to Prince Town, a scraggly hamlet of an inn, a few cottages, and a tollgate. Their journey was almost at an end, for the prison lay just beyond this isolated little assemblage of stones.

A brief pause in front of the inn, which the sign proclaimed to be "The Plume of Feathers," so that the commander could rush inside and quench his thirst, and then the march resumed. Once past the inn, they saw the gray granite wall of the prison in the distance. The sight of that massive, impregnable barrier brought a great depression of the entire column of prisoners. All talk ceased. The men walked silently, and their feet began to shuffle through the mud in the fashion of the aged. It was as if they were trying to hold themselves back, to delay for another moment passing through that solid bulwark that would separate them from homeland and loved ones.

As they approached the prison, the great wall seemed to loom ever higher. They realized that it towered almost twenty feet and was constructed of masonry that looked strong enough to resist a lightning bolt hurled by the devil himself.

Without another halt, the column marched through the prison's main gate. It was surmounted by an archway of granite on which was inscribed a motto in Latin.

"*Parcere subjectis*," pronounced Will Howard, his eyes upon the archway. "To spare the conquered. Like most mottoes, I suppose this one is generally ignored."

Ahead of them was still another wall, a lower one, with another gate open to receive them. They hardly had time to fix this sight in their minds when they were shepherded through still another gate and finally into a large, bare yard. Here they were halted and left to stand for fifteen minutes or more while their soldier-guards eyed them with an amused contempt and various prison officials circled around them and examined the column.

"Come to attention, Americans, for the commander of the depot!" shouted a tall sergeant. "Silence in the ranks, you scum!"

Before them appeared an angular and somewhat elderly man in the uniform of a British naval captain. He stood before them and appeared to be awaiting their silence, although in fact not a man had uttered a word since passing through the first of the several gates.

"American prisoners," the captain called in a thin, reedy voice, "I welcome you to the Depot for Prisoners of War at Dartmoor. I am Isaac Congreve, post captain, His Majesty's Navy. I am the agent for the prisoners on Dartmoor. This means that I command this depot. As with any military command, we must have discipline. We have rules; they will be enforced. Follow my rules and you will do well. Break my rules, and we shall see to it that you are made uncomfortable.

"You will be fed adequately, as follows: each day—one-and-a-half pounds of soft bread per prisoner. A half-pound of fresh beef per day, except on Wednesday and Friday, when you will receive one pound of pickled herrings and one pound of potatoes. Sometimes, for variety, you will be given a pound of pickled codfish instead of herrings. Monday and Tuesday: one-half pound of cabbage or turnips; Thursday, Saturday, and Sunday: one ounce of scotch barley, one-third ounce salt, one-fourth ounce onion."

"Good Lord," whispered Will Howard, "they mean to starve us. That is enough for only one meal a day."

"Some of you may be of more robust appetite," the captain continued, as if responding to the whisper, "and—if you have the means—you are free to purchase additional food from the vendors in the yard. The market will be open each day from nine to noon, except of course on Sunday."

"*If* you have the means," Will Howard whispered angrily. "We have no money, and he knows it." A nearby soldier turned and gave him a warning glance.

"You will be fed now and provisioned for sleep," Congreve went on. "In the morning, we shall tally and register you and make you acquainted with your new home upon the moor. Carry on!" He turned on his heel and was gone.

Ahead, beyond still another gate, rose a series of massive buildings of three floors, ranged in a huge semicircle. They were built of the same brooding granite as everything else in this portion of the world. Toward one of the great granite piles the column now was marched, toward Number Four prison, which would be their home, if such it could be called, for many months to come.

As they walked into the prison, Uriah's control came near to deserting him and he almost wept, for it was here that the true horror of his situation became real to him. The interior of the cavernous, rectangular structure was dark and gloomy like a ship's orlop deck, and almost as damp. The high gray walls were masses of solid, wet granite, broken only by a series of small windows about nine feet apart. The floor was cold, moist stone. There was no glass in the windows, and wood shutters were thrown back to let in the scant light of the fading day.

"Line up, you renegades and rebels, line up for your bedding!" screamed the same sergeant, whose voice was beginning to grate on all the prisoners. A line formed down the middle of the depressingly ugly hall. As it slowly moved past tables heaped with provisions, each prisoner was given a hammock, a bed bag filled with straw, some flock made of chopped rags, a rough and foul-smelling blanket, some rope yarns with which to sling the hammock, a wooden spoon, a tin pot, and—to every six men—a three-gallon bucket.

Along either side of the vast room were two rows of iron stanchions, from which hammock hooks projected. To these, the hammocks were hung, as on the berth deck of a man-of-war. It was necessary to hang the hammocks in two tiers because of the number of prisoners, which meant that those occupying the upper tier had to step on the lower hammocks to climb up, a feat—when the lower was occupied—sure to bring forth angry curses and sometimes blows from the resident of the lower berth. In some of the prisons, they discovered later, three tiers of hammocks were employed, which produced proportionately more hostility.

After the hammocks were hung and personal boxes and trunks stowed, the weary, dispirited, and filthy prisoners from the brig *Argus* were given some bread, a tin of pickled fish, and water to wash it down. Then they found their way in the dark to the primitive head in the yard with its overpowering stench that almost knocked them down as they walked in.

It was barely past sundown, but they had been given no candles and Number Four already was dark. The Americans, hardly exchanging a word among themselves, climbed into their hammocks and lay sleepless, each of them wondering how he would be able to survive captivity in such a place.

The hammocks were pressed so tightly together that it was difficult to escape from one if the adjoining two were occupied. Each man had but nine inches of width, but this was compensated for by the luxury of eight feet in length. Thus, an exceedingly tall, exceedingly thin American would have rested in ease. For everyone else, sleeping was an abomination until their bodies began to grow accustomed to the tiny space.

A night of fitful sleep, erratic as a fluky wind, ended before sunrise. Turnkeys unlocked and slammed open the huge wood doors and walked the length of the hall, yelling, "Tumble up and turn out! Tumble up and turn out for tally!"

The prisoners, their eyes red, their faces streaked with dirt and defeat, stumbled outside to the prison yard. A small stream flowed quietly through the open ground, emptying first into a stone fountain and then into a sort of pool which, it transpired, was the bathing area for the prisoners. The entire depot was built on a slope. On the hillside above them, they could see an elevated fountain that apparently fed the streams that were dug through each of the prison yards and provided water for drinking and washing.

The inhabitants of Number Four were told to stand fast in the yard and wait. They shivered in the early morning chill that, before they were awakened, had caused them to press their skimpy blankets tightly around themselves in the hammocks. No stoves or fires were visible in Number Four. If there was any heat in the prison, it had not been apparent during those shivering hours before sunup.

As the grayness of dawn filled the yard, a group of officials entered and set up tables and chairs. Then each prisoner was called individually to report. It was near two hours before Uriah's turn came, and by then he was stiff with cold and his stomach hurt from hunger. He walked awkwardly forward, his knees feeling like boards of pine.

"Your name, prisoner?"

"Uriah Phillips Levy."

"Take off your shirt."

He stood bare-chested, shivering, while his height was taken and recorded next to his name and he was carefully checked for distinguishing features or marks. Should he escape, such information would help in his recapture. He put his shirt back on and awaited the rest of the interrogation.

"Your age?"

"Twenty-one years."

"Place of birth?"

"Philadelphia, State of Pennsylvania, United States of America."

"Your vessel when captured?"

"The brig-sloop *Argus*, Captain William Henry Allen."

"Your station aboard the vessel?"

"Assistant sailing master and prize master."

"Very well. Return to the line. Next man!"

When the tally was completed and the prisoners were dismissed, most of them returned to the prison hall. They were confined to that gloomy room, or its counterpart on the second floor, or to the yard outside. A series of intersecting walls, of which there seemed to be endless numbers in this place, prevented them from crossing to any of the adjoining prisons.

Uriah sat on his hammock, his boots restlessly scraping the slimy stone floor. He was soon joined by Will Howard Allen, whose hammock was several rows distant.

"A most joyous view, eh, Will?" said Uriah. "I have seen more pleasant prospects in some West Indies sewers."

"I agree," said Will Howard. "And I am kicking myself, for I have just turned down a chance to get out of here."

"Oh? How so?"

"When I told them at the table that I was a lieutenant, they said that commissioned officers have the right to accept a parole. They are housed in private lodgings in nearby towns. I think one was called Ashburton and another was Okehampton, or something like that. They are given an allowance of one shilling, sixpence a day on which to live. They have the right to walk one mile in either direction along the highway. There is an early evening curfew, and they must report here to the Depot twice a week for roll call."

"God, Will, it sounds like heaven. Why on earth didn't you accept? At least you'd have a fire in your room and some decent food."

"I don't know why. But I felt it would be wrong somehow to go off and leave my shipmates. I just couldn't do it. However, I reserve the right to change my mind." He looked up at the high stone walls. "I don't know how long I can stand this place without going insane."

"That is exactly what I have been wondering about myself," replied Uriah.

"You think this is so bad?" The question came in a voice so rough and coarse that it sounded like gravel running across a dirty spar deck. A broad-shouldered old gunner sat on the hammock across from them. He had been listening carefully to their conversation for want of anything better to do.

"You think this is so bad?" he repeated. "Well, it *is* bad, goddamn bad. But you should have been with us on the hulks. Then you'd know what bad really is."

"The hulks?" repeated Will Howard.

"Yes, sir. Hulks in Plymouth Harbor. We was kept for weeks on a rotting old frigate afore we was moved up here. We was kept in the hold, down with the water casks. There was thick mud on the deck, and that was where we sat and slept and ate. They fed us a half-pound or so of salt beef a day and some ship's bread that was so full of weevils you couldn't knock 'em all out. You either ate 'em or did without the bread. In the mornings, they gave us a treat—what they called cocoa, but it was water that had been touched up agin' a tin of cocoa. That hold was so low that no man could walk straight up, and the taller among us had to walk almost bent over in two. And they hardly ever give us any light. When we came out, we was blind as bats for a time. After that, comin' here didn't seem too bad at all, I kin promise you."

"Those bastards!" muttered Will Howard. "That sounds just like their prison ships in New York during the Revolution. They haven't changed a bit!"

"They have a special hate for us Yanks," said the gunner. "The Frogs in the other prisons are allowed to walk around and visit other buildings and yards. Hell, they got a real Frenchtown over there, with markets and schools and variety shows. But not us. No, sir. Americans have to stay in their own prisons and their own yards. You was right, Lieutenant. They ain't changed one bit."

• • •

Dartmoor Prison
November 6, 1813

Dearest Mama,

I am writing this letter with the hope that now, at last, it will be possible for us to get mail back to our families. We have made contact finally with one Beasley, an American in London who is designated the agent in England for American prisoners and is supposed to represent our interests. He has been seemingly reluctant to do much in our behalf, but now says he will do all possible to see that our mail makes its way, via neutral ships, to our dear ones.

I know you are distressed at what has happened and worry greatly about me. Please be assured that I am well and am tolerating this imprisonment better than I thought I might. Obviously this is not a place of luxury, but we are not mistreated. I hasten to tell you that I am healthy.

Let me describe a bit of our life here. This letter will prove to be a lengthy one, I fear, but I want to tell you as much as I can because there could be a change in the rules and the mail stopped.

Our time is passed in Prison No. 4, one of seven such buildings in this establishment. Each prison has two floors for the prisoners and above them is a cockloft, which is empty and used for promenades, for theatricals, lectures, and so on. All of this is contained in a space of some 30 acres, surrounded by a great wall. Within that is a lesser wall, atop which are posted sentries every 20 feet or so, who walk night and day with loaded musket. There are a series of wires connected to bells, so that any sentry immediately can sound an alarm if necessary.

In a yard beyond the inner circle, people from nearby towns conduct a market each day and sell food and clothes. We have little money among us for such buys, but Beasley promises that we can soon expect an allowance from the American government. That will be a blessing, for the prison food is rather scant and most of us are noticeably thinner.

We wear our own clothing, which is getting threadbare and worn. The prison issues us a ridiculous costume: a cap, shirt, trousers, vest, yellow jacket, a pair of wool socks, and shoes made of list with wooden soles. The clothes are emblazoned with a symbol called the King's broad arrow and the huge letters T.O. (standing for Transport Office) to properly brand us as prisoners of the King. Very few Americans will wear such garb and so we remain in our own clothes so long as they last.

Each prison is extended by a cookhouse, where our banquets are prepared, and by a cachot (or "black hole" as we call it), a sort of dungeon where troublemakers are sent. Do not worry. I have given them no cause for anger and I have not seen the inside of the cachot. Certain wild Frenchmen are frequent guests in the cachot. It goes hard for them. They have little light there and only straw to sleep on. They get only bread and water.

Speaking of the French, they are an amazing people. We are allowed now to visit the other prisons and thereby have come to know our fellow prisoners from France, some of whom have been here since the place was opened four years ago. They have built a society like that of a French city. They run schools, have entertainments, and have developed a thriving business with scrimshaw and other homemade items, which they trade to the market people for food and clothes.

The French even have different social classes. Their officers are referred to as "Les Lords" and their workers, the carvers of scrimshaw, teachers, etc., as "Les Labourers." The idlers are called "Les Indifferents" and the gamblers are "Les Minables." The pitiful bottom class are "Les Romains," the unsuccessful gamblers who have bet away everything they owned. Many of them now go stark naked except for a blanket thrown over them with two holes for the arms. Some have even gambled away their daily food ration, and they survive by eating garbage and begging crumbs from their fellows.

I am giving thought to taking instruction in French and perhaps also in fencing. That will have to await our allowance from the U.S. government, for everything here is sold at a price; nothing is given away.

The black prisoners are kept together in a separate prison. They are ruled by a magnificent figure of a man—a Negro near 7 feet high who is called "Bad Dick." He carries a huge club with him wherever he goes. Any one of his subjects who disagrees with him receives a chastisement that he won't ever forget. Thus Bad Dick rules a peaceable kingdom, for there are few who would risk disturbing his temper. I have visited their church services (for want of else to do) and it is a most amazing sight: the black prisoners sitting transfixed while another huge man screams and yells at them and Bad Dick patrols the aisles with his club, looking for any sign of laughter or inattention. I, too, gave the speaker my full measure of mind, for fear of that menacing club if I so much as looked away.

Speaking of services, I have made a search for other Hebrew prisoners in hopes that a minyan might meet for services. So *far, there is lacking a minyan. By asking about, I have talked with Morris Russell, William Wolf, Manuel Joseph, and Levi Myers Harby of Charleston (who has met Cousin Mordecai). They are Israelites all. We meet now and again to recite some prayers and to talk, but lacking the number for a minyan we cannot say the Kaddish or the Kedusha or the Borchu, much to our regret and disappointment. Had we a few more men here, we could have a real congregation.*

If the good Lord is even aware that I am here, I think he forgives me for not properly observing Shabbat and the other holidays, which pass unnoticed. It is almost impossible here to follow the laws of our religion, but in my heart I observe them, as ever our family has. I try not to eat any forbidden foods and have done so only when the food has been unidentified and unrecognizeable.

What do you hear from cousin Mordecai the Diplomat? I'm sure that by now he has all of North Africa under the spell of his witty tongue. I have heard nothing from him, of course, since he sailed last May on his mission.

It is not only news of Mordecai that I miss. We are cut off here from most news of the war, although some passes through these walls somehow. We have prisoners designated (and paid) as criers and it is their duty to gather the news from new arrivals, guards, and any other source and to cry it throughout the prisons. An occasional English newspaper also is smuggled in and we read those, but we doubt that the reports in those newspapers are true. The newspapers in England said little about it, but we have been excited by reports of a great victory won by Commodore Perry over a British fleet on Lake Erie. We pray that the rumor is true, for command of the Great Lakes will be significant in the course of this war. We just heard yesterday that an American general named Harrison has led our army to victories in Canada. That is welcome news, indeed, for our army has not covered itself with glory in the war to date.

I am so glad that I never have taken up the affliction of tobacco, for the lack of it seems to be a terrible curse to those so afflicted. We lack money to buy such luxuries and those men who desperately need their tobacco are driven to extreme lengths. Some have sold their clothes and their daily beef for tobacco. If they have naught left to sell, they find a pocket that once carried their tobacco and then chew the pocket. When that is done, they find a piece of tarred rope or wood and chew on that. My only addiction is to food and our daily ration answers that need, if just barely.

The great passer of time in this place is gambling, a recreation to which I devote only small attention. It serves to take the minds of the men, for a little while at least, away from their captivity and worry over their families at home. Bets here are taken on everything. Men will bet on the weight of a sentry or how many steps the sentry will take before he turns about.

Very popular are the rat races. Here is how it works: someone will place a bit of food in the middle of a bare floor and everyone retreats to watch. Soon the rats begin to slowly creep to the food. Each bettor selects his own rat. When the rats are gathered around the food, someone raises a shout. The rats rush back to their holes and the first to reach the wall is a winner. The rats have become known as individuals and some fleet ones have developed cults of followers. The French tell stories of the great speed of an old gray rat that they named "Père Ratapon." I have witnessed weevil races aboard ship, but it never was so well organized as this.

The most popular gambling pursuit here, however, is the game of Keno, which is played for hours and hours, sometimes all night long. A card costs a penny and about 30 gamblers play at a time. The proprietor of the table calls out the numbers in a strange rhythmic speech that somehow is understood by all. I hear it all night as I try to sleep.

So this is life at Dartmoor Prison. It is a hard life, cer-

tainly not one I would choose, but it is endurable and so I will endure it until our country's glorious victory to come. You must endure it too and though I know you must worry, please do not grieve. I will be home and kissing you hello before too much longer. Give my love to my brothers and sisters, to Grandmother, to my aunts, uncles, cousins, and friends, and remind them that they have the love and are always in the thoughts of,

Your Uriah

January 1814

"I have about reached the end of my rope, Uriah. I may well pack it in. I can stand no more of this."

"It is no disgrace for you to accept parole, Will Howard. Most of the other officers have done so. You would only be getting your due as an officer."

They were walking as briskly as half-frozen limbs would allow, back and forth along the 150-foot-long cockloft of Prison Number Four, hoping against hope that the rapid movement would bring some heat back into their bodies. Despite the blankets wrapped around their shoulders, the lips of both men were bluish and trembling with the cold. They walked in a sort of twilight, for only half the shutters were opened on the windows in a feeble effort to hold out the wind.

"If only I could sit by a fire . . . if only for just a few minutes," muttered Will Howard. "Then perhaps I could feel my toes once again."

"Take the parole, Will Howard, if you still can. Lodgings in Ashburton would give you a far better life than you have here. I would take it, if I stood in your shoes."

"I may do just that. I never did like the cold. Even the fires of hell would seem welcome after this. No wonder we see more and more empty hammocks in the hall. Men are signing into the British service rather than spend another day at this."

"That I would never do," Uriah said, with a touch of his old spirit. "To fight against my own country? I would rather freeze here on their damned moors! And I would spit on any man who did consider it."

"As much as I hate to say it," groaned Allen, "I have to go outside. I can't hold it any longer."

"I have the same problem. My bladder is swollen like a spinnaker."

They descended the stone stairs to the main floor and gingerly opened one of the massive wooden doors to the yard. Outside, snow was piled in great drifts that reached near the top of the wall. Even the sentries had deserted their posts in the cruelty of this Devonshire winter and did their guarding from the barracks. It was, the prisoners were told, the worst winter that had been seen for a half-century. The streams in the prison yards were frozen hard, and the only source of water was the snow that bulked high in the yards. With the roads blocked by drifts, the market people could not come to vend their wares and the prison provisioners from Tavistock and Plymouth were unable to replenish supplies. Fortunately an ample supply of salt beef had been laid in, and each day's menu was austerely simple: beef and snow.

A rough path had been hammered through the snow by thousands of feet from the prison door to the open latrine at the edge of the yard. The cold was almost unbearable as the two men, alone in their misery, stopped to urinate. Uriah hated this place. As foul-smelling and evil as most ships' heads were, they were like ornate Spanish brothels when compared to this stinking hole. At the other end of the latrine, several straddle holes had been dug, over which the men would stand or crouch and evacuate their bowels. For one prone to constipation, as was Uriah, the pure obscene degradation of such facilities made him tighten his bowels more than ever.

"What think you of Shortland?" asked Will Howard, as they picked their way through the snow and returned to Number Four. Captain Thomas Shortland, Royal Navy, had replaced Congreve as the depot commander just before Christmas. The rumor chain had it that Shortland was known through the navy for his iron discipline and his love of the cat as punishment.

"His talks to us indicate that he is a man of discipline, as they say. Yet he seems fair enough. He has promised to see to it that Beasley at long last does his job and gets our allowance for us from our government. I think we'll have to wait and see about Captain Shortland. Perhaps he is not the devil they have pictured him."

"God, I hope you're right. It seems that the embargo will be his main form of punishment, with the market people prevented from coming in. That would hurt the French more than us, for we haven't money to buy anything as it is."

Will Howard walked down the alley between long rows of hammocks and pulled his coarse blanket tighter around his shoulders. "God, maybe it would have been better to let our bladders burst than to have gone out into that wind. I am colder now than I was before we went out, and even then I had no feeling in half my body. I tell you, Uriah, I am soon to request parole for myself. It's either that or I'll take a Taylor dive!"

Young Taylor, son of a New York captain, had reached the limit of his endurance weeks before. He had climbed to the top of the stanchions, near the ceiling of the great hall, tied a rope around his neck, and dove into the air. Ever since, taking a "Taylor dive" had become the exit of last resort for the men of Number Four.

May 1814

"*Moi! Moi!*" De Guissac had always insisted that the word be pronounced sharply, with the lips parting abruptly to give the word a properly percussive sound.

"*Moi! Moi!*" Uriah said it several more times to get it right. His teacher had departed only a week ago, but Uriah already missed him greatly.

He put down his French textbook and leaned back. He sat in the sun in the yard of Number Four, his back against the cold stone wall. Ah, this heat felt good on his chest. He coughed once and felt the usual pain shoot across his lungs. Like almost every other prisoner at Dartmoor, Uriah carried bodily souvenirs of the diabolical winter: a lasting cough or perennial sniffles, if not actual pneumonia.

But the winter had ended at last, and spring had come with its torrential rains that left the prison buildings smoking with damp. There was not a man there who would not gladly accept the endless rains as a substitute for the savage winter that had left many men in a state of near-insanity from the sustained exposure to bitter cold.

The easing of winter's blows had been accompanied by another sort of mercy for the American prisoners: they began finally to receive money from their government. Beasley, the agent in London, made his long-delayed appearance at the office of Captain Shortland and announced that he had been authorized to provide one pence, halfpenny per day for each American to buy tobacco and soap. A few weeks later, he returned to report that an additional penny per day would be provided to purchase coffee.

Some of the Americans wasted no time in taking their new-found wealth to the gaming tables. Others put the allowance to its intended use and rushed to the marketplace to satisfy their long craving for tobacco.

Yet others were more enterprising. They accumulated their allowances and then put them to use in earning still more by following the example of the French and setting themselves up in trade. Before long, the mess areas of the American prisons had blossomed into town markets, with the rough eating tables serving during nonmeal hours as the shopkeepers' benches and stalls. For one like Uriah, who did not use tobacco, there was money at last to supplement the prison's near-starvation diet. He could visit the open market and buy fruits and vegetables from the Devonshire market people or he could patronize the prisoner-entrepreneurs who had set up shop in his own hall.

Oh, what a delightful change it was for Uriah to enjoy hot plum-gudgeons for breakfast—little fried cones of salt fish and potato. For just a penny, one was a treat on a cold morning. And for dinner, if he could lay his hand on two pence, he could buy a pint of freco—a thin stew with a bit of meat and some potato, thickened by barley and cooked with bone marrow. Though his mother would not deign even to have such stuff in her kitchen, he would eat it with pleasure here, for it verily warmed the joints. If he was rich with the savings of several days, he could invest four pence in a pint of lobscouse, a heavier stew with much more meat. And to wash it down—good hot coffee brewed of burnt bread crusts or burnt peas. No, it was not really good, but it was hot and strong and bracing to a man who had survived a winter drinking naught but melted snow.

One American prisoner was rich with prize money earned aboard a Limey frigate. He had been impressed and served for years in the British Navy, then was jailed like many others for refusing to take up arms against his own countrymen. With his wealth, he bought several hundred books from a Plymouth peddler and opened Dartmoor's first rental library. For Uriah, this was another major advance toward making prison life bearable. As his body began to regain some of its lost weight, so his mind was soothed and healed by the availability of books to help pass the long, dreary hours. He had read his own worn copy of Bowditch again and again, to the point where he could recite from memory some of the tables of astronomic data for navigational use. Now he could delve into classics of English literature and regain a measure of serenity.

Even the life of the mind and spirit began to burgeon at Dartmoor. Two drama groups announced themselves, one of white men and the other of dark, and began to offer plays in the spacious cocklofts of the prisons. Just two nights earlier, Uriah had sat in wonder at a presentation by the black company of *Romeo and Juliet*, with the part of the virginal maiden played entrancingly by a muscular black man of well over six feet in height. The white group, known as the Dartmoor Thespian Company, reserved the women's parts for boys, of whom there were many in this cruel prison, who were put in dresses for the occasion.

His new affluence—the regular allowance from the government—enabled Uriah to partake of still another luxury: education. The walls were thick with notices offering instruction: languages of many lands, or the principles of navigation, or even reading, writing, and arithmetic—each of them available for a price ranging from six pence weekly to a shilling monthly.

One of the most favored classes was the one in the manly art of self-defense, as taught by Bad Dick, king of the black men's prison. Most of his students were white, and he taught them with enthusiasm in the cockloft of Prison Number Seven, laying his club aside but never removing his bearskin hat as he coached them in the rudiments of pugilism. Uriah bought two weeks of instruction from Bad Dick and earned that worthy's praise by sparring with him for two three-minute rounds.

About that time, Uriah also met and became a student of André de Guissac, a swarthy, big-chested master of a French privateer that had been taken by a British sloop only after a bloody deck fight. De Guissac promised Uriah that he would make him so fluent in French that, within a few weeks, he would be equipped to seduce the most beautiful women of Paris. The progress was not quite as fast as promised, but de Guissac proved to be a patient, skilled, and inspirational teacher. With the aid of an old textbook, he had Uriah understanding simple phrases within days and had him speaking haltingly, yet with growing confidence within weeks. They soon became fast friends. De Guissac insisted that Uriah promise to visit him in Marseilles on some future day after the British had been defeated.

De Guissac left Dartmoor shortly after Napoleon's abdication on April 11. Now that there was some promise of peace between these old and mortal enemies, the English were setting free large groups of French prisoners each day and marching them downhill to Plymouth, where they would board ships for home.

"I will not leave them with a kiss of thanks, *mon ami*," de Guissac had vowed to Uriah. "I will spit in their eyes as I walk through that stone archway." De Guissac had related many long, bitter stories to Uriah about the five years he had been imprisoned at Dartmoor and about the repeated cruelties inflicted on the Frenchmen by their guards.

Nothing could raise de Guissac to such fury, however, as the memory of the winter of 1809–10. The Dartmoor winter, as always, made survival difficult, but in that winter an outbreak of virulent measles had swept through the prisons. By spring, almost five hundred French prisoners had died. The corpses were carried by other prisoners to the dead house in the prison hospital. Then they were loaded into wagons and taken outside the walls. They were dumped into a mass grave—a wide, shallow trench—and then covered over.

"Those pagan bastards!" de Guissac would snarl, his eyes filling with tears. "They buried my comrades without so much as a prayer, without even a final word from a priest. They sent their souls to heaven without the last rites of the church, without so much as a blessing. Ah, *mon ami*, if I meet one of them outside this place, anywhere, I promise you I shall strangle him on the spot!"

Now this big, dark Frenchman—who would patiently sit for hours and drill Uriah over and over in French verbs in all their infuriating variety—probably was striding across the soil of his homeland once again. He would not be vertical for long, he had assured Uriah. "I must make up for five years of deprivation," he said with a laugh. "If my hand were a woman, it would have been impregnated thousands of times in these years."

Uriah sat alone in the sun and paged slowly through the ancient textbook of French grammar, which was shedding pages like a head of lettuce. He already missed his exuberant teacher, who had brightened the dullness of the hours by roaring out French sea chanteys in his husky voice. They had parted with a fierce hug, and de Guissac had kissed Uriah resoundingly on both cheeks.

"The next time I see you, *mon ami*, you must be able to speak with me entirely in the beautiful words of France," he said as they parted. "Then, together, we will go to a house of whores and bounce the night away on lustful women. It will be *magnifique!*"

October 1814

The crier's voice was hoarse and strident as he moved slowly down the aisle between the hammocks, shouting his news: "Washington City falls! The worst has happened! The British have landed and burned our capital! Madison and the government have fled! The war has turned!"

Uriah came racing down the aisle from a tavern in the mess area, where he had been about to buy lunch. "What is that, man? What is that you say?"

The crier was weary and sore of spirit. He answered in a soft voice that broke with emotion and exhaustion.

"It is true," he said. "The Limeys told us and we didn't believe it, but the committee has secured a New York newspaper by bribe. It is confirmed. The British fleet landed on Maryland shore in August and marched on Washington City. They captured it almost without a fight and burned the Capitol and the White House. Madison and the cabinet and Congress have fled somewhere to the west. The war still is waged, but they have taken our capital."

"Good God!" Uriah said. "If they take any more of our cities, it will be over. We'll have to surrender."

The crier looked at this young prisoner who stood before him, his face pale with rage and grief, his chin trembling with emotion. The bad news obviously had left him heartbroken. The crier felt a surge of pity. He tried to think of better tidings to give the lad a brace.

"There is some good news," he said softly. "Our sloop *Peacock*, under Master Commandant Warrington, has beaten the brig-sloop *Epervier* off the coast of Georgia. The British ship was carrying over one hundred thousand dollars in specie. They say the *Peacock* now is roaming St. George's Channel and taking one British merchant prize after another. Just like the old *Argus*."

Uriah nodded. Aye, just like the old *Argus*. Roaming the English home waters and setting fear in the hearts of the King and his ministers. For the first time in weeks, he thought again of Captain Allen and Will Howard Allen and Will Watson and Inderwick. And wonderful, silly Simon McDeal. His eyes filled with tears, and he strove to choke back the sobs in his throat.

He regained a measure of control and sought to change the direction of the talk. "How goes the war on land?" he asked.

The crier shook his head. "We don't know. It is hard to get word. The guards say that now that Boney has been beaten, they are pouring English soldiers from Europe into America. There have been some battles along the Canada border, at Chippewa and a place called Lundy's Lane. But it's harder to figger what happened there. Both sides claim they have won. Oh, yes. One more thing. There's a rumor we hear that says we have won a great naval battle on Lake Champlain. Commodore McDonough, it was, who has beaten the English off Plattsburg. But the guards here won't answer when they are asked about that. We offer 'em the usual bribes, but they won't talk about Champlain. Which must mean it's true."

Yes, thought Uriah, *it must be true. Thank God that someone, somewhere, is fighting to regain the national honor that went up in the smoke of Washington City.*

December 1814

Uriah sat shivering on the edge of his hammock. He stared dully into space. He had thought of making his way out into the pelting sleet and across the yard to the cockloft of Number Seven to rent a new book, but his heart wasn't in it. He wore every stitch of clothing that he owned and sat with his blanket wrapped tight around him. Yet he still was half-frozen. He was tired of reading, he was tired of studying his French grammar, and he was tired of being cold and wet. He was tired of living.

How could he face yet another winter in this hole? Could he possibly live through four more months of this numbing, brain-freezing cold, of the perpetual wetness, of the paralyzing snow? He retched when he thought of having to feed again on naught but salt beef and snow. For the roads surely would be blocked and the provisioners would not be able to get through the high drifts. The five thousand American prisoners would be forced again to subsist on the grim, minuscule prison food: the unvarying tin of stringy, tough beef and the cup of slowly melting snow to satisfy a parched throat. He wished Will Howard were here with him, for it would be more bearable if they had each other to complain to. But Will had long since requested parole and now was in lodgings at Moretonhamp-stead. And de Guissac—ah, what Uriah would give to have that big Frenchman here at his side to keep his mind off the cold with long, incredibly detailed tales of the women he had known in Marseilles.

But they were not here. There were some men around him whom he considered comrades, but many of them were recent ar-rivals whom he scarcely knew. He did not feel like talking to any of them today. He just wanted to be warm. He would give his soul to the devil now for just the chance to be warm once again.

Oh, the rumors of peace were making the rounds again, as they had almost since the first day he had passed through Dartmoor's stone archway. Sixteen months later, he put no credence in them. The war would continue forever, and he would be here forever. There were negotiations going on in Ghent, in Belgium, the rumors said. Ah, but Uriah well knew that the so-called American peace commissioners—Quincy Adams and Gallatin and the others—had been wandering about Europe for a year-and-a-half in search of peace . . . to no avail. Why was there any reason now to believe they would succeed?

For no reason, suddenly, incredibly, Uriah felt in his mouth the taste of his mother's plum pudding. It had been his special favorite when he was a boy. He put his head down. *I hope she is still alive*, he thought. *I hope I will see her again.*

"Levy."

The voice was soft, so soft that he didn't hear it at first.

"Levy." It was repeated. Uriah looked up, no interest in his face. It was a sergeant in the crimson tunic and shiny gold buttons of the Seventh-Eighth Regiment of the British Army. Two burly troopers stood behind him, for no guard would come into one of the stone prisons without a protective escort.

"You are Uriah Phillips Levy, sailing master?"

Uriah's eyebrows rose. *What was this?* "I am," he answered, and slowly rose to his feet, his legs clumsy with cold.

"Get your things and report to the depot commander's office. At once!"

This was unheard of. What had he done? Prisoners in nearby hammocks looked at him curiously. If a prisoner was to be punished—and Uriah could think of no rules he had broken—the punishment would be administered in the yard of the man's own prison, or he was roughly thrust into the cachot at the end of the building. *What could this be?*

Uriah began to tremble with the cold and with fear. He gathered his few personal possessions, including his Bowditch and his French grammar, and pushed them into a gunnysack that had helped to keep off the cold during the bitter nights in his hammock. His mind tried to work, but he could not think. *What could be the reason for this summons?*

"What have I done?" he finally managed to stammer through quaking lips.

"You are going home," said the sergeant. "Back to your country."

"Home?" Uriah wasn't sure he had heard aright. Was this a delusion? "Going home? You say I am going to my home, to Philadelphia?"

The sergeant nodded curtly, and they began walking slowly past the rows of hammocks toward the door. Other prisoners, most of them buried under their blankets in search of warmth, still peered curiously out at them.

"Then . . . then, the war has ended?" he asked in a querulous voice.

"No, the war goes on," the sergeant answered, "though the peace talks continue in Belgium and the word is that an agreement is near. No, the war goes on, but an exchange of petty officers has been negotiated and your name has been drawn. If Jew peddlers have a god, yours was smiling on you this day."

The slight passed unheard. Uriah stepped through the great wooden door of Number Four and outside into the frigid air. The sleet had ceased, but a slate-gray sky showed low, scudding clouds that promised snow. A flock of birds came across the prison buildings, beating hard against the punishing wind. A thin, broken layer of ice covered the stream in the yard. Uriah shook his head again. He had heard, but he couldn't completely believe. Was this all a dream? Was he to be free at last?

A few minutes later, he stood before a young officer in the outer office of Captain Shortland's quarters. Uriah held his gunnysack tightly in front of him with both hands as if afraid they would try to pull it away. The officer finished writing on a document before him and then signed his name in large, bold strokes with a great flourish.

For the first time since Uriah had been brought before him, the young aide-de-camp looked up.

"Sailing Master, here is your discharge from the depot. Lose it at your peril, because if you are stopped on the highway and cannot produce your papers, you will be returned here. Do you understand?"

Uriah nodded. "Yes, sir. Yes, I understand. Do not lose my papers."

"Very well. You are to make your way to Plymouth. Just walk back down the same highway that brought you here, through Yelverton and on downslope. In Plymouth, look up Mr. Nathaniel Ingraham, the cartel agent. He will see to your lodging and food until a cartel ship is ready to return you to the United States. A schooner is expected within the week. You should be on your way in just a few days."

"Yes, sir. In just a few days." Uriah still was trying to sort all this out, to order in his mind all these unexpected new facts. He could think of nothing else to say, except to repeat what he had been told.

"You seem exceptionally dull-witted for a sailing master," snapped the officer. "Remember the name of the agent: Nathaniel

Ingraham. You'll find him in Stockshire Alley in Plymouth."

Ten minutes later, the discharged prisoner walked slowly through the stone archway at the depot entrance and stopped in the roadway for a moment to get his bearings. Over there was the village of Prince Town. So he must go that way, for the road to Plymouth went through Prince Town and then turned south. He started to walk, then stopped again. Should he return for a moment to Number Four and say farewell to his comrades? He had not even had time to say good-bye. They had taken him away so fast.

He looked up at the great wall, the monstrous outer wall of the Dartmoor Depot, and at the gray, ugly prison buildings looming starkly above it.

No, he decided. *No. Never will I enter that wall again, for any reason. They will have to kill me to get me inside that wall again.*

He turned, threw his sack over his shoulder, and began making his lone way up the highway to the town, where he would take the turn for home.

11

Philadelphia, 1815

The sound of voices from downstairs woke him instantly. He heard the excited words of his little brother Jonas punctuating the lower tones of adult voices. He could not make out what they were saying. He stretched slowly and luxuriously in his bed and pondered the pattern of sunlight on the far wall.

The murmuring below turned to conversation at the foot of the stairs and then the noise of shoes pounding up toward his room. Soon the family came trooping in, full of smiles and arm-waving gaiety. Little Jonas led the way, closely followed by his mother.

"Uriah, Uriah!" the boy piped. "We have news! The war is over! Peace is here!"

Uriah stared, openmouthed. He turned to his mother, his brows raised in question.

Rachel Levy nodded excitedly several times. "It's true, Uriah," she said. "Word has just come from New York. An English sloop, the *Favourite*, has sailed in under a flag of truce. It brought copies of a treaty signed at Ghent in Belgium. The war was ended on the day before Christmas."

Uriah took a deep breath. "So it has finally come. You say the peace was signed before Christmas? That means that Jackson's great victory at New Orleans came after the war actually ended. What a waste of men's lives!"

"Uriah, don't dwell on the bitterness," his mother warned him. "This is a great day, son. They say that huge crowds are in the streets of New York, cheering and raising huzzahs and ringing bells and firing cannon! And the sailors have gathered on the docks and are preparing the merchant ships for sailing again."

He stood up and embraced his mother, who seemed surprised by his reaction. "I'm as glad as any man that the war is over," he assured her. "But I wonder what we have gained by it. Many good men died—some of them my dear comrades—and the war finally has come sputtering to an end, in deadlock. What have we gained? What have we proven? Madison agreed months ago, I am told, that he would sign a peace treaty that did not mention impressment. My God! That was our main reason for fighting this war! And he lets them off so lightly. It's disgraceful!"

"Perhaps, Uriah, we should consider ourselves lucky." It was the voice of Uriah's brother Benjamin, always methodical, always reflective, who had stood quietly at the door, watching the emotions on Uriah's face as he was given the news of peace. "I have heard that England was preparing to send Wellington to our shores to take command of their armies. If that had happened, only God knows what might have been our fate. Madison might have been sent into exile with Bonaparte."

"I'm just grateful that my son is home and safe," Rachel Levy said quietly, "and I hope he'll stay with us now."

Commodore Alexander Murray pored over the requisitions on his big desk, shifting them back and forth in his field of vision in a vain effort to make the tiny, narrow-spaced writing stand out bold and clear. How he hated this damned office work! But here he was, and each of these miserable requisitions must be studied, checked, and approved or disapproved.

His slow perusal of the long, detailed forms gave Uriah a chance to study the ship's models scattered about the large office with its big window overlooking the Delaware and the Navy Yard docks. There was the great *Constitution* and his old friend the *United States*, which had been built just a few yards from where he now sat. And another fine frigate, the *Constellation*. And that brig . . . why, that was the *Argus*! He would know it anywhere. His eyes caressed the fine lines of that noble vessel that now rode under the English flag somewhere in Europe.

"You look wide-eyed, Sailing Master. Have you found fault with one of my fine models, then?" The commodore's words startled him back into the here and now. Before Uriah could offer an apology for his lack of attention, the commodore continued, "Ah, you stare at the *Argus*. I understand. Your old ship. It tugs at our heart, does it not, to see again—even in miniature—the ladies of the sea to whom we gave our hearts. Especially when it is unlikely that we shall see them again. I have the same pangs when I see a painting or a model of the *Chesapeake* or even the old *Philadelphia*."

The commodore cleared his throat. "Well, Sailing Master, I apologize for keeping you waiting." He picked up Uriah's file, which had been delivered from the Navy Department in Washington, and quickly riffled through it.

"I suppose you are enjoying your reunion with your family and the chance to see old friends and companions?" the commodore asked, looking up from the file. "You deserve a recuperation after your adventures at Dartmoor. Fearsome place, fearsome! I don't envy your time there. Well, then, what are your plans, Sailing Master?"

Uriah looked at the commodore in some surprise. "Sir, I had expected you to tell me my plans. I am assigned to you temporarily, pending my transfer to a ship's berth. It was my hope that you might be ready to tell me now what that berth will be."

The commodore smiled benignly. "Oh no, young man, oh no. It's not that simple. So you plan to remain in the navy, do you?"

"Yes, sir. Over my family's strong objections, I fear, but that is what I have decided. I have an offer to join John Coulter's fleet again as a master or even in his office. My mother begs me to take it. But it is the navy for me. I decided that at Dartmoor, and I see no reason to change my mind now that I'm home. I can think of no greater honor than spending my life in the navy of my country." He suddenly felt embarrassed though he meant every word.

"Well said, Sailing Master!" the commodore shouted. "The navy needs good men like you. And a sailing master is worth his weight in gold!"

"Thank you, sir. Now, is it possible to learn today where I will be assigned?"

"As I said, Mr. Levy, it is not so simple. Remember you are but one of many. At the start of the late war, the navy listed twelve captains. Now we have thirty. At the start of the war, we had five thousand able and ordinary seamen and boys. Now we have twelve thousand. This is a big navy, Sailing Master. And most of these men are requesting new assignments. There aren't that many to go around. There will be. But not yet."

"Then, Commodore, do I understand that you have no assignment for me?"

"Correct, Sailing Master. And none contemplated for some time to come. But do not despair. You must be patient. Your pay of four hundred dollars per year will of course continue. Enjoy yourself! Rest with your family in your own home. Walk the streets of Philadelphia once more and breathe the sweet air of home. Your day will come, Sailing Master, never fear. Your day will come."

Uriah felt like shouting at this pompous yet kindly old commodore that he had had a life's worth of sitting at Dartmoor. He was a navy man with skill and experience to spare. Why must it be wasted with more sitting?

"Commodore," he ventured. One more try: "If you will forgive my impertinence—there are rumors afoot among my navy friends that Commodore Bainbridge will form a new squadron and sail to the Mediterranean to teach a lesson to the Barbary States. I would beg for a chance to be within that squadron. Is there any possibility, sir? I would give anything to go with Bainbridge!"

"No, no. No chance. There are hundreds applying ahead of you." The commodore shook his head impatiently.

Commodore Murray studied the intense young man in sailing master's garb as he stood before him. The disappointment was etched clearly on his face. Ah, these young bloods . . . spoiling for battle, for the excitement of the chase! This young fellow had been home from prison scarcely a month and here he was, pounding for a chance to sail away again.

"I have a thought, Mr. Levy, that perhaps will console you a mite. You must have seen on the stocks in my yard this fine new liner a-building. She is the *Franklin*, 74. We expect to launch her in late summer or early fall at the latest. A beautiful ship . . . almost 188 feet between perpendiculars. I have been inking in the names of those who will fill her berths. But there still are open spaces. The post of second sailing master is open. Suppose I ink you in as second master on the *Franklin*? And then, let us see what we shall see. It will depend finally, of course, on the commander of the *Franklin*."

"Is the commander assigned yet, Commodore?"

"Yes, it will be Captain Stewart, if we can ever get word to him in the Atlantic that the war is over. He and the *Constitution* are still out there, hunting for British prizes."

"I would be honored to serve under Captain Stewart, sir."

"Well, Mr. Levy, let's hope that it will all work out. I would suggest you visit the *Franklin* and get to know her while she's being finished. And when Captain Stewart arrives to take over his ship, we'll put the question to him. If he concurs, you will be second master on the *Franklin*."

"I will await the day with much anticipation, Commodore." Uriah raised his fore-and-aft hat in salute, said a final word of thanks, and left the office. He hurried into the yard where the ship-of-the-line *Franklin* rose, majestic on her stocks. She had been designed and was being built by Samuel Humphreys, son of the revered old Joshua. She was kin, then, to the *United States*. In a remote way, she was even kin to him. He walked over to make her acquaintance.

The orchestra had played a minuet and a cotillion and now was bouncing its way through a hearty mazurka. Uriah pivoted and whirled in the paces of the dance, wishing all the while that an intermission would be called. Oh, he tolerated dancing well enough and was nimble on his feet. But he longed to be able to stand alongside Anne once again and feel the soft skin of her arm under his fingers as he guided her to the refreshment table.

The Assembly Room at Oeller's was packed to its limits tonight for the colorful Patriots Ball, which was a cornerstone of Philadelphia's social life. People came hurrying back to the city from ocean shore vacations so as not to miss it. Under the great crystal chandeliers with their glowing tapers, the crowd barely found the space to step through the dances. Adding dash and marvelous color to the assemblage were the many brilliant military uniforms, for this was an evening to honor the brave men of the services, and they were out in force.

Uriah was resplendent in his sailing master's formal uniform, the rich blue tunic setting off the gleaming white trousers and the shiny black boots.

Anne looked so beautiful that it almost hurt him to gaze upon her. Her dark brown hair hung in wavy strands down her back. Her white ball gown seemed to him whiter than all the others and more tastefully adorned with silken flowers. Her brown eyes shone with merriment and happiness, for she loved to dance and to sing and to laugh with her friends.

He was so proud to be with her on this night that he could hardly believe his good fortune. She had confided to him that she had received no fewer than six invitations to the Patriots Ball, and she had chosen him as her escort! The rejected suitors all were here this evening, some with other girls and some alone. Uriah had been the recipient of more than one hateful stare as he danced. He knew those malevolent glares came from those who envied him his great good fortune.

Uriah was captivated by Anne Stahr; he readily admitted it. She was witty and bright and very, very beautiful. And Christian. Uriah remained determined to marry within his own Israelite faith. He had promised his grandfather that he always would remain a Hebrew. *Nothing will drive me away,* he had vowed to himself, *no matter what the temptation.* But Anne was quite a temptation.

In any case, he would remind himself, *I'm not the only man in her life. She has other swains, some of them navy men like myself. It would be unlikely that she would choose me from among so many.*

Still, this evening, he was the one at her side, admiring her loveliness and enjoying her company. Uriah noted to his great relief that the orchestra seemed to be tacking into the final chorus of the endless mazurka. He was making a turn to his left when he was suddenly shoved rudely and roughly from behind. Although not breaking out of the dance, he turned his head. Behind him, arms akimbo and a cool smile on his lips, was William Potter, a big lieutenant who, like Uriah, was assigned to the Navy Yard while awaiting a new assignment.

Uriah nodded to him in a friendly way and murmured, "I beg your pardon, Lieutenant."

Potter continued to stare at him for a moment and then said loudly, "I hope to God you're a better navigator aboard ship than you are on the dancing floor!"

Uriah's face reddened. Other dancers turned at the sound of Potter's voice.

"I said I beg your pardon," Uriah replied, this time a bit louder. Then he turned and continued his dancing. He glanced at Anne, who smiled at him and raised her eyebrows in sympathy. Potter seemed to sway a bit, and it appeared that he was well on his way to being drunk.

The orchestra had played barely another bar of the lilting Polish tune when Uriah again was shoved from behind, this time hard enough to knock him off balance. He stopped dancing this time and again turned. Potter stood before him, grinning happily.

Uriah could sense what was coming. The last thing he wanted

was to create a nasty scene before this audience of leading citizens and especially before Anne. But he wondered if it could be avoided. Potter was seeking trouble, and Potter was one of those who was angry with him over Anne Stahr, for he had been one of the rejected escorts for this evening.

"I have begged your pardon once," Uriah said firmly. "I will not beg it again. I trust that you will watch your step and that it will not happen a third time."

Potter's grin vanished. His face went white. His voice exploded in an angry bellow that silenced all other sounds on the dancing floor, "Why, you damned cowardly Jew, why don't you get out of here? You're a disgrace to that uniform!"

The dancing had stopped. Everyone had turned to watch the drama. In another confused second, the orchestra had ceased playing.

Uriah saw a red mist before his eyes. A searing, consuming fury filled his brain. His stomach contracted as if it were gripped by a giant hand.

From somewhere behind him, he heard Anne's soft, urgent voice: "Uriah, please, ignore him. He's a drunken boor. Let's leave now, Uriah!"

He did not turn away from Potter. He heard himself speak and was surprised that his voice sounded so calm and controlled: "Sir, that I am a Jew I neither deny nor regret. If I am a coward, that fact was not made known to the enemy in the late war. And as to this uniform, I do not besmirch it with drunken insults as you do now."

There were low murmurs of approval from the crowd. Potter laughed loudly, as if Uriah's response had been ridiculous. Then he shouted again, "You damned Jew, you don't belong here! Go peddle your clothes!" He had barely uttered the last words when Uriah stepped forward and slapped Potter resoundingly across the mouth. A startled "Ooh!" went up from the witnesses.

Another lieutenant stepped to Potter's side. "You're drunk, Bill," he said. "Let's clear out of here."

Potter spoke again, and this time his voice was measured: "My second will call upon you tomorrow," he said to Uriah. "You'll pay with your life for this insult."

"Uriah, please!" Anne was pulling hard at Uriah's arm. He turned and walked with her toward the door, the crowd falling back to make an aisle for them.

The same lieutenant who had accompanied Potter to the ball would be his chief second. He appeared before Uriah at the Navy Yard in midmorning and told him that Potter still demanded satisfaction and had issued a challenge.

"The man obviously was drunk and carried a grudge against me," Uriah said. "I am willing to overlook his insults if he wishes to consider the incident closed."

The second shook his head. "You struck him in public, Sailing Master. He has every right to demand satisfaction, and he does. Do you refuse to meet him on the field of honor?"

"Of course not. I fear no man. I accept his challenge."

Uriah had no desire to duel this man or any other man. He always had regarded dueling deaths as a terrible waste of lives, sacrifices to moments of heat and anger, moments that otherwise would be quickly forgotten. But he also knew that the code of honor had special meaning for American military officers. It was a long and respected tradition. An officer who refused a challenge would be branded throughout the service as a coward. He had not slept the night before, knowing that this challenge would be hurled at him in the morning. He was afraid, though he had great confidence in his own skill with a pistol. But he had not for a moment considered refusing the challenge. That would be unthinkable.

The second continued with the arrangements: "Your choice of weapons, Sailing Master?"

"I select pistols."

"Very well. On the Camden grounds at dawn tomorrow, if that is satisfactory. Here is my card. Please have your second contact me today and we will conclude the arrangements. Good day, Sailing Master."

Who should he ask to serve as his friend? Uriah tried to think, while his head began to fill with tactics for the duel. He sat down, took a breath, and forced himself to slow up, to consider with care.

He settled, after running down a long mental list of friends and relatives, on Aaron Marks, a big young merchant with whom he had become friends over the last months. Aaron was cool under pressure and was no stranger to pistols. He would see well enough to Uriah's interests. He left the Navy Yard to seek Aaron out.

In late afternoon, Aaron came to him to report. "It is all set, Uriah," he said solemnly. "Dawn tomorrow on the Camden side, in the oak grove. Pistols at twelve paces. By the way, be sure to wear a black stock and cravat so you won't show any linen. That will make it harder for his aim. Is there anything more I can do for you now?"

Uriah shook his head. "No, Aaron, thank you. Just hold this to yourself, please. I do not want my mother or my brothers and sisters to know of it. If I fall, they'll know soon enough. And if I am lucky, I'll tell them in my own time and my own way."

"Very well, my friend. You can count on me. I'll come by for you just before light tomorrow. I'll have a boat arranged and someone to row us across the river. Try to get some sleep tonight."

At that, Uriah could not refrain from a smile. *Sleep? Did any man sleep the night before a duel, knowing that there was a half-chance that tonight would be his last?* No, he did not expect to sleep. But he would have long, quiet hours in his bed to think about his life and the many hopes that he still held for the rest of it.

It was cold and damp under the tall oaks on the Jersey shore of the river. A thin dawn mist lent a sense of tranquility. Here men came often to kill each other, knowing they would not be hampered. In Penn's land, back across the gray-brown water, the laws against dueling were taken more seriously and strictly enforced.

Uriah and his second walked slowly across the marshy ground toward the clearing—the well-known dueling ground—a hundred yards in from the riverbank. They adjusted their steps to match the pace of Potter and his second, who walked in similar fashion a few hundred feet to their right. They would see to it that they arrived at the ground at the same time, for it was considered ungentlemanly and a violation of the code to keep one's opponent waiting.

A doctor with a bag of instruments stepped out from under the trees. Uriah recognized him as a navy surgeon from the yard. He wondered idly whether Potter and his second had solicited the surgeon to be here. And would he minister only to Potter and perhaps allow Uriah to lie bleeding to death? Or was he a dispassionate observer, willing to tend anyone needing his skills?

Uriah swallowed once or twice in an effort to get some moisture into his mouth. He licked his lips. *So this is what it was like to stand and face death head-on?* He often had wondered how it felt and how he would stand up to it. Now he was experiencing it. He was surprised that he felt almost nothing—certainly no abject fear or panic. He was strangely calm, though he could feel his heart pounding.

Following Aaron's suggestion, he had dressed in dark clothing. His black stock and cravat were complemented by dark brown trousers. He even wore black gloves so that Potter would have nothing light to help his eye. A quick glance across the grove had shown him that his opponent was dressed in much the same way.

They reached the clearing and stopped. Potter and his friend were halted at the opposite side. Then Lieutenant Morse, Potter's second, came striding over to them. Aaron opened the case of pistols he was carrying and displayed the two weapons in their velvet beds.

"The pistols are fully loaded, sir," Aaron said to the lieutenant. "Would you like me to draw out the charges so you may inspect?"

"That will not be necessary, sir," Morse said, impatience in his tone.

Aaron then produced a small canister of powder and carefully filled each priming pan as Morse watched. As the last of the powder went into the second pan, Aaron looked at Morse. "Is that satisfactory, sir?" he asked. Upon receiving a nod in answer, he continued, "Then please take your choice of weapons, sir." Morse selected one of the pistols, turned, and carried it to Potter. In accordance with custom, neither duelist had looked directly at the other since arriving here at the ground. Each combatant stood off to one side and stared off into the distance, leaving the morbid details to the seconds.

Marks and Morse then stepped off the twelve paces. Each second then went to his principal and brought him to the proper place. For the first time since their dancing floor encounter, the two duelists looked into each other's face. Uriah was expressionless. Potter was red-faced, obviously still angry. His mouth was working.

"Gentlemen," Morse announced, "all is prepared. It is my duty to ask you now, before any action, whether it is not possible to compose your differences and thereby prevent the possible loss of life and shedding of blood?"

Uriah made no response. It was not up to him. Potter first shook his head and then replied loudly, "Never! I will avenge his insult. I will have this Jew's head, I promise!"

"Very well then," said Morse. "Please turn your backs." The duelists faced in opposite directions. "I will say loudly, 'One . . . two . . . three . . . Fire!' On the command to fire, you will turn and fire as you are ready. Is that clear?" Hearing no question or objection, he walked slowly to the side.

In those last seconds, as he stood waiting for the portentous voice to begin its count, Uriah quickly whispered the words of the *Shema*. As they filtered through his lips, he desperately tried to remember what else Aaron had drummed into him on the boat coming across the dark, steamy river. Be sure to turn your shoulder toward him to cut down his target area. *What else? Damn it, what else?*

Even in the damp grass, he could hear—perhaps he imagined it—the soft footsteps as Morse walked out of the line of fire. There were several seconds of silence. Then: "One . . . two . . . three . . . Fire!"

Uriah swung quickly round and raised his pistol. He pointed his right shoulder at Potter, giving him only a side silhouette at which to aim. He had just found Potter at the tip of his pistol's barrel when he heard a bang. A puff of gray-blue smoke burst from Potter's weapon. The red-faced lieutenant obviously had fired from the hip at the instant he had whirled around. His aim was very bad, and Uriah neither heard the ball sing as it passed by nor did he feel its wind.

Uriah took a deep breath. Potter stood squarely in front of him, waiting, his empty pistol hanging uselessly in his hand. Uriah looked at him for a long moment, then slowly raised his barrel and fired into the air.

The seconds came running up, along with a hard-eyed Philadelphia lawyer—a veteran duelist—who had been appointed referee by consent of both sides. After a quick glance at the combatants, the referee loudly proclaimed, "Neither gentleman has been struck."

Potter was enraged. "Damn it, man," he screamed to Morse, "bring me some powder and a cartridge! I need to reload!" Morse walked to his valise and prepared to comply.

Aaron Marks stepped forward. "One moment, Lieutenant!" he said, sharply. "My principal has stood your principal's fire, and he has deliberately fired his own pistol into the air. Honor has been satisfied. Both parties must now leave the ground."

"Oh no, oh no!" shouted Potter. "I demand satisfaction. Reload, Jew, or I shall brand you a coward throughout Philadelphia and the navy as well!"

Marks spoke then to Lieutenant Morse, for Potter obviously was too hysterical to make the decision. "Morse, you know full well—or should—that the code calls for the parties to leave the ground. Your principal had his shot and missed. It was not returned. Is he to be given opportunity after opportunity? Let us be done with this."

Morse nodded but did not reply. He knew well enough that the code provided that a duelist must be satisfied when his life has thus been spared and must agree that the affair is over.

"Let him have his shot. Let him shoot until doomsday for all I care!"

They all turned to face Uriah, who until now had said nothing after the shots were fired. He had no more desire to shoot again or to be shot at again than he had the first time. But he realized that this matter must somehow be resolved or there would be no end of it.

The pistols quickly were reloaded. The duelists were replaced on their measured positions. The instructions were repeated. The entire charade began again with Marks this time droning out the commands and then the order to fire.

Again Potter took no chance on being the second to fire. He whirled immediately and crouched slightly, pulling his trigger as he bent his knees. The bang and the puff of smoke were followed almost instantly by a high whine above Uriah's head as if the fastest insect ever created by God had just flown past. The ball had been closer this time; its buzzing song had testified to that, but it was well high. *Tit for tat*, he thought to himself. He took careful aim this time and fired just above Potter's head.

The combatants and their seconds met in the middle. Potter loudly demanded a third round. Marks protested furiously, but Uriah again agreed. The reloading proceeded, and the duelists returned to their places.

"Have done with it," Marks pleaded with Uriah as he handed him the pistol. "At least wound him this time, for if you do not, he will surely kill you. No matter how poor a shooter he is, he will kill you if you keep giving him more chances. End this thing, Uriah. End it now!"

At the command to fire, Potter raised his pistol more carefully than before and took aim. Down the barrel, he saw Uriah slowly raise his own pistol and bring it to bear on the target. The mouth of the pistol gaped like a cavern and it seemed to point right between his eyes. Potter became unnerved. He forgot that he must slowly squeeze his own trigger and instead rapidly jerked it.

The ball sang a louder tune this time, and Uriah felt a stinging pain in his right ear. He knew he had escaped death once more, but he had felt its hot touch. This could not continue.

Uriah fired his pistol, and Potter jumped backward as if hit by a club. Then, a confused expression on his face, he crumpled to the ground.

The surgeon hurried to the prone figure, followed by the referee and the seconds. The surgeon hastily examined Potter. Then he sat back on his haunches, looked up at those gathered around him, and announced, "This man is dead."

Uriah stood alone, rooted to the spot from which he had fired. His arms hung limply at his side, the pistol still smoking in his hand. He shook his head, wondering if he had heard correctly. Waves of nausea swept over him.

Marks came to him and put his arm about his shoulder. "Come, Uriah, let's return to the boat. It's all over. Let's leave this place."

Uriah looked forlornly at him. "I killed him and I didn't even intend to. I sought only to hit him in the leg. What a stupid way for a man to die: by a mistaken aim. Stupid. Stupid."

The pistol still hung, unnoticed, in his hand. He walked with Marks back across the marshy bank to the waiting skiff.

Commodore Murray stroked his chin and assumed the mien of a prophet who was about to issue a pronouncement. "Bear in mind this word of advice, Sailing Master: If ever again you fight a duel, choose an opponent with no family to avenge him, else you never will be free of challenges."

This was said in jest, but he looked across at Uriah and saw no trace of a responsive smile.

"Ah, Sailing Master, just a small joke and I apologize for it. I can see you are troubled by the aftermath of your encounter at Camden, and I understand your feelings. A duel is never pleasant, even for the survivor, as I know full well. Who is it that has challenged you now, an uncle of Potter?"

"No sir, a cousin. He demands satisfaction for his cousin's death. I don't wish to fight him, but I will, rather than be branded as afraid."

"Yes. Yes, of course. Of course you are ready to answer the challenge. But this becomes ridiculous, doesn't it? Do you know this cousin? Have you ever offended him?"

"I have never met him, sir."

"As I thought. Very well. I will not allow my young officers to become targets for every hothead in Philadelphia. I have composed this order to you, Sailing Master, and I expect it to be obeyed. I shall read it to you and then I expect you to carry it upon your person until the day when your ship sails and you no longer are assigned to me." He cleared his throat with an ear-splitting rasp, then pulled a sheet of paper from a pile of documents at the side of his huge desk and began to read:

Navy Yard, June 25, 1816

Sir—It having been notified to me, that a challenge has been sent to you by some unknown person, I, as commanding navy officer on this station, command you not to notice it, in any manner, at your peril. The recent affair that you have been involved in, ought to guard you against similar transactions; and if repeated by you whilst under my command, you must abide the consequences.

Your most obedient, A. Murray

The commodore folded the document and handed it across the desk to Uriah, who rose from his chair to receive it.

"Bear in mind, Sailing Master," the commodore said, the ends of his mouth curling down as if in emphasis, "that this order is both a direction to desist from accepting the challenge of this excited cousin and also a warning that I don't want you becoming bloated with your success and getting into constant scrapes. You are enjoying some acclaim, I gather. Even the newspapers have saluted you for striking down a bully who would not accept an honorable compromise. Very well, then. But do not make a habit of it, sir. It will not go well with you, if you do."

"Sir, I abhor dueling. I fought Potter because I could avoid it only at the expense of my honor and that was too high a price to pay. I do not love killing, Commodore, and I won't seek such adventures in the future, I promise you. But in fairness, I must add: If my bravery is questioned and my religion insulted by some other poltroon, I will respond to that as I did to Potter. I have no intention of turning my back and running."

"Understood, sir. Understood."

"May I ask, Commodore, will I receive punishment from the navy because of the duel? The man that I killed was, after all, a navy lieutenant. Obviously the navy has taken notice of the affair."

"Obviously," said Murray, dryly. "I have conducted my own investigation at the request of the Navy Department. The facts were quite plain; there was no difference in the testimony of the eyewitnesses. You did not seek the fight and you fired twice into the air in an effort to end it honorably, without the shedding of blood. I hold you blameless, Sailing Master, and have so reported to Washington City."

"Thank you, Commodore. That's a great relief to me. I wish the civil authorities were so understanding."

"They are bringing action against you? For what?"

"The officials in Jersey have taken no notice of the affair. It would seem that Pennsylvania officials would have no jurisdiction. But they are planning, I am told, to bring charges against me of challenging to fight a duel, though of course I issued no such challenge. I am told it will be taken to the grand jury."

"I see. Well, keep me informed of the situation." Murray looked grave and again stroked his chin. "Things will work out, Sailing Master. Life will appear much brighter to you in a few months, when all this has been cleared away."

"I hope so, Commodore. I surely hope so."

Uriah stretched his arms and yawned widely. *Lord, what a bore!* Sunday morning aboard a beached battleship. Nothing could be more quiet or tranquil . . . or utterly deadly in its silent idleness. He looked over the port bulwarks at the Navy Yard. Even the usually bustling docks were empty, barren in the pink glow that promised another hot day.

His watch as officer of the deck was almost over. In a few minutes, he would hear the big feet of Ben Page pound up the aft hatchway ladder and then the broad shoulders would fly into view and Ben would stride aft to relieve him. Ben had the knack of remaining in the wardroom or in his cabin until the last possible fraction of a second, then of racing madly to the quarterdeck or other assigned station and arriving there just as the last grains ran out of the sand glass. It had become almost a sport among the officers of the *Franklin* to test Ben's mettle, but he never was known to be late for duty. Or early.

So it was on this vacant, drowsy Sunday morning. Uriah edged closer to the glass and made a game of it. Just as the last clump of grains dipped into the slot, the pounding was heard from the hatch and then Ben's big form was charging across the quarterdeck.

"I relieve you, Sailing Master," he announced, the usual wide grin on his face.

"I thank you, sir," responded Uriah. "The deck is yours."

"What goeth, Uriah? Enemy frigates sighted? A pirate squadron cruising up the Delaware? How many times were we called to quarters during the night? I must have slept through all the action."

"Lieutenant, I have visited cemeteries where there was more action than on this deck last night. Another few weeks on the beach and they'll have to teach us again which are the guns and which the masts."

"One of these days, Uriah, we'll sail down the bay in all our glory, every rag set to the stun'sails, and we'll terrorize the world with our awesome might."

"I just hope I'll not yet be old and feeble when that day finally comes. Now, with your permission, Lieutenant, I'll go below and have myself a spot of breakfast."

"Permission granted, Second Sailing Master. Mind the coffee, though. It tastes worse than grapeshot this morning."

Uriah smiled and shook his head as he went down the ladder. One of the consolations of this long, tedious stretch of port duty while the *Franklin* finished her preparations for an extended cruise was the good fellowship of the officers. They were a fine bunch and skilled seamen all. Captain Stewart was known throughout the navy as a tough fighter who would show the enemy no quarter, but also as a fair, if demanding, commanding officer. And the other officers—Charlie Morgan, the first luff; Ben Page; Frank Smith; Sam Magunder; the other lieutenants; Kearney the surgeon; Barstow the first master—all were able, pleasant men. They had become his comrades, and he had begun to think of them with the loyalty and emotion he still kept for his old mates of the *Argus*. If he had any problem on the *Franklin*, it was with the several marine officers. They were cold and unfriendly to him. He had the feeling that they had conspired to be sullen to him, though he knew that was foolish. He had had no trouble with any of them. Their duties were separate enough that their contact was limited. Yet each of them seemed to go out of his way to ignore him and to avoid conversing with him. He sighed as he descended the last few rungs of the ladder to the berth deck. He wouldn't worry about it. He would do his own job. Everything else would take care of itself.

The wardroom tables were a mess, filled with the soiled plates and crumpled napkins of earlier breakfasts. Two mess boys walked slowly about the cabin, stopping now and then to clear away some rubbish, but mostly conversing in low tones with each other. The room was empty save for a table over at the side, at which sat Lieutenants Bond and Cooper of the marines, who were talking over the last of their coffee. They glanced at Uriah as he entered the wardroom, looked at each other for a moment, then resumed their talk. Uriah sat alone at a table across the room and prepared to place an order for his breakfast.

After several minutes, no one had come to clear his table of its litter or to see what he would have to eat. Uriah called over to one of the loafing boys: "Mess boy, clear away these dirty dishes, can't you?"

The two boys gave each other an irritated look and started toward his table. Then Lieutenant Bond stood up and called out, "Stop, you boys, I gave you no order! Mr. Levy, I will thank you to let the boys alone. You have nothing to do with the tables being set for breakfast. I am the caterer."

Uriah saw that this could blossom into an ugly incident if it went on. But he had to stand his ground. There was no call for Bond to speak to him in this manner in front of the mess boys.

"Lieutenant, I simply ordered the boys to clear this table. As you see, it is filthy with trash. I said nothing to them about breakfast. You are presumptuous, sir, in dictating what I should do."

Bond took several quick strides and stopped a few feet from Uriah. "Nothing to do with breakfast, you say? Why, you are a damned liar!"

His instincts almost led Uriah to swing his fist into Bond's mouth. But he checked himself, remembering Commodore Murray's stern warning against getting into another situation that might lead to a challenge. He was in enough trouble, as it was, over the Potter affair. What could he do? Back down? He could feel the heat in his face and knew it was red with fury and shame. The mess boys stared at him, openmouthed, waiting to see what he would do.

"Sir," he said in measured tones, "do I understand that you tell me I lie?"

Bond smiled. "I repeat myself, sir: You are a damned liar!"

"Well, Lieutenant, I return you the compliment. You, sir, are a liar of the worst stripe and you are no gentleman!"

Bond now was within inches of Uriah, and the two angry men stood, staring into each other's eyes, their fists clenched. Cooper came hurrying over, ready to pry them apart if they came to blows.

"How dare you insult your better, Levy!" Bond said evenly, the trace of a smile still on his lip. "You will hear more of this, you rascal! And I warn you not to order these boys about any further, for if you do, I will countermand it."

"I'll order the boys whenever I please."

"You'll look damned foolish if you do, for they will not obey you."

"Bond, I have as much right to give orders to the boys as you or any other officer on this ship. They had *better* obey me, or I'll know the reason why not!"

"Levy, you will pay for this insolence. It's just what we expect from your kind. But you will pay for it."

Bond turned to Cooper. "You are my witness to this insolence and insubordination. Come on, let's find the first luff." Without another glance at Uriah, they left the wardroom. He heard their feet climbing the hatchway ladder.

"Boy, come here now and clean this table as I told you!" The two mess boys, realizing that this angry man was not to be further trifled with, hurried to his table and began to clear it, their arms and legs moving like frightened sticks.

Uriah sat and stared miserably at the wardroom bulkhead. *Now what?* It had been a quiet morning and had boded nothing more than another boring, uneventful day. Suddenly, with no warning, with no provocation of which he was aware, this hostility had exploded upon him. He sighed. His appetite, lusty when he had come below, was gone.

The joint court-martial of Lieutenant Francis A. Bond of the U.S. Marine Corps and Sailing Master Uriah P. Levy of the U.S. Navy was on mutually preferred charges of ungentlemanly and unofficer-like conduct and behavior. It was held on a blistering hot afternoon in the great cabin of the ship-of-the-line *Franklin*, which still rested at its accustomed berth at the Navy Yard wharf in Philadelphia.

The cabin was like a stifling closet. The air was heavy and oppressive and didn't move a whit, although every available window had been thrown open. Even in the shaded cabin, the air seemed to burn as if afire. Sweat beaded the angry brow of Captain Charles Stewart, commanding officer of the *Franklin*, who was clearly irritated at having to serve as trial officer for this hearing.

"This is ridiculous nonsense, this business," he grunted softly to an aide, "and I will make short shrift of it. These two petulant boys can settle their dispute without forcing me to choke here for lack of air. Lord, what a tempest in a teapot. And mighty hot tea, at that."

Testimony of the principals and the witnesses was brief and to the point; Captain Stewart saw to that. There was little dispute as to the facts of the exchange between Bond and Levy. The sailing master claimed he was innocent of any wrongdoing and had been surprised by the sudden verbal assault upon him. Bond, when he testified, accused Levy of interfering in the operation of the mess and of insulting and branding as a liar an officer of the ship.

The testimony was completed and all were beginning to taste the cold ale that awaited them at a wharfside tavern. Sailing Master Levy, however, requested permission to make a closing statement to the court. Captain Stewart made little effort to conceal his groan of displeasure. "Mr. Levy, must you?" he said. The sailing master requested the court's indulgence and said he had a statement to get into the record. He took out a thick paper document, the product of hours of sweaty labor, and began to read. Captain Stewart mopped his damp face with a kerchief and raised his eyes to heaven for relief.

"I do not mean to offer this paper as a defense," Uriah began, "but to expose the motives and cause of my conduct. . . . The offense offered to me by Lieutenant Bond was of so violent a character and without excuse, yet I did not proceed hostilely to complain of it. I did believe that when reflection occurred, whatever cause produced it, he would have done or said something to have soothed my violated feelings. But no. His temper was unyielding and the offer of a mutual friend to effect an accommodation on honorable terms was presented to him and rejected. . . ."

The members of the court tried their level best to listen attentively to the long closing argument of the sailing master, but the heat and swamplike humidity made this almost impossible. Their victory was in keeping awake despite supreme temptation. Captain Stewart appeared almost in a stupor, his face red, his mouth open to catch any vagrant breeze.

At length, the sailing master finally having subsided, the members of the court retired to weigh the testimony and arguments. Their deliberations were brief, but they remained a bit longer than necessary to breathe deeply of the fresh air on the quarterdeck. Then, after a hasty stop at the scuttle for a drink of water, they returned to the cabin.

Captain Stewart sat behind his desk, cleared his throat, and announced the verdict:

"After making deliberation on the testimony adduced, and the defense of the accused, the court finds Lieutenant Francis A. Bond of the Marine Corps and Sailing Master Uriah P. Levy guilty of the charge and sentences them both to be reprimanded by the Honorable Secretary of the Navy."

As both defendants stood with faces showing irritation and disappointment, Captain Stewart hastily declared the court-martial at an end. The members of the court and their aides vacated the cabin in seconds and showed undue haste in hurrying across the wharf to the tavern for the glasses of ale and chilled cider beer that had been crazing their minds all the long afternoon.

The following day, when he was accosted by a midshipman and told that he should report immediately to the captain on the quarterdeck, Uriah was sure that now the hammer finally would fall. This was what he had feared all during the long, sleepless night that now left him groggy and eye-heavy. Captain Stewart would tell him that his conviction rendered him unfit to serve on the *Franklin* and he must take to the beach immediately and seek another berth.

When he got to the quarterdeck, the captain was standing near the wheel and gazing up. He looked inordinately pleased about something.

"Look there, Mr. Levy," he said as Uriah came before him and raised his hat in salute. "Look at the cut of that new mizzen topsail. Isn't that a true work of art? We've got our best suit on her today, at long last. We'll set them one by one and have a look. I want you to study them and let me know what you think."

"Aye, aye, sir."

The captain continued to study the mizzen topsail, watching it grab strongly for the wind in spite of being triple reefed. Uriah stood nearby in puzzlement, wondering if he had been dismissed. What about the expected order to depart the ship? Could it be that . . . ?

"Oh, Mr. Levy." The captain turned to him again and Uriah felt his heart beating with a thud. Now it would come. "As to the proceedings in the cabin yesterday, I wouldn't let it disturb me if I were you. Happens to the best of us. You wouldn't be much of a sailor without a reprimand or two in your official file. God knows, I have more than my share in mine. Don't take it too seriously. If I were you, I'd make it a point to avoid Lieutenant Bond for a time. He's a bit of a prig, but a decent sort. He'll cool down eventually and it will be forgotten. I expect good things of both of you when we get to sea, so don't let this cause any lasting hard feeling between you."

Uriah felt jubilation rush through his body like a cooling torrent.

"Then, sir, if I may be so bold as to ask: You are saying that this finding of guilty and the official reprimand . . . they will not do any harm to my hopes for a career in the navy? They will not be held against me?"

Stewart laughed loudly. "Oh, Lord no. God, if I was on an evaluation board, I'd be mighty suspicious of a sailor without at least one reprimand. Shows a lack of gumption in my book. No, no. As a matter of fact, Mr. Levy, this reminds me of something I had been meaning to tell you. Are you aware that the navy has a new policy that states that sailing masters of extraordinary merit and for extraordinary services may be promoted to the rank of lieutenant?"

"No sir, I was not aware."

"Yes. Well, it has just taken effect. Caused a big storm, don't you know. Older midshipmen are protesting that the new rule will retard their own chances for promotion. They're angry as hell about it."

"Sir, do you suggest that I might be considered for commission as lieutenant under this new rule?"

"I suggest that very thing, Mr. Levy. You created a fine record in your service on the *Argus*, and you conducted yourself with honor during your imprisonment by the enemy. I have been impressed by your seamanship during our months together on the *Franklin*.

I think you have a chance. I would encourage you to apply, and I would endorse such application."

"Captain, I am deeply grateful. I had no idea. I had thought that the best I could aspire to was a career as sailing master. This opens a whole new world of possibility for me. I will apply at once!"

"Do that, Mr. Levy, do that. And luck to you!"

It clearly was the house of a victorious warrior. On the wall, in frames of dark wood, were the gleaming presentation swords Commodore Stephen Decatur had received from his grateful government. The spoils of victory were everywhere: magnificent paintings of the *United States* and its vanquished foe, the *Macedonian*. Paintings of the *President*, the *Guerierre*, the *Chesapeake* . . . even a fire-lit view of the doomed *Philadelphia*, which he had destroyed so long ago. Ship models filled the room in which Uriah sat waiting, so many of them that he did not have time to identify them all.

In the moments since the footsteps of the servant had receded down the hallway, Uriah had been sitting in this fantastic museum of a library and looking around him in awe. *With his prize money and his gifts,* Uriah thought to himself, *a navy commander is really not so badly off. So long, that is, as he wins.*

"Sailing Master Levy! How good of you to call!" Decatur's voice was just as Uriah remembered it from their last meeting in Philadelphia before the war: low-pitched, rather quiet . . . yet somehow incisive and penetrating. It was the kind of voice that could pierce the conversation of a crowd and cause all others to fall silent, to hear what this commanding figure might have to say.

The commodore walked into the room and extended his hand. He wore civilian clothes, a black coat over pearl-gray pantaloons. He looked much the same as before, the only sign of age being some wrinkles about his eyes. His hair and beard still were dark and showed no gray. His intense black eyes burned in a face that hinted at paleness despite the dark coloring.

"I am honored, Commodore, that you would remember me and allow me to call," Uriah replied.

"Sit down, sit down. Make yourself comfortable, Uriah. It has been a long time since our last meeting. Seems to me that Charlie Stewart was with us when we last talked. Am I correct?"

"Yes, Commodore. You introduced me to Captain Stewart in a coffeehouse in Philadelphia. And now he is my commander on the *Franklin*."

Decatur smiled. "Yes, I know. I read his report on your recent, ah, altercation with some mulish marine lieutenant. Ah, those damned marines. Clumping around the decks with their heavy boots and waking up all the sleepers on the berth deck below. We sailors have to live with 'em, but we don't have to like 'em, eh, Levy? Ah, but they're good fighters . . . at least, most of them."

The servant returned then with a silver tray bearing glasses and a magnificent crystal decanter of claret. Uriah seldom drank, but he took a glass and sipped slowly.

"Whatever happened with that duel you fought last year in Philly?" Decatur asked. "I heard that they were bringing you to trial on some fool charge or another."

Uriah was amazed that Decatur was aware of his troubles. Of course, the navy was a great conduit for gossip, especially among the officers stationed at various American navy yards and harbors. But still, he couldn't believe that his own scrape had come to the ears of this famous commodore.

"It all ended well, sir, I'm glad to report. I was quickly found not guilty by a jury after all the facts had been given—the fact that the other man challenged me, and also that I tried to avoid killing him by firing in the air. A group of Philadelphia citizens submitted a petition to the attorney general on my behalf and this was shown to the jury."

"Well, that's good. Good. As for me, I would welcome a duel these days if it would bring a little excitement into my life. God, I would give anything to get to sea again! I thirst for the taste of salt in my throat. Instead I sit here like a plutocrat in my mansion on

Presidents' Square. Oh, we commissioners live well, my friend. Porter has 150 acres and a huge house on a hill above the city. Rodgers has a small castle on Greenleaf Point with slaves running all over the place. At least he lives within view of the Navy Yard and can look from his house and imagine himself on a quarterdeck again."

"I have heard so much of these men, Commodore. Of course, I'll be meeting all of them in two days."

"Ah yes, yes! You're applying for a lieutenancy. And you'll be coming before us in two days, you say? Well, never fear, our examinations haven't killed anyone yet. You'll survive." He paused and smiled knowingly. "You want to know your chances of success, eh, my friend? Well, I should say they are quite good so long as you answer respectfully and don't make any hideous mistakes when you are asked a few simple-minded questions."

"Of course, sir. I understand."

Decatur glanced at him and touched a small napkin to his lips. "One thing, Levy. A small warning. A remark or two that I have heard—from whom is not important—seems to indicate that you are gaining a reputation in the navy as a hothead, a bit of a troublemaker. Now, most of the good fighting men I have known have had similar reputations, so it's nothing to be ashamed about. But I caution you: You should expect to encounter some difficulties now and then on the basis of this reputation. Some commanders will have you under severe scrutiny from the moment you first set foot on their deck. If you cough too loudly some night, they will take it as an insult and have you up on charges."

"Sir, this report is deeply disturbing to me. I have done nothing to merit such repute. I fought a duel that was forced upon me. I did not intend to kill the man. And the court-martial was the result of insults that I had not earned and that no man of honor would sit quietly and accept."

"Levy, I do not argue your facts. I only tell you what I have heard. To be forewarned is to be forearmed."

"Yes, sir. I will bear your words in mind."

"Have you any other concern that I can help you with?" Decatur asked. Uriah got the impression that the interview was being brought to a close. "Or did you merely wish to pay a social call on me?"

"Well, Commodore, there was a reason for this call. I hesitate to bother you with this, but I have petitioned the Department numerous times and my requests go unheeded."

"Yes?"

"Sir, I have been assigned to the *Franklin* for almost a year. Except for a few cruises down the river and a couple of short sea trials, we have done nothing but sit at the Philadelphia Yard and tinker with the rigging and with the load plan and try on new suits of sail. Sir, I too am desperate to get to sea. I did not join the navy to serve my years on the beach. Can you do anything to get me on a ship that will be cruising?"

"You're not alone, Levy. I hear such complaints all the time. We are at peace, and the government once again has lost its concern for the navy. A few vessels are cruising, but most are tied up at one yard or another. Our officers and men are growing restive, but what can we do? Congress says the money cannot be found right now, but give them time and they'll scratch it up somewhere.

"Levy, my advice to you is to stay where you are. You're on a good ship with a fine commander. The *Franklin* is having some problems getting tuned up—Charlie has kept me well informed of them—but they will be solved. All of us are like flies stuck in a bowl of molasses, Levy. It is an effort to take even a single step. But we must keep trying. Stay with the *Franklin*, Levy. You will be walking a wet deck again soon, I promise you."

Decatur walked him to the door, a courtesy that Uriah appreciated. He, a sailing master lacking even commissioned rank, was being shown the deference due an honored guest by this world-famous hero.

"As to your impatience with your own lot, Mr. Levy," Decatur said at the door after they had shaken hands, "I repeat my advice: Keep your confidence in Charlie Stewart and you won't be sorry. He will not fail you."

The interview on his request for a lieutenancy was over. It had been so brief, so lacking in any drama, that Uriah felt somewhat let down. He was, however, entirely pleased with the outcome. He had not written a speech. He had been expressly told that such would be neither requested nor permitted. He had collected words and thoughts in his head so as to be prepared to deliver, if circumstances warranted, a stirring remark on his love for his country and its navy and upon his determination to devote his life to those causes. He must admit, now that it was over, that he had been looking forward to offering these sentiments and to the warm approbation that he knew would follow.

But there had been no opportunity for stirring professions of patriotism. The interview had been desultory, wholly routine. The three vaunted members of the Board of Commissioners— Commodores Porter, Rodgers, and Decatur—appeared entirely bored with the proceedings and anxious to bring them to a conclusion, as the noon hour was rapidly approaching. A few questions were put to him about his service on the *Argus* and his recent months aboard the *Franklin*. And that was all.

A certificate of good conduct from Commodore Murray in Philadelphia also was submitted, along with two letters of endorsement, one from Captain Charles Stewart and the other from the officers of the *Franklin*.

The three commodores conferred briefly and privately. Then Commodore Rodgers, president of the Board of Commissioners, announced, "Thank you, Sailing Master. You have presented yourself well. We shall convey our recommendation to Secretary Crowninshield and you will be notified by him. This hearing is adjourned."

Everyone in the hearing room rose in respect. Just before the commissioners departed by a side door, Uriah glanced over to Decatur, who sat at Rodgers's left. The commodore returned his glance, and his face broke into a broad smile. Uriah fought to keep a smile of exultation from spreading on his own face.

As Uriah walked alone down the front steps of the Navy Building, calculating in his head the probable cost of a new lieutenant's dress uniform, he heard himself hailed.

"Uriah, you old rascal! You rogue of a sailing master, where have you been keeping yourself?"

He turned his head, looked down to the street's edge, and then raced forward with a glad roar: "Will Howard Allen, you ragtag! I'm glad to see you!"

The two old shipmates heartily shook hands and then enveloped each other in a warm bear hug. Will Howard was accompanied by another man, who stood aside, looking a bit nonplussed at the enthusiasm and noise of their reunion.

"Lord, Uriah, the last time I saw you, you had blue lips and were shaking so badly that your face looked a blur. I have thought of you often since and wondered when you finally were freed from the hell-hole."

"It was long enough at Dartmoor, Will Howard, long enough. I had enough months in prison to last me a lifetime, I assure you. What brings you to Washington City? Are you stationed here?"

"No, no. I am here to see a few people in the Department about finding a sea berth for me. I am rotting away on the beach. Damn me, I need to smell salt air again. Unfortunately, my so-called friends in high places seemed notably cool to my hopes this morning. They told me to wait my turn. Damned lubber clerks! And now I am showing gentle Ben here a bit of our national capital, such as it is. Oh Lord, I'm sorry about my manners. Ben, let me introduce you to Uriah Levy, a grand shipmate of mine on the *Argus* and a fellow sufferer at Dartmoor. Uriah, meet Ben Butler, aspiring attorney and my dashing brother-in-law."

Uriah shook hands with Butler, a handsome, rather regal young man with thin lips and a long aquiline nose.

"You look young to be a lawyer, Mr. Butler."

"I'm twenty-one years, Mr. Levy, and not quite a lawyer yet. I've been reading law with Martin Van Buren in Albany, and I plan to apply to the bar later this year. With luck, I'll be practicing with Mr. Van Buren."

"He looks entirely too young to be a husband, too," Will Howard said, as he threw his arm around young Butler's shoulder. "But my sister tells me that he is proving entirely adequate in that undertaking. And you, Uriah? Have you been captured yet by some beautiful young lady?"

Uriah smiled and shook his head. "Not yet. I have been agile and elusive. There was a time last year when I thought my day had come, but she tired of my indecision and feared my plans to go back to sea."

"Too bad, too bad. Come, Uriah, lunch with us! We'll have a bite at a restaurant and then take a carriage up to the Capitol. My young relative here is mad to see our esteemed Congress at work. I have warned him that one sight of that roomful of dunderheaded politicians will scar him for life, but he insists on seeing for himself. Why don't you join us?"

"Thank you, Will Howard, but I can't. I am taking the first coach back to Philadelphia. My mother is waiting anxiously to hear my news."

"Oh, what news is that?"

"I am applying for a lieutenancy. I appeared before the commissioners this morning. There was no decision, of course, but I think it looks good."

"Well, good for you! Lieutenant Levy, eh? You'll have your own frigate before we know it. I predict it. That's good news, Uriah, good news indeed. Come then, walk with us a way and give me a few moments at least to size you up again. In our careers, long separations are the rule, as you know, and it may be many years before we see one another again."

They walked slowly in the bracing, sun-filled air of this clear winter's day. They walked past the White House and up Pennsylvania Avenue. The sound of hammers rang out from the president's house as workmen completed the rebuilding that had begun after war's end. A gracious new mansion was coming into being from the dark ruin that had been left by the invading British. Meanwhile, President and Mrs. Madison had been forced to live for the past eighteen months in rented lodgings in the Seven Buildings at Pennsylvania and Nineteenth Street. Monroe, after his inauguration, also would reside in rented quarters until the White House was ready for him, probably sometime in the fall.

"Have you seen any of the *Argus* crew since we've been home?" Uriah asked as they walked along the side of the rut-filled avenue. The street was quiet at this midday hour; the government offices, which provided employment for almost all the local residents, were in session from 10 a.m. to 3 p.m., and there were few carriages rolling during these hours.

"Not since the Court of Inquiry," answered Will Howard. "I run into Inderwick the surgeon every now and then. But I never see the others."

"Tell me about the Court of Inquiry."

"Well, they sought a reason for the defeat of the *Argus*, but could come up with little answer except that the officers and men were mortally tired from our day and night pursuit of prizes. Did you know that the prizes taken by the *Argus* were valued at between two and three million dollars? It is a record almost unparalleled in warfare on the sea. Much of the hearing was consumed with the rumor of the wine. Had you heard about that?"

"I have heard people refer to it. I had no idea what they were talking about."

Allen shook his head angrily. "Somehow a rumor went about that we had captured a prize carrying a large quantity of fine Oporto wine just before we encountered the *Pelican*. And that our people had gotten into the wine and were too drunk to put up a decent fight. God, what rubbish! First of all, there was no such prize from Oporto. And anyone with even a small knowledge of Captain Allen and the discipline aboard his ship would know that no such debauchery would have been allowed. No, Uriah, there were no drunkards firing the *Argus*'s guns that fateful day. There were two other reasons for our defeat and these were no rumors."

"And those were—?"

"You may recall that, since we had used up a good bit of our powder on the cruise, the captain ordered us to take aboard a quantity of powder from one of our prizes that was bound to South America when we took her. Since the captured powder lay uppermost in our magazines, the gunner used it to fill a number of cylinders. Long after the *Pelican* battle, Will Watson learned that this captured powder had been defective. It had been condemned by the British Navy and was being shipped to South America for sale there. I was aware that our firing seemed to have very little effect on the *Pelican*. Now I know why."

"You mentioned *two* reasons for our defeat."

"The other, and perhaps the more significant, was the loss of the captain. When he fell to the deck and then was carried below . . . well, you could palpably feel the difference on the ship. Will Watson tried his best and God knows so did I when I took command. But the heart had gone from our men when they saw the captain fall. Oh, they went through the motions. There was little cowardice shown. But we were done for when we lost the captain."

"What a man he was," said Uriah.

"Aye. And the final irony of this tragic drama came after the war. The captain's brother applied to the government for the captain's proper share of prize money. Can you believe they turned him down?"

"No! In God's name, why?"

"They gave no reason. Our U.S. Senate, in its righteous wisdom, merely said no. These are the great men that lawyer-to-be Butler here is so anxious to see in their deliberations. Those fat fools!"

They had walked by now several hundred yards down The Avenue from the president's house. A small white-painted tavern across the road flew the black-and-white silhouette of a coach and team on a wooden sign nailed to a high pole.

"I must leave you here," Uriah said. "Across the way is the coach stop, and it should be here within the hour. But come visit me, Will Howard. Somehow we must not lose each other in time. And you, too, Ben. You are welcome at my home always."

"Luck to you, Uriah, keep the wind at your back!" Will Howard said, warmly embracing him once more.

As Uriah watched them continue down the avenue, a wave of sadness swept over him. God only knew when he would again see Will Howard or any other of his dear comrades from the *Argus*. He studied for a moment the white pattern of his breath upon the cold air. Then he ducked into the tavern to warm himself before the Philadelphia coach arrived.

12

Mediterranean Squadron, 1818

The wind was brisk from the starboard beam. The *Franklin* was close-hauled and pounding happily through the green sea, her head nodding rhythmically, as if in deference to the creaming waves crashing past her bows. They were south of Cape Gata now and driving easily through a part of the Mediterranean that Uriah had expected to be more troublesome.

If the wind stayed fair and remained abeam—the *Franklin's* best point of sailing—they likely would raise Syracuse harbor in Sicily several days earlier than the captain had estimated.

Uriah's eyes rose to the main top, where the broad pennant of a commodore floated regally. Viewing that streaming bougee gave pride to every man-jack aboard. It meant that their ship was a flagship, the vessel of a squadron commander. Captain Stewart had been named to command the U.S. Mediterranean Squadron and was now entitled to be called "Commodore Stewart" and to fly the broad pennant from his main. At Syracuse harbor, the ships of the squadron even now were assembling to await his arrival.

Uriah turned to the quartermaster at the helm. "Bring her two points farther off the wind," he commanded.

"Two points farther off the wind, sir," acknowledged the helmsman.

A voice spoke in his ear. "Mr. Levy, keep a good watch on those stuns'l booms lest we overstrain 'em. This wind is freshening." It was the commodore.

"Aye, aye, sir."

Uriah raised his hat in salute and moved toward the lee side of the quarterdeck as protocol required, but the commodore raised his hand and stopped him. "Stay, Mr. Levy," he said. "I would speak with you."

"Aye, aye, sir."

"My compliments to the first lieutenant," the commodore said, "and tell him, if you please, that I would like a scrub-hammock morning tomorrow. Those hammocks are looking darker every day. I begin to detect an aroma as I walk past the nettings. Let's clean 'em up."

"Aye, aye, sir. Shall I tell him now?"

"No, no. Just pass the word when next you see him."

Commodore Stewart took off his hat and let the wind freshen his light red hair. He cleared his throat and came to the point of what he wanted to discuss with Uriah.

"Mr. Levy, as you know, you are listed on our roll as a supernumerary because we did not have space in our regular complement for another lieutenant. You have been with me for well over a year now. Nonetheless, I am forced to list you among the extra officers I am carrying to stock the ships of the squadron when we reach Sicily."

"Yes sir, I am aware of that."

"I wish you could remain with the *Franklin*, Mr. Levy. You have served me well. But a complement is a complement, and the navy does not permit us to exceed the set number. So a supernumerary you must remain. When we reach rendezvous, I shall send you to another vessel in the squadron."

Uriah felt a tug of disappointment. He had hoped that one of the *Franklin*'s lieutenants might request a transfer and leave an opening for him. But it hadn't happened. He hated to leave the *Franklin*. He had formed bonds of friendship with his wardroom comrades, and he had deep respect for this captain. But this was life in the navy, and he had to accept whatever was handed to him.

"Have you decided upon my new berth, Commodore?"

"Yes. We'll put you on the *United States*. They have need for a third lieutenant."

"I would be proud to serve on that lady, sir." He was unsure whether he should go on, but the commodore seemed in a mood for conversation: "It may sound strange, sir, but I have had a special feeling for the *United States*. I used to visit her in Philadelphia when she was being built in Joshua Humphreys's shipyard and I watched her take shape. I used to tell my grandfather that some day I would own her and take her to sea."

Commodore Stewart did not laugh. "Oh, she's a grand old frigate, that lady," he said. "They used to insult her and call her 'the old wagon' because she was so slow. But a funny thing happened. Someone made an error in her trim when she was provisioned for a cruise one time and she sailed rather low by the head. And they found that such a trim had brought back her speed. The old wagon turned like magic into the speedy lady again. Quite by accident. No one laughs at her now. I was her fourth luff, you know, on her maiden cruise. I'll always love that lady."

"Who commands the *United States* now, sir?"

"Captain Crane. William Montgomery Crane. He was a midshipman on the *United States* on that same maiden cruise in '98. Now he occupies her great cabin. I think you'll find him a just commander."

"I'll look forward to it, sir."

"Mr. Levy! To the commodore's cabin at once! At a gallop, man! He is in a towering rage!"

The urgent command of Ben Page caught Uriah by surprise. He was at the *Franklin*'s port bulwark, supervising the search of a bum boat that had drawn alongside to sell vegetables and fruit to the tars. Such peddler boats needed careful checking to be sure they were not also vending liquor to the thirsty seamen. Uriah was watching the master's mate and his men conduct such a search when Lieutenant Page's shouts broke the air.

The *Franklin* lay at anchor in the spacious harbor of Syracuse, Sicily. Around her—their masts thickly filling the sky like a porcupine's quills—hovered the other ships of the Mediterranean Squadron. The waters between the vessels were busy with launches and gigs plying their routes and bum boats offering their wares.

Lord, what could he have done? Uriah raced aft on the spar deck to the hatch. He hurtled down the ladder so fast that he came close to pitching headlong to the lower gun deck, a fall that had killed more than one man. Finding his balance again, he completed the descent and scurried back to the commodore's cabin, with its two marine guards standing watch at the door. His mind moved back through his own recent watches to seek possible errors. Had he forgotten to relay an order to the first luff? What could he have done?

Despite his shaking hands, Uriah knocked firmly at the cabin door. The "Come!" that sounded from within was more a bellow than a command and did not serve to ease his concern. He entered the cabin. Commodore Stewart sat at his writing desk. His usually pale complexion was red with anger. Uriah stood before him and raised his hat in salute. "Reporting as ordered, sir," he said.

"Sit, Levy!" the commodore snapped. He motioned to a nearby chair, which Uriah lifted over to a place near the desk. The commodore picked up a paper from his desk and handed it to Uriah. "Read!" he commanded.

The paper was a letter written in small, immaculate penmanship. The signature was that of Captain William M. Crane, commander of the *United States*. The letter asked respectfully, yet firmly, that the assignment of Lieutenant Uriah P. Levy to the *United States* be revoked. The wardroom mess of the *United States* had presented a petition to him, Captain Crane wrote, requesting that the captain ask for such a revocation on the grounds that Lieutenant

Levy surely would interrupt the prevailing harmony in that mess. Crane's letter went on to mention the court-martial conviction of Lieutenant Levy and his subsequent reprimand by the secretary of the navy, the fact that he had killed a navy officer in a duel, and cited reports that Levy had been singularly unpopular among his fellow officers and the midshipmen aboard the *Franklin*.

Crane's terse letter concluded with these words: "Considerations of a personal nature render Lieutenant Levy particularly objectionable, and I trust he will not be forced upon me."

It was signed "Respectfully" by "Wm. Crane, Captain, United States."

Uriah read the letter with astonishment that a commodore's order of assignment could be so blithely opposed. His initial wonder was quickly submerged under a growing rage as he realized the personal indignity he had suffered, the insult that had been hurled at him. He swallowed a time or two, trying to calm his anger enough to say something to the commodore, who sat watching him. Was the commodore's anger directed at *him* for causing Stewart the embarrassment of receiving such a request?

"Those insufferable snobs!" The commodore's voice was choked with his own rage, and his words quickly answered Uriah's questions. "They are so proud that their frigate is a 'gentlemen's ship' because all its officers were commissioned as midshipmen and none came from the ranks as you did. A lieutenant such as you comes along, up from master, and they cry that you will hamper the harmony of their mess. God, what rubbish!"

"I fear, sir, that there is more to it than that," Uriah replied quietly. "Their objections go further than my never having been a middie."

Stewart needed no hints as to his meaning. He nodded tersely. "Yes, I shouldn't wonder if you're right," he said. "Well, by God, Mr. Levy, you are speaking to the commander of the Mediterranean Squadron of the Navy of the United States of America"—his voice had risen again to a bellow—"and no snobbish bastards on any ship in that squadron will tell me where to assign my men! And, by the living, punishing Lord of us all, they will never have the temerity to defy my orders to them! Here, read my reply to Crane." He handed Uriah another sheet of paper.

> *Sir: The preservation of harmony among the officers of the squadron, as well as between the officers in their respective ships, is of primary importance, and can only be effected by the strictest discipline. And should any officer's conduct be such as to destroy the harmony prevailing, every means in my power will be readily afforded to punish and correct him. Imaginary objections having no solid existence or growing out of malicious report ought not and can never divert the commander-in-chief from what he considers his duty. For all personal feelings have no other existence and should be forgotten in all cases of public duty. All orders should not only be obeyed with alacrity but with cheerfulness. As all legal orders are obligatory, it is expected that they will be executed with promptness, and not considered as oppressions or forced.*

> *Should you be possessed of a knowledge of any conduct on the part of Lt. Levy which would render him unworthy of the commission he holds, I would at the request of any commander represent it to the government. As your letter contains no specific notice of his misconduct, I can find nothing therein whereupon to find a reason for countermanding the order or changing his destination.*

> *I am*
> *Your obedient servant,*
> *Charles Stewart*

The message was clear enough: The assignment would not be revoked. But Uriah wished that the tone of the letter was more reflective of Stewart's anger, of the bellowing that still seemed to echo in this cabin. He personally would have derived much satisfaction from a stinging reprimand to Crane. Nonetheless, this dispatch informed Crane that he would have Mr. Levy as his third lieutenant, whether his wardroom mess approved or not.

The commodore saw that Uriah had finished reading the reply. "Now, Mr. Levy," he said, "get your gear packed as soon as possible and have a gig take you over to the *United States*. Present this dispatch to Captain Crane." He cleared his throat and managed a slight smile. "With my compliments, of course."

One and a half hours later, farewells behind him, Uriah sat stiffly in the sternsheets of a gig and watched the bulk of the *United States* loom up ever greater before him as he was rowed across the harbor.

He wondered, as he studied the well-remembered lines of the frigate, whether he had made a dreadful mistake. Should he have asked the commodore to accede to Crane's request and revoke the transfer? If Crane's letter told the truth and the wardroom officers indeed had asked that he be turned back, then how could he hope to find acceptance on the *United States*? If they hated him already—before even having met him—for coming to his lieutenancy from the rank of sailing master, then how could he serve with them in harmony and earn their friendship? If they hated him for being a Hebrew—and that was the unexpressed objection that was conveyed by Crane's letter—how could he possibly change their minds?

One thing was for sure: If he *had* asked Stewart to honor Crane's request, the commodore would have exploded all over again and would have lost whatever respect he had gained for Uriah during his nearly two years' service on the *Franklin*. No, he was glad he had not asked that his transfer be quashed. Whatever unhappiness lay in store for him aboard the frigate, he had done the right thing in keeping his mouth shut. He was prepared to take what came.

Uriah came through the frigate's entry port and requested permission from the officer of the deck to see the captain. After a short wait, he was led to the berth deck and the captain's cabin. He knocked on the door but could not hear an order to enter. He stood awkwardly in the passageway and waited. A marine sentry stood alongside the door, but gave him no clue or guidance and merely stared straight ahead.

He knew little about Crane personally, but had heard no ill of him. He had been spoken of, as Stewart had suggested, as a fair and honorable commander. Uriah knew he would soon put this opinion to a test.

The order to "Come!" was so softly spoken that Uriah wasn't completely sure he had heard it. He was uncertain whether to open the door or not. He glanced instinctively at the marine sentry, who continued to stare straight ahead, but nodded curtly. Uriah opened the door and entered the cabin.

Captain Crane sat in a large, rather ornate chair at the rear of the cabin, reading a newspaper by the light of the huge windows in the stern. Uriah stood before him and waited. When Crane slightly raised his head, Uriah lifted his hat in salute.

"Lieutenant Uriah P. Levy, sir, reporting as assigned." He handed the captain the reply from Commodore Stewart. Crane read the note without the slightest show of expression. He then silently folded the paper and dropped it to the floor. Then for the first time, the captain looked directly up at Uriah.

"I presently have as many officers on the *United States* as I need or want, Lieutenant," Captain Crane said. "You therefore will report back to the *Franklin* at once."

Uriah was stunned. This was flagrant insubordination! Crane was directly disobeying the commodore's order.

"But, sir . . . ," he began limply, "the . . . commodore has just. . . ."

"Did you not hear my order?" Crane said sharply. "I told you to get back at once to the *Franklin*! You are not wanted on this frigate. Sentry! Take this man to the officer of the deck and tell him I want a boat manned to row him back to the flagship!" Crane then picked up his newspaper and resumed his reading. Uriah again lifted his hat in a departing salute, but the captain neither looked up nor acknowledged it.

The ride back to the *Franklin* was a sour and agonizing one. Uriah would for the rest of his life remember these few minutes with a sense of outrage. He had been callously, bluntly rejected by fellow officers who had no justification for so doing. And he was being sent, humiliated, to carry this rejection back with him.

Commodore Stewart said little to Uriah when the lieutenant reported again to the *Franklin's* great cabin and told him what had transpired. His red face and abrupt, choppy gestures, however, told all that was necessary about Stewart's cold fury. He told Uriah to sit and called for his clerk.

Facing the cabin, his face grave, hands locked behind him in true quarterdeck style, the commodore dictated two letters to his clerk. The first, he told Uriah, must be shown to Captain Crane, but Uriah was henceforth to keep it in his possession for use when needed. The second letter also was to be handed to Captain Crane.

The first letter read,

> *Commodore Stewart assures Mr. Levy that the reports existing against him at the time he applied for an appointment to the* Franklin *were cleared up by the documents and reasons of Mr. Levy, perfectly to the satisfaction of Commodore Stewart as well as the Government of the United States.*

> *Commodore Stewart also assures Mr. Levy that he has not removed him from the ship under his command in consequence of any reports of his officers but, in conformity with the views of the Government, in having the officers attached to the Squadron distributed in such a manner as to afford them the best opportunity to acquire experience in the service—the principal object of employing either the ships or officers in the navy. When an officer is to be removed from one ship to another, the course the commodore will pursue will be to remove a junior officer, unless the nature of the case should require otherwise.*

"Mark that a true copy, Mr. Weaver," ordered the commodore, "and sign it yourself as my chief aide."

There was a marked change in the commodore's voice when he dictated the second letter. His words came out in short, stentorian bursts, like rapid musket fire:

> *To William A. Crane, commanding the Frigate* United States

Sir—Lieutenant U. P. Levy will report to you for duty on board the frigate United States *under your command. It is not without regret that a second order is found necessary to change the position of one officer in this squadron.*

He took the completed note from his clerk, read it over, affixed his signature with a flourish, and handed it with no further word to Uriah.

As Uriah raised his hat and prepared to leave the cabin again, Stewart clapped him resoundingly on the shoulder, a gesture of support and encouragement. Uriah wished that the red-haired commodore could be at his side when he reported again to the *United States*.

In less than an hour, he stood again in the great cabin of that frigate and presented the two documents to Captain Crane. The captain slowly read through them both, again without expression. He handed the longer statement back to Uriah, as the clerk had requested on the margin.

Then Crane said calmly, "So be it," and returned to the book he was reading. He offered no welcome to his ship nor any other information.

Uriah, expecting some such response this time, was not ruffled. He stood in place for a moment, waiting. Then he asked, "Shall I take my gear to the wardroom, Captain?"

"You might as well, Mr. Levy," answered Crane, without looking up. Uriah raised his hat in salute, of which the captain took no notice, and returned to the spar deck to pick up his gear.

It was the duty of each new officer on a ship, after presenting his papers to the commander, to report as soon as possible to the ship's first lieutenant and make himself available for duty. So it was that, after depositing his gear in a corner of the frigate's wardroom pending assignment of his cabin, Uriah confronted First Lieutenant Jones in the spar deck waist where he was finishing a scathing reprimand to a work party that had been too lazily polishing brightwork.

Thomas ap Catesby Jones was a small, spare man. Utterly unprepossessing, he might have been taken for a store clerk or a harried village postmaster. He was bareheaded, and his broad brow evidenced a rising hairline. He walked about the deck with a leaping stride, a bandy rooster of a man.

This Tom Jones was one of the navy's legendary younger officers. Indeed, some had called Tom Jones the unsung hero of Jackson's great triumph at New Orleans. His resistance on Lake Bourgne, the approach to the city, with only 25 guns and fewer than two hundred men, had won valuable time for Jackson to integrate reinforcements and set up additional gun batteries. A few days later came Jackson's smashing defeat of the redcoats.

Uriah well knew Jones's history. It did not ease his trepidation as he stood to the side and waited for the first luff to complete his tongue-lashing of the lazy tars. *It was one thing to be unwanted by your shipmates*, he thought to himself; *it was worse when one of them was one of the navy's finest fighters and probably one of its great leaders of the future.*

The first lieutenant finally released the work party and turned round to resume his inspection of the spar deck. Uriah stood before him and raised his hat.

"Lieutenant Uriah P. Levy, sir, reporting for duty as third lieutenant aboard this ship."

Jones did not answer immediately. He nodded. Then he studied Uriah intently, looking him over from boot tip to hair.

Then he nodded again and stuck out his hand. "Welcome aboard, Mr. Levy. Glad to have you with us!"

Uriah gratefully took the offered hand and shook it vigorously. There was warmth and sincere welcome in that voice. Could it be that Jones was not one of those in league against him?

The first lieutenant invited him to walk with him along the deck. He instructed Uriah about his duties and gave him a cabin assignment. Jones had a deep voice and seemed to choose his words carefully so as not to use one more than necessary. Uriah had the impression that Jones would rather be silent than speak, if given a choice.

After nearly ten minutes of pleasant chat, Jones ordered that a boat be brought alongside for him to go ashore. He said good-bye to Uriah and prepared to climb down to the boat.

Uriah took a deep breath. "Mr. Jones, before you go, may I ask your advice?"

"My advice, Mr. Levy? On what?"

"Sir, I have been informed that the wardroom officers of this ship have petitioned the captain to refuse to accept me. I have done nothing to merit such treatment. What can I do? I wish to serve here in harmony and to do a good job."

"Your information was correct, Mr. Levy, I regret to say. I can tell you that I had no part of this action nor did I approve of it. These are good men, these officers; I think you will find them so. Give them a chance to know you and you them. I think the situation will iron itself out. Do your duty and conduct yourself as a gentleman, and they will learn that they acted in error. As for me, sir, I can tell you just this: I care not how you came to your lieutenancy nor, for that matter, whether you are God-fearing or heathen. Follow orders, serve with diligence and honor, and we shall do well together. Now—forgive me, I must go over to Syracuse and see to our provisioning."

He jauntily bounced over to the entry port and swung gracefully down the falls and into the gig that awaited him. Before stepping into the sternsheets, he carefully examined the white canvas fendoffs to be sure they were spotless. Satisfied, he sat down for the passage to shore.

Uriah stood at the hammock nettings and watched the gig pull away from the frigate. He felt better than he had since Commodore Stewart had first told him of the hostility toward him on the *United States*. Whatever lay ahead for him, at least there was one officer of open mind aboard who would judge him for what he was. He felt assurance that Lieutenant Jones would come to be his friend. One man on his side. He was grateful for that much.

•••

It had been as horrible as ever. The fact that he had witnessed several floggings by now made it no easier for Uriah to stand at yet another, but stand he did. He no longer had to look away to avoid becoming publicly sick. He had hardened himself enough that he could look directly at the bare back of the prisoner and watch the white flesh being torn into long strips of red, bleeding meat. He could look now and fight back the hot acids coming up into his mouth. But he could not quench his feeling of outrage and horror that his navy must resort to such cruelty.

A middle-aged gunner's mate had returned drunk from shore leave and was accused of making insulting remarks to the officer of the deck. Crane set the man's punishment at three dozen lashes of the cat. The sentence was carried out under a bright morning sun. A midshipman, who could not have been more than fourteen years, stood next to Uriah in the formation and loudly whispered encouragement to the boatswain's mate wielding the cat: "Strike him harder, you fool! Kill him, kill him! You are letting the bastard off too lightly!"

After two and a half dozen strokes of the lash, the gunner's mate fainted. Crane calmly ordered that buckets of water be poured over his head. The prisoner returned to a groggy awareness. Then the captain told the boatswain's mate to complete the punishment. A river of blood poured down the prisoner's back, staining his trousers and dribbling in red rivulets onto the deck. Finally it was completed. The moaning sailor was cut down and carried below for ministrations by the surgeon.

The ship's company was dismissed. Those officers who were off-watch climbed down to the wardroom for coffee and talk. Uriah went among them, intending to fill a coffee mug and take it to his cabin. He had some letters to write, although his mind was still too full of the gore and screaming on the spar deck. He doubted that he could concentrate on the letters.

"Well, Levy, how did you like the show?"

The question surprised him, for it came from Lavalette, a lieutenant who had not spoken three words to him, except for official communication, in the months he had been aboard this frigate. Uriah had little doubt that Lavalette had been among those opposing his appointment. He had been cold to Uriah to the point of surliness. Why the sudden overture now?

"Did you say 'show,' Lavalette? A pretty word for such a horror. I gave it no applause."

"Oh, really?" Lavalette moved forward, a grin on his face. Obviously he had expected such a reply. Heads throughout the wardroom turned their way. "You disapprove of our primitive means of punishment in the navy, do you, Levy? It is too savage for your tender soul, is it?"

"It is savage, yes, and does not belong in the navy of a free country. And it is also illegal."

"Oh, and how is that?"

"The law provides that no commander may order more than twelve lashes on his own authority without a proper court-martial. I'm sure that you well know that fact, Lavalette."

"I'm sure the captain will be pleased to know that we have a Philadelphia lawyer among our lieutenants and that he has indicted the good captain for violation of the navy regulations. But surely the lawyer must also know that the captain can assess twelve lashes on each charge. Each of that drunken slob's words to the officer of the deck could be considered a separate charge."

"A mere sham, Lavalette, as you know. A way to dodge the law."

"You are a loud-mouthed boor, Levy, and your offensiveness is exceeded only by your ignorance of the very laws you so loudly quote!" It was a new voice. The speaker was Charles McCauley, an aristocratic sort who was the second lieutenant. His face was crimson. He stood at a table across the room and fairly shouted his words: "If you knew what you were talking about, you would realize that Article 32 of the Articles of War states that 'All crimes committed by persons belonging to the Navy, which are not specified in the foregoing articles, shall be punished according to the laws and customs in such cases at sea.' The captain of a ship, Levy, is the god of that ship. And I will listen to no officer or sailor on a ship call down my captain as a lawbreaker! Do you understand me?"

Lavalette again: "If you find the captain's methods so odious, Levy, why don't you simply leave the *United States*? We will not weep at your passing. God, we would set off fireworks." A midshipman passing through the wardroom giggled loudly.

Uriah fought hard to control himself. He wanted to leap on Lavalette and beat his head against the bulkhead and then make for McCauley. He would take great pleasure in bloodying his foul mouth. But he knew this would avail him nothing save more grief. He took a long breath, clenched his fists, and tried to keep his voice calm.

"I go where the navy sends me, and it has chosen to send me here. I will stay and do the best that I can."

"Ah, the gallant, loyal navy man." It was McCauley again. His voice no longer came in a shout. It had resumed its typical acid-tinged sarcasm, the tone of a feudal lord upbraiding a servant. "Yes, you are a dedicated officer, are you not, Levy? A veteran of the fabled *Argus*. Tell us again, you lucky fellow, how it came to pass that you managed to jump ship just in time to avoid going into battle against the *Pelican*? What a marvelous stroke of luck! You missed the whole fight, yet you are able to boast and brag about your service with the great *Argus*. Tell us, O Mighty Warrior!"

"I would welcome a chance, sir, to prove to you that I am no coward. I would welcome the chance to meet you upon any field, at any time, with any weapons. Then, lieutenant, we would see who is a coward and who is not."

Lavalette pounded his empty mug on the table. "Did I hear correctly, my friends? Did I hear a challenge, or did my ears deceive me? Has this loud, rude, and disrespectful fellow not violated the law he professes to respect by issuing a challenge to a fellow officer?"

"There has been no challenge and no violation!" First Lieutenant Jones spit the words out angrily as he entered the wardroom. "Take your seats, all of you, and close your mouths! There has been enough blood spilled this day because of someone shooting off his mouth. Belay it!" Jones's sudden appearance and his angry tones immediately brought the exchange to an end. The officers filled their mugs and took their seats. Lavalette pounded McCauley on the back, and they laughed together.

Uriah sat by himself at one end of an empty wardroom table. His coffee was cold by now, but he was too tense and upset to walk to the grate and refill his mug from the huge pot. Obviously it had been only a matter of time until something like this should occur. How could he continue to function on a ship where he was hated by his fellow officers?

Jones took a seat beside Uriah. He sipped slowly from his steaming mug. "What happened?" he asked quietly.

"I was asked my thoughts about the flogging and I gave them," Uriah answered wearily. "One thing led to another."

"I'm glad I happened to walk in. In another minute you'd have been at each other's throats."

"I'm glad you came in, too, Tom. The way the captain feels about me, if I got in trouble with McCauley, he'd probably have me keel-hauled . . . or worse."

"I won't be walking into such situations much longer."

"What do you mean?"

"I'm being transferred. My orders have just arrived. They're sending me to the Washington Navy Yard; they have some problems there, and they say that I can do some good. I'll be taking passage on the first available ship."

"Good Lord. That means McCauley will become first luff, right?"

"That's the way it looks. He's a favorite of Crane."

"My life will be a hell on this ship. Your friendship and fairness have been the only things that have kept me going these months. With you gone, I'll have no one even to talk to. They shun me in the wardroom and speak to me on deck only when they're forced to. It will be like purgatory."

Jones took another sip from his mug and nodded in agreement. "I don't envy you, Uriah. It will be bad. You must try to hold your temper despite their provocations. Stay out of trouble. They'll be doing everything possible to bait you so they can get you off this frigate."

"Why? Why in God's name do they hate me so?"

Jones looked at him curiously. "Surely you can't have much doubt about that. When they came to me and asked me to join them in the petition to keep you from coming aboard, I asked them the nature of their objection to you. They said that you had been commissioned from the ranks and thereby were taking a berth that rightfully should have gone to a senior midshipman with the proper background of a gentleman. And . . ."

"And?"

"And . . . they said you were a damned Jew and they would not have a damned Jew serving with them."

"It doesn't surprise me. I assumed that was behind their dislike of me. And I suppose McCauley and Lavalette were among the ringleaders?"

"You suppose correctly. I'll give you some advice, Uriah. Keep your fists at your sides and clap a stopper on your jaw. In short, keep out of trouble despite their baiting. That's the only way you can triumph over them. Soon enough you'll be sent to a new ship."

"Yes," Uriah responded, bitterness in his voice, "and I'll probably find more of the same there."

"No, I don't think so. People like McCauley and Lavalette are not everywhere in the navy. Oh, there are enough of them. But you'll find enough others who will judge you simply as a man, not as Jew or Christian or heathen."

"I hope you're right, Tom. A lot of people told me I was a fool to cast my lot with the navy. They warned me this would happen. I still hope to prove them wrong. But . . . sometimes I wonder."

These last few minutes on watch always dragged with miserable slowness, like a battleship in a dead calm. It was pitch-black on the spar deck, which made it more difficult for Uriah to fight off sleep.

God help him if he was found sleeping on duty as officer of the deck. He would be crucified. The thought of this stirred him fully awake. He took a big lungful of the damp night air. The *United States* had returned two days earlier to the harbor at Syracuse after a short, uneventful cruise and now hung drowsily from her anchor chain. Uriah wondered if he himself was growing dull and complacent in this navy at peace.

Thwack!

The sound startled him. *What was it?* Then it came again, a loud smacking sound.

He walked rapidly down the dark, almost deserted spar deck toward the source of the sound, which seemed to be somewhere near the main hatch. Then he heard the cries—or was it laughter?—of two of the ship's boys as they came scrambling up the hatchway ladder. A man's voice, angry and strident, followed them.

As Uriah approached the hatch, the boys climbed onto the spar deck. One of them was limping and appeared to be crying. A moment later, a big boatswain's mate named Joseph Porter came charging up behind them, wildly swinging a rope end. The boys, like frightened deer, landed lightly upon the deck, then gathered themselves to run into the darkness. They saw Uriah approaching, knew that he had seen them, and came quickly to a stop. In another instant, Porter was standing alongside, panting hard.

Uriah was incensed at such treatment of mere children.

"Porter!" he shouted.

"Sir?"

"Why do you whip these boys in that manner?"

Porter's answer was given in a high whine, a near-falsetto. Uriah took it as an insolent attempt to mimic his own rather high-pitched voice.

"Why do I whip these boys in what manner, sir?" Porter sang out.

Uriah was enraged. He slapped the big sailor hard across the mouth. "That will teach you not to be insolent to an officer!" he shouted.

Without another word and without asking permission, Porter strode back to the hatchway and descended below decks. The boys, faces full of fear, stood for a moment. Then they, too, vanished in the darkness.

In a few minutes, Porter was back on the spar deck, accompanied by Lieutenant McCauley.

"Mr. Levy!" McCauley shouted. "How dare you strike this man and falsely accuse him of whipping the sideboys?"

This was unheard of! To reprimand a fellow officer in the presence of a seaman? It was a violation of every rule of navy protocol.

Uriah bit his lip, but he could not stomach such treatment.

"Sir," he said, "I will not be called to account this way in front of this boatswain."

"Mr. Levy, I will call you to account any time that I please and in front of whomever I please. Is that clear?"

"What is clear, Mr. McCauley, is that you treat me with the greatest disrespect and in a manner not suited to any officer in this navy!"

"You will hear more of this night, Mr. Levy. You may count on that."

The court-martial of Lieutenant Uriah P. Levy was held aboard the frigate *United States* in Syracuse harbor. It began at 10 a.m. and was completed by 10:35 a.m. A prompt verdict was promised by Captain William Montgomery Crane, commander of the *United States* and president of the court-martial.

Although it was a cold, cloudy, windswept day, the proceedings took place upon the quarterdeck. A great oaken table had been carried up from the wardroom to serve as the bench for the members of the court, who were two captains from other ships of the squadron, in addition to Crane. A gaggle of curious crew members hovered about the perimeter of the court-martial area for a time. Then, bored, they moved on about their business. Uriah felt sure that Crane had placed the trial here on the open deck, rather than in his cabin, in order to deepen his humiliation by allowing idle members of the crew to witness the proceedings.

As the three members of the court conferred, heads together, on the procedure to be followed, Uriah sat in a chair placed squarely before them and wondered how this second court-martial would affect his already problematical career. If, as Decatur had warned him, his reputation was in question at the Navy Department after the unfortunate duel and his first trial on the *Franklin*, then what would his name be worth now, after this?

Crane called the court to order. He solemnly intoned the charges: disobedience of orders, contempt of a superior officer, and unofficer-like conduct. He then called upon McCauley, who had lodged the charges. The first lieutenant testified as to the incident on the spar deck on the late night of October 8. He gave much emphasis to the heated and contemptuous manner with which Lieutenant Levy had addressed him during the confrontation. He further testified that Levy had denied striking the boatswain's mate and admitted only to an attempt to strike him. Uriah sat rigid in his chair at this outright perjury, but he was helpless to interfere.

McCauley and two other officers who followed as witnesses told the court that Lieutenant Levy was strongly disliked by his fellow officers on the *United States* and had earned the reputation of a habitual liar.

The next witness was the aggrieved boatswain's mate. Porter wore a big smile and seemed to vastly enjoy his brief moment in the limelight. He knew that he was in friendly territory. He gave his version of the incident:

"On the evening of the eighth of October, after relieving the watch, I was told by Midshipman Alexander to go and start the two messenger boys of the watch on deck with a lantern that he might muster the watch. I found them lying down behind the ladder of the main hatch and I called to them and, striking with a rope's end upon the second step of the ladder, told them to 'go on deck, boys.' One run up with a lantern. The other had sprained his ankle previously and was a long time getting up. Mr. Levy sung out, 'Porter!' I answered, 'Sir?' He asked me, 'How came you to flog them boys so, you damned rascal?' 'What boys, sir?' says I. Says he, 'Do you repeat my words?' And with that, he drawed off and struck me.'"

Except for Porter's minor amendments of the words that actually had been spoken on the deck, his account was substantially true. On the day after the incident, Uriah had tracked down the two frightened boys. His questioning of them made it clear that Porter had not actually struck them, but was merely pounding hard on the ladder with his colt to speed up their progress. The lad who had been wincing had indeed suffered from a painful ankle for several days. His careful, patient interrogation of the two lads made it clear that they had not been bribed or coerced into their stories. They were telling the truth. Uriah had asked to see McCauley, told the results of his questioning, and apologized for the incident, stating that it all had been an unfortunate misunderstanding. The first lieutenant refused to accept the apology. He told Uriah that his conduct to a superior officer had been unacceptable and that he planned to bring formal charges against him.

Uriah then was called forward and sworn and asked to give his version of the event. He had known from the outset that his cause was lost, but he nonetheless had painstakingly written a statement in his defense. He spoke clearly and vigorously as he pleaded his case:

"It is in evidence that one of the small messenger boys was running upon deck in that degree of hurry that usually attends alarm, that another came limping on deck in tears and evidently much hurt and that this was immediately subsequent to several blows that were struck, which the evidence now shows were on the steps of the ladder.

"I was officer of the deck at the same time and was aloft on the quarter and near the mizzenmast. From the evidence of these circumstances, I concluded that Porter, the boatswain's mate who I had heard ordered to start them up, had been whipping them with his cat more severely than is proper for children like them. This was something so wanton in a stout, able-bodied man like him to be flogging little boys like them, which I heard indicated, that I was incensed and, slipping quickly to the head of the ladder, I demanded of him imperatively, 'Why are you are whipping these boys in this manner?' and his reply, although not in proof, I solemnly declare was in precise and sneering recapitulation of my own words. I believed at the moment he had unmercifully and cruelly whipped the boys and this insolence confirmed me in the belief and I gave him a slap with the back of my hand, not to punish him but to check his insolence by reminding him of his inferiority.

"I was soon after reprimanded by Mr. McCauley, not privately but in the presence of this very Porter, who stood, as was natural for a man of his degree, exulting in having brought me to account. I could not tolerate the suffering and the humiliation of a reprimand when it had the appearance of being done to gratify the sentiment of an inferior. That I should have been excited is natural, but I do not deny that it was unofficer-like to have addressed Mr. McCauley with unusual warmth of force."

Uriah felt a wave of nausea sweep over him as he read these humble words of apology and explanation. Although he stood rigidly at attention as he read, he knew that his words had forced him to his knees. Yet he felt he had no choice. He had been wrong in his accusation of Porter, though he still thought the seaman's insolence had merited the slap across the mouth. He had been wrong, too, in entering a heated exchange with the ship's first lieutenant, no matter what the provocation. In any such exchange, he well knew, right would rest with the superior officer. He knew there was no chance of his acquittal. His only question concerned the severity of the punishment.

Crane and the other two captains, having heard all the testimony, put their heads together for two or three minutes. There was much nodding and whispering and not a sign of disagreement. The three judges suddenly resumed their upright posture, each godlike in his place, and Crane called Uriah forward again to receive the verdict of the court.

The captain cleared his throat, then slowly and quite loudly enunciated the decision: "The court having duly deliberated upon all testimony in the case, as well that adduced in support of the charge as that offered in the defense with the statement of the prisoner, the court are of the opinion that the charges and specifications exhibited by Lieutenant Charles L. McCauley against Lieutenant Uriah P. Levy are proved, and that said Levy is guilty of disobedience of orders, contempt of his superior officers, and unofficer-like conduct. The court, having maturely considered of the said Levy's several offenses, do adjudge that said Levy shall be dismissed from the USS Frigate *United States* and not allowed to serve on board hereof—and that he shall be publicly reprimanded by the commander in chief, at such time and place and in such terms and manner as he shall deem meet and proper. This court is now adjourned."

Uriah leaned back on the cot in his cabin and slowly read, trying to enjoy the batch of letters from home. The arrival of the dispatch ship with naval paper and mail for the Mediterranean Squadron had brought rousing cheers from all the ships of Commodore Stewart's vast armada, but no one was more pleased than Uriah to hear that the mail schooner had come. Letters from home represented a delightful break in an onerous daily routine that made him feel more prisoner than officer.

Since his conviction and the court's decision that he was to be removed from the *United States*, he had been stripped of all duties aboard the frigate, although he still was due the prerogatives of an officer. He was free to roam the ship as he pleased and even to go ashore when the *United States* was in port, but he was given no responsibilities and could not issue orders to any crewman. He was, more than ever before, in a state of exile aboard his own ship—shunned by the other officers as an untouchable and virtually ignored by the crew. He ate in the wardroom as always, but sat by himself at the end of the table. He was seldom addressed by another officer and then only when it was unavoidable. He made little effort to converse with anyone. This state of near nonexistence would continue until the frigate completed its tour in the Mediterranean and returned to America, where he would leave the ship at the first port of call.

A friend from the *Franklin* had told Uriah in a Syracuse tavern that his conviction and punishment had been disapproved by the commodore. The report greatly cheered Uriah, even though its practical effect was nil. It meant at least that Stewart had reviewed the case record and the testimony and felt that, if the conviction itself was not unjust, the severity of the punishment certainly was. He was told further that the commodore had sent the case back home for review by higher authorities and ultimately by the president himself.

Meanwhile, however, he had to sit alone on the *United States*, a veritable pariah. He had no idea how long this would continue, although the report was that the *United States* probably would sail for home in the spring.

The *Guerriere*, 44, was one of the navy's newer frigates, having been rushed to completion in the war and launched in June of '14. She was a Philadelphia-built ship, constructed in the yard of Joseph and Francis Grice. This new *Guerriere* had been given the same name as the British frigate destroyed by Hull and the *Constitution* in August 1812. The U.S. Navy sometimes did this sort of thing, both a tribute to the gallantry of the vanquished foe and a bit of belated boasting on the conquest. She had something of a history of her own by now: she had been Decatur's flagship in 1815 and had killed Rais Hammida, the Algerian admiral who had kept the Mediterranean in thrall.

Uriah sat rigidly in a chair in the great cabin of the U.S. frigate *Guerriere* and studied the frames and planking of the ship, trying without success to divert his depression. Under normal conditions, Uriah might have been looking about him with curiosity, studying the ship's construction, seeking evidence of the Grices' creativity. But on this black day, such things were of little consequence to him.

It was not to be believed! For the third time in little more than two years, he sat in a defendant's seat and awaited the start of his own trial. For the third time, a petty incident had suddenly, almost without warning, mushroomed into a sheet of charges against him— and, no doubt, still another parade of witnesses ready to swear to his lack of truth, lack of courtesy, lack of seamanship, and general unworthiness to serve as an officer of the United States Navy.

It was thanks to Commodore Stewart that this latest court-martial had been removed from the *United States* to the more neutral arena of the *Guerriere* and that Captain Crane had not been assigned as one of the court-martial officers. In fact, though, the three grim-faced, narrow-eyed captains who stared balefully at Uriah as he sat before them promised little more sympathy than Crane would have offered.

Oh, he had brought much of this latest travail upon himself. He knew that. His temper again had led him into great trouble. Now those who always had hated him and called him "the Jew hustler" and other such terms . . . now they likely would get their way. Uriah knew full well that one does not survive courts-martial forever. This might be the one to throw him out of the navy, once and for all.

The president of the court-martial called the proceedings to order and requested that the charges be read. A lieutenant whose face looked vaguely familiar to Uriah stepped forward and began to read in a droning monotone:

"Charge first: Using provoking and reproachful words contrary to the fifteenth article of an Act entitled 'An Act for the Better Government of the Navy of the United States.'

"Specification: for that the said Levy, at Messina in the Island of Sicily, on or about the twenty-first day of January, 1819, did falsely, wickedly, and maliciously utter and publish in divers places and in the hearing of divers persons, officers of the Navy and others, the following false, scandalous, opprobrious, and slanderous words of and concerning the said Williamson, to wit: 'He is a coward, scoundrel, poltroon, and no gentleman' or words to that effect, and the said Levy, to give the wider circulation and effect to the said false and malicious slander, went about in taverns on shore and at divers mess-tables in the squadron and sedulously, busily, wickedly, falsely, and maliciously did utter and repeat aforesaid mischievous and slanderous words, or words to that effect of and concerning the said Williamson.

"Charge second: Treating with contempt his superior, being in the execution of his office, contrary to the thirteenth article of said Act.

"Specification: For that said Williamson on the said twenty-first day of January was attached to the Frigate *United States* then lying in the harbor of Messina aforesaid and was on duty as officer of the deck of said Frigate and the said Levy being a junior and inferior officer to said Williamson was attached to the same ship, but off duty and under an arrest waiting the sentence of a court-martial and the said Levy requested the said Williamson to have a boat manned for him, but before this could be done, the said Levy came on deck. . . ."

After a time, Uriah simply stopped listening. He closed his eyes. The droning voice was fading, blending into a muted refrain of all the charges against him at all his trials, with a speaking chorus of navy lieutenants chanting softly to him: "Dirty Jew, be gone! Go from our midst. You are not one of us."

This whole incident had begun as softly as the flutter of gull wings. Bored witless by his enforced exile aboard the *United States*, Uriah had decided to take advantage of a mild Thursday afternoon by walking around the town of Messina and perhaps buying a trinket for his mother. He had directed a ship's boy to have a boat manned to row him to shore. On being summoned by the boy, he had boarded the waiting boat. This brought down on his head a stream of abuse from the officer of the deck, Lieutenant Jonathan Williamson, who shouted that the waiting boat was not for him and he was to remove himself at once. A confrontation ensued upon the deck. The frightened boy now denied that he had told Lieutenant

Levy that the waiting boat was for him. Within seconds, the two lieutenants were screaming epithets at each other.

The incidents of the next few hours were forever shrouded in a haze of red mist whenever Uriah tried to sort them out in his mind. The harassment he had suffered for months at the hands of those who should have been his friends, the shame and degradation he felt . . . these combined now to hurl him out of control, into a mindless rage. First, he dashed to his cabin and angrily wrote a note to Williamson, demanding that the officer of the deck make "such concessions as the case requires" in the presence of those who had witnessed the argument or else that the two of them should meet, face to face, at the Navy Yard on the following morning. He took the note and rushed back to Williamson, who refused to accept it. Uriah then strode furiously to the wardroom, where the latest incident of the "Jew lieutenant" already was the big topic over the coffee mugs. There he demanded that McCauley, the first lieutenant, read the note aloud. He, too, coldly refused. Uriah then read the note at the top of his own lungs to the crowded wardroom.

As soon as he had finished the reading, he turned and walked back up to the spar deck, where he coolly approached Williamson again and, hand on sword, demanded that a cutter be readied for him. Williamson gave him no argument this time and had the cutter made ready.

Uriah was rowed to the quay at Messina and proceeded to walk, white-faced, eyes ablaze, to every waterfront tavern he could find. In each one, he screamed for the attention of the noisy crowd and then bellowed the words of his challenge to Williamson to the astounded and amused audience.

When the entire row of taverns had been so informed, the red-hot fury now beginning to ebb, he calmly returned to his cutter and was rowed back to the *United States*. He returned to his cabin and sat stoically on his cot, to wait for a summons from Captain Crane and the announcement that new charges were being lodged against him.

・・・

The prosecution began its case by summoning a series of witnesses, each of whom testified to the general reputation enjoyed by said Levy for untruthfulness. McCauley rehashed the earlier court-martial and charged that Levy then had lied about the facts in his testimony. Lieutenant William Weaver described in excruciating detail a dispute between Levy and himself aboard the *Franklin* over a large beefsteak and whether Levy had requested a mess boy to broil it for him. James P. Oellers testified, "Levy has repeatedly represented to my knowledge that he has commanded ships and brigs out of Philadelphia and I think I can safely swear that he never commanded anything other than a small schooner out of there." Elijah Peck told with a flourish of a dispute as to whether Levy had directed the quartermaster to strike the bell eight without first getting permission from the first lieutenant.

Williamson was called and gave his account of the happenings on the spar deck and the dispute over the boat. The ship's boy shakily testified that Lieutenant Levy must have misunderstood him to say the waiting boat was for him. Other witnesses eagerly told of Uriah's outbursts in the wardroom and in the waterfront dives of Messina.

When Uriah finally was asked if he wished to call any witnesses, he told the court that he would limit his defense to a statement. He took several pages of closely lined notes from his pocket. He knew that his chance of acquittal was almost nil. There were too many who had spoken against him and no one who was willing to speak for him. The specific charges were almost incidental. It was their golden chance to rid themselves of the infidel among them and they were making the most of it. He was determined, however, to state his case. He would not stand mute before these accusers. Even though his judges might sit with closed ears, his words would be taken down by the two agile ship's clerks, working in relays. Those words would go into the transcript of the case and would be read by the commodore and eventually by the powers in Washington

City. He had labored for six days on these notes and had silently rehearsed his statement many times in the long night hours when sleep was slow to come.

First he reviewed the incident with Williamson from his own perspective. He then took up the issue of his own honesty: "As far as my vice of lying is concerned, the witnesses torture the most innocent circumstances into abundant proofs of guilt. It will hardly be necessary to draw the recollection of the court to the evident view of prejudice and unfriendliness which pervaded the testimony of those who have impeached my veracity."

The planks of the *Guerriere* creaked shrilly and the sound of pounding feet came from overhead as a group of tars engaged in some skylarking on the spar deck. The presiding officer, with a sharp, angry flick of his hand, sent a lieutenant scurrying above to demand silence.

The intrusion gave Uriah a moment to take a breath and to consider for the last time the question that had been tearing him apart for days. Should he continue with the other things that he felt compelled to say? Or should he end his statement now, on that note of mild rebuttal?

No. No. He decided again, for the last time, that he would let them hear the real issue in this case. He picked up his notes again, stared for a moment at the three hearing officers, and continued his statement:

"There is one other appeal to your consideration, gentlemen, which I hope to make in terms which you will not deem unmanly.

"I am an object of common reproach. I am of that faith which has never been endured in Christendom 'til the Constitution of the United States raised us to a level with our fellow citizens of every religious denomination. I need not apprise you that I have been designated in the language of idle scorn, 'The Jew.' Perhaps I have been thus reproached by those who recognize neither the God of Moses or of Christ. May I not say that I have been marked out to common contempt as a Jew until the slow unmoving finger of scorn hath drawn a circle 'round me that includes all friendships and companions and attachments and all the blandishments of life and leaves me isolated and alone in the very midst of society."

His voice became quieter now and of a husky timbre, as his throat showed the strain of the day and of his emotions. He knew he held the court's rapt attention, for all three of the judges perceptibly leaned forward to better hear his next words:

"To be a Jew as the world now stands is an act of faith that no Christian martyrdom can exceed—for in every corner of the earth but one it consists of this: to be excluded from almost every advantage of society. Although the sufferers of my race have had the trust and confidence of all their Christian revilers as their commercial agents throughout the world, they have been cut off from some of the most substantial benefits of the social compact in Europe. They could not inherit or devise at law, and they could not 'til lately sit as jurors or testify as witnesses. These heartrending, cruel distinctions that seemed adamant have been gradually and imperceptibly worn down by the resistless current of time. They have in no instance been voluntarily obliterated by an act of Christian charity.

"I beg to make the most solemn appeal to the pure and heavenly spirit of universal toleration that pervades the Constitution of the United States, in the presence of this court that has its existence under that Constitution: that before a court-martial in the American Navy, whoever may be the party arraigned, be he Jew or Gentile, Christian or pagan, he shall have that justice done him which forms the essential principle of the best maxim of all their codes—'Do unto others as ye would have them do unto you.'"

There was no sound in the cabin after Uriah completed his statement. He stood still for a moment. Only when he began folding his papers and returning them to his pocket did the spell break and once again rustling and throat clearing were heard around him. The president of the court declared a brief adjournment so that he and his colleagues could consider the evidence.

Uriah turned and started for the door to climb to the spar deck and visit the ship's head. He passed McCauley, who stood nearby and gazed at him with contempt.

"Irrelevant, Levy," he hissed loudly. "Utter, irrelevant shit!"

Uriah's face reddened but he kept his hands at his sides and continued walking, determined to avoid another fracas that would kill off any last lingering hope.

The members of the court closeted themselves in the small sleeping cabin of the *Guerriere's* captain. Their deliberations took three-quarters of an hour, a longer time than usually required for a decision. When they finally strode back into the great cabin to announce their verdict, none of them looked at Uriah.

The president of the court cleared his throat and read slowly from a paper before him:

"The Court are of the opinion that all charges exhibited by Lieutenant Williamson against Lieutenant Levy are proved, but lest an injury in the public opinion be done him, which is not intended, the Court finds that though instances of falsehood have been proved, none have been made of sufficient importance to sustain the second specification under the third charge, that said Levy is addicted to the vice of lying."

Silence again lay like a blanket in the cabin as all present awaited the assessment of punishment. The president coughed once and proceeded:

"And the Court, having considered of the offenses of the said Uriah P. Levy under all the circumstances as proved against him, do adjudge that the said Uriah P. Levy be cashiered out of the Naval Service of the United States and that his sentence be carried into full and complete effect as soon as may be after the same shall be approved of by the President of the United States."

Uriah, his face impassive, said nothing. As the president intoned the adjournment of the court-martial, Uriah lifted his hat in salute to the Honorable Court.

"Do you wish me to arrange your transfer to another ship, Mr. Levy?"

Commodore Stewart sat at ease behind his desk, his boots

sprawled atop the thick pile of documents and dispatches that flooded across the great oak table.

Uriah shook his head. "No sir, thank you. I appreciate the offer, but the solitary life I have lived aboard the *United States* may as well continue to the end of the game. At least there I know each of my enemies. I can listen for the footsteps and knife in the dark, as the saying goes."

"Yes. Well, you won't have to put up with that much longer. I can tell you in confidence that we'll be casting off for home in a few months. You should be ashore at Norfolk by June."

"Yes, sir."

"And what do you plan to do then?"

"I'm not sure, Commodore. First, return home to Philadelphia and try to explain to my family why I have been kicked out of the navy. Then, I suppose, look for work and also speak with a lawyer as to a pursuit of my rights in this matter. I am of the belief that I have a remedy at law."

"That might be ill-advised, Levy. The navy does not take kindly to its justice being questioned in the civilian courts. But . . . you must do what you must do."

The commodore sat silently for several minutes, his fingers spread thoughtfully across his lips, his eyes staring into the distance. Then he looked at Uriah and spoke again: "Mr. Levy, I doubt that I am wise in telling you this, for it may give you false hope. Weigh what I tell you with caution. I am told by people in position to know that President Monroe has carefully reviewed your previous court-martial—the affair with Lieutenant McCauley—and that the president agrees with me that the trial was rather irregular and the sentence was out of proportion to the charge. You can anticipate receiving word soon that your previous punishment has been set aside."

"That is good news, sir. But that merely restores me to duty on the *United States* as third lieutenant. Of what good is that if I am thrown out of the navy now?"

"None at all, of course, if the decision to cashier you is upheld upon review. But this word from Washington City makes us believe that there is a chance of similar action on this finding as well."

New hope exploded with a sharp burst in Uriah's chest. "Then, Commodore, you really think I have a good chance to get this verdict overturned?"

Stewart held up a warning hand. "I did not say that, Mr. Levy. I said merely that a decision in your favor in that earlier court-martial would suggest there is a chance of a similar decision in the later one. The prejudices against you that were operative in the earlier trial were apparent again in the last one. That will not be lost on Monroe. He is more astute than many give him credit for. God knows, though, when such a decision by Monroe can be expected. He has other, slightly more important matters on his mind, you know. As you know, the House is controlled by free-soil men and the Senate by the advocates of slavery. They are in deadlock. Alabama and Missouri are seeking admission to the Union and the antislavery men are demanding that Missouri be admitted as a free state. The nation is in turmoil and tempers are high. To expect that Monroe will put all that aside to give prompt review to your case is pure insanity. You may have to wait quite awhile."

"And while I wait, I am in disgrace and done with the navy."

"So it must be, Mr. Levy. And I counsel you to keep the peace while you wait and keep your temper sealed and your mouth closed—things that have sometimes eluded you in the past. It might be best if you absented yourself for a time . . . perhaps took a trip abroad. The more contact you have now with navy men who know of your troubles—some of whom may indeed be glorying in your tribulations—the more likely it is that another incident will occur. And each of these incidents, Mr. Levy, is another nail in the coffin of your career."

"I understand, Commodore. I thank you for your advice. I promise it will be heeded."

* * *

"What has happened to you, Uriah? What have you become?"

Uriah looked at his mother's pale face and tried to understand her question. They sat together in the big, sunny kitchen of the old house in Philadelphia and sipped strong coffee. It was their first quiet moment together since his homecoming. The house had been filled with the noisy greetings of his brothers and sisters and aunts, uncles, and cousins who had flooded into the house as news of his return spread.

Uriah had become a minor hero in the Jewish communities of the United States and especially to the Jews of his home city. He was one of only a few Hebrews who had begun a career in the military services and now ranked with the highest of them. His well-publicized months on the legendary *Argus*, his imprisonment at Dartmoor, his service with the faraway Mediterranean Squadron— all of these made him somewhat of a celebrity among his people. His troubles in the navy also were well known, but he was held blameless by his relatives and friends, who ascribed every problem that he had encountered to bigotry.

Those troubles, in fact, tended to inflate his reputation even more. He was becoming a symbol of his people's stubborn fight for full acceptance in American society. Every bit of news about him that reached Philadelphia was quickly carried from house to house and then was discussed and analyzed at the synagogue on the Sabbath as the worshippers enjoyed some air on the front steps. When it was known that Lieutenant U. P. Levy had returned home, his mother's parlor was jammed with visitors who came to shake his hand and hear about his adventures and tribulations.

On this warm morning, distant murmurs of western thunder gave promise of afternoon storms. The tide of visitors would begin anew before sunset and continue through the evening, but now it was quiet in the house, and mother and son finally had a chance to talk.

"What do you mean, Mama? What have I become? I am the same as always."

She shook her head sadly. "Then why do I hear again and again that you are in trouble with the navy? You never were a trouble-maker. Suddenly you are famous for fighting and killing people in duels and for having a grand temper. Is this a good repute to have? No, you are not the same. You must have changed, if these stories are true."

"I don't know what stories you've heard, Mama. If I am famous, it is a fame that I would rather do without. My ambition is still the same—to serve my country with my abilities in seamanship and combat. Yes, I've had troubles. But they've been due mostly to dislike of me that I have not earned. I've lost my head at times and talked more than I should and sometimes in the wrong places. I regret it. It has hurt my cause. But that is not the real source of the trouble. They hate me because I'm a Jew and only because of that. If my name was Biddle or Smith, there would be no problem, I assure you."

"Son, I can understand what you have been facing. But you have made the situation much worse by your reaction. Uriah, don't you think I know about people who hate Jews? I've seen such people all my life. I heard their remarks often enough in the store. So did your father and your grandfather. 'So much for this clock, Mrs. Levy? You won't sell it for less? Why do you Jews try to grab all the world's money, Mrs. Levy?' Oh, I've heard such things right enough. And what is to be done? You keep your mouth closed and you turn away. And soon enough they leave. If you answer back, they will just speak more of their hate. That's what we must do, Uriah. Keep our mouths closed and turn away."

Uriah shook his head vehemently. "No, Mama. I won't turn away from them."

"What will you do, then?" she asked. "Will you go through life fighting duels and going on trial and destroying yourself? Is that what you want?"

"Mama, when I was very young, I was taught to be proud to be a Jew and never to shame myself by denying my heritage. I'm also proud to be an American, and I'm every bit as good an American as a Christian is. As a citizen, I'm entitled to every right and privilege of an American. If anyone tries to withhold such rights and privileges from me because I am a Jew, then I will demand my proper due. I will not be silent. I will not keep my mouth closed and turn away. If I do that, then I concede victory to them. The men who founded our country had a vision of a nation unique in this world—a nation where every man is equal under the law. It is Jefferson's dream. If I don't fight for that same dream, Mama, I am helping destroy it."

"They will ruin you, Uriah. I am sorely afraid they will ruin you."

"Don't you know who taught me these lessons, Mama? Who implanted these thoughts in my mind?"

For the first time, his mother smiled. "Of course I know. Do you know how many times have I heard him make these same speeches?"

"Then surely you must understand what I feel and how I must live my life. Papa was right. To be a good American, you cannot keep quiet and turn the other cheek. You have to stand up and demand what is truly yours. The United States Navy never heard of Jonas Phillips, but by God they will be made aware of his grandson!"

She sat silent for a long time, staring down at her coffee. The thick brown liquid was untouched, cold.

"What will you do now, Uriah? I would like to keep you home. But I know that John Coulter wants you to captain his ship, and I suppose he will lure you back to sea."

He studied her face and understood the appeal she was making. She had aged perceptibly since his last visit home. Her hair was bone-gray now, and her face was deeply lined. He was not unaware that her years were slipping away and that it hurt her to see her children scatter across the globe, not to be seen for months at a time. His older brother Louis and his younger brother Morton had begun careers in the merchant fleet and were off at sea right now. Faithful Benjamin and Joseph still operated the family store, selling and repairing clocks as their father had done, assisted by Isaac, who now was nineteen years. Fanny and Jonas were the babies of the brood, and they were no longer babies—Fanny being almost sixteen and Jonas nearing his bar mitzvah—but they were young enough yet to need their mother's attentions and bring a sparkle to her eye.

"I plan to speak with John Coulter, Mama, and to see what he offers. But I am not intending to go to sea for John. Not now, at least."

"Then what will you do? You say it may be years before a final decision is made on your dismissal from the navy."

"I don't know. But I've been advised to get away for a while and to keep myself distant from the navy and its officers. It's good advice. I can't risk getting into another scrape now. Anyway, I have always wanted to see France. I've picked up a bit of the language. And I have some good friends there from my time at Dartmoor. I promised I would find them after the war and pay them a visit."

"You are not leaving right away?"

He laughed. "No, Mama. I'll be here for a few weeks at least."

"There are some new families in town. They have beautiful daughters. . . ."

He roared with glee. "Give up on me, Mama. I am wed to the navy. No woman would have me. I am never home."

She sighed and frowned. "In a few years you'll be thirty, Uriah. If you don't wed soon, no woman will have you because you're too old. Let them bring their daughters over to meet you. Everyone wants to meet you. Perhaps one of them . . ."

"All right, all right. I'll meet them with pleasure. And I'll turn on all my charms."

"Good. And will you do one more thing for me? Little Jonas has been talking about going to sea. He even speaks of running away as you did and becoming a cabin boy on some ship. Please, Uriah, speak to him. He'll listen to you. He worships you. He must finish his schooling. I don't want him to leave so soon, as you did."

"Of course, Mama. I'll speak to him. The sea is like a fever in your blood and young boys in a port city like this are easily caught by it. It may not help, but I'll speak to Jonas as strongly as I can. One cabin boy is enough for any family."

13

Paris, 1819

He lay on his back in bed, planning his day as he stared at the drab walls whose color reminded him of dried blood. It was very fortunate, Uriah told himself, that late autumn was so mild in Paris. Had he been confined more by bad weather to this grim boardinghouse bedroom, he surely would have gone mad. But the spirits of autumn had favored him with gentle, sunlit days and temperate nights. He had taken full advantage of the bountiful offering by roaming the streets and byways of Paris from morning to midnight. He returned to this monastic chamber in a hillside house on the Rue de l'Arbalete only to sleep and to bathe and change clothes. Otherwise he was out, walking under the chestnut trees, breathing the air of a place that seemed to him not only foreign but even exotic. He could not get enough of Paris.

His first act upon arrival three weeks before had been to find the house of Victor Pichot, a comrade from the prisons at Dartmoor, who had begged him to seek him out whenever he came to Paris after the war. Pichot was there as he had promised to be, heavier now by fifty pounds and festooned with a long gray beard, but the same hearty, kind baker as of old. He had known Uriah instantly, had greeted him at the door with a cry of joy, a hug awesome in its power, and kisses on both cheeks.

They had a noisy reunion over lunch, with Uriah trying his rusty French on Victor's eight children, who screamed with laughter at his odd accent and his fumbling efforts to remember the nouns that evaded his memory's grasp. They understood enough, though, to give him hope that his hard-won beginner's competence in the French tongue would suffice to keep him fed, clothed, and housed while he explored the legendary capital.

The meal over, Victor walked with Uriah—a long loaf of Victor's fresh bread under his arm—to the University Quarter to help him find a place to stay. In this gloomy section between the Val-de-Grace and the Pantheon, Victor told him, he could find a variety of accommodations to suit his purse, since almost every one of the rough stone houses was a family boardinghouse.

"You can take a grand first-floor apartment and pay six hundred francs a month," he told Uriah, "or you can climb up to the attic and find a place to sleep for merely forty francs. Or you can find something in-between."

"Well, at those prices this young American will have to do without the apartment. Let us find a decent room that I can afford."

And so they had come to the big house on the Rue de l'Arbalete where the landlady was a friend of Victor's cousin. With the baker's help, they bargained to an agreement on a small but clean second-story room for forty-five francs a month including meals.

"Take it," urged Victor, "for despite the stink of *soupe-aux-choux* in the house, she is known as a fine cook. Anyway, you'll eat most of your dinners in the traiteurs, but you'll get a hot breakfast here and a palatable dinner, should you decide to stay home of an evening."

They parted then, with Victor exacting a promise that Uriah would come for dinner on the next evening and with his assurance that his oldest son would bring Uriah's luggage over from Victor's house within minutes.

The tenants of Mme. Arindais were a mixed lot: several medical and law students whom Uriah found to be a cynical and rather superior lot, a group of gentle elderly people who gazed at him across the dining room table with expressions of perpetual wonderment, and a debonair physician who seemed quite out of place here, but nonetheless consumed inspired amounts of food at each sitting.

After the initial introductions and a few more halting efforts at French conversation, Uriah spent little time with his fellow boarders. He was here to see Paris after all, and see it he would! His days were filled with sightseeing: museums, palaces, and magnificent gardens. He walked the lush paths of the Tuileries and the Luxembourg Gardens. He watched the military reviews in the Champ de Mars and strolled in fascination across the Place Vendôme, with its column coated with the brass melted down from cannon captured in Napoleon's wars. As the sun set, he would return to his room, bathe, and change into fresh clothing. Then he would head for the Palais Royal to find a new traiteur for his dinner. The ground floor of the vast Palais was covered with fine restaurants, hundreds of them it was said. He ate at a different place each evening. Each traiteur offered dozens of tasty dishes—the variety was unbelievable—and he could get a fine meal with a pint of wine for three francs or less.

After dinner he would go upstairs in this magnificent old palace of the Orleans family and watch the activity in the gambling dens, where men and women stood elbow to elbow and wagered in high excitement. Except for a bit of whist now and then, Uriah seldom played but was content to watch the panorama of interesting humanity at the gaming tables. When he became bored with this, he had only to wander further in the palace. There always were lectures being given in the spacious rooms above the gambling dens, and the literary societies of Paris regularly met there. His comprehension of French was improving each day.

He was alone, yet not lonely. There was too much fascination in all this for him to feel any sense of isolation. That might come later, but for now he was an innocent abroad and an untiring audience for the sights and people of this city of delights.

And if the solitary wandering became a bit oppressive and the lack of companionship a touch melancholy, he had only to find one of the many brothels in the Palais Royal, for it also housed Paris's finest collection of whores, and purchase an hour of companionship. He did not often visit whores. When he did, his sense of guilt afterward was very strong. But, like any man on long stretches at sea, his body sometimes compelled him to seek relief, so the commercial variety of love was not wholly unknown to him.

Ah, but such pleasures of the evening were long hours away yet. On this sun-dappled morning, all of Paris beckoned to him. Today he would stride up the hill of Montmartre and then north to the site where legend told that the missionary St. Denis had walked, his severed head under his arm after his decapitation by the Romans at Montmartre, and found the place that God had chosen for his burial.

First, though, there would be time to find one of the delightful cafes under the chestnut trees of the Champs Elysées and to sit in the warm sunshine and sip fragrant coffee as the splendid women of Paris promenaded past or gazed languidly at him from their carriages. It was a forenoon treat never to be missed.

In a few minutes, he sat at such a café, the coffee pungent in his nostrils, and admired the marvelous view. Never had he seen such a variety of vehicles as daily paraded past here. He recognized barouches, berlins, pose chaises, caleches, tilburys. There were dozens of other types that he could not identify. *Paris must be the carriage capital of the world,* he thought, for the Parisians loved to roam their city and its suburbs, looking avidly at one another and now and then at their storied buildings and monuments. Some of them deigned to walk, but the typical Parisian much preferred to flit about in his shiny carriage.

A particularly ornate coach with postillions and a cargo of two saucy young women, their noses held imperiously high, was coming down the avenue. Uriah decided to summon his waiter to refill his cup. He would ask him the identity of these high-nosed young beauties.

Just as he raised his arm and was about to call "*Garçon!*" the air was torn by a hoarse shout that startled everyone in the café, yet to Uriah somehow had a vaguely reassuring tone of familiarity:

"Ooriah! Ooriah! *Mon Dieu!* You are here at last! *Mon ami!* At last! *Mon ami!*"

Along with all the other patrons, Uriah turned to find the source of the joyous bellowing. Before he could even pivot in his chair, he found himself lifted bodily upward, caught in the embrace of what seemed to be a gigantic bear. Held up in the air like a baby by his adoring father, Uriah was terrified for an instant; then all emotions blended into utter astonishment, as he looked downward into the grinning, black-bearded face of André de Guissac, his comrade and teacher from the dread days of Dartmoor.

The air was filled with a flood of French words, spoken so fast and with such emotion that Uriah could understand only a fragmented word or two. De Guissac suddenly stopped talking then and lowered Uriah to his chest, where he hugged him warmly for a long time and then gently planted two wet kisses of welcome on his cheeks before setting him back on his feet.

That done, de Guissac turned to the beaming audience of café patrons and proceeded to give them a rapid-fire explanation of his friendship with this young American seaman and how together they had surmounted the cruel treatment of their British captors. When he finished, his arms waving dramatically with the final words, all the tables burst into wild applause.

De Guissac turned back to Uriah and began to interrogate him, his arms still semaphoring with excitement, his French impossible for Uriah to comprehend. Finally, laughing, Uriah forced his friend to silence.

"You taught me something of your language," he said, "but you are speaking so fast now that even another Frenchman could not understand. You were not *that* good a teacher, you know."

"And *you* were not that good a pupil," de Guissac responded in English. "When I get excited, no language will do but my own. *Mon ami,* the God himself must have brought us together this day! It is amazing that I have found you like this. What are you doing in Paris? How long will you stay? Why did you not try to find me? Were you going to return to America without even seeing the comrade who was so near and dear to you in our captivity?"

Uriah laughed again and put his hand on de Guissac's big shoulder. "My dear old friend," he said, "I did not forget our agreement. I was looking forward eagerly to seeing you . . . when I got to Marseilles. How was I to know that you were in Paris?"

De Guissac looked blankly at him. "I did not inform you that I was moving to Paris? *Mon Dieu*, I have lived here for three years now. Ah well, the God above us all has rectified my mistake by making sure that we found each other."

Uriah became aware of someone else standing by and listening with amusement to their conversation. His eyes focused on a young woman in a white cashmere gown. She was smiling with obvious delight at the emotional reunion of the two men. Her teeth were white and even. She had ash-blonde hair that drifted loosely to her shoulders in the careless arrangement that was the morning fashion for Parisiennes. As his eyes studied her face, Uriah was startled at her loveliness. He thought he never had seen such a beautiful face. Yet there was something artless, guileless, about it—a tender innocence—that set it apart from the sophisticated, almost cynical features of the ladies who promenaded constantly past the café. And her eyes . . . her eyes were as blue as the morning sky.

De Guissac continued to pour out his gratitude over the unexpected reunion and to punctuate his words by pounding Uriah lovingly about the shoulders and ribs. The American found his gaze drawn back again and again to the haunting beauty of de Guissac's companion. But she was so young! She could not have been more than eighteen—twenty years at most. Yet she accompanied a man more than twenty years her elder. This could mean only one thing: she must be a courtesan, for no young woman could be interested in a man so much older for reasons of love, even such a charming womanizer as the privateer captain from Marseilles.

At thirty, Uriah considered himself very much a man of the world, yet he found himself offended that such a magnificent young girl of the apparent innocence could be a prostitute, entertaining and bedding men old enough to be her father. He was hardly a moralist . . . yet this was wrong, and somehow repugnant. If de Guissac wanted to display his oft-boasted prowess at spearing women, let it properly be with whores of a suitable age, of a dignified maturity.

"Where are you staying, Uriah?"

Uriah's mind remained for a moment on the injustice of the young woman's situation; he had to force himself back to consider the question.

"Oh, I am in a boardinghouse on the Left Bank. A nice place in the University Quarter. It serves me well enough."

"Come, we will pick up your things. You will move in with me, immediately!"

"Wait, wait, my friend. My rent is paid until the end of December. There is no way she will give it back. Anyway, I am satisfied with my place. It is clean and warm. And I am not there very much."

"Very well. But come the end of December, you will move to my house. You are my son and my brother! I will not have you living with strangers. Now, stand here while I find a cab. We will go to my house for lunch and spend the afternoon completing our histories for each other. Then, tonight, I am taking you to the Hotel d'Angleterre in the Rue Montmartre for a fabulous dinner. I hate all Englishmen, as you know, but the English lady Mrs. Brown sets the finest table in all Paris. You will see, you will see!" He raised a finger as a gesture to wait and then hurried off toward the street in search of a vacant cab.

As he passed the young woman standing patiently behind him, he muttered to her, "Talk to him, talk to him. Make him welcome."

She took a couple of steps toward Uriah, but stood shyly, not knowing what to say. A slight smile still rested on her lips. Uriah stared her full in the face, adrift and overwhelmed by her young, sweet face. He looked so long into her fire-blue eyes that he felt himself growing dizzy.

Finally, awkward in the silence, he felt constrained to speak. "Good day," he said solemnly. "I am Uriah." He was suddenly shame-faced to realize he had spoken in English and that she probably had not understood a word.

Before he could search his memory for the same words in French, however, she answered him in English with a charming French accent: "Good day, Uriah. I am Elise." She said no more, but nodded in friendly fashion and again smiled happily.

"You . . . you have known him long?" Uriah said, pointing toward de Guissac, who ran nimbly in the street trying to flag the attention of busy coachmen who paid him no mind in the crowded late-morning traffic.

Elise's eyes widened for a moment and Uriah thought he would gladly drown in those blue pools. Then she nodded, the small enigmatic smile again at her lips. "Yes, for quite awhile. He is very good to me."

"Yes, I shouldn't wonder," Uriah answered, a touch of disdain in his voice. "Have you been . . . at this . . . very long?"

"At this?" She asked, her eyebrows raised. "At what?"

"Well . . . I mean . . ." Uriah coughed and cleared his throat. Why had he asked her that? It was none of his concern. "I mean . . . uh . . . being a companion to men like my friend there. You seem very young for . . . such a profession."

"I am not so young as I look," Elise answered, a touch of defiance in her voice. "I am twenty; I am old enough to make my own way in the world."

"You will forgive me, Mademoiselle, for saying this, but you belong at home in the care of loving parents who will protect you from the evils of the world. You have no business being out here on the streets."

"But Monsieur," she protested softly, "I am well protected by such stalwart companions as yourself and M. de Guissac, am I not?"

Their conversation was ended by another bellowing shout from de Guissac who had found a vacant hack and was urging them to hurry to the curb.

Uriah sat jammed against the side of the carriage, de Guissac in the middle, and the girl Elise pressed against the other side. The seat was made for two, but they had to take what they could get and the tightness was soon forgotten in the animated conversation.

"How long will you be here, my friend?" asked de Guissac.

"My stay is indefinite," Uriah answered. "I am waiting to hear the outcome of some troubles I have had with the navy. If the verdict is favorable, then of course I will return immediately and seek a new berth aboard ship. If not, I don't know. Meanwhile I am enjoying life and this beautiful city. So long as my money holds out, I am a temporary Frenchman."

"*Magnifique!* I will show you France as you have never seen it or dreamed of seeing it!"

"But what has brought you to Paris, André? I thought you were going to spend the remainder of your life in Marseilles. That's what you told me at Dartmoor. You were going to own the largest fleet of merchantmen on the southern coast, you said, and show the Limeys how a fleet should be run."

"Ah, plans change, *mon ami*, as life plays its tricks."

Uriah was amazed at the change in de Guissac's voice. It had suddenly become lifeless and flat; all the animation was gone.

"I had such plans in 1814, it is true," the big Frenchman went on. "But everything changed when my beloved wife died, soon after I was sent home from prison. I felt I must put my back to Marseilles and all its memories. I would begin anew in Paris. A fresh slate, you know. I do own ships—not so large a fleet as I had vowed—but large enough. The British know me as a hard competitor. And if we war with them again, I will be back out privateering as before. No, Marseilles is fading into the past now. Only memories remain there for me. Only memories. But surely Elise told you something of that."

Uriah thought at first he had misunderstood. *Did he say Elise? What would his beautiful young courtesan know of de Guissac's old life in Marseilles and of the painful memories he had left there?

Elise's voice was heard, partly choked with laughter. "Ah, but I did not discuss such things with Monsieur Uriah. We spent our time discussing my . . . ah . . . profession, instead."

De Guissac looked at her, puzzled. "Profession? What profession?"

Uriah felt a sense of misgiving growing in the pit of his stomach.

Elise went on: "He was chiding me for spending my days on the streets of Paris, on the arms of men such as yourself, instead of being in the warm embrace of Mama and Papa at home where I belong."

De Guissac exploded. "Elise, you little devil! You didn't introduce yourself—"

The cab was filled with the sound of Elise's laughter . . . like pealing chimes . . . like water flowing downhill over smooth stones.

"Uriah, dear friend, my daughter has victimized you with her penchant for a joke. Please be introduced to Elise de Guissac, my loving and much-loved daughter, who has known only my arm to lean on and who is very much in the embrace and protection of myself, her loving papa and mama at one time. I apologize for her rudeness in not introducing herself."

Uriah hunkered down in the seat, his face red with shame. Elise's laughter still filled the air. It wavered for a moment and threatened to slide down toward silence, then she glanced across and saw his crimson face and her musical laugh rang out again.

Her laughter strangely was like balm to his embarrassment. He found himself feeling better because she was enjoying his discomfiture so much. He looked across de Guissac's ample front at her lovely face and watched her continue to laugh, her eyes filled with tears. God, she was beautiful.

On the first day they met, Uriah had been smitten by Elise de Guissac. On the second day he was captivated by her, and on the third day entranced. Within a week after their first, confused meeting, he was hopelessly, eternally in love with her.

André de Guissac quickly noticed the worshipful way in which his young American friend beheld his daughter. He looked with interest for her reaction and saw how she blushed when Uriah spoke to her and how patiently she endured his plodding efforts to speak French. The father did not need long to realize that his daughter, who had been pleasant yet aloof with most of her young swains, already was remarkably fond of Uriah.

De Guissac was not displeased. Uriah Levy had struck him in Dartmoor as a brave, resourceful, and honorable young naval officer. He had a good mind and was imbued with love of country. If this sudden flare of emotion should result eventually in a match, de Guissac decided, he would not oppose it. Oh, he would not push them together; Elise never would stand for that. But he could help a bit. He directed his daughter to show their visitor all the sights of Paris, for only a young person would know what another young person would care to see. Meanwhile, he would plan attractions for all of them to enjoy in the evenings: a performance at the Opéra Comique, perhaps, or a play at the Odéon.

Elise studied literature at the Sorbonne, but she somehow found time between her classes to proudly show Uriah the length and breadth and the soul of Paris. Although she had lived in the capital with her father for only a few years, she had been coming to the city since she was a small child and knew it as intimately as a born Parisienne. She was inordinately proud of France and of being a Frenchwoman. It was a joy to her to display the stunning beauty of Paris to this earnest young American who listened to her words with rapt attention and who seldom took his eyes from her face as she spoke. It soon dawned upon her that he seldom took his eyes from her face even when she was not speaking.

In the cold, sun-dappled days, bundled well against the sharp wind, they walked among the great monument buildings of Paris. She made him stand for long minutes in the street before the gleaming white Palais du Louvre as she told of its long and tumultuous history. Then they hurried, laughing, into the building that the King's ministers demanded be called the Musée Central des Arts. Rubbing their hands together to restore the blood, they walked down the great galleries of the Louvre and studied one legendary art treasure after another until Uriah begged for mercy and a chance to sit down.

"Come, my Republican friend," she said, after a brief rest. "I will take you to the house of a king." They walked across the Tuileries gardens and into the Tuileries Palace of Louis XVIII.

Although Elise had grown up in Marseilles under Napoleon's rule—and had dutifully learned all the songs and paeans to the emperor as a child—she did not consider herself a Bonapartist, but neither was she a Royalist. Rather she was a Frenchwoman who exulted in her country's triumphs and despaired over its debacles. As they went from place to place, she related the history of France with the same passion and commitment she would have shown if describing the life of her own dear father.

Paris had burrowed in for the winter. The days were dark and melancholy: rain one day, snow the next, fog the next. The streets were silent, save for the muted skitter of an occasional carriage.

It was no weather for sightseeing. Besides, Uriah by now had a nodding acquaintance with every old stone in the city. During the hours when Elise was attending her lectures at the Sorbonne, he sat brooding—sunken in loneliness—reading books and writing letters home to pass the time until he could see her again. When she returned, his day began. They would sit for hours in front of the fire in de Guissac's salon and hold hands and talk. Father and daughter continually begged him to move into their home, but pride made him refuse: he did not want to chance becoming a guest who overstayed his welcome and so he maintained his small room in the boardinghouse on the Rue de l'Arbalete. But most of his waking hours were spent at the de Guissac house in the fashionable Faubourg Saint-Germain.

The time for history lectures and monumental descriptions had come and passed. Now the two young people spent their hours together exchanging confidences, sharing hopes and dreams. They gave each other their biographies and what they hated most and what they most adored. Each told long, funny stories about their respective families, and each gasped with laughter while describing the one very strange relative who provides comic relief in every family. She talked of her mother and of how much she missed her, and he gently wiped away her tears.

On this day in February, as sleet rattled loudly against the window, they talked of sad and happy things as they usually did. And then Uriah carefully took Elise's face in his hands and kissed her, his lips touching hers so softly that it was like a zephyr. Their arms came around each other and their kiss deepened and everything around them was forgotten.

"Have you seen the newspaper? I thought you should know of this."

De Guissac entered the dining room of the boardinghouse and threw off his cloak on this mild April morning. He held a Paris newspaper in his hand, and there was a grave look on his face. Uriah sat alone at the long table, finishing his morning coffee. The students had made their noisy departure for their lectures and even the physician of the ravenous appetite finally had satiated himself and taken his leave. Quiet had returned to the dining room and Uriah had been reflecting pleasantly on his plans to meet Elise later in the day when her father had walked unexpectedly into the room.

"You haven't heard the news, then?" asked de Guissac.

"What news?"

"Your friend, the great Commodore Decatur. He is dead. Killed in a duel."

"What? My God!"

Uriah grabbed the newspaper and tried to find the article, but his comprehension of written French was still poor and he quickly gave up the effort.

"What happened?" he implored. "Who killed him?"

De Guissac shook his head ruefully. "It is a tragedy. Such a great man of the sea. It was Barron, you see, the Commodore James Barron who killed him."

"Barron? The Barron of the *Chesapeake* who surrendered to the *Leopard*? That cowardly cur?"

De Guissac nodded. "The same. Barron had accused Decatur of

insulting him and they had exchanged threatening letters. Finally they met on a field near Washington City about a month ago. Both were wounded. Decatur suffered greatly for twelve hours and then died.

"Ah, but this great commodore got the funeral he merited," de Guissac continued, consulting the newspaper for the facts and reading them aloud. "Ships off Washington and Norfolk fired their guns every thirty minutes for many hours. Congress was adjourned to attend the funeral rites. Mrs. Decatur says her husband was murdered and has begged your president to promise that Barron never will have another command. It is too, too sad."

Uriah sat in silence, staring glumly into space. De Guissac sat next to him. "What will this mean to your chances of being reinstated by the navy? To lose a friend in such a high place!"

"I don't know. I was told that the decision on my case would be made eventually by the president himself, not by the Board of Commissioners. But I am not thinking about that now. I am thinking only of a very great man who has been brought down by an inferior. My navy . . . my country . . . has suffered a terrible loss!"

Hotel Grenville was considered to be one of London's finest hostelries; he found it to be overpriced, cold, and burdened with a most unfriendly staff. Uriah had come to London to meet with and study the drawings of Sir Robert Seppings, the British Navy's chief constructor, who had designed a new circular stern that would be much stronger than the traditional square stern and would increase the firing capability of a man-of-war. He glanced at the pile of papers on the table in his hotel room. They comprised his long, detailed reports to the secretary of the navy on what he had seen and been told in France and England on the latest innovations in shipbuilding. He would dispatch them on the first ship to the United States. If he were returned to the navy, his knowledge of these advances might stand him in good stead in the future.

Now, his hand weary with writer's cramp, he struggled to complete a long letter to Mordecai, the first he had written in several months. He sat, wrapped in thought, bereft of words, because he had come to the most difficult portion of the letter. He felt he must confide in his cousin, not so much to ask his counsel, but more to gain the relief of unburdening himself to a loved friend. He picked up the pen and continued to write:

And so, dear cousin, I am caught in a great turmoil of the heart. All my life I have vowed never to marry out and indeed I have scorned those who did. Rather than marry out, I used to bravely say, I rather would remain a hardy bachelor. I could not be disloyal to my ancestral faith. And I am not unmindful of promises that we both made to our beloved grandfather, who worried so that we would someday abandon Judaism.

Yet, now my test has come and I am weak and wavering. Never did I think I would meet a girl like this one. Just looking at her takes my breath and besides she is wise and witty and full of joy. And she gives me joy, for she loves me as much as I do her. Here, in London, I ache for the sight of her and for the sound of her voice, though we have been apart only for a week. It is the same whenever I am away from her. I have made short trips to see France, as I had planned when I left Philadelphia, but also to regain my balance, my proportions. To see, in other words, whether I still would long for Elise when I was outside her spell, far from her perfume, unable to see her smile. My experiments have failed. I have not been able to get away from her, no matter where I went. Everywhere her eyes followed me, her arms beckoned to me. I am truly in love and distance does not change it.

Dear God, what shall I do? Is it possible that she would take up our faith? I have not had the courage to broach it to her. I think it is hopeless. She is a devout Catholic and attends mass each day. She knows of course that I am an Israelite. We have spoken of it a time or two and she has asked me a few questions about our ways and practices. But it is a mild curi-

osity, nothing more. I know that she would not move across the line. Never. Yet I fear that I cannot give her up.

All of which serves to remind me that another Shabbat is two days past and I have not gone to services in months. I am ashamed. This Shabbat, when I am again in Paris, I will go to the Spanish-Portuguese esnoga and pray for guidance in this problem. Which also serves to remind me that I shall soon be in Paris and there Elise waits for me. My heart pounds at the thought. You, confirmed in your bachelorhood, may think me silly and lovesick. I confess to being both.

They clung together in the warm bed like two green ferns entwined together in a garden of delight. Her hair was pressed against his cheek and he could smell its freshness. Her arms were wrapped tightly around him as if she feared he would break away from her and never return. He took her hand and pressed it to his lips, reassuring her that he never would leave.

He still could not believe that she was here with him in his bed and that they had made love together for the first, wonderful time. It was all like a dream—a familiar dream, for he had thought of it, longed for it, so many times.

It had been the slight rustle of her gown that had made him raise his head from the pillow; he had almost been asleep. The door to his room already was closing, but he could see her outlined against the dim light of the hallway lamp and he knew at once that it was Elise.

"What is it?" he said, startled. "Is something—" She interrupted him, her soft voice cutting like a saber through the darkness: "Shush, my love. There is nothing wrong. Now that I am here, all is well."

In the darkness, he could hear her removing her clothing. Before he could think of consequences or dangers or moral compunctions, she was in bed with him, her lithe body pressed against him in desire.

Though both were fiery with passion, there yet was a sweetness, a gentleness about their lovemaking that would always remain in his memory. It was as if they both wanted to give, rather than to take. It was tender and unhurried. She cried out softly in pain when he entered her and the membrane ruptured, but when he started in dismay, she quickly reassured him and begged him not to stop. She wrapped her long legs around his body and they came together as if two beings had transcended their duality and become unitary.

She moaned low with her lust and whispered how much she loved him. And when he climaxed, she too shuddered with her orgasm and her arms went tightly around his neck as if to confirm her satisfaction, her fulfillment.

"I would have waited, you know," he said afterward, as they lay, sated and peaceful, in the dark. "I never would have demanded this of you. I am your first lover. That is quite a responsibility."

"A woman's first love should only be a man she loves very much," Elise answered. "There is nobody else I shall ever love as I love you, Uriah. If I had not come here tonight, or some other night, I would regret it for the rest of my life. Now I have a beautiful memory that never can be taken away."

"How did you get here?" asked Uriah. "It is late. The streets are dangerous for a woman alone."

"It was all carefully planned," she answered, and he could sense that she was smiling with the success of her plot. "Papa left today for Marseilles on a business trip, and I told the servants that I would spend the night with my friend Claudette. And so, dear handsome Claudette, I sent our valet for a cab and came here to you. A gentle knock at the front door, a gift of two francs to the porter, and *voilà*! I appeared at your bed."

"You are a devil!"

"No, I am a woman in love. And it is time that I am with my lover."

"It will be the first of many wonderful times, Elise. I promise you. We shall be together forever."

There was a noticeable change in her voice. There was an edge of sadness. The deviltry was gone. "Whatever will be, my love," she whispered, "let us think only of tonight. Tomorrow will take care of itself. Tonight, we are together and we have each other. You see how much I love you? Already I begin to hunger for you again."

She moved atop him and began to slide back and forth, tantalizing him, arousing him anew. Her lips came to his, and both their mouths opened in yearning.

Above them the elm trees shivered lightly in the wind, a slightly foreboding sound warning that autumn was climbing the slope of the hill. Here at the crest, though, the sun yet was warm and summer hovered a while longer. Below them all of Paris sprawled quietly in the peaceful afternoon, lovely old domes poking up here and there from the sea of low roofs. The only sounds reaching them from the city below were the clopping of horses as coaches intermittently passed. Even the usually strident voices of the vendors seemed subdued, in respect of Sunday.

Under Napoleon, Elise had explained to him, Sunday was decreed to be a day like any other and shopkeepers were ordered to stay open and do business. With the restoration of King Louis, however, all activity had ceased on the Lord's Day. On such days, Paris seemed almost eerily quiet, as if the population had left. But with the passage of time since the King's edict, some shops again had begun doing business on Sunday and the vendors again walked the avenues. Yet there still was a feeling of homage in the air, as if Parisians were determined to give the Lord at least something of his due.

Here on the crest of Montmartre, under the great windmill that stood on the height, they sat and held hands, enjoying the peace and silence and the lovely view. They talked little. There was no need for talk. It was enough that they were together and very much in love.

Both were dressed in finery, for they had enjoyed an afternoon promenade along the left bank of the Seine and it was necessary to wear their finest costumes lest they look out of place. She wore her beautiful white cashmere gown with exotic Persian embroidery. He had put on his finest linen shirt, pearl-gray trousers, a crisp white pique waistcoat, and a light blue coat. He was shod in gleaming patent leather boots and on his hands were white deerskin gloves, newly bought at six francs the pair, though he had removed them now and slapped them idly against his palm.

"The sun is sinking quickly," she said. "The day is almost gone. I wish it would last much longer. I wish it could last forever."

"Every day I am with you seems too short," he replied.

She put her hand to her mouth in consternation. "Oh, I forgot! I had so many things planned to show you today, and we have lost the time. I wanted to take you to the Jardin des Plantes to see the zoological garden. We have missed that in all our touring. It is quite marvelous. They have lions, a wolf, a panther, and several bears."

"I would much rather stay here on Montmartre with you and just enjoy being together," answered Uriah. "It is so peaceful here."

"Yes, today it is peaceful. But it was not always so. This city has lived through so much history that every square foot can tell its own story of ancient tragedy. Right where we are sitting—on this little white bench resting quietly among the elm trees—right here was a terrible battle in March of 1814, when the emperor was barely holding on and the Russian army stood just outside the gates. On this quiet peaceful hilltop, sixteen thousand Frenchmen died, and our enemies lost almost as many."

Uriah looked around him, gazing at the paths and lawns with new respect. Many brave men had died on this slope, fighting for their flags.

Elise did not want to speak of solemn things on this tranquil day of love. To change the subject, she pointed to the nearby church and its spire, on which was fixed an optical telegraph with its two giant arms.

"Do you know," she said, "that they say it is possible by using the chain of telegraphs to get a message from Paris all the way to the shore of the Mediterranean in less than fifteen minutes? It is a miracle, no? To speak across such great distances in so little time! The world is changing, my love."

He smiled as he looked at the tall mast with its crossbeam and arms, one of hundreds placed on heights throughout France.

"I remember well my introduction to the telegraph," he said. "I was aboard the brig *Argus* and we sailed along the coast of England, and those arms were twirling away, letting our enemies know that we were coming. We would have given much then for less progress in the world. Surprise was our ally; we did not want to be announced like guests at a ball."

They were silent again. The branches above them dipped in the freshening wind. He knew the weather was changing. By tomorrow rain probably would be streaming down. Elise shivered. He put his arm about her and hugged her tightly to him. In a few minutes more they must leave, lest she catch cold.

"I would like to speak to you . . . about our future," he said.

She looked at him, alarm in her eyes. "No," she pleaded. "Not now. Not today. It is so beautiful here. Let us just sit and enjoy what is left of the day."

"But why?" he asked. "I mean to speak only of happy things. I want to ask you to share my life forever. I could never part from you. I want to ask you to marry me. I love you so very much, Elise."

"It cannot be, Uriah," she whispered. "You know it cannot be." She took his hand in both her hands and squeezed it so tightly that he was startled by the force of her grasp.

He was stunned and frightened by her reaction. He had expected joy and a squeal of pleasure, a laughing embrace, a tearful assent. Instead Elise looked down at her hands. On her face was pain.

"What do you mean? Surely you cannot mean that. How can you make such a decision so quickly? You did not even think about it."

"Think about it?" Her eyes were filled with tears. "Do you really believe I have not thought about this? I have thought of almost nothing else since we first met. How many nights I have cried myself to sleep thinking of this and trying to find some solution. There is no solution. There is no happy ending to our love story, *mon cher.* An ending, yes. But not a happy one."

"I simply cannot understand what you are saying!" His face was pale, and he could feel beads of perspiration on his brow. "What is the matter? You have said you loved me. And you know . . . you must know how much I love you."

"Neither of us could have any doubt about the other's love," she said softly. "But love is not enough, dear Uriah. We are from different spheres . . . from different—I don't know the proper word in English."

"You mean because I am not a Christian. Because I am a Hebrew."

There was a hint of a nod. "Yes, that is part of it. Do not mistake my words, Uriah. I do not love you any the less because you are of the faith of Abraham. I respect your people because your religion was the mother of mine, and without it, mine would not exist. I bear no hatred in my soul for your religion. I swear it. And I swear to you that I never have spoken with tight teeth of someone going to the Jews to borrow money or to sell old furniture in the hateful way that some of my friends speak. I never have felt dislike for your people."

"Then why will you not marry a man of this people?" There was a hard edge to his voice. He was hurt and willing to challenge her.

She rubbed her cold hands together and then wrapped her fingers tightly about each other and put them to her lips as if trying desperately to find the proper words in a language not her own.

"I said before that this is just one of the reasons," she whispered. "Perhaps you did not hear me. Will you become a Catholic to marry me?"

He sighed and looked down at his boots. "I would do anything for you, but this I cannot do. It has to do with a promise I made many years ago to a man I loved very much. I cannot break that vow. I cannot leave Judaism. Would you consider . . . there are ways, you know, for a Christian person to become a Hebrew."

There was a tight smile upon her lips. "You know I could not. I thought for a time, when I was perhaps twelve years, of entering the convent. I did not, but I still retain the holy fire. Jesus is my personal savior. Without him, I could not live."

"Then could we not live as we are? Each of us worshipping in our own way? Tell me why that could not be."

"Yes, my love. It is possible, it could be. But where? Where would this be?"

He was confused. Why should she raise this question? "Why, in the United States, of course. In Philadelphia, perhaps . . . or more likely in New York City, which is becoming the great city of my country. We can decide that together. That is a minor question."

"No, my love, it is not minor. It is altogether major to me. Uriah, I could not live away from France. I don't know if you will be able to understand this, but my heart would break if I could not live in my own land. I could not stand it."

"I never dreamed this would be a problem! I thought you would go wherever I should go."

Tears glistened in her eyes. "I knew you would not be able to understand this," she murmured. "That is why I have so long dreaded this day. You must think, in your deepest heart, that I really do not love you when I say such things, but I swear to you that I do love you with all my heart. Never again will I be able to love a man as I do you, Uriah. But I am a Frenchwoman, and I also love my country very much . . . even more, I suppose, than the usual Frenchwoman. I do not know what made me this way. Perhaps it was my father. This big, strong man who is afraid of no other man—he cries whenever he sees the flag of France. Perhaps it was living alone with my mother while my father was captive held in an English prison. Whatever made me this way, I am what I am. I could not think of leaving France."

He nodded curtly. "Then it is settled," he said. "I will live in France with you."

"Will you?" she asked, knowingly. "When the day comes that you are restored to duty in the American Navy, will you be content to remain here in a foreign land while others man your ships and fight your battles? If I know you, and I think I do, you could not do this. You love the United States with the same fervor with which I love France. You would never be happy here, as I could not be happy there. It just cannot be."

He got slowly to his feet. The afternoon light was almost gone now. "I suppose we had better go," he said. "It is growing colder and you have no wrap."

Uriah sat like a statue, the parchment dangling from his fingers. He sat rigidly, his knees pressed together, on a settee in de Guissac's salon, awaiting Elise's return from the Sorbonne, when his old comrade walked into the room.

"What is it, Uriah?" asked de Guissac, alarmed at his friend's empty stare. "Is there some bad news?"

Uriah shook his head slightly as if to break up his thoughts. "It is news, though by no means bad. The royal mail carrier has just brought me a letter from an old navy friend of mine in Washington City. He met President Monroe at a fete and managed to ask him about my trial and my sentence. The president was in a jubilant mood because of his confidence that he would easily be reelected. In any case, the president was happy and talkative, and he told my friend that he agrees with the secretary of the navy that my punishment was excessive. He is going to disapprove the sentence of the court-martial and order me returned to duty. I should receive official notice of this within a month or two."

De Guissac threw his arms into the air. "But—but, that is wonderful my friend! It is what you have hoped and prayed for! You will be going back to the navy and resume your career. Why do you look so miserable? You should be shouting the news from the windows!"

Uriah looked at him. "Yes, I should, shouldn't I? Why, then, do I feel so empty, knowing that as soon as I receive the notice, I must take ship for home?"

De Guissac put a huge hand on the younger man's shoulder. "Of course. I understand. But perhaps she will change her mind and agree to go back with you."

Uriah emphatically shook his head. "No," he said. "Not Elise.

Even if she would change her mind, she could not. I understand her. The same sort of blood flows in both our veins. I could not stay here. She cannot go there. This is our fate."

"I will speak to her," de Guissac said.

"Thank you, André, but do not. It would only upset her. There is nothing that can be done for us."

She lay tightly against him as she had on their first such night together. Her body fit perfectly against his own—curve joining curve, angle meeting angle, as if they were two parts of a whole, rejoined after long separation.

There was no desire to make love on this night. They clung to each other in a last effort to prevent time and distance from tearing them apart, fighting a battle that would be lost on the morrow. He could feel her tears falling on his cheeks, then sliding down as if they were his own.

"Remember this always, Uriah," she said in a choked voice. "Remember that no matter what happens, I shall always be yours and you shall always be mine. Though each of us may marry others and have children by them, never forget that we belong to each other. I beg this of you."

"I will not forget, Elise. I pledge you."

"And you will come to see me?"

"I'll come as often as I can. I don't know where I shall be, but somehow I'll find a way to return to Paris as often as possible."

"My father will miss you, too," she said. "He loves you like a son."

"I will miss him as much."

Uriah sighed and gently brushed a blonde hair back from her eyes as Elise began to cry softly again. "I cannot believe," he said, "that I will not see you tomorrow, that we will not be meeting for luncheon, that we will not go for a promenade in the afternoon. That I will be miles away from you, on the open sea."

14

They stood now on the larboard side of the quarterdeck of the frigate *Cyane*. A small group of ship's officers had retreated to the starboard quarter at their approach and stood watching and listening.

"She bellies well in the high surf, Mr. Levy." Commander Elliott threw the words back over his right shoulder as he raced up the gangplank to his quarterdeck. Commander Elliott seemed perpetually in a hurry and made every motion at top speed.

"Yes, sir. Thank you, sir," responded Uriah, following in the wake of his commanding officer.

"Nice and dry, too, Mr. Levy. A good, tight gig. A capital job, capital! That's as nice a whale boat as ever I've seen."

"Yes, sir. Again, thank you, sir."

"Where did you come up with the design, Levy?" Commander Elliott asked. "That boat is a bit different from any whale boat I've seen before."

"Oh, I just combined a few of my own ideas with the whale boats I knew as a boy on the Delaware. It's a bit different, I agree."

"You have quite a talent for design and construction, Mr. Levy. I wager our carpenters would have been lost without your supervision on this job. Perhaps you've missed your true calling."

"Thank you, sir, but I'm quite happy doing what I'm doing."

"Yes, yes, of course. Glad to have you with me, Levy. It's nice to have a first luff with well-rounded experience for a change. I've had my fill of officers who have only been aloft once or twice in their entire lives. There's something to be said for making an officer from the ranks, eh? Well, that's all, Mr. Levy. Carry on. And thank you again for creating such a nice new gig for me."

"Welcome, sir."

As the *Cyane's* captain went below to his cabin, the nearby group of officers stirred and exchanged amused looks.

"Gawd, I almost expected the captain to kiss him on the lips," said one of them.

"Sickening, wasn't it?" posed Frank Ellery, the third lieutenant. "I think the old man's afraid of the Jew. He heaps praise on him night and day 'til it makes you want to puke all over the planking. I think he's afraid the Jew will cut him into small pieces unless he keeps telling him how great he is."

Ellery's friend, William Spencer, the second luff, nodded in agreement. "That hustler better not be impertinent with me again, as he has a couple of times. Rank or not, I'll kick him in the mouth."

"Watch it, here he comes," warned Jackson, a young midshipman.

Uriah walked over to the group and nodded to them. Some curt nods were received in return.

"Gentlemen, though we are in port, I see no reason for standing idly on the quarterdeck," Uriah told them. His tone was soft, but its firmness was plain. "There are work parties to be supervised, are there not?"

"We watched your whale boat, Mr. Levy," said Spencer. "An admirable performance, admirable!" he continued, in obvious imitation of the captain's repetitious praise.

Uriah knew he was being ragged. He did not respond to the sarcasm but merely nodded again.

"But how could it *not* be admirable, Mr. Spencer?" chimed in Ellery. "The whale boat was constructed of pieces stolen by the carpenters, under Mr. Levy's experienced direction, from every other vessel in the squadron. Each of our sister ships has given of herself to make Mr. Levy's admirable whale boat."

"Ah yes, true, Mr. Ellery." The others in the group had trouble restraining their smiles as Spencer took up his cue. "But remember that our first lieutenant is a past master at appropriating navy property. Why, did you not see his fine new shaving box of mahogany? Such a fine piece of wood is not navy issue. It became Mr. Levy's property when some poor quartermaster was not looking."

"That will be quite enough, you two jackanapes," Uriah snapped. "I can countenance ragging, but I will not listen to outright lies. That mahogany was purchased by me at the Brazilian shipyard yonder, and I have the bill of sale in my cabin to prove it."

"Are you calling me a liar, you scoundrel?" Ellery stepped to within a few inches of Uriah, his face crimson with anger. Other hands tried to pull him back, but he would not be restrained.

"Indeed, sir, you are a liar and you have proved it within the last few minutes. You also are a rascal and a jackass and wanting every quality of a gentleman." Uriah's face also was red with rage, but he kept his voice low and even. Ellery clearly heard him, but the others were not sure exactly what he had said.

"If you were not my superior—," Ellery virtually spat the words into Uriah's face.

"Forget my rank, Ellery! I will gladly waive the privileges of rank and will meet you anywhere you choose with weapons of your choice. You are a lying bastard, and I tell you that in front of your companions and fellow comedians."

Spencer reached around in front of Ellery and physically pulled him backward, away from his rival. "Break it off, Frank! He is a cutthroat and would as soon kill you as look at you. He is well known for such conduct. He has said enough for you to prefer charges anyway. Get your revenge through the law."

Ellery had struggled briefly against the tight grip across his chest, then he relaxed. "Of course," he said, never taking his eyes from Uriah's face. "I shall go to the captain immediately and lodge charges. This sort doesn't belong in the navy anyway, and one more court-martial should do it. I would never duel such a person, no matter the provocation. Dueling is only for gentlemen, not for bloodthirsty ruffians."

A half-hour later, Uriah sat in the cabin of his commanding officer and received the strongest rebuke he ever had taken from the usually mild Elliott.

"You have only played into their hands, Levy. For God's sake, man, didn't you see that? They bait you and you respond. Why are you so brilliant about seamanship and so all-fired stupid about other things?"

Uriah was crestfallen. "You're right, sir. It was stupid. I am plagued with a quick tongue and a ready temper, and they get the best of me."

Elliott angrily shook his head. "You need a leavening of wit, man! You have no sense of humor. For God's sake, stop taking yourself so seriously! They were idiots for getting on you like that, but you were a double idiot for turning it into a challenge. I know your reputation . . . everyone in the navy knows it. But until now we have had peace on this ship, and I thought perhaps you had changed your ways. You're a damned fine officer, Levy. Probably the best first lieutenant I've ever had. But your temper and your sensitivity won't allow you to profit from your ability. You're never out of trouble long enough."

Uriah sighed deeply. "Yes, sir. I guess it took me by surprise. I have had little truck with Ellery and Spencer since I came aboard, but I never knew they were so hostile to me. Had I seen that, perhaps I would have been better prepared for their ragging. I . . . I thought that I had left such nonsense behind me when I left the *North Carolina*."

"You had trouble on the *North Carolina*? I didn't hear of that."

"No sir, no trouble," Uriah hastily explained. "There was no trouble because I knew what to expect, so I kept to myself and scarcely exchanged a word with the other officers except in the line of duty.

You see, soon after I went aboard the liner, a friend of mine—Isaac Mayo, the flag lieutenant—told me that the officers had asked him to join them in a move to keep me off the ship. When Isaac asked them the reason, their answer was that I was a 'damned Jew.' That was the only reason. Isaac is a decent man, and he told them that he would oppose their move and that they had no right to exclude me. Once I knew about that, I was watchful for trouble and managed to avoid it. But here, on the *Cyane*, I had supposed I was accepted as a brother officer. Obviously I was wrong. I was taken by surprise today. I apologize to you, Captain. I'm sorry it happened."

Elliott was mollified now. He leaned back in his chair and put his hands behind his head. "Very well then, Mr. Levy. Guard yourself to see that there is no repetition. I have advised Ellery to give himself some time to cool down. I have asked him to wait a few weeks before making a final decision on whether to prefer charges against you. Good God! Rio de Janeiro is one of the finest liberty ports this frigate will ever touch. Why can't we just enjoy our exotic surroundings here and do our work without all this raging? Guard yourself, sir, and I shall try to see that the others do so. Perhaps peace will return to the *Cyane* and we can get some enjoyment from this port."

Uriah was well satisfied with himself. He had spent a productive day supervising repair work on the *Cyane*'s mainmast, which had been troublesome ever since the frigate had joined the Brazil Squadron a half-year earlier. Now, in this extended call at Rio de Janeiro, there finally was some time to unstep the mast and get to its problems. He kept his work detail hopping all day long as they unbent the sails and sent down the studding-sail booms and the topgallant yards, then housed the topgallant mast. All the rigging was overhauled and replaced where necessary, mended where possible. Just as the sailors were envisioning an end to the detail and perhaps being allowed to loaf for the remainder of the watch, Uriah ordered them to the foremast to repeat the process. The groans were almost audible, but they knew better than to openly oppose this tireless officer who had never been known to order a flogging on this frigate, but whose tongue could by itself cut the hide of a malingerer.

Finally, well into the first dog-watch, the work was done and the men were sent below. They had stayed at their jobs long past the termination of their regular watch, and Uriah had promised them the reward of a free day on the morrow and shore liberty for all. He had the captain's permission to thus reward them for their hard day's work, even though they were not of the quarter-watch that would normally be on liberty for the morrow, for only one-fourth of the *Cyane's* crew was allowed to be on shore at a time. The rest were charged with garrisoning the ship. So off they would go to-morrow, whoring with frenzy until that was drained from them and then drinking themselves into insensibility. The lucky ones would stagger back to the ship without being robbed or maimed en route. Others would lay somewhere in the street until a search party led by scowling midshipmen found them and carried them back to the frigate. Commander Elliott was a tolerant captain and they would not be punished for their indiscretion unless they cursed or—God help 'em—struck a superior in their drunkenness. Then they would face the full wrath of the navy, and the green bags holding the nine-tailed cats would be pulled from their closet.

As for Uriah, he had had enough of sightseeing. Tomorrow he would seek out the marine corporal assigned as ship's librarian and request him to empty out the cask containing the books so that he could choose one or two. His time below would be spent writing a few letters and reading in his cabin.

He sat now in the wardroom, enjoying a mug of coffee and going over in his mind the now-completed day's work. He was confident that the problems with the main mast had been fixed. It had been a day well spent.

"Did you catch a look at the emperor's launch today, Mr. Levy? It passed just off our port quarter. I saw him plain as day." The speaker was Peter Turner, a midshipman who had carried on several friend-ly conversations with Uriah. He was mature for his tender years, a willing worker and eager to learn about the sea.

"Yes, I noticed him go by. He has been in the Navy Yard almost every day. The Brazilians are fitting out a battle squadron to put down an insurrection at St. Catherine's, I believe."

"He looked friendly as could be. I almost expected him to wave at us."

"Steward! Goddamn it, where are you? I want my coffee!" Uriah and the midshipman broke off their exchange and looked across the wardroom at the source of the angry shout. It was Phelps, a hotheaded lieutenant often found in the company of Spencer and Ellery. Indeed, Spencer was just sitting down alongside him.

"You damned steward! Get your ass in here! Where the hell are you?" Phelps continued his caterwauling and banged an empty mug loudly on the table.

Spencer looked over at Uriah and the midshipman. "Obviously someone has dismissed the steward. Isn't that typical? He got himself well fixed with coffee and then dismissed the steward so no one else could have any. This pushy fellow is always taking such liberties, Phelps, or hadn't you noticed?"

Uriah clenched his lips tightly. He was bound to avoid another incident with this rogue. His hands gripped his mug and his knuckles went white.

"Is he speaking to you, sir?" asked Turner innocently. "I did not see you dismiss the steward. In fact, I saw him passing to the scuttlebutt to get water for the mess."

"Never mind, Turner," Uriah said softly. "They are not interested in the truth."

"We are afflicted with a hustler on this ship, Mr. Phelps," Spencer loudly continued. "We have a peddler among us who has not the manners of an officer and a gentleman but belongs with a cart of old clothes, selling his wares. He dismissed the steward not out of malice but out of sheer ignorance. His type is not used to dealing with servants."

Uriah saw red. The comments were too piercing to be ignored. There was a limit. He slowly got to his feet and walked toward Spencer, who rose to wait for him.

"Mr. Spencer, I shall say this one time only: I did not dismiss the steward. He will be back momentarily and will serve you your precious coffee."

"If you cannot speak the truth, Levy, I suggest you be quiet. If you continue in this manner, I shall be forced to gag you."

Uriah's lips peeled back from his teeth in doglike fury. He stuck his face but a few inches from Spencer's. "If you care to," he said softly, "you certainly may try to do that."

Spencer took a step back and then screamed out, "God damn you, you hustler, I told you to be quiet!"

Uriah knew the significance of the words coming out of his throat, but he could do nothing to dam them up. "Let us settle this on shore, sir, with the weapons of your choice. Then one of us will be shut up for all time to come."

Spencer's demeanor changed instantly. He carried a tight, satisfied smile on his mouth. "You will live to regret that challenge, Levy. I would not dirty my hands on a duel with such as you. But the navy will handle you. And good riddance, I must say." He and Phelps then turned and left the wardroom.

Uriah, still shaking in rage, sat down to collect himself. Well, he was in for it now. Had it all been set up? A scene beautifully played out for his benefit? If so, it had worked to perfection. He had taken the bait again.

One hour later, Uriah stood silently in the captain's cabin as Commander Elliott coldly informed him that both Spencer and Ellery had officially proferred charges against him—charges of conduct unbecoming an officer and a gentleman. His court-martial would have to wait until the *Cyane* returned to the United States, Elliott said, for there was no time on this voyage to prepare and conduct such a hearing. But a court-martial there would be. It was only a matter of time.

He spent the last few minutes of his watch as officer of the deck just standing at the larboard bulwark and letting the beauty of Rio de Janeiro soak over him like a healing balm. Oh, they had been tethered in this harbor long enough to make any good navy man restless, and the old-timers among the crew were grousing that the *Cyane* soon would ground on her own beef bones if they didn't set sail and get to sea. He shared their restlessness. But there was no harbor in the world any easier on the eyes, and it was a relief to come on deck and see those green peaks looming over the frigate's masts. They were a sight for weary eyes.

Uriah seldom had taken advantage of his chances to go ashore in Rio; he had far too much work aboard the *Cyane* and afterward was too tired to do much except head for his berth. Today, however, he would stroll down the long wharf and into the city. Perhaps this would take his mind off his latest trouble. He must shop for trinkets, too, for his mother, grandmother, and sisters, for any day now the order would come from Commodore Creighton to weigh anchor.

His eyes took the same route along the crags that they had taken a thousand times before in these last few days, yet a sight of which he never tired. There was Pão de Acúcar, the conelike peak that the sailors called "Sugar Loaf," looking down upon the narrow harbor entrance like a stern teacher. And over there, much higher even than the Pão, was "The Corcovado," whose rocky head reared up what Uriah judged to be well over two thousand feet above the sea. The great landmark for men approaching from the sea, however, was "The Cavea," another great rock with a curiously flat top. It bore the same name given by Portuguese sailors to a sail on their ships for its resemblance to that cloth.

These vertical fingers of rock loomed suddenly, dramatically, above the city built mostly on a seaside plain. Narrow mountain spurs extended out into the plain, and in the picturesque valleys between, Rio was beginning to push out, away from the sea.

The young emperor of Brazil had made a wise choice in declaring Rio as the capital of his newly independent nation. Its bay was monstrous and could provide anchorage for all the ships of all the world's navies. Yet this great lagoon, sixteen miles long, could be entered only through a single gate just one mile wide between the threatening faces of Pão de Acućar on the west and Pico do Papagaio on the east. Threatening faces were not enough against foreign marauders: the Portuguese who had settled this place also had built the Fortress of Santa Cruz on one side of the entrance and the Fort of São João on the other. Gliding through that narrow door under double-reefed sails, any experienced hand on a man-of-war would throw nervous glances as he passed under all those formidable cannon on either side. They could blow an enemy ship to bits with hardly a second thought, for there was no place to hide. Sailors prayed for good weather when they drew near to Rio anchorage, for the entrance to that harbor became a ship-killer whenever a storm blew from the south or southwest. When such a storm roared, a deep bar would cause high swells to explode into the air, and many ships had smashed one side or the other.

American ships, though, had naught to fear from the forts' cannon. The emperor welcomed the Yankees to his capital city. Had not the United States been the first foreign state to recognize Brazil's independence? U.S. warships now were frequent callers to this harbor and were met in friendly fashion.

The *Cyane's* bell had just been struck, the new watch was set, and the off-watch was sent below. Most of the men in the off-watch had by now seen enough of Rio, though the younger ones never seemed to quench their thirst for rum nor appease their hunger for whores. The veterans, during hours off-watch, contented themselves with making fancy shirts or perfecting their scrimshaw. One of them was a capable tattooer and set up his colors and tools on the forecastle. He was well patronized by his mates and accumulated a tidy profit on each cruise.

The piercing sound of the pipes split the air, and the boatswain's mates stood at the fore and aft hatches shouting down, "Ahoy, fore and aft! Larboard quarter-watch, prepare to go ashore on liberty!" The pounding of feet resonated up from the berth deck as young sailors rushed early to their ale and rum and women.

Uriah waited until the first rush had passed the gangplank and then he walked slowly down the plank to the wharf. He had coolly turned the deck over to Lieutenant Phelps, and that worthy had taken and returned his salute without a word, only a dark stare. *So be it*, Uriah thought. *Let us confine our exchanges only to necessary business and I'll do far better in staying out of scrapes.*

The wooden wharf extended for almost a mile. Behind him, as he walked toward the nearby city, the wharf entered a Brazilian navy yard, the source of the polished mahogany over which that bastard Spencer had made such a fuss. Liberty parties of Brazilian sailors often strolled past the *Cyane's* mooring place on their own way to the saloons and whorehouses.

A lone Brazilian sailor came past Uriah now, but this fellow was at a dead run and his gasping breath could be plainly heard as he ran. About sixty feet ahead of Uriah on the wharf, another American preceded him toward the city's edge. It was John Moore, easily recognized by his tall, thin figure, a midshipman and close friend of Peter Turner. The Brazilian sailor, now between Uriah and Moore, stopped suddenly and looked back down the wharf toward the navy yard. A look of horror came over his face. He ran quickly down to Moore, stopped him with a hail, and began an animated conversation with him. Moore, too, looked back down the wharf. A pounding of feet came from behind. Uriah turned about and saw a party of about ten more Brazilian sailors led by an officer, his sword drawn and gleaming in the sun. They swerved to avoid running over Uriah and continued down the wharf to where Moore and the Brazilian sailor were halted. The party quickly surrounded the two men, and the officer began screaming at them in Portuguese, the tone indicating imprecations and threats.

Uriah quickened his pace and came up to the group. Moore's face lighted with relief when he saw him.

"Moore, what's happening here?" Uriah barked.

At the sound of his voice, the Brazilian officer—Uriah was not familiar with their emblems of rank, but judged him to be at the level of a master commandant—turned his attention to the new arrival and began to harangue him, his volume only slightly lower than before in deference to Uriah's maturity and higher rank.

"Damn it, Moore," Uriah shouted again. "Tell me what is the problem!"

"Sir, this man says he is an American and was taken by a Brazilian press gang. He says he was forced into their navy and wants to come aboard the *Cyane* for refuge."

The Brazilian officer suddenly stopped screaming and looked from Moore to Uriah and back again, as if awaiting a decision from them.

"By God, it's true," pleaded the escaping sailor. "I was off the brig *Alicia* out of New Bedford. I got drunk in a whorehouse and the next thing I knew I was in this monkey suit and waking up in their navy yard brig. I'm a Yankee, sir, from Fairhaven, Massachusetts, and I want to go home!"

There was not a trace of a foreign accent in the sailor's voice. He spoke with the twang of a born New Englander. Uriah had no choice but to believe him.

"Mr. Moore," he said softly to the midshipman, "I suggest we turn slowly and walk with our friend here back down the wharf to the *Cyane*'s gangplank. If we act deliberately, perhaps they will not try to stop us."

They turned slowly all right, but at the first step the Brazilian party grabbed them and a fierce fight broke out. Moore savagely pushed the Brazilian officer in the chest and drove him back a step or two. But the furious commander regained his balance and charged forward with a howl of rage, bringing his sword flashing downward toward the midshipman. Uriah, acting on instinct, raised his hand and deflected the sword blade away from the midshipman's skull. He felt a searing pain in his hand and saw in a quick sideward look that the sword had glanced off his palm and left a long gash that was filling with blood. The sword did not plunge again, though, because the escapee from Massachusetts had grabbed the officer from behind and was using one arm to put his neck in a vise while the other kept a tight grip on the officer's sword arm.

The Brazilian sailors were unarmed and were raining blows on Uriah and Moore, each of whom stood his ground and fiercely exchanged punches with the sailors. Uriah desperately understood that it was only a matter of seconds until the Brazilians came to their senses and stopped swinging their fists in order to use their superior numbers to wrestle them to the wharf floor.

At that moment, however, the air was rent by the shrill sound of banshee yells and a force of some twenty-five sailors from the *Cyane* came running toward the fight. Several of them swung heavy belaying pins. They made short work of the Brazilians, grabbing them and hurling them aside. In another moment, all fighting had stopped and the two groups stood staring malevolently at each other, separated by a charged no-man's-land of perhaps ten feet.

"Now, gentlemen," Uriah said calmly, though he winced a bit from the fiery pain in his hand, "let us escort our American friend here back to our ship and arrange an audience for him with the captain."

They walked back down the wharf toward their frigate, and as the distance between them and the Brazilians widened, the air was rent by the piercing voice of the Brazilian officer hurling colorful Portuguese curses.

In answer, one of the American boys began to loudly sing, and soon all the others joined in the chorus:

> *Heart of oak are our ships, jolly tars are our men,*
> *We always are ready: Steady, boys, steady,*
> *To fight and to conquer, again and again.*

As they walked up the gangplank of the *Cyane*, the sailors on watch were loudly cheering and waving their caps in the air. They had watched the brief battle from vantage places on the larboard shrouds.

"Lieutenant Levy, let me look at that hand. It must be attended to." It was the voice of the *Cyane's* surgeon. Uriah followed the surgeon down to sickbay, in the bow section of the berth deck, and had his wound cleaned and bandaged by the doctor.

In the wardroom that evening, after the meal had been finished and the officers waited for the stewards to clear the dirty dishes, Lieutenant Cross—the fourth lieutenant—stood up and raised his wine glass.

"Here is a toast to our intrepid first luff," he said, "who interposed himself today between the body of our midshipman and the sword of an enemy. It was a heroic deed, Mr. Levy, and we toast your bravery and your continued good health!"

Shouts of "Hear, hear!" rang through the wardroom, and the officers lifted their glasses to drink. Uriah noticed that Phelps willingly joined the toast. Spencer and Ellery were ashore and absent from the wardroom.

Afterward a game of whist was begun on the wardroom table. Uriah declined an invitation to play. His hand still pained him, and he headed for his cabin for a bit of reading and then bed.

Phelps approached him on the way.

"Levy, Midshipman Moore has been telling everyone within the sound of his voice how you saved his life today. He said his head would have been split down the middle like a melon had you not interfered. It was a damned brave thing to do, and I congratulate you."

Uriah did not know quite how to respond. "Thank you, Phelps," he said.

"I want you to know," Phelps continued, "that I think you have been ill-treated these past days and that I am among those guilty. I apologize to you and I promise to speak in your behalf at the court-martial, whenever that may be."

"I appreciate that, Phelps," Uriah answered. He shook Phelps's proffered hand with his own left hand, his right being encased in a bloody bandage that wanted changing.

It is a good way to end a day, Uriah thought, *with one fewer enemy in the world.*

"I want every cask inspected, Master-at-Arms, every damned cask!" shouted Uriah across the quarterdeck to the entry port. Master-at-Arms Sutcliff, who was responsible much as a constable for the maintenance of law and order among the crew, threw a resigned look back at the first lieutenant and nodded wearily. His weak "Aye, aye, sir" was barely heard.

The water wagon stood on the wharf, below the gangplank, and members of the *Cyane*'s crew were gathered around it, ready to unload the heavy casks and carry them aboard. They would be lugged down to the hold and there emptied into the great wooden ship's casks that held almost one hundred thousand gallons, enough for a voyage of six months.

Sailors on a man-of-war would go to any lengths to smuggle liquor on board to supplement their daily grog ration. Their thirst was unquenchable. It was the duty of the officer of the deck to direct the master-at-arms and his deputies, the marine corporals, in a careful search when any supplies were brought onto the ship to be sure that no illegal drink was smuggled on board as well. The men were ingenious in developing stratagems. They were known to use reeds to siphon the milk from a coconut and to fill it with spirits before it came aboard. They would bribe a peddler on one of the wagons bringing food to the ship to tie a bottle of rum to the ship below the waterline so that it could be retrieved later by the sailor. Each sailor returning from shore liberty of course was carefully searched by the master-at-arms before he could come back aboard. Why, the crafty devils had even been known to hide bottles or skins full of liquor in the bottom of a water cask so they could stealthily retrieve it as the water was being emptied in the hold.

The master-at-arms would tap each cask and taste it to be sure water was the true content, and several of the casks needed probing with an oar to make certain a bottle or skin was not hidden therein.

Uriah was obsessed with the need for keeping such smuggled drink away from the men, and he gave the master-at-arms no rest when he walked the quarterdeck. A sailor found smuggling would be sternly dealt with: Uriah would deny him his grog ration for a week, which to that ever-thirsty tar would be worse punishment than sixteen lashes of the cat. Other officers, if they stood as officer of the deck, might order the rascal to be flogged. Uriah could not bring himself to do so, no matter how much he hated the perpetual haze of semi-intoxication in which many sailors existed on board.

"Lieutenant Levy, my God, sir, that barge is making right for us!" It was Oldfather, a hardened quartermaster who never seemed to lose his calm, but now showed a strange panic in his voice. He had been stationed on the poop with a glass to watch for the return of the captain, who had been summoned to Commodore Creighton's flagship in the harbor for an "All Captains" council. It was the quartermaster's duty to keep watch for the captain's returning gig and to warn the officer of the deck, who would sound the call. A very proper ceremony of return was in order for the captain, with the boatswain's mates tweeting their pipes at the gangway and carefully formed lines of side boys and marine sentries. All the officers must hasten to the quarterdeck and form up in a tight line to greet their captain's return with hats in hands.

But what was this? The return of the captain's gig would not send a graybeard like Oldfather into such wild excitement. Uriah trotted to the gangway to inquire. After a brief word with the quartermaster, he grabbed the glass and put it to his eye to see for himself.

What he saw was the gigantic and colorful barge of Dom Pedro, emperor of Brazil. The barge could be seen almost every day in this harbor and no longer aroused much interest among the officers and men of the *Cyane*, but this day was different. There was no doubt about it; the barge was moving in brisk lunges through the water, directly for the starboard quarter of the American frigate. It was evident that the emperor of Brazil was about to come aboard.

A sickening thought came to Uriah. Had he created an international incident with his repulse of the Brazilian press gang? If so, this would sink his navy career for sure and for all time. A wave of nausea brought a flush of hot liquid up into his throat. He forced it back and fought to concentrate on the task at hand. He had a royal visitor coming aboard with no captain to greet him and other officers and crew scattered from stem to stern.

"Drummer, beat to quarters!" Uriah screamed at the top of his lungs.

The marine drummer, having heard this order only before gun drills and boarding practice at sea, was afraid to comply, fearful that somehow he had misunderstood.

"To quarters, sir?" the marine shouted back. "Did you say 'beat to quarters'?"

"God damn it, man, beat to quarters *now!*" shouted a frantic Uriah in return. "Do not question my order!"

The drummer immediately began sounding the short, rolling drumbeat that had chilled the blood of fighting men in the navies of many countries. From throughout the *Cyane*, crewmen and officers came running, some in states of near nakedness.

"Mr. Phelps, Mr. Ellery, get your divisions up on the shrouds in some semblance of order! They should be prepared to cheer on command. Mr. Spencer, load starboard guns seven and nine with blank cartridge only and be prepared to fire salutes on command! Sergeant of Marines, form your sentries in the drill for reception of a commodore at the starboard entry port. If they are not formed up in two minutes, I'll throw your balls to the sharks tonight!"

When a royal personage visited an American man-of-war, as Uriah knew from his cruises in the Mediterranean, he should be greeted at the gangway by the vessel's captain in full-dress uniform, with the ship's officers assembled behind him, their gleaming swords drawn and raised to form an aisle of silvery honor. The ship's band should be playing martial airs. The hundreds of members of the ship's crew should be arrayed precisely on the shrouds, dressed in their cleanest uniforms, every hair in place, every face wiped free of grime, lips twisted in forced smiles of welcome.

Well, most of that was impossible on this day, but the emperor would get the best that the *Cyane* could give, considering the lack of warning. The members of the ship's band had rushed into position near the entry port and were hastily tuning up, ready to give their all.

Uriah turned his attention back to the barge, which was rapidly nearing the *Cyane*'s quarter. The huge boat was rowed by at least twenty black slaves. In a strange process peculiar to Brazil, the oarsmen all stood upright at the conclusion of each stroke, then dropped back down to their seats with a loud, moaning sound. The mass groan, intense in its rhythm, now was clearly audible. In the sternsheets of the barge, protected by a silken canopy emblazoned with the yellow and green colors of his new country, sat the emperor. A few attendants hovered about him.

As soon as the barge thudded against the side of the *Cyane*, the vigilant Oldfather turned and signaled Uriah. A few quick, quiet orders were given. The captain of marines shouted, "Present arms!" and the muskets with fixed bayonets on the shoulders of the marines were brought down vertically in front of the men's chests. The boatswain's mates shrilled at the pipes, and the marine drummers, four of the ship's regular complement of six, roared out in salute.

As the head of the emperor appeared above the starboard bulwarks, more orders were passed and the noise of the pipes suddenly faded away, the drums sounded their final ruffles, the two starboard guns boomed their own salute, and the marine fifers and drummers began to play "Heart of Oak."

Uriah, his knees weak and wishing he were somewhere else, stepped forward to greet Emperor Dom Pedro and welcome him to the United States Navy frigate *Cyane*.

He was a youngish man, this new, self-proclaimed ruler of Brazil, of pleasant mien, tending slightly to plumpness. He wore gleaming white pantaloons that looked fresh from the tailor's bench and a brilliant green coat with yellow filigree. Several small, tasteful medals were pinned to his chest. The attendants scurried busily in his wake, fluttering about like worried jungle birds.

Despite the friendly, almost weak demeanor of this young man, who looked little past twenty years in age, Uriah knew that he was no party to trifle with. This was the same young man who, when ordered by his father King John VI to return to Portugal for "more political education" less than four years earlier, stood instead on the Plain of Ipiranga and declared Brazil an independent nation, with himself as its emperor and Rio de Janeiro as its capital. Oh, he looked harmless enough, but inside there was steel. Uriah knew that this emperor was quick to make demands and was very short of temper when his demands were not met. He gave every promise of becoming a despot of the first rank, and Uriah had no desire whatsoever to provoke him.

As ranking officer aboard, he stepped up, introduced himself to the emperor, who nodded pleasantly, and then proceeded to introduce him to the other officers. Uriah had no idea whether the emperor understood English but he went on with the introductions, and the young ruler kept smiling and nodding in greeting.

When the introductions were finished, the officers stood silent and the crew hung curiously from the shrouds above them, all watching to see the purpose of this unexpected and highly irregular visit. Uriah did not know what else to say or do, so he also merely stood and awaited the emperor's pleasure.

Dom Pedro said a few soft words in Portuguese and looked at Uriah. When he obviously did not comprehend, the emperor smiled and tried again, this time in French. Uriah sighed with relief. At least there would be communication.

In the midst of the ship's officers stood the *Cyane's* "professor," the teacher who instructed the ship's boys in the primer and several times a week lectured to the midshipmen on navigation and gunnery. His name was Haddaman, and he was addressed as "Captain Haddaman" in respect of his past service in an Austrian army regiment. He was fluent in French and quietly translated the ensuing conversation to the officers gathered around him.

"Ah, you understand French," the emperor said to Uriah. "I am not proficient in English and feared that we would have to talk with signal flags."

"I know some French, Your Majesty," Uriah answered, "and will do all in my power to make you at home aboard our ship and to carry out your wishes."

The emperor nodded with a slight smile. His eyes dropped to the white bandage around Uriah's right hand.

"So," he said. "You are the angry lieutenant who dispersed my naval delegation on the wharf. It is you that I have come here to see."

Dear God, Uriah thought, *it is just what I had feared. He is going to personally take me prisoner.*

"I am the party who was involved in the incident, Your Majesty. I am at your command," he said.

"How is your hand?"

"It is well enough, Your Majesty. Our surgeon closed the wound. It was not serious."

"Good, good. You are a brave man, and the quarrel was regrettable. I have sternly reprimanded the officer responsible. In fact, he is now on his way to the district of Tejuco, where he will join my loyal subjects there in hunting for diamonds on the Rio Belmonte. He is not fit to wear the uniform of my royal navy."

Uriah did not know what to say, so he said nothing. But a great relief was surging through his vitals like a tidal wave.

"The entire incident," the emperor continued, "has caused me to realize that we have no business forcing your countrymen into our service against their will. Your president Adams is my great and good friend. And was it not his predecessor, the great president Monroe, who warned the nations of Europe to keep away from our part of the world and who was first among all the leaders of the earth in extending the hand of friendship to my new empire? Why should I insult these friends? Please convey to your president my apologies for the wrongs that have been done to your sailors and tell him it will no longer be done."

"I . . . I shall certainly do that, Your Majesty."

The conversation then took a decidedly odd turn. The emperor proceeded to subject Uriah to a detailed interrogation about himself: where he hailed from, when he had gone to sea, how long he had been in the navy, how long he had held his present rank. Uriah wondered if he would be questioned about his forebears and would be forced to tell this son of the king of Portugal that his ancestors had been refugees from the savage Inquisition in that land. But the questioning suddenly ended.

"My royal navy is expanding rapidly," the emperor declared. "My greatest need is for good officers. I am getting the best in the world because I reward them accordingly. Do you know Thomas Cochrane of England? They call him Lord . . . uh, Lord Dundonald, I believe. He is now my admiral. I will continue to bring such great seaman to Brazil. Have you seen my new frigate? It was built in your country, you know. It will carry 60 guns, and it will throw fear into the hearts of all my enemies.

"You have great courage," the emperor continued without a pause. "You obviously have the ability to command a large ship, else you would not be in command of such a ship as this one. You are just the sort of man I want to command my mighty ships. I invite you to join me in the building of my great empire."

The sudden offer brought an amazed gasp from the *Cyane's* officers as Professor Haddaman translated the emperor's words. Uriah, too, almost gasped in the emperor's face. He fought to hide his astonishment. He began framing a reply.

Uriah cleared his throat and wet his lips. He paused, grasping in his mind for the best words. Then he proceeded to give his answer. He spoke slowly and enunciated clearly so there was no chance he would be misunderstood. He hoped his command of French was equal to the task.

As slowly, as carefully, Professor Haddaman rendered the translation of Uriah's words to the officers, who bent toward him so as to better hear him.

"Lieutenant Levy answers," Haddaman whispered, "as follows: 'Your Majesty, I say this with great appreciation for the honor you have just accorded me with your offer and with great respect for you and for your empire. But, Your Majesty, I love my country with all my heart and could serve no other flag. And I love the navy of my country and never could desert it. With the deepest respect, Your Majesty, I tell you that I would rather be a cabin boy in the navy of the United States of America than to wear the uniform of a captain in the navy of any other nation in the world.'"

The officers held their breath as they heard Uriah's words repeated.

Later, after the emperor and his party had rowed away, the news of Uriah's reply spread through the crew like flames through a burning sail. That night, as he climbed up to the deck for a breath of air after evening mess, he found, to his surprise, all the ship's crew assembled and awaiting him. They exploded with cheers and huzzahs that soared up over the green peaks and reverberated across the crowded harbor.

He thought of Elise. He looked at the sapphire sea and thought longingly of Elise. He thought of her eyes that were bluer even than this indigo ocean on which the *Cyane* rolled softly, awaiting even a vagrant breeze. He was off-watch, for the forenoon watch had just been called and the hammocks had been piped up to their nettings atop the bulwarks. *The hammocks are looking gray*, he thought. He would suggest a scrub-hammock morning to the captain.

Only a few minutes before, morning quarters had been called and the ship's chaplain had offered the morning prayer. Uriah welcomed the morning and evening prayer and even the chapel on Sunday morning for they served as daily reminders of Elise. Whenever he heard the chaplain's voice intoning the prayer, with its Christian feeling, it turned his mind back to Elise. He saw her kneeling at Mass, fingering her rosary. Oh, it was an image an Israelite man should not carry in his heart, he knew, but it was this memory that the foredeck prayer always evoked. After the prayer, the ship's officers had to come up to the quarterdeck, one by one, and report to the first lieutenant that all their men were properly at quarters. The ceremony, conducted in near-silence, turned his mind back to the ship and to his duties, and he found the picture of Elise fading back into the morning light. But it would come back soon enough, to haunt him at intervals during the day. In the evening, quarters again would be called and the prayer would echo once more. And Elise would gently walk before his eyes and smile bewitchingly at him.

God, how he missed her! How he longed to see her once again and to hold her! He did not dare allow his thoughts to dwell on Elise when he lay on his cot, for such ghosts would drive him insane.

He knew she was married; she had told him when they last met in Paris that she would marry a kind and generous man who would give her the stable home she craved, though in her heart, he would always be her one true love.

He could not bear to think of her living with another man and calling him husband and making love with him. Whenever he did think of it, he fought to dismiss it quickly, for the thought invariably brought a twist of pain to his stomach as his guts knotted and spun. He knew if he dwelled on this, it would make him sick; he would be holding down a berth in sick bay.

So instead he would remember Elise in the Bois de Boulogne, Elise walking with him along the Seine, Elise sitting with him in the dusk on Montmartre. He remembered Elise in his arms, kissing him and assuring him that she'd always be his. These thoughts were torment enough; he could not stand anything worse.

God only knew when he would see her again. The *Cyane* had touched every definable port on the Brazilian coast, then had meandered northward to Guiana, then to Jamaica, and recently to Cuba. Now she was cruising southward again, slipping aimlessly through the doldrums—on patrol against some unknown enemy even though the world was at peace, with even the pirates of the Caribbean slinking back into their dens. The cruise seemed endless; the officers and men were bored to death. The heat and the insects made their coast-wise passages a horror. Still they eased their way farther south, following their orders, toward far-distant Buenos Aires and another squadron rendezvous.

"Mr. Levy, the coincidence is amazing, is it not? Positively amazing! One would think it is the direct hand of God."

Uriah was startled out of his reverie. The slatelike blue surface of the ocean had put him into a near trance. "What is it, Mr. Turner?" he asked of the midshipman who had hailed him. "What is this amazing coincidence of which you speak?"

"Why, sir, the news of Jefferson and Adams. And on the very same day." He held up an English-language newspaper that he had purchased in Havana, but had not unfolded to read until a few minutes before.

"What news is this?"

"You have not heard, Mr. Levy? Jefferson and John Adams have died on the very same day, and that on July Fourth last—the fiftieth anniversary of our independence. Isn't that truly amazing? Two of our Founding Fathers breathing their last on Independence Day."

Uriah had gone white. Peter Turner was so busy announcing the news and proclaiming the strange coincidence that he did not notice until he heard a gasp. He looked up in surprise. Lieutenant Levy had buried his head in his hands and was quite obviously sobbing.

Turner was astonished at the flood of emotion. He looked around, embarrassed, but the two men stood alone on the larboard side of the foredeck. He had never seen Mr. Levy show any emotion, except for occasional flashes of anger. Certainly he did not seem a sentimental sort. Now he stood here on the deck and openly wept.

"I am sorry, Mr. Turner," Uriah finally said. "I apologize for this display. Mr. Jefferson, you see, had been a great hero since I was a child. To me he was the greatest American and ever will be. I cannot conceive of the United States without him."

"I quite understand, sir," Turner said, not really understanding at all.

Uriah found a handkerchief and dried his eyes. *Dear God, Jefferson is dead.* He could not remember the last time he had cried like this. He could not remember crying when his own father had died.

• • •

November 1, 1827

United States Navy Court Martial No. 454, Philadelphia Navy Yard
Charge: Conduct unbecoming an officer and a gentleman
  Specification 1st: That the said Lt. Uriah P. Levy did, on the 19th day of June in the year 1826, use towards Lt. William A. Spencer of the Navy aforesaid, provoking and reproachful words.

Specification 2nd: That the said Lt. Uriah P. Levy, on the 7th day of June in the year 1826, on the quarterdeck of the U.S. Ship Cyane, did use provoking and reproachful words to Lt. Frank Ellery, also the said Navy, and did then and there offer to waive his rank and fight a duel with the said Lt. Ellery.

Specification 3rd: That the said Lt. Uriah P. Levy, on the 19th day of June in the year 1826, did, in the presence and hearing of many of the officers and crew of the U.S. Ship Cyane, invite the said Lt. William A. Spencer to fight a duel.

Finding and Sentence of the Court: After maturely deliberating upon the charges, the evidence, and the defense, the court is of the opinion and does pronounce and declare that the first specification is so far proved as that the accused used provoking words; not proved as to the reproachful words. That the second specification is so far proved as that the accused did, at the time and place specified, offer to waive rank, and the residue of the specification is not proved. That the third specification is proved, with the exception of the "crew."

The court is of the opinion and does therefore adjudge and declare that the accused is guilty of so much of the charge as sets forth that the conduct of the accused was unbecoming an officer and not guilty of the residue.

The court does, therefore, sentence and adjudge that the accused be reprimanded by the Secretary of the Navy, and that the sentence and reprimand be read publicly on the quarterdeck of every vessel in the Navy in commission and at every Navy Yard in the United States. The court feels it necessary to state that the sentence thus awarded to the accused for the offenses of which he is convicted, in particular, for giving a public challenge on shipboard to another officer, and for offering to waive rank with a junior officer in a controversy arising out of points of duty (offenses which the court deems highly objectionable and detrimental to the service) has been rendered thus mild in consequence of the extent of the provocation to be found in the highly improper con-

duct of Lts. Spencer and Ellery, of which the court cannot consent
to pass over without this marked expression of its disapprobation.

(signed) Wm. Bainbridge, C. Morris, J. Orde Creighton,
S. Cassin, James Renshaw, Alex S. Wadsworth,
Henry E. Ballard, W. B. Shubrick, D. Conner.

Uriah's teeth still chattered from the cold, although he had been indoors for more than fifteen minutes. When finally he was ushered into the office of the commandant, his limbs moved stiffly, a souvenir of the bitterly cold day and of his long walk from home to the Navy Yard. He should have hired a carriage. He hoped that he would thaw quickly so that he could state his case without mumbling through half-frozen lips.

Fortunately he was given several more minutes to stand in silence before the commandant's desk until that worthy raised his head from the papers before him. The pause gave Uriah additional time to warm his face and also to study the features of the man who sat before him.

Commodore James Barron had occupied this office for almost four years. The slayer of Decatur had fought and connived after the duel to be restored to a post of authority and honor. Prominent Virginia politicians took up his cause with President Monroe and requested not only Barron's reinstatement to navy duty but also a presidential pardon for an old charge: that Barron had cursed his own country in a long-ago conversation with a British diplomat.

Barron had lived in Denmark during the War of 1812, sitting out his suspension of five years for his role in the humiliation of the *Chesapeake* by the *Leopard*. He turned out to have skill as an inventor and secured more than a dozen patents on his ideas, among them a spinning machine and a lock cutter. But inventing brought him little money, and he lived in near destitution in Europe, relying on charity from American friends and from the U.S. consul. The navy tried very hard to forget him and refused to answer his letters. Barron finally returned to the United States and began a persistent campaign for restoration to duty, a campaign that barely faltered during the furor over his killing of Decatur. Finally, just before Monroe left the White House, Barron won his victory: he was given his first command since 1807, commandant of the Philadelphia Navy Yard.

Suddenly he looked up and, without even a pause to greet Uriah, launched the exchange: "What is it you want this time, Lieutenant Levy?"

Uriah was surprised at his tone. Though they had been introduced a time or two, he had never before met with the commodore in his office.

"Sir, I wish to inquire as to when I might expect a duty assignment. I have already been—"

"Levy, have I not made myself plain? I have answered each of your requests for sea duty, have I not? There are no berths to be had. Your continued petitions are beginning to exhaust my patience. I will not entertain any more from you, Lieutenant."

"Sir, may I just point out that I have held this rank for almost eleven years. I have some seniority. It has been more than six months since my tour on the *Cyane* ended. I want to go back to sea."

Barron's face went cherry red. "Damn it, Levy, we *all* want to go back to sea! They don't need us! Can't you get that through your head? Last year, the sloop of war *Porpoise* sent its boats against Greek pirates and recaptured an English brig. Bravo! That was our only action since the last of the pirate wars in the Caribbean. The navy is sunk into peacetime hibernation, Levy, and we are sunk with it. My God, you whine about having been in rank for eleven years. There are *midshipmen* twice your age—twice your age, man!—who have never achieved their lieutenancies. We are down to less than three hundred officers now and only five thousand sailors and boys. We have three or four frigates at sea; almost everything else sits in port or is rotting away somewhere. Look out my office window: the great battleship *Pennsylvania*—pierced for 132 guns, the strongest man-of-war in the world if she's ever finished, sits under a canopy.

They've been building her for six years and they're not even half finished."

Uriah knew his cause was hopeless, but he foolishly made one more effort: "Sir, I am aware of all that, but I thought—"

"You did *not* think, Levy. You merely pushed your way, as is your wont. Your reputation is not for thinking, but only for fighting. You remind me of David Porter, a fine seaman but a hothead with a mouth that never knew when to close. And what is he now? The admiral of the Mexican Navy. The admiral of the Indians. That's the way you'll end up, Levy, in the service of some foreign despot, if you do not curb your tongue!"

"Commodore, I had my chance for such high rank and refused it."

"Enough, sir! Do not provoke me with insolence! I tell you there is no place for you on a ship of this navy, and I want to hear no more from you on the subject."

"Very well, Commodore. If that is the case, I respectfully request six months' leave. I am no good to the navy or to myself rotting away here. I plan to travel to Europe and to study the latest developments in the navies there. In that way perhaps I still can be of some use to my country."

"Mr. Levy, your request for leave is granted. I would go further and extend your leave indefinitely, if that be your wish."

Uriah winced at the lashing words. His innate respect for those who wore the braid of higher rank wrestled in Uriah's mind with his dislike for this man whose cowardice—or, at best, indecision—when in command of the *Chesapeake* had caused William Henry Allen to weep in shame when telling of it on the *Argus* long years ago. And this man, the killer of a true American hero, Stephen Decatur, was deciding on his future in the U.S. Navy, and there was nothing Uriah could do.

15

Uncle Naph fairly salivated as he described the bounteous feast awaiting them. "It is the rage of Manhattan, Uriah," he said as they walked up Broadway. "Two brothers newly come to our shores, John and Peter Delmonico, from Venetia, I think, or was it Tuscany? Well, whatever, their restaurant has taken the city by storm. You have never tasted food like this, my boy!"

Though he had aged noticeably in the last few years, Naphtali Phillips still lived with an overweening enthusiasm for each moment. Some, at least, thought it overweening, for he had had his share of tragedy. He had sat by his wife's bed and watched her slowly die of yellow fever in the great epidemic of '22. And he had watched the newspaper that he loved like a child also die slowly, the ledgers growing ever more red with the paper's hemorrhage. Finally he lost control of the paper and was forced to declare himself bankrupt. Through all this travail, his spirit never had flagged. After the death of his beloved Rachel, he took her sister Esther as his wife and his home life became normal again. Despairing of returning to the newspaper business with its ever more savage competition and invective, he made use of his political friendships to secure a post as appraiser in the New York Customs Office. He regarded the job not as a political sinecure but as a position of honor, and he gave to it the same energies that had gone into his beloved *National Advocate*.

"Getting back to your request for my advice, Uriah, I am hardly an authority on finding success in life," Uncle Naph said as they walked to the restaurant in the brisk March wind tempered by a warming noontime sun. "All I can do," he continued, "is to advise you to do the things that I would do if I were your age. And that can be summed up in but a few words: New York City . . . and real estate."

"I take that to mean that you recommend I move permanently to New York."

"I do indeed, Nephew! This is the city of the future. I am positive of that. Oh, I know how much your dear mother would like you to settle down in Philadelphia and to take a wife and father many children. And were it not for the special conditions here, I would advise you to do just that."

Uriah nodded, "Yes, I am strongly tempted to go back home. My old friend John Coulter, the shipowner, has prospered through these years, and he begs me to come back and rejoin his firm. I invested some money with him years ago, and it has grown to a goodly sum."

"And what of the navy, Uriah? Are you considering leaving the service?"

"Never, Uncle Naph! I'll stay in the navy for the rest of my life, unless they tire of hearing of my scrapes and decide to cashier me. My soul belongs to the navy. But, meanwhile, I remain on leave, and there seems no prospect that I'll be called back any time soon. So I must make some decisions about where I will live and what I will do with myself. I won't just sit and get fat on my navy pay. I must find something to do, and if I can earn some money in the process, well and good."

"Then I say again, my boy, New York and real estate! That is your answer!" Uncle Naph waved his walking stick in the air to emphasize his point.

"Uriah, you cannot imagine the change that has occurred here since the opening of the Erie Canal. That big ditch is making New York the commerce capital of the western world! Why, in just a few months after the canal opened, more than five hundred merchants started new businesses in the city. Rents are going through the roof! The city prospers, Nephew! Have you seen the two houses with marble fronts on Broadway? There are houses on Water Street that are lit with gas, and there is talk that Beekman, Fulton, and Wall will have gas streetlights by 1830 . . . perhaps all streets south of Fourteenth.

"Oh, we have our problems, of course. Irishers and Germans are pouring in from Europe, and some of them are having trouble settling down. A lot of people hate the 'Paddies,' as they call them, but they'll simmer down and become good citizens like all the other newcomers. This is a booming city. It has its share of brawlers, but it booms nonetheless! Have you lately walked or ridden to the northern outskirts, Uriah? The outskirts keep moving farther north! In '22, when the fever struck us, Greenwich Village was a country hamlet with cow-paths for roads. Everybody ran up there to hide from the plague, and they slept in the fields. Well, today only a few open lots separate New York City from Greenwich Village. We grow, Uriah, quickly and northward, ever northward. Do you see my point?"

"I think so, Uncle Naph," Uriah responded. "Obviously the growth must always be to the north, since the city sits on a long, narrow island. And you are suggesting that I invest in real estate in the path of this advance?"

"Exactly, my boy, exactly. You will make a confounded fortune if you follow my thinking. Look at the movement of our Hebrew brethren. We number about one thousand souls now—double the number of three years ago—and they, like everyone else, are moving to the north. It's called Midtown, these streets on either side of Broadway, and that's where the people want to live. The Israelites with money live on Charlton, Greene, upper Greenwich . . . the poorer ones live east of Broadway on Houston, Lispenard, Canal.

Some of those poor, old people still cling to their homes on Water and Pearl and the bottom of Greenwich Street. But the future lies to the north."

"Do you recommend vacant land or buildings?"

"Either would be safe and profitable as an investment, Uriah. But I suggest buildings, especially rooming houses and small hotels. That is where the real money is. Look at the Franklin House, at Broadway and Dey. Always packed, always full. Young married women can't get good servants and don't want to care for a house all by themselves. So what do they do? Move into a good boarding-house or a hotel."

"But how would I manage such property if I were called back to sea?"

"Simple enough, my boy. There are men who do such managing for you. I can point you to some good and honest ones. They collect rents and take care of needed repairs—all for an insignificant fee."

"It sounds good, Uncle. I was told just the other day of some rooming houses for sale on Duane Street, north of City Hall. I'll look into it."

"That's right, my boy! And remember the motto: Buy cheap and sell dear. The movement of the population will be ever to the north. If you keep buying and then selling at a profit, always keeping just ahead of the rolling tide, I know you will prosper. It's time to start making plans for your future."

• • •

Hotel d'Angleterre
Rue Montmartre, Paris
January 22, 1829

Dear Cousin Mordecai,

Mazel tov and a great host of hosannahs to you and Rebecca upon the birth of little Manuel Mordecai Noah. Your joyous letter reached me here just yesterday. I was greatly thrilled to learn that you have a son and heir. He must be near to a month old by now and no doubt orating with all the skill and volume of his illustrious father. My love and congratulations to Rebecca and a kiss to the baby from his faraway cousin. I shall look for a clever present for him the next time I visit the shops at the Palais Royal.

Paris is still Paris, as glorious as ever. I am situated in a nice little hotel run by an English lady, who provides fine food and clean rooms. I am keeping busy visiting French navy installations and journeying often to England as well. My long and brilliant reports go in steady stream to our Navy Department, but whether any of the commissioners choose to read them is a question. I get an occasional letter of thanks for my efforts, but nothing to indicate that the information I am sending is being used in any significant way.

I was forced to enter a hospital here shortly after my arrival, due to a recurrence of my old stomach trouble. The doctor, a kindly old man named Monsieur Garon, told me that he would operate if I wished, but that it probably would not cure me. My troubles are an inheritance from my months at Dartmoor and my years feasting on salt beef at sea. I am better of late.

I have confided in you as to my unhappy and blighted love for Elise de Guissac. Now that I am in Paris, things do not seem so unhappy or blighted. Elise visits me almost every day. Our love is as before. Nothing has changed. We cannot be seen together in public, of course. Elise insists that we be circumspect, but beyond that, our love blossoms as much as ever. Each day that she leaves my room, I despair until I see her again. Our love is true, there is no question of that. Yet the fact remains that she is married to another and I am able to see her only every few years. She does not seem to get older, only more beautiful. I had dinner last night with her father, my old friend André de Guissac. He knows everything, of course. He assures me that Elise's husband, though many years her senior, is a good man and treats her with deference and consideration. I thank God that she is content and well cared for. I am grateful to be allowed to see her still and to give her my love and to accept hers.

I, too, was elated at the news of Andrew Jackson's election. He seems a true man of the people, in the style of Jefferson. I think he will be an honest and worthy president. If he has promised you the post of Surveyor and collector of the New York Port, I'm sure his word will be good. I am happy for your fine fortune.

You will remember, perhaps, my old dream of sponsoring the creation of a fine statue of Mr. Jefferson and of presenting it to our government as a symbol of the love and esteem in which the late, great president is held by myself and by all our people. I discussed it with Elise and she suggested that I go to see a friend of hers, a noted sculptor named Pierre-Jean David d'Angers, who is known simply as David. He is quite famous and well regarded here. To give an idea of his quality, he made the figures for the pediment of the Panthéon, which depicts the leading figures of France in a group around a figure of "La Patrie."

I visited his studio with a letter of introduction from Elise. He is eccentric, as are all artists, but was friendly and pleasant. I spoke to him of my idea and he seemed interested, especially at the prospect of having his work displayed in a place of honor in the United States. He would not give me a price, but only hinted at the fee for such a commission. It is ample, but my new wealth leads me to believe that I can manage it. He has seen Thomas Sully's portrait of Jefferson at Lafayette's home and was delighted to hear the Marquis is willing to loan the painting for the purpose of making a statue. I have made plans to visit Lafayette at the Chateau de la Grange this Sunday to renew our friendship and remind him of his promise about the painting.

Unfortunately, all this will not be consummated quickly.

David is extremely busy with commissions and says it probably will be near to two years before he could even think of beginning the Jefferson statue.

My property dealings in New York City are turning out very well. Each day I bless Uncle Naph for his sound advice. I have sold one of the houses I purchased on Duane Street for a tidy profit and have bought another on Sullivan Street. My agent, Mr. Osburn, assures me that the other properties are in good condition and full of tenants. With all rooms rented, each of these buildings is capable of bringing me as much as $175 a month. Such income, when added to my Navy pay, relieves me of any serious financial concerns. In fact, should the city's prosperity (and thus my own) continue in this fashion, I venture to say that I will amass a considerable fortune over time. Of course I help my mother and grandmother and sometimes my brothers and sisters when they are in need, but there is ample left over for me.

Flushed with my growing fortune, I decided to replenish my wardrobe on a recent visit to London and came away with a new frock coat (broadcloth with a velvet collar), two suits of linen, pantaloons of silk jersey and wool, and fancy pleated shirts. I also played the dandy to the fullest by purchasing a walking stick with ivory knob. When next I promenade in the Champs Elysées, I expect to draw all eyes. I will only miss Elise at my side, in person as well as spirit.

Faithfully, your cousin,
U. P. Levy

Usually after making love, Elise, sated, catlike, sank back among the pillows and lay languorously, emitting long sighs of satisfaction.

On this day, though, she sprawled silently at the side of the bed, her back to Uriah, shaking with muffled sobs. Uriah was puzzled and alarmed.

"What is the matter, Elise?" he asked. "Why do you cry? Are you all right?"

She did not answer him but turned toward him, her sobbing heard clearly now, and embraced him convulsively. Her arms went tightly around his waist, and she buried her face in his chest.

"What is wrong, dearest?" he persisted. "Tell me! You frighten me with your crying."

It took her several minutes to regain a measure of control, but gradually the sobbing diminished to weak sniffles, although the tears continued to drift down her pale cheeks.

"I cannot stop thinking that you will be leaving me in two more weeks," she finally admitted. "I have been dreading this almost since the day you arrived, but then, at least, I could console myself that it was far off. But as each day passed, it has occupied my mind more and more."

He nodded, understanding her misery and sharing it. He put his arm around her shoulders and tenderly stroked her cheek. "I know. But I shall return. You know I shall always return to you."

"Return?" Her voice blazed with sudden anger. "Return in a year, or two, or three? Am I to be consoled by that? Do you know what it is like for me to wait so long to see you? Two years is a lifetime, Uriah! I can't bear it when you leave me. It takes all my strength to keep from leaving my husband and running after you. For days after you leave, I take to my bed . . . unable to eat . . . uninterested in living."

"He does not wonder about that?" Uriah asked.

"He is a wise man as well as a good man. But never does he ask," she replied. "He understands all too well."

There were moments of silence, then, as they lay quietly and stared at the ceiling.

"How long will it be this time, Uriah?" Elise finally asked. "How long must I wait this time?"

He looked at her and kissed her gently on the lips, unwilling to upset her again, yet unwilling also to lie to her. "God only knows," he answered. "I must go back to Washington City to press for a sea assignment and also to New York to check upon my investments. If I go back to sea, there is no telling when I will return—as you know full well."

"And the chances of that?"

He sighed. "Probably not too good. All the navy officers are scrambling and fighting for berths on men-of-war. My service record is good enough, but I have more than my share of enemies in the Department, and they are ever ready to point to my list of troubles. If the choice lies between another officer and myself, I can be sure of being passed over."

"Then why don't you stay with me in Paris? You can occupy your time in cultivating David d'Angers and reminding him of your commission. Otherwise, he probably will forget all about it and begin some other work that will take him years to complete."

Uriah smiled at her clumsy effort at persuasion. "I must take my chances on that," he answered. "But I have no chance whatsoever at a new assignment unless I go to Washington City every month and press my application. If I am not there to badger them, they would be only too glad to list me as 'waiting for orders' for the rest of my life. My only hope, Elise, is to go there and politely annoy them until they give me what I want."

"It is always what *you* want," she said quietly. "Always the ships and the sea, before everything else . . . destroying everything else."

He sat up in bed now, silent and full of resentment. He cursed himself for refusing to remain in France with Elise, yet he knew that any other choice would have made him as unhappy as he was at this moment.

"You chose to marry someone else, Elise," he said coldly.

"What would you have me do? Grow old alone, waiting for you to visit me now and then? My father is aging. I am an only child. I have no one else. Uriah, try to understand: I cannot bear the thought of spending my life all alone, waiting for a letter to come from you, telling me that you are now in Japan or Russia. I am not brave enough for that. No, not brave at all."

"I do not understand," he said miserably. "You promised that I would be the only one you loved, and I have vowed that to you. Is all that forgotten now? Or do you break promises as easily as you have broken my heart?"

"Uriah, I have neither forgotten nor changed," murmured Elise, understanding his pain and ignoring for a moment her own. "All will be well. Whatever happens, we will still have each other, and that will last forever. You're never alone, my love. I am always with you. As you are with me."

Paris, 1832 (three years later)

As he completed his morning toilet, Uriah was surprised to find himself thinking more of his recent forays into English and French dockyards than of his imminent reunion with Elise. Just one scent of her perfume, though, and one sight of the dimple in her right cheek or the fire-blue of her eyes and all else would fade into a gray nothingness and his mind, as well as his arms, would be full of naught but Elise.

In keeping with his ever-increasing affluence, Uriah was quartered on this trip at the Hotel Villedot. It was an undue extravagance, he kept telling himself, but he had desired a taste of Parisian luxury, and this the Villedot provided in ample measure. He looked about him at the silken tapestries bedecking his room, the gold and white decor, the Sybaritic four-poster bed. This was elegance that had not been offered at the Angleterre or any other of the modest Paris hotels that he had habited.

Shortly after his arrival on the previous day, he had sent a note to Elise by messenger to the home of her father, stating merely that he had arrived and his place of domicile. There were no words of endearment or any suggested time for their meeting, lest the note fall into the wrong hands. He knew that he would soon hear her knock at the door. It would not be long before they would be together in the large hotel bed, clasping each other with longing and desire.

He stood at the mirror and trimmed his lush, curling mustache, noting with some dismay that several more gray strands were evident. Then he put a thick lather on his cheeks and brought out his razor, thwacking the blade several times on the strop to get a fine, sharp edge.

As he shaved, his mind again floated away from Elise and back to his recent inquiries in England and France. He had completed as much of his business as possible before coming to Paris, for it always upset Elise when he had to leave her for several days to visit some navy yard in Marseilles or L'Orient.

The hesitant knock on the door of his suite startled Uriah, and he came near to breaking off the button that he was fastening on his waistcoat. He hastened to the door but realized almost instantly that it had not been Elise's characteristic, jaunty knock, the signal rap that had become a code between them over these years. No, this had been a tentative knuckling of the door by someone who had approached with deference—and Elise was anything but deferential.

He opened the door to find André de Guissac himself, filling the door frame with his larger-than-life figure, though slightly more stooped than Uriah had remembered. His thick beard and hair had gone completely white. He grabbed Uriah in one of his big bear hugs and immediately broke into deep, heart-wrenching sobs.

"It grieves me to come to you today but I cannot spare you," he said.

Grieves? What choice of words is this?

"She has left us, Ooriah," de Guissac moaned. "She has left us both." His eyes reddened, and large tears welled up in them.

"What are you saying?" Uriah demanded, his voice quavering.

"Elise is dead. Two months ago! She has left us both to be with God!"

The room began to whirl rapidly before Uriah's eyes. A tide of acid rose into his throat, and the old pain stabbed hard at his gut.

"I . . . I cannot believe it," Uriah gasped. "Elise is young and strong! She has not had a sick day in her life. How can it be? This cannot be true!"

De Guissac bowed his head and looked at the floor. "She sleeps now in Père Lachaise cemetery. You are free to go there and visit her yourself."

"Tell me, please, what happened?" he said, helping de Guissac into an armchair.

"A sudden fever, fearsome and unyielding. She had been laughing and gay, romping with her child, when it struck. She took to her bed and the heat rose in her like the furnace of purgatory. Doctors were summoned immediately. They were the best that money could provide, all of them professors at the medical college. They did everything for her that they knew to do, but to no avail. She died less than forty-eight hours after she was stricken."

"My God," Uriah murmured. "My God." With one hand he unknowingly rubbed his stomach, which felt as if someone were squeezing him from the inside. Staggering to a chair, he sat down and began to breathe slowly, deeply, rhythmically. He felt a field of black edging into his vision, and he would not permit himself to faint.

The two men sat silently for several minutes, pondering the awful fate they shared, unable to speak any further. Images of Elise's face—laughing, always laughing—kept floating before Uriah's eyes. He saw the brightness of her hair and the shimmering blue of her eyes and found it hard to believe that she was not actually standing before him, beckoning to him, as of old.

"She was my treasure!" the old man wailed, and Uriah jumped up to embrace him.

Slowly the pain in Uriah's gut began to ebb. He was beginning to think again, even though the thoughts were all bitter and full of pain.

"You mentioned a child," Uriah finally said.

De Guissac nodded, and a slight smile came to his lips. "Yes. Her little daughter, Giselle. She just had her second birthday in November, a bright and loving little girl. She is the light of our lives. She is the image of Elise." His voice faltered slightly as he said her name.

A daughter, two-and-a-half years old! He had not known. Why

hadn't she told him? Perhaps she wanted to tell him in person. Could it be . . . was it possible the child was his?

"May I meet . . . your little Giselle sometime?"

"*Mon ami*, I think not," de Guissac said thoughtfully. "She is everything to her father . . . and now she is all he has."

"Does he know about me?" Uriah asked. "Does he know who I am?"

"He knew about you and how much you meant to Elise since the day she accepted his proposal of marriage. She told him everything from the start—except, of course, the intimate secrets that belonged only to you and to her! Elise would have it no other way. My daughter, she was the most honest person I have ever known," her father said. "But he also knew that she longed for a home and a family that you could not give her. And he felt that every day with her was a blessing from God."

"Each time Elise came to me, do you think he knew?"

"I do not know! How could I know? Never would I ask my daughter such a question! But I believe he knew. And that he loved her very much."

"Did she have a good life with him?" Uriah asked with trembling lips.

"*Oui*, she did," he responded. "*Mon ami*, I love you like a son. But you both made your choices! *Mes enfants*, so stubborn! If it were me, *bien sur*, I would have moved heaven and earth to be with the one I love!"

With this, Uriah broke down completely. Now de Guissac was comforting him as they cried in each other's arms.

"You are a strong man, Ooriah," he finally said, patting him on the back. "I am sure you will prosper. *Moi*, I am not sure that I can go on without her."

"But you have a granddaughter who needs you, André. You must continue for her."

De Guissac nodded and sighed. "Yes, that is true. Little Giselle will save me, if anyone can. I bid you *au revoir*, Ooriah. You are always welcome at my house. We are old friends, like always, bound together by our love—and now by our loss."

Exhausted by his task, de Guissac got up to leave. They hugged for a long time, then the door closed softly behind him.

Uriah walked, dreamlike, to a chair by the window. Outside the clatter of horses' hooves mingled with the strident cries of the hawkers. He did not hear. He sat, his face buried in his hands. Afternoon came, reigned, and weakened. The light outside began to fade. The street cries died away, and twilight descended upon Paris. The room grew dark. He sat still, hands covering his face, unmoving.

For weeks after learning of Elise's death, Uriah existed in a stupor, wandering the streets of Paris for hours at a time, unseeing, unspeaking. He was like a great ship becalmed in the doldrums of the ocean, drifting vacantly with the random tides. In later years he had almost no memory of those tortured weeks: they were a blank, unmarked space in his mind's calendar.

Every few days he bestirred himself enough to purchase a small bouquet from a sidewalk vendor and to go to Père Lachaise. There he would sit alone on a white marble bench across from Elise's grave until the closing hour came nigh and a caretaker gently told him that he must leave.

Each night his sleep was tormented by dreams. Elise was a constant visitor, always dressed in white cashmere, as she was on the day they had first met, always smiling and happy, more beautiful than he could endure. He would awaken moaning, lamenting that the dream had ended and that she had been taken from him again. Then he would weep convulsively for his lost love.

There were other dreams. They came almost as a relief, for Elise's face was not there to scourge him. A recurrent nightmare found him sitting on the foc's'l of a stinking, rotting coaster with Old Sails, his mentor in those long-dead times when he was a boy aboard the *New Jerusalem*. Sails looked just the same, but it was Uriah who had grown old. The two old sailors sat together, alone on a ship that sailed itself toward impending death upon the shoals. And the old companions cried together because they only had each other; there was no one left on the beach to mourn for them. And the ship beat on, its sails slatting obscenely in the rising gale.

On a bright morning early in June, he had sat in his hotel room, unshaven and ungroomed, staring blankly at the walls, wondering how to get through the long hours of the day. He could not remember when he had eaten his last meal, but he must have found food somewhere, for he still lived, though his clothes hung loosely upon him.

He ignored the knock at the door. After another knock went unanswered the door was opened, and two men walked in. André de Guissac was accompanied by a smaller man with wild, wiry hair. Uriah looked at them without interest. He knew that second man from somewhere, but he could not place him and did not care to make the effort.

De Guissac put his hands to his cheeks in dismay when he saw Uriah and his condition. He had not seen him in two weeks, and there had been a noticeable deterioration. His cheeks were sunken, his eyes glazed.

Without a word, de Guissac walked to Uriah and put his arms around him, holding him for a long time in a manly embrace.

After a time, when emotions had subsided and they all sat in chairs near the windows, de Guissac patiently explained to Uriah that his companion was the famed sculptor David d'Angers. He did not reveal that this morning's visit was the result of a long discussion the previous day between him and David about Uriah and his inconsolable grief. They agreed that steps must be taken to save him, or he soon would be dead, from suicide or sheer despair.

The mourning father, himself still numb with grief, pondered ways of helping the stricken man who had been like a son to him and who had loved Elise with a sweetness that matched his own. For the first time since Elise's death, he felt ideas stirring within him— plans, tactics. Elise had told him of Uriah's dream of commissioning a statue of Jefferson, a large statue to be displayed in a place of honor in America to honor the great man who deserved such homage. She had been so moved when Uriah spoke about it that she provided an introduction to David. Now de Guissac himself visited the great sculptor and implored him to begin working on the Jefferson statue immediately. Uriah had money, de Guissac had assured him; he could pay any price. And with all the forcefulness of his younger self, de Guissac convinced David to accompany him on a visit to Uriah the very next day.

It was a painful, difficult meeting in Uriah's hotel suite. Uriah said little, merely sat quietly, listened without protesting, and perhaps comprehended.

Then David began to explain his ideas for the statue of Jefferson. His voice took on a warm glow as he talked, as he began to lose himself in the expression of his creativity. For the first time, a sign of life came to Uriah's face. His eyes seemed to focus on David, and he folded his arms in the position of an attentive man.

The statue would, as Uriah had wanted, follow the Thomas Sully painting of Jefferson owned by the Marquis de Lafayette. The Marquis had once agreed to loan it to David for this purpose. David planned to sculpt Jefferson in a standing position, looking off into the distance, his face deep in thought. His right arm would cross his chest, and his right hand would bear a quill pen. His left hand would hold a scroll representing the Declaration of Independence that Jefferson was writing. It would be a massive work of art, and a great one, David assured Uriah.

Uriah softly cleared his throat and then ventured a comment. "I would hope," he said, "that the scroll might be unrolled, to indicate that the writing of the Declaration was not yet completed, just as the dreams of which the Declaration speaks are not yet complete."

David did not generally welcome artistic suggestions from his patrons. He had been known to abandon a commission at the slightest hint of control by the wealthy merchant or grande dame who retained him. De Guissac glanced anxiously at David's face for signals of annoyance.

Instead, the sculptor responded quietly, "It will be as you wish, Lieutenant."

···

It was, in the end, the statue that saved him—saved him from total despair, black hopelessness, and eventually from lunacy.

As the statue came gradually into being over the next six months—from first tentative sketches to the final clay model—so Uriah Levy gradually found his way back to life and to health. He visited David at his studio at least once a week—a privilege the sculptor had extended to very few patrons in the past. Uriah was delighted with what he saw and was fulsome in his praise; David basked in the approval and invited him to return often to watch the progress.

Oh, he was never long without vagrant pictures of Elise in his mind. They came and went quickly, like lovely butterflies. But her fleeting presence now was like a balm; it did not wound him again and again as in the first months. His thoughts of her were now like brief reunions, except for the moments of acute pain that broke through with the realization that she had left him forever.

On several visits to David's studio, Uriah was accompanied by the Marquis de Lafayette, who had honored his promise to make the portrait of Jefferson available for as long as needed.

The clay model was impressive, Lafayette acknowledged when this stage in the process was completed. It took the Sully painting several leagues further in expression and gave the figure of Jefferson a prodigious humanity, a looming resonance that the portrait had not conveyed.

"I think dear Thomas would be pleased with his statue," Lafayette said, later over lunch. "I think it would appeal to his sense of simplicity and order, even though he was a modest man and uncaring of such homage."

"I hope so, Marquis," Uriah answered. "I hope he would approve, and I hope the American people will take the statue to their heart."

"Where do you plan to display it?"

"I don't know, for it's not my place to say. I will present it to Congress as a gift from myself. They will designate the place, but I hope it will be somewhere in the Capitol building. Perhaps in the great rotunda."

"Ah, *oui*, that would be a magnificent site for the figure. Tell me, Uriah, have you been to Monticello of late?"

Uriah paused, surprised at the turn in the conversation.

"Jefferson's home in Virginia? Why, no, I have never been there."

"Never to Monticello? A pity, my friend. It is a glorious place—a resting place for angels. At least it was glorious. I have heard that Monticello has come upon sad and lonely days. That is why I asked if you have been there of late . . . so that you could tell me how things are there now."

"What has happened to it?"

"Alas, Good Tom was deeply in debt when he died. He proposed to sell some of his land by lottery, but the scheme aroused a great public outcry and citizens began to send their own gifts to the great man. Tom was deeply moved by this outpouring of money from the people he so loved. He died at peace in the belief that his debts were retired. But the money, generous as it was, proved insufficient to clear all the obligations. Much of Tom's personal property was sold after his death. He left Monticello to his daughter, Martha. But her own husband, Thomas Randolph, died a short time later, and she was left with very little, certainly not enough to keep up Monticello. The estate was only a shadow of what it had been: Tom had once owned as much as thirty thousand acres, but most of it had been sold, and Martha eventually inherited only about six hundred acres surrounding the house. Her own state of affairs forced her sadly to seek a buyer for Monticello. She put it up for sale, but no matter its great beauty, no matter its proud history, there were no takers. Martha was forced to lower the price again and again. Finally, she disposed of it . . . to a local man from Charlottesville—a chemist, I believe. He paid a ridiculous pittance for the estate, and, I am told, has set out to ruin it by tearing out the trees and lawns to engage in some wild-eyed scheme involving silkworms. It is such a tragedy."

Lafayette took a sip of wine and shook his head in great sadness.

Uriah felt a flood of anger rise within him. "My God, that is terrible news," he said. "I have always felt that the homes of our great men must be preserved for the sake of history. I was sickened, when I returned to Philadelphia after the late war, to find that Ben Franklin's home had been destroyed. *But Jefferson?* My God, if there is any place in all the United States that should be treasured, it surely is Monticello. It should be a national shrine—a memorial to the hero who lived there."

The conversation was going just as Lafayette had hoped.

"Do I dare suggest . . . Would you consider taking such a historic role, my dear friend?" Lafayette mused aloud. "Perhaps this seems forward on my part, but it would appear you meet all the qualifications."

"I promise that I will consider it, Marquis. I can promise no more than that."

16

Andrew Stevenson of Virginia, Speaker of the United States House of Representatives, cleared his throat and glanced down again at the paper in his hand, which he was about to communicate to the House. *Most unusual*, he told himself . . . *unusual and, somehow, irregular.* Well, it was a slow and rather drowsy Tuesday afternoon. The Twenty-Third Congress was grinding its way through a maze of routine business as it neared the end of its First Session. Perhaps the strange offer in his hand would provide the pestering newspaper reporters with a few words to write. Their readers were sick of Jackson's bitter feud with Nick Biddle and his Bank of the United States and with the interminable speeches and debates on the floors of both Houses over whether to recharter the bank.

"The honorable House will come to order," Stevenson intoned, pounding his gavel upon its wooden block. A buzz of inane conversation filled the air, even though only half the House members were present, for the day's calendar showed no matter of great urgency.

"I have before me," Stevenson shouted, for shouting was necessary to be heard, "the following communication. It reads as follows: 'Sir, I enclose you a letter, which I request you to do me the kindness to present to the House of Representatives with such resolutions and remarks as you may deem most proper. It is a tender of a colossal statue in bronze of the immortal Jefferson to my country.' The note is signed: 'With great respect. Your very humble servant, U. P. Levy, Lieutenant, U.S. Navy.'"

The House members looked at each other in puzzlement. A colossal statue? From some lieutenant? What is this strange business?

Stevenson pounded his gavel again. "Gentlemen, if I may proceed? Here, then, is the text of the message to the House from Lieutenant Levy." Stevenson read,

> I beg leave to present through you, my fellow citizens of the United States, a colossal bronze statue of Thomas Jefferson, author of our Declaration of Independence.
>
> This statue was executed under my eye in Paris by the celebrated David d'Angers and Honoré Gonon and much admired for the fidelity of its likeness to the great original, as well as the plain republic simplicity of the whole design.
>
> It is with pride and satisfaction that I am enabled to offer this tribute of my regard to the people of the United States through their representatives, and I am sure that such disposition will be made of it as boasts correspondence with the illustrious author of our Declaration of Independence and the profound veneration with which his memory is cherished by the American people.

Congressman William Archer, Stevenson's fellow Virginian, turned to his neighbor and complained, "Who is this fellow Levy? Have you heard of him? A damned young lieutenant: A touch of gall in such a gesture, if you ask me."

Speaker Stevenson again addressed the House:

"I might add, gentlemen, that I met briefly with Lieutenant Levy when he delivered the communication. He is a native of Philadelphia and currently a resident of New York City. He is a veteran of more than twenty years' service in the navy and saw action in the War of 1812 and was an officer aboard the legendary brig *Argus*. He commissioned this statue with his own funds as a tribute to Mr. Jefferson, whom he greatly admires and reveres, and oversaw its modeling and casting in bronze in Paris while on leave and awaiting orders. He arranged with the navy to provide conveyance from Europe for the statue, and it came aboard the flagship of Commodore Isaac Hull. Lieutenant Levy meanwhile went to Philadelphia to commission and supervise the carving of a handsome pedestal of four varieties of marble for the display of this statue in any location deemed suitable and proper by this honorable Congress. He then met the statue upon its arrival at Norfolk and personally escorted its travel to Washington City. He also tells me that he brought with him from Europe a clay model of the Jefferson statue that he presented to the Common Council of the City of New York as a gift from himself to his city of residence and which is now displayed in the City Hall."

"Mr. Speaker, a question," came a powerful voice from the well of the House. "Where stands now this colossal statue?"

"It stands now, sir, in the great rotunda of this Capitol, where you and all other honorable members of Congress may inspect it to their hearts' delight."

"Gad," muttered Congressman Archer, "he has already deposited the monster on us before we can say yea or nay? Gall, I tell you, damnable gall!"

Stevenson held a hurried, whispered conference with the venerable clerk of the House, Matthew St. Clair Clarke. Stevenson nodded, glad to be rid of the issue. He was dreadfully tired and wished only to bring the day's business to an early end.

"I am informed that Lieutenant Levy's offer was taken up by the Senate yesterday and was referred by them to the Joint Committee on the Library of Congress for its due consideration. I will entertain a motion that we do the same."

City of Washington
March 27, 1834

Dear Sir,

I have been instructed by the Joint Library Committee of the two houses of Congress to express to you their thanks for the present you have made to the people of the United States in

*the colossal bronze statue of Thomas Jefferson. It is every way
fit and proper that the statue of the author of the Declaration
of American Independence should find a place at its Capitol.
This would doubtlessly, sooner or later, have been ordered by
the Representatives of the States and the people. You, sir, have
only anticipated their action, and have manifested, in so doing, a devotion to the principles contained in that celebrated
instrument, equally felt by all classes of your fellow citizens.*

> *I have the honor to be,*
> *With sentiments of great respect,*
> *Your most obedient servant,*
> *Asher Robbins, Chairman*

The letter from Senator Robbins was both genial and appreciative.
This did not surprise Uriah, for he had met the elderly senator from
Rhode Island at a party a few days earlier and found him to be a
warm and gentle man. They had quickly found a mutual bond of
interest: Robbins was also on the Senate Naval Affairs Committee.
The courtly Robbins listened with interest to Uriah's thoughts on
the future direction of the navy and told him his opinions were well
reasoned and valuable.

Uriah was not unaware of the subtle interplay of politics that
would be involved in his offer of the statue to his country. Nothing
was accomplished in Washington City these days without the hard
realities of party politics being somehow involved. It was a fact of
life. Nothing was simple in this government, not even the generous
offer, no strings attached, of a beautiful statue by one of the world's
finest sculptors. Politics inevitably would be a factor. He hoped
Robbins's support on the committee would carry the day.

Almost a year later, Uriah sat alone in the near-deserted public gallery of the House of Representatives. The long and tedious First Session, which had begun in March of the previous year, was within a
few hours of its end. The weary congressmen had only to dispose of

the remaining odds and ends of business; then they could gratefully disperse to their homes. One of those odd bits of unfinished business was the matter of a statue proffered by an unknown (and rather cheeky, many thought) navy lieutenant.

The members of Congress, their curiosity piqued by this strange offer, had not hesitated to ask questions about the prospective donor. They heard graphic stories of Levy's many courts-martial, of his reputation as a hothead and a duelist. Depending upon their sources at the Navy Department, they heard that Uriah was a most able seaman and a brave fighter who had been William Henry Allen's right-hand man on the *Argus* . . . or that he was an insubordinate, pushy Jew who was never satisfied and always a source of discontent and trouble aboard a ship.

The windows of the chamber were thrown open to catch any stray breeze, and flies swarmed about the public gallery. On this sleepy Friday afternoon, Uriah probably was the most wide-awake person in the House chamber, for he had been told by friends in the New York delegation that the matter of the statue would certainly be disposed of today.

Uriah was aware that the representatives held various sentiments about his proposed gift, and indeed, that some were unalterably opposed to acceptance. Such opposition hurt him but did not surprise him; he was not naïve in the ways of Washington politics. He also harbored no illusions about his clouded reputation or about the hostility evoked in some whenever a Hebrew was involved. Yet he could not help feeling chagrined: his gift was sincerely offered, with no hidden implications. It was a gesture, pure and simple, of his love for Jefferson and for the United States. That such a gift should be the subject of debate and skepticism was deeply troubling to him.

"Mr. Speaker!"

Uriah leaned forward in his seat. It was Congressman Everett of Massachusetts who sought recognition.

"The Chair recognizes the honorable gentleman from Massachusetts."

Everett spoke, as usual, with great dignity and formality: "Mr. Speaker, the Joint Committee on the Library of Congress, of which

I have the honor to be a member, has duly considered the offer of Lieutenant U. P. Levy of the navy to present, through the two houses of Congress, to the people of the United States, a colossal bronze statue of Thomas Jefferson, made in Paris by the noted French sculptor David d'Angers. The Joint Committee on the Library hereby reports out the question to the House of Representatives for final decision, yea or nay, and further recommends that, if accepted, the statue be placed in the center of the square in the eastern front of the Capitol. I move that the House resolve to accept the statue and that it be placed in accord with the Committee's recommendation."

A dispassionate and dry presentation, Uriah thought. Though it was an affirmation, it lacked any semblance of enthusiasm.

The Speaker threw the resolution into debate. Little evidence of interest could be seen on the floor. Congressmen walked the aisles, chatting with their friends, and gleefully recounting their plans for the recess. A few stared vacantly ahead, seemingly unaware of anything that was said.

Archer of Virginia called for the floor. "I confess, Mr. Speaker," he began, "that I have some objections to the resolution. It is an admirable gesture on the part of this navy officer. But I conceive that, if Congress desires to have such a statue of my distinguished fellow Virginian on display in the Capitol, it certainly would be more consistent with propriety for the Congress to procure such a statue itself than to be indebted for it to any person whatever. I also must point out that, as Congress already has resolved to erect a statue in honor of the good and great father of our country, the immortal Washington, which statue is now in process of execution, discretion demands that no other statue of any other man should be set up in the Capitol until that duty is performed which this Congress already has resolved be done. One final word, Mr. Speaker: I have been informed by sources of the highest qualifications in art that the statue offered in this resolution is not of that finished order which, if a statue is to be put up at all in the grounds of the Capitol, it ought to be. It is my hope, therefore, Mr. Speaker, that the resolution pending before us will not be passed. I would like to move that it be laid upon the table, but refrain from doing so only because such action would prevent some honorable member from replying to my remarks."

Uriah hoped that another member of this august body might jump to his feet and respond to Archer in a fiery defense of the statue. But there was no fire in the House of Representatives today, for the desire to put the dust of Washington City behind them for a few months was uppermost in the minds of its members.

A few brief comments were heard. Two or three representatives mildly suggested that it would do no harm to accept the statue, while one or two others seconded Archer's objections.

Mr. Lane of Indiana was recognized and said only this: "I trust that the House will not reject the resolution merely because the statue has been presented by a lieutenant rather than a commander." A low tide of laughter rose in the House, and a few members called out, "Hear, hear!"

After all, pointed out Mr. Clay of Alabama, "We must remember that the adoption of the resolution will not prevent this House hereafter from either erecting another statue of Mr. Jefferson or from changing the site that now is contemplated for display of the statue by David."

On this note of the faintest praise, the resolution was brought to a vote and was approved by the House of Representatives, sixty-nine ayes to fifty-five nays.

Uriah set back in his chair. The House proceeded to other business. He felt no elation, only relief. *How could it be*, he wondered, *that such an openhearted gift came within fourteen votes of rejection?* In the dark months in Paris, he had often lifted his thoughts by dreaming about this glorious day in the United States Congress. Now the day was here, but there was little glory in it.

The resolution would still have to be considered by the Senate. He had less concern about that body, for months ago the Senate had voted to concur in the report of the Joint Committee on the Library, with its recommendation for placing the statue on the Capitol square. Tomorrow the entire affair would be concluded, the statue would belong at last to the United States, and he would be relieved to have the affair concluded.

"Senator Robbins, a word, sir, if you please?"

The old senator, walking briskly down the broad carpeted hallway outside the Senate chamber, stopped and turned to see who hailed him. Uriah, breathing hard from his half-run down the long corridor, came up to him.

"Ah, Lieutenant, a good day to you, sir."

"Senator, I have just come down from the gallery. Sir, I am dismayed by what the Senate has just done on the matter of my statue. Perhaps I misunderstood. Can you explain to me what has happened?"

"I can see, Lieutenant, by your face that you are indeed upset. Well, let me counsel you and perhaps you will feel better about things. In short, my friend, the Senate has voted to table the resolution accepting your statue."

"But—but, the session is to end in a day or two. What does this mean? Does it mean they have turned down my offer? When will it be resolved? Why have they done this to me?"

"Calm yourself, my friend. The situation is not as bleak as it may appear. Since the Senate approved my committee's report on the statue in May, some of the senators have had second thoughts. I am not sure why. Perhaps they oppose you on political grounds. Perhaps they question the rectitude of accepting such a private gift. They were in no mood today for long debate on this or anything else. They want to go home. So when Senator Porter moved to lay the resolution on the table, it was approved without further argument."

"But when will the matter be taken up again?"

"I don't know. I assume it will be taken off the table sometime during the next session. Until then, it remains in limbo."

Uriah shook his head in frustration. "And my statue? What happens to my statue?"

Senator Robbins smiled and clapped Uriah on the arm. "Why, son, your statue is sitting proudly in the Capitol rotunda. Do you think that anyone will trouble himself to move it away? Of course not! The rotunda is the best place for it anyway. It should not be outside, prey to the weather and the birds. Rest easy, Lieutenant Levy, you have what you wanted. Your statue stands in the rotunda, and there it will remain, no matter when Congress takes up the resolution again."

"This is hardly the way I planned it. I had hoped the Congress would appreciate. . . ."

"Son, let me give you a word of wisdom. Politics is the art of the attainable. To be a political man means to compromise. Such is the way government works. Your statue has been neither rejected nor accepted. Yet it stands in the rotunda of the Capitol, where you wanted it to be. And there it will remain. Accept your victory, then, in good spirit."

"It seems hardly a victory, Senator."

"Lieutenant, give thanks that you are not in politics, for such pallid victories are about all we politicians can hope for."

17

Monticello. Monticello. The name itself rippled and sang across the tongue like a fine wine.

From the moment Uriah had reined the horse into the entrance road and his carriage began bouncing along the rutted way, he had felt Jefferson beside him. Uriah was not usually one to think of ghosts, but he could not deny the overpowering feeling that Jefferson was riding with him, guiding him along with the patronizing good humor of any proud landowner.

Uriah had been unable to keep Monticello out of his mind since his talk with Lafayette in Paris. The thought of owning the "little mountain," of actually living in this place that to him was hallowed, had haunted his sleep ever since the old Marquis had proposed it to him. It seemed far-fetched, almost preposterous, yet he could not keep from thinking about it. He made some discreet inquiries in Washington City, while awaiting the decision of Congress on the disposition of his statue, and learned that the estate had been allowed to fall into near-ruin by its present owner. Old friends of Jefferson were still making a quiet effort to raise money to buy Monticello back and present it to his daughter as a token of esteem, but the task was slow and hard.

Now that the statue was ensconced in a secure, if reluctant, home,

Uriah decided to personally investigate the fate of Monticello. He had had enough of strange dreams in which he wandered across the vast lawns of a place that he knew was Monticello, though he never had been there. He resolved at last to hunt up the owner and to find out for himself whether the estate really was for sale and how dear it would come. Then he could assess whether his fantasy could be touched with reality.

He took a slow coach from Washington City for the journey of 110 miles to Charlottesville. There he rested for a day and enjoyed the vistas of Jefferson's own university. Then he rented a horse and carriage from a livery and began a leisurely climb of the mountain south of the town. He stopped at Michie's Tavern, halfway up the slope, for a glass of cold cider and with the aim also of picking up some more information about Monticello's owner and his intentions. But the barman was taciturn and unresponsive, willing only to give Uriah curt directions to the road up to Monticello. He finished his cider and quickly returned to his carriage.

It was, he estimated, a distance of two to three miles from where he had crossed the Rivanna River, a pretty little stream in the valley below, to the top of the mountain. He did not hurry the old gray gelding pulling his carriage, for it was a mellow day and he wanted to take things in fully. An occasional patch of corn provided the only breaks in the thick forest that covered the mountain's lower slopes.

Following the barman's muttered directions, Uriah drove in leisurely style along rough roads that circled their way about the rise, climbing patiently toward the top. These were part of Jefferson's system of roundabouts, as he called them. There were four roads circling the mount, each two hundred feet or so removed from its neighboring road, but connecting here and there by other roads or walking paths. Jefferson carefully had designed the network of roads so as to provide, in their full stretch, a ride or hike of some seven miles through the lush forest.

Breaks in the trees and vistas of sky told him that the mountain's summit and his destination were not far off. Uriah glanced to his left and then suddenly pulled back on the reins. He took a deep breath and climbed down from the carriage to walk a few steps through the trees and view the last resting place of Thomas Jefferson.

It was a small square of ground, perhaps one hundred feet on each side, bordered by a stone wall. The plot appeared untended and was in a state of nature, with trees and bushes fighting for space among large boulders. Uriah, reluctant to tread upon a burial place, kept to the outside of the wall and walked its length, reading the gravestones. It was at the far end of the rustic yard that he found Mr. Jefferson's grave, marked by a simple gray monument. On one side of him was the grave of Martha Jefferson, who had preceded her husband in death by forty-four years, and on the other side lay one of their four dead daughters. Of their six children, only one still lived, and she was far away, residing with her daughter in Boston.

Uriah took off his hat in respect and stood silently at the stone wall, paying homage to the man he had so long loved, though never had they exchanged a word. The linden trees sang in the spring breeze; the birds chorused through the deep woods across the road. There were no sounds of man at all. Uriah felt as if there were no other soul within many miles.

The words on the monument were few and had been chosen by Jefferson himself:

Here was buried Thomas Jefferson
Author of the Declaration of Independence, of the
Statute of Virginia for Religious Freedom, and
Father of the University of Virginia
April 13, 1743 – July 4, 1826

This was how Jefferson had wanted to be remembered, Uriah thought. He did not mention his election twice as President of the United States, but he did cite the statute that affirmed "our civil rights have no dependence on our religious opinions, more than our opinions in physics or geometry." Only a few unadorned words, yet what worlds of meaning they conveyed. *How Jews throughout history would have celebrated had a monarch ever proclaimed such words! How suddenly would their lives have changed!* With these words, the tall Virginian of reddish hair had changed the world forever.

Uriah stood silently before Jefferson's grave for a long time. Others were buried in the square: relatives and old friends of Jefferson, but Uriah had no eyes for the other stones. Once he had found what he sought, he remained as if rooted. Then, with one last look at the monument, he returned to the carriage and resumed his journey up the final few yards of winding road to the top of the hill.

The house was everything he had expected it to be. He was moved by its beauty, even in its shabby and unkempt state. Monticello had an imperishable grandeur. She was a *grande dame* fallen on hard times, clothed in rags and covered with dirt, but still lovely, her beauty reaching out tremulously, shimmering seductively in the spring light.

Here, to the top of this mountain, Jefferson had walked as a boy when his family lived at Shadwell, a half-mile or so distant. The mountain belonged to his father, but in the boy's mind it was his own secret place. He came here to read, to study his Latin and Greek lessons, to sit for hours gazing dreamily at the sublime scenes spread out in the distance. Shadwell, its twenty-five hundred acres and thirty slaves, became his at the age of fourteen when his father died, but it was his "little mountain," his Monticello, that ever was at the center of his dreams, the place where someday he would live out his years. A decade after he became the master of Shadwell, he decided to begin work on the mountaintop and set to building the roundabout roads so that he could have easy access to the summit. When the access was his, he began digging away the pointed top of the mountain so that he could create in its place a level lawn more than twelve acres in size, a man-made garden in the sky almost eight hundred feet above the level of the sea. It made no difference to him that logic and reality demanded that houses be built in valleys and hollows, not on mountaintops. By 1769 he had refined his architectural drawings enough to please himself at last, so that carpenters could begin work on the house that haunted his mind's eye.

In 1772 he married a beautiful young widow named Martha Wayles Skelton, whom he had wooed by playing the violin to her harpsichord. He brought her home to Monticello on a bitter-cold, snow-choked night when the family and servants were asleep and the house was closed and dark. They had spent the night in an outbuilding, which was known forever after as the "honeymoon cottage."

Uriah stood on the east lawn of Monticello and gazed up at the silent house with its graceful columned portico and wondered, as he had so many times before, how he—a lowly lieutenant in the navy with little prospect of advancement and who, indeed, had not even held a navy berth in almost eight years—had the effrontery to think of himself owning so grand a place. Such mansions were for heroic commodores who had triumphs over enemy armadas and had come home to parades and receptions, then had retired to their majestic estates.

He walked up to the door and tried it, but it was locked. He looked through a broken pane of glass and saw an elaborate lobby. A filthy rug, or the remains of one, was piled at the side of a dusty floor.

He turned away from the portico and returned to the east lawn, which was high with weeds. The gravel walks across the lawn were pocked with holes, and a mound of trash lay undisturbed halfway between the house and the drive. Gaping openings on the lawn marked places where trees had apparently been uprooted.

Uriah circled back around the south side of the building, past the long, low wing that extended westward at a right angle to the house. As he followed a walk past a row of mulberry trees, he saw an elderly black man on his knees in the remnants of what had been a much larger vegetable garden. The man had been there when Uriah had driven his carriage past the garden, but had not been easily visible.

"Good day, suh," the man said as Uriah approached him. He lifted his broad-brimmed hat respectfully.

"And good day to you," Uriah answered. "Can you tell me: Is

there any way I may get into the house? I'd like to see its condition."

"Naw suh," the man said and shook his head vigorously. "Naw suh. Massa James, he keeps the key and he won't let anyone in. He don' even wan' us to go in and clean up. It mus' be a fright by now, I reckon."

"Have you lived here long?" Uriah asked.

"Oh, yas suh, yas suh. I belong to Massa Tom since I was a little boy . . . and then to Miss Martha after Massa Tom done pass. And since Massa James bought the farm, I done belong to him."

"That would be Barclay, who owns Monticello now?"

"Yas suh, that's Massa James. He hardly ever comes up from town anymore, though. Me and the other people here, we jus' sittin' and waitin'."

"How do you get food?"

"Oh, we grows plenty to eat here. And Massa James sends us up some meat ever so often. Ain't bad. Ain't bad 'tall." He looked fondly at the terrace with its black loam. "Afore Massa Tom done pass, this here was a right pretty garden. He liked to set here, he did, and watch the crops grow and look out there at the hills. Sometimes, I swear I think I still see Massa Tom a-sittin' right down there on the slope." He shook his head and laughed to himself.

Uriah straightened up and let his eyes roam out to the southern horizon. He luxuriated in the same view that Jefferson had so loved. The country stretched before him for a good fifty miles: thick woods, farms and plantations, a few houses. And in the great distance, the blue-shrouded summits of the Allegheny Mountains, or the Blue Ridge, as some called them. They formed a noble silhouette against the sky, a glorious far border to the grandest vista Uriah ever had seen.

He bid farewell to the old slave and resumed his walk around the buildings, studying the design and trying to imagine Jefferson's motives when he first put pen to paper to lay out his plan. He knew that Jefferson had wanted to avoid the motley collection of service buildings that always congregated about the great house of a plantation. And so he had ingeniously planned the two colonnaded wings of the house that stretched around like enveloping arms. Underneath these wings, he cleverly hid the services: the kitchens, the smoke room, the dairy, the servants' quarters, the wine room and the wareroom and the cider room. Somehow, with crafty sweeps of his pen and straightedge, he found room under these spidery terraces for his stables, too, and a laundry and an icehouse, and even a carriage house—all of them as neatly hidden from view as if they did not really exist. At the end of each long arm, in polite symmetry, were two small houses, one of them the "honeymoon cottage," and the other, on the north side, the building that had been Jefferson's hideaway office.

Uriah passed behind the honeymoon cottage and walked back up the incline to another, larger lawn. His breath caught in his throat again as he saw the house plainly from the west lawn for the first time. It was even grander than from the other side. Above the tall columns of the western portico hovered an octagonal room topped by a dome that glowed like a great melon. The soft, gentle circle of the dome was a contrast to the strong, classic planes of the portico and the house itself.

He walked to the far end of the great expanse of the western lawn. From there he looked again at the fabled house. Oh, it was balm to the eyes, was it not? No amount of maltreatment or want of care could destroy this place—nor its essence—for it had been designed and built with such love that it could not be defeated. The love of its builder poured across the lawn in waves, down the scraggly grass, past the uprooted trees and the piles of waste, to the lone visitor at the end, who stood in wonder.

On the first available coach, Uriah traveled to Fredericksburg to seek out Thomas Hall, the sympathetic friend of the Jefferson family who was endeavoring to raise money to put Monticello back into the hands of Martha Randolph, Jefferson's last surviving child.

"How goes your campaign, Mr. Hall?" asked Uriah boldly.

"It goes slowly and painfully, Lieutenant Levy," Hall responded, a bit put off by his caller's bluntness.

"Sir, I have just come from Monticello and found it in a deplorable state of disrepair and unconcern, but no less a place of honor and great beauty. I have every hope your campaign will meet with success. I, as much as anyone, would like to see Monticello remain in the hands of the Jefferson family. But in the event your campaign does not succeed, I mean to buy Monticello myself."

Hall was stunned. "You, sir? What is your stake in this?"

"My only stake, sir, is in seeing that this home of our greatest American is kept in a manner befitting its history. It should be a shrine to him—and if I must live there to oversee it, then so be it— but I shall make sure that it will be done and properly so."

Hall paused and studied his caller closely as if to take his true measure. "A most worthy objective, Lieutenant. But would you not agree that it could more faithfully be carried out by the daughter and other heirs of that great man . . . that they who lived there in its times of glory are the only ones qualified to renew such glory?"

Uriah sighed. "Mr. Hall, I'm sure you think me some brash interloper who has some scheme in mind to turn Monticello into a glorious profit. Nothing of the kind. My only motive is to honor him. Yes, I would agree that it would be best if Mrs. Randolph were again to live at Monticello and her children after her. But she did live there and could not sustain it. Now she lives with Mrs. Coolidge in Boston, and her own health is not good, I am told. Tell me, sir: Let us suppose that you succeed in buying Monticello back for Mrs. Randolph. I would lead the applause and, by the way, I would myself contribute to your fund. But once that fine deed is done, then what? How does Mrs. Randolph maintain the farm? She could not do so before, and I warrant her finances are less now than then. Must this grand home be put through the same auction all over again and once more be sold to the highest bidder, even though he be someone who cares little about who lived there? No, sir, I say let it fall to someone who loves Jefferson above all men and who will treat his home as his own home and will care for it with all the kindness that he himself would have lavished there."

"I see you are most intent on this, Lieutenant Levy," Hall said quietly.

"Yes, sir, most intent. I have no wish to stand in your way, and I sincerely wish you luck in your efforts. But if the help that you seek does not fill the sails, then I must step in. I will take it myself and thus ensure that its future will be a proper one."

"How long will you give me, Lieutenant, to seek a successful conclusion?"

"One more year, sir. I promise you that I will not step in until one year from now. But if by then you have been unable to buy Monticello for Mrs. Randolph, I will do all I can to be its owner. In that event, I hope that she will understand my purpose. In fact, I promise that I will travel to Boston to tell her and explain myself."

"Very well, sir," Hall concluded and stood up to terminate the meeting. "I wish myself luck, and if that not be forthcoming, I wish you the same." The two men shook hands, politely if not warmly, and Uriah left the house.

James T. Barclay, a big and resolute man, wore on his face a perpetual glower that had so marked his features that the corners of his lips turned downward in an eternal scowl. His sour appearance was well matched by his cold and unfriendly spirit.

Though Uriah sat across an oaken table from him in Barclay's Charlottesville house, the host did not deign to offer his guest so much as a goblet of cold water, much less a cup of tea or a glass of wine. He was hardly more generous with his words than he was with his drink. Uriah found himself sitting through long moments of silence between occasional clipped conversation.

Barclay was a broad-shouldered man whose powerful body had lately gone to fat. His rust-colored hair was tinged with gray. His wife, tall as her husband but thin and frightened-looking, busied herself in the kitchen, stopping her chores every now and again to peer curiously into the parlor.

Barclay had apprenticed as a chemist and had spent many of his years as a medicine maker. He was ambitious for bigger things, though, and one of his ideas was to take the old Jefferson place, clear away its encumbering trees and gardens, plant long rows of mulberry trees, and make his fortune by growing silkworms whose cocoons would be his passage to a finer life. He carefully hoarded his money for such an opportunity and eventually had a tidy sum laid by. He waited and bided his time while Martha Jefferson Randolph anxiously sought buyers for Monticello, all the while still living there with her four sons, four daughters, and grandchildren. Her funds declined alarmingly fast and she knew she must leave this beloved home, but no one wanted to buy. She asked more than seventy thousand dollars at first—in the late months of 1828—but there were no takers. Her asking price went lower and lower, attracting a nibble here and there but no serious biters. Three years after she first put Monticello on the block, the watchful, patient Barclay agreed to take it off her hands—the five hundred acres that still were left from the original tract of thirty thousand acres—for the price of seven thousand dollars. Mrs. Randolph was glad to get the money. She was almost destitute, and Barclay had agreed to throw in a small house in Charlottesville, where she would take up residence. But after several months in the house, Martha Randolph left Virginia forever and moved to Boston to live with her daughter, Ellen Coolidge.

Alas, James Barclay's fortune-making silkworms were easy prey for mosquitoes and other insects, and his silk farm was a short-lived enterprise. He visited Monticello less and less often, and soon his visits stopped almost entirely. To his credit, he saw to it that his small group of slaves on the mountaintop was fed and under roof, but beyond that he wanted nothing more to do with Monticello except to sell it. He had found new hope for himself in the Bible and was dreaming new dreams of going out to the world as a missionary to spread the tidings. Once he disposed of that farm on the mountain and regained his investment, he and his wife would be off to do God's work.

He was disappointed to find that this Jew calling upon him, who purported to be an officer in the federal navy, would not consider buying all the acreage but wanted only part.

"You want the best part, you know, with the house and all," growled Barclay when Uriah had made clear his intention. "You'd better be prepared to pay a choice price, for that's the choice of the farm."

"I realize that, Mr. Barclay," Uriah answered, "and I am prepared to give you a fair price."

"Meanin'?"

"Meaning, I offer you two thousand dollars for 250 acres."

"Pshaw, I wouldn't take a penny less'n three thousand dollars. Why, man, that is the top of the mountain you're askin' to buy. A mountaintop allays goes for top dollar."

"Nonsense," Uriah snapped. "You're not dealing with a child here. Water must be carted up there from the river at the bottom. The place is in a state of ruin and would cost me thousands more to fix up, though I would gladly do it. The best of the trees have been torn out, and the garden, what's left of it, is a shambles. I haven't been inside the house, but I expect it is more of the same. I must see the inside, by the way, before I will sign any papers."

Again, a long silence. Barclay kept his eyes focused on the polished surface of the table. Finally: "It ain't so bad as all that. We did some movin' around, is all."

Uriah tried to restrain himself, but his irritation at this despoiler churned over the dam. "It is the home of a founder of our country and the author of its holiest writ. It deserves far better." Barclay looked up at him in apparent surprise. "You talkin' 'bout Tom Jefferson? Why, he was an unbeliever—an atheist. He tried his best to make this country godless. I knowed Tom since he came back here from Washington City in eighteen and nine. Was nothin' special about Tom Jefferson. His old farm is just a piece of land to me, like any other. Nothin' more."

Uriah's face reddened, but he tried to maintain control. "Yes," he said quietly, "I could tell that when I visited Monticello. I will give you twenty-two hundred dollars, Mr. Barclay, and that is the best I can do."

"I see you're good at jewin' down like all the rest of your folks, Levy, but it ain't gonna work with me. I'll take twenty-eight hundred dollars and never a penny less."

A few more minutes—separated by long, awkward pauses—and they had agreed on a price of twenty-seven hundred dollars for the transfer of acreage ranging somewhere, depending on a survey, of 218 to 223 acres. The purchase would include all the land in a great circle surrounding the house at the top of the mountain, with the sole exception of the small burial ground, title to which had been carefully retained by Martha Randolph. No matter how desperate her need, she could never permit the graves of her parents and her brother and sisters to fall into alien hands.

They shook hands on the deal and then got up to go out to Barclay's gig for the ride back up the mountain to inspect the inside of the closed house. Uriah knew that the interior would be as deplorably run down as everything else, but he also knew for certain that he wanted to complete this transaction and that nothing he would see in the old house would dissuade him.

As they walked down the steps from the porch of the white frame house, Barclay said, "If you accept the house and want to go ahead, I'll have my lawyer draw up a deed of conveyance. We should be ready to sign within a couple of weeks or so." For the first time since Uriah had met him, Barclay drew his lips apart in a tight smile. "Now the hard part comes," he said.

"And what is that, sir?" asked Uriah.

"Why, convincing my wife, Julia, that I didn't get snoickered on this deal."

• • •

"Oh, Uriah, it is so grand I cannot believe it."

Rachel Levy stood in the entrance hall of Monticello and let her eyes travel over the faded splendor of the mansion. She was frightfully weary. She was sixty-seven years now, and her health was not robust. The trip from Philadelphia had seemed to her longer and harder than any journey she had ever taken. But she was determined to hide her exhaustion from her son, who had been telling her for days of this great thrill she had in store when they reached Monticello and saw the magnificent estate that now belonged to him.

Oh, it truly was grand; he had not lied. But it was in need of a good scrubbing, that was plain, and probably a painting as well. She knew that Uriah had not brought her here to be a scrubber, but she also knew that she could not sit idly while this gracious house so wanted the care of a dutiful mistress. And, strangely, some of the weariness seemed to dissipate as she began to lay plans in her mind for the proper restoration of Monticello.

"Mama, look at this!" Uriah was virtually leaping from place to place in his excitement. "Look at the beautiful floor in the parlor. Those squares are wild cherry, and the borders are beech wood. See the contrast of the colors? And, look, here is Mr. Jefferson's seven-day clock . . . and look there at the cannonballs used as weights for the clock. And over there is his bust of Voltaire! And in the next room is a coffee urn that Mr. Jefferson designed himself—a most beautiful object!"

Rachel smiled wearily, held up her hand in protest, and carefully sat in a spindly-looking chair in the foyer. "Please, 'Riah," she said, "give me a chance to catch my breath. I've only just arrived. There is time to see everything. I must get to my room and begin unpacking. Tonight is Shabbat, remember. I must get the candles and see to dinner."

Uriah laughed like a boy and placed his hands on her shoulders. "Forgive me, Mama, but I am so excited to have you here with me, and I want you to see everything. Anyway, what is this talk about seeing to dinner? We have a fine cook named Aggy who will take care of all our meals. Never fear."

"Will she also say my Shabbat prayers for me? Some things I must do for myself. And we'll see how she is in the kitchen." She paused, and a worried look came to her face. "This Aggy—she's a slave woman?"

"Yes, Mama."

"Uriah, must you keep slaves here? Oh, your grandfather would be so unhappy over this . . . and your father as well."

"Mr. Jefferson kept slaves, Mama."

"But you are not Mr. Jefferson, or have you forgotten that? You belong to a tradition that regards slavery as evil."

"I know, Mama, I have kept only a small number of them, the ones who have lived here all their lives. These people are better off staying here and working for me than trying to find new places. And I need them to care for the estate."

Suddenly, without a word or a knock, an angular, dour-looking white man, dressed in dusty work clothing, entered the foyer.

"Mr. Levy, we're done planting those lindens on the south lawn edge," he said. "Can I turn the people loose for the day?"

"Yes, Mr. Wheeler," Uriah answered. "Come over, sir, and meet my mother. I have just brought her from Philadelphia. She'll be staying here with me. Mama, meet Mr. Wheeler, my superintendent."

They were about of an age, these two work-weary people, and they exchanged polite, if stolid nods. Joel Wheeler was like most of the Scotch, Irish, and Germans who populated the small farms of this piedmont, and whatever he had gained in his life had been hard-won. He smiled seldom and was slow to warm to any stranger. In the weeks since he had come here to live, Uriah had been neither visited nor welcomed by a single neighbor. These people were dirt farmers with loam under their nails. They bore little resemblance to the genial aristocrats of the tidewater, who were known for their lavish hospitality and generosity.

Rachel Levy was tolerant of people and their diverse ways. She had not worked for years behind the counters of her father's and her husband's stores without becoming sensitive to the foibles of her customers. She understood immediately that she and her son were considered foreigners, interlopers, by the people of these mountain slopes and valleys, and she knew it would be a long time before this changed, if indeed it ever would. Instinctively she understood why Mr. Wheeler did not show any warmth when he was introduced to her, just as he showed no gladness that his employer had just returned from an absence of two and a half weeks. Instead, he had posed a routine question to Uriah, as if it had been only five minutes since they had last conversed.

They sat together, mother and son, in the fading light as Shabbat came to Middle Virginia. They sat on two straight chairs that Uriah had carried down the walk to the path below the south wing of the house. He had wanted them to sit here after dinner so that his mother could enjoy the glorious scene as the distant blue peaks slowly submerged into night. It was his own favorite time of day and his favorite vista at Monticello. He was sure it would be hers as well. A whitish-blue light still hovered about the far peaks, but it was perceptibly graying with each moment's passage and soon would fade into blackness. A few stars could be seen, and Uriah identified them in his mind, testing his old navigation skills, measuring them now against the sharpness he had prided himself on at sea. He had been a gifted hand with a sextant, seldom in error, always certain of the ship's position on the chart. He hoped that all the years on the beach hadn't dulled those skills, though he knew that, inevitably, they had.

Finally he broached the subject he had planned to raise all along.

"Do you like it here, Mama?" he asked.

She hesitated before answering. "It's a beautiful place, I grant. But I don't know if I could ever live here permanently. I am a stranger here, with no one save you even to talk with. Is there even a synagogue in this country?"

"Yes, I think there is, in Richmond. But I am not talking only of Monticello. I don't plan to spend the entire year here myself. The winters are harsh and it is very chill on this mountain, and the house depends entirely on fires for its heat. I plan to live here only from spring to early fall each year, though I will have to come down a time or two each winter to check on things. No, the rest of the year I'll be in New York to see to my properties there. I have my eye on a fine house on St. Mark's Place, a wonderful area near the new university in Washington Square. It will be a wonderful home, Mama, and I want you with me. Please say you will think on it."

"Of course, Uriah, I'll think upon it. It's sweet of you to want me to be with you." She paused and studied his face in the twilight. "Does . . . does all that you tell me now mean that you have given up thoughts of going back to sea?"

"Given up? No, Mama, I'll never give up. That is my career, my life."

She looked puzzled. "But you are talking about our fine life together, in New York City, and here at Monticello. How then—"

"Mama, all I can do is plan to live my life as best I can without the navy. But I never will give up trying to return to sea. I know the odds are great against me. But I do have some good and influential friends in the navy and in the Congress. Of course I have enemies in both places, too, and they do their best to keep me ashore. So, I will plan a happy life for us both, at Monticello and in New York. And in the back of my heart, I will keep hoping . . . that someday they will call me again."

They sat then in silence in the lowering dark, watching as the green dells below them were gently enfolded by the night.

She sat in her favorite place: on the south gallery, outside the honeymoon cottage. Here she could look out at the blue mountains she had come to love so much. For two years now Rachel Levy had been coming to Monticello to spend the warm months with Uriah in the house that he was restoring.

Fall was coming early to Virginia this year. A spirited breeze played about her, and she was glad for the heavy shawl that Aggy had insisted she wear around her shoulders. The sumac and maples on the hillside below her already were turning to flame. Golden hickory trees and sassafras were slowly, gently, giving the valley hints of the coming winter bleakness.

Unaccountably, Rachel found herself thinking of Michael Levy, the husband who had been gone from her for more than twenty-five years. God, was it possible that so many years had come and gone since she had said her last farewells to him? She missed him. She no longer thought of him so often, but when she did it was with all the old longing. She had been a widow for nigh onto half her life. She raised her eyes to the blue summits in the distance and thought of happy days in the house on Cherry Street, days when her father still was alive and turned up almost every afternoon to take little Uriah and Mordecai by the hand and lead them off on another of their private adventures.

She was shaken from her sweet memories by the pounding of footsteps down the long gallery behind her. She turned and saw her son running toward her, excitedly waving a paper. She knew at once what it was and that the dreaded time was at hand. A few months ago Uriah had received a letter from the secretary of the navy informing him of his promotion to the rank of master commandant, an intermediate rank between captain and lieutenant. As a commander, he could serve as captain on a sloop or brig. After twenty years as a lieutenant, he could finally command his own ship. His orders, she knew, would inevitably follow.

"It's come, Mama, finally!" Uriah shouted as he drew near. "I have been given a sloop! I've been assigned to be captain of the *Vandalia*. She will be a commodore's flagship! Even with a commodore peering at my backbone every minute, it will be a wonderful assignment! I'll be right in the center of everything! After all these years, they've given me a ship of my own at last!"

Rachel Levy smiled gently, despite herself, despite her anticipation of loneliness. As much as she hated the sea for taking her sons far from her—Uriah, Morton, Benjamin, and even her youngest, Jonas—how could she begrudge Uriah this moment of happiness?

18

The Vandalia, *1838*

If a ship indeed could be compared to a lady, then the only apt comparison for the USS *Vandalia* would be to a toothless hag sitting in a gutter in the midst of her own excrement.

Uriah felt his stomach seize within him as he walked slowly down the pier and the ship he would command grew larger and larger, filling his eyes with her ugliness. He thought for a moment that he would lose his lunch, so deep was his disappointment and dismay.

The *Vandalia* appeared to hug the dock tightly lest she sink. Her planks looked rotten, and her rigging was so frayed that a loud whisper on deck would snap it all into a spider's web of ribbons.

What in God's name had so ruined this corvette that had been launched with high hopes only ten years before? Had she been given no maintenance? Had her crews been blind to overlook the long, slow decay? And this—this wreck was to be his first major command? Someone must be playing a terrible joke. Or was this better laid to someone's thirst for revenge, some unseen old enemy in the Navy Department?

He did not board the vessel. He strode back and forth along the dock and took her measure, studying every foot of her. His feeling of panic and nausea had lasted for only a moment, then it was gone.

Now he took careful note of all her shortcomings and began to plan what must be done.

The *Vandalia* was a Philadelphia ship, launched there in 1828 and finished the year after. By the sight of her now, she never again had looked so good as when she first had tasted the Delaware River on her launch day. She was about 125 feet in length, he judged, with a beam exceeding 33 feet. He was sure that she could not make more than ten knots with every stitch of sail set. He counted eight 32-pound carronades on the side facing the dock and two long 9-pounders. So she was carrying 20 guns in all and probably shouldn't have been so heavily loaded.

For a long time he studied her lines. He decided she was poorly designed, with an afterbody much too full. He wondered if Sam Humphreys had designed her. No, Sam would have known better. All of these sloops built in the 1820s were slow, ungainly sailers and couldn't hold a candle to the sloops built during the War of 1812. The later ones had greater displacement by far, but they were not long enough to cut cleanly through the water. The philosophy of the navy still called for loading down each ship with as much heavy armament as it could bear without breaking its back. So the corvettes like the *Vandalia* slogged their way through the ocean like sail-bearing boulders.

At least, he thought with a trace of a grin, *the* Vandalia *had a shapely ass*. She was one of the first U.S. Navy ships to be built with the round stern that the British, heeding the words of Sir Robert Seppings, had been employing for years.

God, she would need months of work before she would be fit to go to sea. She must be careened and smoked out and caulked and rerigged and her masts restepped. But would he be given time for such a radical overhaul? And what was this crazy talk about the *Vandalia* being the flagship for Commodore Dallas? She was not fit to be the flagship for a squadron of garbage scows.

When finally he walked up the gangplank and stepped onto the flush-decked waist of the *Vandalia*, she seemed almost deserted save for a pair of groggy sailors lazily polishing some brightwork. No officer was in sight to properly greet the corvette's new commander.

"OFFICER OF THE DECK!" he screamed at the top of his lungs, the bellow shrilling across the quiet deck, frightening in equal measure the two grimy seamen and the gulls hovering about the mainmast. There was a long moment of silence, then the sound of rushing footsteps was heard from the aft companionway. A tall young lieutenant burst through the hatchway, rubbing sleep from his eyes as he ran. He came to a stop in front of Uriah and raised his hat in salute.

"Sir, Lieutenant David Sharp, officer of the deck."

Uriah eyed him coldly and did not acknowledge the salute.

"The officer of the deck," he said in a voice like cold steel, "is to be on deck while on watch and not in his berth. Is that quite clear?"

"Yes sir," said Sharp, his voice barely audible.

"I am Master Commandant Uriah P. Levy, ordered to take command of this vessel. Lieutenant, where are the ship's officers and midshipmen? Where in God's name are all the people?"

"Why . . . why, ashore, sir. They are either off-watch or . . . or doing ship's business ashore."

"Ah, I see. Now it is quite clear why this corvette is rotting away. The crew has so much navy business to do ashore that it has no time to see to the ship. Very unusual. Perhaps we have a crew of soldiers and marines better suited to land than to water."

"Ah . . ." Lieutenant Sharp, still not sure this wasn't all an unpleasant dream, did not know what to say.

"Who has commanded this corvette until now, Lieutenant Sharp?"

"Sir, the first lieutenant is Lieutenant George Hooe, and he has been acting commander pending the arrival of . . . our new commander . . . of yourself, sir."

"And Lieutenant Hooe is, I am confident, among those ashore?"

"Yes, sir."

"Lieutenant Sharp, take whatever men are aboard and form a shore party. I want all officers, midshipmen, men, and boys aboard this ship within the half-hour. Do you understand?"

"But, sir, there must be dozens of taverns—"

"Within the half-hour, Lieutenant."

"Aye, aye, sir."

Forty-five minutes later, virtually all the 180 officers and men of the USS *Vandalia*, in various states of sobriety and dress, stood bewildered on the spar deck of the corvette and listened to an address by their new commander.

The rather high-pitched voice of Master Commandant Levy took on the piercing tone of a bosun's whistle as it sliced through the alcoholic fume covering the deck. Only occasionally did it rise into shrillness, when his temper came near to boiling over, but for the most part he kept himself in control in spite of his highly agitated state.

"Henceforth and so long as we remain in port," he said, "we shall be made into four quarter-watches, only one of which shall be on shore at a time. The duration of shore liberty will be twenty-four hours. The other three quarter-watches will garrison the corvette. There will, I assure you, be ample work to keep you from becoming bored.

"In the event a member of this crew returns to the ship in a condition of drunkenness, he shall be taken below and lashed into his hammock. If he be contentious and disrespectful, he shall be sewn into his hammock and left there until he comes to his senses. If a member of this crew shall be repeatedly guilty of such infractions, there will be additional penalties.

"Henceforth, when I board this vessel, I expect a quartermaster to duly alert the officer of the deck. I expect further to be properly piped aboard by a boatswain's mates and to proceed through a lane of sideboys. I expect the officers aboard to await me upon the quarterdeck. I will accept no less!"

Lieutenant Hooe, standing at the head of the assembled officers, flushed noticeably at this pointed reminder of the discourteous way in which the new commander had been received a short time earlier.

"Now some general rules: The ship's crew are to be messed in messes of ten each—the men by themselves and the petty officers by themselves. The men of different messes are, on every Monday morning, to appoint one of their messmates to keep their berth, cooking utensils, etc., clean and in proper order during the coming week. The time by the glass must be regularly attended to, as well by night as by day, and the bell must be struck every half-hour. The decks are to be washed in the morning watch. The gun-carriages, port sills, quick work, head and head rails, channels, sides, and all other woodwork must be well washed, and great care must be taken that the decks are well dried. While we are in port, the necessary boats are to be lowered down after the decks are washed, the yards neatly squared, ropes hauled taut, and not a rope yarn to be seen flying about the yards or rigging. The hammocks will be neatly stowed, and we will pipe to breakfast at 8 a.m. precisely."

As Uriah went on with his emphatic pronouncements, an old sheet-anchor-man turned to his mate and whispered, "He's got the bit in his teeth, this one, eh? This captain knows his business."

"Aye," his companion muttered, "he wears a quarterdeck face as if he really means it."

"The master-at-arms," Uriah continued, "is to keep a list of the boys and their clothes and to have a special eye on their conduct, habits, and cleanliness. Every morning at 7 a.m., he is to take care that they are assembled in the gangway for inspection by himself and one of the ship's corporals. Whether we are at sea or in harbor, the first lieutenant is to visit throughout the ship at 10 a.m. and see that the tiers, cockpit, wings, store rooms, passages, etc., are clean and in a proper condition and report to the captain as ready for his inspection. The midshipmen and master's mates are required to sling in hammocks, which are to be brought on deck and taken down at the same time the ship's crew's are. Four minutes and no more will be allowed for piping hammocks up 'til they are completely stowed; the same time will be allowed for taking them down and slinging them up.

"Pay special attention to this: Boats and men returning from shore are to be very strictly examined by the master-at-arms and ship's corporal, under the inspection of the officer of the deck, who will be held responsible for any liquor that may find its way on board during his watch; any liquor found in the boats or on the men, being obtained without permission, is to be thrown overboard and the person or persons found guilty of bringing it on board to be put in the charge of the master-at-arms and reported forthwith to the captain."

At this, an audible hum of mixed protest and astonishment rose from the deck. There had been a great liberality in the past, which had permitted liquor to flow like a mountain stream aboard this ship. As a result, few of the men ever were fully sober. The murmur was quickly quieted by a frosty look from the new commander.

"That is enough for right now," Uriah concluded. "We shall meet each day like this until I have finished explaining to you my rules and regulations for a man-of-war. Now, I will see the officers in my cabin." He looked around him with an expression of great distaste, as if he had smelled a long-dead fish. "This deck looks as if it has not seen a holystone in weeks. All leave for today is cancelled. I want brushes, brooms, and stones at work upon this deck, with lots of purser's soap. First Lieutenant, dismiss the ship's company!"

As he went below decks to meet his officers, Uriah congratulated himself for having made things clear to all in his first minutes as commander of this vessel. This would be a taut ship, or he would sooner see it at the bottom of Pensacola Harbor. He wondered if he had made the same impression upon the company as had Captain William Henry Allen when he had promulgated the rules and regulations for the brig *Argus* almost thirty years before—a speech that still echoed clearly in Uriah's mind on this late day.

The *Vandalia*'s officers came, one by one, down the aft companionway and into the captain's cabin, and Uriah had a chance to study them more carefully. It took him only a few minutes' perusal to see that the decrepit corvette in which they stood was a mirror reflection of this slovenly cadre of officers. Most of them, fresh from the waterfront taverns, were unshaven and red-eyed; their uniforms were wrinkled and stained. The cheek of one of the lieutenants still bore the rouge stains left by the tavern wench he had been fondling when called abruptly back to his ship. This was a group of men bereft of leadership until now, Uriah saw, and thus easily victimized by boredom and thirst.

Uriah did not trouble to make any remarks of welcome to his officers, nor to indulge in friendly repartee. Instead he launched into a terse recital of his rules for the governance of the *Vandalia*, with special emphasis on the accountability of her officers. They stared bleakly back at him, these dull-eyed, sullen epauletteers, without expression of either protest or approval. The only exception was Lieutenant Hooe, the erstwhile interim commander, a tall, blond young man of aristocratic mien whose face bore an unchanging look of distaste.

"Now, gentlemen, a word about punishment aboard this vessel," Uriah continued. "I intend to have tight discipline at all times, but such discipline will be enforced through a punishment system that you will find to be unique and, I trust, most effective. I emphasize that all determination of punishment on the *Vandalia* will be mine and mine alone. Is that clear? No man aboard this ship will be disciplined or punished without my knowledge and approval. And that includes the use of the colt by petty officers."

For the first time a reaction had been evoked. A murmur of surprise drifted across the cabin, but quickly hushed under a strong look from the commander. Then he went on:

"I mean to prove on this corvette, gentlemen, a long-held belief of mine: that the use of the lash is almost always unnecessary to maintain good discipline aboard a navy ship. Therefore, the use of the lash as punishment aboard the *Vandalia* will be forbidden, except in the most extreme of circumstances."

Now there was more than a murmur. There were low groans of displeasure and a few loudly whispered curses.

"With all respect, sir." Lieutenant Hooe stepped forward, a small, thin smile of condescension on his lips. "Sir, such an edict is unprecedented. We are dealing with rabble here, and they cannot be controlled, much less well-ordered, without the threat of flogging hanging over them."

"Rabble, Lieutenant Hooe? I think not, although in a few cases the term may be deserved. The American sailor is a good man for the most part. A bit too thirsty for grog, perhaps, but a loyal man who wants to give his best. There are other ways to get that best out of him, while keeping the cats in their bag. There are ways of dealing with their minds that will be more effective than lashing them and most certainly will not leave them scarred for life. As you must know, Lieutenant Hooe, Article 32 of the Articles of War gives me, as commander of this vessel, broad discretion to punish 'according to the laws and customs in such cases at sea.' Well enough, we shall make our own customs. For example, if a member of the crew is found to be in a drunk and disorderly condition, he will be brought to the mast like anyone else charged with an infraction. For punishment, he will carry for three days hanging from his neck a wooden bottle that publicly labels him 'drunkard.' Likewise, any man caught stealing will wear for a week a similar wooden placard proclaiming him, in large black letters, 'thief.' If men are found in a fight, they will be ordered to ingest a tankard of cold ocean water to cool their blood. Such, gentlemen, will be the order of punishment on this vessel. You will find, I am sure, that the lashing of their shipmates' tongues will punish them far more profoundly than would the kiss of a cat. Yet they will be left whole and ready for a new fresh start."

The officers, as Uriah spoke, had turned to each other with looks of astonishment. Never had they heard such drivel! Perhaps he only jested. God, there would be no semblance of discipline on this ship; the scum soon would be masters of their betters!

"I mean no disrespect, Commander Levy." Again it was Hooe stepping forward. "But, sir, this plan is madness and doomed to disaster. These are rough and stupid men, unused to privilege and, indeed, unresponsive to it. We will have no control over the crew if you persist in this incredible ambition!"

Uriah could not have been blamed if he had responded sharply to such blatant disagreement from a subordinate. But he had anticipated such reactions from his officers, and the anticipation aided him in answering calmly, if no less firmly: "The key word in what you said, Lieutenant Hooe, was that the sailors aboard this ship are *men*. Yes, they are free-born Americans and entitled to all the privileges of free men. Until I am proven wrong, they will be treated as such. And I shall not be proven wrong. Further, the officers of this ship will show the men the common courtesy of addressing them by their names when giving an order or otherwise speaking to them. In other words, I don't want to hear you hailing the captain of the foretop as 'You,' but rather as 'Jones' or 'Smith.' They have names—use them!"

"My God," murmured Lieutenant Sharp, his mouth wide in disbelief.

"Gentlemen, I have served on many ships in twenty-six years in the navy that have done it the old way. I have seen the entire watch of a frigate—some two hundred men—beaten with the colt because a drunken lieutenant did not like the cut of one man's jib. I have seen men beaten into bloody meat with thirty lashes or more, even though the law, as you must know, prohibits a captain from ordering more than twelve strokes for any offense short of a capital crime without approval of a court-martial. Yet this law is flaunted more than obeyed. It is a bad system, gentlemen, and I will not have it on my ship. I repeat, gentlemen, this will be a well-ordered ship, and such order commences with the officers, who will obey my directives to the fullest measure of compliance! I hope that is quite clear. Now, gentlemen, you are dismissed."

Captain Alexander James Dallas, commodore of the West Indies Squadron of the United States Navy, pushed himself wearily away from his desk in his little office at the Pensacola Navy Base. Just back from a tiring, arduous, utterly boring cruise, he was faced on this gray and solemn Monday morning with a high stack of papers to be gone through and duly marked for approval or disapproval.

And before him, obviously eager to begin an oral report of infinite duration and no doubt a litany of complaints, was the commander of the sloop of war *Vandalia*.

"I see by your file that you are a Philadelphian, Commander Levy." Ah, perhaps a bit of social intercourse might delay for a while the flood of complaints and permit the commodore to get his eyes fully open.

"Yes, sir, born and raised there."

"Myself as well. Though I have hardly been back there since I left for the late war."

"I have been told, sir, that you fought with Decatur."

"Indeed, yes. I was but a green lieutenant when I commanded the schooner *Spitfire* in Decatur's Mediterranean Squadron in '15 when we paid the Dey of Algiers a 'friendly' visit. Ah, those were glorious times!"

"Indeed they were, sir."

Dallas heaved a long sigh for Decatur's sad fate and for the bygone days of a carefree young officer and also for the necessity of getting to the tedious business at hand.

"Well, Commander, you requested an interview to report on your ship. How does the *Vandalia*?"

"She does measurably better, Commodore. I am grateful for the time you have allowed me in port to improve her. She is a much different ship than she was two months ago."

"Well, I'm glad to hear that, Commander. Last summer, some of our mechanics were advising me to scrap her. You say she is seaworthy again?"

"Very nearly so, Commodore. Another two months or so and she'll be ready for sea. Since I last saw you, we have unbent all sails, sent down all yards and booms, housed the masts, and careened ship. We removed everything inside the vessel, including her ballast, and set a strong fire of charcoal, brimstone, and bark. Every trace of smoke coming out was followed up by caulking and pasting of each open seam. All rotted wood, of which there was a goodly share, was then replaced. After that, we fully scraped the corvette—decks, masts, and booms and on her side down to the waterline. We then scraped, varnished, and painted the entire inside of the vessel down to the orlop. All rust was scraped from chains, bolts, and fastenings, and coal-tar was spread upon all ironwork, including anchors and ring-bolts. All brass was cleaned and polished, something that apparently had not been done in weeks. We have gone over each inch of rigging, both standing and running, and have brought down the unfit rigging and rove new in its place. All masts, of course, were restepped. I neglected to say earlier that the corvette's bottom was freshly coppered as well."

"Well," said Commodore Dallas with a smile, "it seems that you have kept busy. It seems in fact as if you have constructed a new ship. You have learned well the trick of our Navy Department, which, unable to secure funds from Congress for new ships, scraps an old vessel, rebuilds her from keel to truck, and lists it on the invoices as 'maintenance.'"

"Yes, sir," said Uriah, not knowing if he was being praised or reprimanded.

"Very well, Commander Levy," Dallas said, his voice indicating that the interview was almost done. "You have made much progress. I commend you. As you know, the *Vandalia* had been designated the flagship for my squadron, but when I saw her in the summer, I knew that she'd be lucky to get out of the harbor without sinking, much less carry my bougee. I almost gave the order to scrap her. I'm glad now that I didn't. I must say, Commander, that you leave me pleasantly surprised."

"Why is that, sir?"

"I had been told I would have my hands full with you. I don't mind telling you that some people in this navy dislike you heartily. I suspect that you were assigned to the *Vandalia* in part because some of those people figured it would get the best of you."

"I'm glad to have the chance to prove them wrong, Commodore."

"I will ask this for your own good, Levy, and beg you to understand that I ask it only for your benefit and without malice in mind:

Did it ever occur to you that some of the hardships in your navy career have come because of your reputation as a malcontent, as a constant bellyacher . . . and not because of personal hatred for you, or because of the religion that you profess? Have you given thought to that possibility?"

Uriah paused before answering. He must choose his words carefully. He would do anything to preserve the feeling of amity that presently filled this office.

"Sir, I have had this pointed out to me before. And perhaps there is justice in it. But I was taught as a child to stand up for my rights as an American. And when I feel my rights have been denied to me, yes, I complain and do whatever else must be done. I know it hasn't made my life any easier, but I would not do things differently."

"Very well, Commander. Your own conscience must guide you. All I see is that you have taken a wreck of a ship and, in a short time, put her back into serviceable condition. You are doing all that I can ask. Keep it up, and let me know how you're progressing. When will the *Vandalia* be ready for sea?"

"Within another two months, sir. In six more weeks, if we are lucky and not too disturbed by the weather."

"Good, good. Mexico is in ferment. Our diplomats and our citizens are facing increasing harassment there. I suspect you can look forward to a cruise in the Gulf before too long. Now, Commander, if that is all—"

"Sir, one request, if I may?"

Dallas sighed in annoyance. The interview had been pleasant and encouraging, but he had no more time for it. He had two months' accumulation of paperwork awaiting him. "Yes?" he said, rather curtly.

"With your permission, sir," Uriah said, "I would like to paint the guns of my ship a bright blue."

"You what? What color did you say, Commander?"

"A bright blue, sir. I know it is highly irregular, Commodore, but—"

"Explain yourself, sir. It is indeed highly irregular. I've never heard of any such thing!"

"Sir, in improving the *Vandalia* I have followed all existing rules as to color: the inside of the bulwarks are white, as are the sills of the deck structures; the masts and bowsprit are black; we have a band of white molding along our gun ports. Even the ship's boats conform to regulations, with white hulls and black gunwales. Only our guns await painting: they were terribly rusted and we have scraped them and oiled the carriages. I ask your approval, then, to paint the guns a bright blue."

"But regulations call for black cannon. If you feel the need for color, use red tompions. I have seen that done before."

"Sir, let me explain my motive. With this ship that was on her last legs, I also inherited a crew that seemed to be the castaways and rejects of the entire navy. Most of them were in a state of perpetual drunkenness. They had been so beaten down by the navy that all sense of pride was gone from them. Even the lash no longer held terror for them. We have slowly begun to change that, sir. I have instituted a new punishment system that dispenses with the lash, except in the worst cases, and we have had none such since I took command. The people of the *Vandalia* are beginning to act like men once again, rather than animals. The other day, when we completed the re-stepping of the foremast, they actually cheered that the job had been completed and done well. Oh, there is still much to do—that's why we will need another two months to be sea-ready. They are horrible yet at the guns and couldn't hit a floating barrel if it were across their berth deck. But they are coming, sir, I promise you."

"And? What in God's name has all that to do with blue guns?"

"Sir, I want the men of the *Vandalia* to feel that they serve on a special ship, a ship that is known to the other vessels of the squadron as a taut ship and a good sailer. I want the *Vandalia* to be noticed and to be talked about. My crew then will feel they are a part of something special. For too long, they have gone unseen, unheeded by the navy. They have had no more identity than the rats and cock-roaches in the bilge."

"Your blue guns will make them a laughingstock, Commander."

"Perhaps at first, sir. But it will give them notice. They will get attention and so will their ship. And this will spur them to compete with the other ships so that the laughter will turn to respect. Soon, I promise you, the *Vandalia* will come up to the mark as well as any vessel in the squadron."

"I see. Very well, Commander Levy. I have been told about your gamble in forsaking flogging as punishment. I think you may live to regret that, but it is your decision to make. So I'll let you make this decision as well. Paint your guns blue, Commander, but I pray you, not too bright. When the squadron sails in formation and I look at the *Vandalia* through my glass, I have no wish to be blinded by so garish a color. Understood?"

"Aye, aye, sir. Understood."

It was but a brief incident on the dock, lasting no more than a few seconds, and was quickly forgotten by all those involved except for one silent witness who was keeping careful watch on the commander of the *Vandalia* for the time when a case might be made against him.

Darkness was just falling. Uriah was weary and thirsty from a long day's work in which he supervised the ship's carpenter and a crew of helpers in building, from castoff old materials, a fine new whaleboat that would serve the *Vandalia* as a captain's gig. On the stern of the new gig was painted in bold letters the name "Argus" to honor the legendary brig that never strayed far from the commander's memories.

Now he had departed the ship and walked briskly down the dock toward a nearby tavern called the Waister's Retreat, where he intended to have a mug of coffee and perhaps a glass of claret. He was but a hundred yards or so past the *Vandalia*'s bowsprit when he was suddenly faced with a rough-looking party led by a grizzled, pock-faced tavern keeper named Antonio Collins. Uriah had taken a lodging room at Collin's tavern when he had first come to Pensacola, but had moved out as soon as he saw the filth of the place and the manner in which the barmaids and Collins himself systematically robbed the pockets of drunken sailors as they sprawled across the wet tables. He had given the tavern keeper a tongue-lashing as he left and had promised to seek him out if ever a *Vandalia* man was robbed on his premises.

He had not encountered Collins again in the intervening weeks, but now the stocky landlord boldly stood in his path with three grinning companions at his back.

"Get out of my way, Collins," Uriah said with no preliminaries and a stern look in his eye.

"Not 'til you pay me the money what's coming to me," Collins shouted.

"What money? I paid you in full for the two miserable nights I spent under your roof. I don't owe you a cent."

"You owed me for the week; that was the rule. You still owe me five nights' rent."

"There was no such agreement, you damned liar!" Uriah retorted.

"You Jews have all the world's money," Collins said with a laugh. "It won't hurt you to give a poor man what's owed him."

Uriah would have slapped the man across the mouth for such a remark, but he knew that the oaf's companions would jump him and there would be a brawl in the street. He would be thrashed, he knew, by sheer weight of numbers, but that didn't deter him. The thing that held him back was the certain knowledge that the Pensacola newspaper would headline a navy officer wrestling in the dirt with a group of local longshoremen.

"Collins," he yelled, "you are a damned rascal and a blackguard! Go on your way and I'll go on mine. Another word from you and I'll—"

There were no more words from Collins, but instead he suddenly lunged forward and his hand shot toward Uriah's face. His hand was not clenched into a fist, but his thumb and index finger were extended together as if he meant to grab Uriah's nose and twist it in contempt.

Uriah's own hand whipped across and smacked the other's hand away. Then he reached for his sword and drew it several inches out of the scabbard, the metallic sound making a slash in the twilight quiet.

"If this is what you want," Uriah said, a jagged hoarseness in his voice, "then so be it. I'll run at least two of you through before you can get me down. And my call will quickly bring help from my ship over there. The choice is yours, you sons of bitches!"

The tavern gang was silent for a moment. Then two of Collins's companions took a step back. One of them said, "Come on, Tony, let's go. It ain't worth it."

"Yeah," another stevedore chimed in, "I ain't gettin' cut to settle your fight, Collins."

In another second, Collins and his group had turned and walked back the other way. The tavern keeper threw a last hate-filled look back at Uriah, but he said no more.

Uriah took a long breath and returned the sword to its home. A movement behind him caused him to whirl nervously. A uniformed figure moved out of the shadow of a loading hut. It was Lieutenant George Mason Hooe.

"Was there a problem here, Commander?" he asked.

"Almost," Uriah answered. "A ruffian named Collins accosted me and attempted to pull my nose."

"He is still alive?" Hooe asked, as if innocent of the whole affair.

"I had no cause to kill him. When I warned him against further insult, he and his friends left. He did not actually touch me."

"Well, Commander," Hooe replied, "as long as you have allowed the fellow to go on living, I would think your only recourse is to go to the civilian authorities and prefer charges. Certainly such a lowlife should not be allowed to get off scot-free from such an action. Insult to the uniform and all that, sir." His words were casual enough, but his eyes bored into Uriah's with a look both defiant and condemning.

"Yes, Lieutenant, I am aware of what is involved. I will consider going to the civilian authorities. Now goodnight, sir."

Uriah resumed his stroll toward the Waister's Retreat. *How long had Hooe been standing there*, he wondered, *watching the altercation?* And he also wondered, if a brawl had begun, would the first lieutenant have come to his aid or just remained in the shadow as an amused observer?

Uriah awoke some time after midnight and lay silently on his cot, awaiting sleep's return and listening to the ship's music—the play of the wind across the rigging and the tremulous creaking of the wooden seams as the *Vandalia* leaned into a freshening wind. Perhaps it was the many earlier cruises spent in watch and watch—four hours on watch, four hours below—but he could not adapt well to the luxury given a ship's commander of spending the entire night in his cabin. He always had been a light sleeper, and the changes of watch during the night always roused him right along with the lowliest seaman, even though he had every right to bury his head under his pillow and get quickly back to sleep.

Well, he mused now, perhaps it was his old habit of watch and watch or perhaps it was the salted beef tongue and pickled cabbage that had composed his dinner. His stomach had been troubling him again of late, and the *Vandalia's* cooks were not the most expert he ever had encountered.

It was a warm night, and the cabin was stuffy. He decided to pull on his clothes and take a turn or two about the spar deck. As he came up the companionway and through the aft hatch, the officer of the deck, Lieutenant Sharp, was walking past and was startled by his sudden appearance. Sharp raised his hat, his eyebrows high in question.

Uriah did not feel an explanation of his presence was necessary. He said nothing but walked to the binnacle and, in the light of the two lanterns, perused the traverse board and the slate that served as a deck log.

"I see we were making almost eight when you last heaved the

log," he said, almost to himself. "If this wind continues to freshen, Mr. Sharp, you should consider getting the studding sails in."

"Aye, aye, sir."

Uriah looked up at the sails and watched them draw for a moment or two, then he began a slow walk along the weather side of the spar deck. The larboard watch was on deck, and its members huddled in small groups along the bulwarks, talking in soft voices or sleeping. They had no particular duty during these quiet hours, except when it was necessary to tack or make sail or take in sail. Otherwise they were permitted to lounge on the deck or in the tops to which they were assigned. Silence was the rule, but it was a rule only casually enforced, and the men talked among themselves except when an officer drew near. Thus, as Uriah paced along the deck, the hum of conversation would fade away ahead of him and then renew itself to his rear as the men saw that he was not stopping, but merely passing on into the darkness. A few sailors startled in surprise to see their commander on the deck at this hour, but no one was brazen enough to address him, much less question his presence. They merely stared silently as he passed.

As he drew near the forecastle and was giving some thought to a quick visit to the head before making the turn and heading aft once again, he was puzzled by a rhythmic pounding sound that echoed dully. At first he thought it might be a sail slatting, but he knew almost at once that this was not the sound he was hearing. He rounded the foremast and, as he moved across to the lee side of the deck, he spied a small group of figures in the darkness at the forward lee bulwark. It was from there that the pounding sound was coming.

Curious, he slowed his pace and crossed the deck. He was careful to make no sound. As he came closer to the bulwark, with his eyes having become accustomed to the dark by now, he could distinguish those in the group.

Two burly petty officers, legs braced firmly, grasped the arms of a seaman who stood, or rather hung, between them. Next to them was the tall figure of Lieutenant Hooe, his back to Uriah. Not a word was spoken, but Hooe reared back and pounded his fist sharply into the sailor's chest, then cocked his arm again and smashed the man in the face. Now Uriah understood that the steady drumlike sound he had heard down the deck was the sound of Hooe's fists pounding repeatedly into the man's body. The sailor's legs were wobbly and there was a stream of blood running down his face, but he neither groaned, wept, nor begged for mercy. He stood silently, if shakily, and took the blows.

The petty officers looked thunderstruck as they recognized Uriah striding toward them, a look of fury on his face, but they did not release the man held between them. Hooe had pulled his arm back for yet another punch when Uriah's voice cut across the deck like a cold knife through warm spit: "Hold up, you! What is this? Stop at once! You two, take that man to sick bay at once and roust out the surgeon to see to him! At once, do you hear?"

The petty officers glanced quickly at Hooe but wasted no further time. They half-walked, half-carried the semiconscious sailor to the fore hatchway and led him below. As they passed from view, the sailor for the first time let out a loud, anguished groan of pain and misery.

Uriah turned to face Hooe. He fought to control his rage and to keep his voice from sliding up the scale into a piercing treble. "How dare you, Mr. Hooe." he said. "What is the meaning of this?"

Hooe was breathing hard with his exertion and the surprise of his commander's unexpected appearance. He took a breath or two before answering.

"The bastard had it coming, sir," he said. "He was insubordinate and disrespectful. I warned him more than once."

"This was in direct violation of my orders, Mr. Hooe, and you knew that. We have a system of discipline for dealing with such cases."

"Your 'system,' as you call it, Commander, is of no value in dealing with scum like this. They understand only the fist or the cat. Nothing more. Even the colt is too soft for the likes of him."

"Hooe, you push me too far! I have warned you more than once about punishing men illegally behind my back. I will not tolerate this. You are confined to your cabin until we return to Pensacola."

Hooe nodded coldly. "Very well, sir. But how will you work the ship? You have already put Pennington in his cabin for drinking too much. You'll soon have no lieutenants left."

"That is my concern, Mr. Hooe, and not yours. I have well-trained midshipmen who are ready and willing to act as lieutenant. The ship will be worked, Mr. Hooe, never fear. Now get to your cabin and not another word! And I promise you, when we anchor at Pensacola, you'll answer for this by facing charges. You'll be off my ship for good, and I'll do my best to see you out of the navy, for it does not need your ilk. Now get below!"

Uriah walked back to the lee bulwark and stared out at the inky water. He could hear the surf gurgling past the *Vandalia*'s forefoot. There were loud splashes off the port bow, and he imagined a school of dolphins frolicking in the spring night air. He stood and breathed deeply and waited for his heart to stop pounding. There would be no more sleep for him this night.

•••

U.S. *Ship* Vandalia
Off the Laguna de Los Terminos
April 23, 1839

Dear Mama,

I am sorry that it has been so long since I last wrote, but I have been most busy and also have been cruising off the Mexican coast, where the unsettled conditions caused me to fear that a letter posted to you would never reach you. Today the purser and I are leaving the ship for a time and there is a brig anchored nearby that is Norfolk-bound. I am sending the let-

ter with them and hope it will reach you soon and will find you in good health and humor.

I am well. In fact, I am gloriously well. I have never been happier in all my life than in the last weeks. I am doing what God intended me to do and am doing it well. No man could ask for more.

I don't know where to begin, but let me try to give you a fair and true accounting of our voyage so far. We sailed from Pensacola on February 3 last with a ship and crew that were like new (with one or two exceptions, as I shall relate). One night after we sailed, one of my lieutenants fell overboard in a heavy sea and was lost. It is my opinion that he was in a drunken state at the time for he was a heavy drinker and had been known to smuggle intoxicants aboard although I had expressly forbidden it. I took a bright and dutiful Passed Midshipman named John Moffat and made him an Acting Lieutenant to fill the place. I caught another officer, Lieutenant Sharp, drunk on watch and threatened him with the direst punishment unless he would take a temperance pledge, which he did and has faithfully adhered to since.

In general my new system of discipline on the Vandalia is working even better than I had hoped. I have told you of the wood placards that I hang upon the drunks and the thieves. They have the effect I had hoped and such infractions have greatly lessened.

We sailed for twelve days across the Gulf and then lay off the Rio del Norte for another seven. The American consul at Matamoros had messaged that our citizens there feared for their lives and were not being properly protected by the Mexican authorities. I could not take my corvette up the river to the city due to shoals, so put a number of my men in our 29-foot launch and two of our cutters, armed them to the teeth, and led them in a fast row up the river. We took the town by surprise and our little show of force evidently impressed the

Mexican governor for he promised the consul in my presence that the Americans would have no more to fear. We weighed anchor on February 22 and proceeded southward. After cruising the area for several days, we sailed for Tampico, off which we arrived on the 7th. I put myself in touch at once with the American consul, who was most fearful that a General Bustamente and his army were nearing the town and would sack it. He requested that a naval force be sent to his aid and I promised to convey his request post-haste and did so via the next vessel bound for Pensacola.

We lay from March 17 to April 11 at Vera Cruz, then sailed eastward across the Bay of Campeche to the Laguna de los Terminos in the area known as Yucatan. Our consul here also had a tale of woe to tell, a tale of American citizens being at the mercy of Mexican cutthroats with little help or protection from the Mexican government. A local general was the culprit and I resolved to call upon him and demand proper respect for our flag and its citizens. I brought the Vandalia close in to the shore and armed my men and took them into the city with me to call upon the general. I demanded of him that money stolen from Americans be returned and that he sign an agreement to protect them in the future. He blustered and protested, but I told him that if he resisted, my ship would draw in and fire into his city and would cause great ruination. He quickly capitulated, asking in return only that I provide him with whiskey, a navy officer's uniform, and a ceremony at which we would extend our mutual respects. I agreed, and we had a nice little ceremony in the town square and sealed our undying friendship with a drink of the whiskey.

We will weigh anchor tomorrow at dawn and sail northward, probably to arrive in Pensacola, if the winds are fair, by the end of the month. I know that Monticello is coming into its finest season soon and I wish I could be there with you, but I know I shall be detained in Pensacola until our next cruise begins. My ship's bottom must be scraped and I must *supervise that, as well as her provisioning for a new cruise. Commodore Dallas has been succeeded as commodore of the West Indian Squadron by Commodore William Shubrick. I do not know him or what he has in mind for my ship.*

I must close now. My purser awaits me and we will go ashore today to say farewells to Mr. Thomas, the consul. By the time this letter reaches you, I should be nearing, or with luck be in, the harbor of Pensacola.

My deepest love to you and to all my family,

Your loving son,
Uriah

It always was exhilarating to ride up the now-familiar mountain road to Monticello, and he felt now the warm sense of homecoming surging through him, but the feeling was restrained this time by the urgency of his mission. He spurred his horse up the last furlong of his journey. The woods all around him were ablaze in pink and orange and white, the mountain exultant with blooming azalea, rhododendron, dogwood, and mountain laurel. He was drowned in beauty and he was not blind to it, but his mind was on other things and he could not take the time to enjoy it as he usually did.

The message had been handed to him at Pensacola just as he was supervising the running of the larboard guns over to starboard and the double-breeching of the other guns to enable the *Vandalia* to be heaved over so that the scraping of her bottom could begin.

The note was terse and to the point, written in Joel Wheeler's scraggly hand: "Come at once. Your mother is sick. Do not delay."

As soon as he had read the note, Uriah put Lieutenant Sharp in command of the work on the *Vandalia* and ran to the squadron commander's office to arrange an emergency leave. With Shubrick away on a cruise, the formalities were minimal, and in less than an hour he had his leave paper in hand and was off to hire a coach to begin the frantic ride to Virginia. Through Alabama and Georgia and the Carolinas they ran, Uriah urging the coachman always for more speed, stopping long enough only to rest the horses. Uriah begged the reluctant coachman to leave his horses at a Charlotte livery and pick up a fresh team there, rather than take the time for another rest. The coachman agreed on payment of a large bribe. Finally, two hours past dawn, they reached Charlottesville, where Uriah dismissed the coachman and picked up a saddle horse for the final dash up the mountain.

As he approached across the lawn, a tallish man came out of the west door and stood on the porch between the two center columns of the portico. He stood with his hands behind his back like a commander on quarterdeck. *This must be the doctor*, Uriah thought.

As Uriah crossed the last thirty feet of grass between them, the man on the porch straightened up, as if now certain of the identity of the newcomer, and began walking down the steps toward him.

"Uriah?" said the man. "Don't you recognize me?"

"Jonas? My God, Jonas, is it really you?"

"It is Jonas. Have I changed so much that you are in doubt?"

The two brothers embraced and held each other in a bear hug for long moments. When they parted, Uriah grasped his brother's shoulders and looked him over from top to bottom. "My God, your golden curls have disappeared," he said, "and I detect that you are starting to go bald."

"I'm far from bald," Jonas said with a smile. "The wiser I get, the broader my forehead becomes, that's all. Anyway, I was only fifteen when you last saw me. Now I'm past thirty and look like an old sailor should look."

"How's Mama?" Uriah asked. "Is she improved? Is a doctor attending her?"

The smile faded from Jonas's lips. He shook his head.

A pain of dread raced like a spike of errant wind through Uriah's gut.

"She is dead, Uriah. I'm sorry. She died five days ago."

"Oh, God, no. Not Mama. No." His knees went weak, and he sat down upon the topmost step. Jonas sat next to him and placed his arm around his older brother. They sat in silence for several minutes.

"What happened, Jonas?" Uriah finally asked.

"It was her lungs and her throat, 'Riah. She coughed a lot and had trouble in breathing. The doctor seemed a good man and he treated her kindly, but he told us she was ailing badly in the chest and that he could not save her. He gave her some medicine that helped her breathe easier, but she grew weaker and weaker."

"How long have you been here?"

"Just over a week. Wheeler didn't know if you were still out on a cruise when Mama took sick, so he wrote to Amelia in New York. I happened to be in the city, so she asked me to rush down here. Mama was very bad off when I arrived, but she recognized me and was glad to see me. She kept asking for you, so Wheeler found a man leaving for Pensacola and had him take a note to you. I'm sorry you didn't find out in time to see her before she died."

Uriah nodded. His eyes had filled with tears when he heard that his mother had asked for him in her last agonies. *At least she had not died among strangers*, he thought. At least her youngest child had been there to hold her hand and comfort her.

"Where is she, Jonas? Where did you take Mama?"

"We buried her down there, 'Riah." He pointed off to his left, in the direction of the south gallery. "We buried her on the slope down there, next to the path that goes down the hill to Jefferson's grave. The mulberry walk, Wheeler calls it. I didn't know what to do. I thought of taking her back to Philadelphia and burying her with Father, in Mikveh Israel's cemetery on Spruce Street, but Aggy kept telling me how much Mama loved it here, how she loved to look out at the mountains and valleys here. . . . I didn't know what to do, 'Riah, so we put her in a plain pine box and buried her here. Did I do wrong, do you think?"

Uriah patted his brother's back reassuringly. "No, Jonas, you didn't do anything wrong. Mama did love it here. Were any words said over her? Did you say the Kaddish?"

"You know I did, 'Riah. I wouldn't neglect to do that. I found a man in Richmond, an older man who knows Jewish law and all the prayers. He came up here with me and made sure everything was done right. He chanted the *Moley Rachamim* and helped me say the burial Kaddish."

"I'm glad, Jonas. You did well. You took care of everything. Let's walk down there. I want to see her grave and I want to say my own Kaddish for her. I know she'd want me to do that."

The brothers rose from the steps on the great portico beneath Jefferson's graceful dome and made their way slowly across the lawn, past the honeymoon cottage and down the slope to the final resting place of Rachel Phillips Levy.

Acting Lieutenant John Moffat turned over again on his cot and wished again that sleep would come to him. But it was hot and airless in his tiny cabin off the *Vandalia*'s wardroom. To make things worse, his head buzzed with plans for the coming day. Captain Levy had ordered him to take a boat and proceed into Galveston Island at first light in order to take observations for the latitude and longitude of the lighthouse there. It was a formidable responsibility for a passed midshipman like himself, and Moffat lay sleepless, making plans for his mission. The captain was a stickler for correct charts, and he had the *Vandalia*'s officers busy projecting new ones all the time, for the existing charts were far from precise. The latitude and longitude given on the navy's charts for Galveston Port were, the captain insisted, as much as thirty-five miles off. The only way to see them corrected was to make new ones and do the job right.

The charting task kept the ship busy and reasonably content, for their cruising orders from Commodore Shubrick had been vague. They were to sail to Galveston and thence southward, keeping alert for any signs of slaving and, if such were seen, to confiscate the ships and their contents. They were to cruise as far as Matamoros, make sure that all was well with the Americans there, and then beat back to Pensacola. It would be a cruise of perhaps two months, barring unexpected delays or problems.

Of course, they had more to do than chart. The captain always was jealous of the fighting skills of his ship, and he preached to his officers the dictum of Captain William Henry Allen that the great guns must be worked each day if the ship was to remain a fighting force. So at least once each day, the drums roared out their call to quarters and the *Vandalia* became again a fighting ship of war, her sixteen carronades booming their defiant song out across the startled waves.

The *Vandalia* was a well-ordered ship, Moffat assured himself as he fought for sleep in his hot cabin, under an able and fair, if demanding, captain. He never had known a Jew before now, but he was proud to be serving under this one.

The ship lurched violently, and Moffat was thrown hard against the bulkhead, his skull rebounding smartly off the rough wood. A lurch had occurred a few moments earlier, but Moffat had paid little attention, so engrossed was he in planning his charting mission at daybreak. This time, though, he was startled into attention. *There! There it was again!* A sharp, angular lurch. But how could this be? They were anchored in six-and-a-half fathoms of water off Galveston. Moffat quickly pulled on his clothing and climbed the aft companionway to the spar deck to see what might be amiss.

As he ascended through the hatchway and came up on deck, two sounds caught his ear: the droning howl of a rising wind that had the makings of a gale and the pounding of feet on the deck. Then from the darkness to his left came a piercing yell from Lieutenant Downes, the corvette's new first lieutenant. "Sound the alarm!" he screamed. "We're dragging! Beat to quarters!"

In less than a minute, the ship was filled with the chilling sounds of the drums beating out the old "Heart of Oak" rhythm. Meanwhile, the boatswain's mates were bellowing down the hatchways to the watch below to rise and man their stations.

"How can I help, sir?" Moffat inquired of Downes.

"Run and get the captain! I need him! That damned lookout fell asleep, and we've dragged our anchor. There's a gale blowing up and we're into five fathoms. There's a bank of only two and a half fathoms right around here somewhere, and we'll be up on it any minute!"

Before Moffat could turn and take a step back toward the hatchway, he was aware of a new presence at his side. Captain Levy had thrown a coat around his night clothing and stood on his quarterdeck, looking speculatively at the sky and the ominous flashes of lightning to the western horizon.

"I have the con, Mr. Downes," Uriah said calmly. "Man the capstan and heave up the stream anchor. And put the fore and aft sails on her."

The commands were given in a soft voice, yet it was freighted with authority. Downes jumped to carry out the captain's bidding, and in another minute the deck resounded with the cries of "To the bars, my hearties! Heave hard, boys, heave hard! Up anchor, boys! Heave!"

As soon as the cry came from the forecastle—"Up and down, sir!"—Uriah sent men running aloft to reef the topsails.

The dark spar deck was filled with running men and the pounding of bare feet on the planks, but over all was a sense of assurance and calm. This crew moved with the celerity of men well-trained and unshirking.

"Heave hard, lads, bring 'im up!" came the shout again from the ship's waist. In a few moments the anchor showed his head above the dark waves, and the crew prepared to hook the five-thousand-pound mass of black metal to the cathead.

The *Vandalia* was gaining steering way as the wind filled her fore and aft sails. The wind continued to rise and occasional thunder rumble could be heard. In the last few minutes, the wind had veered and now came smacking at them from the south.

"Helmsman, down helm," Uriah ordered.

"Down helm, sir," repeated the man at the wheel. He spun the great wooden wheel, and the *Vandalia* responded almost instantly, slowly turning her bow into the raging wind.

"Full and by," came the next command.

"Full and by, sir." The helmsman, a graybeard quartermaster who had steered through hundreds of storms like this, kept an eagle eye on the fore and aft sails. He would bring her as close up to the wind as he dared, but those sails must not begin to slat, lest the ship be taken aback and go out of control.

"She's right on the edge," Uriah noted, more to himself than to the helmsman. "Keep her there."

"Aye, aye, sir. On the edge it is!"

"Steer sou' sou'west."

"Aye, sir, sou' sou'west."

The *Vandalia* was pitching and rearing like a wounded animal in the screaming wind and plunging surf, but she was moving perceptibly ahead, through the blackness and the blizzardlike spray, into the safety of deeper water. She was defying the storm and holding like a determined lioness to her own course.

"Mr. Downes!" Uriah called. "Give me double-reefed topsails!"

"Aye, sir! Topmen aloft: Double-reef your topsails!" Downes shouted.

Again the deck reverberated with pounding feet as the topmen poured up the shrouds and out upon the wet yards. They would earn their keep this night, these limber boys of the ratlines and foot-ropes, for they would set sail and reef sail upon a pitching perch that reared like a wild bronco. Yet they went to their work with a will, for they understood that their captain already had steered them away from the mortal danger of shoal and reef and bank and out to the refuge of the deepwater ocean. Here the *Vandalia* would be in her element; here she could master almost any storm that nature deigned to hurl upon her.

First Lieutenant Downes looked perceptibly relieved as he stood upon the rolling, heaving quarterdeck and watched the corvette hurry out to safe water. He could not help wondering, though, if he would draw the blame for the ship dragging her anchor while he was officer of the deck. It was the lookout in the chains who was the real culprit, and Downes knew that the captain would come down hard on the man. The law allowed a death sentence in such cases, but his captain would never go that far. The sailor might have a flogging in store, however, and this from a captain who hated the lash as much as any common seaman. The lookout, by closing his eyes on duty, had endangered his ship and the lives of all his shipmates. It would not go lightly with him.

"Tell me something, Mr. Downes," Moffat asked as the ship quieted down. "Explain to me why the captain put the helm down and turned the ship into the wind. I would think that the most prudent course would have been to run before the wind and get the ship into deeper water as quickly as possible. It seems to me that he did it the hard way."

"That's where you are wrong, Mr. Moffat." Downes smiled, though his smile could not be seen by Moffat in the darkness. "There were two lessons for you to learn from this little bit of action tonight. The captain first called for the fore and aft sails to give him steering way. Had he taken time to set the square sails, we would have gone up on the bank for sure. Then he called for down helm and sent us into the wind. Another very wise decision. Had we scudded before the wind, we'd have been at the wind's mercy and the following sea would have thrown us every which way. Those waves are very high, and they would have been *behind* us, which means they could have blanketed our sails and robbed us of way. No, the captain instead faced the storm like a man and steered us full-and-by. This way, you see, instead of turning the weakest part of a ship—the stern—to this wind, he turned the strongest part—the bow. And by doing so, he made it much easier to close-reef the topsails when he got the time to do so."

"Yes, I see," Moffat said. "I never thought of those things."

"You'll learn plenty by watching this captain of ours, lad. He's a calm head in a pinch. I saw that about him very soon after I came aboard. Captain Levy is a mighty cool customer."

It had been altogether too perfect a Sunday. At precisely five bells in the afternoon watch, Uriah sighed, aware that he was feeling total contentment, and he told himself that surely something would happen to mar his peace and tranquility. He believed that all life and nature operated in a system of cycles and balances. *When things became too luxuriously tranquil,* he assured himself, *fate would act to restore its equilibrium and something would occur to provide strife.*

The *Vandalia* glided under easy sail across the middle of the Gulf of Mexico. The water looked and felt like a giant blue tabletop, and there was hardly a roll or pitch to be noticed. The sky was an eggshell blue, and the only clouds to be seen were a few scattered puffballs that posed not even a remote threat to the general air of peace.

"Captain, excuse me. One of the midshipmen wishes to bring charges against a boy." It was Lieutenant Downes, standing before his commander with raised hat. *I knew it,* Uriah thought. *It was too peaceful to last, too good.*

"What is the problem, Mr. Downes?"

"Sir, Midshipman Ammen reported to me in the wardroom that he had given an order to a boy named John Thompson and that the boy responded by mimicking Midshipman Ammen and therefore mocking him, and that further the boy has been in the habit of so mocking this midshipman. Mr. Ammen wishes to prefer charges against the boy."

"Is this midshipman reliable, Mr. Downes, or is he the type of reefer to be malicious to a ship's boy?"

"I would say he is reliable, Captain, if a trifle overbearing. But I don't think he would prefer charges unless the boy had been extremely disrespectful."

"Very well," Uriah answered, with a touch of exasperation in his tone. "Bring the boy up to the mast and order the ship's company to assemble. We shall get to the bottom of this matter in short order."

Downes hurried off to carry out the order. Within a few minutes, the officers and crew were assembled around the mainmast, awaiting with an air of glee the trial and punishment of one of their shipmates. Indeed they had begun to yawn and stretch in the laziness of the afternoon, and the thought of an inquiry at the mainmast and later one of the captain's unique punishments brought a bit of invigoration back into their day.

John Thompson, an English-born lad of fifteen or sixteen years, stood bareheaded, his face pale with fear, in the center of the crowd and waited for his commander to appear. The sailors called the center of the circle the "bull-ring," and there a miscreant stood and received the taunts and jibes of his shipmates. Cruel reminders of the sad fate in store for him poured past John Thompson's ears, for sailors were a tough and thick lot and not inclined to show mercy to one of tender age or for any other reason.

"You'll taste the cat's tongue more than once before this day is over," called an old sheet-anchor man, cackling with eagerness through toothless gums. "Feel your healthy back now, lad, for never again will it feel so good!"

John Thompson winced at the sour warning, and his chin trembled as he fought to hold the tears. A sailor named Van Ness, also an Englishman and one who had befriended the boy, came up to him and patted him on the shoulder and whispered some encouragement to him, which brought a new torrent of catcalls from the bystanders. "Kiss him, won't you, Van Ness, and dry his tears!" screamed a giraffelike main-top-man, over six feet high and weighing less than 130 pounds.

The noise and taunts suddenly stopped as the crowd parted to make an aisle and Captain Levy passed to the mainmast, followed by his somber officers.

The hearing took but a few minutes. Midshipman Ammen repeated his account. Uriah turned to John Thompson: "Was the midshipman's story correct, sir? Do you wish to challenge any of his facts? Were you guilty of the behavior Mr. Ammen has cited?"

In a voice audible only to his captain, John Thompson admitted his misdeed; he made no effort to deny the accusation.

"And, Thompson, is it correct that you have mimicked the midshipman in the past, that this was not the first such occurrence?"

The boy nodded and softly admitted that this also was true.

Uriah shook his head wearily. He stared at the boy for several minutes, contemplating a while longer the idea that had occurred to him in his cabin as he was donning his coat and sword before coming to the mainmast. Then he nodded, certain that his idea was sound.

"John Thompson, we have ascertained that the accusation brought against you by Midshipman Ammen is substantially proven. Punishment is in order." About him he sensed the circle of seamen drawing closer, as if almost tasting the blood that surely would flow from the tender skin of this misguided Limey boy.

"Thompson," Uriah continued, "we must teach you never to mimic a superior officer again. If you must act like a parrot, we will treat you like a parrot. Master-at-Arms! Take this boy and lean him over that gun!"

John Thompson's mouth opened in sheer panic and he murmured, "Oh, my God!"

Quickly the boy was seized up and bent over a larboard carronade. The master-at-arms was about to rip off the boy's shirt when he was halted by another order from the captain.

"You boys there—I want you to pull Thompson's trousers down to his knees!"

A great hubbub went around the deck as the sailors exclaimed aloud at the unusual order and passed the word to those further back in the crowd, who had not heard. Sprigs of laughter blossomed in the mob.

Two trembling boys ran up to obey the order and pulled Thompson's trousers down to the level of his knees. The startling whiteness of his lean buttocks formed a great contrast to his sun-bronzed arms and neck. The ship's officers exchanged glances of surprise and, in one or two cases, consternation. Was this some diabolical new punishment to be inflicted on this careless boy, or had their captain taken leave of his senses?

"Now, Boatswain Whitaker," Uriah called out, "I want you to bring a pot of tar and some oakum." The supplies were quickly brought. "Master-at-Arms, take some tar on the oakum and place a small circle of it on each of Thompson's buttocks." The burly master-at-arms, a strange look on his face, carried out the order.

"Gunner Dewey!"

"Aye, sir?"

"Do you still have your parrot?" Uriah asked.

"I do, Captain."

"Very well. Go to your cabin and pluck some colorful feathers from your parrot. Bring those feathers here and stick them in the tar on the boy Thompson's nether parts. Thompson, do you hear?"

"I hear, sir," came Thompson's muffled voice.

"You will stride about this deck for ten minutes, wearing your colorful plumage, with your pants hanging about your knees. Perhaps this will persuade you that you are a man and that you no longer wish to be a parrot. Mr. Downes, dismiss the ship's company!"

The captain's order to dismiss was almost drowned out by the great roar of surprise and laughter that filled the air when the men understood the true nature of the punishment. It had never been seen by them before, but most of them had to admit that it certainly should cure John Thompson of his desire to mimic the voice or actions of any superior.

As the men left the mainmast, they hurled fresh new taunts at the boy huddled over the breech of the carronade.

"Flap your wings and fly, little bird!" shouted one.

"Polly wanna cracker?" screamed another, choking with laughter.

John Thompson slumped over the carronade and sobbed. Tears flowed with relief because he would not be flogged and with humiliation at his public disgrace. *Thank you, Lord*, he said to himself. *Thank you, Lord.*

A quarter-hour later, after the tar had been scrubbed away and the pants clewed up again, into their proper place, John Thompson joined his friends on the berth deck and their laughter drew forth his own. He knew he was lucky to be left whole, and he knew he had learned a worthy lesson.

There was no laughter, though, in the cabin of Midshipman

Daniel Ammen. He seethed at the light punishment given to the insolent boy who had mocked him. *Such an offense would have been worth a dozen lashes on any well-run ship*, he told himself. The *Vandalia* is a travesty of discipline, a ship without order under the command of a weakling Jew who cannot bear the sight of blood. He pulled a sheet of paper from his cabinet and his quill pen and ink pot. He must record all the events of this incident. It would make good reading for his friend, Lieutenant George Mason Hooe, who had warned him that he could expect the worst from this corvette and its cowardly commander.

There was fire in Uriah's eye and in his heart as he entered the outer office of Commodore William Shubrick and prepared to demand an audience with that worthy. He would tolerate no more of this treatment, even if it meant facing a charge of insubordination.

The *Vandalia* had anchored again off Pensacola on the fourth day of August. Uriah was pleased with the cruise. It had been an uneventful voyage, and the corvette had not had to fire a cartridge in anger, nor—except for the brief crisis with a dragging anchor at Galveston—did she have to face any perilous storms, under-deck blazes, or other hazards of the life at sea. There had been no trials or tests to speak of, yet Uriah felt that his ship was much better for the cruise. The men had worked hard, and their state of readiness for battle had advanced measurably. It was a taut ship, he felt, and a willing crew. He would not hesitate to take them into battle; they knew what was to be done and they were ready to do it. He was proud of what they had accomplished in these months.

He was not unhappy either about the surprising publicity that had been given to his new system of discipline. It had brought favorable comment in several newspapers, after word of the novel punishment regime was spread across the beach by his officers and crew. Navy men were constantly moving from one port to another, and the word traveled with them. A newspaper in Norfolk had referred to Uriah's innovations as "a great moral reform," and he had been elevated to near-sainthood in New York by his cousin Morde-cai's *Evening Star*, which had lauded him for banishing the lash and the colt, except in the most extreme cases.

Oh, he knew the publicity also was causing him harm. There were many navy officers who were unbreakably wedded to the old ways: the punishment menu copied from the British Navy that went all the way back in history to the tyranny of the Stuart kings.

Such officers were convinced beyond any argument that the common sailor was worth no more than a horse turd and that the only way to teach him right from wrong was to peel his skin with a leather thong. It was the older officers, mostly, who preached this doctrine with all the fervor of an evangelist, and they would hear or heed no other doctrine. Strangely, the other center of pro-flogging sentiment in the navy was among the midshipmen. Those callow youths—many of them still too young to raise face whiskers and themselves immune from any punishment stiffer than confinement to their cabins or being sent aloft to furl a sail—those arrogant young despots loved to hear the whistle of a cat through the air and the agonized screams of a bleeding sailor. As they took on years and as they began to sicken at flogging after flogging on the ships in which they sailed, they gradually would change and most would open themselves to newer and better ways of ensuring respect and discipline from the ship's people.

Meanwhile the reports of Uriah's novel methods and his abjura-tion of the cat spread like a plague through the navy. He knew that his name was being cursed again in many quarters and also saluted, if perhaps secretly, in some.

He had been back from his Gulf of Mexico cruise for a month. He had submitted, as navy practice required, a detailed report on the cruise, along with his ship's log, to Commodore Shubrick for his review. It had been his expectation that after a few days in port he would be summoned by the commodore for a friendly chat about his mission completed, some instructions for the refurbishing and reprovisioning of the *Vandalia* for its next cruise, and perhaps a hint or two as to what that next assignment might entail. Uriah was confident that the meeting would be a pleasant one, for the cruise just finished had been uneventful and, by the standard of peacetime cruises, successful. There had been no incidents to mar the record, no breakdowns in crew performance, no major problems with the ship or its equipage. He had looked forward to his first meeting with William Shubrick and perhaps to discussing with him the current state of the navy and its agonizingly slow transition into the new age of steam.

But there was no meeting. His report produced naught but silence from the commodore's office, and his log was returned to him unmarked, save only for small precise letters in a lower corner to show that Shubrick had indeed inspected and initialed the book.

Puzzled, yet not wishing to impose his presence when he had not been summoned, Uriah set his crew to work varnishing and painting the lower decks of the corvette. When they were done with that, they set up the rigging again and replaced the chafing gear. He would have set them to carrying food and water casks aboard, except that he was not authorized to draw provisions without orders from the commodore.

Pensacola still baked in summer heat, for early September brought no taste of fall there but only a continuation of August's inferno. Uriah spent his days trying to keep busy and to keep his men busy aboard the *Vandalia*. His nights passed slowly in one of the harbor's many rooming houses, where he rolled over and over again for hours on end trying to discover a cool spot somewhere on the fevered sheet, like an explorer seeking a circle of shade in a broad desert.

Three days prior, a communication of sorts finally had come from the commodore. It was a one-sentence note directing Uriah to cease the practice of having his midshipmen pull the oars on a ship's boat. Shubrick did not even sign the missive, but only initialed it.

Uriah read the commodore's note as great currents of sweat poured down his face. The brief order so infuriated him that he was hard put not to send the runner back with a crisp verbal response. But he controlled his impulse and went instead to his cabin, where he wrote out a brief, well-reasoned note to Shubrick. He explained carefully that the purpose of such duty for the midshipmen was to further their education in small-boat handling, which in turn would improve their seamanship. It also would benefit their physical well-being, he said, and by no means was intended as a punitive or reproachful exercise. He signed the note with a flourish and ordered Midshipman Charles Hager to carry the note promptly to the commodore's office. (Uriah thought this an appropriate little touch, although he wondered if the commodore would appreciate it.) A day went by with no further word. Then, today, the same runner from the commodore appeared again on the *Vandalia*'s gangplank and reported a new communication for the ship's captain.

This note from Shubrick was a bit more loquacious than the first, but equally as blunt: "The midshipmen are sent on board ship in order that they may learn the duties of officers and I am of the opinion that pulling an oar is no part of such duties: it tends also to lessen that personal respect for them on the part of the crew which should be promoted by all proper means. You will discontinue the practice in the future."

Uriah strode into the outer office of the commodore, part of his suite in a small whitewashed building about one hundred feet back from the water's edge. The second note had been the final straw! No word for weeks, not even the courtesy of an interview. Then, this curt, peremptory order! As captain, he had the responsibility of educating and training the midshipmen assigned to his ship. There was nothing in naval regulations prohibiting him from sitting middies at the sweeps. God knows, it was not done in a cruel or vindictive way and represented nothing more odious than was the common, everyday lot of ordinary seamen. He would not stand for Shubrick's implication that he had been unfair or cruel in his treatment of his midshipmen, and he would demand a meeting with Shubrick to have this out. Perhaps, in such a meeting, he might be able to ascertain the reason for his being ignored by his commodore ever since he last had dropped anchor in this harbor.

He told his business to the commodore's clerk, and that officious little man knew by the look on this commander's face not to trifle with him or put him off. Instead he dashed into another office and beseeched the help of the commodore's aide.

Lieutenant Silas Blair was a chubby, agreeable young man with a large, bushy mustache. He greeted Uriah with disarming friendliness and urged him to come into his office for a moment to enjoy a cooling glass of wine. Uriah, reluctant to divert from his objective, agreed, if only to give himself a moment to calm down and regain his wit before facing the commodore himself.

Alas, said Lieutenant Blair, his smile offsetting his expression of regret, it would not be possible for Commander Levy to see the commodore, for the commodore had left only this morning aboard his flagship for a week's cruise to Cuba. Could his aide be of any help?

Uriah, glad to have a temporary outlet for his anger even though he knew that a lowly lieutenant could do nothing to solve his problem, explained the dispute over the midshipmen to Blair and briefly argued his own position.

Lieutenant Blair, fully aware of the issue, for he had written the two short notes at the commodore's order, listened sympathetically and nodded at all the proper times. He then explained politely that he could not assist the commander in this question, which must be taken up directly with the commodore.

"Commander Levy," Blair said, after a moment's pause, "if I may make a suggestion to you?"

"I would be glad for your advice as to how to proceed, Lieutenant."

The ingratiating smile left Blair's face, and he became serious. He admired the captain of the *Vandalia* for his efforts to end flogging and decided on the spur of the moment to help him avoid a profitless confrontation with Shubrick.

"Commander," Blair went on, "I would suggest that you refrain from debating the commodore on this matter when he returns next week. I suggest that, sir, because the issue is moot now."

"How do you mean, Lieutenant? I don't understand."

"Sir, orders now are being written in this office, which should be in your hands within the next three days. You will be instructed to scrape the *Vandalia*'s bottom and continue your varnishing and painting until completed. Your request for four new carronades has been approved, and you will install those guns, when received here, upon your corvette. Upon completion of this work, but in no case any later than the twentieth day of October, you are ordered to weigh anchor and to sail the *Vandalia* to the Gosport Navy Yard, where you will be relieved of her command."

Uriah felt the blood drain from his face. His stomach began to twist with the old, familiar spasmodic pain. "Relieved? I—I am to be relieved as captain of the *Vandalia*?"

"Exactly, sir. And that's why it would not be in your best interest to express to the commodore when he returns your feelings about the midshipmen. They will be under your command for only a few more weeks, so the issue—as I said—is a moot one."

"Why . . . why am I being relieved of command, Lieutenant? I have had this ship for only about a year. I . . . I have just barely begun to make her into the fine ship she could be."

"I cannot say, Commander. The commodore indicated no reason to me. But he was most definite about the orders. I can tell you this much about Commodore Shubrick, sir: he brooks no disagreement with his orders. I suggest, Commander, that it would not be wise for you to question him concerning them."

"And a new assignment, Lieutenant? Am I to be given another ship?"

"That is, of course, up to the Navy Department, sir. But I believe that you are to be returned to the status of 'Waiting for Orders.'"

"I see. Consigned, once again to the waiting list. I thought . . . I had hoped that was all behind me."

"I'm sorry, Commander. That is all I can tell you."

Uriah stood up and took his handsome blue and gold, fore-and-aft hat from under his arm. "Yes. Thank you, Lieutenant, for your courtesy. I must return to my ship now. We'd better start on that below-decks work if we are to be ready to sail by twenty October."

Without another word, he squared his hat firmly on his head, lifted the scabbard of his sword, and strode from the office as purposefully as he had entered it.

19

It arrived innocently enough in the familiar envelope with the seal of the Department of the Navy. Uriah had been sitting at a table in his second-floor parlor, looking out at the thick white snow falling placidly on St. Mark's Place. He had been preparing a sheet of orders for spring planting at Monticello, to be posted to Joel Wheeler in the morning, but his attention had wandered as he began remembering the loveliness of spring on his Virginia mountain. It seemed so far away, in miles and in time, from this snow-choked street in the middle of New York City.

When Maureen, the young Irish maid, nervously brought him the envelope that had just come to the door by messenger, he thought little of it. He had been sending the Department a series of proposals for sea trials and tests to be administered to the *Missouri* and the *Mississippi*, the two huge war steamships being readied for launching. All he ever received from the bigwigs in Washington City was a polite acknowledgment of his suggestions. Then he would hear no more. Well, let them ignore him, he was used to that. He would continue to send in his unsolicited ideas. Sooner or later, something would bear fruit.

He tore open the envelope with its blue seal. Usually the acknowledgment message was a terse sentence or two, but this time he was surprised to find a cover letter and several pages of documents:

Navy Department
February 11, 1842

Sir:

You are hereby directed to report, on or before the 4th day of April 1842, to the Commander of Naval Forces at the Port of Baltimore for the convening of Court Martial Number 795. You are to be prepared to defend yourself against the charges listed herewith, which have been lodged against you on the basis of information supplied to this department by Lieutenant George Mason Hooe.

I am respectfully,
Your obedient servant,
Abel P. Upshur

Uriah sat, incredulous, the letter dangling from his fingertips, which hung almost to the floor. The other papers had fallen unnoticed to the carpet. He stared unseeing at the white panorama outside. A teamster's wagon pounded past on the street below, but he didn't even hear the burly driver scream curses at his horses as they struggled to find their footing on the slick surface.

My God, it was happening all over again! He couldn't believe it: his sixth time to stand before the hostile glares of a court of high officers. He had thought this was all behind him, a bitter memory from younger, more tempestuous days, when he was quick to anger and ever ready to fight.

What in God's name had he done on the *Vandalia* to merit a trial? It had been a quiet, peaceful, and productive cruise. Hooe had been a cruel, bullying officer; he had been thrown off the corvette and forced to stand trial for his actions and, indeed, had earned a hard reprimand from the court. How had he managed to twist things around since then and to contrive accusations against the one who had condemned him in the first place?

The old grinding pain churning again in his vitals, Uriah picked up the supporting documents from the floor and slowly began to read them:

Charge 1st: Scandalous and cruel conduct, unbecoming an officer and a gentleman.

Specification: In this, that the said Commander Uriah P. Levy, being then in command of the United States Ship Vandalia, *did, on or about the 7th day of July 1839, cause John Thompson, a boy serving on said ship* Vandalia, *to be seized to a gun, his trousers to be let down, and a quantity of tar to be applied to his naked skin. Such punishment being highly scandalous and unbecoming the dignity of an officer to inflict, and in violation of the 3rd and 30th articles of the 1st section of the Act of Congress, entitled 'An Act for the Better Government of the Navy of the United States,' approved 23rd April 1800.*

Charge 2nd: Scandalous conduct, unbecoming an officer and a gentleman and tending to the destruction of good morals.

Specification 1st: In this, that said Uriah P. Levy, being then in the town of Pensacola, for the purpose of taking command of the United States Ship Vandalia, *did, on or about the 23rd day of November 1838, in the most public street in said town, call Antoine Collins, a citizen of Pensacola, a 'blackguard' or a 'damned blackguard,' or words to that effect; whereupon the said Collins did wring said Levy's nose violently without meeting any resistance. The conduct on the part of said commander, Uriah P. Levy, being 'scandalous and unbecoming an officer and a gentleman, tending to the destruction of good morals' as charged and in violation of the 3rd article of the 1st section. . . .*

So that was it! This was about the boy mimic who had been strikingly, yet humanely disciplined and had laughed about it later. As for Antoine Collins, the thug of a boardinghouse keeper who was keen for a fight on a Pensacola dock, he had beat a hasty retreat at sight of Uriah's ready sword; there was no need for further action to meet the demands of honor. Uriah almost laughed, in spite of the pain gnawing at his gut, in spite of the hot flush in his face. How did the jackals strain to produce a mouse! How the villains did labor to find some whimper of scandal to bring him to his knees!

The incident with Collins had occurred almost three-and-a-half years ago. Why would they bring this up in a court-martial now? If he had indeed committed crimes against the better government of the navy, why had they waited so long to bring him to the bar of justice? For these petty incidents, would he now face a board of accusers? Uriah's head burned with the struggle of seeking out a political motive for his new troubles, but he could not find one that made any sense. No, the answer was not in party politics but surely could be found in navy politics. The old unforgiving enemies still were after him. Dark, faceless figures, they hovered in the halls of the Navy Building and bided their time until they could strike at him again. It never would end. They would keep coming after him until he lowered his flag.

He took a deep breath. If he must fight these unseen foes until he died, then he would fight them with his last breath. He would not haul down his colors. They gave him no peace, but he never had surrendered to them and he never would.

He reread the charges and specifications, then picked up a pen and started making notes toward his defense.

Baltimore, 1842

The members of the court deliberated in an anteroom. Uriah sat in the hot, dusty little hearing room in the Baltimore federal building and awaited their verdict. He exchanged a few desultory words with his counsel, Ben Butler, but neither man had much to say. Even the fiery and always voluble Mordecai Manuel Noah, who had come down from New York City to attend the court-martial, sat silently in the first spectator row behind them.

What was there to say? They had done their best and presented a persuasive case. But Uriah had the strong feeling that it all had been to no avail. He could tell by Ben's subdued manner that the lawyer felt the same way. The six captains who made up the court had listened impassively to the testimony and had asked few questions. It seemed to Uriah that they had made up their minds before they ever walked into this dry, stifling room.

Ben Butler had presented Uriah's case with quiet dignity, taking the tack that the charges were so overstated and exaggerated as to be beneath contempt. Uriah could not have wanted a better planned or argued defense. Butler, his old friend and brother-in-law of his former shipmate Howard Allen, was one of the nation's most distinguished lawyers, having served as attorney general under Jackson and Van Buren and briefly had been secretary of war as well.

The president of the court was Captain John B. Nicholson. Uriah wondered if Nicholson knew he had served on the *Argus* under William Henry Allen. Nicholson and Allen had been officers under Decatur on the *United States* in its glorious triumph over the *Macedonian*. *Ah, what difference did it make?* Uriah shook his head in self-derision. That odd bit of history surely would not influence Nicholson's vote.

Far more disturbing was the presence of Captain Eli A. Lavalette. Uriah remembered him well; there was a special niche in his memory for his tormentors. Lavalette had been a fellow lieutenant on the frigate *United States* in 1818, when Uriah had been transferred to that great ship over the vehement protest of her commander, Captain Crane. Lavalette had been hostile to him throughout Uriah's sixteen months aboard the frigate and had left no doubt that he resented his presence in the wardroom. There was no question in Uriah's mind that Lavalette would vote against him.

The other members of the court were Captains Bolton, Turner, Keever, and Stringham. Their names were familiar to Uriah, but he had no personal knowledge of them. In theory, one didn't know how they might vote. In fact, though, their gray faces and cool stares told him full well that they had no sympathy for him or his case.

Hooe had taken the stand and testified calmly and dispassionately, yet in a manner that made clear his contempt for his former commander. He condemned Uriah's failure to use long-standing man-of-war discipline as fatal to good order aboard the *Vandalia*. He testified as to what he knew of the tarring of the boy John Thompson and related his observation of Uriah's encounter with the tavern keeper Antoine Collins in Pensacola. In Hooe's account, however, Collins had viciously wrung Uriah's nose and the commander had cravenly failed to take any action in return.

In turn, Uriah testified concerning the skirmish with Collins and made it clear that he had offered to do battle, only to have the barman and his stevedore friends suddenly retreat. It was clear to everyone in the courtroom that Hooe had no way of proving his allegations. Collins himself had long since died in a drunken brawl. Hooe could provide no one to corroborate his account, which Uriah emphatically denied.

No, the real problem was the charge involving discipline of the ship's boy. Butler had made this clear to Uriah over dinner after the first day's testimony. There were plenty of witnesses who would agree as to the facts of the discipline. Uriah himself would concede the truth of the allegations.

What they could not foresee—indeed, what they could in no way influence—was the court's judgment of the discipline. Had it been physically harmless, yet psychologically effective, as Uriah claimed? Or had it been a horrible degradation for John Thompson, a punishment that fell far beyond the pale of navy discipline? That was the key question in this charge. Unfortunately the boy John Thompson made no appearance. He had left the navy at the end of his enlistment, and all efforts to locate him had failed.

Winder, the judge advocate, argued passionately that the boy had been permanently scarred by the incident, for he had been horribly humiliated and shamed. The punishment, along with other unorthodox disciplines Uriah had introduced, had so shocked and outraged the *Vandalia*'s crew, Winder argued, that it brought the ship to a state of near mutiny.

Uriah testified that, on the contrary, the *Vandalia* had been a happy, well-ordered ship with an efficient crew and that his new system of discipline had earned wide approbation from newspapers and magazines. Several officers of the *Vandalia* testified and confirmed his statements, though some admitted under cross-examination that their former commander seemed odd at times, with his strange, if effective, methods of discipline and other actions, such as having the guns painted bright blue.

With the agreement of Ben Butler, Uriah delivered his own final argument. The navy, he pointed out, had issued in 1831 a circular that stated, "Flogging is recommended to be discontinued, when practicable, by courts as well as officers, and some badge of disgrace, fine, etc., substituted where discretion exists."

"Did I not explicitly follow the navy's recommendation," he asked, "and substitute a badge of disgrace for the cut of the lash across the boy's naked back? My system of discipline was a mild and moral system, which sinks deep into the heart without the necessity of lacerating the body. The intention was to use light punishments for subordinate offenses, to create shame and regret by proper examples and salutary reproofs.

"The judge advocate and the vengeful officer who has lodged these charges have said that the *Vandalia* was brought near to mutiny by my discipline. This is a blatant lie. No ship in the navy had a better or more orderly set of men; none obeyed orders more cheerfully. In no ship was there less severe punishment, and in none less manifestation of mutiny and disaffection. If I am to be censured for this course, it does not shake my faith in the system, nor my conviction that finally it will be the universal and successful one for the government of the navy."

As soon as the officers of the court walked back into the hearing room, Ben Butler—wise in the ways of juries—knew that he had lost his case. All of the officers averted their gaze from the defendant, except for Captain Lavalette, who peered evenly at Uriah, a slight smile on his thin lips.

Captain Nicholson stood, cleared his throat, and read the court's verdict:

"As to Charge the Second, with its specifications concerning the

incident with one Antoine Collins, this court finds the charge to be
without merit and hereby orders the dismissal of this charge.

"As to Charge the First, concerning the punishment given to the
boy John Thompson on the United States Ship *Vandalia* on or about
the seventh day of July 1839, this court finds that the specification
of the First Charge is proven and that of the First Charge, the accused is guilty. The court, having passed upon the charge and specification, proceeded to take into consideration what sentence should
be adjudged and, after mature deliberation, the court does adjudge
and sentence that Commander U. P. Levy be, and that he is thereby,
dismissed from the Navy of the United States."

There was utter silence in the hearing room. The participants in
the court-martial and the small band of spectators sat as if transfixed. Then, without a word or look between them, the members of
the court stood up as one and left the room. Even Captain Lavalette
wasted no more glances, whether of scorn or pleasure, upon Uriah,
but marched with the others, silently as wraiths, through the door
behind the platform.

Uriah did not rise as they left, though such a sign of respect was
required. He sat and stared ahead, his face ashen.

Ben Butler covered his face with his hands for a moment, then
took them away and murmured to himself: "The punishment did
not fit the offense. There was no justice here today." The clerks began wiping their pens and folding their papers into brown covers.
They glanced momentarily at the face of the defendant, saw its vacant, wounded stare, and then looked away.

Mordecai Noah was standing now beside Uriah and put his hand
lightly on his cousin's shoulder. "I am off immediately to Washington City," he said. "I will see Tyler. I will make him understand. This
verdict requires the president's approval. Tyler will understand everything that is behind your persecution, I promise you."

For the first time since the verdict was announced, Uriah seemed
to come back to life, but he slowly shook his head. "I'm afraid it's
hopeless, Mordecai," he said. "They finally have succeeded in getting rid of me."

Mordecai shook his head emphatically. "It's *not* over, Uriah," he vowed. "You have my word. We have reserves they have not even dreamed of."

Washington City, 1842

"Come on in, Commander, and set yourself."

The words were softly spoken, yet they carried across the quiet room with the force of an order shouted from a quarterdeck. Whether gently voiced, or not, the words were said by the president of the United States and thus brought instant response.

"Yes, Mr. President. Thank you, sir." Uriah walked quickly to a small settee, sat, and made himself as comfortable as possible, given his quaking knees and trembling hands. He put his cocked hat on his lap and felt it twitching as it followed the temblors of his limbs.

He was surprised at the homely nature of the president's office. It looked more like a small guest parlor in a wealthy farmer's home, with its red velvet settee and its deep, comfortable reading chairs. Only the big oaken desk gave evidence of the important business conducted here. The room was in the eastern part of the White House second floor and was in a suite of three or four rooms in which the president and his small staff worked.

It was a sunny day and warm. The choking dampness of Washington summers had not yet descended upon the city, and the afternoon was pleasant, with a soft breeze blowing through the open windows and pushing back the white, gauzelike draperies.

After motioning Uriah to a seat with a slight smile and nod of greeting, President Tyler had turned his attention back to a document on his desk. Uriah sat nervously and waited, awed in the presence of the leader of his country and curious and even somewhat frightened as to the reason for his summons. He did not doubt that it had to do with his court-martial in Baltimore, but why on earth would the president call him in? It was unthinkable that Tyler would personally dismiss him from the navy. Surely such a thing never had been done! Or had it? Even Cousin Mordecai could not explain the summons; he merely had carried the word to Uriah that the president wished him to call at the White House at his earliest convenience.

He watched the president as he read at his desk. A thin-faced man with narrow lips, his sandy hair was skimpy and his forehead was wide. His chin was rather weak and gave him the look of a countryman. He was dressed all in black, save for a gleaming white shirt whose high collar-points framed his face and gave further emphasis to his pointy chin. A cravat of black velvet encircled his neck, held his head stiffly up, and gave him the somber look of a small-town undertaker. Finally he looked up and directly at Uriah.

"Well, Commander Levy, so this is what you are in the flesh."

The president's voice, in its Virginia drawl, again was softly spoken, yet it startled Uriah so that he almost jumped to his feet.

"It . . . it is a pleasure to meet you, Mr. President."

"Likewise, Commander. I've read so much about you in recent weeks that my curiosity got the best of me. I had to see what manner of man you really are."

Uriah did not know how to take this. Was he being held up to scorn? He did not know what to say, so he said nothing, but nodded politely.

"They really have turned heaven and earth to do you in, haven't they, Commander? They have been so anxious to cashier you that I thought you must be Satan Incarnate until I read your history and talked to a few people at the Navy Building and in Congress. You've had more than your share of problems, haven't you, Commander?"

"Yes, Mr. President. I have had some troubles."

The president laughed, a dry, grating laugh. "Well, that's a nice way to put it. Troubles, eh? Persecution's more like it. Appears to me that you're a loner of sorts, an independent sort of cuss. And the navy bigwigs don't easily tolerate that. They prefer to think of the navy as a very exclusive club . . . for officers, that is. You must be of the right background to be taken in, and then you must follow the gentlemen's code to succeed. Appears to me that you're sort of an outsider in the club, and they don't care much for outsiders."

Uriah began to relax. His knees quieted down. He realized now the president was sympathizing with him, even taking his side. For the first time since the beginning of the trial in Baltimore, a surge of optimism swept over him.

"Well, I don't like to see them badgering any man like that, and certainly not a fellow Virginian," the president continued.

The comment brought a smile to Uriah's face for the first time. "Only an adopted Virginian, Mr. President," he said.

"Yes, yes, I know, but a Virginian nonetheless. I'm told you've done good things with Jefferson's old place. Appears to me you saved that place from going to seed by stepping in when you did. The state owes you a vote of thanks."

"I appreciate that, Mr. President."

"I know well enough what it's like to be a loner," President Tyler continued. "You a political man, Commander?"

"No, not really, Mr. President." He wondered if Tyler, a Whig like Cousin Mordecai, knew of his lifelong support of the Democrats, going back to Jefferson's time.

"Well, the political man understands that I am a rarity these days, a president without a party. How I got myself into this predicament, I don't rightly know, but here I am. Each of my nine predecessors in this chair was supported by a loyal party, but here John Tyler sits, having left his Democratic birthright behind and now scorned by the Whigs who elected him because he wouldn't do their will. Impeachment is the word they threaten me with. Impeachment! Why, those jackanapes! I may be a rebel, as they claim, but by Jehovah I won't let Henry Clay and the Whig businessmen run this country in my name!

"Commander, did you know that after I vetoed Clay's insidious attempt to raise tariffs, a mob of hoodlums actually attacked this house and threw rocks through the windows? I've been burned in effigy, cursed to my face, and generally scorned, Commander. All for the sake of a few principles! But I suppose you know as much about such things as I do. I'm pleased by your efforts to eliminate flogging from navy ships. They hate you for it at the Navy Building, but I fully support you, if that's any comfort."

"It is a great comfort indeed, Mr. President."

A faint thrill shot through Uriah's chest. Now, at last, he would hear what fate the president had for him.

The president began shuffling through the great pile of papers and documents on his desk. "Where is that fool thing?" he muttered. "Ah, here it is. I guess the best way to tell you this, Commander, is to read you this letter that I've written to the Navy Court that called for your dismissal from the service. I'm sending a copy to Secretary Upshur, of course. Let me see. . . . 'I have read the argument of the court in this case with great pleasure and have examined the record with care, and if my convictions force me to differ in opinion with the court it arises from no disrespect to it, or indisposition to sustain its authority,' et cetera, et cetera. 'The argument of the court may be conclusive to show that Captain Levy should undergo some punishment, but I cannot but differ from it as to the extent of the punishment' and so on, and so on.

"I go on to state, Commander, that you acted in full observance of the old directive of the secretary of the navy to discontinue flogging whenever practicable and to substitute some badge of disgrace or fine. I also note that the ship commander has discretion as to the substitution of punishment. And I go on to state—and I'm rather proud of this language, Commander, takes me back to my lawyerin' days—'If, under the pretense of substituting a milder punishment he resorted to one which malice alone could suggest, he would deserve the severest condemnation. No such motive or feeling is ascribed to Captain Levy. He meant to affix temporarily to the boy a badge of disgrace in order to correct a bad habit and to teach him and others that the habit of mimicry is that of the parrot whose feathers he wore. The badge was worn only for a few minutes. No harm was done to the person, no blood made to flow, as from the application of the cat. And no cruelty was exercised, unless the reasoning of the court be such that this badge of disgrace was more cruel than corporal punishment.' Which brings us, Commander, to these concluding words and I apologize to you for making you wait so long to hear the decision that I know you are most anxious to hear:

"'Captain Levy erred by resorting to an extremely disgraceful punishment, I admit, and in order to protect the service from its repetition in the future he should be punished. While, therefore, in the absence of any bad motives on his part, I cannot concur with the court in approving the extreme sentence of expulsion from the navy, yet a modified sentence under the law is what is due to the Service, and I therefore mitigate the sentence of Captain Levy from dismissal from the Service to suspension without pay for the period of twelve months.' And I will now sign this letter and give it to my clerks for transmittal."

Uriah was flooded with relief. He had hoped somehow that the president would completely overturn the verdict of the court and order him acquitted and thereby vindicated. He felt a pang of disappointment at the destruction of this hope, but the momentary feeling was overwhelmed by his gratitude that he had, in the main, won presidential support for his contention that the boy's punishment was a trivial error and that his transgression called for a relatively light sentence.

The president obviously read his thoughts. After signing his "John Tyler" to the letter with a flourish, he looked up and said, "You understand, Commander, that I could not bring myself to totally reverse the court's decision and let you go scot-free. I would have a navy rebellion on my hands were I to do that, and I have enough troubles to deal with as it is. It was that court that was responsible for deciding the facts of the case and I must allow them that power. But, having done so, I also could not stand clear and let them punish you far beyond any limit of true justice. My punishment should not pain you too much. I understand that the navy has not seen fit to employ your services of late. Another year ashore won't do you any irreparable harm. Do you get me, Commander?"

"I do, Mr. President. And I am most grateful for your understanding of my predicament. I accept your decision with gratitude."

The president gave him a long look and then spoke again: "The navy has been unjust to you all these years, Commander. Even a blind man can see that. Oh, I know you think it's all because you're a son of Moses—and maybe much of it does stem from that. But I sense that you also are unloved by your fellows for other reasons. They still hold against you that you did not enter as a midshipman, as almost all of them did. It is 'the gentleman's way,' they say. And your open talk against flogging has raised their ire. I sometimes think they hate you more for that than anything else. They see themselves as the last remnants of the aristocracy, standing fast on their quarterdecks with a mob of unwashed rabble teeming down below them and waiting for a chance to mutiny. They're afraid that without the power of the lash, they are sure to be overrun. They view themselves like the French nobles faced by a horde of angry Jacobins. They're brave fighters, these navy officers, and great patriots, but in a strange way, they're frightened men. And you want to take away what they regard as their only weapon against the fears that possess them. Is it any wonder, Commander, that they dislike you so and keep throwing up barricades in your way?"

"No, sir. It is not surprising that they hate me so."

"You have been ill-treated, Commander, and your record sheet has been unfairly blemished. I'm going to do what I can to make it up to you. This nation owes you that much. As soon as the necessary vacancies appear, you'll see what I mean. But beyond that, I cannot do any more for you. I believe very strongly in a proper definition of powers, Commander, and I live by that rule. I never interfere with my military men in the employment of their personnel, for to do it would be to set up a precedent most unwise. I must leave such decisions to them, as harmful as such decisions may sometimes be to deserving individuals such as yourself. Do you have my drift, Commander?"

"I understand, Mr. President. And once again, I am most grateful for your sentiments."

Uriah walked down the thickly carpeted second-floor hallway on his way to the great staircase that would take him back down to the White House door. His knees still were shaky from the emotions of the last few minutes and from the sheer excitement of having met privately with the president.

If he had heard the president correctly, as he was sure he had, he could expect to receive a promotion to captain—the navy's highest rank—sometime in the near future when a necessary vacancy had occurred. For years he had dreamed of attaining his captaincy, but such dreams had been virtually abandoned since the onset of his latest troubles. Now this exalted rank, the station of Preble, Decatur, Hull, and Rodgers, was nearly in his grasp. Thus the president planned to compensate him for the treatment he had received from the navy through these last thirty years.

But beyond the promotion, the president would not go. Uriah might well rot on the beach for the rest of his life, never again to receive the command of a ship or, for that matter, even the command of a navy yard. The president would not interfere in the operation of the navy by ordering it how to assign its officers. And despite the likely implication of this policy for himself, Uriah knew that he agreed with it. The navy could not function if politicians were to decide how and by whom its daily tasks were to be done.

He would have the glory and prestige and the magnificent uniform, with its nine central buttons and its eagle-bearing epaulets, of a navy captain. But, likely, that is all he would have. The navy would turn its back on him from this day onward.

Two years and one month after his meeting with the president, the long-awaited letter arrived:

May 4, 1844

To the Senate of the United States:

I nominate Uriah P. Levy, now a Commander, to be a Captain in the Navy from the 29th day of March 1844, to fill a vacancy occasioned by the death of Commodore E. P. Kennedy.
John Tyler

Part III
Captain Levy

20

May 11, 1846

To: Hon. George Bancroft, Secretary, U.S. Navy

Sir: Mexico having declared war against us, I respectfully solicit that I may be employed in any service in which I can be useful to our country. I have the honor to be, very respectfully,

Your obedient servant,
U. P. Levy, Captain

Navy Department, May 13, 1846

To: Capt. Uriah P. Levy, New York

Captain—Your letter of the 11th instant has been received, and your application to be employed on any service in which you can be useful, is noted.

I am, respectfully yours,
George Bancroft

New York, June 14, 1846

To: Hon. George Bancroft, Secretary, U.S. Navy

Sir—I learn from the Norfolk paper that the Pennsylvania, Delaware, Independence, and Brandywine are to be fitted out for sea without delay. I therefore very respectfully solicit that you will be pleased to favor me with the command of either of the named ships, or any other which in your wisdom you may feel disposed to honor me with. I trust that my great anxiety to be afloat will be attributed to proper and patriotic motives. My term of life is short, and this will be the only opportunity which will offer when I am fit to serve my country a second time when in a state of war. With this feeling, I do hope and trust that you will take my claim into favorable consideration by granting my request.

With great respect, Sir,
I am your very obedient servant,
U. P. Levy, Captain

Navy Department, June 14, 1846

To: Capt. Uriah P. Levy, New York

Captain—Your letter of the 14th instant has been received, and your request that you be considered for command of the Pennsylvania, Delaware, Independence, or Brandywine has been noted.

I am, respectfully yours,
George Bancroft

A cold mixture of sleet and rain slanted across the sky in long, tangential sheets. Unthinkingly, Uriah lifted the collar of his lounging jacket and shuddered as he pictured himself walking the spar deck in such a miserable freezing downpour. He forgot for a moment that he sat warm and protected from the pelting sheets in his second-floor study overlooking St. Mark's Place. All about him were the memories, the beloved trinkets of his navy service: models of the ships on which he had served and paintings of the great frigates *United States* and *Constitution*, framed charts that he had drawn himself or had supervised, glassed-in bookshelves with his library of volumes on navigation and seamanship.

God, this was a sullen and altogether hopeless day! He called to one of the maids to bring him a mug of hot coffee. The glance out upon the drenched, icy street had started him to shivering, and he felt the cold that had taken away all his vigor for the past week reasserting itself. His head ached and his throat was beginning to burn.

He sat and thumbed passively through his folder of correspondence with the navy—his "failure file," as he called it—his requests for assignment and copies of letters that his friends and political allies had sent in his behalf. Neatly fastened together in a separate bundle were the replies from the navy: polite, cool, ever noncommittal.

The war with Mexico had been under way for nine months now, and there had been no summons for him from the navy. The navy already had seen its share of action. John Sloat had commanded the Pacific Squadron; shortly after war was declared, his ships and men had captured Monterey and San Francisco. Soon after that, the frigate *Congress* had taken San Pedro, the port of Los Angeles, and the headquarters for the Mexican officials in California. Captain Robert Field Stockton had replaced the ailing Sloat as commodore of the Pacific Squadron and quickly mustered a force of sailors and marines to march unopposed into Los Angeles. The Mexicans had managed to regain the city after a time, but Stockton had formed another force early in January and had fought his way back into Los Angeles, regaining the city and causing heavy enemy casualties.

To his chagrin, Uriah learned that his old, implacable foe, Captain Eli Lavalette, was in command of the frigate *Congress*, which, along with the *Portsmouth*, bombarded and captured the town of Guaymas. Then Lavalette had joined the *Independence*, Captain Shubrick, and the *Portsmouth*, Commander Montgomery, and the three ships landed a powerful force of six hundred sailors and marines at Mazatlan and took the city without a fight. The American flag was raised over the important port, and Lavalette was named to head the occupation government for the city.

On the other side of the war, in the Gulf of Mexico, Captain David Conner commanded a U.S. squadron of fifteen ships with the 44-gun frigate *Potomac* as his flagship. Early in November, Conner captured Tampico and a week later his men pulled and burned a Mexican vessel laden with ammunition. These heroic men were off the brig *Somers*. Only a few weeks after this exploit, the *Somers* sank during a chase, and forty of her men were drowned.

Oh, there was action aplenty, but not for U. P. Levy, Captain. His constant stream of requests for assignment went unheeded and sometimes unanswered. He sat in his house in New York City and traced the progress of the war on maps in his study. Even his brother Jonas had found a place in the war by hiring out to the army as captain of a steamship used to transport soldiers and supplies. Uriah wondered sometimes if he might find a similar place. But he had no desire to serve on a steamboat, and anyway he was a captain in the United States Navy and he could not bring himself to hire out as a seagoing officer in civilian clothes. By God, he had not served for thirty-four years in the navy to go crawling to the army for a job as captain of a steam-belching carrier of soldiers and victuals!

President Polk had assured Congress and the nation, when war was declared, that the fighting would be over in three or four months. Well, it was long past that time now, but Uriah was convinced that the war would indeed end soon. Winfield Scott and Zachary Taylor were able generals, and without a doubt they would soon be marching at the head of their triumphant armies into Vera Cruz and Mexico City. It would all end in a glorious victory, but he would have no share in the glory. His war would be fought looking out a window at the rooftops of New York City.

I am more businessman now than navy man, Uriah thought bitterly, as he stared at the roiling sky and watched gray fragments of cloud scud back and forth before a darting, ever-shifting wind. *Most people have even forgotten that I hold a captaincy and regard me simply as a successful landlord.*

He was well regarded in business, for sure. Just last year, Moses Beach had published another edition of his popular *Wealth and Biography of the Wealthy Citizens of New York City* and had estimated the value of Uriah's properties at $250,000. Uriah had thought the figure slightly high, but it was not far off. Friends had congratulated him on being included in the volume, and the bolder ones had ragged him about his reputed wealth. His mail each day brought him requests for loans and propositions for investment. His companions at the whist table looked at him with increased respect. Several mamas from Shearith Israel sent discreet overtures to him via intermediaries concerning unmarried daughters or nieces. He would have sacrificed all of it in a minute for the command of a squadron or even of a large frigate in this war with the Mexicans.

He pulled from a compartment in his desk a sheet of stationery with his name embossed across the top in fancy golden curlicues. He picked up a pen, dipped it in the well, and thought for a moment, then slowly began to write. *Another ridiculous, forlorn attempt,* he thought, chiding himself. But attempt he must. . . .

New York, February 26, 1847

To: Honorable John Y. Mason, Secretary of the Navy

Sir: Understanding that a vessel of war may be detailed for the conveyance of food to the distressed people of Ireland, I beg permission should the government select a vessel for that purpose to tender my services to take command of her, having already intimated to the committee not only my willingness to render my service, but at the same time to devote all my pay during the performance of this duty in aid of the benevolent object in view. I have the honor to be, very respectfully,

Your obedient servant,
U. P. Levy, Captain

A few days later, a letter was received from Secretary Mason indicating that Uriah's request had been read and noted.

New York City, 1851

"How is he today, Becky?" Uriah asked Cousin Mordecai's usually cheerful wife.

Rebecca Noah's face was pale, and there were dark blotches under her eyes. But her voice was strong and carried a surge of optimism . . . or perhaps it was faith.

"He does well enough today, 'Riah. He wrote a short article this morning for the *Messenger*, and he spent ten minutes telling me what a Jew-hating blackguard was James Gordon Bennett. So his spirits were high enough. But . . ." Her voice trailed away and, for the first time since she had opened the door for Uriah, there was a look of fear in her eyes.

"Yes?"

"It's the strangest thing. His memory seems to . . . come and go. The doctor has assured me that the paralytic shock has not affected his mind and yet. . . ."

"He doesn't remember some things?"

"He does, and then he doesn't. A few days from now, you see, it will be five years since our dear Daniel was killed. Somehow Mordecai knows that, for he has talked much about Daniel yesterday and today. But he thinks that Daniel still lives and . . . and he reminds me to warn the boy to be careful out in the street. It is as if he is trying so hard to prevent the accident from happening. Then he suddenly remembers and he says, 'Oh, yes, I remember now. Our little Daniel is gone; he died in my arms.' And then, a few minutes later, he'll be talking about Daniel again and urging me to look out for the boy when he crosses the street. It is sad, 'Riah, so very sad." Her composure began to break again and her eyes filled up with tears.

Uriah put his rough hands on her cheeks and kissed her gently on the forehead. "These are difficult days, Becky, but let us pray he'll recover. The doctor said that Mordecai has a good chance to be himself again if there are no more shocks.

"I know, 'Riah, I know. I repeat the doctor's words to myself a hundred times a day. It helps me when I get frightened about him."

"May I go into him now?"

"Of course. He's always happy to see you. He loves to reminisce with you about the old times. It brings a smile to his face."

Mordecai was propped up in his bed, eyeglasses tilted haphazardly on his brow, perusing a newspaper. He did not look ill or weak, save that his usually florid face was more waxen than pink. His mouth was slightly twisted in what first seemed to be a sardonic grimace, but was really an aftereffect of the paralytic shock he had suffered. That, and a bit of awkwardness with his left hand, was the only residue of the illness.

"About time you arrived," Mordecai said, not taking his eyes off the newspaper. "I've been saving up all sorts of witty observations for you. I haven't seen you in so long I thought you perhaps had joined the Navy of All the Russias."

"Hardly," Uriah answered with a smile. "I can't stand the smell of beet soup and cabbage. You look well today, Cousin."

"I was feeling fine until I began reading more of Bennett's garbage. Now my stomach is filled with bile and my bowels are cold with anger. That bastard! I gave him his start in journalism, you know, on my old *Enquirer*. I hired him to replace Graham when he was killed in a duel. I would better have shot Bennett and found some way to resurrect Graham. He has labeled me a descendant of Judas Iscariot, you know, and he accuses our people of secretly conspiring against the Christians. One of these days, when my strength returns, I'll march down there and call him out."

"I thought you were opposed to dueling since your own narrow escape in Charleston."

"True enough, but if I must die, what a glorious way to go: to put a bullet in Bennett's heart just as his shot is piercing my own! I would be enshrined in a pantheon for doing that deed."

"Let us not speak of death. You're getting stronger and sassier every day. You should be concentrating on getting back on your feet and returning to your job. Your paper needs you."

"Yes, and so do you, Cousin. When I think of all the work I did last year editing your articles against flogging! You might be grand on the quarterdeck of a man o' war, 'Riah, but at the helm of a pen, you run aground."

"That's why I employ you as amanuensis for my articles," Uriah responded without rancor. "I supply the ideas and the experience and you supply the elegant sentences. Anyway, it's the result that counts. We make a fine team."

"We do, don't we?" Mordecai said, smiling. "We have churned out some interesting papers together and raised an eyebrow here and there."

There was a long silence then, but there was no discomfort in it. These men, who had spent their entire lives in close touch, could enjoy moments of rest and thought as much as garrulous exchanges.

"Tomorrow night you'll come for Shabbat dinner, Uriah. It will be our first real Shabbat since I was taken sick. I want you to be with us."

"Of course, Mordecai. I'll be delighted, as always."

"It hardly seems like a real Shabbat around here now, with the children grown up and scattered. Manuel Mordecai is in California, you know, and Jacob has been elected justice of the peace in St. Paul. Robert is wandering somewhere in Europe; he has the wanderlust, that lad, and seems fated to be a rover. And my little bird, my little Zipporah, is still in boarding school in Schenectady. Ah, how I miss that little bird! She is sixteen years, you know, and quite a young lady. But if you come tomorrow night, 'Riah, that will make it seem more like old times. Uncle Naph and Aunt Esther will be here, too."

"It will be nice. As you said, like old times."

"Except that my little Daniel will not be there to receive my blessing. He is dead, you know, 'Riah. Killed under the wheels of a teamster's wagon . . . dead in the street before my house."

"I know, Mordecai," replied Uriah, gently.

"We need our own hospital, 'Riah, to care for Israelite people who are hurt or sick. They would have taken my Daniel to such a hospital, but we did not have one. He died in my very arms, you know. As soon as I get my strength back, I am calling a meeting to plan the building of a Hebrew hospital in this city, where our people can return to health among their own kind. Where they can eat kosher food and can lay tefillin without having to endure the ridicule of other patients and even the nurses. My Hebrew Benevolent Society will build such a hospital!" He had risen from his pillow and his face had grown suddenly flushed. Uriah urged him to lie back and calm himself.

"It's all right, it's all right," Mordecai said. "I become excited because my Israelite brothers exasperate me so. They fight each other more than they work together. My God, 'Riah, we number sixteen thousand souls in this city now, and it takes a miracle to get them to work together on something. The English Jews hate the German Jews and they both hate the Polish Jews and all of them hate us Sephardim, who continue to believe that we stand far above them all. It is ridiculous! Do you remember, 'Riah, when we first came to New York and there were less than five hundred of our people here and we all worshipped together in our sweet little shul on Mill Street? Now we number in the thousands and there are shuls everywhere—each little group must have their own. Our Shearith Israel gave birth to B'nai Jeshurun, and B'nai Jeshurun begat Anshe Chesed, and Anshe Chesed begat Sha'are Zedek, and Sha'are Zedek begat Sha'ar Hashamayim, and Sha'ar Hashamayim begat Rodeph Shalom, and then Beth Israel. My God, I can't even remember them all! And now we are flooded with Jews from Germany who want to change our worship to evoke more respect from the Gentiles! So they begat Emanu-El. First they move into an old church building and then they install an organ to accompany their choir, and they have even voted to no longer build a sukkah for the harvest festival. Some among them are calling for the abolition of *aliyot*—they want only their ministers to read the Torah. The members will not be called up. Next thing you know, they'll be seating men and women together! Our traditions are beginning to die, 'Riah. We must have a Hebrew hospital so that our people at least can die with a smile on their lips!"

"I'm sure it will be a fine hospital, Mordecai."

"Fine, yes, fine, *if* we can get our people to stop fighting each other and to unite for once."

"They all respect you, Mordecai, they will listen to you."

"I want to go to the Holy Land, 'Riah," Mordecai said suddenly.

"What?"

"Just once, before I die, I want to walk on the sacred soil of my ancestors. My own people laughed at me when I spoke of the restoration to Palestine. But I swear it will come! Did you know that the Turks finally have granted permission for the building of a synagogue in Jerusalem? Do you know what this means? It is a sign, Cousin! A sign that the hour of redemption is near at hand! I want to be there, 'Riah, when the cornerstone is laid for that shul. I want to be there, for I know that the Messiah will not be far behind."

"I hope you will be there, Mordecai, if that is what you want."

Again there was a long silence, broken only by Mordecai's audible breathing. He lay back on his pillow and stared at the ceiling, as if planning his next words.

"Uriah?" Mordecai spoke again, his voice soft now and questioning. "Do you ever think about Grandfather?"

The question caught Uriah by surprise. "Yes, Mordecai, I think of Grandfather now and then."

"Do you think he would be proud of us? I mean, of what we have become, of what we have done with our lives?"

"I don't know, Mordecai. I hope so."

"Oh, what a great man he was, our grandfather! I loved him so much. I hope somehow he knows, 'Riah, that I have tried hard to be a good American and also a good Jew. That is what he required of us. Do you remember? That is what he always demanded of us."

"Only God knows whether we have succeeded, Mordecai. But we certainly have tried, both of us."

Mordecai smiled again, but it was a strangely secret smile, inward, to himself. "There is an old saying—perhaps from the Talmud, I don't know—that God rewards a man not for what he achieves, but for what he *attempts*. I hope that Grandfather knows how much we have attempted."

"I'm sure he knows, Mordecai. And approves."

"You'll come to dinner tomorrow night, 'Riah? It is Shabbat, you know. I want you here. All my children will be at my table again. It will do my heart good to give them my blessing once again. You will be with us, won't you?"

"I'll be here, Mordecai. I'll be with you for Shabbat."

The funeral of Mordecai Manuel Noah brought forth the greatest outpouring of grief in the history of the Jewish community of New York City. He died peacefully six days after another paralytic shock had left him unable to speak or move. In those six days, he had lain in his bed and stared into the distance while friends and family hovered tearfully about him, not knowing if he could see or hear them, or whether he was capable of thought any longer. Uriah sat by his bed for hours at a stretch, holding his hand and speaking softly to him, consoling, quieting his fears. Finally, mercifully, he closed his eyes and was gone.

At four o'clock in the afternoon, they carried his body from the house and laid the coffin in the waiting hearse. Thousands of New Yorkers, mostly Jews, but with a generous number of Christians as well—many of the city's leading political figures among them— lined the sidewalks along Broadway for blocks on either side of the Noah house.

The mourners walked slowly down the steps and stood behind

the hearse: Rebecca and her six surviving children, ranging from twenty-two-year-old Manuel Mordecai to seven-year-old Lionel. The older ones had been summoned by telegraph just after the fatal stroke, and even the wandering Robert had by coincidence just returned from Europe. Mordecai's unmarried sister Judith, Uriah, Uncle Naph and Aunt Esther, and various other members of the clan took their places in the mourning line.

The hearse began its solemn procession along Broadway. Behind the black vehicle drawn by two black horses, the friends and admirers of the dead man took their places and walked down the street. Many members of the Hebrew Benevolent Society, which Mordecai had led for many years, were there, along with delegations from the "Noah Lodge" of B'nai Israel, B'nai Brith, the Young Men's Hebrew Benevolent and Fuel Association, the Society of Mutual Love, the German Hebrew Benevolent Society, and many others. Each of the city's synagogues was represented by officers and congregants.

When the hearse reached the Shearith Israel burying ground on the south side of Twenty-First Street, it was obvious that the immense crowd would prevent the traditional Sephardi rite of circuits around the coffin inside the tiny chapel. So the circuits were conducted outdoors, in sight of the hundreds of spectators who had accompanied the hearse in its slow travel along Broadway. Rebecca Noah and her children were ushered to the chairs where they would sit during the service. Afterward, Rebecca and her daughter Zipporah, Judith Noah, and the other women of the family would walk over to the chapel and wait there so that, in accordance with Sephardi custom, they could be spared the final pain of watching the plain coffin lowered into the grave.

The burial service was conducted by Jacques Judah Lyons, the *hazzan* of Shearith Israel, and then a moving oration was given by Dr. Morris Raphall, the rabbi-preacher of B'nai Jeshurun. The participation of the two men, brought together by their respect for the deceased, overlay a vast undercurrent of rivalry and disagreement. Raphall's B'nai Jeshurun had been in 1825 the original breakaway congregation from the mother synagogue and now was Shearith Israel's chief rival for the prestige synagogue among New York's Jews. Mordecai would have appreciated the irony of the collaboration.

As Uriah waited his turn to throw a handful of earth into the grave, he saw a perfect image of Mordecai's face before him. He could have sworn that he heard his cousin's familiar voice sing out, "Damn it, 'Riah, this is the biggest crowd I ever drew! The least they could have done is let me stand up and take a bow!"

He was early for his meeting. This day in May was bright and mild. The noonday sun poured warmth on him and tiny beads of sweat glistened on his upper lip and forehead. Uriah walked slowly amid the bustle of the South Street docks and hungrily studied the ships in all their variety.

He came down often to these docks and at other times to the walks on the Battery and to the equally busy docks along the Hudson. Here at least he could smell the ocean again and see shrouds and sails and tackles. For hours at a time he walked these water-edge streets, talking shop with the sailors and staring appraisingly, enviously at the vessels that bore those men beyond the horizon. It was the closest he could come to the place he most longed to be: the quarterdeck of a man-of-war. But this, the navy denied him. So he had to be what the sailors called a "damn-my-eyes-tar," a beached sailor who talks navy lingo to make himself feel still part of the game. He studied the ships in the river and sought their strengths and weaknesses and let his eyes travel their lines as if he watched the body of a desirable woman. What else was left to him? Oh, he could taste the ocean by taking passage on some belching steamship, but this held no appeal to him. He longed to get out under sail again and to walk the deck planks as a commander, not an anonymous traveler among a hundred others.

Steamships! God, they were taking over the world! Over there, at a dock not five hundred feet distant, was the Collins steamer *Bal-*

tic, which several times had crossed the Atlantic in less than ten days, averaging some thirteen knots. Off to his left was the steamer *Bay State*, which voyaged between her South Street dock and New England ports, and to his right was the steamer *Hendrick Hudson*, running between New York and Albany. Wasn't it just the other day that steamers were limited to river runs, for everyone knew they could never supplant the great sailing ships on the blue oceans? No, it wasn't just the other day, by God! Uriah added the years in his head and was stunned to realize that thirteen years had passed since the British steamer *Sirius* barged one night into New York harbor and became the first foreign steam vessel to call at an American port. And just a day later, to the roar of spectators on the shore, had come the *Great Western*, over 230 feet long and weighing sixteen hundred tons. A monster she was, belching smoke from her huge stacks. She had spit into the face of the savage winds that breasted her throughout the passage and had tied up at her South Street pier only fifteen days after departing her English home.

There were more than sixty docks along the East River now and more than fifty along the Hudson, and most of them berthed ships that carried a high smokestack, along with a mast or two with furled sails upon the yards.

It was a sad time for any seagoing man who had grown up under canvas. The day of the sailing ship was passing, and any man with sense could see that. But it wasn't over yet, thank God! There were clipper ships on the high seas that still could show their tails to these smoke pots! The Black Ball Line had a clipper called *Champion of the Seas*, which some sailors boasted could make twenty knots if conditions were right. Let any propeller-pushed tub match that!

The navy still hadn't given up on sailing ships. The old captured frigate *Macedonian* was being nicely converted into a 24-gun corvette. And two more of the 1820-type frigates, the *Sabine* and the *Santee*, were still being built, though the work had been plodding along for years. Navy men talked of plans afoot to take more of the great old frigates and razee them into big corvettes. Last year, when the navy had sent the Grinnell Expedition to the polar region in search of Sir John Franklin, it was the sailing brigs *Advance* and *Rescue* they had ordered up for the trip, not any steamers.

But the handwriting was on the wall. It was only a matter of time. But Uriah hoped that the time would eke its way past. If the great ships of white canvas must pass from the scene, then let it be after he was gone, so that he would not be forced to witness their death. He could not imagine the sea without them.

He sighed and leaned against a pillar of boxes on the dock and studied the line of buildings across the river, on Brooklyn Heights. He had seen that bluff when it was covered with green trees, broken only here and there by a house. Now Brooklyn was a flourishing little city with more than eighty thousand people. A hoarse whistle drew his eyes to the ferry, hurrying back to Peck Slip from Fulton Street in Brooklyn. Its deck was black with people and wagons. Right above the ferry, high on the Brooklyn bluff, was Four Chimneys, the great mansion of old Hezekiah Beers Pierrepont, the distiller of Anchor Gin, who had given Robert Fulton the money to start the world's first steam ferry. Well, the ferry still ran straight and true across the East River, but Fulton and Pierrepont were gone now, and the fine old mansion house soon would join them. The huge manse, where Washington had stayed after the disastrous Battle of Long Island in 1776, was to be torn down to make room for a street.

Uriah had looked forward to this luncheon engagement, but now he found himself depressed, freighted with sadness. It had been a poor year so far, with Mordecai's death in March. And the navy continued to ignore him and apparently would do so forever. He had allowed himself to think too much about the navy and ships and the sea. Whenever he lapsed into such thoughts, he became depressed. He wondered whether anything was left for him in life. Is this the way he must live out his years: collecting rents, buying and selling properties, walking the South Street docks and envying the young men who climbed out on the footropes and waved gaily to him as their ships slid down the river and out to sea? By God, this was no way for a sailing man to finish his life!

He pulled the letter from the inside pocket of his suit coat and looked at it again. It was a copy of the letter he had written in January to William A. Graham, President Fillmore's secretary of the navy. Graham's one-line reply was typically perfunctory. He kept them in the same envelope. Could he bring himself to ask his luncheon companion to intercede for him? And would that worthy agree to do so? And did he have the power to help?

In any case, he would show the exchange of letters to the senator. Perhaps he would take an interest in Uriah's case. John Dix had tried faithfully to help while he sat in the Senate, but to no avail. But John Hale of New Hampshire was a stronger voice, and perhaps he could move the navy. It would do no harm to try.

Uriah pulled his big gold watch from his pocket. Two minutes to meridian. He must move fast or he would be late. One must never keep a United States senator waiting.

"So, Captain Levy, we meet at last."

"Senator Hale, it's an honor to greet you."

"Sit, sir, and peruse the menu. We'll order lunch and make our acquaintance."

The senator from New Hampshire was an imposing figure of a man: almost six feet high and sporting a wide bulge around his middle that attested to a good life. His voice was deep and resonant.

"Captain, may I present my chief clerk, Mr. Winston P. Woods? We are homeward bound to New Hampshire for a few days, then on to Boston."

"What part of New Hampshire are you from?" Uriah asked out of courtesy, though he knew as little of that state's interior as he did of Inner Arabia.

"I am from Dover, near the border of Maine and near the seacoast," the senator answered. "Mr. Woods here is a Contoocook River man and lives within the shadow of glorious Mount Monadnock near the town of Jaffrey."

Winston P. Woods was a small, thin man with slick brown hair combed carefully back across his head like a profusion of railroad tracks. He seemed interested in the inhabitants of nearby tables and glanced regularly over his shoulder as if eavesdropping on other conversations.

"I was most flattered, Senator, to receive your letter suggesting that we meet here for lunch," Uriah said, "but I confess I was surprised at your choice of restaurants. Sweet's is decent enough for fish, but there are many better places. But you seemed most insistent on Sweet's."

"Indeed, Captain, you're right! I have a taste for flounder right enough, but I have my eye out for other things and Mr. Woods here has his ear cocked. Everyone knows that this Sweet's is a gathering place for the so-called blackbirds, the owners and masters of slave ships who keep plying their nefarious trade in spite of our laws. We're on the lookout for them today, Mr. Woods and I, and if we spot any such rascals, I assure you I will have a word with them and then will summon the watch and demand their arrest. As a sailing man, Captain, you might know some of them. You'll point them out to me, won't you?"

Uriah nodded vacantly, though he had no intention of pointing his finger at any man in this squalid riverside café with its tried fish nets hanging from the walls. He would not be found later in some alley with his throat cut. Let the senator point his own finger.

An old waiter, clad in a dirty apron that once had been white, came to their table and took their orders. All three of them ordered fish, the only item on the menu that bore even a taint of respectability.

"I said I was bound for Boston, Captain Levy," continued Senator Hale, "and there I will carry on my fight against the obnoxious Fugitive Slave Act that came to us with the Compromise of 1850. This pretense of a law says that a man or woman accused of being a runaway slave has no right to give evidence, to receive trial by jury, or even the protection of habeas corpus. Early this year a man named Frederick Wilkins, also known as Shadrach, was arrested in Boston and accused of having run away from slavery in Virginia. He faced a certain trip to Virginia, since the new law denied him a chance to defend himself against the charge. Before anything could be done, however, he was broken from the courthouse by a group of Negroes and carried off into hiding. A friend of mine called it the noblest act since the Boston Tea Party. Four of those rescuers are soon to go on trial for their action in freeing Shadrach. I have been engaged by the Boston Vigilance Committee to serve as cocounsel in their defense. My colleague, by the way, is Richard Henry Dana, Jr. I trust you have read his famous book about his life at sea?"

"I have indeed, Senator, and found it most interesting. It brought back to me my early years on merchant ships before I joined the navy."

A rough-looking party of seamen sat down at the next table and ordered tankards of ale. Winston P. Woods lowered his head conspiratorially and listened to every word uttered by the grizzled sailors, awaiting any talk of "black ivory," the term used by slavers to refer to their pitiful human cargoes.

"How stand you on the slavery question, Captain?" asked the senator.

"I take no strong position, sir, though I regard slavery as an unquestioned evil. Other things have been occupying my attention and have kept me from making a study of the arguments, so as to know whether to favor the gradualists or the immediatists."

"Ah, Captain," the senator said with a huge sigh, "there is only one position to take. We must have immediate abolition and thereby purge our national soul! I heard a Boston reverend state that 'the doctrine of immediate emancipation is nothing more or less than that of immediate repentance, applied to this particular sin.' That is God's truth. You hold slaves at Monticello, do you not, Captain?"

"I have a few, Senator. I promise you they are treated with kindness and given good food and decent houses. I constantly entreat my superintendent to look after them and see to their needs."

"'Their greatest need, Captain Levy, is to be free." The senator said this quietly, softly; there was no nag in his tone. "I wish, sir, that you would have the chance to hear, as I have heard many times, the voices of such former slaves as Frederick Douglass or Harriet

Tubman or Sojourner Truth tell of their lives under this accursed condition. Or Miss Sara Grimké, a white lady of South Carolina, who offers horrible testimony of having seen many slaves, both men and women, whipped to near-death and of having seen their teeth pulled as punishment and heavy iron collars thrown around their necks. Such descriptions, I think, would cause you hastily to support our antislavery cause with all the emotion that we do."

"There is no argument between us on this, Senator," Uriah replied, as the luncheon plates were placed before them. "I know your long and proud record as a fighter against slavery and that you were ejected from the Democratic Party because of your courageous stand. I admire you for all that. But I am a patriot, as I know you are, and I worry about the peace of our nation in the fierce arguments over this issue. I know that twenty years ago, when Nat Turner and his men killed more than sixty white people in my adopted state of Virginia, William Lloyd Garrison, the leader of your movement, approved the act and called it the first strike in the war against a nation of oppressors. And I know that Wendell Phillips, another one of your orators, calls upon Negroes to rise up in insurrection and war. How can I support such men who cry for the blood of my countrymen?"

Senator Hale nodded, thoughtfully. "They are hot bloods, no question of that. They are fanatics, obsessed men, and certainly they do not speak for me, or for most of us in the movement, when they issue such calls. But they are driven to it, Captain . . . driven to it by the fear that nothing will ever be done to end this black stain on our honor as a nation. The South stands firm. And well-meaning, cowardly men throughout the North say, 'Yes, yes, of course, but not now. Someday.' And so, Garrison and the others are driven almost to insanity in their frustration, and they shriek for blood. But cooler heads will prevail. Let me tell you a little story, Captain. At an abolitionist meeting in Faneuil Hall in Boston, Frederick Douglass made an impassioned speech in which he cried that there was no hope of justice from the white man; that Negroes must rise up and shed blood if they were to redeem themselves. As he finished, a great silence came over the audience as it sat thunderstruck, contemplating those awful words. Then Sojourner Truth, that magnificent tall black woman, stood up and her voice boomed out over the hall, 'Frederick, is God dead?' In those simple words, she restored common sense to the agenda."

For several minutes, they ate in silence. Even the chief clerk abandoned his mouselike surveillance of the next table and turned with a will to his boiled cod.

"Well, Captain," Senator Hale began again, "I did not ask you here to convert you to my position on slavery, though that would be a fine day's work. No, my purpose in calling you to lunch with me was merely to thank you for inspiring me in our mutual fight against that other evil of our time: the flogging of navy men at sea."

"It is I who must bear thanks, Senator. It was you who carried the day, after long years of trying."

"Seven years in all, Captain, ever since I first entered the House of Representatives in '43. Each year I would persuade my own colleagues to approve the abolition of corporal punishment in the navy, and each year the Senate would reject it. But after I came to the Senate in '47, I was able to force the issue out in the open."

"You mean when you persuaded the Senate to request the numbers of men punished from the navy?"

"Quite so. That was the action that brought light upon this hidden evil. The supporters of flogging claimed that it was used only for the most serious offenses, but the figures showed that in just two months of 1847, seventy-seven men were whipped on the *United States* and seventy on the *Cumberland*, more than forty men each on the *Jamestown*, the *Marion*, and the *Ohio*. Scandalous! Almost all of them received the maximum of twelve lashes each, and for such minor infractions as cooking up a poor meal or failing to be properly dressed. I told the Senate that this was barbarism, abolished by the army but allowed to continue in the navy. The sailor was degraded like a dog! Those figures gave us the opening we needed to launch our campaign. By the way, yours was a stroke of genius in mailing the lashes to members of the Senate. Many of them never had seen a cat before. Perhaps it was my long-standing argument with them over slavery, but it was my colleagues from the South who most strongly fought me over the abolition of whipping.

"Well, in any event, those southern senators argued the navy's discipline would crumble without the lash. The only alternatives for minor offenses would be the extremes of death, on the one hand, or mere confinement, which they said the miscreants would welcome as a vacation from work. I took pleasure in reminding them, sir, of your voyage on the *Vandalia*, when you proved beyond refute that the lash is not needed to maintain discipline. I quoted at length from your most excellent articles against flogging in several newspapers and magazines. There was also a magnificent series of articles, anonymously written, in the *Democratic Review* that was most useful to me. It is rumored that you were the unnamed author, Captain. Is that a fact?"

"Not completely, Senator," Uriah responded. "Those articles were actually written by Dr. John Lockwood, a former navy surgeon and more recently a professor at the new naval academy. But I contributed information to Dr. Lockwood that was incorporated in the articles, and I saw to it that a copy was sent to each member of Congress."

"Well, the evil is ended—forever, I hope. It was a close fight. After hearing me harp on the subject year after year, the Senate finally agreed, by twenty-five votes to twenty-three, to retain my rider abolishing flogging in the naval appropriation bill. It was a great day. You want to know what in my opinion decided that vote, Captain?"

"Yes, sir."

"When Senator Mason of Virginia moved to delete my rider from the bill, he argued very persuasively that the unique situation of ships at sea—far from jails or courts-martial—forced the used of the lash as punishment. He said also that only a few seamen were so punished. I quickly replied that the ship-of-the-line *Pennsylvania* had not been to sea for many years, but had been tied to the shore and served as receiving ship at the Norfolk Navy Yard. Yet during

1848, 239 men were whipped aboard the *Pennsylvania*. The senators laughed aloud when I remarked this. Then the laughter died away as they realized the import of what I had just said. Soon after, the vote was taken and we won.

"I have been receiving petitions of thanks from naval crews ever since, Captain, and from officers as well. Captain Long of the frigate *Mississippi*, for instance, wrote me that flogging always was as painful for him to inflict as for the sailor to receive. The sailors on the *Germantown* have pooled their money and sent me a handsome medal for my efforts. Well, Captain Levy, you should share in all such plaudits. You preceded me in fighting the good fight. Now that the battle has been won, you should stand with me to take the glory."

"The honor in this we can happily share, Senator. The important thing is that you have passed a law that changes the life of all American sailors for the better. Now they will be treated with the dignity that is the right of every American fighting man. The history books will note that day last September as a watershed in the annals of our navy."

"Then let the history books list your name alongside my own, Captain, as the parents of this humane reform!"

Forty-five minutes later they parted, firm friends now. Uriah realized as he walked northward along the docks toward home that he had totally forgotten to show Senator Hale the correspondence with the navy over his latest request for duty. He resolved to write the senator about his problem on this very day. He could always use another strong voice in his behalf.

21

New York City, 1853

"Lord in heaven, it looks like the castle of the pharaoh of Egypt!"

Uriah laughed in delight at his sister's excitement.

"It is no castle, Fanny," he said, "only a great water tank. But built in grand and glorious style, eh?"

"In our Jamaica," commented Virginia, Fanny's younger daughter, "everyone drank pure water from wells and we had no need of huge castles to hold the water. Explain to me, Uriah, why New York needs such a thing."

The three of them had stopped for a moment on the Fifth Avenue sidewalk to gaze upon the looming masonry walls of the central distributing reservoir, which had become—in its eleven years of existence—one of the city's prime curiosities for visitors.

"Watering a city of six hundred thousand people is no easy task, Ginny," Uriah responded. "We used to have sour, dirty water, as bad as that coming from casks in the holds of ships on which I've sailed. Whether you got water from the Manhattan Company or from a public pump, it was equally bad. Those living to the north could buy water from Knapp's Spring, which was somewhat better, and the very wealthy had theirs brought in casks from better wells in the country. But for most New Yorkers, the water was terrible. Finally the experts decided that water from the Croton River, forty miles north, would solve our problem. So a dam was built up there to form a lake, and pipes were laid to bring the water down to the city. They needed something in which to store the water, and so they built this Egyptian temple, which is fifty feet high and has walls twenty-five feet thick. They say it can hold 20 million gallons. The promenade atop the walls offers one of the best views of the city. We'll go up there one day."

"On a cooler day than this, I pray," sighed Fanny, who suffered terribly from New York's stifling summer. Her many years of residence in Jamaica had not rendered her immune to nature's summer furnace. In Jamaica, of course, anyone of sound mind did not walk in the midday heat, and certainly not on a scorching pavement, but instead reclined in a cool, dark house and thus survived.

"As a proper guide for your sightseeing," Uriah continued, "I must add the fact that, in order to build this reservoir, they first had to dig up and remove the bones of one hundred thousand bodies that had been buried on this site, which for years was a potter's field."

"Those poor souls!" Virginia cried. "What ever did they do with them?"

"Removed them to Wards Island, far up the East River at Hell Gate, and buried them again. It was worth all the effort. Ever since the new water system opened, we have had clean water and all of it that we need. And it certainly has improved my own fortunes."

"How is that, Brother?" asked Fanny.

"It brought fire insurance rates far down, which was a boon to every owner of buildings such as myself. It also helped raise real estate values even higher. Each time I raise my glass, I give thanks for the wisdom of those engineers. I toast them with a goblet of pure white water from inside these battlements that stand before us."

"Uriah, I'm melting away! Come, I'm so anxious to see the World's Fair that I can't contain myself! Let's be off!" Virginia was striding up the sidewalk, her short legs working gallantly as she playfully took her uncle's arm and began tugging him along with her.

"Virginia!" huffed her mother. "It's not ladylike!" Uriah only laughed.

"Uriah, if you keep us here in the hot sun much longer, I shall have so much water on my face that I shall no longer even resemble a lady," Virginia complained with a mock pout on her face, but as usual her laughing tone belied any hauteur and beguiled Uriah with its faint singsong accent of Jamaica mixed with a delicate British intonation.

"I'm sorry, Ginny," he said with a smile. "I forgot that you might not be interested in my history lesson. Let's be off, then! The entrance is right over there."

Uriah had been acting as their leader on many sightseeing and shopping expeditions in these past weeks. He did it partly because they were his relatives and newcomers to New York, so they could get acquainted with their new home. He also had to admit, when he took time to ponder the events of a busy day with his sister and niece, that he was spending so much time with them for another reason as well: he found young Virginia absolutely charming. Her sweetness and vivacity, her enthusiasm and ever-present curiosity were like a tonic to him—a renewal of youthful freshness in a life that for a long time now had turned sodden with increasing age and continual disappointment.

His sister Frances, who had been called Fanny by everyone ever since her birth, was twelve years younger than him. She had been born soon after he returned from his first voyage as a cabin boy, and he always remembered her as a plump, ever-smiling infant. He had trouble connecting this short, stout, middle-aged woman with the baby he had known in the house on Cherry Street. He had been far away from home as she grew into womanhood and, like most of his brothers and sisters, she had been more a stranger to him than some of his friends and former shipmates.

Fanny had been little more than a girl when she was married to Abraham Lopez of Jamaica, whom she had met and swiftly come to love when he was a visitor to Philadelphia. She moved with him to Kingston, and there they had lived in peace and prosperity for many years and birthed a son and two daughters.

Virginia, now a month shy of her eighteenth birthday, had been sent a few years before to a fashionable school in Birkenhead, England. She had left Jamaica with her father rich, respected, and brimming with confidence in himself and his fellow men. She had returned home, a year before now, to find him broken and sick. He had stood bond for a close friend and the friend's speculations had crashed. Abraham Lopez made good his bond, paid off all his friend's debts, and ruined himself in so doing.

Fanny Lopez didn't know what to do, but instinctively she realized that their time in Jamaica had ended; they must return to the United States to stand within the comforting ring of the family. Their older children—George Washington Lopez and Abigail, who had married Daniel Peixotto of one of the old, respected Sephardi families—had preceded them to America. It was time for Fanny, too, to lead her family back home.

They sailed to New York and had tearful reunions with long-separated loved ones. Fanny found succor in the arms of her older sisters Eliza and Amelia, and brother Joseph traveled up from Baltimore to greet her. Jonas, the youngest of the brothers and sisters, who was now living in Washington City with his wife—also a Frances called Fanny—came to join the reunion as well.

But of all the family, it was Uriah to whom Fanny cleaved. And this was especially so when, a few months after their arrival in New York, Abraham Lopez died, still despondent over his losses and sudden turn in fortune.

When Abraham died, Uriah invited Fanny and Virginia to live with him in his big house in St. Mark's Place. They could remain as long as they cared to, he told them, for he had plenty of room and servants to attend to their needs. And he would welcome the sound of family voices in his home again. Fanny, bewildered and almost totally impoverished by now, immediately accepted the offer.

Virginia's buoyant personality soon recovered from the shock of her father's death and her numerous dislocations, and she became a talkative sprite in the house, fond of teasing her uncle and deflating his sometimes rather pompous air. Short and buxom like her mother, Virginia had a pretty face and reveled in fashion. She never declined her uncle's offer to take her shopping and showered him with hugs and kisses after every buying expedition. The salesmen at the Arnold Constable Store and Lord & Taylor's, Tiffany's, and Eder Haughwout's chinaware store were always thrilled to see her enter their doors with a buying gleam in her eyes and a doting uncle at her heels.

And when Virginia was not busy adding to her wardrobe or the house furnishings, Uriah managed to entice both mother and daughter to join him for more sightseeing, or another lecture or concert. On one evening, it would be a hack ride to Franconi's Hippodrome on Madison Square to watch the spectacular chariot races under the great canvas roof that spanned the huge enclosure without encumbering pillars or posts. On another night, they'd attend a charitable ball at Niblo's Garden, where Uriah amazed Virginia with his zest and skill at the polkas and quadrilles. After a night or two of rest, they would be off again—to Purdy's National Theatre on the Bowery, or a lecture on Jewish history by Dr. Merzbacher at the Touro Literary Institute on Broome Street and afterward to a soda water shop for refreshment.

And on this particular day in the simmering middle of August, they were bound for New York's newest and most spectacular attraction: the World's Fair, the "Exhibition of the Industry of All Nations," in the Crystal Palace, its fabulous house of glass. President Franklin Pierce had formally opened the fair a month before, and New Yorkers had been talking of nothing else ever since. Most of them were deferring their visits until the weather cooled a bit, but whether they had been there or not, everyone talked incessantly of the Crystal Palace and its amazing contents.

Located just to the west of the great reservoir, the fair building—named for and modeled after London's Crystal Palace—was built in four long sections that crisscrossed each other. The enormous domed structure built of iron and glass soared seventy-six feet into the sky and was likened by some to a huge greenhouse. Inside were thousands of *objets d'art* and industrial items from all over the world. An interior elevated railway system carried visitors about the huge structure, and at the various way stations they could disembark to see Gobelin tapestries, Sevres china, armor from the Tower of London, and hundreds of works of art.

"Uriah," Virginia begged him, "will you allow us also to visit the tower yon and to ride the lifting platform in it? I am told that you can see a hundred miles from the top."

He smiled again at her eagerness. "The Latting Tower? Yes, we'll give it a look if you still have energy left after the Crystal Palace. I doubt that we'll see quite so far, but it will be fun to ride the platform to the top." The wooden tower rose more than three hundred feet into the sky and was one of several tourist attractions that had blossomed around the fair itself.

"Come on, then!" Virginia called and quickened her step. "There is a whole world to see and only a day to see it! Come, Momma! Come, Uriah! The world awaits us!"

As soon as he sat down in the parlor opposite his sister, Uriah could tell that she was nervous and worried.

"Fanny?" he said. "Why so grave? Your daughter becomes eighteen years today. You should be full of smiles. I have a marvelous celebration planned for tonight. We shall have a fine kosher dinner at Joseph Ochs's dining room, and then we'll attend a concert by the Swiss Bell Ringers. You'll be amazed at their music, amazed!"

"Uriah, I have just come from Dr. Abrahams."

"You have seen Simeon? Are you ill? What is it, Fanny?"

She lowered her gaze for a moment as if considering how to tell him. Then she raised it and smiled wanly. "No, I'm not ill. At least, not now. But there are problems. It's my heart, Uriah. It has troubled me for years, on and off. Every now and again, I have spells. But it always passes. However, Dr. Abrahams—a very kind man, by the way—listened long and hard to my heart and says that it does not sound good. There are strange skips in the way it beats, he says."

"What does this mean, Fanny? How bad is it?"

Her chin began to tremble a bit. "He says that I must take care not to overexert and that I must rest a good deal. Beyond that, he says, he cannot be sure what will happen. But . . . but he does not think that I will live to see sixty."

"Fanny! My dear girl! I don't know what to say."

"There is nothing to say, Uriah. I must take all the care I can. And I must make plans."

"Plans?"

"My dear brother, I am dreadfully worried about my daughter and what will become of her after I'm gone."

"Dear Fanny, please do not concern yourself! You know that I will always care for Virginia and see that she is provided for."

"I know that, Uriah, and I'm grateful! But I fear that isn't good enough."

"Why not?"

"Virginia presents herself as a very sophisticated young woman. But underneath all the effervescence and laughter, she is a child—a vulnerable, credulous child. And she will be taken advantage of. I know it and I fear it."

"Fanny, you can be sure I will watch—"

"Uriah, in Jamaica . . . there was a boy. A ne'er-do-well. A lad from one of Jamaica's best and wealthiest Kingston families. Virginia fell madly in love with him and would have run away with him in a minute. Fortunately for all of us, before that could happen, he was arrested for failing to pay his gaming debts. Later they found that he had stolen money from his father's friends. He sits now in a Kingston jail. She is so innocent . . . so trusting! If I am not here to watch over her, I know she will fall into bad company. I feel it in my bones. Oh, I know you think that you could prevent that. But you are her uncle and not her parent. She can be so headstrong! I don't think she will heed you, Uriah."

"Then what can be done?"

"We must find a husband for Virginia. And quickly."

Uriah smiled. "So, you wish me to be a matchmaker? Very well, I'll look for a proper husband for Ginny. It shouldn't be too difficult. She is charming and lovely. And she has a good head."

To his surprise, Fanny shook her head emphatically.

"It's not so simple, Brother. Virginia never would agree to an arranged marriage. She would insist that she must fall in love first, and God only knows who she might select. The good Sephardi families of New York would have little interest in Virginia, for our fortune is gone and we are not established socially. You yourself have told us that the families of Shearith Israel constantly marry with each other and have little interest in anyone else. To them we are outsiders—and poor ones at that. Who knows when Virginia would fall in love? And when it happens, it might well be with someone of whom I never would approve."

"Well, Fanny," Uriah said with a small shrug of his shoulders, "I suppose we must just leave some things up to God."

"No, Uriah," she said firmly. "I have a solution. I have been thinking about it all day. I want *you* to marry my daughter."

Uriah was not sure he had heard right. His eyes widened with surprise. He peered at her intensely to see if she joked with him, but it was obvious that this was not the time or place for humor.

"Fanny, how could you be serious? She is my niece. And she is only a child. To her I'm an old man, like a grandfather."

"She adores you, Uriah. She worships you! You are her hero. I see that, as only a mother's eye can see."

Uriah shook his head in irritation. He still could not believe what he was hearing. "If she looks at me with admiration, it is because I am a loved old uncle and perhaps she has been told exaggerated stories of my navy service. She does not look at me in the way you imply. Fanny, this whole idea is preposterous!"

"I know this sounds like a strange notion to you," she went on. "Perhaps it is a fanciful notion, or even a lunatic one. But please listen to me for a moment more. I must be very frank. You are—what? Sixty years, now?"

"I was sixty-one in April."

"Very well: sixty-one. I pray you will live until a hundred, but that is not likely. When your time comes, as God wills it, Virginia will still be a young woman, but she will be much more settled then and sure of her own mind. I know that you will educate her well. And, if I may continue to speak honestly, she will be left well provided for and able to live without having to accept the first man who beckons her to the marriage canopy. Oh, Uriah, she will be so much more ready for life if she first has the advantage of at least several years as your dear companion. I will not be here to look after her; I pray that you will do it for me. And meanwhile she will look after you and provide you a warm and loving home. You will no longer be alone. Mama always worried so much about you being alone, and so do I."

"Good Lord, Fanny, can you imagine what people would say? I would be on every tongue in the city."

"I don't care about that, Uriah. Let them talk. They'll get used to the idea."

"But why must there be a marriage? Why could not Virginia continue to live with me—as my ward—after you . . . after. . . ."

"A young girl living in this house with you, chaperoned only by Irish servant girls? And you worry about malicious tongues? Think how they would wag with such an arrangement! It would be a scandal! No, it's impossible!"

"Fanny, for God's sake, she is my niece. How could I marry her?"

"I have asked a few people who know of such things. They think it is perfectly legal, though unusual. They see nothing illegal about it."

"In the eyes of the state law, perhaps not. But according to Jewish law? I would not go against the Jewish law, Fanny, not even for you. I would not disgrace Virginia in the *esnoga*, nor myself for that matter."

"Very well then. Will you speak to Hazzan Lyons and get his ruling? Will you do that much for me?"

He sighed and shook his head again. "Very well, if you insist. I'll ask the *hazzan*. And if he says it is forbidden, then that will be the end of it."

Fanny nodded in agreement. She could not restrain a slight smile. She was sure of her ground, for one of her friends was well versed in Jewish law and had given her reason for confidence. And she smiled because her brother had made a major concession: he no longer dismissed the idea out of hand.

Neither was Fanny worried about his eventual decision. She had seen the loneliness in his eyes. She had seen him sitting alone in his study, staring morosely out the window at the dull sky. And she had seen his face light like a lamp when Virginia waltzed into the room. She had watched the age drop from his body like a discarded robe when he walked the street with his niece and exchanged teasing banter with her. Virginia had brought laughter back into Uriah's life. Could he give that up now? Could he chance losing her to someone else? Fanny was quite confident. It would be the perfect solution, and she could, one day not too far off, die in peace. Her brother would see the logic of it all, and his heart would carry him the rest of the way.

They were married on the morning of the last Sunday in October in the grand parlor of Uriah's house on St. Mark's Place. Although all the fine old Chippendale and Heppelwhite chairs and the Sheraton desk had been moved out of the big room, it still was crowded beyond comfort with family members and friends.

Virginia had wept when she learned that they could not be married in the sanctuary of Shearith Israel, for marriage in the synagogue had been the custom in her native Jamaica, and she sobbed to her mother that her marriage otherwise would not seem legal. But the elders of Shearith Israel had long before banned all nuptials in the *esnoga* after unruly crowds of spectators—Jews and Gentiles alike—had come uninvited to prominent weddings and damaged the furniture as well as the solemnity.

Uriah stood in an anteroom and waited for the appearance of his young bride. He studied the happy faces of the guests seated in tight rows of chairs in his parlor. How good it was to see so many of the family gathered together, brought back by this ancient ceremonial that would entwine two tendrils of the very same family tree. *Perhaps it was the novelty*, he thought, that had taken them from their scattered homes to this reunion.

No, that was unkind, he told himself. They seemed happy for him and relieved that the old warhorse of the clan at last had found a partner. Fanny had sprung into action as soon as the date was set and had sprayed letters and telegrams like confetti to every member of the family whom she could locate. Despite the short notice, they had responded to a degree that astounded Uriah. He loved and honored them all, but he had been a distant kinsman—kept far away by career and, he must admit, somewhat by choice, because he was a private man and did not much cleave to relatives. He had not expected them now to descend upon his house in such numbers, but he was glad to see them here.

All his living brothers and sisters were in this room today, save for Isaac, who had not responded to the invitation and perhaps had never received it. His eldest sister, Eliza, sat in the front row with three of her five children. Brothers Benjamin and Joseph were in the second row with their wives. The youngest of the family, Jonas, had been asked to be best man. Of the ten children of Michael and Rachel Levy, only the two other seagoing brothers were no longer living: Louis, dead at the hands of his own mutinous crewman in Havana harbor, and Morton, lost at sea on a doomed brig out of New Orleans. But a son of Morton's, named Uriah Phillips after his uncle, sat proudly today with the rest of the family and was his lost father's proxy.

Dear little Fanny bustled frantically around the house like a honeybee, flitting between her alternating roles of hostess and tear-brimmed mother of the bride. She wore a becoming pink gown and looked like a dawn-struck little cloud, scudding lightly from one room to the next, checking a detail here, solving a problem there, directing the servant girls and urging the cook to new peaks of ingenuity.

Uriah, wearing his magnificent captain's dress uniform for the first time in months, caught the eye of Rebecca Noah, Mordecai's widow, and gave her a smile and nod. She smiled in return, a good and warming smile that told him she was glad for him. She sat with Judith, Mordecai's sister, and her daughter Zipporah, who was now a beautiful young woman of eighteen years.

It was time: Uriah started, almost in fright, as he came back to the present moment. Hazzan Lyons quietly took his place under the bridal canopy, and Uriah walked out to join him. There was a great rustling in the parlor as all the family members turned in their chairs to watch the entrance of the bride. Uriah saw his bride enter the parlor on the arm of her brother. Fanny walked proudly at her other elbow.

Virginia, heavily veiled, could nonetheless be seen to smile gaily as she walked down the narrow aisle to the huppah. Once under the canopy, however, she began to cry softly and continued to do so throughout the brief ceremony. It was not because of Uriah; she married him freely and without reservation. But the gathering of family members and her mother's tears brought back painful memories of her dead father, and it was for him that she cried. If only that gentle, sad man could have been here to see her wed!

While the Seven Benedictions were recited by the *hazzan*, Uriah suddenly was filled with the strange, powerful sensation that it was Elise who stood next to him in the white gown of a bride. The feeling was so strong that he was almost convinced and he came near to calling her name in a burst of emotion and surprise. Then he heard Virginia stifle a sob, and the illusion vanished. Had it been Elise alongside him, he knew, there would have been no tears. She would have been laughing with joy and whispering irreverent things to him, for she found happiness in the most sentimental moments and even in the midst of them would not be sad. She would have a smile to his nervous face.

They drank from the goblet of wine, and then Uriah stamped upon the glass wrapped in cloth that had been slipped under his foot. The spectators called out a hearty "Mazel tov!" and it was all over.

As required by custom, Uriah took his bride to another room for a few quiet moments together before they reappeared for the wedding luncheon. He kissed her gently on the cheeks and wiped away her tears. He promised her that all would be well and that they would have a happy life together. And they both understood that he was the one needing reassurance, for he still was not sure that, in taking his young niece as his wife, he had not broken some obscure, yet primal law of man and God.

They sat together in the upstairs sitting room, just two months after their wedding, as if they had been married for fifty years, half hearing the sleet flick against the windows, each dreamily engaged in the pastime of a winter's night. Virginia busied herself with her knitting, stopping only now and then to glance at her husband and to remind herself how fortunate she was, being married to such a man.

For his part, Uriah went over the week's reports from his building managers and pondered the progress of the winter repairs under way on some of his properties. He was not like some of the city's landlords who paid no need to their buildings or their tenants except diligently to collect the rents. No, Uriah was proud that his buildings were kept in good repair. In part this was because he thought of his tenants much as the people on a ship under his command: they were human beings and surely entitled to live in a place that was warm, dry, clean, and as free as possible from ravaging insects. Alongside his very real compassion for his tenants was his conviction that good maintenance of his properties was good sense and good business; it made for buildings that better stood the onslaughts of time and thus would continue to produce healthy incomes for that much longer.

So Uriah kept busy a small army of craftsmen and supervisors, chipping and painting and sealing and patching his buildings, doing everything to them short of careening them and scraping their bottoms that is done to keep a ship in fine sailing fettle.

The rattle of the sleet against the window glass grew louder. It was a foul night, and the morrow promised fouler yet. It was a good night to be home. He began to run over in his head the roster of his properties. He amazed himself that he could keep the list sharp in his memory, though it changed every few weeks as he bought or sold. But keep it he could, and he would pull it out of his mind's corner and run it past every so often. It reassured him, it calmed him. It was good warmth against the chill of a sleet-struck night.

Duane Street: No. 70. The litany slowly began unrolling in his mind, a silent roster of buildings, each with its own personality: *Division Street: 163, 163½, 165, 165½. Canal Street: 493. Houston Street: 49, 81, 83. Laurens: No. 162. A bad actor, that one. Needed a new roof, and soon.* He must give some thought to selling the Laurens building. It was falling apart before his eyes. *MacDougal Street: No. 8. Sullivan: 78, 80, 82. Thompson: No. 105. Greenwich: 653, 657. Broome: No. 219. Rivington Street: 80A, 80B, 80H, 80I, 80K, 80L. Goerick: 428.*

Many of his tenants now were Jews. The Israelite community in New York had swelled with the great influx from Middle Europe that had followed the slow death of the liberal revolutions of the late forties. It was the Bohemians, Germans, and Bavarians who populated Uriah's buildings now. They worshipped at Anshe Chesed and Sha'are Zedek, or at Emanu-El, which called itself a "temple" rather than a synagogue and soon would be moving into a much larger building on Twelfth Street.

"Uriah?" Virginia's call was soft, yet it startled him. He had been deep in his thoughts and perhaps even had dozed off. Her voice had brought him fully awake.

"Yes, my dear, what is it?"

"Uriah, I mean to share your bed tonight."

He did not reply for a time. He was taken aback; he had not

expected this. They were alone in the house for the first time since their marriage. Fanny had left in the morning to spend a few days with her older daughter, Abigail Peixotto. They were alone, save for the Irish servant girls who had scurried about the lower regions of the house like distant mice as they put away the last of the dinner utensils and by now had locked the doors and doused the lamps and had retired sleepily to their own rooms.

"Ginny, what are you saying?"

"I am saying, my dear husband, that I am your wife and I mean to share your bed tonight as any good wife, and that I shall do so from this night forward. I was wrong to have waited so long as it is."

"But, Virginia, your mother—"

"My mother is not here. Anyway, I have made my feelings quite clear to her. Why do you think she decided to visit Abigail and David right now? She wanted us to be alone to have the honeymoon we should have taken when we were married."

"But . . . I'm sure she didn't intend—"

"Uriah Levy, I don't give a fig what my mother intended! I did not marry you because I perceived you as a kindly old grandfather who would buy me candies and bonnets. I married you because I love you very much and I shall be a wife to you, not a ward. Beginning tonight. Mama will continue, I hope, to make her home with us for the rest of her days—may God make them many—but she will not live here as a chaperone. I was foolish to keep sharing her suite after our wedding. I should have moved into your room on the very first night. But Mama was right here . . . and I was shy. And you said nothing to the contrary."

"My God, Virginia, I never thought that you would expect . . . that you would want to. . . . My God, I am old enough to be your grandfather. And I'm your uncle, to boot!"

"You're twice the man of any boy my own age. And you are no longer my uncle, Uriah! I absolve you of that relationship forever. Our *ketuba* makes it very plain: you are my husband. I want no token marriage. I mean to be your true wife, by night as well as by day! Hear me well, Uriah Levy!"

He could not help smiling at her emphatic tone and the look on her face that would brook no opposition. Lord, she had taken him so by surprise! How could he possibly make love to this . . . this child? And yet, he could not lie to himself: he felt that old telltale heating in his loins.

"Ginny, perhaps this is the time to talk with you about another matter that has been on my mind. To set things straight with you, so there will be no hurt or broken hearts, that sort of thing. What I mean to say is this: I will do my best to be a good husband to you and to make a good life for you. But I may not always be here with you. It has been almost fifteen years since I was last favored by the navy with a command. But I remain a captain on the active list, and though I am written on their roster as 'waiting for duty,' the fact is that I have been and will continue to do all in my power to seek another assignment. When that assignment comes, I must go away—perhaps for as long as two or three years. I will remain your husband, of course, but I cannot then be at your side. You must clearly understand this, for my assignment could come at any time. Just last week I sent another letter off to the Navy Department requesting their consideration."

She sighed and shook her head in puzzlement. "Uriah, why? Why, in heaven's name? You are past sixty. Why continue to beg them to put you to sea on some creaking old ship? You have a new life here with me! Please put that other life behind you. It was good in its time, but that time is past."

"No, Virginia, no, never. You must understand. I am a navy man! This is my life. I am an officer in the navy of the greatest country in the world. Think how many aspire to such a place! I cannot give it up! I am still young in mind and body. Older men than I command ships-of-the-line and squadrons. My greatest navy days are yet to come, I know it! Any day now, I will get the message from Washington City. You must be prepared, my dear. You must live here with your mother and wait for me. For such is the fate of a navy wife."

She did not argue further. She had seen the fire in his eyes; he burned with fervor for his nation, for his navy. It was unquenched yet, after all the repudiation, all the ignominy. No words of hers could change it. She knew, with the innate wisdom of a wife, when further argument was useless.

"Uriah," she said, "it is time for us to be in bed."

Surprised, he pulled his gold watch from the pocket of his waist-coat. "But, my dear, it is not yet nine o'clock."

She did not look at him, but rose and began putting her knitting into its gingham bag. "Nonetheless," she answered, "a husband and wife should be abed by now. That is the custom of my Jamaica, and I prefer that we follow it."

Both of them knew, of course, that it was no such thing.

22

New York City
May 23, 1854

The Hon. J. C. Dobbin
Secretary of the Navy

It is understood here that the Department is about to dispatch a strong force for the protection of our commerce in the North Sea. Should this be true, I very respectfully solicit that you will do justice to my very long deferred claims to a command. All I ask is a due proportion of service in common with my Brother Officers.

With great respect, I am, sir.
Your obedient servant,
U. P. Levy, Captain

St. Mark's Place, New York
August 25, 1855

Hon. J. C. Dobbin
Secretary of the Navy

Sir: The command of the squadron on the coast of Brazil, and the Navy Yard here, will be vacant by limitation this fall. I am the next captain in rank on the register, entitled to the command of a squadron or a station; and being capable of performing, promptly and efficiently all my duties, both on sea and on shore, I therefore respectfully solicit that, as an act of justice long deferred, you will confer the appointment of either of these commands on me.

Your obedient servant,
U. P. Levy, Captain

New York City, 1855

Whenever an envelope bearing the familiar blue seal of the Navy Department rested among his morning mail, Uriah followed a little ritual before opening it. Although the communication from the navy always was uppermost in his mind, he would set aside the envelope from Washington City and first go slowly, meticulously, through the other mail. It was as if he desired to clear all inconsequential matters from his agenda and to resolve any tasks relating to his properties that arose from the morning correspondence. Then he would turn to the letter from the navy and give it his full attention. For years now he had done it thus, saving the navy letter for last, hoping against hope that somehow his latest request had found a sympathetic ear and that he would get his coveted command.

When he came across the navy envelope in today's batch of mail, he set it at the corner of the desk in his study. Then he proceeded to examine with precise care every other envelope in the small stack. It was a typical day's ration: two invitations to parties; the latest issue of a navy magazine; a notice of a meeting of Sampson Simson's North American Relief Society, which aided poor Jews in Palestine; an invitation to a concert sponsored by the Young Men's Hebrew Benevolent Society; and a polite note from a tenant thanking him for repairing the roof on one of the buildings on Houston Street.

Uriah methodically read each communication and then placed it in the proper pile: to be filed, to be answered, or to be given to Virginia for reply.

His reading and sorting completed, he was ready at last to give his clear mind to the letter from the navy. He held the envelope in his hand, knowing that he was acting like a child, and tried for a moment to predict the words inside. Then he took a deep breath, sliced open the envelope with his letter blade, and unfolded the letter to read,

Navy Department
Sept. 13, 1855

Mr. Uriah P. Levy, Late Captain
U.S. Navy

Sir: The Board of Naval Officers assembled under the "Act to Promote the Efficiency of the Navy," approved Feb. 23, 1855, having reported you as one of the officers who should, in their judgment, be stricken from the rolls of the Navy, and the finding of the Board having been approved by the President, it becomes my duty to inform you that accordingly, your name is stricken from the rolls of the Navy.

I am respectfully,
Your obedient servant,
J. C. Dobbin

Virginia came to him about an hour later, wondering why he had not come down for luncheon. She found him sitting at his desk, staring into space, his face white as alabaster. The letter rested in his lap.

"Uriah!" she cried as she hurried to him. "What is it? Are you ill? Dearest, what has happened? Can you hear me? Can you move?"

His face slowly came to life again, and he looked blankly up at her. His eyes were wide, as if he had seen something that filled him with awe. But his voice, when he finally answered her, was weak like an old man's and flat as a tropical sea in the doldrums.

"They have finally done it," he murmured. "They have destroyed me."

"What has happened?" Virginia repeated, kneeling before him, her arms frantically clasping his knees. "Who has done something to you? Tell me!"

"They have accomplished their end at last," he continued in the same lifeless tone. "They have branded me unfit and thrown me out. I have lost everything for which I have worked. It is over. . . . I am finished."

She looked down and saw the letter in his lap. As she unfolded it and slowly began to read it, she heard the first sounds of his sobs. In a moment more, he was weeping openly, unashamedly. Virginia, her face now as pale as his, understood at last. She gently brought him to his feet and embraced him as he cried in great, gasping coughs. She caressed his arms and shoulders and crooned softly to him, as she would to a child.

The following day he was wan from lack of sleep and still white-faced from emotion and fatigue. But his fighting soul had revived, with amazing speed. In the afternoon of this warm, sunny Sunday, Uriah sat at his desk and made notes for his plan of action. He had, in the blackest moments of the long night, made up his mind to give battle to this damnable board, to the secretary of the navy himself, to the president if necessary, in order to overturn a decision that reeked of bigotry, that was so palpably wrong and lacking in proof.

The purpose of the infamous Board of Fifteen, its reason for existence, was not to shorten the roll of the navy's officer corps. No, its task—as specified by Congress—was to weed out the unfit, the drunk, the incompetent. They had placed *him* in such ignominious company. Well, by God, then let them prove their case! He had the right of any American citizen to a hearing, to be proven unfit, incompetent. They had no such proof. That, by God, he knew. He would demand his rights—as a navy captain and as an American. In the darkness of his bedchamber, while Virginia snored softly alongside him, he lay and began framing his arguments.

In the morning, though he had not slept, his mind was clear and his resolve to fight his dismissal grew ever stronger. Virginia was surprised and heartened that he ate a bountiful breakfast. He had not eaten since breakfast of the previous day, and he was hungry. Now he ate with the gusto of a young man.

After breakfast, he paid a call upon his old friend, John Dix, the former U.S. senator from New York. He knew Dix had a fine legal mind and wanted to get his reaction to the crisis. Uriah brought the fateful letter from Secretary Dobbin and quickly explained the Board of Fifteen and its mission.

Dix listened silently, read the letter several times, and then told Uriah that his immediate reaction—without having recourse to the Act of February 1855 that had established the board—was that such a body, operating in secrecy and failing to give its victims a chance to face their accusers or hear the evidence against them, probably was illegal. He advised Uriah to hold his fire for the time being, but to request more information from the navy, and particularly to ask the grounds on which the decision had been made. If such information was given to him (and Dix predicted that the navy would refuse to do so), he would at least have something on which to base a challenge. If they refused to give him the information, he would be in a position to raise legal questions on the constitutionality of the board's action.

Uriah walked back home almost jauntily. If it was a fight they wanted, he would give it to them! He had been forced to fight ever since he had taken his oath as sailing master, forty-three years before. So be it! He would do battle once again.

He sat down at his desk to compose a reply to Secretary Dobbin. He wanted them to know that he was shocked and infuriated by their action, but he must not let his rage spoil his tactics. He would follow John Dix's advice and demand, as his right, the board's reasons for cashiering him.

He began slowly, precisely, to write. He told Dobbin of his horror at the action of the board and emphasized that he had not any expectation of being a victim of the Fifteen because he knew that the board's purview was limited to officers not competent. He must know the grounds on which the board had acted, he wrote, and then added, "I cannot think it but hard that, without crime or fault—without charges or trial or notice, and by the fact of a tribunal sitting in secret—I should be ignominiously deprived of the commission I had gained by so many years of toil and peril."

In less than a week, Dobbin replied:

Navy Department
Sept. 18, 1855

U. P. Levy, Esq.,
Late of U.S. Navy
New York

Sir: I have received your letter of the 16th instant, asking the grounds upon which the judgment of the Naval Board was based in your case. The Board, in accordance with the law, merely reported the names of the officers who, in their judgment, were affected by the law, without assigning any reasons. I am therefore not in possession of the grounds on which they based their action, and am unable to comply with your request. I am, respectfully,

Your obedient servant,
J. C. Dobbin

As soon as he received Dobbin's letter, Uriah went to his desk and composed another letter to the secretary, respectfully requesting a copy of all charges and reports on file against him, from the date of his captain's commission to the day of his removal from the service, and also the date of all applications for service that he had submitted during the same period.

Again he received a prompt reply from Washington City:

Navy Department
Sept. 24, 1855

U. P. Levy, Esq.
New York

Sir: Your letter of the 23rd instant has been received. In reply, I have to inform you that the charges that have been made against you officially were made prior to your captaincy. Since that period the secretaries of the Navy have not seen fit to assign you any duty, for which, it is true, you have made frequent applications.

I am respectfully
Your obedient servant,
J. C. Dobbin

"It would seem to me," Ben Butler said, "that they have committed a patent violation of their authority."

"I'm glad to hear you say so, Ben," responded Uriah. "But tell me how you come to say it."

"Why, Dobbin virtually admitted in his last letter to you that the board's decision was based on charges lodged against you *prior* to your promotion to captain. Yet, the Act of February 28, 1855, charges this board with identifying those officers who are unfit for further service as of the date of the Act. Things that happened in your career years ago should certainly have no bearing on a decision as to whether you presently are fit for duty. And yet it would seem that the board took precisely such history into account in ruling you unfit."

The two old friends sat in the large, commodious law office of Ben Butler in an elegant, three-story building just off Wall Street.

There, with his son, William Howard Allen Butler, he engaged quietly and most rewardingly in the practice of corporate law.

Ben had aged badly. He was thick and looked nervous and ill, though his manner was as soft and gracious as ever. His hair stood out in wild gray tufts above his high forehead and served to further emphasize his long, pointed jaw. His narrow nose above thin lips gave him a look of severity, but Uriah knew this to be misleading: this was a kind, quiet man, devoted to his family and his church, and loyal beyond any duty of his profession to his clients.

"You say you have just returned from the capital, Uriah. Tell me what else you determined about this board, and its work."

"'The Board of Fifteen,' as it is known, was composed of the following"—Uriah took a slip of paper from his coat pocket to refresh his memory—"Captains William B. Shubrick, Matthew Calbraith Perry, Charles McCauley, C. K. Stribling, and Abraham Bigelow. I am acquainted with several of the captains, one or two of the commanders, and none of the lieutenants. The board was appointed early in June 1855 and commenced its secret deliberations on June 20. It continued to meet daily until July 26, when it submitted its infernal black list to Secretary Dobbin.

"The names, with no other supporting data or reasons for inclusion on the list, were then passed on to President Pierce, who signed his approval. The list included 201 names of officers said to be incapacitated for further duty. Of this total, the board recommended that 49 be dismissed from the service, that 81 be retired on furlough pay, and that the remaining 71 be retired on leave-of-absence pay."

"Would you explain the distinction to me, please?" asked Butler.

"A retirement on leave-of-absence pay is a retirement on full pay and is designed for officers deemed to have served well and with fidelity. There were 14 captains so designated, among them my old and dear friends, Commodores Charles Stewart and Thomas ap Catesby Jones and Charlie Skinner, now a commodore. There were nine other captains removed from the active list and designated as 'reserved on furlough,' which carries an allowance of one-half pay.

And, finally, there were three captains designated simply as unfit for duty and ordered dropped from the service, with no further pay. They were John P. Zantzinger, William Ramsey, and myself. There were, of course, several commanders, lieutenants, and sailing masters also cashiered in the same fashion. Interestingly, one of the dismissed lieutenants was a Lawrence Pennington, an officer that I suspended from duty for drunkenness aboard the *Vandalia* in '39. Yet my cruise on the *Vandalia* was probably among the things this board held against me."

"And you say this Board of Fifteen met in secret throughout and gave you and the other officers on the list no chance whatever to be told of their concerns about you, or to answer in your defense?"

"That is precisely true, Ben. And I'm not the only one on the list who is fighting back. Washington is full of talk that many officers are preparing to challenge this cruel and unjust action. There is talk of lawsuits galore."

Butler put his fingers to his lips and sat thoughtfully for a long time. Uriah wanted to comment further, but he knew that his friend was running the legal ramifications of the case through his mind. This was no time to interrupt him.

"No," came Butler's soft voice finally. "I don't think a judicial remedy is the best answer. One can always seek equity in a court of law, of course; that is every citizen's right. But the navy will argue that its internal governance is an administrative matter and that it must be free to work its own ship, as it were. No, I think a faster and much more effective remedy could be gained in the Congress."

"How?" asked Uriah.

"By persuading the Congress that an injustice has been perpetrated in its name and to rectify this by passing amendatory legislation."

"You mean—to cancel the action of this board?"

Butler slowly shook his head. "I doubt that Congress would have the courage to do that. After all, they passed the Act to appoint this board in the first place and they don't want to look like fools. But

I think they might be persuaded to require that each officer dismissed from the service be given the right to a proper hearing. In other words, the navy would be forced to decide each case on its merits, rather than in this slapdash manner that has been done."

"Then I would have a chance for vindication?"

"A chance, yes. But, Uriah, it would be a long and hard fight. You would have to spend a good deal of money. You would need outstanding legal counsel. You would need to locate and bring to the hearing witnesses who would testify in your behalf as to all the controversial elements in your long career. Merely locating such witnesses would be expensive in itself."

"I can afford it, Ben. I would have no reservations."

"It's not just the money, my friend. You would have to devote months, perhaps years to the preparation of your case. Everything else would have to wait. Your wife probably will become furious with you. Your business will suffer. Worst of all, you'll fill up with hope and yet face the possibility of a verdict against you. And that, I'm afraid, would end it, once and for all. I don't see much possibility of a successful appeal in this matter. Even with all the furor this board has caused, I'm sure the president will not dare to overrule a tribunal's verdict. In short, you would fight this great battle and then possibly find that it ends in naught but tragedy. That is the chance you would have to take."

"But it is a chance I must take, Ben. You bring me to the main question that brought me here today. Dare I hope that you will agree to be my counsel in this matter and to guide me in this long fight? I pray that you will say yes."

Butler sighed, stood up, and walked to the window. He looked out at the traffic passing in the street below for several silent minutes, then turned back to Uriah.

"I did not doubt that you came here to ask me that, Uriah," he said. "I'm flattered, of course, that you would want me to lead your defense in a matter that means so very much to you. But I don't see how I could do it. In two months I shall be sixty years old. I have cut my law practice to the bone. Since Harriet died two years ago, my own health has not been good. I tire easily. I do not feel strong. I have been staying on here only to see my son Allen established in this practice. It is my intention to retire in the very near future. Surely there are others as well qualified as myself to help you."

Uriah felt disappointment surge through him. "There is no one in whom I have greater faith, Ben, than you. No one whom I respect more, as a lawyer and as a man. I have talked about this at great length with John Dix and also with Senator Crittenden of Kentucky, who has been most friendly to me. They warned me that I must have a lawyer who knows Washington City, who knows the way the government works, and who knows many officials there. There is no one else with your qualifications, Ben. I beg you to reconsider."

"If 'knowledge of Washington officials' is a way of saying 'political influence,'" Butler said with a smile, "I am afraid you would find me wanting. I left the Democratic Party recently, you know, and now side with the new Republican Party. I suspect that my former colleagues regard me now with loathing."

"It's not your influence that I need, Ben. It's your character, your integrity. I know why you bolted from the Democratic Party. I was among the crowd in City Hall Park last year when you spoke out against the repeal of the Missouri Compromise and against the so-called Kansas-Nebraska Act introduced by Stephen Douglas and his cohorts to replace it. It is bad enough that history has bestowed slavery on our South; we should never allow it to spread to the western territories. It is because you are the man you are—one who would leave his party for his principles—that I want you as my lawyer. For my case also involves questions of human dignity and liberty under our laws. It is because I am a Jew that all this trouble has befallen me."

"Uriah, are you certain of that? Are you quite certain that religious prejudice against you has led to all this? Have you evidence?" Butler quite sternly pointed his finger at Uriah as he asked the questions.

"Evidence? Not much. But I will swear on the flag of my country, which I love more than life itself, that this is the real issue in my case, as it has been throughout my navy life. I am a Jew, hated, despised, even feared. And for them—these rascals in the navy who stand in the shadows and do their dirty work—I am unfit to be in their midst. This is the real reason. Ben, I beg you—help me to fight this evil! If they do it to me, they will do it to others after me. It will never end. It does not belong in the United States. It must be stopped!"

"Uriah, let me think it over some more and speak to my son," Ben said after a long silence. "I'll give you my answer as soon as possible."

···

New York City
Tuesday, October 23, 1855

My dear Uriah:

After prayerful contemplation and thorough discussion of the matter with my sons and daughters, I have come at last to the conclusion that I must take your case. My conscience will permit me to do no other. A great wrong has been committed and I shall do all in my power to set it aright.

We have two tasks immediately before us:

First, I ask you to notify all your relatives, friends, and acquaintances, far and wide, of what has happened to you. Send them a copy of Secretary Dobbin's letter announcing your dismissal. We want them to contact their congressmen and urge that you receive justice. I am informed that many of the 201 officers on the list are doing the same and members of Congress are being besieged with requests for corrective legislation.

Second, we must begin work immediately on a memorial to Congress asking a remedy. I suggest that you plan to report to my office at 10:00 A.M. on Friday next and we shall commence to prepare such a memorial.

Sincerely yours,
Benjamin P. Butler

●●●

New York City, 1857

"But damn it all, Ben, this delay is intolerable! I thought it would all have been settled by now!"

They sat in the gilded bar of the Astor House and looked out upon the throngs of people milling about on Broadway. Ben carefully had requested a secluded corner table, for he knew that Uriah was agitated and impatient.

Ben Butler slowly sipped his glass of claret. He well could understand Uriah's irritation, but the fact is that they had made good progress. In January, Congress approved an amendment to the 1855 Act, "To Promote the Efficiency of the Navy," based on Uriah's campaign in concert with others. The amendatory act provided that any officer who had been dropped, furloughed, or retired by the Board of Fifteen could demand and receive a full-scale court of inquiry to judge his case. At these proceedings both sides would have the right to summon and examine witnesses under oath. And in April, the new secretary of the navy, Isaac Toucey, appointed the first judges to the Naval Court of Inquiry created for the purpose of making such investigations. But here it was July, and not one case had been tried.

"Uriah, you should know Washington by now and how it works. They make molasses look like a racehorse. It is the nature of officials to fiddle around, and that's what they are doing: fiddling around."

"But the court was appointed in April and was charged by

Toucey to begin as soon as possible! Why have we heard nothing from them?"

"For one thing, there have been some maneuverings concerning the court. I do not know who is behind it or why it has been done. For some reason, Captain Lawrence Kearney was detached from the court soon after he was named its president. And then, to further complicate things, Captain John Newton died a few weeks ago. Captain George Storer is the only one of the three judges remaining and apparently will be named president."

"Good God."

"I did all I could, Uriah, to make known to the Department your eagerness for your hearing. But you must remember that yours will be only one of many hearings. The court, whenever its membership is determined, will have its hands full. We must wait our turn. We dare not put pressure on them to be placed at the head of the list; it would most certainly prejudice our case. We must simply wait our turn."

"Ben, have you any idea when we can expect to be heard? Can you give me any hope?"

"My best guess, based on what little I could pick up around the Navy Department, would be sometime late in the year, most likely by Christmas, I should think."

"Very well, Ben," Uriah sighed, pulling out his big gold watch and studying the time. "I must be leaving soon. I promised Virginia I'd be home early. She is sad because all her friends have boasted to her of attending Laura Keene's Varieties Theater, and we cannot because we are still in mourning. Plays and concerts are not possible for us yet."

It was only six months since Fanny Lopez, Uriah's youngest sister and Virginia's mother, had died after several months of illness from her weak heart. He and Virginia were observing the traditional year of mourning for her.

"Your little wife does well then, I trust?" Ben asked compassionately.

"Yes, with the aid of New York's merchants and dressmakers,

whom she feels to have been ordained by God to restore her happiness. Her latest rage is this—what is he called?—this . . . interior designer, George Platt. She is wheedling me to hire him to redecorate our house. I resist with all my strength, though I know that sooner or later, she'll have her way. Now that her spirit has returned, she is like a dithering child, casting my money everywhere she goes."

Ben nodded, understandingly, and a broad smile came to his usually solemn lips.

Uriah also smiled, despite himself. "She keeps my life light and full of noise and excitement. And she keeps my mind off my old troubles—at least for a time. She prevents me, I must confess, from feeling old. If the pace does not kill me, I probably will live another forty years."

Uriah frowned as he thought again of the lack of developments in Washington. "The waiting gets harder to bear as each additional week passes. Ben, you will let me know as soon as you pick up any news? As soon as there is even a whisper of when we will go to court?"

"I promise, Uriah. The instant I hear anything, I will have a messenger on his way to you with the news in hand. I promise faithfully."

23

It began in the most perfunctory way: Commodore Storer softly rapped his gavel one time and then directed the judge advocate, Robert R. Little, to step forward.

"Judge Advocate," Storer directed, "kindly read the charge to this court."

Little, a small, bespectacled man, cleared his throat and read from a paper in his hand:

"This document is addressed to Commodore George W. Storer and is from the Navy Department and bears the date of November 9, 1857. It reads as follows: 'Sir, Captain Uriah P. Levy, a captain in the Navy, dropped by the operation of the Act of February 23, 1855, having made a written request in conformity with the Act of January 16, 1857, entitled "An Act to Amend An Act to Promote the Efficiency of the Navy," the Court of Inquiry of which you are president is hereby directed to investigate the physical, mental, professional and moral fitness of the said Uriah P. Levy for the Navy service and to transmit the records of its proceedings and finding in his case to this Department. I am respectfully your obedient servant.' The letter is signed by Isaac Toucey, secretary of the navy."

The little hearing room on the uppermost floor of the three-story Navy Building was dusty and hot, even though the air outside was chilly on this November morning. The several rows of seats for spectators were almost empty, save for two or three Department clerks watching out of curiosity before beginning their office duties and a couple of newspaper reporters. Virginia sat directly behind Uriah in the front row of chairs. Jonas had indicated he would be on hand but had not yet arrived.

Uriah sat at a table with his counsel, Ben Butler, Philip Phillips, and T. M. Blount, an associate of Phillips. The judge advocate had a comparable table across the way. The court's clerk had his own little desk, piled high with tablets of paper, fresh pens, and spare bottles of ink, at which that worthy noted down in some code comprehensible only to him every word that was uttered.

On the dais, behind a long desk that commanded the room, sat the members of the court: Captains Storer, Louis M. Goldsborough, and J. B. Montgomery. Each wore the formal dress uniform of his rank. Their faces wore a look of gravity, in keeping with the importance and difficulty of the task confronting them.

"May it please the court?" Ben Butler had risen and addressed the bench.

"Yes, sir?" acknowledged Storer, one eyebrow raised quizzically.

"Sir, I am B. F. Butler, chief counsel for Captain Levy. We regret that Captain Levy finds it necessary to submit a challenge to the membership of Captain Goldsborough on this court."

"State the reason for this challenge, if you please, Mr. Butler."

"Commodore, Captain Levy submits this challenge on the grounds that Captain Goldsborough is junior to him in point of service in rank, and also on the grounds that Captain Goldsborough was promoted to the rank of captain by action of the so-called Board of Fifteen, that is, the very same board formed under the Act of February 28, 1855, which caused the retirement of more than two hundred officers of the navy, among them this selfsame Captain U. P. Levy. On these grounds, sir, we respectfully challenge Captain Goldsborough's membership on this court and request that he be removed from this court and another member named in his place."

Commodore Storer sighed and then nodded curtly. He conferred in a quick whisper with the other two captains and then turned back to the hearing room. "Very well," he said. "This challenge is deserving of the court's deliberation. This court of inquiry will stand in recess until two days from now—Saturday, November 14—at which time we will announce our decision on this challenge. This court is now recessed."

And so it ended, seven minutes after it had begun. His day in court, for which Uriah had waited for more than two years, had come at last and, before more than a handful of breaths had been taken, had sputtered to a halt.

When the august members of the Court of Inquiry entered the hearing room two days later, Uriah knew his challenge had been successful. As the three captains took their places behind the long desk on the raised platform, it became obvious to all that a new face was among them and that the newcomer took the center chair.

"Who is he?" asked Ben, turning quickly to Uriah and whispering urgently.

"Commodore Lawrence Kearney, now of the New York Navy Yard," Uriah answered. "I think we have won our point."

Commodore Kearney tapped his gavel on the desk and the room immediately stilled. There were a few more spectators sitting in the rows of chairs today. A newspaper reporter pulled a sheaf of papers from his pocket and a sharpened lead and prepared to take notes on the proceedings. Jonas was present today also and sat with Virginia behind Uriah and his attorneys.

"The challenge submitted by Captain Levy to the membership of Captain Goldsborough on this court," Kearney announced, "has been carefully considered by the court and it has been upheld. Captain Goldsborough therefore has been removed from the court. Secretary Toucey has reappointed me as a member of this court and in addition has designated me as president of the court. Captains Storer and Montgomery will serve as the other members. We will dispense with the reading of Mr. Toucey's directive to me, unless there is objection."

While the necessary oaths were taken, Uriah had the time to study Commodore Kearney, whose role would be so important during the days ahead. Small of stature, yet husky and powerful, Kearney was known to Uriah mostly by reputation, though they had met and briefly conversed at navy gatherings over the years. Kearney was highly regarded by his fellow officers, as much for his skill as a diplomat as for his seamanship.

Perhaps it was merely intuitive on his part, but Uriah felt greatly comforted that Kearney sat in the president's chair.

"Mr. President," Ben Butler said in his soft, firm voice, "on behalf of Captain Levy, we respectfully request that the government take the initiative in this inquiry."

Again Kearney quickly turned to his fellows and received their nodded approval. He turned back to the room and replied, "Your request is granted. Judge Advocate, please begin the presentation of the government's case."

Judge Advocate Little caught up a great mass of papers from his table and approached the bench. Now, finally, the Navy Department would be forced to state its reasons for denying this man his honored rank and consigning him to oblivion.

"I will begin, if it please the court," Little said, "by producing evidence concerning an encounter by United States Gunboat No. 158, otherwise known as the *Revenge*, under the command of Captain U. P. Levy, with the Spanish ship *Voluntaria*, Captain De Oligorius De Los Ciretos, on January 7, 1823. Following that, I intend to produce evidence concerning a series of courts-martial, in various years, in which Captain Levy was the accused."

"There we go," Ben muttered, "just as we expected." He rose quickly.

"Mr. President, if it pleases the court, I should like to reserve the right, until after the judge advocate has presented the evidence to which he refers, to submit my objection to the use of such evidence in this proceeding."

"Very well, Mr. Butler," Kearney replied. "You may reserve such right of objection. Please proceed, Mr. Little."

And so it began, the dreary recitation by the judge advocate of the long record of Uriah's troubles in the navy, beginning with the brief altercation between *Gunboat No. 158*, the first ship commanded by Levy, and the Spanish sloop-of-war *Voluntaria* off Cuba, investigated by a court of inquiry in 1823, and then going back further, to 1816, the dispute between Uriah and Lieutenant Francis Bond on the *Franklin* and the subsequent court-martial. Each of the six old courts-martial was reprised in as fine detail as the records permitted; each charge and specification was carefully read, each verdict loudly enunciated. Little read the records in a monotone, his voice taking on color and emotion only in those passages where Uriah was found guilty of the charges against him. The reading continued through the last court-martial stemming from the tar-and-feather punishment of the boy on the *Vandalia*.

The reading proceeded without interruption, except for a few occasions when Ben Butler, who was closely following his own records of the courts-martial, felt that Little had been remiss in giving a full history of what had transpired. A time or two, the judge advocate somehow neglected to mention that the other officer involved, countercharged by Uriah in a dispute, also was found guilty and also was punished by the court. Ben quickly rose at each such moment and insisted the record give full account.

The long, detailed recounting of the records by the judge advocate had taken most of the day. Ben Butler rose again to state his client's objections to the admission of all the records introduced by the judge advocate. The 1823 court inquiry findings on the *Voluntaria* incident had been reviewed by the president, who had decided that a court-martial was not warranted. As for the six courts-martial—the crux of the judge advocate's case—to cite them as evidence is illegal because it relates to collateral facts and is therefore inadmissible under the laws of evidence. The only question before the court, according to the law, Ben argued, is Uriah Levy's present fitness for the naval service as a captain, the rank he attained in 1844 with the approval of Congress.

Commodore Kearney announced that the court would give the objection its due consideration and adjourned the hearing until the following morning. The judge advocate stepped forward to protest that he had not been given a chance to answer the objection, but Kearney put up a warning hand.

"In due time, Judge Advocate," he said firmly. "You will have your say in the morning. We stand adjourned."

Judge Advocate Little took only a moment to respond to Ben's objection of the previous day. "There is no doubt," Little said, "that a candidate for office or high rank who has many times been tried and convicted on very grave offenses must stand the examination of such records, for they bear strongly on his fitness. Retired officers who have *not* been court-martialed have used the fact to be restored to service. Such records do most certainly affect the question of his present fitness."

The members of the court retired briefly to an anteroom to consider both the objection and the government's response.

"Can we win this dispute?" Uriah asked Ben.

"Most unlikely that they'll sustain us," Ben answered. "Those records make up most of their case against you. They'll have a hard time proving you're incompetent, though they'll probably produce a few witnesses to swear that you always were. Without those records, though, they have a lost cause and they know it. The captains are not lawyers, and my claims of illegal evidence fell on deaf ears, I fear. But I never expected to win this little skirmish; it was necessary to get our objection on the record."

Returning to the dias, Kearney pounded his gavel one time and quickly announced the result of the captains' conference: "The decision of the court is that the said records are competent evidence in this investigation, as offered by the judge advocate. Gentlemen, let us proceed. Judge Advocate, call your first witness."

"I call Commodore Matthew Calbraith Perry!" Little announced with authority.

"Well, they are hauling out their big guns right at the start," Ben remarked. The famous Commodore Perry, fresh from his triumph in opening Japan to trade with America, was a younger brother of the heroic and still-mourned Commodore Oliver Hazard Perry.

As Perry walked to the witness stand and turned to take the oath, Uriah had a chance to study him and to wonder what he might have to say against him. Uriah hardly knew the man, although they had served together briefly somewhere; he was not certain where. What, then, would Matthew Calbraith Perry possibly say against him?

"Mr. President, if it please the court," Judge Advocate Little said, "I plan to call a series of witnesses—Commodore Perry being the first—and will put to said witnesses the following series of questions: First, how long have you known U. P. Levy? Have you ever served with him—when, where, and how long, and state your relative positions. Second, from such acquaintance with him, state whether his temper and disposition are such as in your judgment to promote good order and discipline in the service. Third, state whether you have observed him sufficiently to enable you to determine his most prominent characteristics. If so, what are they? And fourth, do you know what his general reputation is in the navy in respect to those qualities of mind, character, and temperament necessary to ensure proper respect for the rank and position of captain in the navy? If so, what is it?"

"Very well, Judge Advocate," Kearney answered from the bench. "And at the conclusion of each witness's testimony, I will ask the clerk to read back the testimony to the witness and hear the witness pronounce the record 'correct' before we proceed with the hearing."

The questions were put to Commodore Perry, who testified that he had served with Uriah on the *North Carolina* in 1824. Beyond that, he had not much to offer, except the opinion that Uriah was "nothing remarkable, rather impulsive and eccentric and fond of speaking of himself and his professional requirements." Perry then added, "By the fact that he has not been employed for many years by the government in the position to which his grade would entitle him, I am led to the inevitable conclusion that he has thus been rendered unfit for the proper performance of the duties of a captain in the United States Navy."

As soon as Perry's last word had left his mouth, Ben Butler was on his feet to lodge a vigorous objection. "Instead of testifying to my client's general reputation in the navy, as called for in the question, Perry gives his own personal opinion or conclusions. While admitting his own knowledge is meager, he gives his opinion founded on supposed incidents in his career. The uncalled-for opinion of the witness is founded in part on the navy's nonemployment of U. P. Levy because he does not know the reason for it."

Kearney had a whispered consultation with his fellows, Storer and Montgomery, and then turned back to face Butler. "It by no means follows that an answer of a witness is not admissible evidence because it may have been given under a misapprehension of the question," Kearney responded. "A part of said answer was called for by the question. A witness often misunderstands and goes beyond a question, and this often obviates the necessity of putting in another question, but it is not necessarily a reason for excluding that portion of the answer that is not called for. If the extra material is unimportant or irrelevant, the court so considers it in estimating its weight. Objection overruled."

Ben sat down and leaned over to Uriah. "That was the biggest pile of gibberish I've ever heard. The man is out of his depth in the legality of this case. The most serious thing is that we lost the argument."

"It was important?"

"It means that they're going to allow the government to present a parade of famous officers, most of whom hardly know you, and they're going to say bad things about you based on their personal opinions, not on the facts. It's utter nonsense! Let's just pray that it doesn't harm us too much."

The government witnesses continued: a succession of commodores and captains, most of whom had not laid eyes on Uriah in years and never had known him well.

Commodore Silas H. Stringham, who had served with Uriah on the *Cyane* in the Mediterranean in 1825: "His temper and disposition are not such as to promote good order and discipline. He was very vain, interfered in conversations, made statements not credited as fact. He was sent home by the commodore because he was so disagreeable to the other officers. He was always in difficulty in the ships he was on. His mind did not seem to be well balanced. I did not consider him much a practical seaman."

Captain Charles McCauley, who had spent six months with Uriah on the frigate *United States* in 1818 and had not seen him since: "He was generally disliked on the ship."

Ben quickly rose to remind the court that McCauley, too, had been one of the captains on the Board of Fifteen who had voted to dismiss Uriah from the service and therefore would be most unlikely to say anything in his defense on this day.

Commodore William B. Shubrick, who had taken command of the West Indies Squadron when Uriah brought the *Vandalia* back to Pensacola and who shortly after took the ship away from him: "As an example of his incompetence to command, I was obliged to remove the senior lieutenant of his ship because of their constant bickering. His midshipmen complain he made them do duty not proper for them. He performed his duties satisfactorily, but his reputation was low."

Again Butler rose to remind the court that Commodore Shubrick also had sat on the Board of Fifteen and was this day merely justifying and defending his actions as a member of that board.

Next came Commodore Eli A. F. Lavalette, who had commanded the frigate *Congress* in the late war with Mexico and had played major roles in the captures of Guaymas and Mazatlan: "I knew U. P. Levy for about a year prior to 1818 on the frigate *United States*. His temper and disposition did not promote good order. He was quarrelsome and insubordinate. His reputation is low."

Lavalette was forced to make one interesting concession during Ben's brief cross-examination. Yes, he, Commodore Lavalette, had risen to his present esteemed rank from a beginning as a sailing master. And, yes, it was quite true that navy officers who had entered the service in this fashion did encounter quite a bit of prejudice from their fellow officers owing to their humble origin as a master.

Captain G. J. Van Brunt was the next government witness: "I have known U. P. Levy since 1821. We spent six months together on the *Spark*. His temper and disposition were not conducive to good order. His reputation was not good."

Captain William Mervine, who had commanded the 44-gun frigate *Savannah* in the Mexican War and had led a party of marines and sailors in the capture of Monterrey, was the government's last witness. This worthy testified that he had known Uriah since 1822, when they had served together for three or four months aboard the *Cyane*. Then he brought wide smiles to the faces of Uriah and his counsel when he testified, in response to the judge advocate's questions, "I don't know Mr. Levy's reputation, but I have heard rumors of petty, trifling matters. I know nothing of my own knowledge to his disadvantage as an officer and a gentleman."

The exasperated look on the judge advocate's face even brought a small smile to the face of Commodore Kearney, who struggled to retain his judicial equanimity.

"The government rests its case, Mr. President," announced the judge advocate.

"So there it is," Ben whispered to Uriah, "that is their case. A bunch of witnesses who haven't seen you in thirty years or more, relying on hearsay and their obviously decrepit memories. Their case rises and falls on the old courts-martial. That is really all they have."

The week's recess requested by the defense and granted by the court had been put to good use by Uriah's legal staff. Telegrams and, in a few cases, personal messengers were sent to cities and naval bases all along the eastern coast to gather in the many witnesses who had agreed to speak in Uriah's behalf. Each of the witnesses arrived as promised, and now the defense stood ready to offer its own case.

When Commodore Charles Stewart came forward to take his

oath, he let no one in the hearing room doubt for a moment that they were in the presence of a great man. He walked with the easy hauteur of one who knows his high station in history and who is quite aware that everyone else also knows. He had been a captain in the navy for more than fifty years, since the early years of the century when there had been only a dozen or so of such rank. This was the man who had fought in the Mediterranean under the immortal Edward Preble. This was the man who had commanded the great old frigate *Constitution* in February 1815 and took her into courageous battle against the British frigate *Cyane* and sloop of war *Levant* and handily defeated them both. For this, Congress had presented him with a gold medal and sword, and he proudly wore them as he strode into this grimy little hearing room in the federal city.

"Mr. President," Ben Butler began, when Commodore Stewart had been seated in the witness chair, "I will ask each witness for the defense the following questions: First, are you acquainted with U. P. Levy, late a captain in the navy? If yes, how long have you known him? Second, has he ever served with you? If yes, when, where, and how long, and what were your relative positions? Third, from what you have known of him, state whether you believe him physically, mentally, professionally, and morally competent to perform the duties of a captain in the navy and fit for said service. Fourth, during your intercourse with him, did you ever discover any such temper or disposition as was calculated to impair his efficiency or mar the harmony of the service?"

Commodore Stewart testified that he had known Uriah since 1816, when Uriah had served under him for two years aboard the *Franklin*.

"Commodore, how would you rate his service under you?"

"He performed his professional duties to my perfect satisfaction."

"Do you think Levy physically, mentally, morally, professionally competent to perform the duties of a captain?"

"Certainly I do. I can't think otherwise of him, having no knowledge of any deficiency in that respect."

"Would you, then, be willing today to give him a command under you?"

"I should have no objection whatever to giving him command of a ship in my squadron or, for that matter, my flagship."

The judge advocate cross-examined with alacrity and courtesy; he knew that this was no witness to harry or badger.

"Sir," he began respectfully, "do you believe Levy to be competent to hold a captaincy today?"

"I think," Stewart answered, "that he is just as competent today as he was in 1817 when I recommended him for promotion to lieutenant. I have never had reason to regret that recommendation."

The judge advocate hastily withdrew.

Butler had one more question on redirect examination. "Commodore, the complaint has been made against Mr. Levy that while in command of the *Vandalia*, he gave his midshipmen improper duties . . . this apparently referring to his requiring them occasionally to row a ship's boat to cause them to be familiar with the use of oars. I ask you: Is this not done in the navy?"

"Some commanders do it, some do not," Stewart replied, rather testily, as if tired of the ignorance of lubbers. "It is hardly a rare practice."

The next witness, Commodore Isaac Mayo, testified that he first met Uriah in the War of 1812, but his only service with him lasted about a month in 1825 aboard the *North Carolina*. He related his memory of that time: "I had returned from recruiting, had been gone about six to eight months, and upon rejoining the ship some of the junior officers asked me if I knew that Levy had been ordered to take passage in the ship. They told me their object was to keep him out of the wardroom. I asked what they had against Levy. They replied that he was a damned Jew, to which I answered that if that was all, I would certainly vote for his admission to the mess. The officers who spoke against him were marine officers Carter and Randolph and a Lieutenant Griffin. Levy took his meals alone aboard the ship and generally retired. He was not a general favorite, some of the officers kept aloof from him, and he did from them. To look at him, I would say that he is physically and mentally competent; professionally, I have never heard it doubted. I considered him a good seaman and a brave man."

Lieutenant Peter Turner, who had been a midshipman on the *Cyane* and had served with Uriah from November 1825 to July 1827, was next called to the stand. Under Butler's gentle prodding, he described at length an incident at Rio de Janeiro in which Uriah had come to the aid of another *Cyane* midshipman when he was attacked near the ship by Brazilians. He also recalled the offer to him of a high post in the Brazilian Navy by Emperor Dom Pedro, and Uriah's ringing affirmation that he would rather be a cabin boy in the Navy of the United States than serve any other nation.

Ben touched only lightly on these incidents, for he knew that they would have little influence on the court, except as reassurances of Uriah's bravery and patriotism. Instead he questioned Lieutenant Turner closely on Uriah's leadership and seamanship and asked him to cite evidence of this.

"There was a whale boat built for a gig for the captain," Turner recalled. "Lieutenant Levy modeled her, planned her, and superintended the work. It was a work of difficulty and one that required knowledge and skill. Our carpenters knew little about it and were dependent entirely upon Lieutenant Levy's knowledge in everything except the labor, even to getting the pieces, picking up one in one place and another in another from different vessels."

"Was the boat a staunch and valuable one?"

"So far as I can recollect, she was a very excellent one."

"Could such a boat have been procured at Rio, or not?"

"At that time, not in my opinion. From my knowledge of whale boats, she was a much better one than whale boats usually are."

"You would consider Mr. Levy qualified as a seaman, then?"

"I consider him very well qualified."

When he returned to his chair, and while the judge advocate conducted a cursory cross-examination of Turner, Ben leaned over to Uriah: "Tomorrow we'll call John Moffat from the *Vandalia*. His testimony is exceedingly important to us. All your other troubles happened many years ago and could easily be dismissed as the peccadilloes of a headstrong young man. But the court-martial involving the *Vandalia* is more damning—it happened less than twenty years ago and you were commanding the vessel. That is their most potent ammunition. We must try to defuse it with Moffat."

"Mr. President," Ben Butler intoned, "I call to the witness stand Lieutenant John N. Moffat."

Moffat looked nervous, ill at ease. In fact he had a slightly unhealthy appearance. Uriah remembered from their time together on the *Vandalia* that Moffat had seemed always to walk a razor's edge between calm and hysteria; he seemed to have only a light touch on his emotions. Yet he had been a capable and dutiful officer and unquestioned in his loyalty. The perspiration that gleamed on Moffat's forehead today was familiar to Uriah: he had seen it numerous times on the quarterdeck. Yet the man always had come through and performed well in moments of crisis.

"Lieutenant Moffat, please describe your acquaintance with Uriah P. Levy."

"I was a passed midshipman aboard the *Vandalia*, Mr. Levy commanding, from October 1838 until November 1839. I served as acting lieutenant and sailing master during that time."

"And during that period of service, did the *Vandalia*, under Mr. Levy's command, sail upon cruises?"

"She did, sir. The first cruise was in the winter season off Tampico, the Rio Bravo, Vera Cruz, and Laguna de Terminos. The second cruise lasted about three months and was between Galveston and the Southwest Pass of the Mississippi, during which time we entered no port."

"Lieutenant, how would you describe the efficiency of the *Vandalia*, under Mr. Levy's command?"

"The ship was efficient in every particular," Moffat asserted, his voice now strong and forthright, his unease apparently subsiding. "He was very much jealous to secure order and efficiency. His orders were very stringent in regard to the officers being exceedingly particular in reference to all matters concerning the duties of the ship. He was perfectly temperate and, so far as I could judge from personal observation, scrupulously moral."

"Was he greatly concerned with the training and education of the midshipmen on the *Vandalia*?"

"Indeed he was. He ordered the purser to furnish the midshipmen with quadrants, Bowditch's navigators, and other needful articles. He watched after their training constantly and ordered them to periodically man the ship's boats so that they would be well-acquainted with the problems of moving a boat by dint of sweeps."

Moffat then was asked to give his own memory of the near-disaster at Galveston, when the *Vandalia* had dragged her anchor. It was Moffat who had first discovered the crisis.

"We came to anchor in the evening about 6 or 7 p.m. in six and a half fathoms of water. At 8 p.m. he sent for me and directed that I should proceed into Galveston Island by daylight for the purpose of obtaining observations for the longitude and latitude of the beacon, or lighthouse. It was incorrectly laid down on the chart. His desire was to have it established correctly, for its application to a chart that I was then projecting by his order. I was consequently excused from watch.

"Sometime after midnight, the vessel began to pitch very heavily, and my anxiety in regard to her holding on to her anchorage became so great that I went on deck. The weather was threatening, and there was a heavy groundswell. I found the man in the chains asleep and his line drawing ahead of the vessel. I soon discovered that she was dragging and was at that time in five fathoms of water. I gave the alarm; all hands were called. The commander, Mr. Levy, took charge of the deck, and while they were heaving up the stream anchor, he put the fore and aft sails upon her. When the anchor was up and down, he gave her the courses and sent the men aloft to reef topsails. This conduct on the occasion was prompt and energetic and, but for that, there is every probability that she would soon have gone ashore on a two-and-a-half-fathom bank in close proximity to us."

"Lieutenant Moffat, would you say that this display of leadership by U. P. Levy was unusual of him, or would you call it typical?"

"He was always cool, collected, prompt, and efficient in every emergency and always was on deck in such cases."

"One more thing, Lieutenant. Please state whether or not he manifested avidity in the acquisition of nautical information, not only for the benefit of the ship, but for that of the naval service in general."

"He did."

"Please look at the lithographed chart, marked O, now shown you. Is it a copy of a chart in the preparation of which you took part? If so, does it correctly set forth the soundings and observations made by order of Captain Levy? State particularly how far the matters contained in it were new."

Moffat looked carefully at the chart for several minutes before answering. More than most witnesses, he was ever mindful of the fact that he was under solemn oath and he was determined to avoid even the slightest error in his statements. Finally he raised his head again and, upon receiving a nod to proceed from Ben, answered, "The original of this chart was made by me. It does set forth correctly the soundings and observations made by order of Captain Levy. The latitude and longitude of Galveston Port in the charts then in use was some thirty-five miles out, as near as I can recollect. The two-and-a-half-fathom bank to the eastward northerly of Galveston was not known to exist. The longitude of the Rio Bravo was also erroneous."

The judge advocate came forward for the cross-examination with a determined set to his jaw. This had been a damaging witness for the prosecution: an obviously intelligent young officer had testified most positively as to the efficiency of the *Vandalia* under Levy's command, and also as to the commander's personal coolness and skill in time of danger. Little could tell that the three members of the court had been impressed. He must do something to counteract this witness; he must at least gain a draw.

"In speaking of Mr. Levy's conduct during the time he commanded the *Vandalia*, do you mean that his conduct and deportment were always such as should, in your judgment, characterize a commander in the navy?" the judge advocate asked.

"On all occasions except one, I did so consider it."

"Was his ordinary deportment or manner, in your judgment, free from objection in one exercising command in the navy?"

Moffat swallowed once or twice. He obviously was debating with himself. Then he answered: "His manner was peculiar, but I can't say that it was objectionable. It might be so to those who were hunting up objections."

Uriah felt his face redden. His manner peculiar? How so? Why did they not force Moffat to explain that remark?

The judge advocate moved in quickly to exploit the slight opening that the witness had offered him: "Was his ordinary deportment when in the performance of duty such as you would approve?"

"It was."

"Was his deportment always such as you would approve, except on the one occasion you before mentioned?"

"Sometimes I did not think it was so, but the occasions were rare and generally from a misconception. When I first knew him, his manner while on duty struck me unpleasantly. That wore off when I knew him better."

"In what respect was his manner peculiar?"

"I cannot answer—save in regard to peculiarities of voice and manner."

Uriah felt his stomach quiver, then subside. Obviously Moffat could not back his comment about peculiarities with any concrete examples. Uriah often had been teased by fellow officers about his rather high-pitched command voice on a quarterdeck. He was certain that was what Moffat had in mind.

"What was the one occasion you mentioned? I do not ask for the details, but a statement of the occasion."

"It was the indecorous punishment of a boy on board the vessel, ordered and superintended by himself."

Little smiled. He had scored a telling point. This, after all, had been the reason for Uriah's most recent court-martial. And even this sincere young lieutenant, who defended his former commander with an open heart, could not justify this bizarre action aboard the *Vandalia*. Little had deftly succeeded in bringing the attention of the court back to the record of courts-martial. He had also, through Moffat, renewed the charge that Levy had displayed an insensitivity ill befitting a commander by his method of punishing the boy. It was time to continue; he must not appear to gloat over his small victory.

"In the performance of ordinary duty, did he, in your judgment, exhibit familiarity with the duties pertaining to his rank?"

"He did."

"Was not his treatment of his officers frequently harsh and his manner to them unkind?"

"I can't say that it was, although I have known him to be very harsh on occasions when there was a presumed neglect of duty."

"Did he or did he not introduce unusual punishments on any other occasions than the one to which you have referred?"

"He did, that were *then* unusual."

"What were they?"

"They were numerous and various."

"Was there anything unusual in the arrangements ordered by him in respect to any of the appointments of the vessel?"

"There were no such unusual arrangements that I recollect. The guns were fitted as is usual. The only peculiarity I recollect about them was in their color, which was blue."

Little again smiled his tiny smile. He would not make the witness elaborate on this last comment. It was enough to see the surprised expressions, the raised eyebrows, on the faces of the three captains sitting in judgment. If there was to be explanation of the blue guns, let the defense counsel attend to that.

"I have no further questions, Mr. President," Little said softly and returned to his chair, quite satisfied that he had at least partially blunted the damage done earlier by Mr. Moffat.

"I have a few more questions on redirect examination, if it please the court," Ben said. He knew he must do something quickly to remove the onus from the now-familiar punishment given to John Thompson, the boy on the *Vandalia*.

"Did not Captain Levy," Ben asked, "while in command of the *Vandalia*, endeavor as far as practicable to dispense with punishment by the lash? Were not the various punishments to which you have referred intended by him, as you believe, as substitutes for the use of the lash?"

"Such was the case, although the lash was not abolished."

"Was not the amount of flogging on board the *Vandalia*, during the time you were there, less in proportion to other vessels in which you served about that time?"

"I never made a comparison and could not, therefore, answer directly to the question."

Ben sighed. *Why could not this man have given a straight answer? Why must he hedge so?* He would make one more effort, but he was certain that Moffat again would evade a definite response.

"Did not the fact of the small number of lashes inflicted on board the *Vandalia* while under Captain Levy's command attract notice on her final return to the U.S. and was it not commented on by the public press?"

"I did not return in the *Vandalia* and therefore do not know as to the comments of the press."

Commodore Kearney interrupted: "Mr. Butler, do you have many more questions for this witness?"

"A few, Mr. President," Ben said, still hoping to recover lost ground.

Kearney nodded. "Gentlemen," he said, "tomorrow is Thursday, November 26. Although we stand under no legal requirement to do so, I propose that we spend tomorrow in recess and give thanks for this nation and its manifold blessings. Many of your home states and mine have proclaimed this Thursday to be a day of giving thanks.

Therefore, unless I hear vehement objection to the contrary, I declare that this hearing shall now stand in recess and shall resume at 9 a.m. on the morning of Friday, two days hence."

Without waiting to hear any objections, Kearney loudly banged the gavel once, and the hearing was suspended.

"The man means 'adjourn,' not 'recess,'" Ben muttered as he began picking up his papers and stuffing them into his briefcase. "He should be more precise with his words if he is to preside over a court of inquiry."

On Friday, Lieutenant Moffat returned to the stand to answer a few more questions from Ben concerning the lack of efficiency and insubordination displayed by some officers on the *Vandalia* when Uriah first had taken command of the corvette. Finally Moffat was excused. As he left the stand, he gratefully wiped his still-glistening brow.

Next Ben called on a long procession of character witnesses to testify as to Uriah's fine qualities as they had known them. The parade of "good-sayers" was to continue all day and through the following day as well. As the first few witnesses testified, Uriah felt a glow of pleasure and a blush of embarrassment at such well-reputed men saying such fine things about him. But after a few such testimonials, he, along with all the others present, became frightfully bored with it all and found it increasingly difficult to sit through. He had to hear each eulogy twice, because after the witness testified, the president insisted that the clerk read his testimony back to him and be sure each word was as originally spoken.

"These things really have little relevance," Ben confided to Uriah during one such read-back, "and, as you can see, the members of the court are paying little heed. We are 'making a record,' to strengthen our presentation in case we have to eventually take an appeal into the civil courts."

Uriah's nephew, Asahel S. Levy, Isaac's son and now a New York attorney, was called to testify as to his uncle's unceasing efforts on behalf of the navy during the years of enforced idleness ashore. Asahel explained his own awareness of his uncle's generous nature: he had lived with Uriah for a time, and his education had largely been supported by him. He described the many articles Uriah had written on naval construction, naval discipline, and the abolition of corporal punishment—articles that had been published in newspapers in New York, Washington City, and Virginia. He described how Uriah had, at his own expense, lithographed and published navigation charts—at a cost of three hundred dollars or more per chart—and had inserted notices in navy and sailing journals that such charts could be obtained from him gratis upon request, and that many were requested. These were things of which Uriah was proud, and he was glad to have them known.

Uriah was suddenly moved by a name and a voice from his youth: Joseph Nones of Philadelphia, the ebullient youth who would hail him on the steps of Mikveh Israel, had followed Uriah to sea and then to the navy. Joe Nones had entered the navy as a midshipman in 1814 at the age of seventeen and had served as an aide to Henry Clay at the peace talks in Belgium. Later he went back to sea with Decatur's fleet in the Mediterranean and took part in the defeat of the Barbary States. He had left the navy in 1821 and became an importer in Philadelphia and later commissioner of deeds in New York City, but he retained a love for the navy and wrote many articles on naval history for the *Army and Navy Journal* and other historical and military publications.

Now gray of hair and beard, Joe Nones cast a warm, appreciative look at Uriah as he testified, "I have repeatedly conversed with officers of our navy respecting Uriah P. Levy, many of whom sailed with him. Generally they all spoke well and favorably of him as a lieutenant and captain, in all that pertains to those conditions. I have known him since our childhood. He is a man of undaunted courage and bravery. He is a true lover of his country; zealous for her honor, interests, and rights; and prompt to maintain the same."

• • •

"Mr. President, I call to the witness stand the Honorable George Bancroft."

There was a rustling in the hearing room as the spectators shifted around to see the distinguished man enter.

"Cross your fingers, Uriah," whispered Philip Phillips, leaning across Ben Butler's empty chair toward his client. "This can be our entire case."

Uriah looked at him intently. A fist flexed itself somewhere deep inside him and then grabbed and compressed the walls of his stomach, "Will he be honest?" he asked Phillips. "Will he state the true facts?"

"All I can say," Phillips answered, "is that he has been most forthcoming in our interviews with him. He is an honorable man. Let us hope that he tells the whole truth now and doesn't hold back."

Bancroft was the epitome of the classical scholar, the truly learned man: thick white hair; a long and full white beard topped by a glorious white handlebar mustache; a dominant, imperious Roman nose; and thin, ascetic lips. He had entered Harvard at age thirteen and graduated at seventeen, then went to Europe to study theology and philology at the University of Göttingen. Weeks before his twentieth birthday, he was awarded the master of arts and doctor of philosophy degrees. He returned to America to teach Greek at Harvard, to preach at churches, and to translate the classics. In 1823 he and an associate founded a school for boys in Northampton, Massachusetts, and he stayed there for eight years. After selling his interest in the school to his partner in 1831 he began what would be his epic work: a multivolume *History of the United States*. It was a great success from the start; it sold well and earned loud applause from the scholarly community.

Politics began to appeal to him; perhaps his widespread renown helped convince him of his own potential as a public servant. He was a delegate to the Democratic National Convention in 1844 and threw his support and influence behind James K. Polk, while he himself was defeated in his try for the governorship of Massachusetts. Polk rewarded Bancroft for his support by naming him secretary of the navy, and he served in that seat from March 10, 1845, to September 8, 1846. While in office he had daringly used the general funds of the Navy Department—overcoming the longtime opposition of Congress—to start a United States Naval Academy at Fort Severn in Annapolis, Maryland. While in office, also, he ignored a number of appeals for assignment from one Uriah P. Levy. Today he would be asked to explain why he had done so.

"Mr. Witness," Ben Butler began, "will you please state your name, your age, and your occupation?"

"My name is George Bancroft. I am fifty-seven years of age. My occupation is at present of a private character."

"And what is your connection, past and present, with the United States Navy?"

"I was secretary of the navy from March 1845 to September 1846. I have had no other connection with the U.S. Navy."

"Would you describe, Mr. Bancroft, the nature of your acquaintanceship with Uriah P. Levy, its duration, and its intensity?"

"I became acquainted with Captain U. P. Levy about March 4, 1845. My acquaintance with Captain Levy was not otherwise intimate than he constantly importuned me, when secretary of the navy, to give him employment suited to his rank, in particular when the war broke out with Mexico in 1846. He was as earnest as an officer could be to get a command during that war."

"Mr. Bancroft, would you give us your estimation of Captain Levy's personal qualities during your term as secretary of the navy? I mean by that, your estimation then of his physical capacity and his professional ability."

Bancroft nodded, then proceeded confidently: "I have always considered the physical capacity and health of Captain Levy to be equal or superior to those commonly possessed by persons of his age. Captain Levy's faculties have seemed to me strong, rather than weak; quick, rather than slow; vigilant, rather than heedless; active, rather than sluggish. I know nothing of their having been impaired, nor do I know anything impeaching his moral character and deportment, his courage, or his patriotism."

"Did Captain Levy ever give you, when you held office, reason to question his competence as a naval officer?"

"When secretary of the navy, I never had cause to doubt, and never doubted, Captain Levy's competence to serve the United States in the grade of captain."

Ben Butler paused and stared into the eyes of his witness. Then he struck home: "Would you explain to us, Mr. Bancroft, why, despite Captain Levy's constant pleas for duty during your term as secretary, you did not see fit to accede to his pleas and give him an assignment?"

Bancroft again did not hesitate. He was a man of surpassing urbanity, and he did not feel he had anything to hide.

"I did not find myself able to give him a command for three reasons: First, the excessive number of officers of his grade made it impossible to employ all those who were fit. Second, the good of the service, moreover, seemed to require bringing forward officers less advanced in years than most of the captains, and the law sanctioned that course. Third, I perceived a strong prejudice in the service against Captain Levy, which seemed to be in a considerable part attributable to his being of the Jewish persuasion. While I as an executive officer had the same liberal views which guided the president and the Senate in commissioning him as a captain, I always endeavored in fitting out ships to have some reference to that harmonious cooperation which is essential to the highest effectiveness."

The point had been made, but Ben Butler could not resist a final sally, a second twist of the blade in the government's case.

"Do I understand you to say, Mr. Bancroft, that you refused Captain Levy a command because you felt that the prejudice against him, as a Jew, would tend to endanger that 'harmonious cooperation' which you sought aboard the navy's ships? Is that correct, sir?"

"'That is correct, Mr. Butler,'" said Bancroft, as he stared levelly into the penetrating eyes of his interrogator.

There was a great hush in the hearing room. Commodore Kearney turned and looked silently into the faces of his fellow judges. They in turn stared back at him. Judge Advocate Little sat quietly and looked down at the papers on the counsel table before him.

So it was out at last! Philip Phillips reached over and squeezed Uriah's arm. George Bancroft had taken the honorable course; he had spoken truth. He had admitted publicly that the religion of a member of the U.S. armed forces had caused the officer to be refused assignment. The dark suspicions that Uriah had held for years about shadowy forces arrayed against him inside the Navy Department had now been confirmed. It had not been, finally, his humble origin as a sailing master, or his sometime bad temper, or his tendency to boastfulness, or even his campaign against flogging. It had all come down to his being a Jew.

Instinctively he always had known it. He had felt it with the ultrasensitive feelers of a Jew in a Gentile world. Now it had been said in the open for all the nation to know.

Uriah sat quietly. He showed no emotion, save for a flushed face. He looked at Bancroft with a gaze mixed of anger and weariness. He stared at this well-born, well-educated, cultivated man of letters and wondered how he could have succumbed to such blatant prejudice, such unseeing hatred. He wondered how the man could have testified so coolly, so calmly, in such measured, almost self-righteous tones, that he had grossly violated, not only the law, but the most essential spirit of a land that promised, nay guaranteed, equal treatment to every man.

Uriah felt no surge of justification at Bancroft's testimony. He felt contempt for people of high station, educated to know better, who winked at the Constitution and ignored it. He felt a bone-deep, all-consuming fatigue. He wished desperately that this draining ordeal would finally end.

Ben did not want to lose the tactical advantage that Bancroft's statement had given him. He quickly introduced a deposition supplied by Captain Francis Hoyt Gregory, who had entered the navy in 1809 as a midshipman and who testified that he had known Uriah P. Levy since 1821: "I do know that there were in years past officers in the navy entertaining strong prejudices against him which, I believe, still exist. I know also that he has friends in the service as well able to judge of his merits who estimate him very differently. So far as my information goes in relation to this matter, the prejudices existing against him originated in his being a Jew."

"We are saving our other star witness for the very end," Ben explained to Uriah, as the judge advocate challenged the deposition with a prosecution interrogatory. "Let it end with such a witness clear and fresh in their minds."

"Mr. President, I call to the witness stand as our final witness Commodore Thomas ap Catesby Jones."

Commodore Jones strode to the witness stand with a vigor that belied his years—a small, wiry, dapper man with a jaunty step and glowing eyes. Five days from now would be the forty-third anniversary of his gallant fight as leader of a few flimsy American gunboats against a fleet of forty-two British launches armed with carronades. Jones had lined his seven vessels across the narrow Malheureux passage in Lake Borgne, outside New Orleans, and watched the English bear down upon them. The resulting fight went into the history books as a British victory, but the heroic defense put up by Jones and his men would never be forgotten. They had given Andy Jackson valuable time to prepare his defense line at New Orleans. Jones had made the English pay well for his defeat: more than twice as many English casualties as American. The commodore to this day still carried a musket ball in his shoulder and metal fragments in his eyes from the British cannon on Lake Borgne.

A little more than three years after that battle, he had been first lieutenant aboard the frigate *United States* in the Mediterranean when a distraught Lieutenant Levy came to him and asked his advice. Levy had been assigned to the frigate by Commodore Stewart, but the commander of the *United States*, William Montgomery Crane, had vehemently rejected him. Crane was angrily overruled by Stewart, and Uriah had remained as an unwelcome addition to the officer list on the frigate. But he had been treated fairly and courteously by Jones, and a friendship developed that had lasted ever since, even though the two old warriors rarely had a chance to meet. Uriah never forgot how Jones had worked to persuade the other officers on the *United States* to forget their hatred and to treat the Jew in their midst with the deference due another officer. Then Tom Jones was transferred back to the States and the situation on the frigate rapidly deteriorated.

Since then, Jones had risen steadily through the ranks. By September 1842 Jones was commodore of the Pacific Squadron, with the old *United States* as his flagship.

Now sixty-seven years old, Jones described himself when he took the witness chair as "sometimes a sailor, sometimes a farmer." He, too, had been a victim of the Board of Fifteen; he, along with Commodore Stewart and Uriah's boyhood friend, Commodore Charles W. Skinner, had been among the fourteen captains placed on "Reserved on Leave Pay" status. But this was a retirement on full pay and was a category reserved for those officers deemed by the Board of Fifteen to have served "well and with fidelity." It was a retirement with honor, prestige, with a salute of "well done." It could not be compared to Uriah's abject dismissal in dishonor.

Commodore Jones testified in short, abrupt, piercing sentences that burst over the hearing room like the *rat-a-tat* of a fast-firing swivel gun on a man-of-war. Known as a man of few words, he was far from silent on this day; in fact, he was much more voluble than the judge advocate would have preferred.

"Commodore, please state your experience with the navy," Ben asked.

"I have been with the navy as midshipman, lieutenant, lieutenant commandant, master commandant, captain, and commander of squadrons from the twenty-second day of November 1805 to the present time, say fifty-two years, lacking one day."

"How long and how well have you known Captain Uriah P. Levy?"

"I have known Captain Levy for forty-one years; I served with him on the frigate *United States*. Since that time, I have known him socially."

"Commodore, would you describe Captain Levy in terms of his qualifications—mentally, physically, and morally?"

"Mentally, in my judgment, Captain Levy has not many equals left in the grade from which he was ejected. I know of no act of immorality chargeable against Captain Levy. Captain Levy is a man of active mind and quick perception, scrupulously jealous of his own and of his country's rights and honor, neither of which I am sure can ever be insulted with impunity in his hearing or presence. While Captain Levy is prompt and always ready to resent insult on proper occasions, I do not think him reckless or heedless. So far as I have had an opportunity for judging, Captain Levy is quick, vigilant, and prompt in the discharge of all public and private duties, and as to patriotism and devotion to his country, her institutions and her interests, I know of no one, in or out of the navy, more truly devoted than Captain Levy."

"While you have not actually served with Captain Levy in many years, Commodore, what have you heard about his performance? I refer particularly to his performance as commander of the *Vandalia*."

"I have always understood that the ship *Vandalia*, when commanded by Captain Levy in the West Indies or Gulf Squadron, was considered the man-of-war of the squadron, although Captain Levy had among his officers the most refractory in the navy at that day."

The judge advocate approached his cross-examination of the witness gingerly, as if he carried a live shell in his hands.

"Was it not true, Commodore Jones," asked the judge advocate, "that Mr. Levy was well known for the many enemies he had made during his career in the navy?"

Commodore Jones smiled, as if he had been awaiting this question. At his smile, the judge advocate perceptibly winced.

Jones took a deep breath and replied in a rush, "Captain Levy, like all high-minded public officers, knowing and faithfully discharging all the duties of their stations, whether in the navy or army, or in political stations, who exact like faithfulness from all around and under them, has made enemies. To the few clamorous opponents thus made, these may be added: the pharisees of the navy, who have late set themselves up as guardians of public and naval morals and who profess to think that an Israelite is not to be tolerated in or out of the navy. And to those may be further added some who can see nothing praiseworthy or meritorious in certain officers introduced into the navy as masters from the merchant service, subsequent to the reorganization of the navy in 1800. It is not surprising that when such influences are active with even a few, that a brave and independent man like Captain Levy, who will neither feign, fawn, nor flatter, should encounter trials and tribulations in the service."

The live shell had exploded and left the judge advocate with face blackened. He was very sorry he had asked the question.

When Commodore Jones had been excused from the witness stand, Ben Butler faced and addressed the bench: "Mr. President, we are in need of additional time to prepare our final argument to the court. I respectfully request the court to order this proceeding adjourned until Thursday, December 17, nine days hence, to allow us sufficient time for such preparation."

Kearney nodded and turned to Little: "Does the judge advocate have any objection to such adjournment?"

"I can well use the time, Mr. President, to work on my own final suggestions to the court."

"Very well. This hearing will stand in recess until December 17 at nine o'clock." He banged his gavel with a strong sense of relief.

"*Adjourning*, damn it, *adjourning*," Ben grumbled to no one in particular. "It's not a recess, it's an *adjournment*."

"The Defense of Uriah P. Levy before the Court of Inquiry Held at Washington City, November and December 1857" rested in neat stacks, a separate copy on the table in front of each of the three attorneys for the defense and in front of Uriah.

After Commodore Kearney gaveled the hearing into session, Ben cleared his throat and stepped forward. "Mr. President, may it please the court: We now prepare to begin our defense. It is a lengthy document: we anticipate that its reading will take several days. The reading will be shared by my cocounsel and myself and, in parts, by Mr. Levy himself."

Two of the judging captains sipped water and then sat back and folded their hands, as if settling in for a long winter.

Ben paused, took a deep breath, then began to read a detailed recounting of Uriah's life, beginning with his childhood in Philadelphia and his service as a cabin boy aboard the *New Jerusalem*. It was the autobiography that Uriah had painfully constructed in his hotel suite after many false starts and long walks through the mud and dust of Washington City. Uriah listened to the parade of familiar episodes, most of it in his own words, although smoothed and rearranged by Ben's agile pen. Yet, as those words were read by another's voice, the story seemed to become a stranger's . . . the story of someone who achieved much in his life, yet somehow had attracted travail as a magnet pulls iron filings.

The reading of Uriah's biography, his nautical experience and education as a seaman, and the history and character of his connection with the naval service took up all of Saturday. Ben's voice was cracking and his throat was raw and sore when his cocounsel, Philip Phillips, took over the presentation.

When court resumed on Monday, the defense undertook a slow, careful examination of each of the courts-martial in which Uriah had been a defendant. If this was to constitute the foundation of the government's case, then it had to be confronted head-on. Phillips and his associate, Blount, divided these readings in order to save Ben's voice and energies as much as possible. Each case was painstakingly reviewed and assessed, the mitigating circumstances in each were fully exposed, and strong emphasis was placed on the punishments imposed, as well as the various presidential actions in overriding or lightening such punishments.

After the courts-martial had been dissected, Phillips and Blount turned to the testimony offered by the handful of prosecution witnesses—the high-ranking naval officers who had assured the court of Uriah's unfitness. In summation, Phillips read Uriah's words as he had written them, with Ben's help, in the first person: "I have shown you that not one of my commanders or superiors ever made a charge against me for disobeying his commands or neglecting my duties. . . . I have shown you that, from my service in the *Argus* in 1813 to my command of the *Vandalia* in 1839, my particular duties were performed to the satisfaction of my commanders, and that in every station I have filled, I have given myself with wholehearted alacrity and vigor to the duties of my profession."

Now it was time to draw this reasoned defense, more than one hundred pages, to its end. But before presenting the closing arguments, Ben addressed the judges directly.

"Mr. President and members of this honorable court," he said softly, "you have patiently listened to us for three days. Our defense soon will be completed. Your forbearance, your courteous attention to our arguments is deeply appreciated. This morning, before bringing this defense to its end, we call upon Mr. Levy himself to read to you the most crucial words of all those we have presented to you. For this, after all, is certainly the issue that has fomented this entire, sad affair."

Uriah stood up, his papers clasped in his hand, and walked to the reading stand squarely in front of Commodore Kearney. His hands were wet with perspiration, but his face was impassive, showing no emotion. It was his quarterdeck face, and he wore it with the familiarity of one who has spent many hours on a man-of-war's spar deck. A naval officer cannot allow his face to reveal his inner thoughts; too many of the ship's people are watching that face for clues.

He looked up and stared for a moment directly into the eyes of each of his judges, in turn: Storer, then Kearney in the middle, then Montgomery. Then, in a voice barely audible to the young clerks leaning forward in the back row, he began:

"My parents were Israelites, and I was nurtured in the faith of my ancestors. In deciding to adhere to it, I have but exercised a right, guaranteed to me by the constitution of my native state, and of the United States—a right given to all men by their maker—a right more precious to each of us than life itself. But, while claiming and exercising this freedom of conscience, I have never failed to acknowledge and respect the like freedom in others. I might safely defy the citation of a single act, in the whole course of my official career, injurious to the religious rights of any other person. Remembering always that the great mass of my fellow citizens were Christians—profoundly grateful to the Christian founders of our Republic, for their justice and liberality to my long-persecuted race—I have earnestly endeavored, in all places and circumstances, to act up to the wise and tolerant spirit of our political institutions. I have been careful to treat every Christian, and especially every Christian under my command, with exemplary justice and ungrudging liberality.

"I have to complain—more in sorrow than in anger do I say it—that in my official experience I have met with little to encourage, though much to frustrate, these conciliatory efforts. At an early day, and especially from the time when it became known to the officers of my age and grade, that I aspired to a lieutenancy—and still more, after I had gained it—I was forced to encounter a large share of the prejudice and hostility by which, for so many ages, the Jew has been pursued. I need not speak to you of the incompatibility of these sentiments with the genius of Christianity or the precepts of its author. You should know this far better than I; but I may ask you to unite with the wisest and best men of our own country and of Europe, in denouncing them, not merely as injurious to the peace and welfare of the community, but as repugnant to every dictate of reason, humanity, and justice. . . .

"Never, on the other hand, was there a man, in the ranks of our profession, against whom, in the breasts of certain members of that profession, prejudices so unjust and yet so strong have so long and so incessantly rankled. Such, too, are the origin and character of these prejudices, as to make them, above all others, the most inveterate and unyielding. The prejudice felt by men of little minds, who think themselves, by accidental circumstance of wealth or ancestors, better than the less favored of their fellows—the prejudice of *caste*, which looks down on the man who, by honest toil, is the maker of his own fortunes—this prejudice is stubborn as well as bitter, and of this I have had, as you have seen by the proofs, my full share. But this is placable and transient compared with that generated and nourished by religious intolerance and bigotry.

"The first article of the amendments to the Constitution of the United States, specially declares, in its first clause, that 'Congress shall make no law respecting an establishment of religion, or prohibiting the free exercise thereof,' thus showing by its place, no less than by its language, how highly freedom of conscience was valued by the founders of our Republic. In the constitutions of several states, now in force, the like provision is contained. Our liberality and justice, in this regard, have been honored by the friends of liberty and human rights throughout the world. An eminent British writer, about thirty years ago, speaking of Americans, put it thusly: 'They have fairly and completely, and probably forever, extinguished that spirit of religious persecution which has been the employment and the curse of mankind for four or five centuries; not only that persecution which imprisons and scourges all religious opinions, but the tyranny of incapacitation, which by disqualifying from civil offices, and cutting a man off from the lawful objections of ambitions, endeavors to strangle religious freedom in silence, and to enjoy all the advantages, without the blood, and noise, and fire of persecution. In this particular, the Americans are at the head of all the nations of the world.'

"Little did the author of this generous tribute to our country suspect that, even while he was penning it, there were those in the American Navy with whom it was a question whether a Jew should be tolerated in the service. Still less did he dream that, at the very moment when, in his own country, Lord John Russell, of the illustrious House of Russell, is about giving himself, with the full assent of his government, to the work of Jewish emancipation, a spectacle like the present should be witnessed in this land of equality and freedom. For with those who would now deny to me, because of my religious faith, the restoration, to which, by half a century of witnesses, I have proved myself entitled, what is it but an attempt to place the professors of this faith under the ban of incapacitation?

"This is the case before you; and, in this view, its importance cannot be overrated. It is the case of every Israelite in the Union. I need not speak to you of their number. They are unsurpassed by any portion of our people in loyalty to the Constitution and to the Union, in their quiet obedience to the laws, and the cheerfulness with which they contribute to the public burdens. Many of them have been distinguished by their liberal donations to the general interests of education and of charity; in some cases, too—of which the name of Judah Touro will remind you—to charities controlled by Christians. And of all my brethren in this land—as well those of foreign birth as of American descent—how rarely does any one of them become a charge on your state or municipal treasuries! How largely do they all contribute to the activities of trade, to the interest of commerce, to the stock of public wealth! Are all these to be proscribed? And is this to be done while we retain in our Constitution the language I have quoted? Is that language to be spoken to the ear, but broken to the hope of my race? Are the thousands of Judah and the tens of thousands of Israel, in their dispersions throughout the earth, who look to America as a land bright with promise—are they now to learn, to their sorrow and dismay, that we, too, have sunk into the mire of religious intolerance and bigotry? And are American Christians now to begin the persecution of the Jews? Of the Jews, who stand among them the representatives of the patriarchs and prophets; of the Jews, to whom were committed the oracles of God; the Jews, from whom these oracles have been received, and who are the living witnesses of their truth; the Jews, from whom came the founder of Christianity; the Jews, to whom, Christians themselves believe, have been made promises of greatness and of glory, in whose fulfillment are bound up the hopes, not merely of the remnant of Israel, but of all the races of man?

"And think not, if you once enter on this career, that it can be limited to the Jew. What is my case today, if you yield to this injustice, may tomorrow be that of the Roman Catholic or the Unitarian; the Episcopalian or the Methodist; the Presbyterian or the Baptist. There is but one safeguard and this is to be found in an honest, wholehearted, inflexible support of the wise, the just, the impartial guarantee of the Constitution. I have the fullest confidence that you will faithfully adhere to this guarantee; and, therefore, with like confidence, I leave my destiny in your hands."

Uriah ended the reading as softly as he had begun it. There was no bombast. He spoke matter of factly, his face stolid, his feelings well controlled. He allowed the words to speak for themselves.

The audience was motionless until Uriah gathered up his papers and turned away from the reading stand. Once they were certain he was finished, a sharp burst of applause cut through the silence, most of it coming from Jonas and his compatriots, a group of prominent people in the Washington Jewish community, leaders in the new Washington Hebrew Congregation that Jonas had helped organize. They had been forewarned by Jonas that this day would bring statements of importance to every Israelite. Now they responded to Uriah's speech with vigorous clapping. The reporters were surprised that so small a group of people could produce so much noise.

The president of the court permitted the show of approval to run its brief course without interference.

As for Uriah, he took no heed of the spectators. He sat down in his accustomed place and stared straight ahead, his back straight as a ramrod. Inside his shirt, his heart pounded like a ship's drum. Ben put his hand upon Uriah's arm in silent applause.

They sat and waited for the judge advocate to offer his closing suggestions to the court. That worthy shuffled his papers and got them in order while Commodore Kearney's face showed increasing irritation.

"He must respond somehow to Uriah's charge of religious bigotry," Ben whispered in a muddle of the defense lawyers and Uriah.

"He must seek to neutralize that charge, to disarm it, if possible."

"He will have a difficult time doing that in light of Bancroft's testimony," responded Phillips. "That was irrefutable evidence that our claim is justified."

"Dare we hope that we shall get a verdict today?" muttered Ben. "Tomorrow is Christmas. If we do not hear a verdict today, we'll have to carry over until Saturday."

"Think of it," said Phillips with a smile. "With all the issues of religious hatred that have been raised in this hearing, think of the fine Christmas gift that this court has within its power to render to us all: Christian and Jew alike."

"I used to warn my children when they were small," Ben answered, "not to count their Christmas gifts until they saw them under the tree on Christmas morn. I would give the same warning to you, Philip."

Commodore Kearney's voice suddenly cut like a lash through the hearing room: "Mr. Little, we surely shall be marking New Year in this room if you are not soon ready to proceed!"

The judge advocate, face reddening, scurried to his feet and brought his papers to the reading stand. He cleared his throat and prepared to address the court.

Little was surprisingly brief. He spent some time in an effort to impeach the testimony of most of Uriah's distinguished character witnesses by emphasizing the inability of "mere citizens and non-military personnel" to reliably estimate Uriah's moral, physical, or professional fitness for duty.

Then, as predicted by Ben, Little confronted the issue of Uriah's alleged incapacitation because of religion:

"It has been urged, with great apparent earnestness, that the action of the retiring board in the case of Mr. Levy and the omissions of the several secretaries of the navy from 1844 to 1855 to assign him employment in his rank of captain were both grounded solely upon unfounded and causeless prejudice; and that the evidence introduced on the part of the government in this investigation is the effect of such prejudice, a prejudice which, it is alleged, is attributable solely to the fact that Mr. Levy is a Jew (or is alleged to be such) and that he entered the service as a sailing master.

"If this be true—if it indeed be the truth that such a prejudice does exist against him as alleged, and that this prejudice is properly attributable to the causes assigned, and has pursued him at every step through a long life, he is indeed a most unfortunate man. But does the remark of the marine, Carter, testified to by Commodore Mayo, and the vague and unsatisfactory inferences and suppositions of the two or three other witnesses who speak of this matter, prove the existence of such a prejudice—and one capable of producing such tremendous results upon the prospects of almost an entire lifetime?

"When we hear those assailed from whom we entertain feelings of partiality, it is natural and easy to attribute such attacks to prejudice, and it is rarely difficult to fancy some reason for such prejudice. If we were told that a single individual, himself a bigot, entertained a feeling of prejudice against Mr. Levy on account of his connection with the Jewish Church (if such a connection does, in fact, exist), it would not be difficult to credit the assertion. But is it credible that the American Navy is composed of such materials that a prejudice so widespread and so disastrous in its effects as that alleged to exist in this case can arise from such a cause, and yet find in it so wide a place? Is the loose and unsatisfactory evidence referred to in support of this allegation sufficient to fasten upon our navy such a stain?

"If a general prejudice exists in the navy against the applicant, growing out of *other* causes than those assigned by Mr. Levy and his learned counsel—for example, the circumstances referred to by Commodore Lavalette, those mentioned by several other witnesses on the part of the government, from the unfavorable reputation in the navy testified to by Commodores Lavalette, Shubrick, Perry, Stringham, and Captain Van Brunt, from the characteristics adverted to by these witnesses and Commodore McCauley, corroborated as they are by the several records of courts-martial . . . from any or all these causes combined—would not even such a prejudice, independent of the facts and circumstances from which it arose, materially impair his efficiency if upon the active list? Whether this opinion governed the action of the several secretaries to grant Mr. Levy's constant applications for a command, we do not know. It seems to have had such effect with at least one of them. Does not the credit, good order, and efficiency of the service demand that even a general prejudice of so inveterate a character as that alleged, growing out of either of the causes last named, should be respected?"

As the judge advocate continued with advice to the court on the various verdicts it had the power to return, Ben again leaned over to Uriah and whispered, "It was a rather weak argument. The only worrisome thing in it was his appeal to the court not to 'stain' the navy with the finding that it harbored widespread feeling against an officer solely because he was a Jew. He was subtly appealing to them to ignore the evidence and instead to defend the navy against any tarnish, no matter if deserved. I hope to God they see clearly what he is asking them to do."

"They are men of honor," Uriah whispered back. "I'm sure of that. I have every confidence that that they'll bring back the verdict that is fairly directed by the evidence."

Ben nodded, out of courtesy if not necessarily agreement. He didn't feel quite the confidence that Uriah felt.

The judge advocate finished. The three captains solemnly retired to an anteroom to consider their verdict. The hearing stood in recess, but a palpable air of tension still hung over the hearing room. Conversation was subdued, still mostly in whispers even though normal conversation was now allowed.

Uriah felt the need to be alone. He walked to the back of the hearing room and out the door, then down the stairway to the floor below. There he stood and gazed out at a nearly deserted Seventeenth Street. The government virtually had closed down for the holiday. Members of Congress had set sail for their homes. The walkways between the Army and Navy Buildings were empty of pedestrians. The silent street and walks made the day seem lonely.

Uriah stood by himself at the window. He was weary, depressed.

He had found himself thinking often of death recently. He continually was assessing his life, adding up his accomplishments and deducting his failures. He kept remembering his talk with Mordecai some short time before his cousin had died. Mordecai had wondered if dear Papa would be proud of them . . . of what they finally had done with their years. Uriah stood now and wondered the same thing. He had given almost his entire life to the navy, yet what did he have to show? Oh, he had attained the service's highest rank, yet sometimes he felt that his last promotion surely must have been a gesture on someone's part, perhaps President Tyler, to appease him for past travails. He did not doubt his capacity to hold the rank of captain. He never had doubted it. But had he really earned it? His combat service consisted totally of the two months less one week on the beloved old *Argus*. He had served out the remainder of that war in Dartmoor Prison. The rest of his career, he had tallied up a few days earlier, consisted of about twelve years of sea duty and another few months of shore duty—this in a career of forty-five years in the navy. The remainder of the time, he had been listed on the rolls as "waiting for orders." That was how he had spent his life: waiting for orders. *Well, Papa, was it a life well spent?* He shook his head and gazed out the window again, a feeling of dismay in his chest.

And yet, he told himself, given the chance that every man covets in his fantasy—the chance to do it all over again—how would he change things? Would he, given that chance, have opened a store in Philadelphia like his merchant grandfather and father? Would he have begun earlier the ownership of properties and devoted his life to accumulating money and doing good works?

He smiled a slightly bitter smile and shook his head again. No, he could not contemplate, even in fantasy, a life away from the sea. Even at this moment, he craved the tang of salt spray, the feel of a stout hawser under his hand, the rise and fall of a well-planked deck under his foot. This was the life for him. His only regret was that he had been denied it for so many of his years.

● ● ●

A sudden silence draped over the hearing room as the door to the anteroom opened and the three captains filed back to their chairs. The clerk's call to order was most unnecessary: the people in the room were anxious to hear the decision. There was no idle chatter, not even nervous whispering.

Ben eyed the captains closely as they entered the room. He saw that two of them threw a long glance at Uriah as they took their seats. His heart lifted. Every experienced trial lawyer is aware that a jury, when carrying back a guilty verdict in a criminal case, tends to avert its eyes from a defendant when it files back into the jury box. It was a good sign, their look at Uriah.

Commodore Kearney pounded his gavel one time and softly spoke: "This court is now ready to announce its decision."

With no command from his lawyers or anyone else, Uriah stood up and faced the court at stiff attention. Whether their verdict would doom him or resurrect him, Uriah, unbidden by anyone, stood to demonstrate his respect for the nation and its navy. They had already reached their verdict; his gesture need not impress them or anyone else. But Uriah let them know, let everyone know, that in his heart he was still a navy officer and would stand, rigidly erect, to hear the orders of his superiors. They could not deny him this last expression of his allegiance.

Commodore Kearney appeared to take no notice of Uriah, but there was a flush to Kearney's cheeks. He read a brief preamble concerning the charge that had been given to the court and a quick summation of the proceedings that had taken place. Then, mercifully, the preliminaries were over. His voice rising in volume, he read the decision:

"And thereupon the court, upon consideration, does find that the said Levy is morally, mentally, physically, and professionally fit for the Naval Service, and does respectfully report that he ought to be restored to the active list of said Navy. In testimony whereof, we have herein to set our hands, this 24th day of December A.D. 1857."

It was over.

He had won.

The hearing room erupted in cheers and applause. The three captains sat back in their chairs and watched the celebration, broad smiles on their faces. The judge advocate, having shrugged his shoulders when he heard the verdict, began gathering up his papers. His thoughts turned to the next such hearing, to begin after New Year's: a lieutenant who had been dismissed by the Board of Fifteen would present his case for reinstatement.

Uriah turned and walked over to Ben, who slowly rose to face him. The two men wrapped their arms about each other and stood there, holding on. Uriah had seen that Ben's eyes were filled with tears. He wished he had the words to thank Ben properly, but he knew he did not. So he said no more, but again put his arms around Ben's thin shoulders.

Virginia came up, still sobbing wildly, and it was her turn for an embrace. Jonas, his cheeks wet, was behind her. Then, gently, Uriah freed himself from their embraces. He strode forward to the dais to shake the hands of the three men who had given his life back to him.

24

The Macedonian, *1858*

If the secretary of the navy had expected Captain U. P. Levy to be humble, obsequious, and full of gratitude for his restoration to rank, he did not know this man. The captain who sat before him in the secretary's office on the first floor of the Navy Building on this windy, sun-dappled April day was far from overflowing with gratitude. He was, in fact, rather irritated.

"Mr. Secretary, I do not demean the command of any vessel of the United States Navy, no matter how humble," Uriah proclaimed, pounding his fist on the arm of his chair for emphasis. "When I received your letter of the April 16, ordering me to command of the *Macedonian*, my first reaction—I admit—was one of surprise and gratitude. One week ago, I turned sixty-six years. I am no longer a young man, though still vigorous. I was not sure I would ever again be favored with a navy command. So I was at first elated when I read your letter. But on reflection, sir, I became more and more downcast. I have, after all, the seniority of fourteen years in my rank. Surely I am entitled to more than the command of a sloop of war. Surely I am entitled to command a squadron or, at the very least, a liner or a large frigate. I have never, in all my years in the navy, questioned an order or an assignment. But, sir, this order I must protest."

Isaac Toucey clasped his hands together firmly on his desk. He was striving hard to maintain his calm and his patience. He sympathized with this man for all the troubles he had encountered. The secretary had not been unhappy when the Court of Inquiry had restored Levy to active status and restored his rank with full seniority. He had thought he was doing him a large favor when he had overlooked his age and his long absence from the sea to give him command of the *Macedonian*, one of the great old ships of the navy, which had been recently rebuilt as a smaller 24-gun corvette.

Toucey had far graver concerns on his mind this morning. He was a loyal Democrat and considered as most ominous the widening schisms inside the party over the slavery issue. President Buchanan had firmly supported the *Dred Scott* decision and was calling for a constitutional amendment to recognize Southern property rights inherent in slaves. The North increasingly had come to perceive the president as a Southern sympathizer, though he himself came of Pennsylvania pioneer stock. And now Buchanan was trying to persuade Congress to accept the Lecompton constitution that permitted slavery in the new state of Kansas. Stephen Douglas was bitterly opposed to this, and adherents were forming around both men. It did not bode well for the party or the nation. Toucey had little time for, or interest in, mollifying this old navy captain who felt shortshrifted by an assignment that had been given to him, in the first place, to placate him for past adversities. But Toucey told himself, as he gripped his fingers together until they were white, *I will hold my temper and give this old man my most beneficial advice.*

"Captain Levy, your protest was noted for the record when your reply to my letter was received. I understand, sir, your desire for greater responsibility than command of a sloop of war would entail. At the moment, however, no such opportunity exists."

"Mr. Toucey, I do not foresee that I will be receiving many more commands in my career. Is this the way it is all to end? On such a minor note?"

Toucey could not help feeling a pang of sympathy for the man who sat before him. His captain's uniform was freshly cleaned and pressed. His boots carried a glistening sheen. He sat tall and stiff in his chair, knees pressed tightly together. His curly hair and his thick mustache had obviously been given a darker color to minimize the white and to keep others' thoughts away from his advancing years.

Toucey deliberated for a moment or two, then gave this answer:

"Captain, it is not customary, as you know, for this Department to discuss future assignments with its commanders. Such discussion would be neither prudent nor intelligent. Yet I am compelled to make a small exception in your case—in recognition of the injustices you have suffered in your career. What I tell you now, sir, I ask you to hold close. It is merely that you should be patient: the end that you seek will eventually be attained."

Uriah gazed for a moment at the secretary, then nodded, understanding. The assignment that he wanted would come to him, then, in time. It had been charted in the plans of the Department. The only question was when. But he dare not ask that. He had been bold enough.

Toucey continued, "I must add only one other thing, Captain, in fairness to you and so you will not get the wrong idea. The object of which I spoke will be yours for only a comparatively short time. We cannot overlook your age. We cannot forget that there are scores of younger captains behind you, clamoring for their just due. But I think you will be satisfied."

Uriah had a strong idea what was in store for him. He had been ordered to prepare the *Macedonian* for sea and then to take it to join the Mediterranean Squadron. The commander of that squadron was now about seventy years old and his health was failing. It was common knowledge that he soon must be replaced. Toucey had given him no clue of the grand assignment that awaited him, but Uriah grew increasingly confident, as he mulled it over, that the Mediterranean Squadron would someday be his. He almost laughed aloud in delight as he thought ahead to the ceremony in which the command would be handed over to him, for his predecessor as commodore of the squadron (and who would for the time being be his superior officer) was Eli A. F. Lavalette, who had been his adversary years ago on the *United States* and who had testified against him at the court of inquiry. He could hardly wait to look upon Lavalette's face in that change-of-command ceremony.

"Captain Levy, you raise another problem for me." Toucey's voice roused him from his reverie. "In your letter of April 26, which was brought to my desk just this morning, you make a most unusual and inconvenient request."

Uriah's face flushed. "I am sorry to trouble you with this, Mr. Secretary, but I felt I had no choice in the matter."

"You request permission to take Mrs. Levy with you on the *Macedonian* on the grounds that she is an orphan and not a native of the United States and would be left in this country without protection in your absence?"

"That is correct, sir."

"Have you no relatives to look after her?"

"There are relatives, Mr. Secretary, but Mrs. Levy is not close to them. She is young and inexperienced, and unfamiliar with American ways. She would live alone and would, I fear, come to harm. She does not manage money well and she tends to be . . . somewhat flighty. I would desperately worry over her welfare, were I to abandon her for a long period of time."

"The navy just does not do this sort of thing, Captain Levy. You know that."

"My request is not without its precedents, Mr. Secretary. I made a careful study of the matter before drafting my letter to you. I respectfully call to your attention the following: When Captain Richard V. Morris was named commodore of the Mediterranean Squadron in the year 1802, the secretary of the navy—Mr. Robert Smith—approved his request that his wife accompany him aboard the frigate *Chesapeake*. And, more recently, the great Commodore Isaac Hull won the permission of Secretary James Paulding to take Mrs. Hull with him on a cruise to Italy aboard the *Ohio*."

"I had not known of Commodore Morris's case," Toucey answered with a hint of a smile, "but I have some knowledge of Commodore Hull's. I know that Commodore Hull took with him, not only Mrs. Hull, but also two of her sisters. I know also that the presence of these ladies stimulated a series of protest petitions to the Department from the officers of the *Ohio*, who charged that Mrs. Hull virtually had assumed command of the vessel. I know that the tempest aboard that ship resulted in three lieutenants being sent back to the United States by the commodore for alleged discourtesy to him or to his lady."

Uriah could not hold back a smile. "Well, I assure you, sir, that Mrs. Levy would be accompanied on the *Macedonian* by no relatives other than myself."

Toucey nodded. He sighed and contemplated his hands. God, he had no time for such triviality! There was danger that his party would dissolve. Indeed, there was danger that the nation would soon be in flames.

"Very well, Captain, let us resolve this matter. Since there is some precedent, I will grant you permission to convey Mrs. Levy aboard the *Macedonian* to the first port in Italy that you touch."

Uriah was grateful, yet still concerned. "I appreciate your compassion, sir. But does this mean that I must eject my wife from the ship at the first such port and leave her to the mercy of strangers in Europe?"

"I will rely on your judgment and good instincts, Captain. Your orders will mention only the first port in Italy, as I have stated. I can do no more than that in public. But if all is serene on the ship and Mrs. Levy's presence does no disservice to the *Macedonian's* performance, I see no reason why she cannot remain with you. But that is between us, as gentlemen, and I do not care to make written record of it."

"My humble thanks, Mr. Secretary. You have made this, for me, a day to be long remembered."

The passage from Key West to Gibraltar lasted from July 22 until August 27 and was pleasant and untoward. Uriah worked his officers hard and constantly preached to them to call the common sailors by their names and to treat them as human beings. The lieutenants expressed little fondness for their taskmaster commander, but they could not deny that he ran a strong ship, an efficient ship.

They had stopped briefly at Gibraltar but were denied permission to land because the Spanish authorities claimed there was yellow fever at Key West. The American consul begged Uriah not to argue the point, for he was dependent upon the Spaniards for his supplies. The *Macedonian* weighed anchor and made an easting to Marseilles. There they anchored on September 6 and stayed for several weeks. Virginia delightedly added to her book the signature of Viscount de Ferdinand Marie Lesseps, who was making plans to construct a canal across the Isthmus of Suez. The new waterway, de Lesseps assured them, would change the trading patterns of the world. His canal company was well provisioned for its task, with a capital stock of $40 million.

Finally, after residing in the *Macedonian's* great cabin for more than three months, Virginia temporarily took her leave. By prearrangement, she met friends from New York in Marseilles and traveled with them to Paris. She would rejoin the *Macedonian* in January. She bade farewell to Uriah at the quay in Marseilles. While she reminded him to take his stomach medicine faithfully each evening, he warned her to mind her money well and not to fall victim to grasping Parisian dress merchants. Then she was gone, and he returned, with a sense of relief, to a corvette left once again to the pure masculinity of its ship's company.

The Mediterranean Squadron was one of America's six principal naval squadrons abroad, the others being the West Indies, the Brazil, the Pacific, the East Indies, and the African Squadron, which was primarily an anti-slaveship patrol. The ships of a squadron did not often sail in force but instead cruised individually over their stations. The vessels of the Mediterranean Squadron spent much of the winter in base at Port Mahon on the island of Minorca. When the weather allowed, they cruised to and fro, to the waters of the Levant, where pirates occasionally made bold to hamper shipping, and to the ports of Egypt and Greece, Turkey and Italy. It was pleasurable duty for the squadron's officers. There were many social events for the visiting ships. Members of the various royal families and government dignitaries often paid formal visits to the vessels to demonstrate their high regard for the United States.

Uriah enjoyed these weeks thoroughly, as much as any time in his entire navy career. He missed Virginia, but he was free now to give all his time to the improvement of his ship and crew, and he did so with joy. Given more time, he would have the *Macedonian* in a condition to satisfy even him.

Ah, how nice it was to enter a cabin put back in a state of Spartan tidiness, free of great piles of skirts and hoops and bonnets, and lacy underthings. From her first moment aboard the corvette, Virginia had moaned over the lack of space for her belongings. She proceeded thereafter to drape her apparel over the huge mahogany table, all six Windsor chairs, and even—before the weather had turned cold—over the big copper stove. Uriah had the constant feeling, when he walked though the door, that he was entering a dressmaker's shop. He couldn't help noticing the looks of distaste on the faces of his officers when they came to the cabin to summon him or to give a report.

Had it been a terrible mistake to take Virginia with him on the corvette? For the life of him, he didn't know. He was glad that he had not left her alone in New York City. Yet her presence here certainly had not been conducive to good order on the ship, and he knew it.

For her part, Virginia enjoyed every minute of it. Though she bewailed the lack of space and the absence of a personal maid, her smile was ever-present and she chattered away amiably with any officer, midshipman, or crew member she could find to listen.

Naples, Italy
September 2, 1859

Dearest Abigail,

I pray that God is taking good care of you and David and the babies and that the coming new year will be pleasant and prosperous for you. I think of you often and miss you.

My adventures of the last months would fill a book. I shall tell them briefly because the Ambassador's carriage will soon be here to fetch me to a gay ball at the Villa D'Estanza!

In January I took passage on a packet (most filthy and uncomfortable) and sailed from Marseilles to Alexandria and there I rejoined Uriah on his ship. That closet of a cabin seemed even smaller to me when I saw it again. I do not know how men stand living on such ships. We remained in Alexandria for four months, leaving only for very short cruises of one or two days. We had a gay time there. The Duke of Edinburgh, second son of Queen Victoria, was visiting Egypt at the time and many balls and entertainments were held in his honor and we were invited to them. La, it was a happy and exciting time! The Duke resided on a British vessel that anchored very near the Macedonian and so we came to know him and he spent time visiting us and we him. He and I played checkers many times, though he always won. Once he claimed victory and I denied it and so I playfully upset the checkerboard, where upon this royal prince got on his knees to pick up the checkers. Uriah came along and witnessed this and chastised me, but the Prince replied, "I am always ready to serve a queen, whether it be my mother or Mrs. Levy, whose sovereignty is undisputed here."

Uriah and I met a Jewish banker from Cairo who has taken us on tours and entertained us royally in his lovely home. I was invited by the Princess to tour the harem of the Khedive and the banker's son, a handsome youth just returned from his education in Paris, tried to convince me to dress him in my clothes and let him accompany me. I of course indignantly refused, though it was a temptation. The Princess gave me a beautiful costume, which I put on, and the ladies of the harem pranced around in my own hoop skirts. The banker took Uriah and me on the first train across the desert, when the railroad was officially opened, and we saw the famed Pyramids.

We left Alexandria in the middle of March and sailed to

Italy. Several days out, we struck a terrible storm and there was much water in our ship. I was terrified! Uriah stayed on deck for hours, supervising the men. They found that the seams of the ship had parted and she badly wanted caulking. It would be done in Italy.

We called briefly at Spezia, Livorno, and Genoa. Then we came here to Naples. Uriah was ordered by Commodore Lavalette to continue to Palermo, Messina, Tripoli, Tunis, Algiers, Marseilles, and back to Genoa, until finally the Macedonian would return to base at Spezia after a cruise of five months or more. And after re-provisioning and a bit of rest, Uriah would be expected to begin another cruise to the eastern Mediterranean.

Before the ship left Naples, I had a talk with Uriah. I told him I could not stand living on the ship much longer and pleaded with him to allow me to escape. He was very cross with me and said he was afraid to set me loose again in Europe for fear I would spend every last penny he owned. I promised him faithfully on bended knees that I would respect my budget if he would permit me to tour Europe.

It has all worked out beautifully! We have become good friends with Ambassador Chandler and his wife (a very motherly woman) and Uriah has agreed to let me take an apartment here and stay for a time, under their watch and care. They will take me with them to Florence soon and probably to Venice as well.

And even better: while in Genoa, we became acquainted with Mr. and Mrs. Leonard Jerome (he is a very wealthy American businessman). They took a great liking to me and have persuaded Uriah to allow them to take me to Paris with them. Then we will all sail together on a packet back to America, where I shall await Uriah's return. Since a tour of duty in the Mediterranean is usually two years and it has been about one-and-a-half years since we embarked, Uriah is quite sure that he will be taking the Macedonian home within the next *six or seven months. So we shall not be parted for too long. I am invited to pass Rosh Hashanah and Yom Kippur with Baron and Baroness Rothschild, who have their own synagogue in their home.*

I suppose I finally have become an adult in Uriah's eyes, for he has consented to trust me to tour Europe and sail home without him. Before leaving, however, he warned me again about overspending on new clothes and said that if I spent my passage money, I would have to work my way back to America on a catamaran! I pray I will mind my pennies this time, for his wrath when I spend too much is something to behold.

La, look at the time! The Ambassador's coach must surely be near and I have to finish my toilet. God bless you all.

Your loving sister,
Virginia

With Virginia in the company of people he trusted, Uriah could focus his attentions on the ship and crew and their next destination: the eastern Mediterranean.

The young lieutenant was properly deferential when he stood before Uriah on the quarterdeck and raised his hat in salute, but his face was red and bore a look of pained indignation.

"Yes, Lieutenant Braden?" Uriah forced patience into his voice. This lieutenant was a foppish nuisance. A product of the school at Annapolis, he had recently come over to the *Macedonian* as a replacement for the fourth lieutenant, who had developed bad lungs and been sent home.

"Captain," Braden began with a rush, "it is my obligation to remind you that I am well trained in all the skills required of my rank and am, in addition, the latest in a long line of Bradens who have served the navy of our country."

To Uriah's astonishment, the lad began to recite a list of his navy ancestors, beginning with his great-grandfather who had seen action with John Paul Jones. After the presentation had moved past that worthy and down to Braden's grandfather, Uriah felt compelled to interrupt.

"I am delighted to know of your distinguished forebears, sir, and assure you I will keep this information well in mind, but I must ask, to what purpose are you telling me all this?"

"Why, sir, in order to state that I have been directed by the first lieutenant to take a boat and crew and go on shore to Jaffa port and there to dig a load of dirt and bring it back in the boat. I have told the first lieutenant that I find this order both incomprehensible and beneath my dignity as an officer. He told me the order came directly from you and that I should take the matter up with you. That I now do, sir."

Uriah regarded the young upstart with wry amusement. At certain times and under certain conditions, the mere suggestion by a junior officer that he questioned orders from the quarterdeck would have triggered Uriah's raging fury. But this day, anchored on a placid, fire-blue sea off the coast of Syrian Palestine, he was in a most enjoyable mood. The weather was balmy, two-thirds of his crew was skylarking in the Arab bazaars on shore, and it was altogether an exceedingly gracious day. Lieutenant John Armintrout Braden was a blithering young snob. He reminded Uriah of some British naval officers—Lord This and Sir That—who had gained their positions through family influence and who barely could find their way to the ship's head, much less navigate the oceans of the world. Braden somehow had managed to stay the course at Annapolis, but God help the navy if ever he took command of a man-of-war.

"You are well informed by the first lieutenant, Mr. Braden," Uriah replied quietly. "The order to secure a boatload of dirt did come directly from me."

"Is it permissible to ask, Captain, of what earthly use has the *Macedonian* for a boatload of Arab dirt?"

"No, it is *not* permissible to ask, Mr. Braden," Uriah answered, and he saw the young officer's eyes widen in dismay. "But since you have the temerity to question my order, I shall enlighten you. The earth in this land may be mere Arab dirt to you, but it is holy soil to my own ancient people. It is considered a blessing to be buried in such soil. Therefore, since most of my fellow Israelites will not have the opportunity to be buried in the Holy Land, I am doing the next best thing for them: I shall bring a load of this holy soil back to America and present it, with my compliments, to my own synagogue in New York City. This will make it possible for a small amount of this soil to be placed in the grave of each person who dies hereafter and will thereby, at least in a small way, satisfy both the Almighty and the deceased. Are you now properly enlightened, Lieutenant?"

Lieutenant Braden stood with mouth open, his jaw having dropped in amazement as the explanation unwound. He had never heard anything so foolish! John Armintrout Braden, a conveyor of burying dirt?

Uriah continued, "Now, Lieutenant, in spite of your noble ancestry and your undoubted talents as an officer, I direct you to carry out my orders and go fetch said dirt. I do not believe it will permanently injure your dignity. You may protest going and you may protest coming back, but go you must, sir."

The exchange had been overheard by three sailors of the afterguard who were polishing brass on the quarterdeck. They stood with broad smiles, thoroughly enjoying the discomfort of the imperious young lieutenant. After a year with this captain, the ship's people idolized Uriah. They well knew his repute as a leader in the fight against flogging. They had found him always ready to listen to their complaints and, though he did not always uphold them, they were certain of a fair hearing. Many times he had fiercely called down an officer for not properly seeing to the welfare or comfort of the men in his division. He was a hard captain, the people said of him, a demanding commander, but a good man, "a sailors' captain."

Lieutenant Braden, redder of face than before, raised his cap again in final salute and left to carry out his assignment. Uriah turned, and his eyes caught the three members of the afterguard in their enjoyment of the little scene. The smiles on the three faces quickly vanished as their commander looked their way.

Still early in the afternoon, Uriah went below to read a packet of dispatches that had been dropped off earlier by the squadron's dispatch steamer. Well satisfied with himself and his day, he sank back into an easy chair in his cabin and put his feet up on a low table. He thought for a moment, before tearing the seal of the packet, about the fabled land off which they were anchored and the history that radiated like incense from its shores. He wished he had the time and the wherewithal to travel this land. He wished he could follow in the steps of the American Navy party that had taken two small boats some twelve years before, put in at the Sea of Galilee, and then descended the sixty miles of the Jordan River to the Dead Sea. There they had established a camp and spent several weeks exploring the area and measuring the geography of the Dead Sea, which they found to be more than thirteen hundred feet below sea level. Ah, he would love to explore Jerusalem and Tiberias and Safed! He wished he could do all that . . . and he wished that Mordecai could be with him to do it—Mordecai, who had predicted that his people would one day regain their ancient homeland, but who, like Moses, had not himself been able to see it.

He shook his head at the memories that flooded his mind. Then he broke the seal on his packet.

Amid the pile of dispatches, supply memoranda, and a new chart or two, was an envelope bearing the familiar cramped, shaky handwriting of Commodore Lavalette. Uriah, wondering why the Commodore had written the communication himself rather than relying on his secretary, opened it first. It read:

Port of Spezia, Italy
November 9, 1859

Captain Levy:

By the time you read this, I shall have departed Spezia and shall be returning aboard my flagship to the United States. I have been directed by Secretary Toucey (see copy of his letter, dated 29 September 1859, enclosed) to hand over all order and instructions to you as senior officer in the Mediterranean, or to leave them for you if you are absent, and thence to return with the Wabash *to New York. I am leaving such orders and instructions for you here, as directed. We are quickly provisioning and expect to pass Gibraltar by the 15th of the month.*

You and I had our problems in the past. I never liked you much and don't know if I do now. But I have come to learn that you are a good officer and run a taut ship. I was glad to have you in my squadron.

I expect to be asked, upon my return home, whether you are fit to succeed me as squadron commander. I shall have no word to say against you.

While the squadron was under my command, there were no general courts-martial and no desertions. I trust you to keep up that record.

I am, sincerely yours,
Eli A. P. Lavalette,
Captain and Commodore

Uriah could not keep his hands from shaking as they held the letter. He stood up and walked to the row of six aft windows and looked out on Jaffa harbor. His knees shook as well.

It was obvious now. Barring some last-minute change of plan, he was to be flag officer of the Mediterranean Squadron. He was to be a commodore. At last, the pinnacle was to be his! He would stand at the very top, with Decatur and Hull and Bainbridge and Rodgers and Charlie Stewart and Tom Jones: the great names of the navy that he had idolized for all his years.

The squadron would not be his for long. He knew that; Toucey had warned him. All right. But he had climbed all the way. If he must soon go back down, so be it. But he would be there.

•••

U.S.S. Macedonian
Genoa, February 23, 1860

The Hon. Isaac Toucey
Secretary of the Navy

Sir: I had the honor to receive on the 19th instant the order of the Honorable Secretary dated January 7th by which I am directed to hoist my flag on the Macedonian *and assume the command of the Mediterranean Squadron when the* Iroquois *shall arrive out and Commander Palmer shall have reported to me for duty. I hoisted my flag on the* Macedonian *and assumed command of the Mediterranean Squadron on the 21st instant.*

Sincerely yours,
U. P. Levy
Captain and Commodore

The clatter of feet on the spar deck above him was plainly audible in the commodore's cabin. The hoarse commands of two boatswains and their mates could be heard periodically through the planking as the officers and men of two ships, the *Iroquois* and the *Macedonian*, assembled on the deck and rigging of the flagship and crowded into formation for the change-of-command ceremony.

Every man jack of them would be wearing his best uniform and would be freshly washed and shaved; the hard-voiced boatswains and their mates would see to that.

The queer sliding sound of band instruments tuning added to the spar-deck din as the marine band prepared for its moment of glory.

Uriah waited in his cabin to be informed that all was in readiness. Then he would make his stately way up the aft hatchway and into the cold air and bright sunshine of the Gulf of Genoa. He would be greeted by the sight of hundreds of sailors massed on the decks and hanging from the rigging. All the officers of both ships would be lined up in full dress, with swords and epaulettes. Uriah would walk past a row of sideboys standing at salute, their white gloves immaculate. Then he would pass down a double row of boatswain's mates, their pipes at mouth. They would salute him with the eerie, sluicing call of the boatswain's pipe that is sweet only to the ear of a navy man. On down the deck he would walk, past the marine guard from both vessels, to the open area in front of the phalanx of officers.

There, Commander Palmer of the *Iroquois*, standing in for Commodore Lavalette, would formally bestow upon Uriah the command of the Mediterranean Squadron.

Uriah sat rigidly, awaiting his summons. He wore his captain's dress uniform, but it was adorned now on the sleeves with the four gold lace stripes of a commodore. The heavy bullion epaulettes now bore an eagle, an anchor, and a silver star, signifying that the wearer of this uniform commanded not merely a single vessel but a squadron of ships.

There was a gentle tap at the cabin door.

"Come!"

"Sir, the ships' companies are assembled and waiting. The ceremony can begin whenever you are ready."

"Very well," Uriah answered. "Tell them I'm on my way."

As Uriah came up the last few rungs of the hatchway, the loud squealing of the boatswain's pipes began. At the instant his foot came down upon the spar deck, the marine drummers pounded out a ruffle, the great percussion somehow blending with the pipes in a beautiful cacophonic harmony. Then the marine fifers joined in, and the skin of every man on the ship prickled at the sound that commenced the passing of the power.

Uriah saw from the corner of his eye, as he walked down the

deck, a sailor standing near the main signal halliards of the *Macedonian*, a cloth ball held carefully in his outstretched hand. It was Uriah's own broad pendant. From this day on, it would fly at the *Macedonian*'s main whenever Uriah was aboard, signifying that this was the vessel of the squadron's flag officer.

In a few moments, as soon as the brief change-of-command ceremony was ended, the signalman would haul this bougee up the *Macedonian*'s mast and thereby signal to all ships that a new commodore had taken the con. Gun captains stood alert for orders, for when the broad pendant broke out into the sunlit air, the *Macedonian* would salute its new leader with thirteen guns, followed by the guns of the *Iroquois*, and then the guns of every other ship in the squadron.

Finally, Sardinian warships in the harbor would fire their own salutes, and the visiting warships of other nations would follow suit. The massive roar of cannon would roll all the way across the Ligurian Sea to the mountains of Corsica and echo back again, like a living memory of the great naval battles of yore.

Uriah came to a halt in the open space before the assembled officers in the corvette's waist. He glanced slowly about him at the mass of white uniforms gleaming on all sides. He took a deep, joyful breath and then came to rigid attention.

The marine band struck up a brief martial air and then fell silent. Commander Palmer strode forward, stopped in front of Captain Levy, and saluted. There was not a sound on the ship. Then Commander Palmer began to read the official order denoting the new squadron commander, Commodore Levy.

Epilogue

The tale has been told for generations in the Levy and Phillips families. According to this tale, after the Civil War began, Commodore Levy repeatedly applied for a new combat command, but his requests were ignored by the Navy Department. Finally, the story says, he managed to secure a private audience with President Lincoln at the White House.

The old warrior, now close to seventy years old, pleaded with the president for the command of a fighting ship so he could help to preserve the Union. The president gently but firmly told him that he was too old for such combat duty.

"Is there nothing I can do to help the cause?" the commodore asked.

"Yes, there is something," Mr. Lincoln replied. "I'd like you to stay here in Washington for a time and sit on the Court-Martial Board." Then a smile came to the president's tired face. "I understand," he said, "that you have had your share of experience in that line."

Before he left the president, the tale goes, Commodore Levy offered all his personal fortune to the government to help pay for the war. Again the president declined, but he told the commodore that his support of the war loan effort would be much appreciated.

Commodore Levy did spend several months in Washington as a member of the Court-Martial Board. Then he and Virginia returned to their home in New York City. In March 1862 Commodore Levy contracted a heavy cold that developed into pneumonia. He fought valiantly for two weeks but finally died in his sleep on March 22.

A military funeral was held on March 25 after a religious service conducted by Hazzan Lyons of Shearith Israel. Four companies of marines served as an escort, and six navy officers were pallbearers. A company of sailors provided a guard of honor as the coffin was carried from the house on St. Mark's Place and taken to a carriage. The solemn cavalcade proceeded to the East River and then aboard a ferry to Brooklyn.

The funeral procession came finally to Shearith Israel's cemetery at Cypress Hills, Long Island, overlooking the waters of Jamaica Bay. There the final rites took place and the mourners made their seven circuits around the coffin, meanwhile reciting the prayers attesting to God's mercy. Just before the coffin was lowered into the grave, three male relatives scattered over it dust from the Holy Land, some Palestine earth that the commodore had brought back home with him on the *Macedonian*.

Afterword

The book that you have just read is a novel. It is neither biography nor a work of history. Therefore, the reader is justified in asking: How much of this story was true? How much of it was an accurate representation of history?

All the major incidents in U. P. Levy's life, as depicted in this book, actually happened. All the major characters, with one significant exception, were real people who played the actual roles attributed to them in the book.

The young French woman, Elise de Guissac (along with her father), was entirely my own creation. She is based, however, upon a real person. Virginia Lopez Levy Ree, near the end of her own long life, told an interviewer that Commodore Levy had fallen deeply in love with a young French woman of noble birth during his stay in France in 1820. They parted because she refused to leave France permanently and he would not forsake his navy career.

As with any biographical novel, most of the dialogue is an imaginative re-creation. The hope always is that such dialogue is a reasonably accurate assumption, based upon all available information, as to what might have been said in the circumstances. Some of the letters reproduced in this book were actually written, while others are fiction and used mainly for narrative purposes. Captain Levy's speech from his defense at the Court of Inquiry in December 1857 is taken from his actual testimony.

The various confrontations and meetings between real people cited were, once again, a mixture of actual incidents verifiable in the historical record and created encounters. One example of the latter is the lunch of Levy and Senator John Parker Hale at Sweet's Restaurant in New York City. This actually was a well-known gathering place for ship captains in the slave trade, but there is no evidence that Levy and Hale ever met there, nor in fact that they ever met. The attitudes and experiences imputed to them in that scene, however, are authentic.

In a few instances I have used my prerogative as a novelist to alter minor historical facts for the sake of drama. One example concerns the highly important testimony given in the Court of Inquiry by former navy secretary George Bancroft and the testimony of Commodore Thomas ap Catesby Jones. Both men actually did testify, but by means of sworn depositions rather than in actual appearance at the hearing. However, the words attributed to them in this book were their actual words, as taken from their depositions, and their actual importance in the case was no less, even though the two men did not really appear in the hearing room.

Another example wherein a question of accuracy might be raised concerns the close relationship described in this book between Levy and his cousin, Mordecai Manual Noah. The information given about both men's lives is factual. They were boys together in Philadelphia, and Noah was indeed raised by his grandparents. We do not really know, however, whether they maintained the intimate, almost brotherly, closeness that my book has posited. There is some evidence to support it: we know, for instance, that Noah assisted Levy with some of his articles on navy matters during the 1840s. We also know they were in close proximity at the start of their lives and were on cordial terms before Noah's death. It does not take too great a leap of the imagination to suggest that their lives were closely intertwined throughout. In any case, Noah was one of the most colorful characters and also one of the most prophetic voices in American Jewish history. I could not have done this book without including him.

This book was possible only because of painstaking research and writing of many scholars and writers, whose hard work—as manifested in books and articles—happily was available to me. I would be greatly remiss if I didn't acknowledge my debt to them and express my deep appreciation. Research for this book was done in many libraries, and I thank the staff members of each of them, with a special word of thanks to the staffs at the American Jewish Historical Society in Waltham, Massachusetts, and the American Jewish Archives in Cincinnati for their cooperation and patient assistance.

It is impossible to list all the books, magazines, and newspapers that provided source material for this novel. I am compelled, however, to offer my gratitude for the following sources. The seminal figure in modern research on the life of Uriah P. Levy was Dr. Abram Kanof. His unearthing of much new information and his long article on Levy published by the American Jewish Historical Society illuminated many heretofore dark corners of that life. The biography of Levy, *Navy Maverick*, by Donovan Fitzpatrick and Saul Saphire, provided a road map and guide for my own independent research. William D. Sanderson's thesis on Levy's life also was most helpful.

A wealth of information on the controversy-filled life of Mordecai Manual Noah was available in *Major Noah* by Isaac Goldberg, long the only book-length biography of Noah, and in Jonathan Sarna's excellent doctoral dissertation on Noah, which more recently was published in expanded form as a book called *Jacksonian Jew.* Of considerable help in tracing the lives and fortunes of the many members of the Levy and Phillips families was Dr. Samuel Rezneck's *The Saga of an American Jewish Family since the Revolution: A History of the Family of Jonas Phillips.*

For general background I relied heavily on the many scholarly publications of the revered pioneer among American Jewish historians, Dr. Jacob Rader Marcus, and my gratitude to him runs deep and strong. Much of my information on early Jewish leaders and communities in Philadelphia and New York City came from two fine volumes, *The History of the Jews of Philadelphia: From Colonial Times to the Age of Jackson* by Edwin Wolf and Maxwell Whiteman and *The Rise of the Jewish Community of New York* by Hyman Grinstein. The great traditions of Shearith Israel Congregation and the special *minhag* (rite) of Sephardic Judaism were made known to me through the writings of Dr. David de Sola Pool, spiritual leader of that historic congregation for so many years. Ever useful as a genealogical source were the compilations found in the invaluable *First American Jewish Families* by Rabbi Malcolm Stern.

I must not fail to express my thanks to Rabbi P. P. Bloch, whose marvelous column on Jewish history in the newspaper *National Jewish Post and Opinion* first sparked my interest in Uriah P. Levy.

Irving Litvag

About the Author

Irving Litvag was a former news writer for the CBS Radio Network and public relations executive. He is the author of two previous books, *Singer in the Shadows: The Strange Story of Patience Worth* and *The Master of Sunnybank: A Biography of Albert Payson Terhun.* A lifelong resident of St. Louis, he completed this novel shortly before his death in 2005.

.